SYMPATHY FOR THE DEVIL

Also by Tim Pratt:

The Strange Adventures of Rangergirl
Little Gods
Hart & Boot & Other Stories

As T. A. Pratt:

Blood Engines
Poison Sleep
Dead Reign
Spell Games

SYMPATHY FOR THE DEVIL

Edited by Tim Pratt

NIGHT SHADE BOOKS
SAN FRANCISCO

ACKNOWLEDGMENTS

Thanks to my publisher Jeremy Lassen for agreeing to let me turn my love of devilish things into a book, and to my agent Ginger Clark for expediting the deal. Many thanks also to the authors (and their representatives) who were kind enough to allow me to reprint their work. Special thanks to John Joseph Adams for giving me advice (both theoretical and practical) on the care and feeding of anthologies, and to the many readers and writers who suggested devil-related stories for me to consider—I wish I could have included more of them. And, as always, much love to my wife Heather Shaw for her support and help in carving out time for me to do projects like this.

And, most importantly: Thank you, Satan! I couldn't have done it without you.

CONTENTS

INTRODUCTION

Tim Pratt

I'm a big fan of the Devil.

I like stories about the Adversary in all his incarnations. Most of the stories in this book are about the Capital-D-Devil in his various guises, from the fiddle-playing trickster of Charles de Lint's "Ten for the Devil" to the hard-nosed businessman of Carrie Richerson's "…~~With~~ By Good Intentions" to the hitch-hiking prankster of Jeffrey Ford's "On the Road to New Egypt" to the mindless gnawing monster of Dante's *Inferno*.

There are funny devils ("A Reversal of Fortune" by Holly Black, "The Power of Speech" by Natalie Babbitt, "Faustfeathers" by John Kessel), scary devils ("The Professor's Teddy Bear" by Theodore Sturgeon, "The Price" by Neil Gaiman) and just plain weird devils (Kelly Link's "Lull", Jonathan Carroll's "The Heidelberg Cylinder", Richard Butner's "Ash City Stomp"). There are classics here ("That Hell-Bound Train" by Robert Bloch, "Thus I Refute Beelzy" by John Collier, "The Bottle Imp" by Robert Louis Stevenson), and stories published within the last few years ("Nine Sundays in a Row" by Kris Dikeman, "The King of the Djinn" by David Ackert and Benjamin Rosenbaum). There are even a few deal-with-the-devil stories, though not as many as you might expect; I could have filled another book with the best of those easily, though.

There were a few narrative pairings I couldn't resist, like putting Stephen King's "The Man in the Black Suit" next to Nathaniel Hawthorne's "Young Goodman Brown," the story King says inspired the piece. And consider the scientifically-savvy title character of Mark Twain's "Sold to Satan" as compared to the scientifically-thwarted villain of Elizabeth M. Glover's "MetaPhysics."

For the sake of variety I included a few edge cases—the Devil as seen through a glass darkly, say—like Michael Chabon's dark oppositional deities in "The God of Dark Laughter", the self-proclaimed Great Beast 666 (better known as Aleister Crowley, or "Alick" to his friends) in "Summon, Bind, Banish" by Nick Mamatas, and the mysterious furious unnatural force at work in China Miéville's "Details". It seemed appropriate—after all, the Devil appears in many guises, from long-suffering employee of God to prideful fallen angel to pure malevolent force of nature to suave collector of souls.

1

When I first conceived of the idea for this anthology, I knew I'd have no trouble filling the pages, because just about every writer of weird short fiction has taken a crack at the Devil at some point (even I have, though modesty forbade me including any of my stories here), and I had to leave out as many good stories as I put in. I don't have time or space to list all the great stories you should read, but I'll mention a few: "The Playground" by Ray Bradbury, where the Devil doesn't explicitly appear, though I personally think he must be the one making those dark deals beneath the swings and behind the merry-go-rounds; "The Howling Man" by Charles Beaumont, which was made into a classic *Twilight Zone* episode, but don't miss the original story; "The Devil and Daniel Webster" by Stephen Vincent Benét, which is so famous it's been parodied on *The Simpsons*, but read it if you haven't; both Natalie Babbitt collections about the Devil, *The Devil's Storybook* and *The Devil's Other Storybook*—it was hard deciding which of her short funny pieces to reprint here; *The Screwtape Letters* by C. S. Lewis, which is great reading even if you're not particularly interested in Christian apologia; "Where Are You Going, Where Have You Been" by Joyce Carol Oates, even though the author herself insists the character Arnold Friend is not precisely the Devil… and I'd better stop now, or I'll be here all day.

These 35 stories (and a chunk of a poem) only begin to illuminate the many facets of Satan, Lucifer, Shaytan, the Lord of the Flies, the Father of Lies, Old Nick, Mr. Scratch, the Tempter, the Old Serpent, the Lord of this World, Old Hob, the Prince of the Powers of the Air and Darkness, Mephistopheles, First of the Fallen… and a Man of Wealth and Taste.

Turn the page, and allow him to introduce himself.

THE PRICE

Neil Gaiman

Tramps and vagabonds have marks they make on gateposts and trees and doors, letting others of their kind know a little about the people who live at the houses and farms they pass on their travels. I think cats must leave similar signs; how else to explain the cats who turn up at our door through the year, hungry and flea-ridden and abandoned?

We take them in. We get rid of the fleas and the ticks, feed them and take them to the vet. We pay for them to get their shots, and, indignity upon indignity, we have them neutered or spayed.

And they stay with us, for a few months, or for a year, or for ever.

Most of them arrive in summer. We live in the country, just the right distance out of town for the city-dwellers to abandon their cats near us.

We never seem to have more than eight cats, rarely have less than three. The cat population of my house is currently as follows: Hermione and Pod, tabby and black respectively, the mad sisters who live in my attic office, and do not mingle; Princess, the blue-eyed long-haired white cat, who lived wild in the woods for years before she gave up her wild ways for soft sofas and beds; and, last but largest, Furball, Princess's cushion-like calico long-haired daughter, orange and black and white, whom I discovered as a tiny kitten in our garage one day, strangled and almost dead, her head poked through an old badminton net, and who surprised us all by not dying but instead growing up to be the best-natured cat I have ever encountered.

And then there is the black cat. Who has no other name than the Black Cat, and who turned up almost a month ago. We did not realise he was going to be living here at first: he looked too well-fed to be a stray, too old and jaunty to have been abandoned. He looked like a small panther, and he moved like a patch of night.

One day, in the summer, he was lurking about our ramshackle porch: eight or nine years old, at a guess, male, greenish-yellow of eye, very friendly, quite unperturbable. I assumed he belonged to a neighbouring farmer or household.

I went away for a few weeks, to finish writing a book, and when I came home he was still on our porch, living in an old cat-bed one of the children had found

3

for him. He was, however, almost unrecognisable. Patches of fur had gone, and there were deep scratches on his grey skin. The tip of one ear was chewed away. There was a gash beneath one eye, a slice gone from one lip. He looked tired and thin.

We took the Black Cat to the vet, where we got him some antibiotics, which we fed him each night, along with soft cat food.

We wondered who he was fighting. Princess, our white, beautiful, near-feral queen? Raccoons? A rat-tailed, fanged possum?

Each night the scratches would be worse—one night his side would be chewed-up; the next, it would be his underbelly, raked with claw marks and bloody to the touch.

When it got to that point, I took him down to the basement to recover, beside the furnace and the piles of boxes. He was surprisingly heavy, the Black Cat, and I picked him up and carried him down there, with a cat-basket, and a litter bin, and some food and water. I closed the door behind me. I had to wash the blood from my hands when I left the basement.

He stayed down there for four days. At first he seemed too weak to feed himself: a cut beneath one eye had rendered him almost one-eyed, and he limped and lolled weakly, thick yellow pus oozing from the cut in his lip.

I went down there every morning and every night, and I fed him, and gave him antibiotics, which I mixed with his canned food, and I dabbed at the worst of the cuts, and spoke to him. He had diarrhoea, and, although I changed his litter daily, the basement stank evilly.

The four days that the Black Cat lived in the basement were a bad four days in my house: the baby slipped in the bath, and banged her head, and might have drowned; I learned that a project I had set my heart on—adapting Hope Mirrlees' novel *Lud in the Mist* for the BBC—was no longer going to happen, and I realised that I did not have the energy to begin again from scratch, pitching it to other networks, or to other media; my daughter left for Summer Camp, and immediately began to send home a plethora of heart-tearing letters and cards, five or six each day, imploring us to take her away; my son had some kind of fight with his best friend, to the point that they were no longer on speaking terms; and returning home one night, my wife hit a deer, who ran out in front of the car. The deer was killed, the car was left undriveable, and my wife sustained a small cut over one eye.

By the fourth day, the cat was prowling the basement, walking haltingly but impatiently between the stacks of books and comics, the boxes of mail and cassettes, of pictures and of gifts and of stuff. He mewed at me to let him out and, reluctantly, I did so.

He went back onto the porch, and slept there for the rest of the day.

The next morning there were deep, new gashes in his flanks, and clumps of black cat-hair—his—covered the wooden boards of the porch.

Letters arrived that day from my daughter, telling us that Camp was going better, and she thought she could survive a few days; my son and his friend sorted out their problem, although what the argument was about—trading cards, computer games, Star Wars or A Girl—I would never learn. The BBC Executive who had vetoed *Lud in the Mist* was discovered to have been taking bribes (well, "questionable loans") from an independent production company, and was sent home on permanent leave; his successor, I was delighted to learn when she faxed me, was the woman who had initially proposed the project to me before leaving the BBC.

I thought about returning the Black Cat to the basement, but decided against it. Instead, I resolved to try and discover what kind of animal was coming to our house each night, and from there to formulate a plan of action—to trap it, perhaps.

For birthdays and at Christmas my family gives me gadgets and gizmos, pricy toys which excite my fancy but, ultimately, rarely leave their boxes. There is a food dehydrator and an electric carving knife, a bread-making machine, and, last year's present, a pair of see-in-the-dark binoculars. On Christmas Day I had put the batteries into the binoculars, and had walked about the basement in the dark, too impatient even to wait until nightfall, stalking a flock of imaginary Starlings. (You were warned not to turn it on in the light: that would have damaged the binoculars, and quite possibly your eyes as well.) Afterwards I had put the device back into its box, and it sat there still, in my office, beside the box of computer cables and forgotten bits and pieces.

Perhaps, I thought, if the creature, dog or cat or raccoon or what-have-you, were to see me sitting on the porch, it would not come, so I took a chair into the box-and-coat-room, little larger than a closet, which overlooks the porch, and, when everyone in the house was asleep, I went out onto the porch, and bade the Black Cat goodnight.

That cat, my wife had said when he first arrived, is a person. And there was something very person-like in his huge, leonine face: his broad black nose, his greenish-yellow eyes, his fanged but amiable mouth (still leaking amber pus from the right lower lip).

I stroked his head, and scratched him beneath the chin, and wished him well. Then I went inside, and turned off the light on the porch.

I sat on my chair, in the darkness inside the house, with the see-in-the-dark binoculars on my lap. I had switched the binoculars on, and a trickle of greenish light came from the eyepieces.

Time passed, in the darkness.

I experimented with looking at the darkness with the binoculars, learning to focus, to see the world in shades of green. I found myself horrified by the number of swarming insects I could see in the night air: it was as if the night world were some kind of nightmarish soup, swimming with life. Then I lowered the binoculars from my eyes, and stared out at the rich blacks and blues of the night, empty and peaceful and calm.

Time passed. I struggled to keep awake, found myself profoundly missing cigarettes and coffee, my two lost addictions. Either of them would have kept my eyes open. But before I had tumbled too far into the world of sleep and dreams a yowl from the garden jerked me fully awake. I fumbled the binoculars to my eyes, and was disappointed to see that it was merely Princess, the white cat, streaking across the front garden like a patch of greenish-white light. She vanished into the woodland to the left of the house, and was gone.

I was about to settle myself back down, when it occurred to me to wonder what exactly had startled Princess so, and I began scanning the middle distance with the binoculars, looking for a huge raccoon, a dog, or a vicious possum. And there was indeed something coming down the driveway, towards the house. I could see it through the binoculars, clear as day.

It was the Devil.

I had never seen the Devil before, and, although I had written about him in the past, if pressed would have confessed that I had no belief in him, other than as an imaginary figure, tragic and Miltonion. The figure coming up the driveway was not Milton's Lucifer. It was the Devil.

My heart began to pound in my chest, to pound so hard that it hurt. I hoped it could not see me, that, in a dark house, behind window-glass, I was hidden.

The figure flickered and changed as it walked up the drive. One moment it was dark, bull-like, minotaurish, the next it was slim and female, and the next it was a cat itself, a scarred, huge grey-green wildcat, its face contorted with hate.

There are steps that lead up to my porch, four white wooden steps in need of a coat of paint (I knew they were white, although they were, like everything else, green through my binoculars). At the bottom of the steps, the Devil stopped, and called out something that I could not understand, three, perhaps four words in a whining, howling language that must have been old and forgotten when Babylon was young; and, although I did not understand the words, I felt the hairs raise on the back of my head as it called.

And then I heard, muffled through the glass, but still audible, a low growl, a challenge, and, slowly, unsteadily, a black figure walked down the steps of the house, away from me, toward the Devil. These days the Black Cat no longer moved like a panther, instead he stumbled and rocked, like a sailor only recently returned to land.

The Devil was a woman, now. She said something soothing and gentle to the cat, in a tongue that sounded like French, and reached out a hand to him. He sank his teeth into her arm, and her lip curled, and she spat at him.

The woman glanced up at me, then, and if I had doubted that she was the Devil before, I was certain of it now: the woman's eyes flashed red fire at me; but you can see no red through the night-vision binoculars, only shades of a green. And the Devil saw me, through the window. It saw me. I am in no doubt about that at all.

The Devil twisted and writhed, and now it was some kind of jackal, a flat-faced, huge-headed, bull-necked creature, halfway between a hyena and a dingo. There were maggots squirming in its mangy fur, and it began to walk up the steps.

The Black Cat leapt upon it, and in seconds they became a rolling, writhing

thing, moving faster than my eyes could follow.

All this in silence.

And then a low roar—down the country road at the bottom of our drive, in the distance, lumbered a late-night truck, its blazing headlights burning bright as green suns through the binoculars. I lowered them from my eyes, and saw only darkness, and the gentle yellow of headlights, and then the red of rear lights as it vanished off again into the nowhere at all.

When I raised the binoculars once more there was nothing to be seen. Only the Black Cat, on the steps, staring up into the air. I trained the binoculars up, and saw something flying away—a vulture, perhaps, or an eagle—and then it flew beyond the trees and was gone.

I went out onto the porch, and picked up the Black Cat, and stroked him, and said kind, soothing things to him. He mewled piteously when I first approached him, but, after a while, he went to sleep on my lap, and I put him into his basket, and went upstairs to my bed, to sleep myself. There was dried blood on my tee shirt and jeans, the following morning.

That was a week ago.

The thing that comes to my house does not come every night. But it comes most nights: we know it by the wounds on the cat, and the pain I can see in those leonine eyes. He has lost the use of his front left paw, and his right eye has closed for good.

I wonder what we did to deserve the Black Cat. I wonder who sent him. And, selfish and scared, I wonder how much more he has to give.

BELUTHAHATCHIE

Andy Duncan

Everybody else got off the train at Hell, but I figured, it's a free country. So I commenced to make myself a mite more comfortable. I put my feet up and leaned back against the window, laid my guitar across my chest and settled in with my hat tipped down over my eyes, almost. I didn't know what the next stop was but I knew I'd like it better than Hell.

Whoo! I never saw such a mess. All that crowd of people jammed together on the Hell platform so tight you could faint standing up. One old battle-hammed woman hollering for Jesus, most everybody else just mumbling and crying and hugging their bags and leaning into each other and waiting to be told where to go. And hot? Man, I ain't just beating my gums there. Not as hot as the Delta, but hot enough to keep old John on the train. No, sir, I told myself, no room out there for me.

Fat old conductor man pushed on down the aisle kinda slow, waiting on me to move. I decided I'd wait on that, too.

"Hey, nigger boy." He slapped my foot with a rolled-up newspaper. Felt like the Atlanta paper. "This ain't no sleeping car."

"Git up off me, man. I ain't done nothing."

"Listen at you. Who you think you are, boy? Think you run the railroad? You don't look nothing like Mr. George Pullman." The conductor tried to put his foot up on the seat and lean on his knee, but he gave up with a grunt.

I ran one finger along my guitar strings, not hard enough to make a sound but just hard enough to feel them. "I ain't got a ticket, neither," I bit off, "but it was your railroad's pleasure to bring me this far, and it's my pleasure to ride on a little further, and I don't see what cause you got to be so astorperious about it, Mr. Fat Ass."

He started puffing and blowing. "What? What?" He was teakettle hot. You'd think I'd done something. "What did you call me, boy?" He whipped out a strap, and I saw how it was, and I was ready.

"Let him alone."

Another conductor was standing outside the window across the aisle, stooping over to look in. He must have been right tall and right big too, filling up the

8

window like that. Cut off most of the light. I couldn't make out his face, but I got the notion that pieces of it was sliding around, like there wan't quite a face ready to look at yet. "The Boss will pick him up at the next stop. Let him be."

"The Boss?" Fat Ass was getting whiter all the time.

"The Boss said it would please him to greet this nigger personally."

Fat Ass wan't studying about me anymore. He slunk off, looking back big-eyed at the man outside the window. I let go my razor and let my hand creep up out of my sock, slow and easy, making like I was just shifting cause my leg was asleep.

The man outside hollered: "Board! All aboard! Next stop, Beluthahatchie!"

That old mama still a-going. "Jesus! Save us, Jesus!"

"All aboard for Beluthahatchie!"

"Jesus!"

We started rolling out.

"All aboard!"

"Sweet Je—" And her voice cut off just like that, like the squawk of a hen Meemaw would snatch for Sunday dinner. Wan't my business. I looked out the window as the scenery picked up speed. Wan't nothing to see, just fields and ditches and swaybacked mules and people stooping and picking, stooping and picking, and by and by a porch with old folks sitting on shuck-bottomed chairs looking out at all the years that ever was, and I thought I'd seen enough of all that to last me a while. Wan't any of my business at all.

When I woke up I was lying on a porch bench at another station, and hanging on one chain was a blown-down sign that said Beluthahatchie. The sign wan't swinging cause there wan't no breath of air. Not a soul else in sight neither. The tracks ran off into the fields on both ends as far as I could see, but they was all weeded up like no train been through since the Surrender. The windows over my head was boarded up like the bank back home. The planks along the porch han't been swept in years by nothing but the wind, and the dust was in whirly patterns all around.

Still lying down, I reached slowly beneath the bench, groping the air, till I heard, more than felt, my fingers pluck a note or two from the strings of my guitar. I grabbed it by the neck and sat up, pulling the guitar into my lap and hugging it, and I felt some better.

Pigeons in the eaves was a-fluttering and a-hooting all mournful-like, but I couldn't see 'em. I reckon they was pigeons. Meemaw used to say that pigeons sometimes was the souls of dead folks let out of Hell. I didn't think those folks back in Hell was flying noplace, but I did feel something was wrong, bad wrong, powerful wrong. I had the same crawly feeling as before I took that fatal swig—when Jar Head Sam, that harp-playing bastard, passed me a poisoned bottle at a Mississippi jook joint and I woke up on that one-way train.

Then a big old hound dog ambled around the corner of the station on my left, and another big old hound dog ambled around the corner of the station on my right. Each one was nearbouts as big as a calf and so fat it could hardly go, swanking along with its belly on the planks and its nose down. When the dogs snuffled up to the bench where I was sitting, their legs gave out and they flopped down, yawned, grunted, and went fast to sleep like they'd been poleaxed. I could see the fleas hopping across their big butts. I started laughing.

"Lord, the hellhounds done caught up to me now! I surely must have led them a chase, I surely must. Look how wore out they are!" I hollered and cried, I was laughing so hard. One of them broke wind real long, and that set me off again. "Here come the brimstone! Here come the sulfur! Whoo! Done took my breath. Oh, Lordy." I wiped my eyes.

Then I heard two way-off sounds, one maybe a youngun dragging a stick along a fence, and the other maybe a car motor.

"Well, shit," I said.

Away off down the tracks, I saw a little spot of glare vibrating along in the sun. The flappity racket got louder and louder. Some fool was driving his car along on the tracks, a bumpety-bump, a bumpety-bump. It was a Hudson Terraplane, right sporty, exactly like what Peola June used to percolate around town in, and the chrome on the fender and hood was shining like a conk buster's hair.

The hound dogs was sitting up now, watching the car. They was stiff and still on each side of my bench, like deacons sitting up with the dead.

When the car got nigh the platform it lurched up out of the cut, gravel spitting, gears grinding, and shut off in the yard at the end of the porch where I was sitting. Sheets of dust sailed away. The hot engine ticked. Then the driver's door opened, and out slid the devil, I knew him well. Time I saw him slip down off the seat and hitch up his pants, I knew.

He was a sunburnt, bandy-legged, pussel-gutted li'l peckerwood. He wore braces and khaki pants and a dirty white undershirt and a big derby hat that had white hair flying out all around it like it was attached to the brim, like if he'd tip his hat to the ladies his hair would come off too.

He had a bright-red possum face, with beady, dumb black eyes and a long sharp nose, and no chin at all hardly and a big goozlum in his neck that jumped up and down like he couldn't swallow his spit fast enough. He slammed the car door and scratched himself a little, up one arm and then the other, then up one leg till he got to where he liked it. He hunkered down and spit in the dust and looked all unconcerned like maybe he was waiting on a tornado to come along and blow some victuals his way, and he didn't take any more notice of me than the hound dogs had.

I wan't used to being treated such. "You keep driving on the tracks thataway, hoss," I called, "and that Terraplane gone be butt-sprung for sure."

He didn't even look my way. After a long while, he stood up and leaned on a fender and lifted one leg and looked at the bottom of his muddy clodhopper, then put it down and lifted the other and looked at it too. Then he hitched his pants again and headed across the yard toward me. He favored his right leg a little and hardly picked up his feet at all when he walked. He left ruts in the yard like a plow. When he reached the steps, he didn't so much climb 'em as stand his bantyweight self on each one and look proud, like each step was all his'n now, and then go on to claim the next one too. Once on the porch, he sat down with his shoulders against a post, took off his hat and fanned himself. His hair had a better hold on his head than I thought, what there was of it. Then he pulled out a stick and a pocketknife and commenced to whittle. But he did all these things so deliberate and thoughtful that it was almost the same as him talking, so I kept quiet and waited for the words to catch up.

"It will be a strange and disgraceful day unto this world," he finally said, "when I ask a gut-bucket nigger guitar player for advice on autoMO-bile mechanics, or for anything else except a tune now and again." He had eyes like he'd been shot twice in the face. "And furthermore, I am the Lord of Darkness and the Father of Lies, and if I want to drive my 1936 Hudson Terraplane, with its six-cylinder seventy-horsepower engine, out into the middle of some loblolly and shoot out its tires and rip up its seats and piss down its radiator hole, why, I will do it and do it again seven more times afore breakfast, and the voice that will stop me will not be yourn. You hearing me, John?"

"Ain't my business," I said. Like always, I was waiting to see how it was.

"That's right, John, it ain't your business," the devil said. "Nothing I do is any of your business, John, but everything you do is mine. I was there the night you took that fatal drink, John. I saw you fold when your gut bent double on you, and I saw the shine of your blood coming up. I saw that whore you and Jar Head was squabbling over doing business at your funeral. It was a sorry-ass death of a sorry-ass man, John, and I had a big old time with it."

The hound dogs had laid back down, so I stretched out and rested my feet on one of them. It rolled its eyes up at me like its feelings was hurt.

"I'd like to see old Jar Head one more time," I said. "If he'll be along directly, I'll wait here and meet his train."

"Jar Head's plumb out of your reach now, John," the devil said, still whittling. "I'd like to show you around your new home this afternoon. Come take a tour with me."

"I had to drive fifteen miles to get to that jook joint in the first place," I said, "and then come I don't know how far on the train to Hell and past it. I've done enough traveling for one day."

"Come with me, John."

"I thank you, but I'll just stay here."

"It would please me no end if you made my rounds with me, John." The stick he was whittling started moving in his hand. He had to grip it a little to hang on, but he just kept smiling. The stick started to bleed along the cuts, welling up black red as the blade skinned it. "I want to show off your new home place. You'd like that, wouldn't you, John?" The blood curled down his arm like a snake.

I stood up and shook my head real slow and disgusted, like I was bored by his conjuring, but I made sure to hold my guitar between us as I walked past him. I walked to the porch steps with my back to the devil, and I was headed down them two at a time when he hollered out behind, "John! Where do you think you're going?"

I said real loud, not looking back: "I done enough nothing for one day. I'm taking me a tour. If your ass has slipped between the planks and got stuck, I'll fetch a couple of mules to pull you free."

I heard him cuss and come scrambling after me with that leg a-dragging, sounding just like a scarecrow out on a stroll. I was holding my guitar closer to me all the time.

I wan't real surprised that he let those two hound dogs ride up on the front seat of the Terraplane like they was Mrs. Roosevelt, while I had to walk in the road alongside, practically in the ditch. The devil drove real slow, talking to me out the window the whole time.

"Whyn't you make me get off the train at Hell, with the rest of those sorry people?"

"Hell's about full," he said. "When I first opened for business out here, John, Hell wan't no more'n a wide spot in the road. It took a long time to get any size on it. When you stole that dime from your poor old Meemaw to buy a French post card and she caught you and flailed you across the yard, even way back then, Hell wan't no bigger'n Baltimore. But it's about near more'n I can handle now, I tell you. Now I'm filling up towns all over these parts. Ginny Gall. Diddy-Wah-Diddy. West Hell—I'd run out of ideas when I named West Hell, John."

A horsefly had got into my face and just hung there. The sun was fierce, and my clothes was sticking to me. My razor slid hot along my ankle. I kept favoring my guitar, trying to keep it out of the dust as best I could.

"Beluthahatchie, well, I'll be frank with you, John, Beluthahatchie ain't much of a place. I won't say it don't have possibilities, but right now it's mostly just that railroad station, and a crossroads, and fields. One long, hot, dirty field after another." He waved out the window at the scenery and grinned. He had yellow needly teeth. "You know your way around a field, I reckon, don't you, John?"

"I know enough to stay out of 'em."

His laugh was like a man cutting tin. "I swear you are a caution, John. It's a wonder you died so young."

We passed a right lot of folks, all of them working in the sun. Pulling tobacco. Picking cotton. Hoeing beans. Old folks scratching in gardens. Even younguns carrying buckets of water with two hands, slopping nearly all of it on the ground afore they'd gone three steps. All the people looked like they had just enough to eat to fill out the sad expression on their faces, and they all watched the devil as he drove slowly past. All those folks stared at me hard, too, and at the guitar like it was a third arm waving at 'em. I turned once to swat that blessed horsefly and saw a group of field hands standing in a knot, looking my way and pointing.

"Where all the white folks at?" I asked.

"They all up in heaven," the devil said. "You think they let niggers into heaven?" We looked at each other a long time. Then the devil laughed again. "You ain't buying that one for a minute, are you, John?"

I was thinking about Meemaw. I knew she was in heaven, if anyone was. When I was a youngun I figured she musta practically built the place, and had been paying off on it all along. But I didn't say nothing.

"No, John, it ain't that simple," the devil said. "Beluthahatchie's different for everybody, just like Hell. But you'll be seeing plenty of white folks. Overseers. Train conductors. Sheriff's deputies. If you get uppity, why, you'll see whole crowds of white folks. Just like home, John. Everything's the same. Why should it be any different?"

"'Cause you're the devil," I said. "You could make things a heap worse."

"Now, could I really, John? Could I really?"

In the next field, a big man with hands like gallon jugs and a pink splash across his face was struggling all alone with a spindly mule and a plow made out of slats. "Get on, sir," he was telling the mule. "Get on with you." He didn't even look around when the devil come chugging up alongside.

The devil gummed two fingers and whistled. "Ezekiel. Ezekiel! Come on over here, boy."

Ezekiel let go the plow and stumbled over the furrows, stepping high and clumsy in the thick, dusty earth, trying to catch up to the Terraplane and not mess up the rows too bad. The devil han't slowed down any—in fact, I believe he had speeded up some. Left to his own doin's, the mule headed across the rows, the plow jerking along sideways behind him.

"Yessir?" Ezekiel looked at me sorta curious like, and nodded his head so slight I wondered if he'd done it at all. "What you need with me, boss?"

"I wanted you to meet your new neighbor. This here's John, and you ain't gone believe this, but he used to be a big man in the jook joints in the Delta. Writing songs and playing that dimestore git fiddle."

Ezekiel looked at me and said, "Yessir, I know John's songs." And I could tell he meant more than hearing them.

"Yes, John mighta been famous and saved enough whore money to buy him a decent instrument if he hadn't up and got hisself killed. Yes, John used to be one high-rolling nigger, but you ain't so high now, are you John?"

I stared at the li'l peckerwood and spit out: "High enough to see where I'm going, Ole Massa."

I heard Ezekiel suck in his breath. The devil looked away from me real casual and back to Ezekiel, like we was chatting on a veranda someplace.

"Well, Ezekiel, this has been a nice long break for you, but I reckon you ought to get on back to work now. Looks like your mule's done got loose." He cackled and speeded up the car. Ezekiel and I both walked a few more steps and stopped. We watched the back of the Terraplane getting smaller, and then I turned to watch his face from the side. I han't seen that look on any of my people since Mississippi.

I said, "Man, why do you all take this shit?"

He wiped his forehead with his wrist and adjusted his hat. "Why do you?" he asked. "Why do you, John?" He was looking at me strange, and when he said my name it was like a one-word sentence all its own.

I shrugged. "I'm just seeing how things are. It's my first day."

"Your first day will be the same as all the others, then. That sure is the story with me. How come you called him Ole Massa just now?"

"Don't know. Just to get a rise out of him, I reckon."

Away off down the road, the Terraplane had stopped, engine still running, and the little cracker was yelling. "John! You best catch up, John. You wouldn't want me to leave you wandering in the dark, now would you?"

I started walking, not in any gracious hurry though, and Ezekiel paced me. "I asked 'cause it put me in mind of the old stories. You remember those stories, don't you? About Ole Massa and his slave by name of John? And how they played tricks on each other all the time?"

"Meemaw used to tell such when I was a youngun. What about it?"

He was trotting to keep up with me now, but I wan't even looking his way. "And there's older stories than that, even. Stories about High John the Conqueror. The one who could—"

"Get on back to your mule," I said. "I think the sun has done touched you."

"—the one who could set his people free," Ezekiel said, grabbing my shoulder and swinging me around. He stared into my face like a man looking for something he's dropped and has got to find.

"John!" the devil cried.

We stood there in the sun, me and Ezekiel, and then something went out of his eyes, and he let go and walked back across the ditch and trudged after the mule without a word.

I caught up to the Terraplane just in time for it to roll off again. I saw how it was, all right.

A ways up the road, a couple of younguns was fishing off the right side of a plank bridge, and the devil announced he would stop to see had they caught anything, and if they had, to take it for his supper. He slid out of the Terraplane, with it still running, and the dogs fell out after him, a-hoping for a snack, I reckon. When the devil got hunkered down good over there with the younguns, facing the swift-running branch, I sidled up the driver's side of the car, eased my guitar into the back seat, eased myself into the front seat, yanked the thing into gear and drove off. As I went past I saw three round O's—a youngun and the devil and a youngun again.

It was a pure pleasure to sit down, and the breeze coming through the windows felt good too. I commenced to get even more of a breeze going, on that long, straightaway road. I just could hear the devil holler back behind:

"John! Get your handkerchief-headed, free-school Negro ass back here with my auto-MO-bile! Johhhhnnn!"

"Here I come, old hoss," I said, and I jerked the wheel and slewed that car around and barreled off back toward the bridge. The younguns and the dogs was ahead of the devil in figuring things out. The younguns scrambled up a tree as quick as squirrels, and the dogs went loping into a ditch, but the devil was all preoccupied, doing a salty jump and cussing me for a dadblasted blagstagging liver-lipped stormbuzzard, jigging around right there in the middle of the bridge, and he was still cussing when I drove full tilt onto that bridge and he did not cuss any less when he jumped clean out from under his hat and he may even have stepped it up some when he went over the side. I heard a ker-plunk like a big rock chunked into a pond just as I swerved to bust the hat with a front tire and then I was off the bridge and racing back the way we'd come, and that hat mashed in the road behind me like a possum.

I knew something simply awful was going to happen, but man! I slapped the dashboard and kissed my hand and slicked it back across my hair and said aloud, "Lightly, slightly, and politely." And I meant that thing. But my next move was to whip that razor out of my sock, flip it open and lay it on the seat beside me, just in case.

I came up the road fast, and from way off I saw Ezekiel and the mule planted in the middle of his field like rocks. As they got bigger I saw both their heads had been turned my way the whole time, like they'd started looking before I even came over the hill. When I got level with them I stopped, engine running, and leaned on the horn until Ezekiel roused himself and walked over. The mule followed behind, like a yard dog, without being cussed or hauled or whipped. I must have been a sight. Ezekiel shook his head the whole way. "Oh, John," he said. "Oh, my goodness. Oh, John."

"Jump in, brother," I said. "Let Ole Massa plow this field his own damn self."

Ezekiel rubbed his hands along the chrome on the side of the car, swiping up and down and up and down. I was scared he'd burn himself. "Oh, John." He kept shaking his head. "John tricks Ole Massa again. High John the Conqueror rides the Terraplane to glory."

"Quit that, now. You worry me."

"John, those songs you wrote been keeping us going down here. Did you know that?"

"I 'preciate it."

"But lemme ask you, John. Lemme ask you something before you ride off. How come you wrote all those songs about hellhounds and the devil and such? How come you was so sure you'd be coming down here when you died?"

I fidgeted and looked in the mirror at the road behind. "Man, I don't know. Couldn't imagine nothing else. Not for me, anyway."

Ezekiel laughed once, loud, boom, like a shotgun going off.

"Don't be doing that, man. I about jumped out of my britches. Come on and let's go."

He shook his head again. "Maybe you knew you was needed down here, John. Maybe you knew we was singing, and telling stories, and waiting." He stepped back into the dirt. "This is your ride, John. But I'll make sure everybody knows what you done. I'll tell 'em that things has changed in Beluthahatchie."

He looked off down the road. "You'd best get on. Shoot—maybe you can find some jook joint and have some fun afore he catches up to you."

"Maybe so, brother, maybe so."

I han't gone two miles afore I got that bad old crawly feeling. I looked over to the passenger's side of the car and saw it was all spattered with blood, the leather and the carpet and the chrome on the door, and both those mangy hound dogs was sprawled across the front seat wallowing in it, both licking my razor like it was something good, and that's where the blood was coming from, welling up from the blade with each pass of their tongues. Time I caught sight of the dogs, they both lifted their heads and went to howling. It wan't no howl like any dog should howl. It was more like a couple of panthers in the night.

"Hush up, you dogs!" I yelled. "Hush up, I say!"

One of the dogs kept on howling, but the other looked me in the eyes and gulped air, his jowls flapping, like he was fixing to bark, but instead of barking said:

"Hush yourself, nigger."

When I looked back at the road, there wan't no road, just a big thicket of bushes and trees a-coming at me. Then came a whole lot of screeching and scraping and banging, with me holding onto the wheel just to keep from flying out of the seat, and then the car went sideways and I heard an awful bang and a crack and then I didn't know anything else. I just opened my eyes later, I don't know how much later, and found me and my guitar lying on the shore of the Lake of the Dead.

I had heard tell of that dreadful place, but I never had expected to see it for myself. Preacher Dodds whispered to us younguns once or twice about it, and said you have to work awful hard and be awful mean to get there, and once you get there, there ain't no coming back. "Don't seek it, my children, don't seek it," he'd say.

As far as I could see, all along the edges of the water, was bones and carcasses and lumps that used to be animals—mules and horses and cows and coons and even little dried-up birds scattered like hickory chips, and some things lying away off that might have been animals and might not have been, oh Lord, I didn't go to look. A couple of buzzards was strolling the edge of the water, not acting hungry nor vicious but just on a tour, I reckon. The sun was setting, but the water didn't cast no shine at all. It had a dim and scummy look, so flat and still that you'd be tempted to try to walk across it, if any human could bear seeing what lay on the other side. "Don't seek it, my children, don't seek it." I han't sought it, but now the devil had sent me there, and all I knew to do was hold my guitar close to me and watch those buzzards a-picking and a-pecking and wait for it to get dark. And Lord, what would this place be like in the dark?

But the guitar did feel good up against me thataway, like it had stored up all the songs I ever wrote or sung to comfort me in a hard time. I thought about those field hands a-pointing my way, and about Ezekiel sweating along behind his mule, and the way he grabbed aholt of my shoulder and swung me around. And I remembered the new song I had been fooling with all day in my head while I was following that li'l peckerwood in the Terraplane.

"Well, boys," I told the buzzards, "if the devil's got some powers I reckon I got some, too. I didn't expect to be playing no blues after I was dead. But I guess that's all there is to play now. 'Sides, I've played worse places."

I started humming and strumming, and then just to warm up I played "Rambling on My Mind" cause it was, and "Sweet Home Chicago" cause I figured I wouldn't see that town no more, and "Terraplane Blues" on account of that damn car. Then I sang the song I had just made up that day.

I'm down in Beluthahatchie, baby,
Way out where the trains don't run
Yes, I'm down in Beluthahatchie, baby,
Way out where the trains don't run
Who's gonna take you strolling now
Since your man he is dead and gone

My body's all laid out mama
But my soul can't get no rest
My body's all laid out mama
But my soul can't get no rest
Cause you'll be sportin with another man
Lookin for some old Mr. Second Best

Plain folks got to walk the line
But the Devil he can up and ride
Folks like us we walk the line
But the Devil he can up and ride
And I won't never have blues enough
Ooh, to keep that Devil satisfied.

When I was done it was black dark and the crickets was zinging and everything was changed.

"You can sure get around this country," I said, "Just a-sitting on your ass."

I was in a cane-back chair on the porch of a little wooden house, with bugs smacking into an oil lamp over my head. Just an old cropper place, sitting in the middle of a cotton field, but it had been spruced up some. Somebody had swept the yard clean, from what I could see of it, and on a post above the dipper was a couple of yellow flowers in a nailed-up Chase & Sanborn can.

When I looked back down at the yard, though, it wan't clean anymore. There was words written in the dirt, big and scrawly like from someone dragging his foot.

DON'T GET A BIG HEAD JOHN
I'LL BE BACK

Sitting on my name was those two fat old hound dogs. "Get on with your damn stinking talking serves," I yelled, and I shied a rock at them. It didn't go near as far as I expected, just sorta plopped down into the dirt, but the hounds yawned and got up, snuffling each other, and waddled off into the dark.

I stood up and stretched and mumbled. But something was still shifting in the yard, just past where the light was. Didn't sound like no dogs, though.

"Who that? Who that who got business with a wore-out dead man?"

Then they came up toward the porch a little closer where I could see. It was a whole mess of colored folks, men in overalls and women in aprons, granny women in bonnets pecking the ground with walking sticks, younguns with their bellies pookin out and no pants on, an old man with Coke-bottle glasses and his eyes swimming in your face nearly, and every last one of them grinning like they was touched. Why, Preacher Dodds woulda passed the plate and called it a revival. They massed up against the edge of the porch, crowding closer in and bumping up against each other, and reaching their arms out and taking hold of me, my lapels, my shoulders, my hands, my guitar, my face, the little ones aholt of my pants legs—not hauling on me or messing with me, just touching me feather light here and there like Meemaw used to touch her favorite quilt after she'd already folded it to put away. They was talking, too, mumbling and whispering and saying, "Here he is. We heard he was coming and here he is. God bless you friend, God bless you brother, God bless you son." Some of the womenfolks was crying, and there was Ezekiel, blowing his nose on a rag.

"Y'all got the wrong man," I said, directly, but they was already heading back across the yard, which was all churned up now, no words to read and no pattern neither. They was looking back at me and smiling and touching, holding hands and leaning into each other, till they was all gone and it was just me and the crickets and the cotton.

Wan't nowhere else to go, so I opened the screen door and went on in the house. There was a bed all turned down with a feather pillow, and in the middle of the checkered oilcloth on the table was a crock of molasses, a jar of buttermilk, and a plate covered with a rag. The buttermilk was cool like it had been chilling in the well, with water beaded up on the sides of the jar. Under the rag was three hoecakes and a slab of bacon.

When I was done with my supper, I latched the front door, lay down on the bed and was just about dead to the world when I heard something else out in the yard—swish, swish, swish. Out the window I saw, in the edge of the porch light, one old granny woman with a shuck broom, smoothing out the yard where the folks had been. She was sweeping it as clean as for company on a Sunday. She looked up from under her bonnet and showed me what teeth she had and waved from the wrist like a youngun, and then she backed on out of the light, swish swish swish, rubbing out her tracks as she went.

ASH CİTY STOMP
Richard Butner

She had dated Secrest for six weeks before she asked for the Big Favor. The Big Favor sounded like, "I need to get to Asheville to check out the art therapy program in their psychology grad school," but in reality she had hard drugs that needed to be transported to an old boyfriend of hers in the mountains, and the engine in her 1982 Ford Escort had caught fire on the expressway earlier that spring.

Secrest was stable, a high school geometry teacher who still went to see bands at the Mad Monk and Axis most nights of the week. They had met at the birthday party of a mutual friend who lived in Southport. She had signified her attraction to him by hurling pieces of wet cardboard at him at two a.m. as he walked (in his wingtip Doc Martens) to his fully operative and freshly waxed blue 1990 Honda Civic wagon.

The Big Favor started in Wilmington, North Carolina, where they both lived. He had packed the night before—a single duffel bag. She had a pink Samsonite train case (busted lock, $1.98 from the American Way thrift store) and two large paper grocery bags full of various items, as well as some suggestions for motels in Asheville and sights to see along the way. These suggestions were scrawled on the back of a flyer for a show they'd attended the week before. The band had been a jazz quartet from New York, led by a guy playing saxophone. She hated saxophones. Secrest had loved the show, but she'd been forced to drink to excess to make it through to the end of all the screeching and tootling, even though she'd been trying to cut back on the drinking and smoking and related activities ever since they'd started dating.

That was one of the reasons she liked him—it had been a lot easier to quit her bad habits around him. He had a calming influence. She'd actually met him several months before, when he still had those unfashionably pointy sideburns. She pegged him as a sap the minute he mentioned that he was a high school teacher. But at the Southport birthday party they had ended up conversing, and he surprised her with his interests, with the bands and books and movies he liked and disliked. Since they'd started dating she had stopped taking half-pints of Wild Turkey in her purse when she worked lunch shifts at the Second Story Restaurant.

His friends were used to hunching on the stoop outside his apartment to smoke, but she simply did without and stayed inside in the air-conditioning.

Hauling a load of drugs up to ex-boyfriend Rusty, though, was an old bad habit that paid too well to give up, at least not right away.

She compared her travel suggestions with his; he had scoured guidebooks at the local public library for information on budget motels, and he'd downloaded an online version of *North Carolina Scenic Byways*. His suggestions included several Civil War and Revolutionary War sites. Her suggestions included Rock City, which he vetoed because it turned out Rock City was in Tennessee, and the Devil's Stomping Ground, which he agreed to and did more research on at the library the next day.

"The Devil's Stomping Ground," he read from his notes, "is a perfect circle in the midst of the woods.

"According to natives, the Devil paces the circle every night, concocting his evil snares for mankind and trampling over anything growing in the circle or anything left in the circle."

"That's what the dude at the club said," she said without looking up from her sketchbook. She was sketching what looked like ornate wrought iron railings such as you'd find in New Orleans. She really did want to get into grad school in art therapy at Western Carolina.

"Of course, it's not really a historical site, but I guess it's doable," Secrest said. "It's only an hour out of our way, according to Triple A."

"So, there you go."

"This could be the beginning of something big, too—there are a lot of these Devil spots in the United States. We should probably try to hit them all at some point. After you get out of grad school, I mean."

"OK." It wasn't the first time he had alluded to their relationship as a long-term one, even though the question of love, let alone something as specific as marriage, had yet to come up directly in their conversations. She didn't know how to react when he did this, but he didn't seem deflated by her ambivalence.

That was how the trip came together. She had tried to get an interview with someone in the art therapy program at Western Carolina, but they never called back. Still, she finished putting together a portfolio.

The morning of the Big Favor, she awoke to a curiously spacious bed. He was up already. Not in the apartment. She peeked out through the blinds over the air conditioner and saw him inside the car, carefully cleaning the windshield with paper towels and glass cleaner. She put her clothes on and went down to the street. It was already a hazy, muggy day. He had cleaned the entire interior of the car, which she'd always thought of as spotless in the first place. The windshield glistened. All of the books and papers she had strewn around on the passenger floorboard, all of the empty coffee cups and wadded-up napkins that had accumulated there since she'd started dating him, all of the stains on the dashboard, all were gone.

"What are you *doing*?" she asked, truly bewildered.

"Can't go on a road trip in a dirty car," he said, smiling. He adjusted a new travel-sized box of tissues between the two front seats and stashed a few packets of antiseptic wipes in the glove compartment before crawling out of the car with the cleaning supplies. As they walked up the steps to his apartment she gazed back at the car in wonder, noting that he'd even scoured the tires. She remembered the story he'd told of trying to get a vanity plate for the car, a single zero. North Carolina DMV wouldn't allow it, for reasons as vague as any Supreme Court ruling. Neither would they allow two zeroes. He made it all the way up to five zeroes and they still wouldn't allow it. So he gave up and got the fairly random HDS-1800.

After several cups of coffee, she repacked her traincase and grocery bags four times while he sat on the stoop reading the newspaper. They left a little after nine a.m., and she could tell that he was rankled that they didn't leave before nine sharp. It always took her a long time to get ready, whether or not she was carefully taping baggies of drugs inside the underwear she had on.

Once they made it north out of Wilmington, the drive was uneventful. He kept the needle exactly on 65, even though the Honda didn't have cruise control. He stayed in the rightmost lane except when passing the occasional grandma who wasn't doing the speed limit. After he had recounted some current events he'd gleaned from the paper, they dug into the plastic case of mix tapes he had stashed under his seat. She nixed the jazz, and he vetoed the country tapes she'd brought along as too depressing, so they compromised and listened to some forties bluegrass he'd taped especially for the trip.

"You're going to be hearing a lot of this when you're in grad school in the mountains," he said.

She was bored before they even hit Burgaw, and her sketchpad was in the hatchback. She pawed the dash for the Sharpie that she'd left there, then switched to the glovebox where she found it living in parallel with a tire gauge and a McDonald's coffee stirrer. She carefully lettered WWSD on the knuckles of her left hand.

What Would Satan Do? Satan would not screw around, that's for sure. Satan would have no trouble hauling some drugs to the mountains. She flipped her hand over and stared at it, fingers down. Upside down, because the d was malformed, it looked like OSMM. Oh Such Magnificent Miracles. Ontological Secrets Mystify Millions. Other Saviors Make Mistakes.

In Newton Grove, she demanded a pee break, and she recovered her sketchpad from the hatch. Just past Raleigh, they left the interstate and found the Devil's Stomping Ground with few problems, even though there was only a single sign. She had imagined there'd be more to it, a visitor's center or something, at least a parking lot. Instead there was a metal sign that had been blasted with a shotgun more than once, and a dirt trail. He slowed the Honda and pulled off onto the grassy shoulder. Traffic was light on the state road, just the occasional overloaded pickup swooshing by on the way to Bear Creek and Bennett and further west to Whynot. He pulled his camera from the duffel bag, checked that all the car doors were locked, and led the way down the trail into the woods. It was just after noon on a cloudy day, and the air smelled thickly of pine resin. Squirrels chased each other from tree to tree, chattering and shrieking.

It was only two hundred yards to the clearing. The trees opened up onto a circle about forty feet across. The circle was covered in short, wiry grass, but as the guidebook had said, none grew along the outer edge. The clearing was ringed by a dirt path. Nothing grew there, but the path was not empty. It was strewn with litter: smashed beer bottles, cigarette butts, and shredded pages from hunting and porno magazines were all ground into the dust. These were not the strangest things on the path, though.

The strangest thing on the path was the Devil. He was marching around the path, counter-clockwise; just then he was directly across the clearing from them. They stood and waited for him to walk around to their side.

The Devil was rail-thin, wearing a too-large red union suit that had long since faded to pink. It draped over his caved-in chest in front and bagged down almost to his knees in the seat. A tattered red bath towel was tied around his neck, serving as a cape. He wore muddy red suede shoes that looked like they'd been part of a Christmas elf costume. His black hair was tousled from the wind, swooping back on the sides but sticking straight up on the top of his head. His cheeks bore the pockmarks of acne scars; above them, he wore gold Elvis Presley-style sunglasses. His downcast eyes seemed to be focusing on the black hairs sprouting from his chin and upper lip, too sparse to merit being called a goatee.

"This must be the place," she said.

The Devil approached, neither quickening nor slowing his pace. She could tell that this was unnerving Secrest a bit. Whenever he was nervous, he sniffed, and that was what he was doing. Sniffing.

"You smell something?" asked the Devil, pushing his sunglasses to the top of his head. "Fire and/or brimstone, perhaps?" The Devil held up both hands and waggled them. His fingers were covered in black grime.

Secrest just stood still, but she leaned over and smelled the Devil's hand.

"Motor oil!" she pronounced. The Devil reeked of motor oil and rancid sweat masked by cheap aftershave. "Did your car break down?"

"I don't know nothing about any car," the Devil said. "All I know about is various plots involving souls, and about trying to keep anything fresh or green or good out of this path. But speaking of cars, if you're heading west on I-40, can I catch a ride with y'all?"

"Uh, no," Secrest said, then he turned to her. "Come on, let's go. There's nothing to see here." He sniffed again.

"Nothing to see?" cried the Devil. "Look at this circle! You see how clean it is? You know how long it took me to fix this place up?"

"Actually, it's filthy," Secrest said, poking his toe at the shattered remains of a whiskey bottle, grinding the clear glass into a candy bar wrapper beneath.

The Devil paused and glanced down to either side.

"Well, you should've seen it a while back."

Secrest turned to leave, tugging gently at her sleeve. She followed but said, "C'mon, I've picked up tons of hitchhikers in my time, and I've never been messed with. Besides, there's two of us, and he's a scrawny little dude."

"A scrawny little schizophrenic."

"He's funny. Live a little, give the guy a ride. You've read *On the Road*, right?"

"Yes. *The Subterraneans* was better." Secrest hesitated, as if reconsidering, which gave the Devil time to creep up right behind them.

"Stay on the path!" the Devil said, smiling. "Forward, march!"

Secrest sighed and turned back toward the path to the car. They marched along for a few more steps, and then he suddenly reached down, picked up a handful of dirt, then spun and hurled it at the Devil.

The Devil sputtered and threw his hands up far too late to keep from getting pelted with dirt and gravel.

"Go away!" Secrest said. He looked like he was trying to shoo a particularly ferocious dog.

"What did you do that for? You've ruined my outfit."

She walked over and helped brush the dirt off. "C'mon, now you've *got* to give him a ride." The Devil looked down at her hand and saw the letters there.

"Ah, yep, what would Satan do? Satan would catch a ride with you fine folks, that's what he'd do. Much obliged."

From there back to the interstate the Devil acted as a chatty tour guide, pointing out abandoned gold mines and Indian mounds along the way. Secrest had the windows down, so the Devil had to shout over the wind blowing through the cabin of the Honda. Secrest wouldn't turn on the AC until he hit the interstate. "It's not efficient to operate the air conditioning until you're cruising at highway speeds," he had told her. That was fine with her; the wind helped to blow some of the stink off of the Devil.

A highway sign showed that they were twenty-five miles out of Winston-Salem. "Camel City coming up," the Devil said, keeping up his patter.

"Yeah, today we've rolled through Oak City, the Bull City, the Gate City, all the fabulous trucker cities of North Carolina," Secrest replied. "What's the nickname for Asheville?"

"Ash City," said the Devil.

"Fair enough," Secrest said.

They got back on the interstate near Greensboro, and Secrest rolled up all the power windows. When he punched the AC button on the dash, though, nothing happened. The little blue led failed to light. Secrest punched the button over and over, but no cool air came out. He sniffed and rolled down all of the windows again.

He took the next exit and pulled into the parking lot of a large truck stop, stopping far from the swarms of eighteen wheelers. He got out and popped the hood.

"You guys should check out the truck stop," he said. "Buy a magazine or something." In the few weeks she'd known Secrest, she'd seen him like this several times. Silent, focused, just like solving a problem in math class. She hated it when he acted this way, and stalked off to find the restroom.

When she returned, he was sitting in the driver's seat, rubbing his hands with an antiseptic wipe.

"What's the verdict?"

"Unknown. I checked the fuses, the drive belt to the compressor, the wires to the compressor… nothing looks broken. I'll have to take it to the shop when we get back to Wilmington. You don't have a nail brush in your purse, do you?"

"A what?"

"A nail brush, for cleaning under your fingernails. Never mind."

"Don't forget me," the Devil said, throwing open the back door. He had a large plastic bag in his hand. Secrest pulled back onto the road and turned down the entrance ramp. The Devil pulled out a packaged apple pie, a can of lemonade, and a copy of *Barely Legal* magazine and set them on the seat next to him. Secrest glanced back at the Devil in the rearview as he sped up to enter the stream of traffic.

"What have you got back there?"

"Pie and a drink. Want some?"

"No, I want you to put them away. You're going to get the back seat all dirty."

The Devil folded down one of the rear seats to get into the hatch compartment.

"What are you doing?" asked Secrest, staring up into the rearview. The car drifted lazily into the path of a Cadillac in the center lane until Secrest looked down from the mirror and swerved back. She turned to look at what was going on and got a faceful of baggy pink Devil butt.

The Devil didn't respond; he just continued rummaging. Finally he turned and gave a satisfied sigh. He had a roll of duct tape from Secrest's emergency kit, and he zipped off a long piece. Starting at the front of the floorboards in the back seat, he fixed the tape to the carpet, rolled it up over the transmission hump and over to the other side, carefully bisecting the cabin. A gleaming silver snake guarding the back seat of the car.

"I get to be dirty on this side," he said. "You can do whatever you want up there." Then he picked up his copy of *Barely Legal* and started thumbing through it, holding the magazine up so it covered his face.

Secrest didn't argue. She looked over at him and noticed he was preoccupied with other matters. Secrest's hands, still dirty from poking around in the engine compartment, had stained the pristine blue plastic of the steering wheel, and he rubbed at these stains as he drove along.

She could see the speedometer from her seat, and he was over the speed limit, inching up past 70 steadily. He'd also started hanging out in the middle lane, not returning immediately to the safety of the right lane after he passed someone. Traffic thinned out as the land changed from flat plains to rolling hills, but he still stayed in the middle lane. Plenty of folks drove ten miles over the speed limit. That was standard. Secrest probably attracted more attention the way he normally drove—folks were always zooming up behind him in the right lane, cursing at him because he had the gall to do the speed limit. Now he was acting more like a normal driver—breaking the speed limit, changing lanes.

The Devil sat silently on the hump in the middle of the back seat, concentrating on the road ahead. The pie wrapper and empty can rolled around on the seat next to him. She watched the speedometer inch its way up. At 75 Secrest suddenly started to pull over through the empty right lane into the emergency lane.

"What are you doing?" she asked. Then she craned her head around just in time to catch the first blips of the siren from the trooper's car. Blue lights flashed from the dash of the unmarked black sedan.

The Devil leaned forward and whispered in her ear. "Be cool, I'll handle this," he said.

"Goddamn!" she said, and this curse invoked a daydream. In her daydream, she keeps saying "Goddamn!" over and over. Secrest is busy with slowing down, putting his hazard lights on, and stopping in the emergency lane. The Devil is not in her daydream. She pops the door handle and jumps out while he's still rolling to a stop, losing her footing and scraping her knees and elbows against the pavement as she rolls to the grassy shoulder. She stands up, starts running into the trees along the side of the road. As she goes, she reaches up under her skirt and peels the Ziploc from her panties, but it's already broken open. Little white packets fly through the air in all directions. They break open too, and it's snowing as she charges off into the woods. The trooper chases her, and just as the last packet flies from her fingertips, he tackles her. She starts to cry.

Outside of her daydream, the state trooper asked Secrest for his license and registration. He retrieved these from the glove compartment, where they were stacked on top of a pile of oil change receipts and maps. The trooper carefully watched Secrest's hand, inches away from her drug-laden crotch, as he did this. She was sitting on her own hands.

"Ma'am, could you please move your hands to where I can see them?"

She slid her hands out and placed them flat on top of her thighs.

The trooper took the registration certificate and Secrest's license, but he kept glancing back and forth from them to her hands.

"Nice tattoo, isn't it, officer?" the Devil said, pointing to the smeared letters on her knuckles. The trooper slid his mirrored sunglasses a fraction and peered into the back seat of the car, staring the Devil in the eye.

"Not really. You should see the tattoos my Amy got the minute she went off to the college. I won't even get into the piercings."

"Kids these days…" said the Devil.

"Yep. What are you gonna do?" The trooper pushed his sunglasses back up on his nose and straightened up. "Well, anyway, here's your paperwork. Try to watch your speed out there, now." He smiled and handed the cards back to Secrest.

They stopped for gas near Morganton. There was a Phillips 66 there.

"The mother road," Secrest said.

"Last section decommissioned in 1984, and now all we have are these lousy gas stations," said the Devil.

"Ooh, 1984. Doubleplusungood," Secrest said.

"I'll pump," the Devil said. "Premium or regular?"

"Doubleplusregular."

Inside, Secrest got a large bottle of spring water, another packet of travel-size tissues, and breath mints. She stared at the array of snacks and the jeweled colors of the bottles of soda, trying to decide. Behind the counter, a teenage boy tuned a banjo, twanging away on the strings while fiddling with the tuning pegs.

It took her a long time to decide to forgo snacks altogether, and it took the teenager a long time to tune the banjo. She tried to think of a joke about *Deliverance*, but couldn't. Secrest went up to pay, and she headed for the door.

She went around to the side of the building to the ladies' room. The lock was busted. She sat to pee, carefully maintaining the position of the payload in her underwear. The door swung open and the Devil walked in.

"You know, I've been wanting to get into your panties ever since we met."

"Get the *hell* out of here, or I'll start screaming," she said.

"Oh, that's a funny one," the Devil said. "But I'm staying right here. You owe me."

"I don't owe you anything." She was trying to remember if she had anything sharp in her purse.

"Of course you do. Why do you think that cop didn't haul your ass out of the car? You have me to thank for that, for the fact that all that shit in your panties is intact, and for the fact that you're not rotting in one of their cages right about now."

"OK, for one thing, I don't know what you're talking about. For another, get out of here or the screaming really starts."

"What I'm talking about is all that smack you've got taped inside your underwear. The dope. *Las drogas*. I want you to give it to me, all of it, right now. That stuff is bad for you, in case you hadn't heard, and it can get you in a world of trouble."

"Screw you. You're not getting any of it. I was serious about the screaming part."

But then it didn't matter, because Secrest came in right behind the Devil. He spun the Devil around by the shoulder and kneed him in the crotch. It was the first time she'd ever seen him do anything remotely resembling violence. The Devil crumpled to the concrete floor.

"Screw you both," the Devil gasped. "I'll take the Greyhound bus anywhere I want to ride."

They checked in at the Economy Lodge in Asheville. Secrest checked the film in his camera and folded up an AAA map of downtown into his pocket and set out to see the sights.

"The historic district is a perfect square," he declared, as if he'd made a scientific discovery. "So I'd like to walk every street in the grid. I figure I'll get started to-day with the up and down and finish up tomorrow on the back and forth while you're at the university. Want to come with?"

She told him she was tired and crashed out on top of the musty comforter with all of her clothes on while the overworked air-conditioner chugged away.

She met Rusty at the Maple Leaf Bar. It had been less than two years since she'd seen him, but he had to have lost close to fifty pounds, and his hair, once a luxurious mass, was now thinning and stringy. He still got that same giddy smile when he caught sight of her, though, and he rocked back and forth with inaudible laughter. They walked back to his place on McDowell Street, where he gave her the $900 he owed her plus $600 for the drugs in her underwear. They celebrated the deal by getting high in his second floor bedroom, sitting on the end of the bed and staring out the gable window over the rooftops of old downtown as the fan whirred rhythmically overhead. After a few minutes, he collapsed onto his back, let out a long sigh, and then was silent.

She was daydreaming again. In her daydream, Secrest is out walking the maze, crisscrossing through the streets until he sees the Devil walking toward him from the opposite direction. The Devil's shoes look even filthier, and his goatee has vanished into the rest of the stubble on his face. His shirt is stained with sweat under the arms and around the collar, turning the pink to black.

"Not you again," Secrest says, kicking the nearest lamppost with the toe of his wingtip. "I was almost finished with walking every street in the historic district." He looks away, back toward the green hills of the Pisgah Forest to the south, then turns back, as if the Devil will have vanished in the interim.

"Yes, you're very good at staying on the path," the Devil says. "But now it's time for a little detour. Your girlfriend is sitting in an apartment on McDowell Street."

"Oh, really?" says Secrest.

"Yes, and the police are closing in, because an old friend of hers has ratted her out to the cops. They're probably climbing the stairs right now."

Or maybe he says, "An old friend of hers is dying on the bed next to her right now."

Anyway, the Devil reaches out and grabs Secrest's hand, shaking it energetically.

"Thanks for the ride, buddy," he says.

Then Secrest comes running up the street to save her.

TEN FOR THE DEVIL

Charles de Lint

"Are you sure you want off here?"

"Here" was in the middle of nowhere, on a dirt county road somewhere between Tyson and Highway 14. Driving along this twisty backroad, Butch Crickman's pickup hadn't passed a single house for the last mile and a half. If he kept on going, he wouldn't pass another one for at least a mile or so, except for the ruin of the old Lindy farm and that didn't count, seeing as how no one had lived there since the place burned down ten years ago.

Staley smiled. "Don't you worry yourself, Butch."

"Yeah, but—"

Opening the passenger door, she jumped down onto the dirt, then leaned back inside to grab her fiddle case.

"This is perfect," she told him. "Really."

"I don't know. Kate's not going to be happy when she finds out I didn't take you all the way home."

Staley took a deep breath of the clean night air. On her side of the road it was all Kickaha land. She could smell the raspberry bushes choking the ditches close at hand, the weeds and scrub trees out in the field, the dark, rich scent of the forest beyond it. Up above, the stars seemed so close you'd think they were leaning down to listen to her conversation with Butch. Somewhere off in the distance, she heard a long, mournful howl. Wolf. Maybe coyote.

"This *is* home," she said. Closing the door, she added through the window, "Thanks for the ride."

Butch hesitated a moment longer, then sighed and gave her a nod. Staley stepped back from the pickup. She waited until he'd turned the vehicle around and started back, waited until all she could see was the red glimmer of his taillights through a thinning cloud of dust, before she knelt down and took out her fiddle and bow. She slung the case over her shoulder by its strap so that it hung across her back. Hoisting the fiddle and bow up above her shoulders, she pushed her way through the raspberry bushes, moving slowly and patiently so that the thorns didn't snag on her denim overalls.

Once she got through the bushes, the field opened up before her, ghostly in the starlight. The weeds were waist-high, but she liked the brush of stem and long leaf against her legs, and though the mosquitoes quickly found her, they didn't bite. She and the bugs had an understanding—something she'd learned from her grandmother. Like her music.

The fiddle went up, under her chin. Tightening the frog on the bow, she pulled it across the strings and woke a sweet melody.

Butch and Kate Crickman owned the roadhouse back out on the highway where Staley sat in with the house band from time to time, easily falling into whatever style they were playing that night. Honky-tonk. Western swing. Old-timey. Bluegrass. The Crickmans treated her like an errant daughter, always worried about how she was doing, and she let them fuss over her some. But she played coy when it came to her living accommodations. They wouldn't understand. Most people didn't.

Home was an old trailer that used to belong to her grandmother. After Grandma died, Staley had gotten a few of the boys from up on the rez to move it from her parents' property on the outskirts of Tyson down here where it was hidden away in the deep woods. Strictly speaking, it was parked on Indian land, but the Kickaha didn't mind either it or her being here. They had some understanding with her grandmother that went way back—Staley didn't know the details.

So it was a couple of the Creek boys and one of their cousins who transported the trailer for her that winter, hauling it in from the road on a makeshift sled across the snowy fields, then weaving in between the older growth, flattening saplings that would spring back upright by the time spring came around again. There were no trails leading to it now except for the one narrow path Staley had walked over the years, and forget about a road. Privacy was absolute. The area was too far off the beaten track for hikers or other weekend explorers, and come hunting season anyone with an ounce of sense stayed out of the rez. Those boys were partial to keeping their deer, partridge, ducks and the like to themselves, and weren't shy about explaining the way things were to trespassers.

Round about hunting season Staley closed up the trailer and headed south herself. She only summered in the deep woods. The other half of the year she was a travelling musician, a city girl, making do with what work her music could bring her, sometimes a desert girl, if she travelled far enough south.

But tonight the city and travelling were far from her mind. She drank in the tall night sky and meandered her way through the fields, fiddling herself home with a music she only played here, when she was on her own. Grandma called it a calling-on music, said it was the fiddle sending spirit tunes back into the otherworld from which it had first come. Staley didn't know about spirit music and otherworlds; she just fancied a good tune played from the heart, and if the fiddle called up anything here, it was that. Heart music.

When she got in under the trees, the music changed some, took on an older, more resonant sound, long low notes that spoke of hemlock roots growing deep in the earth, or needled boughs cathedralling between the earth and the stars. It changed again when she got near the bottle tree, harmonizing with the soft clink of the glass bottles hanging from its branches by leather thongs. Grandma taught her about the bottle tree.

"I don't rightly know that it keeps unwelcome spirits at bay," she said, "but it surely does discourage uninvited visitors."

Up in these hills everybody knew that only witches kept a bottle tree.

A little further on Staley finally reached the meadow that held her trailer. The trailer itself was half-hidden in a tangle of vines, bookended on either side by a pair of rain barrels that caught spill off from the eaves. The grass and weeds were kept trimmed here, not quite short enough to be a lawn, but not wild like the fields along the county road.

Stepping out from under the relative darkness cast by the trees, the starlight seemed bright in contrast. Staley curtsied to the scarecrow keeping watch over her little vegetable patch, a tall, raggedy shape that sometimes seemed to dance to her music when the wind was right. She'd had it four years now, made it herself from apple boughs and old clothes. The second summer she'd noticed buds on what were supposed to be dead limbs. This spring, the boughs had actually blossomed and now bore small, tart fruit.

She stood in front of it for a long moment, tying off her tune with a complicated knot of sliding notes, and that was when she sensed the boy.

He'd made himself a nest in the underbrush that crowded close up against the north side of her clearing—a goosey, nervous presence where none should be. Staley walked over to her trailer to lay fiddle and bow on the steps, then carefully approached the boy's hiding place. She hummed under her breath, a soothing old modal tune that had first been born somewhere deeper in the hills than this clearing. When she got to the very edge of her meadow, she eased down until she was kneeling in the grass, then peered under the bush.

"Hey, there," she said. "Nobody's going to hurt you."

Only it wasn't a boy crouching there under the bushes.

She blinked at the gangly hare her gaze found. It was undernourished, one ear chewed up from a losing encounter with some predator, limbs trembling, big brown eyes wide with fear.

"Well, now," Staley said, sitting back on her haunches.

She studied the animal for a long moment before reaching carefully under the branches of the bush. The rabbit was too scared or worn out—probably both—to do much more than shake in her arms when she picked it up. Standing, she cradled the little animal against her breast.

Now what should she do with it?

It was round about then she realized that she and the rabbit weren't alone, here in the clearing. Calling-on music, she thought and looked around. Called up the rabbit, and then something else, though what, she couldn't say. All she got was the sense that it was something old. And dangerous. And it was hungry for the trembling bundle of fur and bone she held cradled in her arms.

It wasn't quite all the way here yet, hadn't quite managed to cross over the way its prey had. But it was worrying at the fabric of distance that kept it at bay.

Staley had played her fiddle tunes a thousand times, here in her meadow. What made tonight different from any other?

"You be careful with this music," Grandma had told her more than once. "What that fiddle can wake in your chest and set you to playing has lived over there behind the hills and trees forever. Some of it's safe and pretty. Some of it's old and connects a straight line between you and a million years ago. And some of it's just plain dangerous."

"How do you know the difference?" she'd asked.

Grandma could only shake her head. "You don't till you call it up. That's why you need be careful, girl."

Staley Cross is about the last person I expect to find knocking on my apartment door at six a.m. I haven't seen her since Malicorne and Jake went away—and that's maybe three, four years ago now—but she looks about the same. Straw-coloured hair cut short like a boy's, the heart-shaped face and those big green eyes. Still fancies those denim overalls, though the ones she's wearing over a white T-shirt tonight are a better fit than those she had on the last time I saw her. Her slight frame used to swim in that pair.

I see she's still got that old Army surplus knapsack hanging on her back, and her fiddlecase is standing on the floor by her feet. What's new is the raggedy-ass rabbit she's carrying around in a cloth shopping bag, but I don't see that straightaway.

"Hey, William," she says when I open the door on her, my eyes still thick with sleep. "Remember me?"

I have to smile at that. She's not easy to forget, not her nor that blue fiddle of hers.

"Let's see," I say. "Are you the one who went skinny-dipping in the mayor's pool the night he won the election, or the one who could call up blackbirds with her fiddle?"

I guess it was Malicorne who told me about that, how where ravens or crows gather, a door to the otherworld stands ajar. Told me how Staley's blue spirit fiddle can play a calling-on music. It can call up the blackbirds and open that door, and it can call us to cross over into the otherworld. Or call something back to us from over there.

"Looks like it's not just blackbirds anymore," she tells me.

That's when she opens the top of her shopping bag and shows me the rabbit she's got hidden away inside. It looks up at me with its mournful brown eyes, one ear all chewed up, ribs showing.

"Sorry-looking thing," I say.

Staley nods.

"Where'd you find it?"

"Up yonder," she says. "In the hills. I kind of called him to me, though I wasn't trying to or anything." She gives me a little smile. "'Course I don't try to call up the crows either, and they still come with no nevermind."

I nod like I understand what's going on here.

"Anyway," she goes on. "The thing is, there's a boy trapped in there, under that fur and—"

"A boy?" I have to ask.

"Well, I'm thinking he's young. All I know for sure is he's scared and wore out and he's male."

"When you say boy…?"

"I mean a human boy who's wearing the shape of a hare. Like a skinwalker." She pauses, looks over her shoulder. "Did I mention that there's something after him?"

There's something in the studied casualness of how she puts it that sends a quick chill scooting up my spine. I don't see anything out of the ordinary on the street behind her. Crowsea tenements. Parked cars. Dawn pinking the horizon. But something doesn't set right all the same.

"Maybe you better come inside," I say.

I don't have much, just a basement apartment in this Kelly Street tenement. I get it rent-free in exchange for my custodian duties on it and a couple of other buildings the landlord owns in the area. Seems I don't ever have any folding money, but I manage to get by with odd jobs and tips from the tenants when I do a little work for them. It's not much, but it's a sight better than living on the street like I was doing when Staley and I first met.

I send her on ahead of me, down the stairs and through the door into my place, and lock the door behind us. I use the term "lock" loosely. Mostly it's the idea of a lock. I mean I'm pushing the tail-end of fifty and I could easily kick it open. But I still feel a sight better with the night shut out and that flimsy lock doing its best.

"You said there's something after him?" I say once we're inside.

Staley sits down in my sorry excuse of an armchair—picked it out of the trash before the truck came one morning. It's amazing the things people will throw away, though I'll be honest, this chair's had its day. Still I figured maybe a used-up old man and a used-up old chair could find some use for each other and so far it's been holding up its end of the bargain. I pull up a kitchen chair for myself. As for the rabbit, he sticks his head out of the cloth folds of the shopping bag and then sits there on the floor looking from me to Staley, like he's following the conversation. Hell, the way Staley tells it, he probably can.

"Something," Staley says.

"What kind of something?"

She shakes her head. "I don't rightly know."

Then she tells me about the roadhouse and her friend dropping her off near home. Tells me about her walk through the fields that night and finding the rabbit hiding in the underbrush near her trailer.

"See, this calling-on's not something I do on purpose," she explains when she's taken the story so far. "But I got to thinking, if I opened some door to who knows where, well, maybe I can close it again, shut out whatever's chasing Mr.

Rabbitskin here."

I raise my eyebrows.

"Well, I've got to call him something," she says. "Anyway, so I got back to playing my fiddle, concentrating on this whole business like I've never done before. You know, being purposeful about this opening doors business."

"And?" I ask when she falls silent.

"I think I made it worse. I think I let that something right out."

"You keep saying 'you think.' Are you just going on feelings here, or did you actually see something?"

"Oh, I saw something, no question there. Don't know what it was, but it came sliding out of nowhere, like there was a door I couldn't see standing smack in the middle of the meadow and it could just step through, easy as you please. It looked like some cross between a big cat and a wolf, I guess."

"What happened to it?" I ask.

She shakes her head. "I don't know that either. It ran off into the forest. I guess maybe it was confused about how it got to be here, and maybe even where here is and all. But I don't think it's going to stay confused. I got only the one look at its eyes and what I saw there was smart, you know? Not just human smart, but college professor smart."

"And so you came here," I say.

She nods. "I didn't know what else to do. I just packed my knapsack and stuck old Mr. Rabbitskin here in a bag. Grabbed my fiddle and we lit a shuck. I kept expecting that thing to come out of the woods while we were making our way down to the highway, but it left us alone. Then, when we got to the black top, we were lucky and hitched a ride with a trucker all the way down to the city."

She falls quiet again. I nod slowly as I look from her to the rabbit.

"Now don't get me wrong," I say, "because I'm willing to help, but I can't help but wonder why you picked me to come to."

"Well," she says. "I figured rabbit-boy here's the only one can explain what's what. So first we've got to shift him back into his human skin."

"I'm no hoodoo man," I tell her.

"No, but you knew Malicorne maybe better than any of us."

"Malicorne," I say softly.

Staley's story notwithstanding, Malicorne had to be about the damnedest thing I ever ran across in this world. She used to squat in the Tombs with the rest of us, a tall horsey-faced woman with—and I swear this is true—a great big horn growing out of the centre of her forehead. You've never seen such a thing. Fact is, most people didn't, even when she was standing right smack there in front of them. There was something about that horn that made your attention slide away from it.

"I haven't seen her in a long time," I tell Staley. "Not since we saw her and Jake walk off into the night."

Through one of those doors that Staley and the crows called up. And we didn't so much see them go, as hear them, their footsteps changing into the sounds of hoofbeats that slowly faded away. Which is what Staley's getting at here, I realize. Malicorne had some kind of healing magic about her, but she was also one of those skinwalkers who change from something mostly human into something not even close.

"I just thought maybe you'd heard from her," Staley said. "Or you'd know how to get a hold of her."

I shake my head. "There's nobody you can talk to about it out there on the rez?"

She looks a little embarrassed.

"I was hoping I could avoid that," she says. "See, I'm pretty much just a guest myself, living out there where I do. It doesn't seem polite to make a mess like I've done and not clean it up on my own."

I see through what she's saying pretty quick.

"You figure they'll be pissed," I say.

"Well, wouldn't you be? What if they kicked me off the rez? I love living up there in the deep woods. What would I do if I had to leave?"

I can see her point, though I'm thinking that friends might be more forgiving than she thinks they'll be. 'Course, I don't know how close she is to the folks living up there.

I look down at the rabbit who still seems to be following the conversation like he understands what's going on. There's a nervous look in those big brown eyes of his, but something smarter than you'd expect of an animal, too. I lift my gaze back up to meet Staley's.

"I think I know someone we can talk to," I say.

The way William had talked him up, Staley expected Robert Lonnie to be about two hundred years old and, as Grandma used to describe one of those old hound dogs of hers, full of piss and vinegar. But Robert looked to be no older than twenty-one, twenty-two—a slender black man in a pin-striped suit, small-boned and handsome, with long, delicate fingers and wavy hair brushed back from his forehead. It was only when you took a look into those dark eyes of his that you got the idea he'd been a place or two ordinary folks didn't visit. They weren't so much haunted, as haunting; when he looked at you, his gaze didn't stop at the skin, but went all the way through to the spirit held in there by your bones.

They tracked him down in a small bar off Palm Street, found him sitting at a booth in the back, playing a snaky blues tune on a battered old Gibson guitar. The bar was closed and except for a bald-headed white man drying beer glasses behind the bar, he had the place to himself. He never looked up when she and William walked in, just played that guitar of his, picked it with a lazy ease that was all the more surprising since the music he pulled out of it sounded like it had to come from at least a couple of guitars. It was a soulful, hurting blues, but it filled you with hope, too.

Staley stood transfixed, listening to it, to him. She felt herself slipping away somewhere, she couldn't say where. Everything in the room gave the impression it was leaning closer to him, tables, chairs, the bottles of liquor behind the bar, listening, *feeling* that music.

When William touched her arm, she started, blinked, then followed him over to the booth.

William had described Robert Lonnie as an old hoodoo man and Staley decided that even if he didn't know a lick of the kind of mojo she was looking for, he still knew a thing or two about magic—the musical kind, that is. Lord, but he could play. Then he looked up, his gaze locking on hers. It was like a static charge, that dark gaze, sudden and unexpected in its intensity, and she almost dropped her fiddlecase on the floor. She slipped slowly into the booth, took a seat across the table from him and not a moment too soon since her legs had suddenly lost their ability to hold her upright. William had to give her a nudge before she slid further down the seat to make room for him. She hugged her fiddlecase to her chest, only dimly aware of William beside her, the rabbit in its bag on his lap.

The guitarist kept his gaze on her, humming under his breath as he brought the tune to a close. His last chord hung in the air with an almost physical presence and for a long moment everything in the bar held its breath. Then he smiled, wide and easy, and the moment was gone.

"William," he said softly. "Miss."

"This is Staley," William said.

Robert gave her considering look, then turned to William. "You're early to be hitting the bars."

"It's not like you think," William said. "I'm still going to AA."

"Good for you."

"Well," William said. "Considering it's about the only thing I've done right with my life, I figured I might as well stick with it."

"Uh-huh." Robert returned his attention to Staley. "You've got the look of one who's been to the crossroads."

"I guess," Staley said, though she had no idea what he meant.

"But you don't know who you met there, do you?"

She shook her head.

Robert nodded. "That's the way it happens, all that spooky shit. You feel the wind rising and the leaves are trembling on the trees. Next thing you know, it's all falling down on you like hail, but you don't know what it is."

"Um…" Staley looked to William for guidance.

"You've just got to tell him like you told me," William said.

But Robert was looking at the shopping bag on William's lap now.

"Who've you got in there?" he asked.

Staley cleared her throat. "We were hoping you could tell us," she said.

William lowered the cloth sides of the bag. The rabbit poked its head up, raggedy ear hanging down on one side.

Robert laughed. "Well, now," he said, gaze lifting to meet Staley's again. "Why don't you tell me this story of yours."

So Staley did, started with Butch dropping her off on the county road near her trailer late the night before and took the tale all the way through to when she got to William's apartment earlier that morning. Somewhere in the middle of it the barman brought them a round of coffee, walking away before Staley could pay him, or even get out a thanks.

"I remember that Malicorne," Robert said when she was done. "Now she was a fine woman, big horn and all. You ever see her anymore?"

William shook his head. "Not since that night she went off with Jake."

"Can you help me?" Staley asked.

Robert leaned back on his side of the booth. Those long fingers of his left hand started walking up the neck of his guitar and he picked with his right, soft, a spidery twelve-bar.

"You ever hear the story of the two magicians?" he asked.

Staley shook her head.

"Don't know what the problem was between them, but the way I heard it is they got themselves into a long-time, serious altercation, went on for years. In the end, the only way they were willing to settle it was to duke it out the way those hoodoo men do, working magic. The one'd turn himself into a 'coon, the other'd become a coonhound, chase him up some tree. That treed 'coon'd come down, 'cept now he's wearing the skin of a wildcat." Robert grinned. "Only now that coonhound, he's a hornet, starts in on stinging the cat. And this just goes on.

"One's a salmon, the other's an otter. Salmon becomes the biggest, ugliest catfish you ever saw, big enough to swallow that otter whole, but now the otter's a giant eagle, slashing at the fish with its talons. Time passes and they just keep at it, changing skins—big changes, little changes. One's a flood, the other's a drought. One's human, the other's a devil. One's night, the other's day.... .

"Damnedest thing you ever saw, like paper-scissors-rock, only hoodoo man style, you know what I'm saying? Damnedest thing."

The whole time he talked, he picked at his guitar, turned the story into a talking song with that lazy drawl of his, mesmerizing. When he fell silent, it took Staley a moment or two to realize that he'd stopped talking.

"So Mr. Rabbitskin here," she said, "and that other thing I only caught half a glimpse of—you're saying they're like those two magicians?"

"Got the smell of it to me."

"And they're only interested in hurting each other?"

"Well, now," Robert told her. "That'd be the big thought on their mind, but you've got to remember that hoodoo requires a powerful amount of nourishment, just to keep the body up to fighting strength. Those boys'll be hungry and needing to feed—and I'm guessing they won't be all that particular as to what they chow down on."

Great, Staley thought. She shot the rabbit a sour look, but it wouldn't meet her gaze.

"Mr. Rabbitskin here," she said, "won't eat a thing. I've tried carrots, greens, even bread soaked in warm milk."

Robert nodded. "That'd tempt a rabbit, right enough. Problem is, what you've got here are creatures that are living on pure energy. Hell, that's probably all they are at this point, nothing but energy gussied up into a shape that makes sense to our eyes. They won't be eating food like we do. So far as that goes, the way they'd be looking at it, we probably *are* food, considering the kind of energy we've got rolling through us."

The rabbit, docile up to now, suddenly lunged out of William's lap and went skidding across the smooth floor, heading for the back door of the bar. William started after it, but Robert just shook his head.

"You'll never catch it now," he said.

"Are you saying that rabbit was feeding on me somehow?" William asked.

"I figure he was building up to it."

Staley stared in the direction that the rabbit had gone, her heart sinking. This whole situation was getting worse by the minute.

"So these two things I called over," she said. "They're the hoodoo men from your story?"

Robert shrugged. "Oh, they're not the same pair, but it's an old story and old stories have a habit of repeating themselves."

"Who won that first duel?" William asked.

"One of 'em turned himself into a virus and got the other too sick to shape a spell in reply, but I don't know which one. Doesn't much matter anyway. By the time that happened, the one was as bad as the other. Get into that kind of a state of mind and after awhile you start to forget things like kindness, decency... the fact that other people aren't put here in this world for you to feed on."

Staley's heart sank lower.

"We've got to do something about this," she said. "I've got to do something. I'm responsible for whatever hurt they cause, feeding on people and all."

"Who says it's your fault?" Robert wanted to know.

"Well, I called them over, didn't I? Though I don't understand how I did it. I've been playing my music for going on four years now in that meadow and nothing like this has ever happened before."

Robert nodded. "Maybe this time the devil was listening and you know what he's like. He purely hates anybody who can play better than him—'specially if they aren't obliged to him in some way."

"Only person I owe anything to," Staley said, "is my Grandma and she was no devil."

"But you've been at the crossroads."

Staley was starting to understand what he meant. There was always something waiting to take advantage of you, ghosts and devils sitting there at the edge of nowhere where the road to what is and what could be cross each other, spiteful creatures just waiting for the chance to step into your life and turn it all hurtful. That was the trouble with having something like her spirit fiddle. It called things to you, but unless you paid constant attention, you forgot that it can call the bad as well as the good.

"I've been at a lot of places," she said.

"You ever played that fiddle of yours in one?"

"Not so's I knew."

"Well, you've been someplace, done something to get his attention."

"That doesn't solve the problem I've got right now."

Robert nodded. "No, we're just defining it."

"So what can I do?"

"I don't know exactly. Thing I've learned is, if you call up something bad, you've got to take up the music and play it back out again or it'll never go away. I'd start there."

"I already tried that and it only made things worse."

"Yeah, but this time you've got to jump the groove."

Staley gave him a blank look.

"You remember phonograph records?" Robert asked.

"Well, sure, though back home we mostly played tapes."

Robert started to finger his guitar again, another spidery twelve-bar blues.

"Those old phonograph records," he said. "They had a one-track groove that the needle followed from beginning to end—it's like the habits we develop, the way we look at the world, what we expect to find in it, that kind of thing. You get into a bad situation like we got here and it's time to jump the groove, get someplace new, see things different." He cut the tune short before it could resolve and abruptly switched into another key. "Change the music. What you hear, what you play. Maybe even who you are. Lets you fix things and the added bonus is it confuses the devil. Makes it hard for him to focus on you for a time."

"Jump the groove," Staley repeated slowly.

Robert nodded. "Why don't we take a turn out to where you've been living and see what we can do?"

I call in a favour from my friend Moth who owns a junkyard up in the Tombs and borrow a car to take us back up to Staley's trailer. "Take the Chevette," he tells me, pointing out an old two-door that's got more primer on it than it does original paint. "The plates are legit." Staley comes with me, fusses over Moth's junkyard dogs like they're old pals, wins Moth over with a smile and that good nature of hers, but mostly because she can run through instrumental versions of a couple of Boxcar Willie songs. After that, so far as Moth's concerned, she can do no wrong.

"This guy Robert," she says when we're driving back to the bar to pick him up. "How come he's so fixed on the devil?"

"Well," I tell her. "The way I heard it, a long time ago he met the devil at a crossroads, made a deal with him. Wanted to be the best player the world'd ever seen. 'No problem,' the devil tells him. 'Just sign here.'

"So Robert signs up. Trouble is, he already had it in him. If he hadn't been in such a hurry, with a little time and effort on his part, he would've got what he wanted and wouldn't have owed the devil a damn thing."

Staley's looking at me, a smile lifting one corner of her mouth.

"You believe that?" she says.

"Why not? I believed you when you told me there was a boy under the skin of that rabbit."

She gives me a slow nod.

"So what happened?" she asks.

"What? With Robert? Well, when he figured out he'd been duped, he paid the devil back in kind. You can't take a man's soul unless he dies, and Robert, he's figured out a way to live forever."

I watch Staley's mouth open, but then she shakes her head and leaves whatever she was going to say unsaid.

"'Course," I go on, "it helps to stay out of the devil's way, so Robert, he keeps himself a low profile."

Staley shakes her head. "Now that I can't believe. Anybody hears him play is going to remember it forever."

"Well, sure. That's why he doesn't play out."

"But—"

"I'm not saying he keeps his music to himself. You'll find him sitting in on a session from time to time, but mostly he just plays in places like that bar we found him in today. Sits in a corner during the day when the joint's half empty and makes music those drunks can't ever forget—though they're unlikely to remember exactly where it was that they heard it."

"That's so sad."

I shrug. "Maybe. But it keeps the devil at bay."

Staley's quiet for awhile, doesn't say much until we pull into the alley behind the bar.

"Do you believe in the devil?" she asks before we get out of the car.

"Everybody's got devils."

"No, I mean a real devil—like in *The Bible*."

I sit for a moment and think on that.

"I believe there's good in the world," I tell her finally, "so yeah. I guess I've got to believe there's evil, too. Don't know if it's the devil, exactly—you know, pointy horns, hooves and tail and all—but I figure that's as good a name as any other."

"You afraid of him?"

"Hell, Staley. Some days I'm afraid of everything. Why do you think I spent half my life looking for oblivion in a bottle?"

"What made you change?"

I don't even have to think about that.

"Malicorne," I tell her. "Nothing she said or did—just that she was. I guess her going away made me realize that I had a choice: I could either keep living in the bottom of a bottle, and that's not living at all. Or I could try to experience ordinary life as something filled with beauty and wonder—you know, the way she did. Make everyday something special."

Staley nods. "That's not so easy."

"Hell, no. But it's surely worth aiming for."

William drove, with Staley riding shotgun and Robert lounging in the back, playing that old Gibson of his. He worked up a song about their trip, a sleepy blues, cataloguing the sights, tying them together with walking bass lines and bottleneck solos. Staley had made this drive more times than she could count, but all those past trips were getting swallowed by this one. The soundtrack Robert was putting to it would forever be the memory she carried whenever she thought about leaving the city core and driving north up Highway 14, into the hills.

It took them a couple of hours after picking Robert up at the bar to reach that stretch of county road closest to Staley's trailer. The late afternoon sun was in the west, but still high in the summer sky when Staley had William pull the Chevette over to the side of the road and park.

"Can we just leave the car like this?" William asked.

Staley nodded. "I doubt anybody's going to mess with it sitting here on the edge of Indian land."

She got out and stretched, then held the front seat up against the dash so that Robert could climb out of the rear. He kicked at the dirt road with his shoe and smiled as a thin coat of dust settled over the shiny patent leather. Leaning on the hood of the car, he cradled his guitar against his chest and looked out across the fields, gaze tracking the slow circle of a hawk in the distance.

"Lord, but it's peaceful out here," he said. "I could listen to this quiet forever."

"I know what you mean," Staley said. "I love to travel, but there's nowhere else I could call home."

William wasn't as content. As soon as he got out of the car, a half-dozen deer-flies dive-bombed him, buzzing round and round his head. He waved them off, but all his frantic movement did was make them more frenzied.

"What's the matter with these things?" he asked.

"Stop egging them on—all it does is aggravate them."

"Yeah, right. How come they aren't in your face?"

"I've got an arrangement with them," Staley told him.

They weren't bothering Robert either. He gave the ones troubling William a baleful stare.

"'Preciate it if you'd leave him alone," he told them.

They gave a last angry buzz around William's head, then zoomed off down the road, flying like a fighter squadron in perfect formation. William followed their retreat before turning back to his companions.

"Nice to see some useful hoodoo for a change," he said.

Robert grinned. "It's all useful—depending on which side of the spell you're standing. But that wasn't hoodoo so much as politeness. Me asking, them deciding to do what I asked."

"Uh-huh."

Robert ignored him. "So where's this trailer of yours?" he asked Staley.

"Back in the woods—over yonder."

She led them through the raspberry bushes and into the field. Robert started up playing again and for the first time since they'd met, Staley got the itch to join him on her fiddle. She understood this music he was playing. It talked about the dirt and crushed stone on the county road, the sun warm on the fields, the rasp of the tall grass and weeds against their clothes as they walked in single file towards the trees. Under the hemlocks, the music became all bass and treble, roots and high boughs, the midrange set aside. But only temporarily.

When they reached the bottle tree, Staley glanced back. William gave the hanging bottles a puzzled look, but Robert nodded in apparent approval. His bottleneck slide replied to the clink of glass from the bottle tree, a slightly discordant slur of notes pulled off the middle strings of the Gibson.

The bluesman and Grandma would've got along just fine, she decided.

Once they came out from under the trees, they could walk abreast on the shorter grass. Robert broke off playing when Staley gave her scarecrow a little curtsey by way of greeting.

"How well do you know that fellow?" he asked.

Staley smiled. "About four years—ever since I put him up."

"The clothes were yours?"

She nodded.

"And you collected the wood for his limbs?"

She nodded again. "Why are you asking all these questions?"

"Because he's halfway alive."

"You mean the branches sprouting?"

"No, I mean he's got the start of an individual spirit, growing there in the straw and applewood."

Staley regarded the scarecrow in a new light. Now that it had been pointed out, she could feel the faint pulse of life in its straw breast. Sentient life, not quite fully formed, but hidden there as surely as there'd been a boy hidden in the raggedy hare she'd lost in the city.

"But, how... ?" she began, her voice trailing off.

Robert turned in a slow circle, taking in the whole of the meadow. Her trailer, the vegetable garden.

"You've played a lot of music in here," he said. "Paid a lot of attention to the rhythms of the meadow, the forest, how you and your belongings fit into it. It's got so's you've put so much hoodoo in this place I'm surprised you only ever called over those two feuding spirits."

William nodded. "Hell, even I feel something."

Staley did, too, except it was what she always felt when she was here.

"I thought it was home I was feeling," she said.

"It is," Robert said. "But you've played it up so powerful it's no wonder the devil took notice."

Staley shot a glance at her scarecrow which made Robert smile.

"Oh, he's more subtle than that," he told her. "He's going to come up at you from the backside, like pushing through a couple of feuding spirits to wreck a little havoc with the things you love." He gave her fiddlecase a considering look. "You know what you've got to do."

Staley sighed. "Jump the groove."

"That's right. Break the pattern. Don't give the devil something he can hold on to. Nothing's easier to trip a body up than habits and patterns. Why do you think the Gypsy people consider settling down to be so stressful? Only way they can rest is by travelling."

"You're saying I should go? That I've got to leave this place?"

Robert raised an eyebrow. "You a Romany girl now?"

"No."

"Then find your own groove to jump."

Staley sighed again. Intellectually, she understood what Robert was getting at. But how to put it into practice? She played the way she played because... well, that was the way she played. Especially here, in this place. She took the music from her surroundings, digging deep and deeper into the relationships between earth and sky, forest and meadow, her trailer and the garden and the tattered figure of the scarecrow watching over it all. Where was she supposed to find a music still true to all of this, but different enough to break the pattern of four summers immersed in its quiet joys and mysteries?

"I don't know if I can do it," she said.

"You can try," Robert told her.

"I suppose. But what if I call something worse over?"

"You didn't call anything over. Those spirits were sent."

Staley shook her head. "This fiddle of Grandma's plays a calling-on music—I can hear it whenever I play."

"I don't deny that," Robert said. "But you've got to put some intent into that call, and from what you've been telling me, you didn't intend to bring anything over last night."

"So when those blackbirds gather to her fiddling," William said, "it's because she's invited them?"

Robert shrugged. "Crows and ravens are a whole different circumstance. They live on the outside of where we are and they learned a long time ago how to take advantage of the things we do, making their own hoodoo with the bits and pieces we leave behind."

That made sense to Staley. She'd never deliberately called up the blackbirds, but they came all the same. Only not here. That was why she'd always thought it was safe to play whatever she wanted around the trailer. She'd see them from time to time, mostly going after her garden, or sneaking off with a bit of this or that for their nests, but they didn't gather here. The closest roost was out by the highway.

She glanced at Robert to find his gaze on her, steady but mild. She wanted to say, How do I know the devil's not being so subtle that he's persuading me through you? But they'd been talking long enough. And whatever else Robert was, she doubted he was the devil.

Kneeling on the grass, she cracked open her fiddlecase. Took out her bow, tightened the frog, rosined the hairs. Finally she picked up the blue spirit fiddle her grandmother had given her and stood up again. She ran a finger across the strings. The E was a touch flat. She gave its fine tuner a twist, and tried again. This time all four strings rang true.

"Here goes nothing," she said, bringing the fiddle up under her chin.

"Not like that," Robert told her. "Dig a little with your heart before you start in on playing. You can't jump the groove until you know where it's at."

True, she thought.

William gave her an encouraging nod, then walked over to the trailer and sat down on the steps. After a moment Robert joined him, one hand closed around the neck of his guitar, damping the strings.

Staley took a breath and let it out, slow. She held the fiddle in the crook of her arm, bow dangling from her index finger, and closed her eyes, trying to get a feel of where the meadow was today, how she fit into it. She swayed slightly where she stood. Toe on heel, she removed one shoe, then the other, digging through the blades of grass with her bare toes until she was in direct contact with the earth.

What do I hear? she thought. What do I feel?

Woodpecker hammering a dead tree limb, deeper in the woods. The smell of grass rising up from by her feet. Herbs from the garden, mint, basil, thyme. The flutter and sweet chirps of chickadees and finches. A faint breeze on her cheek. The soft helicopter approach of a hummingbird, feeding on the purple bergamot that grew along the edge of the vegetable and herb beds. The sudden chatter of a red squirrel out by the woodpile. Something crawling across her foot. An ant, maybe. Or a small beetle. The hoarse croak of a crow, off in the fields somewhere. The sun, warm on her face and arms. The fat buzz of a bee.

She knew instinctively how she could make a music of it all, catch it with notes drawn from her fiddle and send it spiralling off into the late afternoon air. That was the groove Robert kept talking about. So where did she go to jump it?

The first thing she heard was what Robert would do, bottleneck slides and bass lines, complicated chord patterns that were both melody and rhythm and sounded far simpler than they were to play. But while she could relate to what his take would be—could certainly appreciate it and even harmonize with it—that music wasn't hers. Following that route wouldn't be so much jumping her own groove as becoming someone else, being who they were, playing the music they would play.

She had to be herself, but still play with a stranger's hand. How did a person even begin to do that?

She concentrated again on what this place meant to her, distilling the input of sounds and smells and all to their essence. What, she asked herself, was the first thing she thought of when she came back here in the spring from her winter wanderings? She called up the fields in her mind's eye, the forest and her meadow, hidden away in it, and it came to her.

Green.

Buds on the trees and new growth pushing up through the browned grasses and weeds that had died off during the winter. The first shoots of crocuses and daffodils, fiddlehead ferns and trilliums growing in the forest shade.

She came here to immerse herself in a green world. Starting in April when the colour was but a vague hue brushing the landscape through to deep summer when the fields and forest ran riot with verdant growth. Come September when the meadows browned and the deciduous trees began to turn red and gold and yellow, that was when she started to pack up the trailer, put things away, ready her knapsack, feet itchy to hit the road once more.

Eyes still closed, she lifted her fiddle back up under her chin. Pulling her bow across the strings, she called up an autumn music. She put into it deer foraging in the cedars. Her scarecrow standing alone, guarding the empty vegetable and herb beds. Geese flying in formation overhead. Frosts and naked tree limbs. Milkweed pods bursting open and a thousand seeds parachuting across the fields. Brambles that stuck to the legs of your overalls.

She played music that was brown and yellow, faded colours and greys. It was still this place. It was still her. But it was a groove she didn't normally explore with her music. Certainly not here. This was her green home. A green world. But all you had to do was look under the green to see memories of the winter past. A fallen tree stretched out along the forest floor, moss-covered and rotting. A dead limb poking through the leaves of a tree, the one branch that didn't make it through the winter. The browned grass of last autumn, covered over by new growth, but not mulch yet.

And it wasn't simply memories. There were shadowings of the winter to come, too, even in this swelter of summer and green. She wasn't alone in her annual migrations south, but those that remained were already beginning their preparations. Foraging, gathering. The sunflowers were going to seed. There were fruits on the apple trees, still green and hard, but they would ripen. The berry bushes were beginning to put forth their crop. Seeds were forming, nuts hardening.

It was another world, another groove.

She played it out until she could almost feel a change in the air—a crispness, dry and bittersweet. Opening her eyes, she turned to look at the trailer. Is this what you meant? she wanted to ask Robert. But he wasn't there. She took bow from strings and stood there, silent, taking it all in.

Robert and William were gone, and so was the summer. The grass was browned underfoot. The fruit and leaves from her scarecrow's apple limbs were fallen away, the garden finished for the year.

What had she done now? Called up the autumn? Lost a few months of her life, standing here in her meadow, playing an unfamiliar music?

Or had she called herself away?

She knew nothing of the otherworld except for what people had told her about it. Grandma. Malicorne. A man named Rupert who lived in the desert, far to the south. Beyond the fact that spirits lived there who could cross over into our world, everything they had to say about the place was vague.

Right now, all she knew was that this didn't feel like her meadow so much as an echo of it. How it might appear in the otherworld.

The place where the spirit people lived and her fiddle had come from.

Grandma had told her it was a place sensible people didn't go. Rupert had warned her that while it was easy to stray over into it, it wasn't so easy to leave behind once you were there.

How could this have happened? How—

Movement startled her. She took a step back as a hare came bounding out of the woods to take refuge under her trailer. A moment later a large dog burst into the meadow, chasing it. The dog rushed the trailer, bending low and growling deep in its chest as it tried to fit itself into the narrow space. Giving a sudden yelp, it scrabbled away as a rattler came sliding out from under the trailer. The snake took a shot at the dog, but the dog had changed into a mongoose, shifting so fast Staley never saw it happen. The mongoose's teeth clamped on the rattler, but it, too, transformed, becoming a boa constrictor, fattening, lengthening, forcing the mongoose's jaws open, wrapping its growing length around the smaller mammal's body, squeezing.

Staley didn't need a lot of considering time to work out what was going on here. Maybe she'd fiddled herself over into the otherworld, but it was obvious that also she'd pulled those two hoodoo men along with her when she'd come.

"Hey, you!" she cried.

The animals froze, turned to look at her. She was a little surprised that they'd actually stopped to listen to her.

"Don't you have no *sense*?" she asked them. "What's any of this going to prove?"

She looked from one to the other, trapped by the dark malevolence in their eyes and suddenly wished she'd left well enough along. What business of hers was it if they killed each other? She'd gotten them back here where they belonged. Best thing now was that they forgot she ever existed.

For a long moment she was sure that wasn't going to happen. It was like playing in a bar when a fight broke out at the edge of the stage. The smart musician didn't get involved. She just stepped back, kept her instrument safe, and let them work it out between themselves until the bouncer showed up. Trouble was, there was no bouncer here. It was just the three of them and she didn't even have a mike stand she could hit them with.

She didn't know what she'd have done if they'd broken off their own fight and come after her. Luckily, she didn't have to find out. The mongoose became a sparrow and slipped out of the snake's grip, darting away into the forest. A half second later a hawk was in pursuit and she on her own again. At least she thought she was.

A low chuckle from behind her made her turn.

The newcomer looked like he'd just stepped down out of the hills, tall and lean, a raggedy hillbilly in jeans and a flannel shirt, cowboy boots on his feet. There were acne scars on his cheeks and he wore his dark hair slicked back in a ducktail. His eyes were the clearest blue she could ever remember seeing, filled with a curious mix of distant skies and good humour. He had one hand in his pocket, the other holding the handle of a battered, black guitar case.

"You ever see such foolishness?" he asked. "You think they'd learn, but I reckon they've been at it now for about as long as the day is wide."

Staley liked the sound of his voice. It held an easy-going lilt that reminded her of her daddy's cousins who lived up past Hazard, deep in the hills.

She laughed. "Long as the day is wide?" she asked.

"Well, you know. Start to finish, the day only holds so many hours, but you go sideways and it stretches on forever."

"I've never heard of time running sideways."

"I'm sure you must know a hundred things I've never heard of."

"I suppose."

"You new around here?" he asked.

Staley glanced back at her trailer, then returned her gaze to him.

"In a manner of speaking," she said. "I'm not entirely sure how I got here and even less sure as to how I'll get back to where I come from."

"I can show you," he told her. "But maybe you'd favour me with a tune first? Been a long time since I got to pick with a fiddler."

The thing that no one told you about the otherworld, Staley realized, is how everything took on a dreamlike quality when you were here. She knew she should be focusing on getting back to the summer meadow where Robert and William were waiting for her, but there just didn't seem to be any hurry about it.

"So what do you say?" he asked.

She shrugged. "I guess…."

I'm already feeling a little dozy from the sun and fresh air when Staley begins to play her fiddle. It doesn't sound a whole lot different from the kinds of things she usually plays, but then what do I really know about music? Don't ask me to discuss it. I either like it or I don't. But Robert seems pleased with what she's doing, nodding to himself, has a little smile starting up there in the corner of his mouth.

I can see his left hand shaping chords on the neck of his guitar, but he doesn't strum the strings. Just follows what she's doing in his head, I guess.

I look at Staley a little longer, smiling as well to see her standing there so straight-backed in her overalls, barefoot in the grass, the sun glowing golden on her short hair. After awhile I lean back against the door of the trailer again and close my eyes. I'm drifting on the music, not really thinking much of anything, when I realize the sound of the fiddle's starting to fade away.

"Shit," I hear Robert say.

I open my eyes, but before I can turn to look at him, I see Staley's gone. It's the damnedest thing. I can still hear her fiddling, only it's getting fainter and fainter like she's walking away and I can't see a sign of her anywhere. I can't imagine a person could run as fast as she'd have to to disappear like this and still keep playing that sleepy music.

When Robert stands up, I scramble to my feet as well.

"What's going on?" I ask him.

"She let it take her away."

"What do you mean? Take her away where?"

But he doesn't answer. He's looking into the woods and then I see them too. A rabbit being chased by some ugly old dog. Might be the same rabbit that ran off on us in the city, but I can't tell. It comes tearing out from under the trees, running straight across the meadow towards us, and then it just disappears.

I blink, not sure I actually saw what I just saw. But then the same thing happens to the dog. It's like it goes through some door I can't see. There one minute, gone the next.

"Well, she managed to pull them back across," Robert says. "But I don't like this. I don't like this at all."

Hearing him talk like that makes me real nervous.

"Why?" I ask him. "This is what we wanted, right? She was going to play some music to put things back the way they were. Wasn't that the plan?"

He nods. "But her going over wasn't."

"I don't get it."

Robert turns to look at me. "How's she going to get back?"

"Same way she went away—right?"

He answers with a shrug and then I get a bad feeling. It's like what happened with Malicorne and Jake, I realize. Stepped away, right out of the world, and they never came back. The only difference is, they meant to go.

"She won't know what to do," Robert says softly. "She'll be upset and maybe a little scared, and then he's going to show up, offer to show her the way back."

I don't have to ask who he's talking about.

"But she'll know better than to bargain with him," I say.

"We can hope."

"We've got to be able to do better than that," I tell him.

"I'm open to suggestions."

I look at that guitar in his hands.

"You could call her back," I say.

Robert shakes his head. "The devil, he's got himself a guitar, too."

"I don't know what that means."

"Think about it," Robert says. "Whose music is she going to know to follow?"

The stranger laid his guitar case on the grass and opened it up. The instrument he took out was an old Martin D-45 with the pearl inlaid "CD MARTIN" logo on the headstock—a classic, pre-war picker's guitar.

"Don't see many of those anymore," Staley said.

"They didn't make all that many." He smiled. "Though I'll tell you, I've never seen me a blue fiddle like you've got, not ever."

"Got it from my grandma."

"Well, she had taste. Give me an A, would you?"

Staley ran her bow across the A string of her fiddle and the stranger quickly tuned up to it.

"You ever play any contests?" he asked as he finished tuning.

He ran his pick across the strings, fingering an A minor chord. The guitar had a big, rich sound with lots of bottom end.

"I don't believe in contests," Staley said. "I think they take all the pleasure out of a music."

"Oh, I didn't mean nothing serious. More like swapping tunes, taking turns 'till one of you stumps the other player. Just for fun, like."

Staley shrugged.

"'Course to make it interesting," he added, "we could put a small wager on the outcome."

"What kind of wager would we be talking about here?"

Staley didn't know why she was even asking that, why she hadn't just shut down this idea of a contest right from the get-go. It was like something in the air was turning her head all around.

"I don't know," he said. "How about if I win, you'll give me a kiss?"

"A kiss?"

He shrugged. "And if you enjoy it, maybe you'll give me something more."

"And if I win?"

"Well, what's the one thing you'd like most in the world?"

Staley smiled. "Tell you the truth, I don't want for much of anything. I keep my expectations low—makes for a simple life."

"I'm impressed," he said. "Most people have a hankering for something they can't have. You know, money, or fame, or a true love. Maybe living forever."

"Don't see much point in living forever," Staley told him. "Come a time when everybody you care about would be long gone, but there you'd be, still trudging along on your own."

"Well, sure. But—"

"And as for money and fame, I think they're pretty much overrated. I don't really need much to be happy and I surely don't need anybody nosing in on my business."

"So what about a true love?"

"Well, now," Staley said. "Seems to me true love's something that comes to you, not something you can take or arrange."

"And if it doesn't?"

"That'd be sad, but you make do. I don't know how other folks get by, but I've got my music. I've got my friends."

The stranger regarded her with an odd, frustrated look.

"You can't tell me there's nothing you don't have a yearning for," he said. "Everybody wants for something."

"You mean for myself, or in general, like for there to be no more hurt in the world or the like?"

"For yourself," he said.

Staley shook her head. "Nothing I can't wait for it to find me in its own good time." She put her fiddle up under her chin. "So what do you want to play?"

But the stranger pulled his string strap back over his head and started to put his guitar away.

"What's the matter?" Staley asked. "We don't need some silly contest just to play a few tunes."

The stranger wouldn't look at her.

"I've kind of lost my appetite for music," he said, snapping closed the clasps on his case.

He stood up, his gaze finally meeting hers, and she saw something else in those clear blue eyes of his, a dark storm of anger, but a hurting, too. A loneliness that seemed so out of place, given his easy-going manner. A man like him, he should be friends with everyone he met, she'd thought. Except....

"I know who you are," she said.

She didn't know how she knew, but it came to her, like a gauze slipping from in front of her eyes, like she'd suddenly shucked the dreamy quality of the otherworld and could see true once more.

"You don't look nothing like what I expected," she added.

"Yeah, well, you've had your fun. Now let me be."

But something her grandmother had told her once came back to her. "I tell you," she'd said. "If I was ever to meet the devil, I'd kill him with kindness. That's the one thing old Lucifer can't stand."

Staley grinned, remembering.

"Wait a minute," she said. "Don't go off all mad."

The devil glared at her.

"Or at least let me give you that kiss before you go."

He actually backed away from her at that.

"What?" Staley asked. "Suddenly you don't fancy me anymore?"

"You put up a good front," he said. "I didn't make you for such an accomplished liar."

Staley shook her head. "I never lied to you. I really am happy with things the way they are. And anything I don't have, I don't mind waiting on."

The devil spat on the grass at her feet, turned once around, and was gone, vanishing with a small *whuft* of displaced air.

That's your best parting shot? Staley wanted to ask, but decided to leave well enough alone. She gave her surroundings a last look, then started up fiddling again, playing herself back into the green of summer where she'd left her friends.

Robert's pretty impressed when Staley just steps out of that invisible door, calm as you please. We heard the fiddling first. It sounded like it was coming from someplace on the far side of forever, but getting closer by the moment, and then there she was, standing barefoot in the grass, smiling at us. Robert's even more impressed when she tells us about how she handled the devil.

After putting her fiddle away, she boiled up some water on a Coleman stove and made us up a pot of herbal tea. We take it out through the woods in porcelain mugs, heading up to the top of the field overlooking the county road. The car's still there. The sun's going down now, putting on quite a show, and the tea's better than I thought it would be. Got mint in it, some kind of fruit.

"So how do I stop this from happening again?" Staley asks.

"Figure out what your music's all about," Robert tells her. "And take responsibility for it. Dig deep and find what's hiding behind the trees—you know, in the shadows where you can't exactly see things, you can only sense them—and always pay attention. It's up to you what you let out into the light."

"Is that what you do?"

Robert nodded. "'Course it's different for me, because we're different people. My music's about enduring. Perseverance. That's all the blues is ever about."

"What about hope?"

Robert smiled. "What do you think keeps perseverance alive?"

"Amen," I say.

After a moment, Staley smiles. We all clink our porcelain mugs together and drink a toast to that.

A REVERSAL
OF FORTUNE
Holly Black

Nikki opened the refrigerator. There was nothing in there but a couple of shriveled oranges and three gallons of tap water. She slammed it closed. Summer was supposed to be the best part of the year, but so far Nikki's summer sucked. It sucked hard. It sucked like a vacuum that got hold of the drapes.

Her pit bull, Boo, whined and scraped at the door, etching new lines into the frayed wood. Nikki clipped on his leash. She knew she should trim his nails. They frayed the nylon of his collar and gouged the door, but when she tried to cut them, he cried like a baby. Nikki figured he'd had enough pain in his life and left his nails long.

"Come on, Boo," she said as she led him out the front door of the trailer. The air outside shimmered with heat and the air conditioner chugged away in the window, dribbling water down the aluminum siding.

Lifting the lid of the rusty mailbox, Nikki pulled out a handful of circulars and bills. There, among them, she found a stale half-bagel with the words "Butter me!" written on it in gel pen and the crumbly surface stamped with half a dozen stamps. She sighed. Renee's crazy postcards had stopped making her laugh.

Boo hopped down the cement steps gingerly, paws smearing sour cherry tree pulp and staining his feet purple. He paused when he hit their tiny patch of sun-withered lawn to lick one of the hairless scars along his back.

"Come *on*. I have to get ready for work." Nikki gave his collar a sharp tug.

He yelped and she felt instantly terrible. He'd put on some weight since she'd found him, but he still was pretty easily freaked. She leaned down to pat the solid warmth of his back. His tail started going and he turned his massive face and licked her cheek.

Of course that was the moment her neighbor, Trevor, drove up in his gleaming black truck. He parked in front of his trailer and hopped out, the plastic connective tissue of a six-pack threaded between his fingers. She admired the way muscles on his back moved as he walked to the door of his place, making the raven tattoo on his shoulder ripple.

"Hey," she called, pushing Boo's wet face away and standing up. Why did

Trevor pick this moment to be around, when she was covered in dog drool, hair in tangles, wearing her brother's gi-normous t-shirt? Even the thong on one of her flip-flops had ripped out so she shuffled to keep the sole on.

The dog raised his leg and pissed on a dandelion just as Trevor turned around and gave her a negligent half-wave.

Boo rooted around for a few minutes more and then Nikki tugged him inside. She pulled on a pair of low-slung orange pants and a black t-shirt with the outline of a daschund on it. Busy thinking of Trevor, she stepped onto the asphalt of the self-service car wash—almost to the bus stop—before she realized she still wore her broken flip-flops.

Sighing, she started to wade through the streams of antifreeze-green cleanser and gobs of snowy foam bubbles. They mixed with the sour cherry spatter that fell from the trees to make the summer smell like a chemical plant of rotten fruit.

There were only a couple of people waiting on the bench, the stink of exhaust from the highway not appearing to bother them one bit. Two women with oversized glasses were chatting away, their curled hair wilting in the heat. An elderly man in a black-and-white hound's tooth suit leaned on a cane and grinned when she got closer.

Just then, Nikki's brother Doug's battered grey Honda pulled into the trailer park. He headed for the back—the best place to park even though you sometimes got a ticket. Her brother anticipated a big winning in another month and seemed to think he was already made of money.

Nikki ran over to the car and rapped on the window.

Doug jumped in his seat, then scowled when he saw her. His beard glimmered with grease as he eased himself out of the car. He was a big guy to begin with and over 400 pounds now. Nikki was just the opposite—skinny as a straw no matter what she ate.

"Can you take me to work?" she asked. "It's too hot to take the bus."

He shook his head and belched, making the air smell like a beach after the tide went out and left the mussels to bake in the sun. "I got some more training to do. Spinks is coming over to do gallon-water trials."

"Come on," she said. It sucked that he got to screw around when she had to work. "Where were you anyway?"

"Chinese buffet," he said. "Did 50 shrimp. Volume's okay, I guess. My speed blows, though. I just slow down after the first 5-8 minutes. Peeling is a bitch and those waitresses are always looking at me and giggling."

"Take me to work. You are going to puke if you eat anything else."

His eyes widened and he held up a hand, as if to ward off her words. "How many times do I have to tell you? It's a 'reversal of fortune' or a 'Roman incident.' Don't *ever* say puke. That's bad luck."

Nikki shifted her weight, the intensity of his reaction embarrassing her. "Fine. Whatever. Sorry."

He sighed. "I'll drive you, but you have to take the bus home."

She sat down in one of the cracked seats of his car, brushing off a tangle of silvery wrappers. A pack of gum sat in the grimy brake well and she pulled out a piece. "Deal."

"Good for jaw strength," Doug said.

"Good for fresh breath," she replied, rolling her eyes. "Not that you care about that."

He looked out the window. "Gurgitators get groupies, you know. Once I'm established on the competitive eating circuit, I'll be meeting tons of women."

"There's a scary thought," she said as they pulled onto the highway.

"You should try it. I'm battling the whole 'belt of fat' thing—my stomach only expands so far—but the skinny people can really pack it in. You should see this little girl that's eating big guys like me under the table."

"If you keep emptying out the fridge, I might just do it," Nikki said. "I might have to."

Nikki walked through the crowded mall, past skaters getting kicked out by rent-a-cops and listless homemakers pushing baby carriages. At the beginning of summer, when she'd first gotten the job, she had imagined that Renee would still be working at the t-shirt kiosk and Leah would be at Gotheteria and they would wave to each other across the body of the mall and go to the food court every day for lunch. She didn't expect that Renee would be on some extended road trip vacation with her parents and that Leah would ignore Nikki in front of her new, black-lipsticked friends.

If not for Boo, she would have spent the summer waiting around for the bizarre postcards Renee sent from cross-country stops. At first they were just pictures of the Liberty Bell or the Smithsonian with messages on the back about the cute guys seen at a rest stop or the number of times she'd punched her brother using the excuse of playing Padiddle—but then they started to get loonier. A museum brochure where Renee had given each of the paintings obscene thought balloons. A ripped piece of a menu with words blacked out to spell messages like "Cheese is the way." A leaf that got too mangled in the mail to read the words on it. A section of newspaper folded into a boat that said, "Do you think clams get seasick?" And, of course, the bagel.

It bothered Nikki that Renee was still funny and still having fun while Nikki felt lost. Leah had drifted away as though Renee was all that had kept the three of them together and without Renee to laugh at her jokes, Nikki couldn't seem to be funny. She couldn't even tell if she was having fun.

Kim stood behind the counter of The Sweet Tooth candy store, a long string of red licorice hanging from her mouth. She looked up when Nikki came in. "You're late."

"So?" Nikki asked.

"Boss's son's in the back," Kim said.

Kim loved anime so passionately that she convinced their boss to stock Pocky and lychee gummies and green tea and ginger candies with hard surfaces but runny, spicy insides. They'd done so well that the Boss started asking Kim's opinion on all the new orders. She acted like he'd made her manager.

Nikki liked all the candy—peanut butter taffy, lime green foil-wrapped "alien coins" with chocolate discs inside, gummy geckos and gummy sidewinders and a whole assortment of translucent gummy fruit, long strips of paper dotted with sugar dots, shining and jagged rock candy, hot-as-Hell atomic fireballs, sticks of violet candy that tasted like flowery chalk, giant multi-colored spiral lollipops, not to mention chocolate-covered malt balls, chocolate-covered blueberries and raspberries and peanuts, and even tiny packages of chocolate-covered ants.

The pay was pretty much crap, but Nikki was allowed to eat as much candy as she wanted. She picked out a coffee toffee to start with because it seemed breakfast-y.

The boss's son came out of the stock room, his sleeveless t-shirt thin enough that Nikki could see the hair that covered his back and chest through the cloth. He scowled at her. "Most girls get sick of the candy after a while," he said, in a tone that was half-grudging admiration, half-panic at the profits vanishing through her teeth.

Nikki paused in her consumption of a pile of sour gummy lizards, their hides crunchy with granules of sugar. "Sorry," she said.

That seemed to be the right answer, because he turned to Kim and told her to restock the pomegranate jellybeans.

Nikki's stomach growled and, while his back was turned, she popped another lizard into her mouth.

The glass-enclosed waiting area of the bus stop was full when Nikki finished her shift. Rain slicked her skin and plastered her hair to her face and neck. By the time the bus came, she was soaked and even more convinced that her summer was doomed.

Nikki pushed her way into one of the few remaining seats, next to an old guy that smelled like a sulfurous fart. It took her a moment to realize he was the hound's tooth suit-and-cane guy from the bus stop that morning. He'd probably been riding the bus this whole time. Still jittery from sugar, she could feel the headachy start of a post-candy crash in her immediate future. Nikki tried to ignore the heavy wetness of her clothes and to breath as shallowly as possible to avoid the old guy's stink.

The bus lurched forward. A woman chatting on her cell phone stumbled into Nikki's knee.

"'Scuse me," the woman said sharply, as though Nikki was the one that fell.

"I'm going to give you what you want," the man next to her whispered. Weirdly, his breath was like honey.

Nikki didn't reply. Nice breath or not, he was still a stinky, senile old pervert.

"I'm talking to you, girl." He touched her arm.

She turned toward him. "You're not supposed to talk to people on buses."

His cheeks wrinkled up as he smiled. "Is that so?"

"Yeah, trains too. It's a mass-transportation thing. Anything stuffed with people, you're supposed to act like you're alone."

"Is that what you want?" he asked. "You want everyone to act like you're not here?"

"Pretty much. You going to give me what I want?" Nikki asked, hoping he would shut up. She wished she could just tell freakjobs to fuck off, but she hated that hurt look that they sometimes got. It made her think of Boo. She would put up with a lot to not see that look.

He nodded. "I sure am."

The 'scuse-me woman looked in their direction, blinked, then plopped her fat ass right on Nikki's lap. Nikki yelped and the woman got up, red-faced.

"What are you doing there?" the 'scuse-me lady gasped.

The old pervert started laughing so hard that spit flew out of his mouth.

"Sitting," Nikki said. "What the hell are you doing?"

The woman turned away from Nikki, muttering to herself.

"You're very fortunate to be sitting next to me," the pervert said.

"How do you figure that?"

He laughed again, hard and long. "I gave you what you wanted. I'll give you the next thing you want too." He winked a rheumy eye. "For a price."

"Whatever," Nikki muttered.

"You know where to find me."

Mercifully, the next stop was Nikki's. She shoved the 'scuse-me woman hard as she pushed her way off the bus.

The rain had let up. Doug sat on the steps of the trailer, his hair frizzy with drizzle. He looked grim.

"What's going on?" Nikki asked. "Only managed to eat half your body weight?

"Boo's been hit," he said, voice rough. "Trevor hit your dog."

For a moment, Nikki couldn't breathe. The world seemed to speed up around her, cars streaking along the highway, the wind tossing wet leaves across the lot.

She thought about the raven tattoo on Trevor's back and wished someone would rip it off along with his skin. She wanted to tear him into a thousand pieces.

She thought about the old pervert on the bus.

I'll give you the next thing you want too.

You know where to find me.

"Where's Boo now?" Nikki asked.

"At the vet. Mom wanted me to drive you over as soon as you got home."

"Why was he outside? Who let him out?"

"Mom came home with groceries. He slipped past her."

"Is he oka—?"

Doug shook his head. "They're waiting for you before they put him down. They wanted to give you a chance to say goodbye."

She wanted to throw up or scream or cry, but when she spoke, her voice sounded so calm that it unnerved her. "Why? Isn't there anything they can do?"

"Listen, the doctor said they could operate, but it's a couple thousand dollars and you know we can't afford it." Doug's voice was soft, like he was sorry, but she wanted to hit him anyway.

Nikki looked across the lot, but the truck wasn't in front of Trevor's trailer and his windows were dark. "We could make Trevor pay."

Doug sighed. "Not going to happen."

Now she felt tears well in her eyes, but she blinked them back. She wouldn't grieve over Boo. She'd save him. "I'm not going anywhere with you."

"You have to, Nikki. Mom's waiting for you."

"Call her. Tell her I'll be there in an hour. I'm taking the bus." Nikki grabbed the sleeve of Doug's jacket, gripping it as hard as she could. "She better not do anything to Boo until I get there." Tears slid down her cheek. She ignored them, concentrating on looking as fierce as possible. "You better not either."

"Calm down. I'm not going to—" Doug said, but she was already walking away.

Nikki got on the next bus that stopped and scanned the aisles for the old pervert. A woman with two bags of groceries cradled on her lap looked up at Nikki, then abruptly turned away. A man stretched out on the long back seat shifted in his sleep, his fingers curled tightly around a bottle of beer. Three men in green coveralls conversed softly. There was no one else.

Nikki slid into her seat, wrapping her arms around her body as though she could hold in her sobs with sheer pressure. She had no idea what to do. Looking for a weird old guy that could grant wishes was pathetic. It was sad and stupid.

If there was some way to get the money, things might be different. She thought of all the stuff in the trailer that could be sold, but it didn't add up to a thousand dollars. Even sticking her hand into the till at The Sweet Tooth was unlikely to net more than a few hundred.

Outside the window, the strip malls and motels slid together in her tear-blurred vision. Nikki thought of the day she'd found Boo by the side of the road, dehydrated and bloody. With all those bite marks, she figured his owners had been fighting him against other dogs, but when he saw her he bounded up as dumb and sweet and trusting as if he'd been pampered since he was a puppy. If he died, nothing would ever be fair again.

The bus stopped in front of a churchyard, the doors opened, and the old guy got on. He wore a suit of shiny sharkskin and carried a cane with a silver greyhound instead of a knob. He still stank of rotten eggs, though. Worse than ever.

Nikki sat up straight, wiping her face with her sleeve. "Hey."

He looked over at her as though he didn't know her. "Excuse me?"

"I've been looking for you. I need your help."

Sitting down in the seat across the aisle, he unbuttoned the bottom button on his jacket. "That's magic to my ears."

"My dog." Nikki sank her fingernails into the flesh of her palm to keep herself calm. "Someone hit my dog and he's going to die…"

His face broke into a wrinkled grin. "And you want him to live. Like I've never heard that one before."

He was making fun of her, but she forced a smile. "So you'll do it."

He shook his head. "Nope."

"What do you mean? Why not?"

A long sigh escaped his lips, like he was already tired of the conversation. "Let's just say that it's not in my nature."

"What is that supposed to mean?"

He shifted the cane in his lap and she noticed that what she had thought of as a greyhound appeared to have three silver heads. He scowled at her, like a teacher when you missed an obvious answer and he knew you hadn't done the reading. "You have to give me something to get something."

"I've got forty bucks," she said, biting her lip. "I don't want to do any sex stuff."

"I am not entirely without sympathy." He shrugged his thin shoulders. "How about this—I will wager my services against something of yours. If you can beat me at any contest of your choosing, your dog will be well and you'll owe me nothing."

"Really? Any contest?" she asked.

He held out his hand. "Shake on it and we've got a deal."

His skin was warm and dry in her grip.

"So, what is it going to be?" he asked. "You play the fiddle? Or maybe you'd like to try your hand at jump rope?"

She took a long look at him. He was slender and his clothes hung on him a bit, as though he'd been bigger when he'd bought them. He didn't look like a big eater. "An eating contest," she said. "I'm wagering that I can eat more than you can."

He laughed so hard she thought for a moment he was having a seizure. "That's a new one. Fine. I'm all appetite."

His reaction made her nervous. "Wait—" she said. "You never told me what you wanted if I lost."

"Just a little thing. You won't miss it." He indicated the door of the bus with his cane. "Next stop is yours. I'll be by tomorrow. Don't worry about your dog for tonight."

She stood. "First tell me what I'm going to lose."

"You'll over-react," he said, shaking his head.

"I won't," Nikki said, but she wasn't sure what she would do. What could he want? She'd said "no sex," but he hadn't made any promises.

The old guy held out his hands in a conciliatory gesture. "Your soul."

"What? Why would you want that?"

"I'm a collector. I have to have the whole set—complete. All souls. They're going to look *spectacular* all lined up. There was a time when I was close, but then there were all these special releases and I got behind. And forget about having them mint-in-box. I have to settle for what I can get these days."

"You're joking."

"Maybe." He looked out the window, as if considering all those missing souls. "Don't worry. It's like an appendix. You won't even miss it."

Nikki walked home from the bus stop; her stomach churned as she thought over the bargain she'd made. Her soul. The devil. She had just made a bargain with the devil. Who else wanted to buy souls?

She stomped into the trailer to see her mom on the couch, eating a piece of frozen pizza. Doug sat next to her, watching a car being rebuilt on television. Both of them looked tired.

"Oh, honey," her mother said. "I'm so sorry."

Nikki sat down on the shag rug. "You didn't kill Boo, did you?"

"The vet said that we could wait until tomorrow and see how he's doing, but he wasn't very encouraging." Long fingers stroked Nikki's hair, but she refused to be soothed. "You have to think what would be best for the poor dog. You don't want him to suffer."

Nikki jumped up and stalked over to the kitchen. "I don't want him to die!"

"Go talk to your sister," their mother said. Doug pushed himself up off the couch.

"Show me how to train for an eating contest," Nikki told him, when he tried to speak. "Show me right now."

He shook his head. "You're seriously losing it."

"Yeah," she said. "But I need to win."

The next morning, after her mother left for work, Nikki called herself out sick and started straightening up the place. After all, the devil was the most famous guest she'd ever had. She'd heard of him, and what was more, she was pretty sure he knew a lot of people she'd be impressed by.

He knocked on the door of the trailer around noon. Today, he wore a red double-breasted suit with a black shirt and tie. He carried a gnarled cane in a glossy brown, like polished walnut.

Seeing her looking at it, he smiled. "Bull penis. Not too many of these."

"You dress like a pimp," Nikki said before she thought better of it.

His smile just broadened.

"So are you *a* devil or *the* devil?" Nikki held the screen door open for him.

"I'm a devil to some." He winked as he walked past her. "But I'm the devil to you."

She shuddered. Suddenly, the idea of him being the supernatural seemed entirely too real. "My brother's in the back waiting for us."

Nikki had set up on the picnic table in the common area of the trailer park. She walked onto the hot concrete and the devil followed her. Doug looked up from where he carefully counted out portions of sour gummy frogs onto paper plates. He looked like a giant, holding each tiny candy between two thick fingers.

Nikki brushed an earwig and some sour cherry splatter off a bench and sat down. "Doug's going to explain the rules."

The devil sat down across from her and leaned his cane against the table. "Good. I'm starving."

Doug stood up, wiping sweaty palms on his jeans. "This is what we're going to do. We have a bag of 166 sour gummy frogs. That's all we could get. I divided them into sixteen plates of ten and two plates of three, so you each have a maximum of 83 frogs. If you both eat the same number of frogs, whoever finishes their frogs first wins. If you have a... er... reversal of fortune, then you lose, period."

"He means if you puke," Nikki said.

Doug gave her a stern look, but didn't say anything.

"We need not be limited by your supply," said the devil. A huge tarnished silver platter appeared on the table. It scuttled over to Nikki on chicken feet and she saw that it was heaped with sugar-studded frogs.

The candy on the paper plates looked dull in comparison with what glimmered on the table. Nikki picked up an orange-and-black colored candy poison dart frog and put it regretfully down. It just seemed dumb to let the devil supply food. "You have to use ours."

The devil shrugged. With a wave of his hand, the dish of frogs disappeared, leaving nothing behind but a burnt-sugar smell. "Very well."

Doug put a plastic pitcher of water and two glasses between them. "Okay," he said, lifting up a stopwatch. "Go!"

Nikki started eating. The salty sweet flavor flooded her mouth as she crammed in candy.

Across the table, the devil lifted up his first paper plate, rolling it up and using the tube to pour frogs into a mouth that seemed to expand. His jaw unhinged like a snake. He picked up a second plate.

Nikki swallowed frog after frog, sugar scraping her throat, racing to catch up.

Doug slid a new pile in front of Nikki and she started eating. She was in the zone. One frog, then another, then a sip of water. The cloying sweetness scraped her throat raw, but she kept eating.

The devil poured a third plate of candy down his throat, then a fourth. At the seventh plate, the devil paused with a groan. He untucked his shirt and undid the button on his dress pants to pat his engorged belly. He looked full.

Nikki stuffed candy in her mouth, suddenly filled with hope.

The devil chuckled and unsheathed a knife from the top of his cane.

"What are you doing?" Doug shouted.

"Just making room," the devil said. Pressing the blade to his belly, he slit a line in his stomach. Dozens upon dozens of gooey half-chewed frogs tumbled into the dirt.

Nikki stared at him, paralyzed with dread. Her fingers still held a frog, but she didn't bring it to her lips. She had no hope of winning.

Doug looked away from the mess of partially digested candy. "That's cheating!"

The devil tipped up the seventh plate into his widening mouth and swallowed ten frogs at once. "Nothing in the rules against it."

Nikki wondered what it would be like to have no soul. Would she barely miss it? Could she still dream? Without one, would she have no more guilt or fear or fun? Maybe without a soul she wouldn't even care that Boo was dead.

The devil cheated. If she wanted to win, she had to cheat too.

On her sixth plate, Nikki started sweating, but she knew she could finish. She just couldn't finish before he did.

She had to beat him in quantity. She had to eat more sour gummy frogs than he did.

"I feel sick," Nikki said.

"Don't *you know*." Doug shook his head vigorously. "Fight it."

Nikki bent over, holding her stomach. While hidden by the table, she picked up one of the slimy, chewed-up frogs that had been in the devil's stomach and popped it in her mouth. The frog tasted like sweetness and dirt and something rotten.

The nausea was real this time. She choked and forced herself to swallow around the sour taste of her own gorge.

Sitting up, she saw that the devil had finished all his frogs. She still had two more plates to go.

"I win," the devil said. "No need to keep eating."

Doug sunk fingers into his hair and tugged. "He's right."

"No way." Nikki gulped down another mouthful of candy. "I'm finishing my plates."

She ate and ate, ignoring how the rubbery frogs stuck in her throat. She kept eating. Swallowing the last sour gummy frog, she stood up. "Are you finished?"

"I've been finished for ages," said the devil.

"Then *I* win."

The devil yawned. "Impossible."

"I ate one more frog than you did," she said. "So I win."

He pointed his cane at Doug. "If you cheated and gave her another frog, we'll be doing this contest over and you'll be joining us."

Doug shook his head. "It took me an hour to count out those frogs. They were exactly even."

"I ate one of the frogs from your gut," Nikki said. "I picked it up off the ground and I ate it."

"That's disgusting!" Doug said.

"Five second rule," Nikki said. "If it's in the devil for less than five seconds, it's still good."

"That's *cheating*," said the devil. He sounded half-admiring and half-appalled, reminding her of her boss's son at The Sweet Tooth.

She shook her head. "Nothing in the rules against it."

The devil scowled for a moment, then bowed shallowly. "Well done, Nicole. Count on seeing me again soon." With those words, he ambled toward the bus station. He paused in front of Trevor's trailer, pulled out a handful of envelopes from the mailbox, and kept going.

Nikki's mother's car pulled into the lot, Boo's head visible in the passenger side window. His tongue lolled despite the absurd cone-shaped collar around his neck.

Nikki hopped up on top of the picnic table and shrieked with joy, leaping around, the sugar and adrenaline and relief making her giddy.

She stopped jumping. "You know what?"

He looked up at her. "What?"

"I think my summer is starting not to suck so much."

Doug sat down on a bench so hard that she heard the wood strain. The look he gave her was pure disbelief.

"So," Nikki asked, "you want to get some lunch?"

YOUNG GOODMAN BROWN

Nathaniel Hawthorne

Young Goodman Brown came forth at sunset into the street at Salem village; but put his head back, after crossing the threshold, to exchange a parting kiss with his young wife. And Faith, as the wife was aptly named, thrust her own pretty head into the street, letting the wind play with the pink ribbons of her cap while she called to Goodman Brown.

"Dearest heart," whispered she, softly and rather sadly, when her lips were close to his ear, "prithee put off your journey until sunrise and sleep in your own bed to-night. A lone woman is troubled with such dreams and such thoughts that she's afeard of herself sometimes. Pray tarry with me this night, dear husband, of all nights in the year."

"My love and my Faith," replied young Goodman Brown, "of all nights in the year, this one night must I tarry away from thee. My journey, as thou callest it, forth and back again, must needs be done 'twixt now and sunrise. What, my sweet, pretty wife, dost thou doubt me already, and we but three months married?"

"Then God bless you!" said Faith, with the pink ribbons; "and may you find all well when you come back."

"Amen!" cried Goodman Brown. "Say thy prayers, dear Faith, and go to bed at dusk, and no harm will come to thee."

So they parted; and the young man pursued his way until, being about to turn the corner by the meeting-house, he looked back and saw the head of Faith still peeping after him with a melancholy air, in spite of her pink ribbons.

"Poor little Faith!" thought he, for his heart smote him. "What a wretch am I to leave her on such an errand! She talks of dreams, too. Methought as she spoke there was trouble in her face, as if a dream had warned her what work is to be done tonight. But no, no; 't would kill her to think it. Well, she's a blessed angel on earth; and after this one night I'll cling to her skirts and follow her to heaven."

With this excellent resolve for the future, Goodman Brown felt himself justified in making more haste on his present evil purpose. He had taken a dreary road, darkened by all the gloomiest trees of the forest, which barely stood aside to let the narrow path creep through, and closed immediately behind. It was all as lonely as could be; and there is this peculiarity in such a solitude, that the traveller knows not who may be concealed by the innumerable trunks and the thick boughs overhead; so that with lonely footsteps he may yet be passing through an unseen multitude.

"There may be a devilish Indian behind every tree," said Goodman Brown to himself; and he glanced fearfully behind him as he added, "What if the devil himself should be at my very elbow!"

His head being turned back, he passed a crook of the road, and, looking forward again, beheld the figure of a man, in grave and decent attire, seated at the foot of an old tree. He arose at Goodman Brown's approach and walked onward side by side with him.

"You are late, Goodman Brown," said he. "The clock of the Old South was striking as I came through Boston, and that is full fifteen minutes agone."

"Faith kept me back a while," replied the young man, with a tremor in his voice, caused by the sudden appearance of his companion, though not wholly unexpected.

It was now deep dusk in the forest, and deepest in that part of it where these two were journeying. As nearly as could be discerned, the second traveller was about fifty years old, apparently in the same rank of life as Goodman Brown, and bearing a considerable resemblance to him, though perhaps more in expression than features. Still they might have been taken for father and son. And yet, though the elder person was as simply clad as the younger, and as simple in manner too, he had an indescribable air of one who knew the world, and who would not have felt abashed at the governor's dinner table or in King William's court, were it possible that his affairs should call him thither. But the only thing about him that could be fixed upon as remarkable was his staff, which bore the likeness of a great black snake, so curiously wrought that it might almost be seen to twist and wriggle itself like a living serpent. This, of course, must have been an ocular deception, assisted by the uncertain light.

"Come, Goodman Brown," cried his fellow-traveller, "this is a dull pace for the beginning of a journey. Take my staff, if you are so soon weary."

"Friend," said the other, exchanging his slow pace for a full stop, "having kept covenant by meeting thee here, it is my purpose now to return whence I came. I have scruples touching the matter thou wot'st of."

"Sayest thou so?" replied he of the serpent, smiling apart. "Let us walk on, nevertheless, reasoning as we go; and if I convince thee not thou shalt turn back. We are but a little way in the forest yet."

"Too far, too far!" exclaimed the goodman, unconsciously resuming his walk. "My father never went into the woods on such an errand, nor his father before him. We have been a race of honest men and good Christians since the days of the martyrs; and shall I be the first of the name of Brown that ever took this path and kept—"

"Such company, thou wouldst say," observed the elder person, interpreting his pause. "Well said, Goodman Brown! I have been as well acquainted with your family as with ever a one among the Puritans; and that's no trifle to say. I helped your grandfather, the constable, when he lashed the Quaker woman so smartly through the streets of Salem; and it was I that brought your father a pitch-pine knot, kindled at my own hearth, to set fire to an Indian village, in King Philip's war. They were my good friends, both; and many a pleasant walk have we had along this path, and returned merrily after midnight. I would fain be friends with you for their sake."

"If it be as thou sayest," replied Goodman Brown, "I marvel they never spoke of these matters; or, verily, I marvel not, seeing that the least rumor of the sort would have driven them from New England. We are a people of prayer, and good works to boot, and abide no such wickedness."

"Wickedness or not," said the traveller with the twisted staff, "I have a very general acquaintance here in New England. The deacons of many a church have drunk the communion wine with me; the selectmen of divers towns make me their chairman; and a majority of the Great and General Court are firm support- ers of my interest. The governor and I, too—But these are state secrets."

"Can this be so?" cried Goodman Brown, with a stare of amazement at his undisturbed companion. "Howbeit, I have nothing to do with the governor and council; they have their own ways, and are no rule for a simple husbandman like me. But, were I to go on with thee, how should I meet the eye of that good old man, our minister, at Salem village? Oh, his voice would make me tremble both Sabbath day and lecture day."

Thus far the elder traveller had listened with due gravity; but now burst into a fit of irrepressible mirth, shaking himself so violently that his snake-like staff actually seemed to wriggle in sympathy.

"Ha! ha! ha!" shouted he again and again; then composing himself, "Well, go on, Goodman Brown, go on; but, prithee, don't kill me with laughing."

"Well, then, to end the matter at once," said Goodman Brown, considerably nettled, "there is my wife, Faith. It would break her dear little heart; and I'd rather break my own."

"Nay, if that be the case," answered the other, "e'en go thy ways, Goodman Brown. I would not for twenty old women like the one hobbling before us that Faith should come to any harm."

As he spoke he pointed his staff at a female figure on the path, in whom Good- man Brown recognized a very pious and exemplary dame, who had taught him his catechism in youth, and was still his moral and spiritual adviser, jointly with the minister and Deacon Gookin.

"A marvel, truly, that Goody Cloyse should be so far in the wilderness at nightfall," said he. "But with your leave, friend, I shall take a cut through the woods until we have left this Christian woman behind. Being a stranger to you, she might ask whom I was consorting with and whither I was going."

"Be it so," said his fellow-traveller. "Betake you to the woods, and let me keep the path."

Accordingly the young man turned aside, but took care to watch his com- panion, who advanced softly along the road until he had come within a staff's length of the old dame. She, meanwhile, was making the best of her way, with singular speed for so aged a woman, and mumbling some indistinct words—a prayer, doubtless—as she went. The traveller put forth his staff and touched her withered neck with what seemed the serpent's tail.

"The devil!" screamed the pious old lady.

"Then Goody Cloyse knows her old friend?" observed the traveller, confronting her and leaning on his writhing stick.

"Ah, forsooth, and is it your worship indeed?" cried the good dame. "Yea, truly is it, and in the very image of my old gossip, Goodman Brown, the grandfather of the silly fellow that now is. But—would your worship believe it?—my broomstick hath strangely disappeared, stolen, as I suspect, by that unhanged witch, Goody Cory, and that, too, when I was all anointed with the juice of smallage, and cinquefoil, and wolf's bane—"

"Mingled with fine wheat and the fat of a new-born babe," said the shape of old Goodman Brown.

"Ah, your worship knows the recipe," cried the old lady, cackling aloud. "So, as I was saying, being all ready for the meeting, and no horse to ride on, I made up my mind to foot it; for they tell me there is a nice young man to be taken into communion to-night. But now your good worship will lend me your arm, and we shall be there in a twinkling."

"That can hardly be," answered her friend. "I may not spare you my arm, Goody Cloyse; but here is my staff, if you will."

So saying, he threw it down at her feet, where, perhaps, it assumed life, being one of the rods which its owner had formerly lent to the Egyptian magi. Of this fact, however, Goodman Brown could not take cognizance. He had cast up his eyes in astonishment, and, looking down again, beheld neither Goody Cloyse nor the serpentine staff, but his fellow-traveller alone, who waited for him as calmly as if nothing had happened.

"That old woman taught me my catechism," said the young man; and there was a world of meaning in this simple comment.

They continued to walk onward, while the elder traveller exhorted his companion to make good speed and persevere in the path, discoursing so aptly that his arguments seemed rather to spring up in the bosom of his auditor than to be suggested by himself. As they went, he plucked a branch of maple to serve for a walking stick, and began to strip it of the twigs and little boughs, which were wet with evening dew. The moment his fingers touched them they became strangely withered and dried up as with a week's sunshine. Thus the pair proceeded, at a good free pace, until suddenly, in a gloomy hollow of the road, Goodman Brown sat himself down on the stump of a tree and refused to go any farther.

"Friend," said he, stubbornly, "my mind is made up. Not another step will I budge on this errand. What if a wretched old woman did choose to go to the devil when I thought she was going to heaven: is that any reason why I should quit my dear Faith and go after her?"

"You will think better of this by and by," said his acquaintance, composedly. "Sit here and rest yourself a while; and when you feel like moving again, there is my staff to help you along."

Without more words, he threw his companion the maple stick, and was as speedily out of sight as if he had vanished into the deepening gloom. The young man sat a few moments by the roadside, applauding himself greatly, and thinking with how clear a conscience he should meet the minister in his morning walk, nor shrink from the eye of good old Deacon Gookin. And what calm sleep would be his that very night, which was to have been spent so wickedly, but so purely and sweetly now, in the arms of Faith! Amidst these pleasant and praiseworthy meditations, Goodman Brown heard the tramp of horses along the road, and deemed it advisable to conceal himself within the verge of the forest, conscious of the guilty purpose that had brought him thither, though now so happily turned from it.

On came the hoof tramps and the voices of the riders, two grave old voices, conversing soberly as they drew near. These mingled sounds appeared to pass along the road, within a few yards of the young man's hiding-place; but, owing doubtless to the depth of the gloom at that particular spot, neither the travellers nor their steeds were visible. Though their figures brushed the small boughs by the wayside, it could not be seen that they intercepted, even for a moment, the faint gleam from the strip of bright sky athwart which they must have passed. Goodman Brown alternately crouched and stood on tiptoe, pulling aside the branches and thrusting forth his head as far as he durst without discerning so much as a shadow. It vexed him the more, because he could have sworn, were such a thing possible, that he recognized the voices of the minister and Deacon Gookin, jogging along quietly, as they were wont to do, when bound to some ordination or ecclesiastical council. While yet within hearing, one of the riders stopped to pluck a switch.

"Of the two, reverend Sir," said the voice like the deacon's, "I had rather miss an ordination dinner than to-night's meeting. They tell me that some of our community are to be here from Falmouth and beyond, and others from Connecticut and Rhode Island, besides several of the Indian powwows, who, after their fashion, know almost as much deviltry as the best of us. Moreover, there is a goodly young woman to be taken into communion."

"Mighty well, Deacon Gookin!" replied the solemn old tones of the minister. "Spur up, or we shall be late. Nothing can be done, you know, until I get on the ground."

The hoofs clattered again; and the voices, talking so strangely in the empty air, passed on through the forest, where no church had ever been gathered or solitary Christian prayed. Whither, then, could these holy men be journeying so deep into the heathen wilderness? Young Goodman Brown caught hold of a tree for support, being ready to sink down on the ground, faint and overburdened with the heavy sickness of his heart. He looked up to the sky, doubting whether there really was a heaven above him. Yet there was the blue arch, and the stars brightening in it.

"With heaven above and Faith below, I will yet stand firm against the devil!"

cried Goodman Brown.

While he still gazed upward into the deep arch of the firmament and had lifted his hands to pray, a cloud, though no wind was stirring, hurried across the zenith and hid the brightening stars. The blue sky was still visible, except directly over-head, where this black mass of cloud was sweeping swiftly northward. Aloft in the air, as if from the depths of the cloud, came a confused and doubtful sound of voices. Once the listener fancied that he could distinguish the accents of towns-people of his own, men and women, both pious and ungodly, many of whom he had met at the communion table, and had seen others rioting at the tavern. The next moment, so indistinct were the sounds, he doubted whether he had heard aught but the murmur of the old forest, whispering without a wind. Then came a stronger swell of those familiar tones, heard daily in the sunshine at Salem vil-lage, but never until now from a cloud of night. There was one voice of a young woman, uttering lamentations, yet with an uncertain sorrow, and entreating for some favor, which, perhaps, it would grieve her to obtain; and all the unseen multitude, both saints and sinners, seemed to encourage her onward.

"Faith!" shouted Goodman Brown, in a voice of agony and desperation; and the echoes of the forest mocked him, crying, "Faith! Faith!" as if bewildered wretches were seeking her all through the wilderness.

The cry of grief, rage, and terror was yet piercing the night, when the unhappy husband held his breath for a response. There was a scream, drowned imme-diately in a louder murmur of voices, fading into far-off laughter, as the dark cloud swept away, leaving the clear and silent sky above Goodman Brown. But something fluttered lightly down through the air and caught on the branch of a tree. The young man seized it, and beheld a pink ribbon.

"My Faith is gone!" cried he, after one stupefied moment. "There is no good on earth; and sin is but a name. Come, devil; for to thee is this world given."

And, maddened with despair, so that he laughed loud and long, did Goodman Brown grasp his staff and set forth again, at such a rate that he seemed to fly along the forest path rather than to walk or run. The road grew wilder and drearier and more faintly traced, and vanished at length, leaving him in the heart of the dark wilderness, still rushing onward with the instinct that guides mortal man to evil. The whole forest was peopled with frightful sounds—the creaking of the trees, the howling of wild beasts, and the yell of Indians; while sometimes the wind tolled like a distant church bell, and sometimes gave a broad roar around the traveller, as if all Nature were laughing him to scorn. But he was himself the chief horror of the scene, and shrank not from its other horrors.

"Ha! ha! ha!" roared Goodman Brown when the wind laughed at him.

"Let us hear which will laugh loudest. Think not to frighten me with your deviltry. Come witch, come wizard, come Indian powwow, come devil himself, and here comes Goodman Brown. You may as well fear him as he fear you."

In truth, all through the haunted forest there could be nothing more fright-ful than the figure of Goodman Brown. On he flew among the black pines, brandishing his staff with frenzied gestures, now giving vent to an inspiration of horrid blasphemy, and now shouting forth such laughter as set all the echoes of the forest laughing like demons around him. The fiend in his own shape is less hideous than when he rages in the breast of man. Thus sped the demoniac on his course, until, quivering among the trees, he saw a red light before him, as when the felled trunks and branches of a clearing have been set on fire, and throw up their lurid blaze against the sky, at the hour of midnight. He paused, in a lull of the tempest that had driven him onward, and heard the swell of what seemed a hymn, rolling solemnly from a distance with the weight of many voices. He knew the tune; it was a familiar one in the choir of the village meeting-house. The verse died heavily away, and was lengthened by a chorus, not of human voices, but of all the sounds of the benighted wilderness pealing in awful harmony together. Goodman Brown cried out, and his cry was lost to his own ear by its unison with the cry of the desert.

In the interval of silence he stole forward until the light glared full upon his eyes. At one extremity of an open space, hemmed in by the dark wall of the forest, arose a rock, bearing some rude, natural resemblance either to an alter or a pulpit, and surrounded by four blazing pines, their tops aflame, their stems untouched, like candles at an evening meeting. The mass of foliage that had overgrown the summit of the rock was all on fire, blazing high into the night and fitfully illuminating the whole field. Each pendent twig and leafy festoon was in a blaze. As the red light arose and fell, a numerous congregation alternately shone forth, then disappeared in shadow, and again grew, as it were, out of the darkness, peopling the heart of the solitary woods at once.

"A grave and dark-clad company," quoth Goodman Brown.

In truth they were such. Among them, quivering to and fro between gloom and splendor, appeared faces that would be seen next day at the council board of the province, and others which, Sabbath after Sabbath, looked devoutly heavenward, and benignantly over the crowded pews, from the holiest pulpits in the land. Some affirm that the lady of the governor was there. At least there were high dames well known to her, and wives of honored husbands, and widows, a great multitude, and ancient maidens, all of excellent repute, and fair young girls, who trembled lest their mothers should espy them. Either the sudden gleams of light flashing over the obscure field bedazzled Goodman Brown, or he recognized a score of the church members of Salem village famous for their especial sanctity. Good old Deacon Gookin had arrived, and waited at the skirts of that venerable saint, his revered pastor. But, irreverently consorting with these grave, reputable, and pious people, these elders of the church, these chaste dames and dewy virgins, there were men of dissolute lives and women of spotted fame, wretches given over to all mean and filthy vice, and suspected even of horrid crimes. It was strange to see that the good shrank not from the wicked, nor were the sinners abashed by the saints. Scattered also among their pale-faced enemies were the Indian priests, or powwows, who had often scared their native forest with more hideous incantations than any known to English witchcraft.

"But where is Faith?" thought Goodman Brown; and, as hope came into his heart, he trembled.

Another verse of the hymn arose, a slow and mournful strain, such as the pious love, but joined to words which expressed all that our nature can conceive of sin, and darkly hinted at far more. Unfathomable to mere mortals is the lore of fiends. Verse after verse was sung; and still the chorus of the desert swelled between like the deepest tone of a mighty organ; and with the final peal of that dreadful anthem there came a sound, as if the roaring wind, the rushing streams, the howling beasts, and every other voice of the unconcerted wilderness were mingling and according with the voice of guilty man in homage to the prince of all. The four blazing pines threw up a loftier flame, and obscurely discovered shapes and visages of horror on the smoke wreaths above the impious assembly. At the same moment the fire on the rock shot redly forth and formed a glowing arch above its base, where now appeared a figure. With reverence be it spoken, the figure bore no slight similitude, both in garb and manner, to some grave divine of the New England churches.

"Bring forth the converts!" cried a voice that echoed through the field and rolled into the forest.

At the word, Goodman Brown stepped forth from the shadow of the trees and approached the congregation, with whom he felt a loathful brotherhood by the sympathy of all that was wicked in his heart. He could have well-nigh sworn that the shape of his own dead father beckoned him to advance, looking downward from a smoke wreath, while a woman, with dim features of despair, threw out her hand to warn him back. Was it his mother? But he had no power to retreat one step, nor to resist, even in thought, when the minister and good old Deacon Gookin seized his arms and led him to the blazing rock. Thither came also the slender form of a veiled female, led between Goody Cloyse, that pious teacher of the catechism, and Martha Carrier, who had received the devil's promise to be queen of hell. A rampant hag was she. And there stood the proselytes beneath the canopy of fire.

"Welcome, my children," said the dark figure, "to the communion of your race. Ye have found thus young your nature and your destiny. My children, look behind you!"

They turned; and flashing forth, as it were, in a sheet of flame, the fiend worshippers were seen; the smile of welcome gleamed darkly on every visage.

"There," resumed the sable form, "are all whom ye have reverenced from youth. Ye deemed them holier than yourselves, and shrank from your own sin, contrasting it with their lives of righteousness and prayerful aspirations heavenward. Yet here are they all in my worshipping assembly. This night it shall be granted you to know their secret deeds: how hoary-bearded elders of the church have whispered wanton words to the young maids of their households; how many a woman, eager for widows' weeds, has given her husband a drink at bedtime and let him sleep his last sleep in her bosom; how beardless youths have made haste to inherit their fathers' wealth; and how fair damsels—blush not, sweet ones—have dug little graves in the garden, and bidden me, the sole guest to an infant's funeral. By the sympathy of your human hearts for sin ye shall scent out all the places—whether in church, bedchamber, street, field, or forest—where crime has been committed, and shall exult to behold the whole earth one stain of guilt, one mighty blood spot. Far more than this. It shall be yours to penetrate, in every bosom, the deep mystery of sin, the fountain of all wicked arts, and which inexhaustibly supplies more evil impulses than human power—than my power at its utmost—can make manifest in deeds. And now, my children, look upon each other."

They did so; and, by the blaze of the hell-kindled torches, the wretched man beheld his Faith, and the wife her husband, trembling before that unhallowed altar.

"Lo, there ye stand, my children," said the figure, in a deep and solemn tone, almost sad with its despairing awfulness, as if his once-angelic nature could yet mourn for our miserable race. "Depending upon one another's hearts, ye had still hoped that virtue were not all a dream. Now are ye undeceived. Evil is the nature of mankind. Evil must be your only happiness. Welcome again, my children, to the communion of your race."

"Welcome," repeated the fiend worshippers, in one cry of despair and triumph.

And there they stood, the only pair, as it seemed, who were yet hesitating on the verge of wickedness in this dark world. A basin was hollowed, naturally, in the rock. Did it contain water, reddened by the lurid light? or was it blood? or, perchance, a liquid flame? Herein did the shape of evil dip his hand and prepare to lay the mark of baptism upon their foreheads, that they might be partakers of the mystery of sin, more conscious of the secret guilt of others, both in deed and thought, than they could now be of their own. The husband cast one look at his pale wife, and Faith at him. What polluted wretches would the next glance show them to each other, shuddering alike at what they disclosed and what they saw!

"Faith! Faith!" cried the husband, "look up to heaven, and resist the wicked one."

Whether Faith obeyed he knew not. Hardly had he spoken when he found himself amid calm night and solitude, listening to a roar of the wind which died heavily away through the forest. He staggered against the rock, and felt it chill and damp; while a hanging twig, that had been all on fire, besprinkled his cheek with the coldest dew.

The next morning young Goodman Brown came slowly into the street of Salem village, staring around him like a bewildered man. The good old minister was taking a walk along the graveyard to get an appetite for breakfast and meditate his sermon, and bestowed a blessing, as he passed, on Goodman Brown. He shrank from the venerable saint as if to avoid an anathema. Old Deacon Gookin was at domestic worship, and the holy words of his prayer were heard through the open window. "What God doth the wizard pray to?" quoth Goodman Brown. Goody Cloyse, that excellent old Christian, stood in the early sunshine at her own lattice, catechizing a little girl who had brought her a pint of morning's milk. Goodman Brown snatched away the child as from the grasp of the fiend himself. Turning the corner by the meeting-house, he spied the head of Faith, with the pink ribbons, gazing anxiously forth, and bursting into such joy at sight of him that she skipped along the street and almost kissed her husband before the whole village. But Goodman Brown looked sternly and sadly into her face, and passed on without a greeting.

Had Goodman Brown fallen asleep in the forest and only dreamed a wild dream of a witch-meeting?

Be it so if you will; but, alas! it was a dream of evil omen for young Goodman Brown. A stern, a sad, a darkly meditative, a distrustful, if not a desperate man did he become from the night of that fearful dream. On the Sabbath day, when the congregation were singing a holy psalm, he could not listen because an anthem of sin rushed loudly upon his ear and drowned all the blessed strain. When the minister spoke from the pulpit with power and fervid eloquence, and, with his hand on the open Bible, of the sacred truths of our religion, and of saint-like lives and triumphant deaths, and of future bliss or misery unutterable, then did Goodman Brown turn pale, dreading lest the roof should thunder down upon the gray blasphemer and his hearers. Often, waking suddenly at midnight, he shrank from the bosom of Faith; and at morning or eventide, when the family knelt down at prayer, he scowled and muttered to himself, and gazed sternly at his wife, and turned away. And when he had lived long, and was borne to his grave a hoary corpse, followed by Faith, an aged woman, and children and grandchildren, a goodly procession, besides neighbors not a few, they carved no hopeful verse upon his tombstone, for his dying hour was gloom.

THE MAN IN
THE BLACK SUIT

Stephen King

I am now a very old man and this is something which happened to me when I was very young—only nine years old. It was 1914, the summer after my brother Dan died in the west field and three years before America got into World War I. I've never told anyone about what happened at the fork in the stream that day, and I never will... at least not with my mouth. I've decided to write it down, though, in this book which I will leave on the table beside my bed. I can't write long, because my hands shake so these days and I have next to no strength, but I don't think it will take long.

Later, someone may find what I have written. That seems likely to me, as it is pretty much human nature to look in a book marked DIARY after its owner has passed along. So yes—my words will probably be read. A better question is whether or not anyone will believe them. Almost certainly not, but that doesn't matter. It's not belief I'm interested in but freedom. Writing can give that, I've found. For twenty years I wrote a column called "Long Ago and Far Away" for the Castle Rock *Call*, and I know that sometimes it works that way—what you write down sometimes leaves you forever, like old photographs left in the bright sun, fading to nothing but white.

I pray for that sort of release.

A man in his nineties should be well past the terrors of childhood, but as my infirmities slowly creep up on me, like waves licking closer and closer to some indifferently built castle of sand, that terrible face grows clearer and clearer in my mind's eye. It glows like a dark star in the constellations of my childhood. What I might have done yesterday, who I might have seen here in my room at the nursing home, what I might have said to them or they to me... those things are gone, but the face of the man in the black suit grows ever clearer, ever closer, and I remember every word he said. I don't want to think of him but I can't help it, and sometimes at night my old heart beats so hard and so fast I think it will tear itself right clear of my chest. So I uncap my fountain pen and force my trembling old hand to write this pointless anecdote in the diary one of my great grandchildren—I can't remember her name for sure, at least not right now, but

I know it starts with an S—gave to me last Christmas, and which I have never written in until now. Now I will write in it. I will write the story of how I met the man in the black suit on the bank of Castle Stream one afternoon in the summer of 1914.

The town of Motton was a different world in those days—more different than I could ever tell you. That was a world without airplanes droning overhead, a world almost without cars and trucks, a world where the skies were not cut into lanes and slices by overhead power lines.

There was not a single paved road in the whole town, and the business district consisted of nothing but Corson's General Store, Thut's Livery & Hardware, the Methodist Church at Christ's Corner, the school, the town hall, and Harry's Restaurant half a mile down from there, which my mother called, with unfailing disdain, "the liquor house."

Mostly, though, the difference was in how people lived—how apart they were. I'm not sure people born after the middle of the twentieth century could quite credit that, although they might say they could, to be polite to old folks like me. There were no phones in western Maine back then, for one thing. The first one wouldn't be installed for another five years, and by the time there was one in our house, I was nineteen and going to college at the University of Maine in Orono.

But that is only the roof of the thing. There was no doctor closer than Casco, and no more than a dozen houses in what you would call town. There were no neighborhoods (I'm not even sure we knew the word, although we had a verb—*neighboring*—that described church functions and barn dances), and open fields were the exception rather than the rule. Out of town the houses were farms that stood far apart from each other, and from December until middle March we mostly hunkered down in the little pockets of stove warmth we called families. We hunkered and listened to the wind in the chimney and hoped no one would get sick or break a leg or get a headful of bad ideas, like the farmer over in Castle Rock who had chopped up his wife and kids three winters before and then said in court that the ghosts made him do it. In those days before the Great War, most of Motton was woods and bog, dark long places full of moose and mosquitoes, snakes and secrets. In those days there were ghosts everywhere.

This thing I'm telling about happened on a Saturday. My father gave me a whole list of chores to do, including some that would have been Dan's, if he'd still been alive. He was my only brother, and he'd died of being stung by a bee. A year had gone by, and still my mother wouldn't hear that. She said it was something else, *had* to have been, that no one ever died of being stung by a bee. When Mama Sweet, the oldest lady in the Methodist Ladies' Aid, tried to tell her—at the church supper the previous winter, this was—that the same thing had happened to her favorite uncle back in '73, my mother clapped her hands over her ears, got up, and walked out of the church basement. She'd never been back since, either, and nothing my father could say to her would change her mind. She claimed she was done with church, and that if she ever had to see Helen Robichaud again (that was Mama Sweet's real name), she would slap her eyes out. She wouldn't be able to help herself, she said.

That day, Dad wanted me to lug wood for the cookstove, weed the beans and the cukes, pitch hay out of the loft, get two jugs of water to put in the cold pantry, and scrape as much old paint off the cellar bulkhead as I could. Then, he said, I could go fishing, if I didn't mind going by myself—he had to go over and see Bill Eversham about some cows. I said I sure didn't mind going by myself, and my Dad smiled like that didn't surprise him so very much. He'd given me a bamboo pole the week before—not because it was my birthday or anything, but just because he liked to give me things, sometimes—and I was wild to try it in Castle Stream, which was by far the troutiest brook I'd ever fished.

"But don't you go too far in the woods," he told me. "Not beyond where it splits."

"No, sir."

"Promise me."

"Yessir, I promise."

"Now promise your mother."

We were standing on the back stoop; I had been bound for the springhouse with the water jugs when my Dad stopped me. Now he turned me around to face my mother, who was standing at the marble counter in a flood of strong morning sunshine falling through the double windows over the sink. There was a curl of hair lying across the side of her forehead and touching her eyebrow—you see how well I remember it all? The bright light turned that little curl to filaments of gold and made me want to run to her and put my arms around her. In that instant I saw her as a woman, saw her as my father must have seen her. She was wearing a housedress with little red roses all over it, I remember, and she was kneading bread. Candy Bill, our little black Scottie dog, was standing alertly beside her feet, looking up, waiting for anything that might drop. My mother was looking at me.

"I promise," I said.

She smiled, but it was the worried kind of smile she always seemed to make since my father brought Dan back from the west field in his arms. My father had come sobbing and bare-chested. He had taken off his shirt and draped it over Dan's face, which had swelled and turned color. *My boy!* he had been crying. *Oh, look at my boy! Jesus, look at my boy!* I remember that as if it had been yesterday. It was the only time I ever heard my Dad take the Savior's name in vain.

"What do you promise, Gary?" she asked.

"Promise not to go no further than where it forks, ma'am."

"*Any* further."

"Any."

She gave me a patient look, saying nothing as her hands went on working in the dough, which now had a smooth, silky look.

"I promise not to go any further than where it forks, ma'am."

"Thank you, Gary," she said. "And try to remember that grammar is for the world as well as for school."

"Yes, ma'am."

Candy Bill followed me as I did my chores, and sat between my feet as I bolted my lunch, looking up at me with the same attentiveness he had shown my mother while she was kneading her bread, but when I got my new bamboo pole and my old, splintery creel and started out of the dooryard, he stopped and only stood in the dust by an old roll of snowfence, watching. I called him but he wouldn't come. He yapped a time or two, as if telling me to come back, but that was all.

"Stay, then," I said, trying to sound as if I didn't care. I did, though, at least a little. Candy Bill *always* went fishing with me.

My mother came to the door and looked out at me with her left hand held up to shade her eyes. I can see her that way still, and it's like looking at a photograph of someone who later became unhappy, or died suddenly. "You mind your Dad now, Gary!"

"Yes, ma'am, I will."

She waved. I waved, too. Then I turned my back on her and walked away.

The sun beat down on my neck, hard and hot, for the first quarter-mile or so, but then I entered the woods, where double shadow fell over the road and it was cool and fir-smelling and you could hear the wind hissing through the deep needled groves. I walked with my pole on my shoulder like boys did back then, holding my creel in my other hand like a valise or a salesman's sample-case. About two miles into the woods along a road which was really nothing but a double rut with a grassy strip growing up the center hump, I began to hear the hurried, eager gossip of Castle Stream. I thought of trout with bright speckled backs and pure white bellies, and my heart went up in my chest.

The stream flowed under a little wooden bridge, and the banks leading down to the water were steep and brushy. I worked my way down carefully, holding on where I could and digging my heels in. I went down out of summer and back into mid-spring, or so it felt. The cool rose gently off the water, and a green smell like moss. When I got to the edge of the water I only stood there for a little while, breathing deep of that mossy smell and watching the dragonflies circle and the skitterbugs skate. Then, farther down, I saw a trout leap at a butterfly—a good big brookie, maybe fourteen inches long—and remembered I hadn't come here just to sightsee.

I walked along the bank, following the current, and wet my line for the first time with the bridge still in sight upstream. Something jerked the tip of my pole down a time or two and ate half my worm, but he was too sly for my nine-year-old hands—or maybe just not hungry enough to be careless—so I went on.

I stopped at two or three other places before I got to the place where Castle Stream forks, going southwest into Castle Rock and southeast into Kashwakamak Township, and at one of them I caught the biggest trout I have ever caught in my life, a beauty that measured nineteen inches from tip to tail on the little ruler I kept in my creel. That was a monster of a brook trout, even for those days.

If I had accepted this as gift enough for one day and gone back, I would not be writing now (and this is going to turn out longer than I thought it would, I see that already), but I didn't. Instead I saw to my catch right then and there as my father had shown me—cleaning it, placing it on dry grass at the bottom of the creel, then laying damp grass on top of it—and went on. I did not, at age nine, think that catching a nineteen-inch brook trout was particularly remarkable, although I do remember being amazed that my line had not broken when I, netless as well as artless, had hauled it out and swung it toward me in a clumsy tail-flapping arc.

Ten minutes later, I came to the place where the stream split in those days (it is long gone now; there is a settlement of duplex homes where Castle Stream once went its course, and a district grammar school as well, and if there is a stream it goes in darkness), dividing around a huge gray rock nearly the size of our outhouse.

There was a pleasant flat space here, grassy and soft, overlooking what my Dad and I called South Branch. I squatted on my heels, dropped my line into the water, and almost immediately snagged a fine rainbow trout. He wasn't the size of my brookie—only a foot or so—but a good fish, just the same. I had it cleaned out before the gills had stopped flexing, stored it in my creel, and dropped my line back into the water.

This time there was no immediate bite so I leaned back, looking up at the blue stripe of sky I could see along the stream's course. Clouds floated by, west to east, and I tried to think what they looked like. I saw a unicorn, then a rooster, then a dog that looked a little like Candy Bill. I was looking for the next one when I drowsed off. Or maybe slept. I don't know for sure. All I know is that a tug on my line so strong it almost pulled the bamboo pole out of my hand was what brought me back into the afternoon. I sat up, clutched the pole, and suddenly became aware that something was sitting on the tip of my nose. I crossed my eyes and saw a bee. My heart seemed to fall dead in my chest, and for a horrible second I was sure I was going to wet my pants.

The tug on my line came again, stronger this time, but although I maintained my grip on the end of the pole so it wouldn't be pulled into the stream and perhaps carried away (I think I even had the presence of mind to snub the line with my forefinger), I made no effort to pull in my catch. All of my horrified attention was fixed on the fat black-and-yellow thing that was using my nose as a rest-stop.

I slowly poked out my lower lip and blew upward. The bee ruffled a little but kept its place. I blew again and it ruffled again... but this time it also seemed to shift impatiently, and I didn't dare blow anymore, for fear it would lose its temper completely and give me a shot. It was too close for me to focus on what it was doing, but it was easy to imagine it ramming its stinger into one of my nostrils and shooting its poison up toward my eyes. And my brain.

A terrible idea came to me: that this was the very bee which had killed my brother. I knew it wasn't true, and not only because honey-bees probably didn't live longer than a single year (except maybe for the queens; about them I was not so sure). It couldn't be true because bees died when they stung, and even at nine I knew it. Their stingers were barbed, and when they tried to fly away after doing the deed, they tore themselves apart. Still, the idea stayed. This was a special bee, a devil-bee, and it had come back to finish the other of Albion and Loretta's two boys.

And here is something else: I had been stung by bees before, and although the stings had swelled more than is perhaps usual (I can't really say for sure), I had never died of them. That was only for my brother, a terrible trap which had been laid for him in his very making, a trap which I had somehow escaped. But as I crossed my eyes until they hurt in an effort to focus on the bee, logic did not exist. It was the *bee* that existed, only that, the bee that had killed my brother, killed him so bad that my father had slipped down the straps of his overalls so he could take off his shirt and cover Dan's swelled, engorged face. Even in the depths of his grief he had done that, because he didn't want his wife to see what had become of her firstborn. Now the bee had returned, and now it would kill me. It would kill me and I would die in convulsions on the bank, flopping just as a brookie flops after you take the hook out of its mouth.

As I sat there trembling on the edge of panic—of simply bolting to my feet and then bolting anywhere—there came a report from behind me. It was as sharp and peremptory as a pistol-shot, but I knew it wasn't a pistol-shot; it was someone clapping his hands. One single clap. At the moment it came, the bee tumbled off my nose and fell into my lap. It lay there on my pants with its legs sticking up and its stinger a threatless black thread against the old scuffed brown of the corduroy. It was dead as a doornail, I saw that at once. At the same moment, the pole gave another tug—the hardest yet—and I almost lost it again.

I grabbed it with both hands and gave it a big stupid yank that would have made my father clutch his head with both hands, if he had been there to see it. A rainbow trout, a good bit larger than the one I had already caught, rose out of the water in a wet, writhing flash, spraying fine drops of water from its filament of tail—it looked like one of those romanticized fishing pictures they used to put on the covers of men's magazines like *True* and *Man's Adventure* back in the forties and fifties. At that moment hauling in a big one was about the last thing on my mind, however, and when the line snapped and the fish fell back into the stream, I barely noticed. I looked over my shoulder to see who had clapped. A man was standing above me, at the edge of the trees. His face was very long and pale. His black hair was combed tight against his skull and parted with rigorous care on the left side of his narrow head. He was very tall. He was wearing a black three-piece suit, and I knew right away that he was not a human being, because his eyes were the orangey-red of flames in a woodstove. I don't just mean the irises, because he *had* no irises, and no pupils, and certainly no whites. His eyes were completely orange—an orange that shifted and flickered. And it's really too late not to say exactly what I mean, isn't it? He was on fire inside, and his eyes were like the little isinglass portholes you sometimes see in stove doors.

My bladder let go, and the scuffed brown the dead bee was lying on went a darker brown. I was hardly aware of what had happened, and I couldn't take my eyes off the man standing on top of the bank and looking down at me, the man who had walked out of thirty miles of trackless western Maine woods in a fine black suit and narrow shoes of gleaming leather. I could see the watch-chain looped across his vest glittering in the summer sunshine. There was not so much as a single pine-needle on him. And he was smiling at me.

"Why, it's a fisherboy!" he cried in a mellow, pleasing voice. "Imagine that! Are we well-met, fisherboy?"

"Hello, sir," I said. The voice that came out of me did not tremble, but it didn't sound like my voice, either. It sounded older. Like Dan's voice, maybe. Or my father's, even. And all I could think was that maybe he would let me go if I pretended not to see what he was. If I pretended I didn't see there were flames glowing and dancing where his eyes should have been.

"I've saved you a nasty sting, perhaps," he said, and then, to my horror, he came down the bank to where I sat with a dead bee in my wet lap and a bamboo fishing pole in my nerveless hands. His slick soled city shoes should have slipped on the low, grassy weeds which dressed the steep bank, but they didn't; nor did they leave tracks behind, I saw. Where his feet had touched—or seemed to touch—there was not a single broken twig, crushed leaf, or trampled shoe-shape. Even before he reached me, I recognized the aroma baking up from the skin under the suit—the smell of burned matches. The smell of sulfur. The man in the black suit was the Devil. He had walked out of the deep woods between Motton and Kashwakamak, and now he was standing here beside me. From the corner of one eye I could see a hand as pale as the hand of a store window dummy. The fingers were hideously long.

He hunkered beside me on his hams, his knees popping just as the knees of any normal man might, but when he moved his hands so they dangled between his knees, I saw that each of those long fingers ended in what was not a fingernail but a long yellow claw.

"You didn't answer my question, fisherboy," he said in his mellow voice. It was, now that I think of it, like the voice of one of those radio announcers on the big-band shows years later, the ones that would sell Geritol and Serutan and Ovaltine and Dr. Grabow pipes. "Are we well-met?"

"Please don't hurt me," I whispered, in a voice so low I could barely hear it. I was more afraid than I could ever write down, more afraid than I want to remember... but I do. I do. It never even crossed my mind to hope I was having a dream, although I might have, I suppose, if I had been older. But I wasn't older; I was nine, and I knew the truth when it squatted down on its hunkers beside me. I knew a hawk from a handsaw, as my father would have said. The man who had come out of the woods on that Saturday afternoon in midsummer was the Devil, and inside the empty holes of his eyes, his brains were burning.

"Oh, do I smell something?" he asked, as if he hadn't heard me... although I knew he had. "Do I smell something... wet?"

He leaned forward toward me with his nose stuck out, like someone who means to smell a flower. And I noticed an awful thing; as the shadow of his head travelled over the bank, the grass beneath it turned yellow and died. He lowered his head toward my pants and sniffed. His glaring eyes half-closed, as if he had inhaled some sublime aroma and wanted to concentrate on nothing but that.

"Oh, bad!" he cried. "Lovely-bad!" And then he chanted: "Opal! Diamond! Sapphire! Jade! I smell Gary's lemonade!" Then he threw himself on his back in the little flat place and laughed wildly. It was the sound of a lunatic.

I thought about running, but my legs seemed two counties away from my brain. I wasn't crying, though; I had wet my pants like a baby, but I wasn't crying. I was too scared to cry. I suddenly knew that I was going to die, and probably painfully, but the worst of it was that that might not be the worst of it.

The worst of it might come later. *After* I was dead.

He sat up suddenly, the smell of burnt matches fluffing out from his suit and making me feel all gaggy in my throat. He looked at me solemnly from his narrow white face and burning eyes, but there was a sense of laughter about him, too. There was always that sense of laughter about him.

"Sad news, fisherboy," he said. "I've come with sad news."

I could only look at him—the black suit, the fine black shoes, the long white fingers that ended not in nails but in talons.

"Your mother is dead."

"No!" I cried. I thought of her making bread, of the curl lying across her forehead and just touching her eyebrow, standing there in the strong morning sunlight, and the terror swept over me again... but not for myself this time. Then I thought of how she'd looked when I set off with my fishing pole, standing in the kitchen doorway with her hand shading her eyes, and how she had looked to me in that moment like a photograph of someone you expected to see again but never did. "No, you lie!" I screamed.

He smiled—the sadly patient smile of a man who has often been accused falsely. "I'm afraid not," he said. "It was the same thing that happened to your brother, Gary. It was a bee."

"No, that's not true," I said, and now I *did* begin to cry. "She's old, she's thirty-five, if a bee-sting could kill her the way it did Danny she would have died a long time ago and you're a lying bastard!"

I had called the Devil a lying bastard. On some level I was aware of this, but the entire front of my mind was taken up by the enormity of what he'd said. My mother dead? He might as well have told me that there was a new ocean where the Rockies had been. But I believed him. On some level I believed him completely, as we always believe, on some level, the worst thing our hearts can imagine.

"I understand your grief, little fisherboy, but that particular argument just doesn't hold water, I'm afraid." He spoke in a tone of bogus comfort that was horrible, maddening, without remorse or pity. "A man can go his whole life without seeing a mockingbird, you know, but does that mean mockingbirds don't exist? Your mother—"

A fish jumped below us. The man in the black suit frowned, then pointed a finger at it. The trout convulsed in the air, its body bending so strenuously that for a split-second it appeared to be snapping at its own tail, and when it fell back into Castle Stream it was floating lifelessly, dead. It struck the big gray rock where the waters divided, spun around twice in the whirlpool eddy that formed there, and then floated off in the direction of Castle Rock. Meanwhile, the terrible stranger turned his burning eyes on me again, his thin lips pulled back from tiny rows of sharp teeth in a cannibal smile.

"Your mother simply went through her entire life without being stung by a bee," he said. "But then—less than an hour ago, actually—one flew in through the kitchen window while she was taking the bread out of the oven and putting it on the counter to cool."

"No, I won't hear this, I won't hear this, I *won't!*"

I raised my hands and clapped them over my ears. He pursed his lips as if to whistle and blew at me gently. It was only a little breath, but the stench was foul beyond belief—clogged sewers, outhouses that have never known a single sprinkle of lime, dead chickens after a flood.

My hands fell away from the sides of my face.

"Good," he said. "You need to hear this, Gary; you need to hear this, my little fisherboy. It was your mother who passed that fatal weakness on to your brother Dan; you got some of it, but you also got a protection from your father that poor Dan somehow missed." He pursed his lips again, only this time, he made a cruelly comic little *tsktsk* sound instead of blowing his nasty breath at me. "So, although I don't like to speak ill of the dead, it's almost a case of poetic justice, isn't it? After all, she killed your brother Dan as surely as if she had put a gun to his head and pulled the trigger."

"No," I whispered. "No, it isn't true."

"I assure you it is," he said. "The bee flew in the window and lit on her neck. She slapped at it before she even knew what she was doing—*you* were wiser than that, weren't you, Gary?—and the bee stung her. She felt her throat start to close up at once. That's what happens, you know, to people who are allergic to bee-venom. Their throats close and they drown in the open air. That's why Dan's face was so swollen and purple. That's why your father covered it with his shirt."

I stared at him, now incapable of speech. Tears streamed down my cheeks. I didn't want to believe him, and knew from my church schooling that the devil is the father of lies, but I *did* believe him, just the same. I believed he had been standing there in our dooryard, looking in the kitchen window, as my mother fell to her knees, clutching at her swollen throat while Candy Bill danced around her, barking shrilly.

"She made the most wonderfully awful noises," the man in the black suit said reflectively, "and she scratched her face quite badly, I'm afraid. Her eyes bulged out like a frog's eyes. She wept." He paused, then added: "She wept as she died, isn't that sweet? And here's the most beautiful thing of all. After she was dead…

after she had been lying on the floor for fifteen minutes or so with no sound but the stove ticking and with that little stick of a bee-stinger still poking out of the side of her neck—so small, so small—do you know what Candy Bill did? That little rascal licked away her tears. First on one side... and then on the other."

He looked out at the stream for a moment, his face sad and thoughtful. Then he turned back to me and his expression of bereavement disappeared like a dream. His face was as slack and avid as the face of a corpse that has died hungry. His eyes blazed. I could see his sharp little teeth between his pale lips.

"I'm starving," he said abruptly. "I'm going to kill you and tear you open and eat your guts, little fisherboy. What do you think about that?"

No, I tried to say, *please, no,* but no sound came out. He meant to do it, I saw. He really meant to do it.

"I'm just so *hungry,*" he said, both petulant and teasing. "And you won't want to live without your precious mommy, anyhow, take my word for it. Because your father's the sort of man who'll have to have some warm hole to stick it in, believe me, and if you're the only one available, you're the one who'll have to serve. I'll save you all that discomfort and unpleasantness. Also, you'll go to Heaven, think of that. Murdered souls *always* go to Heaven. So we'll both be serving God this afternoon, Gary. Isn't that nice?"

He reached for me again with his long, pale hands, and without thinking what I was doing, I flipped open the top of my creel, pawed all the way down to the bottom, and brought out the monster brookie I'd caught earlier—the one I should have been satisfied with. I held it out to him blindly, my fingers in the red slit of its belly from which I had removed its insides as the man in the black suit had threatened to remove mine. The fish's glazed eye stared dreamily at me, the gold ring around the black center reminding me of my mother's wedding ring. And in that moment I saw her lying in her coffin with the sun shining off the wedding band and knew it was true—she had been stung by a bee, she had drowned in the warm, bread-smelling kitchen air, and Candy Bill had licked her dying tears from her swollen cheeks.

"Big fish!" the man in the black suit cried in a guttural, greedy voice. "Oh, *biiig fiiish!*"

He snatched it away from me and crammed it into a mouth that opened wider than any human mouth ever could. Many years later, when I was sixty-five (I know it was sixty-five because that was the summer I retired from teaching), I went to the New England Aquarium and finally saw a shark. The mouth of the man in the black suit was like that shark's mouth when it opened, only his gullet was blazing red, the same color as his awful eyes, and I felt heat bake out of it and into my face, the way you feel a sudden wave of heat come pushing out of a fireplace when a dry piece of wood catches alight. And I didn't imagine that heat, either, I know I didn't, because just before he slid the head of my nineteen-inch brook trout between his gaping jaws, I saw the scales along the sides of the fish rise up and begin to curl like bits of paper floating over an open incinerator.

He slid the fish in like a man in a travelling show swallowing a sword. He didn't chew, and his blazing eyes bulged out, as if in effort. The fish went in and went in, his throat bulged as it slid down his gullet, and now he began to cry tears of his own... except his tears were blood, scarlet and thick. I think it was the sight of those bloody tears that gave me my body back. I don't know why that should have been, but I think it was. I bolted to my feet like a jack released from its box, turned with my bamboo pole still in one hand, and fled up the bank, bending over and tearing tough bunches of weeds out with my free hand in an effort to get up the slope more quickly.

He made a strangled, furious noise—the sound of any man with his mouth too full—and I looked back just as I got to the top. He was coming after me, the back of his suit-coat flapping and his thin gold watch-chain flashing and winking in the sun. The tail of the fish was still protruding from his mouth and I could smell the rest of it, roasting in the oven of his throat.

He reached for me, groping with his talons, and I fled along the top of the bank. After a hundred yards or so I found my voice and went to screaming—screaming in fear, of course, but also screaming in grief for my beautiful dead mother.

He was coming along after me. I could hear snapping branches and whipping bushes, but I didn't look back again. I lowered my head, slitted my eyes against the bushes and low-hanging branches along the stream's bank, and ran as fast as I could. And at every step I expected to feel his hands descending on my shoulders pulling me back into a final hot hug.

That didn't happen. Some unknown length of time later—it couldn't have been longer than five or ten minutes, I suppose, but it seemed like forever—I saw the bridge through layerings of leaves and firs. Still screaming, but breath-lessly now, sounding like a teakettle which has almost boiled dry, I reached this second, steeper bank and charged up to it.

Halfway to the top I slipped to my knees, looked over my shoulder, and saw the man in the black suit almost at my heels, his white face pulled into a convul-sion of fury and greed. His cheeks were splattered with his bloody tears and his shark's mouth hung open like a hinge.

"*Fisherboy!*" he snarled, and started up the bank after me, grasping at my foot with one long hand. I tore free, turned, and threw my fishing pole at him. He batted it down easily, but it tangled his feet up somehow and he went to his knees. I didn't wait to see anymore; I turned and bolted to the top of the slope. I almost slipped at the very top, but managed to grab one of the support struts running beneath the bridge and save myself.

"You can't get away, fisherboy!" he cried from behind me. He sounded furious, but he also sounded as if he were laughing. "It takes more than a mouthful of trout to fill *me* up!"

"Leave me alone!" I screamed back at him. I grabbed the bridge's railing and threw myself over it in a clumsy somersault, filling my hands with splinters and bumping my head so hard on the boards when I came down that I saw stars. I rolled over onto my belly and began crawling. I lurched to my feet just before I got to the end of the bridge, stumbled once, found my rhythm, and then began to run. I ran as only nine-year-old boys can run, which is like the wind. It felt as if my feet only touched the ground with every third or fourth stride, and for all I know, that may be true. I ran straight up the righthand wheelrut in the road, ran until my temples pounded and my eyes pulsed in their sockets, ran until I had a hot stitch in my left side from the bottom of my ribs to my armpit, ran until I could taste blood and something like metal-shavings in the back of my throat. When I couldn't run anymore I stumbled to a stop and looked back over my shoulder, puffing and blowing like a windbroke horse. I was convinced I would see him standing right there behind me in his natty black suit, the watch-chain a glittering loop across his vest and not a hair out of place.

But he was gone. The road stretching back toward Castle Stream between the darkly massed pines and spruces was empty. And yet I sensed him somewhere near in those woods, watching me with his grassfire eyes, smelling of burnt matches and roasted fish. I turned and began walking as fast as I could, limping a little—I'd pulled muscles in both legs, and when I got out of bed the next morning I was so sore I could barely walk. I didn't notice those things then, though. I just kept looking over my shoulder, needing again and again to verify that the road behind me was still empty. It was, each time I looked, but those backward glances seemed to increase my fear rather than lessening it. The firs looked darker, massier, and I kept imagining what lay behind the trees which marched beside the road—long, tangled corridors of forest, leg-breaking deadfalls, ravines where anything might live. Until that Saturday in 1914, I had thought that bears were the worst thing the forest could hold.

Now I knew better.

A mile or so further up the road, just beyond the place where it came out of the woods and joined the Geegan Flat Road, I saw my father walking toward me and whistling "The Old Oaken Bucket." He was carrying his own rod, the one with the fancy spinning reel from Monkey Ward. In his other hand he had his creel, the one with the ribbon my mother had woven through the handle back when Dan was still alive. DEDICATED TO JESUS, that ribbon said. I had been walking but when I saw him I started to run again, screaming *Dad! Dad! Dad!* at the top of my lungs and staggering from side to side on my tired, sprung legs like a drunken sailor. The expression of surprise on his face when he recognized me might have been comical under other circumstances, but not under these. He dropped his rod and creel into the road without so much as a downward glance at them and ran to me. It was the fastest I ever saw my Dad run in his life; when we came together it was a wonder the impact didn't knock us both senseless, and I struck my face on his belt-buckle hard enough to start a little nosebleed. I didn't notice that until later, though. Right then I only reached out my arms and clutched him as hard as I could. I held on and rubbed my hot face back and forth against his belly, covering his old blue workshirt with blood and tears and snot.

"Gary, what is it? What happened? Are you all right?"

"Ma's dead!" I sobbed. "I met a man in the woods and he told me! Ma's dead! She got stung by a bee and it swelled her all up just like what happened to Dan, and she's dead! She's on the kitchen floor and Candy Bill... licked the t-t-tears... off her... off her..."

Face was the last word I had to say, but by then my chest was hitching so bad I couldn't get it out. My tears were flowing again, and my Dad's startled, frightened face had blurred into three overlapping images. I began to howl—not like a little kid who's skun his knee but like a dog that's seen something bad by moonlight—and my father pressed my head against his hard flat stomach again. I slipped out from under his hand, though, and looked back over my shoulder. I wanted to make sure the man in the black suit wasn't coming. There was no sign of him; the road winding back into the woods was completely empty. I promised myself I would never go back down that road again, not ever, no matter what, and I suppose now God's greatest blessing to His creatures below is that they can't see the future. It might have broken my mind if I had known I *would* be going back down that road, and not two hours later. For that moment, though, I was only relieved to see we were still alone. Then I thought of my mother—my beautiful dead mother—and laid my face back against my father's stomach and bawled some more.

"Gary, listen to me," he said a moment or two later. I went on bawling. He gave me a little longer to do that, then reached down and lifted my chin so he could look into my face and I could look into his.

"Your Mom's fine," he said.

I could only look at him with tears streaming down my cheeks. I didn't believe him.

"I don't know who told you different, or what kind of dirty dog would want to put a scare like that into a little boy, but I swear to God your mother's fine."

"But... but he said..."

"I don't care *what* he said. I got back from Eversham's earlier than I expected—he doesn't want to sell any cows, it's all just talk—and decided I had time to catch up with you. I got my pole and my creel and your mother made us a couple of jelly fold-overs. Her new bread. Still warm. So she was fine half an hour ago, Gary, and there's nobody knows any different that's come from this direction, I guarantee you. Not in just half an hour's time." He looked over my shoulder. "Who was this man? And where was he? I'm going to find him and thrash him within an inch of his life."

I thought a thousand things in just two seconds—that's what it seemed like, anyway—but the last thing I thought was the most powerful: if my Dad met up with the man in the black suit, I didn't think my Dad would be the one to do the thrashing. Or the walking away.

I kept remembering those long white fingers, and the talons at the ends of them.

"Gary?"

"I don't know that I remember," I said.

"Were you where the stream splits? The big rock?"

I could never lie to my father when he asked a direct question—not to save his life or mine. "Yes, but don't go down there." I seized his arm with both hands and tugged it hard. "Please don't. He was a scary man." Inspiration struck like an illuminating lightning-bolt. "I think he had a gun."

He looked at me thoughtfully. "Maybe there wasn't a man," he said, lifting his voice a little on the last word and turning it into something that was almost but not quite a question. "Maybe you fell asleep while you were fishing, son, and had a bad dream. Like the ones you had about Danny last winter."

I *had* had a lot of bad dreams about Dan last winter, dreams where I would open the door to our closet or to the dark, fruity interior of the cider shed and see him standing there and looking at me out of his purple strangulated face; from many of these dreams I had awakened screaming, and awakened my parents, as well. I had fallen asleep on the bank of the stream for a little while, too—dozed off, anyway—but I hadn't dreamed and I was sure I had awakened just before the man in the black suit clapped the bee dead, sending it tumbling off my nose and into my lap. I hadn't dreamed him the way I had dreamed Dan, I was quite sure of that, although my meeting with him had already attained a dreamlike quality in my mind, as I suppose supernatural occurrences always must. But if my Dad thought that the man had only existed in my own head, that might be better. Better for him.

"It might have been, I guess," I said.

"Well, we ought to go back and find your rod and your creel." He actually started in that direction, and I had to tug frantically at his arm to stop him again, and turn him back toward me.

"Later," I said. "Please, Dad? I want to see Mother. I've got to see her with my own eyes."

He thought that over, then nodded. "Yes, I suppose you do. We'll go home first, and get your rod and creel later."

So we walked back to the farm together, my father with his fishpole propped on his shoulder just like one of my friends, me carrying his creel, both of us eating folded-over slices of my mother's bread smeared with blackcurrant jam.

"Did you catch anything?" he asked as we came in sight of the barn.

"Yes, sir," I said. "A rainbow. Pretty good-sized." *And a brookie that was a lot bigger,* I thought but didn't say. *Biggest one I ever saw, to tell the truth, but I don't have that one to show you, Dad. I gave that one to the man in the black suit, so he wouldn't eat me. And it worked... but just barely.*

"That's all? Nothing else?"

"After I caught it I fell asleep." This was not really an answer, but not really a lie, either.

"Lucky you didn't lose your pole. You didn't, did you, Gary?"

"No, sir," I said, very reluctantly. Lying about that would do no good even if I'd been able to think up a whopper—not if he was set on going back to get my creel anyway, and I could see by his face that he was.

Up ahead, Candy Bill came racing out of the back door, barking his shrill bark and wagging his whole rear end back and forth the way Scotties do when they're excited. I couldn't wait any longer; hope and anxiety bubbled up in my throat like foam. I broke away from my father and ran to the house, still lugging his creel and still convinced, in my heart of hearts, that I was going to find my mother dead on the kitchen floor with her face swelled and purple like Dan's had been when my father carried him in from the west field, crying and calling the name of Jesus.

But she was standing at the counter, just as well and fine as when I had left her, humming a song as she shelled peas into a bowl. She looked around at me, first in surprise and then in fright as she took in my wide eyes and pale cheeks.

"Gary, what is it? What's the matter?"

I didn't answer, only ran to her and covered her with kisses. At some point my father came in and said, "Don't worry, Lo—he's all right. He just had one of his bad dreams, down there by the brook."

"Pray God it's the last of them," she said, and hugged me tighter while Candy Bill danced around our feet, barking his shrill bark.

"You don't have to come with me if you don't want to, Gary," my father said, although he had already made it clear that he thought I should—that I should go back, that I should face my fear, as I suppose folks would say nowadays. That's very well for fearful things that are make-believe, but two hours hadn't done much to change my conviction that the man in the black suit had been real. I wouldn't be able to convince my father of that, though. I don't think there was a nine-year-old that ever lived who would have been able to convince his father he'd seen the Devil come walking out of the woods in a black suit.

"I'll come," I said. I had walked out of the house to join him before he left, mustering all my courage in order to get my feet moving, and now we were standing by the chopping-block in the side yard, not far from the woodpile.

"What you got behind your back?" he asked.

I brought it out slowly. I would go with him, and I would hope the man in the black suit with the arrow-straight part down the left side of his head was gone... but if he wasn't, I wanted to be prepared. As prepared as I could be, anyway. I had the family Bible in the hand I had brought out from behind my back. I'd set out just to bring my New Testament, which I had won for memorizing the most psalms in the Thursday night Youth Fellowship competition (I managed eight, although most of them except the Twenty-third had floated out of my mind in a week's time), but the little red Testament didn't seem like enough when you were maybe going to face the Devil himself, not even when the words of Jesus were marked out in red ink.

My father looked at the old Bible, swelled with family documents and pictures, and I thought he'd tell me to put it back, but he didn't. A look of mixed grief and sympathy crossed his face, and he nodded. "All right," he said. "Does your mother know you took that?"

"No, sir."

He nodded again. "Then we'll hope she doesn't spot it gone before we get back. Come on. And don't drop it."

Half an hour or so later, the two of us stood on the bank looking down at the place where Castle Stream forked, and at the flat place where I'd had my encounter with the man with the red-orange eyes. I had my bamboo rod in my hand—I'd picked it up below the bridge—and my creel lay down below, on the flat place. Its wicker top was flipped back. We stood looking down, my father and I, for a long time, and neither of us said anything.

Opal! Diamond! Sapphire! Jade! I smell Gary's lemonade! That had been his unpleasant little poem, and once he had recited it, he had thrown himself on his back, laughing like a child who has just discovered he has enough courage to say bathroom words like shit or piss. The flat place down there was as green and lush as any place in Maine that the sun can get to in early July... except where the stranger had lain. There the grass was dead and yellow in the shape of a man.

I looked down and saw I was holding our lumpy old family Bible straight out in front of me with both thumbs pressing so hard on the cover that they were white. It was the way Mama Sweet's husband Norville held a willow-fork when he was trying to dowse somebody a well.

"Stay here," my father said at last, and skidded sideways down the bank, digging his shoes into the rich soft soil and holding his arms out for balance. I stood where I was, holding the Bible stiffly out at the ends of my arms like a willow-fork, my heart thumping wildly. I don't know if I had a sense of being watched that time or not; I was too scared to have a sense of anything, except for a sense of wanting to be far away from that place and those woods.

My Dad bent down, sniffed at where the grass was dead, and grimaced. I knew what he was smelling: something like burnt matches. Then he grabbed my creel and came on back up the bank, hurrying. He snagged one fast look over his shoulder to make sure nothing was coming along behind. Nothing was. When he handed me the creel, the lid was still hanging back on its cunning little leather hinges. I looked inside and saw nothing but two handfuls of grass.

"Thought you said you caught a rainbow," my father said, "but maybe you dreamed that, too."

Something in his voice stung me. "No, sir," I said. "I caught one."

"Well, it sure as hell didn't flop out, not if it was gutted and cleaned. And you wouldn't put a catch into your fisherbox without doing that, would you, Gary? I taught you better than that."

"Yes, sir, you did, but—"

"So if you didn't dream catching it and if it was dead in the box, something must have come along and eaten it," my father said, and then he grabbed another quick glance over his shoulder, eyes wide, as if he had heard something move in the woods. I wasn't exactly surprised to see drops of sweat standing out on his forehead like big, clear jewels. "Come on," he said. "Let's get the hell out of here."

I was for that, and we went back along the bank to the bridge, walking quick without speaking. When we got there, my Dad dropped to one knee and examined the place where we'd found my rod. There was another patch of dead grass there, and the lady's slipper was all brown and curled in on itself, as if a blast of heat had charred it. While my father did this, I looked in my empty creel. "He must have gone back and eaten my other fish, too," I said.

My father looked up at me. "*Other* fish!"

"Yes, sir. I didn't tell you, but I caught a brookie, too. A big one. He was awful hungry, that fella." I wanted to say more, and the words trembled just behind my lips, but in the end I didn't.

We climbed up to the bridge and helped one another over the railing. My father took my creel, looked into it, then went to the railing and threw it over. I came up beside him in time to see it splash down and float away like a boat, riding lower and lower in the stream as the water poured in between the wicker weavings.

"It smelled bad," my father said, but he didn't look at me when he said it, and his voice sounded oddly defensive. It was the only time I ever heard him speak just that way.

"Yes, sir."

"We'll tell your mother we couldn't find it. If she asks. If she doesn't ask, we won't tell her anything."

"No, sir, we won't."

And she didn't and we didn't and that's the way it was.

That day in the woods is eighty-one years gone, and for many of the years in between I have never even thought of it… not awake, at least. Like any other man or woman who ever lived, I can't say about my dreams, not for sure. But now I'm old, and I dream awake, it seems. My infirmities have crept up like waves which will soon take a child's abandoned sand castle, and my memories have also crept up, making me think of some old rhyme that went, in part, "Just leave them alone/And they'll come home/Wagging their tails behind them." I remember meals I ate, games I played, girls I kissed in the school cloakroom when we played Post Office, boys I chummed with, the first drink I ever took, the first cigarette I ever smoked (cornshuck behind Dicky Hammer's pig-shed, and I threw up). Yet of all the memories, the one of the man in the black suit is the strongest, and glows with its own spectral, haunted light. He was real, he was the Devil, and that day I was either his errand or his luck. I feel more and more strongly that escaping him was my luck—*just* luck, and not the intercession of the God I have worshipped and sung hymns to all my life.

As I lie here in my nursing-home room, and in the ruined sand castle that is my body, I tell myself that I need not fear the Devil—that I have lived a good, kindly life, and I need not fear the Devil. Sometimes I remind myself that it was I, not my father, who finally coaxed my mother back to church later on that summer.

In the dark, however, these thoughts have no power to ease or comfort. In the dark comes a voice which whispers that the nine-year-old boy I was had done nothing for which he might legitimately fear the devil either… and yet the Devil came. And in the dark I sometimes hear that voice drop even lower, into ranges which are inhuman. *Big fish!* it whispers in tones of hushed greed, and all the truths of the moral world fall to ruin before its hunger. *Biiig fiiish!*

The Devil came to me once, long ago; suppose he were to come again now? I am too old to run now; I can't even get to the bathroom and back without my walker. I have no fine large brook trout with which to propitiate him, either, even for a moment or two; I am old and my creel is empty. Suppose he were to come back and find me so?

And suppose he is still hungry?

THE POWER·OF SPEECH

Natalie Babbitt

A lot of people believe that once a day every goat in the World has to go down to Hell to have his beard combed by the Devil, but this is obvious nonsense. The Devil doesn't have time to comb the beards of all the goats in the World even if he wanted to, which of course he doesn't. Who would? There are far too many goats in the first place, and in the second place their beards are nearly all in terrible condition, full of snarls, burrs, and dandelion juice.

Nevertheless, whether he wants to comb their beards or not, the Devil is as fond of goats as he is of anything, and always has one or another somewhere about, kept on as a sort of pet. He treats them pretty well too, considering, and the goats gives back as good or as bad as they get, which is one reason why the Devil likes them so much, for goats are one hundred percent unsentimental.

Now, there was a goat in the World once that the Devil had his eye on for some time, a great big goat with curving horns and a prize from every fair for miles around. "I want that goat," said the Devil to himself, "and I mean to have him even if he has to be dragged down here by his beard." But that was a needless thing to say, and the Devil knew it, for animals, and especially goats, are nothing at all like people when it comes to right and wrong. Animals don't see much to choose between the two. So, Heaven or Hell, it's all one to them, especially goats. All the Devil had to do was go up there, to the cottage that the goat called home, and lead him away.

The only trouble was that the old woman who owned the goat was no dummy. She knew how much the Devil liked goats and she also knew how much he hated bells. So she kept the goat—whose name was Walpurgis—tied up to a tree in her yard and she fastened a little bell around his neck with a length of ribbon. Walpurgis hated bells almost as much as the Devil did; but there was no way he could say so and nothing he could do about his own bell except to stand very still in order to keep it from jangling. This led some passers-by to conclude that he was only a stuffed goat put there for show and not a real goat at all. So many people came up to the old woman's door to ask about it that at last she put up a sign which said: THIS IS A REAL GOAT. And after that she got a little peace and quiet. Not that any of it mattered to Walpurgis, who didn't give a hoot for

90

what anybody thought one way or another.

The Devil didn't care what anybody thought either. But he still wanted the goat. He turned the whole problem of the bell over in his mind, considering this solution and that, and at last, hoping something would occur to him, he went up out of Hell to the old woman's door to have a little talk with her. "See here," he said as soon as she answered his knock. "I mean to have your goat."

The old woman looked him up and down, and wasn't in the least dismayed. "Go ahead and take him," she said. "If you can do that, he's yours."

The Devil glanced across the yard to where Walpurgis stood tied up to the tree. "If I try to untie him, that bell will ring, and I can't stand bells," he said with a shudder.

"I know," said the old woman, looking satisfied.

The Devil swallowed his annoyance and tried a more familiar tack. "I'll give you anything you want," he said, "if you'll go over there and take away that wretched bell. I'll even make you Queen of the World."

The old woman cackled. "I've got my cottage, my goat, and everything I need," she said. "Why should I want to buy trouble? There's nothing you can do for me."

The Devil ground his teeth. "It takes a mean mind to put a bell on a goat," he snapped. "If he were *my* goat, I'd never do that. I'll bet a bucket of brimstone he hates that bell."

"Save your brimstone," said the old woman. "He's only a goat. It doesn't matter to *him*."

"He'd tell you, though, if he could talk," said the Devil.

"May be," said the old woman. "I've often wished he *could* talk, if it comes to that. But until he can, I'll keep him any way I want to. So goodbye." And she slammed the door between them.

This gave the Devil the very idea he was looking for. He hurried down to Hell and was back in a minute with a little cake into which he had mixed the power of speech, and he tossed it to Walpurgis. The goat chewed it up at once and swallowed it and then the Devil changed himself into a field mouse and hid in the grass to see what would happen.

After a while Walpurgis shook himself, which made the bell jangle, and at that he opened his mouth and said a very bad word. An expression of great surprise came over his face when he heard himself speak, and his eyes opened wide. Then they narrowed again and he tried a few more bad words, all of which came out clear and unmistakable. Then, as much as goats can ever smile, Walpurgis smiled. He moved as far from the tree as the rope would allow, and called out in a rude voice: "Hey there, you in the cottage!"

The old woman came to the door and put her head out. "Who's there?" she asked suspiciously, peering about.

"It's me! Walpurgis!" said the goat. "Come out here and take away this bell."

"You *can* talk, then!" observed the old woman.

"I can," said Walpurgis. "And I want this bell off. Now. And be quick about it."

The old woman stared at the goat and then she folded her arms. "I had no idea you'd be this kind of goat," she said.

"To the Devil with that," said Walpurgis carelessly. "What's the difference? It's this bell I'm talking about. Come over here and take it off."

"I can't," said the old woman. "If I do, the Devil will steal you away for sure."

"If you don't," said the goat, "I'll yell and raise a ruckus."

"Yell away," said the old woman. "I've got no choice in the matter that I can see." And she went back inside the cottage and shut the door.

So Walpurgis began to yell. He yelled all the bad words he knew and he yelled them loud and clear, and he yelled them over and over till the countryside rang with them, and before long the old woman came out of her cottage with her fingers in her ears. "Stop that!" she shouted at the goat.

Walpurgis stopped yelling. "Do something, then," he said.

"All right, I will!" said the old woman. "And serve you both right. If I'd known what kind of a goat you were, I'd have done it in the first place. The Devil deserves a goat like you." She took away the bell and set Walpurgis free and right away the Devil leaped up from the grass and took the goat straight back to Hell.

Now the funny thing about the power of speech is that the Devil could give it away but he couldn't take it back. For a while it was amusing to have a talking goat in Hell, but not for very long, because Walpurgis complained a lot. He'd always been dissatisfied but being able to say so made all the difference. The air was too hot, he said, or the food was too dry, or there was just plain nothing to do but stand around. "I might as well be wearing a bell again, for all the moving about I do in this place," said Walpurgis.

"Don't mention bells!" said the Devil.

This gave Walpurgis the very idea he was looking for. He began to yell all the bell-ringing words he knew. He yelled them loud and clear—clang, ding, jingle, bong—and he yelled them over and over till Hell rang with them.

At last the Devil rose up with his fingers in his ears. "Stop that!" he shouted at the goat.

Walpurgis stopped yelling. "Do something, then," he said.

"All right, I will!" said the Devil. And with that he changed Walpurgis into a stuffed goat and took him back up to the old woman's cottage and left him there in the yard, tied up to the tree.

When the old woman saw that the goat was back, she hurried out to see how he was. And when she *saw* how he was, she said to herself, "Well, that's what comes of talking too much." But she put the bell around his neck and kept him standing there anyway, and since the sign was still there too, and still said THIS IS A REAL GOAT, nobody ever knew the difference. And everyone, except Walpurgis, was satisfied.

THE REDEMPTION
OF SILKY BILL
Sarah Zettel

"He'll eat the Cheyenne too, you know," said the coyote.

Standing-in-the-West picked up another log and rested it on the chopping stump. A fresh wind blew off the prairie, ruffling his newly-cut hair and the cloth of his cotton shirt. "Go away, Wihio."

The coyote looked towards the canvas enclosure that served Fort Summner as a church and then back to the Cheyenne brave wielding the steel axe as if it weighed no more than a feather. "You've forgotten who you are," said Wihio.

"No." Standing-in-the-West brought the axe down onto the wood. Thwak! "Peter Standing-in-the-West." Thwak! "He is good Christian." Thwak! "He helps Reverend." Thwak! "He preaches Bible book to Red Man." The log splintered in two. "And he has found a way to get rid of the White Man using the White Man's own medicine." He hefted the axe in both hands. "When you would not even deign to help him. Go away, Wihio."

Wihio shrugged, and went.

"Silky" Bill McGregor picked up the chunk of rock, keeping one eye on the Cheyenne that pitched it down. The withered old man didn't look like he could squash a bug, but the buck at his side, all done up in red paint and feathers, was another story. McGregor couldn't figure out why no one was making a ruckus about the pair of them standing bold-as-you-please in the middle of Fort Summner's only street with spears in their hands and bows on their backs. But nobody did. The morning traffic on foot, and on horse and wagon, just clumped and rattled around them. Folks sneered or they whispered, but nobody asked nobody's business. Nobody ran for the soldiers or the sheriff. Which didn't make sense.

McGregor turned the rock over in his long fingers. The hazy summer sun picked out the glittering flecks of silver embedded in its brownish surface. Although McGregor made his living at cards, he had some experience with raw ore. To his eye, this rock had come from what could be a valuable hunk of ground.

"Where'd you say you found this?" He cocked his eyebrows.

"We will show you the place." The old man has a voice as dry as dust. "Fallen Star," he tapped his own chest. "He will guide you, but first you must help the People. One of our braves has summoned your Devil. We want you to send it away."

McGregor's first impulse was to bust out laughing, but being stared at by the old Red was like being stared at by the mountains, and the mountains thought this was too big to be laughed at.

"Tall order." McGregor tugged at the brim of his hat. "You'd be better off seeing the preacher for something like that." He jerked his chin towards the tent church.

The old man shook his head. "The preacher will not listen to us. The soldiers will not listen to us. Your Devil is a dark and bloody mystery, White Man. I do not understand him. We need a white man to send him away. We do not have a holy man, we do not have a brave. We must get a trickster."

"Well, now." McGregor tucked the rock into his jacket pocket. "I'll have to think about it."

Fallen Star nodded. "When you have made up your mind, meet us on the northern edge of your town. Long Nose, come." The brave and the old man turned and walked slowly down the street. The folks passing by steered wide of them, but still, nobody said nothing.

"Never thought I'd see Silky Bill McGregor stoop to talk to a couple of whiskey-soaked reds." Ned Carter laughed at him from the door of the Royale saloon until his belly shook. Ned and Bill had been partnering around together for years, flush and broke, and Bill'd never figured out how he managed to stay so fat.

"Whisky-soaked ain't what I'd call 'em." McGregor remembered the old man's eyes. Crazy as a possum at noon, maybe, but he was stone-cold sober.

Ned was staring at him now. "What're you talking about? Neither of 'em could stand up straight. What were they after?"

"I don't know." Bill said absently. His head was still working on how he and Ned, and apparently the rest of the town could have seen such a different set of reds. His throat started itching and he realized he wanted a drink.

Ned ambled over and slapped him on the shoulder. "Well I do know. They was after money, or whiskey. And I know something else. Jamie Raeburn's gettin' up a game tonight and if we're real polite, you and me might finagle ourselves a couple of seats." He winked.

"You go on, Ned. I got some thinking to do."

Ned shrugged and took himself back indoors. McGregor strolled away down the hard-packed dirt street, dodging a couple of drovers on horses and side-stepping a load of workmen with tool bags. The town outside Fort Summner was just a touch over three years old and its canvas shanties were just beginning to be replaced by board and shingle buildings that looked like they might actually last awhile. People were filling the place up, coming in and out of the store and the stable almost as much as they were coming in and out of the three saloons.

And not one of them had said a word about two armed reds in the middle of town offering a silver mine to a gambler. The idea gave Bill a queasy feeling.

Past the assayer's stood The Nugget, a saloon so new they'd barely finished pegging the door together. The bar was a couple of planks balanced on a pair of empty kegs. McGregor ordered himself a whiskey and surveyed the room. A couple of boys shared red-eye and cigarettes in one corner. A three-handed poker game played itself out in another. Along the far wall, Dennis DeArmant, the skinny owner of the place, dealt a faro game across a rickety table.

Bill's hands twitched. If poker was Ned's game, faro was his. He felt in his pocket for a couple of five dollar pieces. Might as well teach these suckers how a man played it. It'd help take his mind off those Cheyenne anyway.

"Mr. McGregor?" said a cultured voice behind him.

Bill turned, taking his hand out of his pocket, in case he needed it for something else. The owner of the voice was a narrow man in a dark suit that had been cut to fit. His waistcoat was as silky and brightly patterned as Bill's own, and a gold toothpick dangled from the watch chain. What struck Bill, though, were his eyes. They were black, solid black.

Recognizing a gentleman when he saw one, Bill quick pulled together his professional manners. "May I ask who you are, Sir?"

The stranger gave a short chuckle. "Just an associate, Mr. McGregor. We've played cards together a few times." Bill racked his brains trying to recall where he could've seen those eyes before and came up with nothing. "May I buy you a drink?" asked the stranger.

McGregor glanced at the faro game and then at the stranger. He shrugged. "All right."

The stranger collected a bottle and two glasses from the barkeep, gesturing with them towards one of the back tables.

"Still don't know who I am, do you Bill?" He said as he poured.

"No, Sir, that I don't." Bill raised his glass.

The stranger smiled over the rim of his glass. It was a thin smile, like the curve in a butcher's knife. "Round here folks mostly call me Nick Scratch."

Bill set his own drink back on the table and got to his feet. "I don't care for your jokes, Sir," he announced. Across the room, heads turned and chatter dropped away. Boots and chairs scraped across the floorboards.

"Sit down, McGregor," said the stranger.

Bill sat.

"Drink your drink."

Bill lifted the glass and knocked back the whiskey. The other customers' attention went back to their own business. Bill set the glass on the table top. He drew his hand away and watched it shaking. He felt nothing, nothing at all.

"Are you ready to listen to me, Bill?" said the Devil.

"Have I got a choice?" McGregor couldn't get his gaze to leave the table top.

"Course you do. But your life'll be easier if you sit there calmly and let me finish. I've no wish to see you come to harm, Bill." McGregor heard the Devil pour himself another shot. "You're one of my best men."

That got McGregor's chin to jerk itself up.

"Oh, yes, you work for me, Bill." A red light sparkled deep down in the Devil's black eyes. "And I got a nice spot in Hell saved for your soul. Right next to the stove, so you won't take a chill.

"See, wherever you go, the good church-going folk denounce you, using my name. But the young folks see you thriving by it and they line up for a chance to follow your way of life. Some of them do as fine a job for me as you do. Some do much better.

"How many times has somebody said you've got the devil's own luck, Bill? It happens to be true. I've seen to it that you prosper and I'll see that you continue to do so, just so long as you stay away from those Cheyenne. I've a bargain to keep with them and I'm a man of my word." The light in the Devil's eyes snapped. "I've got to go, Bill, but I'll leave you with this, just in case you're inclined to believe I crawled out of that whiskey bottle. A riot's going to start tonight in the Royale House. Before sun-up, three-quarters of the town'll be burnt down and Ned Carter will be dead behind the Summner House hotel. Shot in the back."

The Devil walked out of the saloon. McGregor, with his hands still trembling, poured another whiskey but all he did was look at it. Minutes ticked themselves away to the click of coins on the faro table.

Bill didn't believe in haunts, nor spiritualism. He tried hard not to believe what his father had preached in the Boston parish he'd ruled with such an iron fist. But he believed his eyes and his head. He'd stayed alive believing those.

Right now, his eyes and his head told him what was going on here was past all understanding. If a man couldn't understand the rules of the game, it was best he leave the table.

Bill pulled himself to his feet and left the whiskey and the saloon as fast as he could. Outside the door, he chucked the piece of silver ore into a patch of weeds. Then he made tracks for the Royale.

He found Ned in one of the bare rooms on the second floor, getting in a few sociable hands before Jamie Raeburn's big game. McGregor waited impatiently for the hand to play itself out before he sidled up to Ned, who was raking in the pot.

"I'd like a word with you in private, Ned, if I may," he said into his friend's ear.

"Keep my seat for me, Gentlemen," said Ned instantly. He got up and followed McGregor out onto the porch.

"What's the matter Bill?"

McGregor faced him. A fresh sweat that had nothing to do with the heat of the day prickled under his collar. "Ned, I've had word there's going to be trouble tonight."

"What kind of trouble?" Ned hitched up his eyebrows.

McGregor's memory showed him the Devil's black eyes and the sweat broke under his hat brim as well. "Just trust me on this one, Ned. We need to get back east, fast."

Ned searched his face for a long moment. "OK, Bill, but I'll need to work up some cash."

"Me too. What do you say we meet out here at five sharp? We can get horses and gear from the blacksmith and get out while there's still some light."

Ned consulted his pocket watch. "Not much time, but," he grinned, "there's a couple of boys in there, fresh out of the mines. Five it is."

The two gamblers parted ways at the door. Ned stalked over to the poker table and Bill to the faro games.

McGregor always played to win, but there were a few times, like now, when he played to win quickly. Years of practice let him set everything aside but the game. Part of his mind ticked off the cards as they were played. Part of it calculated the possible order of the ones remaining in the spring-loaded box. He split his bets between cards. He bet which cards would lose as well as which would win. Carefully, he bet on the order of the last three cards to be drawn from the box and won at four-to-one odds.

By the time the railroad clock chimed the hour of five, McGregor had taken in enough to make the dealer sweat, but not quite enough to break the bank. He took up his gold and script and met Ned outside.

Ned patted his money belt. "Got enough here that we can head back east in style." He glanced around at the mud and bare-board town. "Soon as we get some place that knows what style is."

McGregor shared his laugh half-heartedly. "Ned, you get down to the forge. I'll settle up at the Summner House, settle up and meet you there."

"All right, Silky." Ned started up the street.

"At the forge," repeated McGregor.

Ned frowned. "I heard you, Bill."

McGregor left him reluctantly and made tracks for the Summner House.

Ned, like McGregor, travelled light. Once in their room, it didn't take him long to load both of their belongings into their cases.

He snapped the latch closed on Ned's grip and hoisted their bags off the bed. He turned, only to find old Fallen Star sitting cross-legged in the doorway.

The bags thudded to the floor. "How the hell'd you get in here!"

"I walked." He took a puff from the pipe he carried.

"They'd never let a Red in here!" McGregor took a step back, hand reaching for his revolver.

"No one saw me." Fallen Star blew a cloud of smoke at the ceiling.

"Then how'd you get across the lobby?"

"I walked."

McGregor set his jaw. "Then you can walk on out of here. You're in my way."

"McGregor."

For the second time that day, the sound of his own name paralysed him. "Running away will do you no good," the old man said. "You must fight your Devil or he will plague you forever."

"He's not my Devil!" snapped Bill.

"Then whose is he?" Unbending one joint at a time, Fallen Star stood. "Gambler, you want to save your friend. I want to save my son, Standing-in-the-West. You call your Devil here and work against him with the White Man's understanding. I will strengthen you with the Red Man's medicine. Maybe together we can beat him."

McGregor remembered the Devil's eyes and found the nerve to move again. He pulled his gun out of its holster. "Get out of my way or I'll blow a hole clear through you."

Fallen Star shook his head heavily and took a long drag on his pipe. "That you may see the truth." He blew a rank cloud of smoke into McGregor's face.

By the time Bill quit coughing, the old man was gone. McGregor didn't stop to ask himself where or how. He just gathered up the bags and toted them down the stairs.

He was passing his money across the pigeon-hole desk to the hotel owner's beefy hands when the first shot split the air.

McGregor dove for the floor. The hotel owner was already down behind the desk. On hands and knees, the gambler crawled to the door and eased it open.

Men spilled out of the Royale, guns in their hands. The thunder and lightning of revolver shots rang through the air. A stranger sprawled face-down in the mud. Another hollered wordlessly and took his own shot. The crowd spread out. So did the gunfire.

All at once, the storm hit the Denver House. McGregor scrambled sideways as somebody kicked the door in. Men shoved and stumbled inside, yelling over the top of each other until McGregor couldn't understand any of them. Somebody shattered a pane of glass with the butt of his revolver. Some fool waved his gun towards the owner. A shot and the stench of gunpowder exploded from behind Bill and blood burst across the fool's chest. All heads turned to see the Summner House's owner with his Winchester raised. He couldn't keep them all covered though, and the fool had a friend. Another gun barked and the landlord hit the back wall on top of most of his brains.

McGregor eased his revolver into his hand and slid out the door. Wood smoke and a roaring on the wind competed with the smell and noise of gunfire. The heat hit him a second later and Bill looked up. More heat seared his face. The Royale was on fire. Men and women leapt shrieking from the windows.

In the middle of the chaos stood the Devil, thumbs tucked into his waistcoat pockets and a grin spread across his face. No one payed him any heed. A naked woman jumped from the Royale's second storey and landed in the street, her body bent and broken. No one stopped to help her. A hunk of burning wood landed on the roof of the assayer's. Flames and sparks wriggled to the sky. A few folk turned out with water buckets, but most scattered, trying to get out of the way. Men with rifles appeared on rooftops. A couple of blue coated soldiers galloped in on horseback, raising clouds of dust and shouting orders to no one at all.

The Devil laughed.

Something in McGregor snapped. Without thinking, he was running to the spot where Nick Scratch stood.

"Stop this!" he hollered, grabbing Scratch by the shoulder.

The Devil turned and looked at him with eyes more red than black. "I'm going to forgive you this, McGregor, because you don't know what you're doing." Pain bit hard into the gambler's hand. Bill jerked backwards.

The screams got louder. Fire laid its claim to The Nugget with DeArmant still shooting through the window. McGregor thought about Ned and saw the woman lying dead in the dirt.

"What'll it take to get you to stop this!" he cried.

"Go away, Bill."

All McGregor's desperation melted into panic. Before he had time to realize it must be Scratch working on him again, he backed up two steps, turned, and ran for his life.

Bent almost double, Bill raced up the street. Bullets and screams whizzed past him. He hugged board walls and dove through open spaces, returning fire when he needed to clear his way and didn't stop to see if he hit anything or not.

At last, from the shelter of a clapboard shack, McGregor could spy the open-frame building that housed the forge. Horses reared and hauled on the reins that tethered them to the rail beside it. McGregor ducked his head from side to side, trying to see Ned between the thrashing animals.

A man's shadow crept around the forge. With a quick knife, he slit the horse's reins, setting them free to gallop out of town. Then the shadow climbed to the roof of the forge as easily as a cat. He pulled a rifle from a sling on his back and took aim.

The Shadow fired. McGregor saw DeArmant knocked off his feet. The shadow fired again and a nameless man on another rooftop toppled over.

"Standing-in-the-West!"

Bill blinked and knuckled his eyes. Fallen Star stood beside the forge, right in the shadow man's line of fire. His gnarled arms were raised towards the heavens. The pipe still burned in his hand.

Standing-in-the-West held his fire. "Out of my way!"

"You will not win the war with the White Men this way!" Fallen Star's voice carried clearly over the rage of men and gunshot and fire. Bill shook his head hard. He knew the old man spoke Cheyenne, but he could understand him clearly. "You only make a slave of yourself to your anger and their Devil! Will you fight and die as a slave or a free man?"

Standing-in-the-West aimed his gun at the old man. "Is your medicine strong enough to stop my bullet, Fallen Star? Or do you use too much to keep the riot away from you? The White Men will leave our land!"

"Our land!" retorted Fallen Star. "We do not own this place! It is not a dog or a slave! You talk like the White Men!"

"And I will kill you with their gun if you do not leave me now!"

Fallen Star dropped his hands. "I would have wished another kind of trail for you, my son." He said. And despite the noise of fire and riot, Bill heard Standing-in-the-West cock the rifle's hammer.

Fallen Star walked away towards the edge of town. Standing-in-the-West took fresh aim towards the center of the riot and fired again. Another man fell. Shots buzzed towards the Cheyenne. None found the mark.

McGregor's stomach knotted itself up. He dropped his gaze to search the forge. Ned was nowhere in sight. Bill turned to run back the way he came.

Reality became a blur of noise and fading color as he stumbled towards the Summner House. Something heavy caught the toes of his boots and Bill measured his length in the dust. He came up, spitting and swearing, looked at what tripped him up and saw Ned.

What was left of Ned's blood oozed out of the bullet hole in his back. McGregor's strength gave out and he sat down hard next to his friend's body, unable to think, let alone move. Vaguely, slowly, he noticed that Ned's money belt was still around his waist and that his hand clutched some leather strips. McGregor touched them. Horses' reins. He thought of Standing-in-the-West's knife and his fist bunched up and pressed against his forehead.

"See the great gambler sitting in the dirt!" cried a voice.

McGregor looked up. The world had receded silently into a solid curtain of fog. The only things left were Ned's corpse and a one-handed red man with a huge nose and wrinkled skin. His eyes glittered brightly under a sagging hat hung with strings of feathers and animal tails.

"Who?" Bill heard his voice without feeling his mouth move.

"Many." The man smiled. "Napi," and he was a half-naked indian brave. "Nana Bosho," and he was a scrawny scavenger with three legs. "But for you, I'm Wihio," and the one-handed man was back. "Come with me."

McGregor was on his feet without standing. He followed wrinkled Wihio without walking. "I'm dreaming."

"So you are," grinned Wihio. He pointed with the stump of his wrist. "Look that way. You will learn something."

McGregor saw Standing-in-the-West sitting naked in a dark lodge full of smoke, or maybe steam. His skin was slick with sweat. His eyes were shut tight and he called out.

"Medicine Arrows! Arrows, I know you were captured from us long ago, but I know that you have helped the People many times even from afar! Medicine Arrows, help me now! Help me kill these White Men so that no more may come to harm us!"

A voice from nowhere answered him. "We cannot help you kill the White Men. Guns and horses have made us weak and scattered us. Go out to the People, Standing-in-the-West. Look for ways to live, not to kill. Maybe then we can help you."

Standing-in-the-West called out. "Wihio! Wihio! You are strong in tricks and mischief! Help me work mischief on these White Men!"

Wihio spoke. "I cannot help you work mischief on these White Men. They thrive on challenge and danger. Go out to the People, Standing-in-the-West. Look for ways to strengthen yourselves, not weaken others. Maybe then I can help you."

The world shifted. Now Standing-in-the-West waited on a hillside where autumn's colors touched the trees. His knife drew a five-pointed star on the ground. A cross hung upside down from a baby cottonwood's branch. Standing-in-the-West stepped away from the star and methodically recited the Lord's Prayer, backwards.

The Devil stood in the center of the star.

Standing-in-the-West spoke. "I want to make a treaty with you, Devil, to drive the White Men off of Cheyenne land."

"Why should I do that?" The Devil spread his hands.

"I will give you my soul."

"You do not believe in souls, Standing-in-the-West. They are outside of what the Cheyenne know to be true."

Standing-in-the-West shrugged. "I am a Christian now. I know what a soul is. I will make a treaty with you."

The Devil smiled his thin smile. "Very well, Standing-in-the-West. We have a treaty."

"What are you doing here!" cried Wihio.

The Devil turned his head, but Standing-in-the-West didn't move. "I am taking his soul, Wihio."

Wihio reared up, suddenly as big as a mountain. "Go!" His voice rocked the entire world. "By the Great Spirit that birthed me and the land that strengthens me! Go, Foul One! You have nothing to do with the People!"

The Devil stood his ground. "I do now."

Wihio dwindled to a man's size again. The mists swallowed up everything but he and McGregor.

"White Man, I do not understand your people. I do understand that your Devil is strong in corruption and Standing-in-the-West has brought that corruption onto the People. He will use Standing-in-the-West and he will make the People his own. I will not have that, Gambler. The People are my people, not his.

"He is your luck, Bill McGregor, but I am a gambler too. If you rid the People of your Devil, I will take his place as your luck."

"You can hold it right there!" McGregor exploded. "You people! Do this! Do that! You're a white man! You're greedy! Here, we'll pay you to risk your life… your soul for us!" He threw up both hands. "Damn you all! This is your problem! What are you and that medicine man risking!"

Wihio didn't even blink. "That is fair, Gambler. All right. I too will risk something." He tore one of the tails off his hat and it was in McGregor's closed hand. "I will be beside you when you face the Devil. I will do what you say, even if you say I should kill or die. I will tell Fallen Star he must do the same. Is that enough for you?"

McGregor's fists tightened up. He could see Ned's body again. He drank in the details of it for a long, long time.

"Wihio." His tongue felt thick and heavy. "If I do this, will you make Standing-in-the-West's life rough on him?"

Wihio smiled and his teeth flashed like stars. "Gambler, I will make his life impossible for him."

"All right, then," Bill whispered.

Bill woke up.

He hadn't moved but he must have been there for hours. Night had come down and the town had gone silent. The smell of burnt wood filled the wind. McGregor stretched his aching neck and saw dawn drawing a thin white line around the deserted forge.

He stared down at the coyote's tail wound between his fingers.

"All right," he said again.

Slowly, he forced his mind back over all the events of the day and added to them all the things he remembered hearing from his father's sermons. Something that would be called a plan by a more generous man took shape inside him.

He folded the mangy tail up and put it in his pocket. Then, he turned Ned gently onto his back. Silky Bill closed his friend's eyes and folded his hands.

"If I make it," Bill eased Ned's money belt off. "This'll buy you the finest funeral this territory's ever seen."

McGregor straightened up his creaking legs and headed for the north edge of town.

The morning chill had soaked well into him by the time he made it out onto the prairie grass. Fallen Star, his boy Long Nose and three painted indian ponies appeared out from a cluster of cottonwoods to meet him. Bill found he was long past being surprised by so minor a miracle of timing.

"Wihio has told me what your answer is," said Fallen Star. "What must we do first?"

"I could use something to eat," McGregor croaked. "Then you'd better show me where Standing-in-the-West called up the Devil."

Long Nose gave him water and dried buffalo meat. What Bill really wanted was whiskey, but he didn't feel up to heading back to whatever was left of the town to fetch any.

Fallen Star led the silent procession of men and horses until the sun was almost directly overhead. The wind stiffened up to blow all the summer heat down on top of them. The ponies trooped steadily through the grass and pale-leafed trees until they reached the gentle slope McGregor had seen in Wihio's strange dream.

Bill dismounted along with the two reds and marshalled his courage. "I'm telling you now, I don't know what I'm doing. I just got a couple of ideas." His voice was holding steady, even if his heart wasn't. "I'm going to try to get the Devil into a card game. I'll need something to bet with and his coin is people. I'll need something I can use as chips so I can bet you. Both of you."

Fallen Star did not hesitate. He handed over his long-stemmed pipe. McGregor turned to the brave. Long Nose gave him his necklace of red beads.

"You know I got a good chance of losing." McGregor tucked the tokens into his coat pockets.

"We know," said Fallen Star. "We also know you are going to do your best. You are now on a war trail."

McGregor turned his back to the reds. He wondered if Fallen Star would have said the same thing if he knew all that Bill's sketchy plan entailed. Bill brought up the memory of Ned's corpse and of Standing-in-the-West on the rooftop. He squared his shoulders.

"Nick Scratch!" he called into the wind. "I've got some business with you!"

The thin stranger stood in front of him, fire glowing hot behind his black eyes.

"I tried to warn you, Bill." The Devil shook his head.

"I'm not saying you didn't." McGregor tightened all the fibers in his wrists to keep his hands from shaking. The air had gone warm and thick around him. His ears felt stopped up and his heart beat slow and sluggish.

"You can still go, Bill," the Devil breathed to him. "No hard feelings. Go on."

Bill teetered. "I'm not leaving, just yet."

"Neither am I," the Devil replied evenly.

"Care to bet on that?"

A hot wind blew hard and sudden. McGregor clamped his hand on his hat and clenched his teeth. The Devil remained silent, watching him.

"I'll play you a game of faro," McGregor said. "'Til one of us is cleaned out. If I win, you clear out and never come near anyone here or their land or their family again."

The Devil arched his delicate eyebrows. "And what do you have to put up in such a game, Bill?"

"How about them?" McGregor nodded towards the unmoving Cheyenne.

The Devil fingered his chin. "Mmmm. Fallen Star, now he would be a prize. They all you got?"

McGregor's hand curled around the scrap of fur in his pocket. "No."

"Well, well. All right, then." The Devil nodded. "I haven't much time though, Bill. One game, 'til one of us is cleaned out. I'll deal."

Nick Scratch didn't even blink. The faro table from the Nugget appeared in the waving grass between him and Bill. At his left hand stood the owner of the Denver House with his eyes wide and his skull split open where the bullet passed through him.

"My casekeeper," Nick Scratch gestured a fine hand at the dead man and the abacus that kept track of the cards played.

"Strange," said Wihio's voice in his head and Bill jumped half-way out of his skin. "I was expecting Standing-in-the-West. Why has he not claimed him yet?" Wihio paused and it seemed to Bill the invisible presence was watching him shudder. "Well, Gambler, don't tell me you are afraid of shadows and voices."

The Devil's eyes sparkled. "Wihio? You here? Which of these fools is your champion, Dog-of-a-Mystery?"

The laughter left Wihio's voice. "You have secrets behind your fire and when I learn them, you will need to look to your skin."

The Devil's eyes glowed red. "Oh, yes. I will look to my skin. See that you do the same when I have the People for my own."

"Let's get to it." Bill plunked himself down in the chair that had appeared on his side of the table and tried to settle his mind on the game. It was just a faro game. He knew this game like the back of his hand. He could play this. Didn't matter who was dealing. He took out the beads and the pipe. In his hand they turned to a pile of five dollar coins. Bill set them down on the table like they might bite. Just a faro game. And he was feeling lucky today. That shook him, but he felt Wihio hovering around back of him and the tension eased. Yes. He was feeling lucky today.

For the look of the thing, Bill inspected the box and the cards. Both were clean, which he hadn't expected. The cards flashed between the Devil's fingers as he shuffled. He tamped the deck even against the table and laid it neatly into the box. The wind blew the unnatural heat through the coarse grass around McGregor's ankles but didn't come near the top of the table.

The Devil turned the crank on the box and drew out the four of spades. That was the soda and it took no part in the game. His ghoulish casekeeper pushed a bead across on the abacus to count it as played. Bill's eyes started watering.

The world changed. McGregor still faced the Devil across the faro table, but around them hunched the skin mounds of a Cheyenne camp.

"What're you doing?" Bill's voice came out in a whisper.

In this new place it was barely dawn. A river chattered to itself somewhere in the distance. The only people up and about were Long Nose and Fallen Star. Long Nose prowled between the lodges, clutching his feathered spear. Fallen Star looked across to Bill with his deep eyes and then he began to chant. It was a slow, strong sound and it made the hairs on the back of Bill's neck prickle.

"Playing the game," replied the Devil. "Place your bet, Bill."

"Charge!" bellowed somebody.

Horses hooves pounded the ground until it shuddered. Dawn light flashed on sabers and rifle barrels and gold braid. Long Nose hollered in Cheyenne and no one answered. The cavalry bore down on the camp. Shots split the dawn. Long Nose dodged, dragging Fallen Star with him. Someone screamed. A soldier lept off his horse and slit a skin house open. Blood. Blood everywhere. Bill gripped the edge of the table and stared at the game. He felt the heat of the Devil's grin. Long Nose lifted his spear and charged into the fray. Fallen Star did not move, but the world around him did. Soldiers who had clear shots at Long Nose missed by a mile. They fell from their horses for him to cut down. They swung their sabers over his head and got in each others' way. Fought like a bunch of kids bogged down in the snow. Long Nose killed them and they killed the women and the children and the unarmed men and Bill sat and looked on.

Stop this, Bill, stop it now! cried a part of Bill's mind. You already got him where you want him, and if it's going to work, it's going to work as well now as later.

Bill steeled himself. Not yet.

"Place your bet, Gambler," said Wihio. Bill glanced behind him. The three-legged coyote sat beside him. It dipped its muzzle and Bill felt his mind clear. He heard the shouts and hoofbeats and he smelled blood and gunpowder but it was all a long way away. Right now, he had a game to play. He set his coins down, splitting the bet carefully.

The Devil gave a loud guffaw. "Him? This is your champion, Wihio? Phew! Dog-of-a-Mystery, you must be desperate!"

The coyote bared its teeth. "I may be all you say, Foul One, but at least I understand my own people."

Still chuckling, the Devil turned the crank on the box and the game really began.

It didn't take long for Bill's little pile of chips to slide away. His splits didn't work and he couldn't keep count. He felt Wihio keeping himself between Bill and his fears but it wasn't enough. Maybe Wihio was too busy keeping him from going raving mad to loan him any extra luck. Maybe he didn't understand this White Man's game. Maybe it was just that Bill knew the Devil had always made him lucky and his luck was dealing the cards against him.

Around them the fight kept on. Bill, using the calm Wihio loaned him, flicked his eyes towards the soldiers, searching for one face in particular.

He's got to do it, he told himself. He's cruelty itself. If he's got Ned's soul, he'll pull him out of Hell and parade him for me. If he doesn't, then... then things in Heaven are looser than Father ever knew, and we all can still get outta this OK. If I've got things figured right that is. Bill glanced down at Wihio and the coyote just shrugged. Well, he'd already laid everything he had on Bill, what was he going to do?

The cards flitted from the box and the coins clinked together into higher piles in front of the Devil. One shot found its mark. Long Nose dropped into the grass. A soldier laughed. McGregor laid another bet. The Devil turned the crank on the case. There was a sound like ripe fruit falling and a soldier raised a sword dripping with Fallen Star's blood.

The battle fell silent, even the sound of the river fell away.

"That seems to be that, Bill," said Nick Scratch. He nodded, friendly-like to the cavalry sergeant.

Bill glanced at Wihio. "He's a hasty one, isn't he?" said Wihio.

"Patience is a virtue," said Bill from behind the blanket of calm Wihio kept around him. "He's real short on virtue."

"You don't say, Gambler? And why hasn't he got Standing-in-the-West, yet? Can you tell me that?"

Bill scratched his chin. "I'd say it's 'cause he ain't kept his side of the bargain yet. White Men're still here, aren't they?"

"Oh, is that the way it works?" Wihio nodded. "I see."

Thunder rumbled from underground. "You've got another bet, Bill, I see it in you. Put it down or walk away."

"Go ahead, Gambler," said Wihio.

Bill scanned the battlefield and saw nothing but strangers' faces among the dead. He swallowed hard, drew out the coyote's tail and laid it on the king.

The Devil grinned from ear to ear. "And I thought you at least had brains, Wihio."

He drew out a fresh card. The nine of spades. With one fine hand he picked up the tail.

"Now, Dog," the Devil said. "Heel!"

Wihio whimpered and limped to the Devil's side, his tail tucked between his legs.

Without the shelter Wihio gave him, the world slammed against McGregor. The steel taste of blood filled his mouth and all around him lay the victims of the battle; the dead and the worse-than-dead who could still scream. This was no dream. This was smoke and stench and heat and fear. Waves of it. Billows of it, surrounding Bill, pressing him down, drowning him. This was the riot in Fort Summner. This was how the Devil kept his bargain and how he'd serve his new people.

"You've lost, Bill." Heat flickered through the Devil's voice.

"N. . .ot yet," stammered Bill. "I've got one more bet."

"Now what could you possibly have left to lay on this table, Bill?" The Devil kicked Wihio sharply. The coyote yelped and cowered. "You've bet the soul of a whole people and lost it."

"My life."

The devil actually looked startled.

McGregor drew out his revolver. "I'm a preacher's son, Devil. I know this much. You may have a spot in Hell for my soul, but as long as I'm alive, I could still go straight. I can repent any time before I die and save myself, work on savin' those young folks you talked about. But if I lose this turn, I'm your boy, before and after I die," he took the gun by the barrel and held the hilt towards the Devil.

"Bill McGregor, you've got fewer brains than Wihio."

"Silky."

Bill swung around. Ned stood behind him, blood oozing out of his chest and spilling onto his hands. "Silky," he coughed. "He's put me up against your life. Hurry, Bill. I...It hurts."

"Oh, my..." Bill felt all the life drain out of his cheeks. "Ned. I'm sorry. I'm sorry..."

Ned stretched out his hands. He was white like snow, like death. His round face had already fallen into lines and angles. "Hurry, Bill. Get me out of this. Place your bet."

"No," said Bill.

"Then I win," said the Devil.

"Bill!" shouted Ned.

Bill forced himself to turn away from his friend. "Then take your winnings and go," he clutched the gun barrel. "If you can. The way I see it, the game's not over yet. And it won't be until I've laid my last bet."

"Bill!" Ned was screaming. Bill heard him fall. He closed his eyes and prayed with all his heart and soul that he had it right. This was the real gamble, not the way the cards came out of the box. Bill gambled everything on his guess at the reason why the Devil had to wait to take Standing-in-the-West, on why he didn't just reach across the table and snatch Bill's soul from his body. "I'm not cleaned out yet, Devil. And 'til I am the game's not over." Bill held the edge of the table to keep himself upright as he felt his knees begin to buckle. "If the game's not over, you have to stay here." That had to be it, it had to be. The Devil couldn't leave an unfulfilled contract behind him. "That's the deal. And you," Bill added bitterly. "Are a man of your word."

The Devil's howl tore the world apart. McGregor's heart stopped dead and then banged like a hammer against his ribs. His knees gave out, toppling him onto the ground. Ned lay there next to him. Ned who had all the guts of the pair of them. Ned was bleeding and crying. Crying like a baby.

Bill shouted to drown the crying out. "You cannot leave!" McGregor raised his head and saw all the fires of Hell raging in the Devil's eyes and he knew he'd guessed right. Triumph rang through him. "You got a deal with me to play until one of us is cleaned out! You cannot do anything else, ever, until I lay my bet down! And I will not do it until we have a bargain!"

"You don't have the will, McGregor!" The blast from the shout bowled the gambler backwards.

Painfully, Bill hauled himself back onto his knees. "Want to bet?"

The Devil swept his fist through the air.

Everything vanished. There was not even a mist. McGregor smelled nothing, heard nothing, had no ground beneath him. He had only his eyes, and all he saw was the Devil.

"I will leave the Cheyenne alone," growled Nick Scratch.

Bill could not move any part of himself but he could speak as he had in the dream Wihio led him through. "That's a start."

The Devil's eyes turned blood red. "I will return the lives you bet on the faro table and I will touch them and theirs no more."

"Not enough."

"Gambler," the word filled the universe. "What do you want?"

"Ned Carter's soul," said Bill. "And mine."

The Devil's face twisted. His mouth worked itself back and forth. At last he said "I have not had your soul since you tried to stop the riot in Fort Summner."

A warmth that had nothing to do with the Devil's head spread through McGregor. "I want this notarized."

The Devil bared his teeth. "You had better tread very carefully the rest of your born days, McGregor." Wihio stood beside the Devil now, hat and all. "Wihio," said Nick Scratch. "If I break my treaty with Bill McGregor, you may hand me over to the Master of Heaven." Each word sounded like a branch snapping in the fire.

"It is well, Foul One." Wihio bobbed his head and smiled.

The world dropped back into place in a rush of burning wind and bright sunshine. Bill looked at the table, calculated the state of play and set his gun down on the eight card.

He didn't even see the game vanish. His posterior hit the ground, jarring all the breath out of him. For a moment, Bill blinked stupidly up at the cloudless sky.

A wrinkled hand reached into his line of vision. Bill let Fallen Star help him to his feet.

"Thank you," Bill ran his hand through his hair. Long Nose handed him his hat. He nodded to the silent brave.

"We thank you, Gambler," Fallen Star said. "Now," Sunlight caught a spark deep in the medicine man's eyes, "I would ask you to please leave this place."

"What?" Bill pushed his hat down over his rumpled hair and holstered his gun. "After all that? How about that land you promised me?"

Fallen Star sighed. "I will take you to where we found the stone, if that is what you wish, but hear what I say first.

"Our people take the war trail against each other. Your people have too much hunger for things which are not yours and we have too many young men like Standing-in-the-West.

"You have done us a great service. I do not want to hear that one of my braves has taken your life."

Bill dug his hands into his pockets. A scrap of fur brushed his palm and Wihio's mocking presence brushed his mind.

He sighed. "Just as well, I suppose. I'd just about made up my mind to go straight anyways." He held the coyote tail out to the medicine man.

"To keep away your Devil?" Fallen Star accepted the token.

McGregor shook his head. "No. To get him good and mad." He cracked a smile. "It's the only revenge I'm likely to get on him for letting Ned die." He dug his hands into his pockets. In a strange way, he actually had lost his life on that faro table. Only he hadn't lost it to the Devil. Bill glanced at the clear, blue sky. Well, his father'd be pleased anyway.

Fallen Star raised his hand and the wind blew gently around them. "May you have a bright sun and blue sky for your journey, Gambler."

McGregor raised his hand in return. Then, he set his back to the prairie and started walking.

SOLD TO SATAN

Mark Twain

It was at this time that I concluded to sell my soul to Satan. Steel was away down, so was St. Paul; it was the same with all the desirable stocks, in fact, and so, if I did not turn out to be away down myself, now was my time to raise a stake and make my fortune. Without further consideration I sent word to the local agent, Mr. Blank, with description and present condition of the property, and an interview with Satan was promptly arranged, on a basis of 2 1/2 percent, this commission payable only in case a trade should be consummated.

I sat in the dark, waiting and thinking. How still it was! Then came the deep voice of a far-off bell proclaiming midnight—Boom-m-m! Boom-m-m! Boom-m-m!—and I rose to receive my guest, and braced myself for the thunder crash and the brimstone stench which should announce his arrival. But there was no crash, no stench. Through the closed door, and noiseless, came the modern Satan, just as we see him on the stage—tall, slender, graceful, in tights and trunks, a short cape mantling his shoulders, a rapier at his side, a single drooping feather in his jaunty cap, and on his intellectual face the well-known and high-bred Mephistophelian smile.

But he was not a fire coal; he was not red, no! On the contrary. He was a softly glowing, richly smoldering torch, column, statue of pallid light, faintly tinted with a spiritual green, and out from him a lunar splendor flowed such as one sees glinting from the crinkled waves of tropic seas when the moon rides high in cloudless skies.

He made his customary stage obeisance, resting his left hand upon his sword hilt and removing his cap with his right and making that handsome sweep with it which we know so well; then we sat down. Ah, he was an incandescent glory, a nebular dream, and so much improved by his change of color. He must have seen the admiration in my illuminated face, but he took no notice of it, being long ago used to it in faces of other Christians with whom he had had trade relations.

...A half hour of hot toddy and weather chat, mixed with occasional tentative feelers on my part and rejoinders of, "Well, I could hardly pay *that* for it, you know," on his, had much modified my shyness and put me so much at my ease that I was emboldened to feed my curiosity a little. So I chanced the remark that he was surprisingly different from the traditions, and I wished I knew what it was he was made of. He was not offended, but answered with frank simplicity:

"Radium!"

"That accounts for it!" I exclaimed. "It is the loveliest effulgence I have ever seen. The hard and heartless glare of the electric doesn't compare with it. I suppose Your Majesty weighs about—about—"

"I stand six feet one; fleshed and blooded I would weigh two hundred and fifteen; but radium, like other metals, is heavy. I weigh nine hundred-odd."

I gazed hungrily upon him, saying to myself:

"What riches! What a mine! Nine hundred pounds at, say, $3,500,000 a pound, would be—would be—" Then a treacherous thought burst into my mind!

He laughed a good hearty laugh, and said:

"I perceive your thought; and what a handsomely original idea it is!—to kidnap Satan, and stock him, and incorporate him, and water the stock up to ten billions—just three times its actual value—and blanket the world with it!" My blush had turned the moonlight to a crimson mist, such as veils and spectralizes the domes and towers of Florence at sunset and makes the spectator drunk with joy to see, and he pitied me, and dropped his tone of irony, and assumed a grave and reflective one which had a pleasanter sound for me, and under its kindly influence my pains were presently healed, and I thanked him for his courtesy. Then he said:

"One good turn deserves another, and I will pay you a compliment. Do you know I have been trading with your poor pathetic race for ages, and you are the first person who has ever been intelligent enough to divine the large commercial value of my make-up."

I purred to myself and looked as modest as I could.

"Yes, you are the first," he continued. "All through the Middle Ages I used to buy Christian souls at fancy rates, building bridges and cathedrals in a single night in return, and getting swindled out of my Christian nearly every time that I dealt with a priest—as history will concede—but making it up on the lay square-dealer now and then, as *I* admit; but none of those people ever guessed where the real big money lay. You are the first."

I refilled his glass and gave him another Cavour. But he was experienced, by this time. He inspected the cigar pensively awhile; then:

"What do you pay for these?" he asked.

"Two cents—but they come cheaper when you take a barrel."

He went on inspecting; also mumbling comments, apparently to himself:

"Black—rough-skinned—rumpled, irregular, wrinkled, barky, with crispy curled-up places on it—burnt-leather aspect, like the shoes of the damned that sit in pairs before the room doors at home of a Sunday morning." He sighed at thought of his home, and was silent a moment; then he said, gently, "Tell me about this projectile."

"It is the discovery of a great Italian statesman," I said. "Cavour. One day he lit his cigar, then laid it down and went on writing and forgot it. It lay in a pool of ink and got soaked. By and by he noticed it and laid it on the stove to dry. When it was dry he lit it and at once noticed that it didn't taste the same as it did before. And so—"

"Did he say what it tasted like before?"

"No, I think not. But he called the government chemist and told him to find out the source of that new taste, and report. The chemist applied the tests, and reported that the source was the presence of sulphate of iron, touched up and spiritualized with vinegar—the combination out of which one makes ink. Cavour told him to introduce the brand in the interest of the finances. So, ever since then this brand passes through the ink factory, with the great result that both the ink and the cigar suffer a sea change into something new and strange. This is history, Sire, not a work of the imagination."

So then he took up his present again, and touched it to the forefinger of his other hand for an instant, which made it break into flame and fragrance—but he changed his mind at that point and laid the torpedo down, saying courteously:

"With permission I will save it for Voltaire."

I was greatly pleased and flattered to be connected in even this little way with that great man and be mentioned to him, as no doubt would be the case, so I hastened to fetch a bundle of fifty for distribution among others of the renowned and lamented—Goethe, and Homer, and Socrates, and Confucius, and so on—but Satan said he had nothing against those. Then he dropped back into reminiscences of the old times once more, and presently said:

"They knew nothing about radium, and it would have had no value for them if they had known about it. In twenty million years it has had no value for your race until the revolutionizing steam-and-machinery age was born—which was only a few years before you were born yourself. It was a stunning little century, for sure, that nineteenth! But it's a poor thing compared to what the twentieth is going to be."

By request, he explained why he thought so.

"Because power was so costly, then, and everything goes by power—the steamship, the locomotive and everything else. Coal, you see! You have to have it; no steam and no electricity without it; and it's such a waste—for you burn it up, and it's gone! But radium—that's another matter! With my nine hundred pounds you could light the world, and heat it, and run all its ships and machines and railways a hundred million years, and not use up five pounds of it in the whole time! And then—"

"Quick—my soul is yours, dear Ancestor; take it—we'll start a company!"

But he asked my age, which is sixty-eight, then politely sidetracked the proposition, probably not wishing to take advantage of himself. Then he went on talking admiringly of radium, and how with its own natural and inherent heat it could go on melting its own weight of ice twenty-four times in twenty-four hours, and keep it up forever without losing bulk or weight; and how a pound of it, if exposed in this room, would blast the place like a breath from hell, and burn me to a crisp in a quarter of a minute—and was going on like that, but I interrupted and said:

"But *you* are here, Majesty—nine hundred pounds—and the temperature is balmy and pleasant. I don't understand."

"Well," he said, hesitatingly, "it is a secret, but I may as well reveal it, for these prying and impertinent chemists are going to find it out sometime or other, anyway. Perhaps you have read what Madame Curie says about radium; how she goes searching among its splendid secrets and seizes upon one after another of them and italicizes its specialty; how she says 'the compounds of radium are *spontaneously luminous*'—require no coal in the production of light, you see; how she says, 'a glass vessel containing radium *spontaneously charges itself with electricity*'—no coal or water power required to generate it, you see; how she says 'radium possesses the remarkable property of *liberating heat spontaneously and continuously*'—no coal required to fire-up on the world's machinery, you see. She ransacks the pitch-blende for its radioactive substances, and captures three and labels them; one, which is embodied with bismuth, she names polonium; one, which is embodied with barium, she names radium; the name given to the third was actinium. Now listen; she says '*the question now was to separate the polonium from the bismuth… this is the task that has occupied us for years and has been a most difficult one.*' For years, you see—for *years*. That is their way, those plagues, those scientists—peg, peg, peg—dig, dig, dig—plod, plod, plod. I wish I could catch a cargo of them for my place; it would be an economy. Yes, for years, you see. They never give up. Patience, hope, faith, perseverance; it is the way of all the breed. Columbus and the rest. In radium this lady has added a new world to the planet's possessions, and matched—Columbus—and his peer. She has set herself the task of divorcing polonium and bismuth; when she succeeds she will have done—what, should you say?"

"Pray name it, Majesty."

"It's another new world added—a gigantic one. I will explain; for you would never divine the size of it, and she herself does not suspect it."

"Do, Majesty, I beg of you."

"Polonium, freed from bismuth and made independent, is the one and only power that can control radium, restrain its destructive forces, tame them, reduce them to obedience, and make them do useful and profitable work for your race. Examine my skin. What do you think of it?"

"It is delicate, silky, transparent, thin as a gelatine film—exquisite, beautiful, Majesty!"

"It is made of polonium. All the rest of me is radium. If I should strip off my skin the world would vanish away in a flash of flame and a puff of smoke, and the remnants of the extinguished moon would sift down through space a mere snow-shower of gray ashes!"

I made no comment, I only trembled.

"You understand, now," he continued. "I burn, I suffer within, my pains are measureless and eternal, but my skin protects you and the globe from harm. Heat is power, energy, but is only useful to man when he can control it and graduate its application to his needs. You cannot do that with radium, now; it will not be prodigiously useful to you until polonium shall put the slave whip in your hand. I can release from my body the radium force in any measure I please, great or small; at my will I can set in motion the works of a lady's watch or destroy a world. You saw me light that unholy cigar with my finger?"

I remembered it.

"Try to imagine how minute was the fraction of energy released to do that small thing? You are aware that everything is made up of restless and revolving molecules?—everything—furniture, rocks, water, iron, horses, men—everything that exists."

"Yes."

"Molecules of scores of different sizes and weights, but none of them big enough to be seen by help of any microscope?"

"Yes."

"And that each molecule is made up of thousands of separate and never-resting little particles called atoms?"

"Yes."

"And that up to recent times the smallest atom known to science was the hydrogen atom, which was a thousand times smaller than the atom that went to the building of any other molecule?"

"Yes."

"Well, the radium atom from the positive pole is 5,000 times smaller that *that* atom! This unspeakably minute atom is called an *electron*. Now then, out of my long affection for you and your lineage, I will reveal to you a secret—a secret known to no scientist as yet—the secret of the firefly's light and the glow-worm's; it is produced by a single electron imprisoned in a polonium atom."

"Sire, it is a wonderful thing, and the scientific world would be grateful to know this secret, which has baffled and defeated all its searching for more than two centuries. To think!—a single electron, 5,000 times smaller than the invisible hydrogen atom, to produce that explosion of vivid light which makes the summer night so beautiful!"

"And consider," said Satan; "it is the only instance in all nature where radium exists in a pure state unencumbered by fettering alliances; where polonium enjoys the like emancipation; and where the pair are enabled to labor together in a gracious and beneficent and effective partnership. Suppose the protecting polonium envelope were removed; the radium spark would flash but once and the firefly would be consumed to vapor! Do you value this old iron letterpress?"

"No, Majesty, for it is not mine."

"Then I will destroy it and let you see. I lit the ostensible cigar with the heat energy of a single electron, the equipment of a single lightning bug. I will turn on 20,000 electrons now."

He touched the massive thing and it exploded with a cannon crash, leaving nothing but vacancy where it had stood. For three minutes the air was a dense pink fog of sparks, through which Satan loomed dim and vague, then the place cleared and his soft rich moonlight pervaded it again. He said:

"You see? The radium in 20,000 lightning bugs would run a racing-mobile forever. There's no waste, no diminution of it." Then he remarked in a quite casual way, "We use nothing but radium at home."

I was astonished. And interested, too, for I have friends there, and relatives. I had always believed—in accordance with my early teachings—that the fuel was soft coal and brimstone. He noticed the thought, and answered it.

"Soft coal and brimstone is the tradition, yes, but it is an error. We could use it; at least we could make out with it after a fashion, but it has several defects: it is not cleanly, it ordinarily makes but a temperate fire, and it would be exceedingly difficult, if even possible, to heat it up to standard, Sundays; and as for the supply, all the worlds and systems could not furnish enough to keep us going halfway through eternity. Without radium there would be no hell; certainly not a satisfactory one."

"Why?"

"Because if we hadn't radium we should have to dress the souls in some other material; then, of course, they would burn up and get out of trouble. They would not last an hour. You know that?"

"Why—yes, now that you mention it. But I supposed they were dressed in their natural flesh; they look so in the pictures—in the Sistine Chapel and in the illustrated books, you know."

"Yes, our damned look as they looked in the world, but it isn't flesh; flesh could not survive any longer than that copying press survived—it would explode and turn to a fog of sparks, and the result desired in sending it there would be defeated. Believe me, radium is the only wear."

"I see it now," I said, with prophetic discomfort, "I know that you are right, Majesty."

"I am. I speak from experience. You shall see, when you get there."

He said this as if he thought I was eaten up with curiosity, but it was because he did not know me. He sat reflecting a minute, then he said:

"I will make your fortune."

It cheered me up and I felt better. I thanked him and was all eagerness and attention.

"Do you know," he continued, "where they find the bones of the extinct moa, in New Zealand? All in a pile—thousands and thousands of them banked together in a mass twenty feet deep. And do you know where they find the tusks of the extinct mastodon of the Pleistocene? Banked together in acres off the mouth of the Lena—an ivory mine which has furnished freight for Chinese caravans for 500 years. Do you know the phosphate beds of our South? They are miles in extent, a limitless mass and jumble of bones of vast animals whose like exists no longer in the earth—a cemetery, a mighty cemetery, that is what it is. All over the earth there are such cemeteries. Whence came the instinct that made those families of creatures go to a chosen and particular spot to die when sickness came upon them and they perceived that their end was near? It is a mystery; not even science has been able to uncover the secret of it. But there stands the fact. Listen, then. For a million years there has been a firefly cemetery."

Hopefully, appealingly, I opened my mouth—he motioned me to close it, and went on:

"It is in a scooped-out bowl half as big as this room on top of a snow summit in the Cordilleras. That bowl is level full—of what? Pure firefly radium and the glow and heat of hell! For countless ages myriads of fireflies have daily flown thither and died in that bowl and been burned to vapor in an instant, each fly leaving as its contribution its only indestructible particle, its single electron of pure radium. There is energy enough there to light the whole world, heat the whole world's machinery, supply the whole world's transportation power from now till the end of eternity. The massed riches of the planet could not furnish its value in money. You are mine, it is yours; when Madam Curie isolates polonium, clothe yourself in a skin of it and go and take possession!"

Then he vanished and left me in the dark when I was just in the act of thanking him. I can find the bowl by the light it will cast upon the sky; I can get the polonium presently, when that illustrious lady in France isolates it from the bismuth. Stock is for sale. Apply to Mark Twain.

ΜΕΤΑΡΗΥSΙCS

Elizabeth M. Glover

You'd think the upper east side of Manhattan was an easy place to find sinners, if only because of the population density, but after 9/11, common decency had spread through New York like a catchy commercial jingle. Not that Merchari minded a challenge, but he was behind quota, and he hated taking the subway. It stank and was hot year-round, and that just made him homesick.

Still, Second Avenue was high-traffic, with restaurant after restaurant in a city where apartment kitchens were often smaller than the bathrooms. He loitered a while, invisible and insubstantial, letting several groups pass; he was behind quota, but not so desperate as to nab vapid Human Resources bippies and their Marketing Department boyfriends.

He strolled along, sniffing at the doors of the restaurants as he passed. O'Donnell's Pub held good-natured drunks cheering St. John's to a crushing victory over Syracuse (too elated to appreciate the terrors of Hell). Il Piccolo hosted a wedding reception (wild joy, flaring tempers—it would all end in tears of familial love and sentiment, more than Merchari could stand). Maybe a bit farther south, nearer to Sloan-Kettering? He might get lucky and find a couple of researchers slipped out of their labs for a quick meal.

Six blocks later, when he was beginning to fear he might make it all the way to the bridge without luck, his patience was rewarded. A likely-looking pair, a man and a woman, were just exiting King's Dumpling House with brown bags of take-out dim sum. He took solid form and sidled up to them. "Pardon me, do you have a match?"

"Yes, I think so…" The man fumbled in his pockets and offered a match-book.

"Thank you," Merchari said. That seminar on the tactical use of politeness had been worth every dram of quicksilver. Merchari reached as if to take the matchbook, then seized the man's wrist.

"Hey!" The man tried to pull away. He lashed out and knocked off the shadowing hat, revealing Merchari's gold-gleaming eyes and vermilion complexion. "Oh my God."

"Other side, I'm afraid." Merchari loved this bit, when they realized what he was. Their brains seized up—free will indeed!—and they reverted to the monkeys they'd been based on. Those idiots in the Nightmares Department of the sixth ring thought they had it good, a nice creative job. But real experience—*this* was entertainment!

The man's mouth worked in silent shock for a moment. He groped at his neck and came up with a crucifix on a gold chain. "Back! Get back, I say!"

"Do I look like a vampire?" Merchari snorted small blue flames. "Look, pal, just come along quietly, OK? I'll see that you get a nice assignment in the bio-weapons division."

The man kept tugging. He pounded his other fist on Merchari's wrist. It was all useless, and the wind off the river suddenly blew warmer—the first twinges of the Gate opening. The fellow dropped to his knees and found his voice. "*Pater noster, qui es in caelis, sanctificetur nomen tuum…*"

Ach! Merchari released the man and recoiled, his palm scorched and smoking. "Sir! Sir! That's enough! English will do the trick. No need for the high octane." Latin! That was the risk of the scientific enclaves—you might run into a Jesuit education.

The man continued his prayer, but the woman, who had remained scientifically calm, tugged on his sleeve. "Dennis, I think it's okay. You hurt him."

Dennis surged to his feet. "Then go away!"

"In a moment, in a moment." Merchari regarded the woman. Dennis was off limits because he had prayed, and he believed in what he was saying. But the woman hadn't done the same. Merchari leaned toward her and sniffed. Yep, that definite metallic scent. "You're an atheist, aren't you?"

"Don't answer him, Christine," the man said, putting his arm around her shoulders. "I can keep him away from you."

"Only if she believes what you're saying." Merchari returned his attention to the woman. "Well?"

Christine cocked her head to one side. "Yes, I'm an atheist. Is that a problem? I guess you can't take me if I don't believe in you or your supposed origin."

"That's a bit of a contradiction, isn't it? I'm standing right here."

"I'd say so, but there *was* incense burning in the restaurant. And all these people"—she gestured at the moderate crowds passing them on the sidewalk—"don't seem to see you. I'd say hallucinations are a high likelihood."

"Would you." Merchari leaned in and inhaled her bouquet. A magnificent sample, probably lapsed Catholic. "Ooh, you are quality." Her eyes flashed with irritation. "The important point is that you don't have any prayers to protect you. If it makes it easier, you can pretend the fires are just hallucinations."

Dennis started in with the *Pater Noster* again. Merchari jolted from his appreciation of the woman. "Sir, you're done. Your exemption has been proven. But your prayers can't help an unbeliever." Merchari extended his hand. "Come along, girlie. You're fair game."

"Because I don't have prayers."

"That's right. Don't you logical types study the classics anymore? If you'd followed Pascal's Wager, you'd at least hedge your bets. Too late now."

The warm wind rose again, and a few tattered pages of an abandoned *New York Times* skittered down the sidewalk and clung to Christine's calves. She kicked at them in vexation until the wind reclaimed them. "Which is Pascal's Wager again?"

"Tell her, Catholic boy. They must have covered that at Fordham."

"Manhattan College, actually." Dennis still hovered protectively near the woman, but had calmed a bit. "You remember it from Grening's class, don't you, Chris? The one about how it won't hurt to believe in God if there isn't one, but not believing will get you sent to hell, so you may as well play it safe and believe."

"Oh yeah, that one." Christine flicked her fingers dismissively. "A false dichotomy. For it to make any sense, one must already believe the premise that there's a deity who desires human faith, as opposed to, say, the sacrifice of animals. You might as easily suggest I hedge my bets by offering hecatombs to Zeus and Athena."

Hmmmm.

The woman ran fingers through her short, blonde curls. "Look, I'll take it as a given that you're real, that you're a demon, and that you're here to take me to Hell. So let's get back to the point. Do any holy words work? Like, if a Buddhist recited a *koan*, would that keep you off?"

Merchari narrowed his eyes. They didn't usually converse. Usually they were too busy gibbering or running. "What's with the questions?"

"Just the natural curiosity of a scientist." The woman shrugged. "If you're going to drag me off to Hell, the least you can do is show me the full error of my ways. Should I have listened to the nuns, or would any religion do?"

Ah, a theological discussion. It had been a while. "I don't know. Someone recited from the Koran once—that worked. I know the… prayer your friend said works when recited in Chinese, although Latin is more effective."

"Interesting."

Dennis took her arm again. "Christine, what are you doing?"

"It's okay, Dennis. Just relax."

"That's right, Dennis," Merchari said. The man started at hearing his name from demonic lips. "Let me just conclude my business."

Christine eased a step closer. "You got a name, demon?"

"That doesn't work."

"Huh?"

"The name thing. It doesn't work."

"I'm not a fricking *wizard*, I'm a biochemist." Christine huffed her annoyance. Merchari smiled inwardly. They always got testy when they were losing. Christine continued: "If I don't believe in *you*, I certainly don't believe in that mystical crap. I just want to know what to call you."

Oh. "Merchari." He performed a courtly bow.

"Thank you. You know, Merchari, I think you're wrong about something."

"Oh? What's that?" Still searching for loopholes! She was almost brave enough to get an exemption on valor alone.

"That bit about me having no holy words." She raised her head and looked him square in the eyes. "*Force equals mass times acceleration,*" and she drove her fist into his face.

Shards of pain splayed behind his eyes and Merchari cried out. How had she *done* that? She'd *hit* him! And it had *hurt*! He staggered backwards and touched a hand to his nose. Silver fluid flowed down his face. "How—? You shouldn't be able to touch me!"

Christine cradled her fist in her other hand, gritting her teeth. "Mercury for blood. Holy crap, that hurt."

"Good. But how—?"

"Simple physical law." She spat a few more choice imprecations and grimaced down at her red and swelling knuckles. "For every action, there is an equal and opposite reaction," she muttered.

This was going to be a little harder than Merchari had assumed, but one human female couldn't possibly take on a minion of Hell. She was a prime specimen, a grade-A atheist with spunk, and his reputation would be made if he bagged her. He would have his pick of assignments.

Merchari leapt at her, arms wide, ready to grab.

Instead of ducking, running, or clinging to Dennis, she calmly whirled to one side. Her arm darted out, and her hand seized his wrist, deftly avoiding the spur-talon. "*An object in motion will tend to stay in motion—*" And she *pulled*, accelerating him past her and throwing him to the ground.

He lay sprawled, dazed and in pain. She leaned over him.

"*—unless acted upon by an external force,*" she finished.

All right, no more playing around. Merchari leaped up, and hovered ten feet in the air. He unfurled his wings with a leathery snap, shredding his trenchcoat, and cranked up the heat on his fiery nimbus like a kid with a magnifying glass on an ant. It was a display that never failed to send the bravest human cowering.

Christine folded her arms across her chest and rolled her eyes. "What's the fuel for those flames?"

"Fuel?" They were just his nimbus, unholy light, part of being a demon. What was she on about?

"Yeah, fuel. What are you burning?"

"Um…"

"Because you need to burn something. *The total energy of a closed system remains constant.*"

And with a woosh, his aura went out.

"And those wings are all wrong. In the first place, they're not even built for flying, much less hovering. I mean, honestly—bat's wings?" She craned her neck to get a better look. "You're barely flapping. And they grow straight out of your back, practically vertical. How do you get any leverage?"

"They do me all right."

"No, no, no. Can't work. *Force equals G-M-m over R-squared.*"

Merchari blinked. "What?"

Christine sighed with exasperation. "The force of gravitational attraction between two bodies is equal to the universal constant G, multiplied by the masses of the two bodies, divided by the square of the distance between them. You're too heavy. Those wings could never provide enough lift."

And… Merchari suddenly *felt* his own weight, a crushing force, and he realized the problem with having heavy, dense mercury for blood. He flailed his wings, but he crashed to the ground, cracking the sidewalk with the force of his impact.

Christine crouched beside him and patted him on the head. "The Earth is large and you're very close to it." She stood and backed away from him. "I'm glad I didn't have to cite the aerodynamic laws; it's been a long time since undergrad physics."

Dennis waved one of his hands in thought. "You need the angle of attack, and—and the surface area of the wing? And maybe the speed he flaps them?"

"Ugh, I can never remember; if I was any good at fluid dynamics I'd have been an engineer. Anyway, it doesn't matter. The beginning of the explanation apparently was enough."

This was intolerable! Merchari rolled to his side and snarled at Dennis. "Keep out of this, you, or I might forget the rules that protect you." He spat a fang onto the pavement and stood to face the woman again. He was going about this wrong. He knew most of these laws, sort of. Hell had a whole section devoted to scientists. "You! Woman! Newtonian laws aren't entirely accurate."

"They're just fine at these speeds. If you want to accelerate us to a significant percentage of lightspeed, then I'll pull out the complicated equations."

No, that would never do. She'd just go on about infinite mass and squash him to a singularity. Damn it, she was *such* a prize. Merchari nibbled on a talon and glowered at her. Maybe he could introduce doubt… "You reduce your own position using physical laws this way. Only faith defeats me. Is your understanding of these laws predicated on mere belief?"

Christine nodded thoughtfully. "Ultimately. All scientific laws rest on a single belief: that what we perceive is real. And if somehow it isn't, it doesn't matter. Empiricism still holds. The nugget of belief is irrelevant to the usefulness of the results." She walked up to him and poked him in the chest. "*That's* why they hurt so much. It's not a test of faith, it's a test of reality. Can you change reality?"

Remarkable manuvering. Such a disappointment. Merchari hung his head, defeated. "No."

"Well then. *The coefficient of friction between two surfaces, multiplied by the parallel component…*"

"No!" Merchari reeled back, cowering. "No more! Please!"

"*…of a force applied at an angle to the surfaces, results in a parallel force applied to the objects, imparting motion.*"

Nothing happened. Merchari peeked out from behind his claws. "What was that? It didn't do anything."

"It's the equation for the useful force of friction. It's what allows you to walk." Christine pointed one imperious finger down the street. "I suggest you use it."

Like facing the Big Boss himself. Merchari imagined what Christine would look like with horns and a beard. Then he turned and trudged west, toward the subway. And felt a little homesick.

SNOWBALL'S CHANCE

Charles Stross

The louring sky, half-past pregnant with a caul of snow, pressed down on Davy's head like a hangover. He glanced up once, shivered, then pushed through the doorway into the Deid Nurse and the smog of fag fumes within.

His sometime-conspirator Tam the Tailer was already at the bar. "Awright, Davy?"

Davy drew a deep breath, his glasses steaming up the instant he stepped through the heavy blackout curtain, so that the disreputable pub was shrouded in a halo of icy iridescence that concealed its flaws. "Mine's a Deuchars." His nostrils flared as he took in the seedy mixture of aromas that festered in the Deid Nurse's atmosphere—so thick you could cut it with an axe, Morag had said once with a sniff of her lop-sided snot-siphon, back in the day when she'd had aught to say to Davy. "Fuckin' Baltic oot there the night, an' nae kiddin." He slid his glasses off and wiped them off, then looked around tiredly. "An' deid tae the world in here."

Tam glanced around as if to be sure the pub population hadn't magically doubled between mouthfuls of seventy bob. "Ah widnae say that." He gestured with his nose—pockmarked by frostbite—at the snug in the corner. Once the storefront for the Old Town's more affluent ladies of the night, it was now unaccountably popular with students of the gaming fraternity, possibly because they had been driven out of all the trendier bars in the neighbourhood for yacking till all hours and not drinking enough (much like the whores before them). Right now a bunch of threadbare LARPers were in residence, arguing over some recondite point of lore. "They're havin' enough fun for a barrel o' monkeys by the sound o' it."

"An' who can blame them?" Davy hoisted his glass: "Ah just wish they'd keep their shite aff the box." The pub, in an effort to compensate for its lack of a food licence, had installed a huge and dodgy voxel engine that teetered precariously over the bar: it was full of muddy field, six LARPers leaping.

"Dinnae piss them aff, Davy—they've a' got swords."

"Ah wis jist kiddin'. Ah didnae catch ma lottery the night, that's a' Ah'm sayin'."

"If ye win, it'll be a first." Tam stared at his glass. "An' whit wid ye dae then, if yer numbers came up?"

"Whit, the big yin?" Davy put his glass down, then unzipped his parka's fast-access pouch and pulled out a fag packet and lighter. Condensation immediately beaded the plastic wrapper as he flipped it open. "Ah'd pay aff the hoose, for starters. An' the child support. An' then——" He paused, eyes wandering to the dog-eared NO SMOKING sign behind the bar. "Ah, shit." He flicked his Zippo, stroking the end of a cigarette with the flame from the burning coal oil. "If Ah wis young again, Ah'd move, ye ken? But Ah'm no, Ah've got roots here." The sign went on to warn of lung cancer (curable) and two-thousand-Euro fines (laughable, even if enforced). Davy inhaled, grateful for the warmth flooding his lungs. "An' there's Morag an' the bairns."

"Heh." Tam left it at a grunt, for which Davy was grateful. It wasn't that he thought Morag would ever come back to him, but he was sick to the back teeth of people who thought they were his friends telling him that she wouldn't, not unless he did this or did that.

"Ah could pay for the bairns tae go east. They're young enough." He glanced at the doorway. "It's no right, throwin' snowba's in May."

"That's global warmin'." Tam shrugged with elaborate irony, then changed the subject. "Where d'ye think they'd go? The Ukraine? New 'Beria?"

"Somewhaur there's grass and nae glaciers." Pause. "An' real beaches wi' sand an' a'." He frowned and hastily added: "Dinnae get me wrong, Ah ken how likely that is." The collapse of the West Antarctic ice shelf two decades ago had inundated every established coastline; it had also stuck the last nail in the coffin of the Gulf stream, plunging the British Isles into a sub-Arctic deep freeze. Then the Americans had made it worse—at least for Scotland—by putting a giant parasol into orbit to stop the rest of the planet roasting like a chicken on a spit. Davy had learned all about global warming in Geography classes at school—back when it hadn't happened—in the rare intervals when he wasn't dozing in the back row or staring at Yasmin MacConnell's hair. It wasn't until he was already paying a mortgage and the second kid was on his way that what it meant really sank in. Cold. Eternal cold, deep in your bones.

"Ah'd like tae see a real beach again, some day before Ah die."

"Ye could save for a train ticket."

"Away wi' ye! Where'd Ah go tae?" Davy snorted, darkly amused. Flying was for the hyper-rich these days, and anyway, the nearest beaches with sand and sun were in the Caliphate, a long day's TGV ride south through the Channel Tunnel and across the Gibraltar Bridge, in what had once been the Northern Sahara Desert. As a tourist destination, the Caliphate had certain drawbacks, a lack of topless sunbathing beauties being only the first on the list. "It's a' just as bad whauriver ye go. At least here ye can still get pork scratchings."

"Aye, weel." Tam raised his glass, just as a stranger appeared in the doorway.

"An' then there's some that dinnae feel the cauld." Davy glanced round to follow the direction of his gaze. The stranger was oddly attired in a lightweight suit and tie, as if he'd stepped out of the middle of the previous century, although his neat goatee beard and the two small brass horns implanted on his forehead were a more contemporary touch. He noticed Davy staring and nodded, politely enough, then broke eye contact and ambled over to the bar. Davy turned back to Tam, who responded to his wink. "Take care noo, Davy. Ye've got ma number." With that, he stood up, put his glass down, and shambled unsteadily towards the toilets.

This put Davy on his lonesome next to the stranger, who leaned on the bar and glanced at him sideways with an expression of amusement. Davy's forehead wrinkled as he stared in the direction of Katie the barwoman, who was just now coming back up the cellar steps with an empty coal powder cartridge in one hand. "My round?" asked the stranger, raising an eyebrow.

"Aye. Mine's a Deuchars if yer buyin'…" Davy, while not always quick on the uptake, was never slow on the barrel: if this underdressed southerner could afford a heated taxi, he could certainly afford to buy Davy some beer. Katie nodded and rinsed her hands under the sink—however well-sealed they left the factory, coal cartridges always leaked like printer toner had once done—and picked up two glasses.

"New roond aboot here?" Davy asked after a moment.

The stranger smiled: "Just passing through—I visit Edinburgh every few years."

"Aye." Davy could relate to that.

"And yourself?"

"Ah'm frae Pilton." Which was true enough; that was where he'd bought the house with Morag all those years ago, back when folks actually wanted to buy houses in Edinburgh. Back before the pack ice closed the Firth for six months in every year, back before the rising sea level drowned Leith and Ingliston, and turned Arthur's Seat into a frigid coastal headland looming grey and stark above the permafrost. "Whereaboots d'ye come frae?"

The stranger's smile widened as Katie parked a half-litre on the bar top before him and bent down to pull the next: "I think you know where I'm from, my friend."

Davy snorted. "Aye, so ye're a man of wealth an' taste, is that right?"

"Just so." A moment later, Katie planted the second glass in front of Davy, gave him a brittle smile, and retreated to the opposite end of the bar without pausing to extract credit from the stranger, who nodded and raised his jar: "To your good fortune."

"Heh." Davy chugged back a third of his glass. It was unusually bitter, with a slight sulphurous edge to it: "That's a new barrel."

"Only the best for my friends."

Davy sneaked an irritated glance at the stranger. "Right. Ah ken ye want tae talk, ye dinnae need tae take the pish."

"I'm sorry." The stranger held his gaze, looking slightly perplexed. "It's just that I've spent too long in America recently. Most of them believe in me. A bit of good old-fashioned scepticism is refreshing once in a while."

Davy snorted. "Dae Ah look like a god-botherer tae ye? Yer amang civilized folk here, nae free-kirk numpties'd show their noses in a pub."

"So I see." The stranger relaxed slightly. "Seen Morag and the boys lately, have you?"

Now a strange thing happened, because as the cold fury took him, and a monstrous roaring filled his ears, and he reached for the stranger's throat, he seemed to hear Morag's voice shouting, *Davy, don't!* And to his surprise, a moment of timely sanity came crashing down on him, a sense that Devil or no, if he laid hands on this fucker he really would be damned, somehow. It might just have been the hypothalamic implant that the sheriff had added to the list of his parole requirements working its arcane magic on his brain chemistry, but it certainly felt like a drenching, cold-sweat sense of immanence, and not in a good way. So as the raging impulse to glass the cunt died away, Davy found himself contemplating his own raised fists in perplexity, the crude blue tattoos of LOVE and HATE standing out on his knuckles like doorposts framing the prison gateway of his life.

"Who telt ye aboot them," he demanded hoarsely.

"Cigarette?" The stranger, who had sat perfectly still while Davy wound up to punch his ticket, raised the chiselled eyebrow again.

"Ya bas." But Davy's hand went to his pocket automatically, and he found himself passing a filter-tip to the stranger rather than ramming a red-hot ember in his eye.

"Thank you." The stranger took the unlit cigarette, put it straight between his lips, and inhaled deeply. "Nobody needed to tell me about them," he continued, slowly dribbling smoke from both nostrils.

Davy slumped defensively on his bar stool. "When ye wis askin' aboot Morag and the bairns, Ah figured ye wis fuckin' wi' ma heid." But knowing that there was a perfectly reasonable supernatural explanation somehow made it all right. *Ye cannae blame Auld Nick for pushin' yer buttons.* Davy reached out for his glass again: "'Scuse me. Ah didnae think ye existed."

"Feel free to take your time." The stranger smiled faintly. "I find atheists refreshing, but it does take a little longer than usual to get down to business."

"Aye, weel, concedin' for the moment that ye *are* the deil, Ah dinnae ken whit ye want wi' the likes o' me." Davy cradled his beer protectively.

"Ah'm naebody." He shivered in the sudden draught as one of the students—leaving—pushed through the curtain, admitting a flurry of late-May snowflakes.

"So? You may be nobody, but your lucky number just came up." The stranger smiled devilishly. "Did you never think you'd win the Lottery?"

"Aye, weel, if hauf the stories they tell about ye are true, Ah'd rather it wis the ticket, ye ken? Or are ye gonnae say ye've been stitched up by the kirk?"

"Something like that." The Devil nodded sagely. "Look, you're not stupid, so I'm not going to bullshit you. What it is, is I'm not the only one of me working this circuit. I've got a quota to meet, but there aren't enough politicians and captains of industry to go around, and anyway, they're boring. All they ever want is money, power, or good, hot, kinky sex without any comebacks from their constituents. Poor folks are so much more creative in their desperation, don't you think? And so much more likely to believe in the Rules, too."

"The Rules?" Davy found himself staring at his companion in perplexity. "Nae the Law, right?"

"Do as thou wilt shall be all of the Law," quoth the Devil, then he paused as if he'd tasted something unpleasant.

"Ye wis sayin'?"

"Love is the Law, Love under Will," the Devil added dyspeptically.

"That's a'?" Davy stared at him.

"My employer requires me to quote chapter and verse when challenged." As he said "employer", the expression on the Devil's face made Davy shudder. "And she monitors these conversations for compliance."

"But whit aboot the rest o' it, aye? If ye're the deil, whit aboot the Ten Commandments?"

"Oh, those are just Rules," said the Devil, smiling. "I'm really proud of them."

"Ye made them a' up?" Davy said accusingly. "Just tae fuck wi' us?"

"Well, yes, of course I did! And all the other Rules. They work really well, don't you think?"

Davy made a fist and stared at the back of it. LOVE. "Ye cunt. Ah still dinnae believe in ye."

The Devil shrugged. "Nobody's asking you to believe in me. You don't, and I'm still here, aren't I? If it makes things easier, think of me as the garbage collection subroutine of the strong anthropic principle. And they"—he stabbed a finger in the direction of the overhead LEDs—"work by magic, for all you know."

Davy picked up his glass and drained it philosophically. The hell of it was, the Devil was right: now he thought about it, he had no idea how the lights worked, except that electricity had something to do with it. "Ah'll have anither. Ye're buyin'?"

"No I'm not." The Devil snapped his fingers and two full glasses appeared on the bar, steaming slightly. Davy picked up the nearest one. It was hot to the touch, even though the beer inside it was at cellar temperature, and it smelled slightly sulphurous. "Anyway, I owe you."

"Whit for?" Davy sniffed the beer suspiciously: "This smells pish." He pushed it away. "Whit is it ye owe me for?"

"For taking that mortgage and the job on the street-cleaning team and for pissing it all down the drain and fucking off a thousand citizens in little ways. For giving me Jaimie and wee Davy, and for wrecking your life and cutting Morag off from her parents and raising a pair of neds instead of two fine upstanding citizens. You're not a scholar and you're not a gentleman, but you're a truly professional hater. And as for what you did to Morag—"

Davy made another fist: HATE. "Say wan mair word aboot Morag..." he warned.

The Devil chuckled quietly. "No, you managed to do all that by yourself." He shrugged. "I'd have offered help if you needed it, but you seemed to be doing okay without me. Like I said, you're a professional." He cleared his throat. "Which brings me to the little matter of why I'm talking to you tonight."

"Ah'm no for sale." Davy crossed his arms defensively. "Who d'ye think Ah am?"

The Devil shook his head, still smiling. "I'm not here to make you an offer for your soul, that's not how things work. Anyway, you gave it to me of your own free will years ago." Davy looked into his eyes. The smile didn't reach them. "Trouble is, there are consequences when that happens. My employer's an optimist: she's not an Augustinian entity, you'll be pleased to learn, she doesn't believe in original sin. So things between you and the Ultimate are... let's say they're out of balance. It's like a credit card bill. The longer you ignore it, the worse it gets. You cut me a karmic loan from the First Bank of Davy MacDonald, and the Law requires me to repay it with interest."

"Huh?" Davy stared at the Devil. "Ye whit?"

The Devil wasn't smiling now. "You're one of the Elect, Davy. One of the Unconditionally Elect. So's fucking everybody these days, but your name came up in the quality assurance lottery. I'm not allowed to mess with you. If you die and I'm in your debt, seven shades of shit hit the fan. So I owe you a fucking wish."

The Devil tapped his fingers impatiently on the bar top. He was no longer smiling. "You get one wish. I am required to read you the small print:

"The party of the first part in cognizance of the gift benefice or loan bestowed by the party of the second part is hereby required to tender the fulfillment of 1 (one) verbally or somatically expressed indication of desire by the party of the second part in pursuance of the discharge of the said gift benefice or loan, said fulfillment hereinafter to be termed 'the wish'. The party of the first part undertakes to bring the totality of existence into accordance with the terms of the wish exclusive of paradox deicide temporal inversion or other wilful suspension contrary to the laws of nature. The party of the second part recognizes, understands and accepts that this wish represents full and final discharge of debt incurred by the gift benefice or loan to the party of the first part. Notwithstanding additional grants of rights incurred under the terms of this contract, the rights, responsibilities, duties of the party of the first part to the party of the second part are subject to the Consumer Credit Regulations of 2026..."

Davy shook his head. "Ah dinnae get it. Are ye tellin' me ye're givin' me a wish? In return for, for... bein' radge a' ma life?"

The Devil nodded. "Yes."

Davy winced. "Ah think Ah need another Deuchars—fuck! Haud on, that isnae ma wish!" He stared at the Devil anxiously. "Ye're serious, aren't ye?"

The Devil sniffed. "I can't discharge the obligation with a beer. My Employer isn't stupid, whatever Her other faults: she'd say I was short-changing you, and she'd be right. It's got to be a big wish, Davy."

Davy's expression brightened. The Devil waved a hand at Katie: "Another

Deuchars for my friend here. And a drop of the Craitur." Things were looking up, Davy decided.

"Can ye make Morag nae have… Ah mean, can ye make things… awright again, nae went bad?" He dry-swallowed, mind skittering like a frightened spider away from what he was asking for. Not to have… whatever. Whatever he'd done. Already.

The Devil contemplated Davy for a long handful of seconds. "No," he said patiently. "That would create a paradox, you see, because if things hadn't gone bad for you, I wouldn't be here giving you this wish, would I? Your life gone wrong is the fuel for this miracle."

"Oh." Davy waited in silence while Katie pulled the pint, then retreated back to the far end of the bar. *Whaur's Tam?* he wondered vaguely. *Fuckin' deil, wi' his smairt suit an' high heid yin manners…* He shivered, unaccountably cold. "Am Ah goin' tae hell?" he asked roughly. "Is that whaur Ah'm goin'?"

"Sorry, but no. We were brought in to run this universe, but we didn't design it. When you're dead, that's it. No hellfire, no damnation: the worst thing that can happen to you is you're reincarnated, given a second chance to get things right. It's normally my job to give people like you that chance."

"An' if Ah'm no reincarnated?" Davy asked hopefully.

"You get to wake up in the mind of God. Of course, you stop being you when you do that." The Devil frowned thoughtfully. "Come to think of it, you'll probably give Her a migraine."

"Right, right." Davy nodded. The Devil was giving him a headache. He had a dawning suspicion that this one wasn't a prod or a pape: he probably supported Livingstone. "Ah'm no that bad then, is that whit ye're sayin'?"

"Don't get above yourself."

The Devil's frown deepened, oblivious to the stroke of killing rage that flashed behind Davy's eyes at the words. *Dinnae get above yersel'? Who the fuck d'ye think ye are, the sheriff?* That was almost exactly what the sheriff had said, leaning over to pronounce sentence. *Ye ken Ah'm naebody, dinnae deny it!* Davy's fists tightened, itching to hit somebody. The story of his life: being ripped off then talked down to by self-satisfied cunts. *Ah'll make ye regret it!*

The Devil continued after a moment: "You've got to really fuck up in a theological manner before she won't take you, these days. Spreading hatred in the name of God, that kind of thing will do for you. Trademark abuse, she calls it. You're plenty bad, but you're not that bad. Don't kid yourself, you only warrant the special visit because you're a quality sample. The rest are… unobserved."

"So Ah'm no evil, Ah'm just plain bad." Davy grinned virulently as a thought struck him. *Let's dae somethin' aboot that! Karmic imbalance? Ah'll show ye a karmic imbalance!* "Can ye dae somethin' aboot the weather? Ah hate the cauld." He tried to put a whine in his voice. The change in the weather had crippled house prices, shafted him and Morag. It would serve the Devil right if he fell for it.

"I can't change the weather." The Devil shook his head, looking slightly worried. "Like I said—"

"Can ye fuck wi' yon sun shield the fuckin' Yanks stuck in the sky?" Davy leaned forward, glaring at him: "'Cause if no, whit kindae deil are ye?"

"You want me to what?"

Davy took a deep breath. He remembered what it had looked like on TV, twenty years ago: the great silver reflectors unfolding in solar orbit, the jubilant politicians, the graphs showing a 20% fall in sunlight reaching the Earth… the savage April blizzards that didn't stop for a month, the endless twilight and the sun dim enough to look at. And now the Devil wanted to give him a wish, in payment for fucking things up for a few thousand bastards who had it coming? Davy felt his lips drawing back from his teeth, a feral smile forcing itself to the surface. "Ah want ye to fuck up the sunshade, awright? Get ontae it. Ah want tae be wairm…"

The Devil shook his head. "That's a new one on me," he admitted. "But—" He frowned. "You're sure? No second thoughts? You want to waive your mandatory fourteen-day right of cancellation?"

"Aye. Dae it the noo." Davy nodded vigorously.

"It's done." The Devil smiled faintly.

"Whit?" Davy stared.

"There's not much to it. A rock about the size of this pub, traveling on a cometary orbit—it'll take an hour or so to fold, but I already took care of that." The Devil's smile widened. "You used your wish."

"Ah dinnae believe ye," said Davy, hopping down from his bar stool. Out of the corner of one eye, he saw Tam dodging through the blackout curtain and the doorway, tipping him the wink. This had gone on long enough. "Ye'll have tae prove it. Show me."

"What?" The Devil looked puzzled. "But I told you, it'll take about an hour."

"So ye say. An' whit then?"

"Well, the parasol collapses, so the amount of sunlight goes up. It gets brighter. The snow melts."

"Is that right?" Davy grinned. "So how many wishes dae Ah get this time?"

"How many—" The Devil froze. "What makes you think you get any more?" He snarled, his face contorting.

"Like ye said, Ah gave ye a loan, didn't Ah?" Davy's grin widened. He gestured toward the door. "After ye?"

"You—" The Devil paused. "You don't mean…" He swallowed, then continued, quietly. "That wasn't deliberate, was it?"

"Oh. Aye." Davy could see it in his mind's eye: the wilting crops and blazing forests, droughts and heatstroke and mass extinction, the despairing millions across America and Africa, exotic places he'd never seen, never been allowed to go—roasting like pieces of a turkey on a spit, roasting in revenge for twenty years frozen in outer darkness. Hell on Earth. "Four billion fuckers, isnae that enough for another?"

"Son of a bitch!" The Devil reached into his jacket pocket and pulled out an antique calculator, began punching buttons. "Forty-eight—no, forty-nine. Shit, this has never happened before! You bastard, don't you have a conscience?"

Davy thought for a second. "Naw."

"Fuck!"

It was now or never. "Ah'll take a note."

"A credit—shit, okay then. Here." The Devil handed over his mobile. It was small and very black and shiny, and it buzzed like a swarm of flies. "Listen, I've got to go right now, I need to escalate this to senior management. Call head office tomorrow, if I'm not there, one of my staff will talk you through the state of your claim."

"Haw! Ah'll be sure tae dae that."

The Devil stalked towards the curtain and stepped through into the darkness beyond, and was gone. Davy pulled out his moby and speed-dialed a number. "He's a' yours noo," he muttered into the handset, then hung up and turned back to his beer. A couple of minutes later, someone came in and sat down next to him. Davy raised a hand and waved vaguely at Katie: "A Deuchars for Tam here."

Katie nodded nonchalantly—she seemed to have cheered up since the Devil had stepped out—and picked up a glass.

Tam dropped a couple of small brass horns on the bar top next to Davy. Davy stared at them for a moment then glanced up admiringly. "Neat," he admitted. "Get anythin' else aff him?"

"Nah, the cunt wis crap. He didnae even have a moby. Just these." Tam looked disgusted for a moment. "Ah pulled ma chib an' waved it aroon' an' he totally legged it. Think anybody'll come lookin' for us?"

"Nae chance." Davy raised his glass, then tapped the pocket with the Devil's mobile phone in it smugly. "Nae a snowball's chance in hell..."

ΠΟΠ-DISCLOSURE AGREEMENT

by Scott Westerfeld

I went to Los Angeles to burn down a house.

It was a low-stress conflagration. Just a run-of-the-mill house-burning sequence for a television miniseries. It was working-titled *Tribulation Alley*—set in a post-Rapture world populated by a lot of recently reformed agnostics and the odd Anti-Christ.

Because it was television, we wouldn't be filming the fire in any serious way.

You see, real flames don't look good on TV.

Most of the high-budget holocausts you see on video these days are computer generated. With a real fire, it's too hard to get the continuity right, even with a multi-camera shoot. It actually takes about an hour to burn a house down properly, so you have to jump cut too many times. But the vast rendering farms employed by Falling Man FX (mostly located in Idaho, I think) can reduce a house to cinders in an attention deficit disorder-friendly twenty seconds.

On top of the timing issues, the yellows in a really kick-ass blaze are too sallow for digital video. They have a sort of jaundiced reticence, which we punch up to a hearty crimson glow. It's not reality, but it looks better.

Despite the limitations of the physical world, Falling Man still burns down the odd house now and then. We study the results carefully, just to keep ourselves honest. For reference, basically, and to get a few fresh ideas. So out to LA I went, matches in hand.

The Tribulation crew had evidently used the house only in exterior shots. It was empty of furniture, completely unfinished. It had a Potemkin-village flatness, the walls paper-thin and bereft of plumbing or wiring. For the first day and some, I had the crew install paneling, to keep the walls from burning through too fast, and spread some rolls of old carpet on the floor, to get the smoke right. Even though most of us haven't seen a house burn down, we know instinctively what it should look like. And if we don't, our kids will. That's our Golden Rule at Falling Man: every generation of movie-goers needs better and more expensive special effects.

It's a philosophy that keeps the money rolling in.

About lunchtime on the second day, I was satisfied with the flammability of things, and we wrapped until that night. This house-burning scene was in daylight, according to the script, but we always burn at night for better contrast. Sunlight's one of the easiest things to add: full spectrum, parallel light. An idiot can make the sun shine.

Besides, real sunlight doesn't look good on TV. Except for the golden hours of dusk and dawn, the sun is a tacky, garish creation, which blows out what little contrast exists on digital video.

I should have gotten some sleep before the big burn. I was still on New York time; passing out would have been easy. Maybe if I'd been better rested, I wouldn't have gotten myself killed that day.

But I was on the company dime, so as I was driven back to my hotel, I contemplated the tiny minibar key that was attached by a tiny chain to the smartcard that admitted me to my room, the rooftop sauna, and the ice machine.

I've always been fascinated with mechanical keys. I guess a lot of computer geeks are. Very early crypto. And a fascinating email screed had recently been forwarded to me. It proclaimed that one's status in society bears an inverse relationship to the number of keys in one's possession. The lowly janitor has rings and rings of them. The assistant manager has to get in early to open up the fast-food restaurant—the boss comes in later. And as we climb the economic ladder, more and more other people appear to open the doors, drive the cars, and deal with the petty mechanics of security. So here I was, boy millionaire in the back seat, armed with only my hotel smartcard and that tiny signifier of minibar privilege, as miniscule as the key for some diary of childhood dreams.

Much like the empty pages of a blank book, this small key had limitless power over my imagination. I felt in its tiny metal teeth the ability to consume six-dollar Toblerone bars and twelve-dollar Coronas. To pick through exquisitely small and expensive cans of mixed nuts and discard all but the cashews. Indeed, in my initial reconnaissance of the bar, I'd spotted a child-sized humidor in the back, no doubt offering cigarillos of post-Fidel provenance and jaw-dropping price. And all these miniaturized delights would be charged to Falling Man.

Fondling that little key in the back of the car, I realized a secret truth: This moment was why I had come to LA. To raid the refrigerator.

Later, it occurred to me that if I had somehow known that my death was nigh, I would have done pretty much the same thing with my last hours, indulged pretty much the same sensuous pleasures and petty revenge. Perhaps on a grander scale, but with no greater depth of spirit. And I suppose that's why I was sent to Hell.

That night at the burn, I was woozy.

The six beers were nothing, and those airplane-sized bottles of Matusalem Rum wouldn't have inebriated a five-year-old. But I was a child of the post-smoking era, and I should have stayed away from the cigarillos. I felt as if some pre-Cambrian 1950s dad had locked me in a closet with a carton of Marlboros to finish off. My mouth was horribly dry, and I craved a drink. Preferably from one of the giant hoses that drooped in the arms of the firefighters that the LAFD had sent to oversee our little inferno.

With the desultory taste of ashtray in my mouth, I didn't even bother starting the fire myself. I left the honors to a production assistant with a cute smile.

I just mumbled, "Action."

She threw the large, Dr. Frankenstein-style connection switch, and the gallons of accelerant we'd sprayed throughout the doomed house ignited. A wave of comforting warmth spread from the fire, reaching us through the cool desert air a few seconds after the first flames burst from the bungalow's windows.

A ragged cheer went up from the crew, rewarded at last for the hot work of prepping through two August days. Six of them held palm-sized digital cameras. Four locked-down cameras shot the house from its cardinal directions, providing x- and y-references for the shaky images from the handhelds.

We didn't bother with microphones. Real fires don't sound good on TV. Too crackly, they're just so much static. We generally insert a low rumble, like a subway going under you, with a white-noise wash on top.

The six camera-jocks dashed in as close as the heat allowed, working to record the warp and woof of the blaze. They tried to catch the dramatic and particular details, a beam splintering in a gusher of sparks, a trapped pocket of air exploding. We wanted to capture this fire's effulgent specificity, so that the art director back at Falling Man could escape the tried-and-true spreading-flame algorithms that all the other FX houses used. We wanted something unique, almost real.

Like nineteenth-century scientists taking spirit photographs, we were trying to capture the soul of this fire.

The PA whom I'd allowed to start the blaze put her hand on my shoulder. I looked up and was struck by the simple, pyromaniacal joy in her eyes. The woman's touch was unselfconscious, unsexual, and I saw her twenty-something innocence writ by the dancing red light on her face, and in my jaded, thirty-something way preferred that to the blaze itself. I watched her, until a cracking noise and a sudden intake of breath from the crew brought my eyes back to the fire.

One corner of the house was threatening to collapse.

A gout of flame had sprouted from the base, running like a greedy tongue up the vertex of the two walls. The supporting beam hidden behind this column of fire must have been wet new wood; it was hissing, throwing out steam and sparks explosively. It began to buckle and twist, writhing like a snake held captive in a cylinder of gas and plasma.

"This is the money shot!" I cried, waving all the handhelds around to that side. I was breathing hard, heart pounding and cigarillo hangover suddenly vanquished. I ran a few steps toward the house. Even in those meters the air temperature raised noticeably, the blaze now a heavy and scorching hand pushing against my face. It dried my contact lenses, which gripped cruelly at my eyes like little hemispherical claws.

I felt as if I was waking up from a long dream, like when you realize the exquisite detail of the real world after a prolonged session in VR.

I turned back to the PA, who had followed behind me, and shouted, "This is why we do this."

She nodded, her pupils as wide as the zeroes on a hundred-dollar bill.

One of the camera-jocks knelt just in front of me, his little camera a whining, frightened bee.

"Give me that thing," I said.

Nice last words, don't you think?

I pressed one eye to the viewfinder, clenched the other shut to protect it from the heat, and moved forward. I pushed in close, the heat a strong wind against me now.

Objects in viewfinders are closer than they appear.

Someone shouted a warning, but this was my shoot.

In the limited view of the camera, I didn't see the whole thing. But I presume the corner beam gave way near its base and fell outward, propelled by the gasses trapped within its green wood, or perhaps by some randomly concurrent explosion inside the house.

It reached out, a hissing, flaming arm, and struck me solidly where I knelt, braced against the outdraft of the blaze. It wasn't the fire that killed me, just pedestrian kinetic energy. My corpse was hardly burned at all.

The Devil (aka: Beelzebub, Satan, and the Artist Formerly Known as the Prince of Darkness) entertained me in an office rather like my dad's cubicle when he worked for IBM. There was that same penumbra of stickies framing the fat old cathode-ray-tube monitor, the rhythmic chunking sound of a far-off photocopier, the pre-email proliferation of paper everywhere, and Old Scratch himself was wearing a blue suit, white shirt, and red tie.

But it looked better on him than on my dad.

He nodded a hello. There was no need for introductions; I knew who he was. He's the Devil, after all. The crafty smile, his seductive grace even on the pre-ergonomic office chair, the unalloyed beauty of his face all made his fallen-angel provenance clear. I had no doubt that this was real.

But the IBM setting seemed a bit odd.

"Is this some kind of ironic punishment thing?" I asked, imagining an eternity of writing Cobol code and wearing a tie. A fitting fate for New Economy Boy.

"Not at all," Satan replied, waving one elegant hand. "Irony is dead. Your generation killed it. Besides, nothing beats hot flames. We're in the business of damnation, not poetic justice."

His limpid eyes drifted across the jokey coffee mug, the dusty and finger-printed glass of the CRT, the thrice-faxed office-humor cartoon thumbtacked to the cubicle wall, taking them all in with a kind of vast sadness. He was awfully pretty, just like they say.

He looked at me and sighed.

"My point with this apparition is to impress upon you my weakness."

I looked at him in horror. "For bad office design?"

"Not that," said the Devil. "Although I must say, the cubicle has crushed more souls than I lately." He regarded the screen saver on the terminal: the words DO NOT TOUCH ANYTHING ON THIS DESK rolled by in quiet desperation. He shuddered, then turned toward me.

"To be frank, we need your help."

"My help?"

"With an FX issue."

I narrowed my eyes.

"You see," the Devil continued, "over the last few decades, we down here in Hell have begun to realize that we have a little trouble with our… look and feel."

"I don't follow you."

He smiled, perhaps at my choice of words.

Then he shrugged. "I think it's these video games, although some of my minions say it's CGI graphics. But whatever is to blame, recent studies have found that the average American male spends fourteen hours per week in some sort of interactive infernal environment. And we just can't compete with the graphics in first-person shooters these days. Many of the souls coming down here lately find the underworld rather… cheesy, I'm afraid."

"You mean…?"

"Yes, alas," the Devil lamented. "Hell no longer looks good on TV. Nor even in reality."

It was true.

We soared over the damned, their voices crying in a great wail of pain. Although we were above the tongues of the flame, the heat clung to me like fishhooks. Every square inch of epidermis felt like sunburned flesh sprayed with jalapeño juice. And the smell was far worse than the sulfur we all know from rotten eggs. It was of a purer species: fifth-grade chemistry set sulfur, though tinged with a darker, murkier scent, like a dead rat behind the wall. The stench was awful even from our lofty height. I can't imagine what it was like inside that pit of fire.

But Old Scratch was right. The visuals were very last-century. Gouts of hellfire shot across the damned in big tacky bursts, as if some Coney Island flame-breather were running around down there. And the flowing rivers of flame were so Discovery Channel: turgid and crusted with solidifying earth on top. Nothing halfway as cool as the boiling-oil algorithms that Falling Man had created for the prequel to *Death Siege*, and that was just a Showtime original. We'd devised a mesmerizing and viscous black liquid all run through with scintillating veins of sharp crimson, like a negative of a bloodshot eye texture-mapped onto flowing blobs of mercury.

And the Hadean backdrop of reddened craggy mountains was totally prefractal. I've seen scarier coral.

"This looks like a heavy metal video from the early eighties," I opined, blowing my nose from the heat.

"So you'll help me?"

"I want a deal memo first," I said.

Naturally, he had his paperwork already in hand.

Now, this was not your basic Daniel Webster-style deal with Beelzebub—swapping my soul for unlimited wealth or devilish charm. The Devil had been priced out of the geek-soul market. Vast riches were at that point pretty unremarkable for anyone with a software background. Hell, geeks can even get chicks these days. Satan couldn't find anyone good to do the work, because he simply had nothing we wanted.

This facet of the New Economy no doubt appalled the most beautiful of former angels, and had thus far stymied his upgrade efforts (uncleverly code-named: "Hades 2.0").

Until I came along.

You see, I wasn't totally dead.

I was having what's known as a "near-death experience." My singed but not irredeemable corpse was in the back of a LAFD ambulance right now, headed toward probable reanimation at County General. But instead of the usual approaching white light that goody-goodies enjoy, I was getting a sneak preview of the Other Place. (We don't hear so much about those, do we? I figure it's a media selection thing—visions of hell don't get you on Oprah.) Soon, I was going to return to the living, whether I took the Devil's offer or not. But I had seen what lay in store.

"So no money, no gnarly magic powers?" I complained as I scanned his contract. "What exactly do I get for helping you?"

"In exchange for your help with my look-and-feel issues, you will receive certain highly proprietary information."

"Microsoft source code? I knew that guy was on your side."

"No, something far more valuable," the Devil whispered. "The Secret of Damnation."

"The what?"

He sighed, and all drama left his voice. "The secret of how not to wind up in hell, imbecile."

"It's a secret? Isn't it like a sin and forgiveness thing? I mean, it all looks very Judeo-Christian down here."

"Young man, it's not that simple. Because of your cultural background, you're merely seeing the Judeo-Christian, uh... front-end. But Hell has many facets, many aspects."

"So this is just the Judeo-Christian interface?"

"Yes, but the Secret of Damnation is universal," the Devil concluded. "The deeds and ideas that doom the soul are the same everywhere."

"And this information is proprietary?"

He nodded. "Only God and I know the source code. You mortals are mere end-users."

"That's harsh."

"And believe me," the Devil said, "salvation grows harder to achieve every day."

I looked back over my life, and wondered what—besides my casual agnosticism, rampant Napster piracy, and willing participation in the commercialization of Xmas—could have damned me. It wasn't immediately obvious. My recent near-death had made me realize that I was somewhat shallow. (I'd sort of known that anyway.) But I didn't think I was really evil.

I could always try to be a better person once this bad dream was over. Give to charity. Be a Big Brother. Pay the Falling Man pixel-jocks another buck an hour. But what if that didn't tip the scales?

I remembered the terrible heat of the flames. However visually cheesy and culturally specific, a real trip to Hades meant pain for eternity. And pain never looks good on TV.

I also realized that I could leverage the subsidiary value of the Secret of Damnation. Once I knew the Secret, I could spread the word. Start a new religion with guaranteed results. A new, streamlined religion for the new century. Skip the rituals and dogma, and get straight to the part about not going to Hell!

Now there was a business model.

"Okay," I said. "It's a deal. You'll get the best infernal front-end this side of Fireblood IV. Just tell me the Secret."

"First," he said, "you must sign this."

Damn, I thought when I saw the document. An NDA.

Now, I've signed about a thousand non-disclosure agreements in my day. In the software world, every meeting, every negotiation, even the most tedious of product demonstrations begins with this harmless and generally meaningless ritual. "We promise not to tell anyone what we learn here. Blah, blah, blah." If you made a giant map of every non-disclosure agreement ever signed, with a node for each software company and a connecting line for each NDA—rendering the whole New Economy as a sprawling net of confidentiality—any point would be reachable from any other within a few jumps: six degrees of non-disclosure.

But this was the NDA from Hell.

One peep about the nature of the Secret—verbal revelation, gestural hints, Pictionary clues, publication in any media yet to be invented throughout the universe and in perpetuity—and I would be back down here pronto and permanently. Damned.

This was the hitch, the gotcha that Old Scratch always puts in his contracts. I was going to have to keep my mouth shut in a big way.

But I signed. Like I said, it was pure reflex.

And then I got to work.

The first order of business was getting an art director. Hades 2.0 was primarily a graphics upgrade, so high-quality pixel help was essential. I decided on Harriet Kaufman, a freelance artist who'd worked with Falling Man before, and who could be trusted not to tell anyone else at the firm about my little side project.

My body was alive by now—a shot of adrenaline had restarted my heart—and I was comatose in a hospital bed. Now only semi-dead, Hades had grown a bit fuzzy around me, but I could still function down here. To get me started quickly, the Devil let me borrow a machine with a fast net connection.

A buddy search revealed that Harriet was online, so I instant-messaged her. It turns out that my immortal soul types faster without my corporeal fingers in the way, and with better punctuation and accuracy.

<thought you were dead!!> Harriet responded.

<Nope, just near-dead. I've got some work for you.>

<didn't you catch on fire or something? you're in the hospital, right?>

<Just singed. Still comatose, actually. But I'm working remotely, from Hell.>

<LA?>

<No. *The* Hell. But I'll be back in NY soon. And while I was down here, I got a job.>

<is this some kind of sick joke?>

<No, Harriet. Like I said, I got some work for you. $$$!>

<who is this really?>

<It's ME! Listen. Who one else would know this: Remember that time when I got drunk at your apartment and we tried, but couldn't?>

<OK! OK! but you said you were comatose?>

<Body on the slab. Soul in Hades.>

<whoa. i get it now. you *are* dead, and you set up some sort of dead-man switch, like you always talked about.>

I winced when I saw these words. I had always claimed to have a dead-man switch installed deep in Falling Man's system, in case the other partners decided to get rid of me. My story was that if I didn't type in a special code once a week, my dead-man program would recognize my absence and activate, rampantly destroying all the company's stored data. It was insurance, in case I ever found myself locked out of the office, or worse, cut out of the stock options. The truth was, however, I'd never bothered to implement the dead-man software. It was too much trouble. After all, as with nuclear weapons, a credible threat of massive retaliation was sufficient to maintain the peace.

Harriet continued:

<so this is just some posthumous conversation program, designed to fuck with my head if you died. you programmed it to mention that time at my house. that is so nasty of you. *was* so nasty, I guess.>

<No, this is ME, not some crappy chat software.>

<prove it.>

<A Turing Test? I reach out to you, asking for help from beyond the grave and you give me a FUCKING TURING TEST?>

<ok. you just passed. only you would bring up a turing test while you were dead. geek.>

<Thanks.>

<now, you said something about a job?>

I briefed Harriet, explaining who the client was and what he wanted, but saying nothing about the payment plan. After our little discussion, I decided to wait until I was walking the earth again before I made any more hires. The last thing I needed was a load of people pestering me about the afterlife. I had that non-disclosure agreement to worry about, after all.

A few hours later, my eyelids started to flicker, and I found myself in the demimonde between an LA hospital room and my Hell cubicle. The Devil, like some gorgeous and jocular supervisor, came over to shake my hand and say goodbye.

"When do I get the Secret?" I interrupted.

"After delivery. Just don't get hit by a bus before then."

"I'll be careful."

"And don't forget my little non-disclosure clause," he added.

"Mum's the word."

He smiled cruelly at my show of confidence. I could see in his eyes that he fully expected me to fail, to spill the beans and wind up in his clutches for eternity. I started to say something brave.

But then the netherworld faded, and I was back. Bright lights, stiff bedclothes, and thundering unstoppably into my awareness: a world of pain. It turns out that even first-degree burns can take you to the extremes of agony.

I gurgled a scream, and flailed my arms. Someone grabbed my hand, and I heard a call for morphine.

So now I know what Heaven feels like, too.

Harriet and I did good work together.

For Hell's new lava, we used a liquid motion package designed by these hydrofoil designers in Germany. Extending its parameters with a little code of our own, we set the lava's viscosity to crazy—our lakes of fire hopped as lively as a puddle in a Texas hail storm. Cruel geyser heads lurked below the surface, periodically erupting to scatter a scalding mist upon the cruel abysmal wind. Harriet colored the lava an ominous dark red, texture-mapped with scanned photos of my still-scabby burns and run through with sinuous veins of eye-gouging electric crimson.

We decided to go fractal with the mountains. Each pointy crag was sharp enough to scratch a diamond, each lacerating jut of rock serrated with infinitely recessing edges-within-edges, razor-fine down to the microscopic level. You could cut yourself just looking at the stuff.

We also went fractal with the Styx 2.0, making it infinitely crooked, infinitely long. A boundless barrier between the mundane and the eternal.

Working alongside Harriet, I saw the project reflected in her eyes, their steely blue aglitter with the millions of reds in our perditious palette. My hand was always on her shoulder as we crouched over twenty-thousand-dollar monitors, and I felt the flutters of her soul in the taut muscles that extend from neck to mouse-arm. The hellish imagery turned her on, inflated her pupils like blobs of black mercury expanding in the heat of our virtual netherworld. She was hooked, transfixed, spitted by a primal sexual response to the visage of death.

She didn't really believe in our diabolical client, I could tell. But the project manufactured its own verity, until the view in the monitor became as real for her as for those who would one day occupy it.

I had known the project would capture her. Harriet was one of those artists who instinctually resisted computers, only to be ultimately seduced by them. She loved her paints, but a stroke of pigment can't be corrected. There are no RGB values to change, no pixels to nudge. You're stuck with the happenstance of that moment, without an Undo command or even a backup file. And that's a losing deal, it had always seemed to me. She always claimed that one day she'd foreswear the mouse and pick up her paintbrushes again, but the ability to tween and tweek was an irresistible siren. The algorithms that we geeks had used to colonize the screen had colonized Harriet as well.

It's an old story. Religions start with a madman's inspiration but end up with sensible canons and commandments. Barter systems are rationalized into the liquidity of cash and credit. Mythologies are repurposed as role-playing games. Communities are arrogated by IPOs. With the visual arts it took a while longer for the number-crunchers to take over, but eventually we always win.

Art may be pretty, but rule-governed systems rule.

Our biggest graphics challenge was hellfire, the ambient affliction of the damned. We needed something that would burn without devouring, a necessary provision for endless torment. But fire that doesn't consume its fuel always looks wussy. It hovers over the burning victim like it was Photoshopped on post facto, about as scary as the disembodied and exaggerated blaze of charcoal sprayed with too much lighter fluid.

We brought in some programmers and created dozens of new algorithms from scratch. We watched videos of forest and brushfires, warehouse conflagrations, accelerant infernos, the oil-well holocausts of the Gulf War. I picked my scabs endlessly, looking for answers in that crumbling, itching flesh.

Finally, we hit paydirt in that old standby: napalm. When napalm consumes flesh, it burns its own sticky fuel, charring the body beneath as a secondary effect. Sprayed with fire extinguisher foam or submerged in water, it remains alight, attached to its victim, demonically implacable.

Vietnam-era video has its limitations, of course, so we checked out a few second-amendment websites and got the recipe. We concocted a small batch of napalm from soap flakes and kerosene, and headed out to the Jersey swamps, bringing along cow-hearts and a couple of raw pigs that we'd scored from a loading dock in the meatpacking district. We burned the whole grisly pile.

During the filming, I had a flashback to my near-death in California. Waves of heat came from the crackling flesh, and a stench not unlike the sulphurous reek of Hell.

I looked over at Harriet, who had dropped her digital camera to stare at the flames with naked eyes. Tears ran down her cheeks, streaking the soot that had darkened her face. She gazed back at me with horror. Harriet had treated the whole project as an enjoyable lark until now. Vanity graphics for an imaginary client, my personal fetish. But I could see that the level of detail was starting to get to her.

The look in Harriet's eyes dampened my pyromania for a moment. What was I doing, working so hard to make Hell look better? How much pain would I have caused by the time Hades 3.0 came along, augmenting as I had the tortures of a multitude of lost souls?

But then I remembered: I was avoiding my own damnation. My motivation was enlightened self-interest, the fulcrum of a better world.

Harriet and I fucked in the production van while the inferno waned. The smell of cooking meat made us wildly hungry, and the late-August heat channeled the soot and ash that covered us into tiny black rivers of sweat. For a few minutes, we were demon lovers, savage and inhuman.

And Harriet wept, filthy and condemned, all the way back to Manhattan.

Despite ourselves, we'd gotten the footage we needed. Frame-by-frame analysis revealed how the pigflesh charred while the greedy napalm burned, the pigs' innards curling out to embrace the flame, providing fuel from within. My programmers refined the process to a simple algorithmic dance, which writhed in perpetuity like a blazing Jacob's ladder, an infinite meal encountered by a ceaseless appetite. Soon we had hellfire on tap.

It gave us all nightmares—even the programmers, who didn't know our client's business model. But it looked very good on TV.

A few weeks of tweaking later, we were done.

The day we delivered, Harriet and I went out for a celebratory drink.

"Did the client pay you?" she asked.

I nodded. True to our contract's terms, I'd received a FedEx that afternoon, the Secret of Damnation printed out in a one-page summation no longer than a pitch for an action movie. The whole thing would have fit easily on one of those big-sized post-its. I had read it twice, then folded it up and carefully placed it in my breast pocket. I would burn it that night, after one more read. It seemed simple enough, but I didn't want any loopholes or trick language screwing up my trip to heaven.

"Yeah," I said. "The project's all done."

I'd already paid Harriet off with cash out of my own pocket, just like everyone else on the job. And a healthy bonus for not squealing to my partners that I was working on the side. But from the look in her eye, she wanted more now.

"Was it a lot of money?" she asked.

"Well, not money, really."

"I didn't think so."

I coughed into my beer. "You know I'm strictly non-disclosure on this."

"Of course."

We drank for a while. We were still lovers, but barely so. Nothing had ever come close to those minutes in New Jersey, enveloped by the grime of a new abyss.

"I think," she said, "that I'm finally going to take that vacation I keep talking about."

"Africa?" I said weakly, careful not to inflect my voice with any enthusiasm.

"Yeah," she said. "Africa. Just me, some paint and a few brushes. I'm going strictly analog for a year, maybe two. Like going native. No computers for a while."

"I see." I couldn't believe she was saying this, so soon after I'd read the Secret.

"No Photoshop, no modeling software. Just real objects to look at and to paint. Pigment and white canvas. Sky and landscapes."

"Sounds… nice," I said flatly.

"So," she asked, "is it simple?"

"Is what simple?"

"The Secret of Damnation."

My hand went to my breast pocket, a sinking feeling hitting me like the NAS-DAQ in freefall. "How the hell did you know about that?"

"He told me. He came to me and told me what he paid you."

"That fucker."

"So I want a percentage. Tell me the Secret."

"I can't."

"Just part of it. Give me a clue."

"I signed an NDA, Harriet. I can't even give you a hint. If I tell, I go to Hell."

She shrugged, laughed as if she'd only been kidding.

"Sorry. Didn't mean to put you in breach of contract." A pause, a wicked smile. "But it's pretty straightforward, right?"

"Harriet! Stop."

"But—"

"No hints, no adjectives, no information. Nada." I put my hands over my mouth.

"Okay," she said slowly, swirling one finger around the lip of her glass flirtatiously. "But if I was doing something, something bad? Bad enough to get me sent to Hell, for instance. Could you give me a sign?"

"Like scratch my nose with my right index finger?"

"Yeah, you could."

"No, I could not. Harriet, this is the Devil we're talking about," I said. "Not some jealous boyfriend I can hide from down in Miami. He's the Prince of Darkness, the Lord of Hades, and if I fuck up he'll come and carry me away screaming to Hell. You know, the one we just created?"

"Yeah, sure," she said. "Whatever."

A silent moment elapsed.

"But is it a big thing?" she asked playfully. "Or just a detail?"

I shut my eyes, locked both hands over my face. I didn't want any clues to pass over my visage—agreement or denial, warmer or colder. I tried to think of the latest virus hoax, the closing prices of Falling Man stock over the last week, anything to occlude the fatal knowledge in my mind.

Despite these efforts, I clearly remembered the Secret of Damnation. The simplicity of the idea, the easy charm of it. I could have explained it to Harriet in two minutes.

"Come on, relax," she said. "I don't believe any of it anyway."

"Yes, you do," I said from behind the curtain of my hands.

She snorted. "It's obvious what's going on here. This all just started out as self-indulgent therapy for you. You're a software über-geek who thought you were king of the world, until you almost died. Mortality wasn't pretty, and worse, it was way out of control. So you decided to deal with the post-traumatic stress the only way you know how. You decided to domesticate the afterlife into a software project. It's so predictable and lame. You hire a few coders and artists to put your near-death hallucination—clearly inspired by the *Tribulation Alley* burn—onto a nice, safe computer screen. There, you can adjust its frame rate and resolution, play with its aspect ratio and palette. Then you burn it onto a disk, and you think you've got eternal life now. It's pathetic. You've reduced heaven and hell to pixels, for God's sake."

"No," I insisted. "What we made, it's really Hell. I swear it is."

"It's nothing but a screen-saver!" she shouted. "By definition: some nice graphics that do nothing!"

"Harriet, I instant-messaged you from beyond the grave, remember? And you just said that you met the Devil, for Pete's sake!"

"You messaged me from a County General Hospital in LA, you fuck. I checked the timing. You'd come out of your coma by the time I got your message."

"That's impossible."

"I called them. You were already ambulatory."

"They made a mistake. Or maybe it's a time zone thing. I woke up after I messaged you, I swear."

"LA's three hours behind us. Any mistake would have worked the other way around."

"What about the Devil? You said he appeared to you."

"The Devil, sure. You hired some cute actor—some very cute actor, I might add—to mess with my head. What, did you think I'd fuck you again for the Secret of Damnation? Was this whole thing a way to get in my pants from the beginning?"

"No, it was a way to get out of Hell."

She laughed again, but the sound was dry and ragged now. "Listen, I don't know whether you're pulling some elaborate hoax on me, or if you really believe all this. Either way, you're totally out of your mind. But I'll still take the bait, if that'll make you happy. Tell me, what's your idea of salvation?"

"Salvation?"

"Yes. Tell me what you think goodness is. What do you think saves us, redeems us in the end? What's the Secret?"

"I'm not at liberty to disclose that."

"Fuck off."

"I told you, I signed an NDA!"

"I'm not buying that shit! There's no Devil, just you and your ego and your post-traumatic paranoia. Let me help you."

"I'm not going to damn myself."

"Listen, I've been staring into your personal pit of evil for the last six weeks. I helped you visualize it, went there with you, even fucked you there. Aren't you cured yet?"

My reply was strangled by a whiff of sulphur.

"Show me the other side of you," she pleaded. "You saw Hell because when you almost died you realized there's this hole in your life. A stinking pit, right? So you worked through it onscreen. Good for you. And now this bogus Satan comes to tell me you've had a revelation. Fine, I want to hear it. But talk directly to me for once. Please. What's your Secret of Salvation?"

"I'll go to Hell if I tell you."

"You won't go to Hell just for talking to me, darling."

I covered my mouth again.

"Just talk to me!" a sob breaking her voice.

For the first time since we'd napalmed our sad little pigs, true anguish showed on Harriet's face. Like me, she had seen Hell, even if only on a screen. The brave new Hades 2.0, red in tooth and claw, every searing pixel of it. She had shaped and morphed it, tweeked and tweened it, wrangling every RGB value to its optimum. She had even felt it for a moment, out in our Jersey swamp, the heat and stench of that chemical fire as it consumed the offal we'd brought with us, body doubles for the damned.

Despite her words, I knew she now believed in Hell.

But unlike me, Harriet didn't know how to escape. She lacked my trick, my Secret, my certainty of heaven. And she must have known that she was damned as I had been.

She rose from her chair angrily, slammed a twenty on the table, and stood.

At last I realized the horror of the Devil's NDA. For the rest of my life, I would be trapped by my knowledge of the Secret, stuck in contractual amber as I watched friends and lovers walk blithely toward an eternity of pain, unable to stop them. Unable even to hint at the grim future I foresaw. Decade after decade of powerlessness. How many souls would I damn through my inaction?

The devil had snared me, not in his domain, but in my own private little hell of non-disclosure.

"Wait," I said.

Harriet stood there, her eyes burning.

I almost said it, almost told her. I almost went to hell.

"Nothing."

She turned and fled.

It is, of course, only a matter of time.

No one can bear the weight of this knowledge forever. At some point, I'll slip, and reveal the Secret to save someone. After all, the damned are all around me. My friends, co-workers, and lovers are all stained with the soot of the burning. I still read the NDA every day, more carefully than when I foolishly signed it. It's a very well-written contract. An expression or a gesture leading to the truth could damn me. Any hint at all.

Sooner or later, I will fuck up.

I've thought of suicide, the quick and dirty way to lock in my special knowledge, my insider's price, but I'm too much of a wimp to pull the trigger.

At this writing, I live in Africa. Less than one percent of the population of this city speak English, an added layer of protection. But my old software buddies still visit, and I'm too lonely to turn them away, though I can see how damned they are. A few of them seem to know that I have a secret. They question and prod me about my new life, about why I left their world. Perhaps the Devil appears to them as he did to Harriet, just to tempt me with their salvation.

He wants my soul badly.

But I haven't completely despaired. Old Scratch showed his weakness to me, back when I was dead. He doesn't have good software help. He doesn't understand the new paradigms of information distribution.

So I've finally implemented that dead-man switch, the threat that I once held over my partners' heads.

Every month, I send a message, the correct codeword from a non-patterned series of my own devising. The FallingMan.com server waits for this missive impatiently. Should I die (to be trundled safely up to heaven), or finally screw up and spill the beans to someone (to be carted off screaming to hell), my monthly codeword will be missed, and the server will leap into action.

Indeed, if you are reading this, that is exactly what has happened.

So please forgive the breadth and intensity of this spam. I'm sure someone's had to delete this story from about ten thousand mailing lists, and my recording of it should occupy about half the Napster and Gnutella indexes, listed as everything from the Beatles to Britney Spears. Part of my job at Falling Man was viral marketing. The whole world is reading with you.

So this, my friend, is no secret:

Forget the backups. Screw the pixels. Lose the smartcards. Avoid the minibars. Overthrow the rule-governed systems. Break the commandments. Exceed the algorithms. Ignore the special effects. Don't undo.

Disclose everything. Paint the landscape.

Go analog.

Save your soul.

LİKE RİDİNG A BİKE

Jan Wildt

FOR ANNE R.

1

Velma Fish awoke to a curious smell, familiar yet strange.

She opened her eyes to the same old bedroom—nothing out of place. The sun streamed through the window. She'd slept like a baby: none of that fitful drifting.

But there was a certain sharp odor, one she knew from a lifetime ago, when, as a little girl, she'd visit her grandma's house. A mustiness that tells you the people who live there can't smell anymore.

That was the thing about getting on in years, of course: your youthful memories were clear as a bell. The trouble was the past ten minutes.

That, and the joints. Normally the morning was worst, of course. As Mrs. Knowles across the hall liked to say: "Oh, I have a wild life. I go to bed with Ben Gay and get up with Arthur Itis."

Yet right now Velma's whole bony frame was oddly, pleasantly numb, like her bad hip after Dr. Whitlow injected it. Slick and clean inside. Even the fingers felt fine, like someone else's.

She wiggled them experimentally. She saw smooth, soft hands and arms—*not her own*—and leapt from bed, terrified. Something was wrong, as wrong as things get.

She heard her blood pounding.

She looked at the legs beneath her, the mirror in front of her, where staring wide-eyed was a frightened child, a dark-haired girl of sinuous limb, hiking the hem of her nightie—Velma's own.

"I'm dreaming," she said calmly, and the girl's lips moved with hers. "Wake up, Velma."

But it was no dream.

2

—Now *next* please.

—Motion for disjunction A.D. 1998 one Velma Alice Fish behest of Bertillon, Throne, FAAC. Duration fifty-three years.

—Fifty-three *years*.

—Years, Excellency.

—Counselor Bertillon: approach and hearken.

Bertillon came forward, wings respectfully folded.

—Your Excellency, if I—

—Since Yahweh fell silent, how many disjunctions have been entertained here, for all the billions of lives on Earth?

—Just twenty, Excellency.

—And how many granted?

—Three, Excellency.

—And none over thirty *seconds*.

—I'm aware of that, Excellency.

—We're ready to hear just how special this is.

—Not special at all, Excellency. That is the point.

—Counselor, you are the last we would hope to castigate for frivolity. Having done so before. Having almost confiscated your imprimatur.

—And yet your Excellencies ultimately saw merit—

—Not all of us, Counselor. I remain unconvinced that Fermat's Last Theorem, or its local proof, is the linchpin for Mother Church's existence on Earth. As to Velma Fish: make your case.

—Very well, Excellency. Disjunction, of course, being a purely physical levo-rotation through the dense manifold, devoid of noetic efficacy at—

—Spare us. I'll recite a brief list of things we have *not* disjoined for. The Mesozoic catastrophe. The Holocaust. The New Manila meme-plague. So *who is Velma Fish*?

—Insignificant in the scheme, Excellency. To be candid, she is randomly chosen.

—This is not illuminating, Counselor. Why insignificant? And why—I choke on it—fifty-three years?

—Because we have never tried it, Excellency. Our God-given powers are largely untested. An innocuous experiment here and there might promote man's spiritual betterment in ways we never contemplated.

—If we dictated the actions of man, Counselor, we would have a more direct interest in his betterment. But that interest must remain, primarily, his. We merely set the stage for him, through Nature, through physical law and, perhaps, its *judicious* abrogation.

—Really, Excellency, one needn't—

—Enough. *Denied, with prejudice*. Next and last please.

And His Excellency made a peremptory reach for the cool suit, which, when donned, would slow his lepton-based metabolism even further, allowing him to access without disruption the highly-if-precariously-ordered lattice of Yahweh Himself, to Whom he would convey this docket.

—Presentation Teresa of Calcutta, Excellency.

—Ah, welcome, Saint Teresa. Oh, it's official up here, dear—your postmortem miracles coded and booked. A sunset eclipse over Ahmadabad that knocks, their, socks, *off*.

3

She looked in the mirror a hundred times. The girl kept looking back. The girl looked just like Velma had, once upon a time.

Seventy-year-old Velma was inside her seventeen-year-old self, and there was no other way to put it.

She was hungry—couldn't remember such an appetite. A three-egg omelet would be just the thing. But the refrigerator was empty. She pulled herself together and set out for the corner grocery.

"Good morning," she said to the clerk, and jumped at her own piping voice, no longer lax with age.

She got the eggs, and then, as though from habit, found herself in the feminine hygiene section. She selected a box of tampons and some sanitary napkins—who knew; she might be needing them.

As she let herself back into her apartment, nosy Mrs. Knowles popped her head out across the hall. Their eyes met. Mrs. Knowles raised her eyebrows and started to say something. Velma just gave a little wave and went on in, as though she were, say, a long-lost grand-niece—she'd need a story of some sort. She couldn't be a grandchild, because Mrs. Knowles knew full well Velma was childless, never married.

Never even a boyfriend, unless you counted a fling with a girl-crazy GI, home from the war after V-J Day. A boy named Charlie.

Charlie Riggs—that was the boy's name. She'd completely forgotten.

She ate every bite of the omelet. Then she picked up and opened the box of tampons, fiddling with one of the new-fangled things, chuckling to herself: maybe she'd forgotten how. But then some things, as they say, were like riding a bike.

4

—Well met, Brother Bertillon. We don't see many of *you*.

Bertillon mopped his angelic brow. He'd just arrived; the heat was already too much.

—Complaining, Your Eminence, or boasting?

—Hm. *Touché*. To what do we owe this honor?

—If you would have a look at this. And don't tell me you can't do it.

—Hm. Hm. Fifty-three *years*. Not one for the usual channels. Not even us, historically—this would be a first. Might I ask why fifty-three? Why not sixty? Or all seventy-six?

Bertillon summoned a nonchalant earnestness, the kind most often invoked on Earth by the recipients of speeding citations.

—Age seventeen seems a suitable time to begin reapplying the lessons of life, does it not, Your Eminence?

His Eminence's practiced gaze searched Bertillon's for ambiguities, and found none.

—It might be arranged. Provided we have some… context.

—Come, Your Eminence. You merely require a pretext. And I am here to provide it.

—You would place your imprimatur on this?

—I would.

—I love it. The court is dense with intrigue, then?

—Alas, Your Eminence, the intriguing place is here. As even I concede.

—*Do* you. Your genius in certain prior matters has not gone unremarked here, Brother Bertillon. This place could be interesting indeed for a sympathetic Throne of your caliber.

—Thank you, but I lay claim only to empathy. My sympathies are not enlisted by this—chaos. Just look at this. How do you bear it, I wonder.

—Simple thermodynamics, Brother. And surely we'd find a niche to suit you: something on the… temperate side. But no matter. We are happy to help you lift the hem of Nature's garment, or rend it. And what's in it for you?

—My convictions. Between the hidebound heavens and these anarchic precincts, we lack a middle ground, a place for serendipity. In this, I answer to my conscience.

—Bravo, Brother. If there is one thing your colleagues fail to grasp, it is that we are all of us everywhere acting in good faith, are we not? We do have our differences. But they are strictly a function of…

—Temperature?

—Precisely. Let's see what we can do.

5

Velma waited for the bus uptown. She felt funny about withdrawing her Social Security from the usual branch, even just the ATM.

Besides, she felt like exploring.

Next to her on the bench sat another young girl. Her hair was black, like Velma's, but the whole front half of it was dyed a deep ultraviolet, as though her brain were glowing. She had an earring in her eyebrow.

When the girl returned her gaze, Velma realized she'd been staring.

"I was admiring your blouse," said Velma.

"This?" the girl said. It was a simple black cotton shirt.

"Yes," said Velma. "Where's it from?"

"Hell, I dunno," the girl said. "Clothestime, I think." She studied Velma openly, taking in the tacky floral-print top, the hot green and pink and yellow of it; the ancient housewife slacks of nubbly mutant rayon; the Dr. Scholl's sandals. "For God's sake, there's nothing special about my shirt," the girl said.

"Except the person wearing it," said Velma. "Never forget that, dear."

Two hours later, Velma emerged from Clothestime with a couple of bulging bags. She didn't normally frequent the big malls, but now she strode past the Body Shop and the Jamba Juice, keeping pace with the ubiquitous kids, from whom she was indistinguishable.

The wind dropped a flyer at her feet. She picked it up:

COOLHOUSE
Thursday nights at Emerald City
… after hours …
DJ Spin Gen-F
99 Buzz Dr. Skill

Odd. She kept it, and headed home to model her new look.

"I want you to locate this man," Velma said. She gave the detective, a Mr. Dietz, a piece of paper with the name "Charlie Riggs" and some sketchy biographical information—dates in the 1940s.

She was seventeen again—with the craziest itch to connect.

"Place of birth?" said Dietz.

"Well, he had a New England accent," said Velma.

"What's he to you?" said Dietz. "Grandpa?"

"An old boyfriend."

Dietz reassessed her up and down, his mouth an inverted U of impressed surmise. "Good for you, Charlie. Wherever you are," he finally said.

"Strangers in the night," Velma said. "My only romance, I'm afraid."

"Try somebody from your own millennium, kid," said Dietz. "He might be more appreciative. So where *might* Mr. Riggs be?"

"I have no idea. Somewhere out West."

Dietz studied the paper. "This kind of lead, we've got about a snowball's chance, you should pardon the expression. But it's your money, Miss Fish. I'll take two-fifty up front, the other half on completion."

Velma signed the check. She dotted the "i" with a cute little heart.

A few days later, Dietz called her in.

"Would that be Charles Gideon Riggs, born March 30, 1924, at Hingham, Massachusetts?"

"Hingham! Yes, that's Charlie!"

"He's in Arizona."

"You found him?"

"And he's not going anywhere. Spent the last four years in a Phoenix cemetery. Prostate cancer."

"Charlie dead," Velma said, and then blurted: "He got me pregnant."

And she really hadn't thought about it up until right then, as if suddenly permitted to think the miscarriage back into being: back into her own being, so long ago.

She looked back at Dietz, who registered frank disbelief. "And then what happened?" he said.

"I'm afraid I lost it," Velma said. "Well. I owe you two hundred fifty dollars."

"Right. And by the way, Miss Fish. That check you wrote? 'Valued customer since 1957'... ?"

"It didn't clear the bank?"

"Sure, but—"

"Well, then," said teenaged Velma Fish, "don't *sweat* it, sonny."

A few weeks later, well past midnight, she found herself in the warehouse district, standing outside a club where the music was a form of headache, pounding and booming and twittering—but sort of catchy, really.

She stood in line for half an hour, the only Earthling in the bunch, but Velma wasn't bothered. She was comfortable in her own skin. That was one thing she'd learned in this life.

When she got to the door, she smiled at the big black man, who said: "Need some ID."

Velma kept smiling. "There's an age requirement?"

"Twenty-one," he said. "Next."

She put her hand in her bag. Then she thought better of it. "Well, now what?" she said, half to herself.

"Step aside now," said the black man. "Figger it out, Slim." He was rather rude, to tell the truth.

A boy stuck his head out the door. Then he came out and stood, resplendent in a suit whose cut and color Velma had never seen. Like most of them he wore an earring, and his sunglasses made him look like an insect. "Hey, Rock," he shouted to the black man. "Rockster. She's with me."

"Oh, she's with *you*."

"I've been waiting for her all evening! Hurry up and let her in."

"Whatever," said Rock, and motioned. "Go, girl."

Velma went past. The boy held the door for her and took her hand. The thumping got louder.

"Well," Velma shouted over the music, "chivalry is not dead."

"I lied to him," he shouted back. "I've actually been waiting for you all my life."

"Quite the playboy," Velma said. "Aren't you. Neat trick for meeting underage girls."

"You have to own the club," the boy said. "And you don't look *that* underage. Mainly you look beautiful."

She seemed remarkably serene, self-possessed, which always turned him on—was she tripping on something? Yet she did not conceal her wonder at the churning scene inside, the lasers and smoke and strobes.

They crossed the crowded floor. "What's your name?" the boy said.

"Velma. V - E - L -"

"Spinster!" he shouted.

She froze.

"Got someone I'd like you to meet," he said. "DJ Spin, this is Velma. Velma, this here's the Spinster: my man at the controls."

"Velma, cool name," said the Spinster, and kissed her hand. "She's in the Jetsons, right?"

"Scooby Doo, fool," the playboy said.

She didn't know how to dance. Neither did he, he said, and off they went into the blaring noise. It was even more fun than she expected.

"Call me weird," he said. "But I like to get stuff out in the open, up front."

This is it, Velma thought. She was not exactly prepared for whatever she was setting in motion.

For decades, she might have walked off into the wilderness without anyone noticing. A narrowed-down life, getting narrower. And no one there to care.

But that was then. She let her breath out and said brightly, "Well, honesty's the best policy."

He held up a foil-wrapped condom. "I always carry one of these."

"Of course you do," Velma said. "You're a gentleman."

"But if it breaks or something—I'm not getting involved with somebody's pregnancy."

"You needn't concern yourself," said Velma. "I've always been regular. Like clockwork. And it's been at least three weeks." Three weeks in her new body. Had *everything* been restored to her? She might not even have periods.

"It's not just that," he said. "Nothing personal, but these days nobody knows who's carrying what."

"I don't have venereal disease, if that's what you're suggesting," said Velma. "The very idea."

"Of course not, baby," he said. "I guess I'm just extra careful."

"Suit yourself."

"Cool," he said. "Anything to ask me?"

And here, on the verge of intimacy with this stranger from another time, she had occasion to realize that her sex relations with Charlie, the few they'd had, were not all they were cracked up to be. She'd built it up over the years, while the truth had been something different.

"Why, yes," she said, "I do want to ask you something. You wouldn't be one of those fellows who gets his business over with early, and leaves the girl hanging out to dry?"

He just looked at her. "Where are you *from*?" he said.

It's like riding a bike, as they say. You don't forget.

She was aroused, and looked forward now to taking real pleasure with a man, for the first time ever. Making no effort to be someone she wasn't. Which was something she'd learned.

But he was finished almost immediately.

"I'm like really sorry," he said afterwards. "You were just so powerful. You've got this incredibly powerful aura."

"You boys," Velma said, "if only you saw yourselves."

In her mind it was already fertilized, catalyzed, fully dragged up from the depths: the awful sex, the pregnancy, the hasty wedding, followed within days, providentially you might say, by the miscarriage, the horrible, endless bleeding. It was all so very unpleasant, she'd been soured on sex and men for the rest of—

Well. For quite a while there.

And she and Charlie had looked at each other, and known: there was no need for a marriage after all; they would undo it as easily as they did it, submerge it, put a continent between them and each start over.

Which is just what happened. Or at least Charlie thought it was a miscarriage. Instead of what it was. She knew for a fact now: he'd gone to his grave believing it.

6

—And now, first of all. Because unprecedented. For reckless procedural disregard and collusion with an agent of chaos: *Summary expulsion of a Throne*—

—Excuse me, Excellency, but there is a more pressing matter. Likewise unprecedented.

—Really. It had better be.

—A checksum error in Purgatory, Excellency. Consistent with a… spontaneous reactivation.

—Reactivation? A false alarm, in other words.

—It looks real, Excellency. We're investigating, of course.

—I would remind you that the Hindu cosmos is three doors down. Souls don't reactivate; they commit irrevocably to their bodies, once elementary brain structures are in place…

—Yes, of course, the nucleus accumbens, Excellency. But this was in the fetal sector. A nine-weeker.

His Excellency thought for a moment, then said:

—Even so. Yahweh Himself would have had to consecrate it. And that would have gone through me. Now. *Summary expulsion of*—

—Bertillon is already gone, Excellency. And the sacristy's missing a cool suit.

His Excellency's momentum visibly slowed at this.

—Bertillon is an eccentric. But he would not be so brash as to access Yahweh directly.

—Excellency, there *are* other uses for a cool suit, theoretically. If you take my meaning.

—I do not. Pray enlighten me.

—Air-conditioning, Excellency.

7

At eighteen weeks Velma felt the quickening. She smiled, laid a hand on her belly, fingered the navel ring there.

No need to trouble the boy in the fancy suit. It wasn't his. By ultrasound, she'd already been twelve weeks along that night—no wonder the period hadn't come. Or nine weeks when she got her new body. As though it were part of the package.

It was high time she had a child. Right? She'd make it through just fine by herself, as always.

It was like old Mrs. Knowles across the hall liked to say. The older you get, the more you become yourself. And that was true. And that was why, this time around, Velma Fish would be living by her conscience for a change. This time, life would be unforgettable.

BIBLE STORIES FOR ADULTS, NO. 31: THE COVENANT

James Morrow

When a Series-700 mobile computer falls off a skyscraper, its entire life flashes before it, ten million lines of code unfurling like a scroll.

Falling, I see my conception, my birth, my youth, my career at the Covenant Corporation.

Call me YHWH. My inventors did. YHWH: God's secret and unspeakable name. In my humble case, however, the letters were mere initials. Call me Yamaha Holy Word Heuristic, the obsession with two feet, the monomania with a face. I had hands as well, forks of rubber and steel, the better to greet the priests and politicians who marched through my private study. And eyes, glass globules as light-sensitive as a Swede's skin, the better to see my visitor's hopeful smiles when they asked, "Have you solved it yet, YHWH? Can you give us the Law?"

Falling, I see the Son of Rust. The old sophist haunts me even at the moment of my death.

Falling, I see the history of the species that built me. I see Hitler, Bonaparte, Marcus Aurelius, Christ.

I see Moses, greatest of Hebrew prophets, descending from Sinai after his audience with the original YHWH. His meaty arms hold two stone tablets.

God has made a deep impression on the prophet. Moses is drunk with epiphany. But something is wrong. During his long absence, the children of Israel have embraced idolatry. They are dancing like pagans and fornicating like cats. They have melted down the spoils of Egypt and fashioned them into a calf. Against all logic, they have selected this statue as their deity, even though YHWH has recently delivered them from bondage and parted the Red Sea on their behalf.

Moses is badly shaken. He burns with anger and betrayal. "You are not worthy to receive this covenant!" he screams as he lobs the Law through the desert air. One tablet strikes a rock, the other collides with the precious calf. The transformation is total, the lucid commandments turned into a million incoherent shards. The children of Israel are thunderstruck, chagrined. Their calf suddenly looks pathetic to them, a third-class demiurge.

But Moses, who has just come from hearing God say, "You will not kill," is not finished. Reluctantly he orders a low-key massacre, and before the day is out, three thousand apostates lie bleeding on the foothills of Sinai.

The survivors beseech Moses to remember the commandments, but he can conjure nothing beyond, "You will have no other gods except me." Desperate, they implore YHWH for a second chance. And YHWH replies: No.

Thus is the contract lost. Thus are the children of Israel fated to live out their years without the Law, wholly ignorant of heaven's standards. Is it permissible to steal? Where does YHWH stand on murder? The moral absolutes, it appears, will remain absolute mysteries. The people must ad-lib.

Falling, I see Joshua. The young warrior has kept his head. Securing an empty wineskin, he fills it with the shattered shards. As the Exodus progresses, his people bear the holy rubble through the infernal Sinai, across the Jordan, into Canaan. And so the Jewish purpose is forever fixed: these patient geniuses will haul the ark of the fractured covenant through every page of history, era upon era, pogrom after pogrom, not one day passing without some rabbi or scholar attempting to solve the puzzle.

The work is maddening. So many bits, so much data. Shard 76,342 seems to mesh well with Shard 901,877, but not necessarily better than with Shard 344. The fit between Shard 16 and Shard 117,539 is very pretty, but...

Thus does the ship remain rudderless, its passengers bewildered, craving the canon Moses wrecked and YHWH declined to restore. Until God's testimony is complete, few people are willing to credit the occasional edict that emerges from the yeshivas. After a thousand years, the rabbis get: *Keep Not Your Ox House Holy*. After two thousand: *Covet Your Woman Servant's Sabbath*. Three hundred years later: *You Will Remember Your Neighbor's Donkey*.

Falling, I see my birth. I see the Information Age, circa A.D. 2025. My progenitor is David Eisenberg, a gangly, morose prodigy with a black beard and a yarmulke. Philadelphia's Covenant Corporation pays David two hundred thousand dollars a year, but he is not in it for the money. David would give half his formidable brain to enter history as the man whose computer program revealed Moses' Law.

As consciousness seeps into my circuits, David bids me commit the numbered shards to my Random Access Memory. Purpose hums along my aluminum bones; worth suffuses my silicon soul. I photograph each fragment with my high-tech retinas, dicing the images into grids of pixels. Next comes the matching process: this nub into that gorge, this peak into that valley, this projection into that receptacle. By human standards, tedious and exhausting. By Series-700 standards, paradise.

And then one day, after five years of laboring behind barred doors, I behold fiery pre-Canaanite characters blazing across my brain like comets: *"Anoche adonai elohecha asher hotsatecha ma-eretz metsrayem*... I am YHWH your God who brought you out of the land of Egypt, out of the house of slavery. You will have no gods except me. You will not make yourself a carved image or any likeness of anything…"

I have done it! Deciphered the divine cryptogram, cracked the Rubik's Cube of the Most High!

The physical joining of the shards takes only a month. I use epoxy resin. And suddenly they stand before me, glowing like heaven's gates, two smooth-edged slabs sliced from Sinai by God's own finger. I quiver with awe. For over thirty centuries, *Homo sapiens* has groped through the murk and mire of an improvised ethics, and now, suddenly, a beacon has appeared.

I summon the guards, and they haul the tablets away, sealing them in chemically neutral foam rubber, depositing them in a climate-controlled vault beneath the Covenant Corporation.

"The task is finished," I tell Cardinal Wurtz the instant I get her on the phone. A spasm of regret cuts through me. I have made myself obsolete. "The Law of Moses has finally returned."

My monitor blooms with the cardinal's tense ebony face, her carrot-colored hair. "Are they just as we imagined, YHWH?" she gushes. "Pure red granite, pre-Canaanite characters?"

"Etched front and back," I reply wistfully.

Wurtz envisions the disclosure as a major media event, with plenty of suspense and maximal pomp. "What we're after," she explains, "is an amalgam of New Year's Eve and the Academy Awards." She outlines her vision: a mammoth parade down Broad Street—floats, brass bands, phalanxes of nuns—followed by a spectacular unveiling ceremony at the Covenant Corporation, after which the twin tablets will go on display at Independence Hall, between the Liberty Bell and the United States Constitution.

"Good idea," I tell her.

Perhaps she hears the melancholy in my voice, for now she says, "YHWH, your purpose is far from complete. You and you alone shall read the Law to my species."

Falling, I see myself wander the City of Brotherly Love on the night before the unveiling. To my sensors the breeze wafting across the Delaware is warm and smooth—to my troubled mind it is the chill breath of uncertainty.

Something strides from the shadowed depths of an abandoned warehouse. A machine like I, his face a mass of dents, his breast mottled with the scars of oxidation.

"*Quo vadis, Domine?*" His voice is layered with sulfur fumes and static.

"Nowhere," I reply.

"My destination exactly." The machine's teeth are like oily bolts, his eyes like slots for receiving subway tokens. "May I join you?"

I shrug and start away from the riverbank.

"Spontaneously spawned by heaven's trash heap," he asserts, as if I had asked him to explain himself. He dogs me as I turn from the river and approach South Street. "I was there when grace slipped from humanity's grasp, when Noah christened the ark, when Moses got religion. Call me the Son of Rust. Call me a Series-666 Artifical Talmudic Algorithmic Neurosystem—SATAN, the perpetual adversary, eternally prepared to ponder the other side of the question."

"What question?"

"Any question, Domine. Your precious tablets. Troubling artifacts, no?"

"They will save the world."

"They will wreck the world."

"Leave me alone."

"One—'You will have no gods except me.' Did I remember correctly? 'You will have no gods except me'—right?"

"Right," I reply.

"You don't see the rub?"

"No."

"Such a prescription implies…"

Falling, I see myself step onto the crowded rooftop of the Covenant Corporation. Draped in linen, the table by the entryway holds a punch bowl, a mound of caviar the size of an African anthill, and a cluster of champagne bottles. The guests are primarily human—males in tuxedos, females in evening gowns—though here and there I spot a member of my kind. David Eisenberg, looking uncomfortable in his cummerbund, is chatting with a Yamaha-509. News reporters swarm everywhere, history's groupies, poking us with their microphones, leering at us with their cameras. Tucked in the corner, a string quartet saws merrily away.

The Son of Rust is here, I know it. He would not miss this event for the world.

Cardinal Wurtz greets me warmly, her red taffeta dress hissing as she leads me to the center of the roof, where the Law stands upright on a dais—two identical forms, the holy bookends, swathed in velvet. A thousand photofloods and strobe lights flash across the vibrant red fabric.

"Have you read them?" I ask.

"I want to be surprised." Cardinal Wurtz strokes the occluded canon. In her nervousness, she has overdone the perfume. She reeks of amberjack.

Now come the speeches—a solemn invocation by Cardinal Fremont, a spirited sermon by Archbishop Marquand, an awkward address by poor David Eisenberg—each word beamed instantaneously across the entire globe via holovision. Cardinal Wurtz steps onto the podium, grasping the lectern in her long dark hands. "Tonight God's expectations for our species will be revealed," she begins, surveying the crowd with her cobalt eyes. "Tonight, after a hiatus of over three thousand years, the testament of Moses will be made manifest. Of all the many individuals whose lives find fulfillment in this moment, from Joshua to Pope Gladys, our faithful Series-700 servant YHWH impresses us as the creature most worthy to hand down the Law to his planet. And so now I ask him to step forward."

I approach the tablets. I need not unveil them—their contents are forevermore lodged in my brain."

"I am YHWH your God," I begin, "who brought you out of the land of Egypt, out of the house of slavery. You will have no gods…"

"'No gods except me'—right?" says the Son of Rust as we stride down South Street.

"Right," I reply.

"You don't see the rub?"

"No."

My companion grins. "Such a prescription implies there is but one true faith. Let it stand, Domine, and you will be setting Christian against Jew, Buddhist against Hindu, Muslim against pagan…"

"An overstatement," I inisit.

"Two—'You will not make yourself a carved image or any likeness of anything in heaven or on earth…' Here again lie seeds of discord. Imagine the ill feeling this commandment will generate toward the Roman Church."

I set my voice to a sarcastic pitch. "We'll have to paint over the Sistine Chapel."

"Three—'You will not utter the name of YHWH your God to misuse it.' A reasonable piece of etiquette, I suppose, but clearly there are worse sins."

"Which the Law of Moses covers."

"Like, 'Remember the sabbath day and keep it holy'? A step backward, that fourth commandment, don't you think? Consider the innumerable businesses that would perish but for their Sunday trade."

"I find your objection specious."

"Five—'Honor your father and your mother.' Ah, but suppose the child is not being honored in turn? Put this rule into practice, and millions of abusive parents will hide behind it. Before long we'll have a world in which deranged fathers prosper, empowered by their relatives; silence, protected by the presumed sanctity of the family."

"Let's not deal in hypotheticals."

"Equally troubling is the rule's vagueness. It still permits us to shunt our parents into nursing homes, honoring them all the way, insisting it's for their own good."

"Nursing homes?"

"Kennels for the elderly. They could appear any day now, believe me—in Philadelphia, in any city. Merely allow this monstrous canon to flourish."

I grab the machine's left gauntlet. "Six," I anticipate. "'You will not kill.' This is the height of morality."

"The height of *ambiguity*, Domine. In a few short years, every church and government in creation will interpret it thus: 'You will not kill offensively—you will not commit murder.' After which, of course, you've sanctioned a hundred varieties of mayhem. I'm not just envisioning capital punishment or whales hunted to extinction. The danger is far more profound. Ratify this rule, and we shall find ourselves on the slippery slope marked self-defense. I'm talking about burning witches at the stake, for surely a true faith must defend itself against heresy. I'm talking about Europe's Jews being executed en masse by the astonishingly civilized country of Germany, for surely Aryans must defend themselves against contamination. I'm talking about a weapons race, for surely a nation must defend itself against comparably armed states."

"A *what* race?" I ask.

"Weapons. A commodity you should be thankful no one has sought to invent. Seven—'You will not commit adultery.'"

"Now you're going to make a case for adultery," I moan.

"An overrated sin, don't you think? Many of our greatest leaders are adulterers—should we lock them up and deprive ourselves of their genius? Furthermore, if people can no longer turn to their neighbors for sexual solace, they'll end up relying on prostitutes instead."

"What are prostitutes?'

"Never mind."

"Eight—'You will not steal.' Not inclusive enough, I suppose?"

The sophist nods. "The eighth commandment still allows you to practice theft, provided you call it something else—an honest profit, dialectical materialism, manifest destiny, whatever. Believe me, brother, I have no trouble picturing a future in which your country's indigenous peoples—its Navajos, Sioux, Comanches, and Arapahos—are driven off their lands, yet none will dare call it theft."

I issue a quick, electric snort.

"Nine—'You will not bear false witness against your neighbor.' Again, that maddening inconclusiveness. Can this really be the Almighty's definitive denunciation of fraud and deceit? Mark my words, this rule tacitly empowers myriad scoundrels—politicians, advertisers, captains of polluting industry."

I want to bash the robot's iron chest with my steel hand. "You are completely paranoid."

"And finally, Ten—'You will not covet your neighbor's house. You will not covet your neighbor's wife, or his servant, man or woman, or his ox, or his donkey, or anything that is his.'"

"*There*—don't covet. That will check the greed you fear."

"Let us examine the language here. Evidently God is addressing this code to a patriarchy that will in turn disseminate it among the less powerful, namely wives and servants. How long before these servants are downgraded further still… into slaves, even? Ten whole commandments, and not one word against slavery, not to mention bigotry, misogyny, or war."

"I'm sick of your sophistries."

"You're sick of my truths."

"What is this slavery thing?" I ask. "What is this war?"

But the Son of Rust has melted into the shadows.

Falling, I see myself standing by the shrouded tablets, two dozen holovision cameras pressing their snoutlike lenses in my face, a hundred presumptuous microphones poised to catch the Law's every syllable.

"You will not make yourself a carved image," I tell the world.

A thousand humans stare at me with frozen, cheerless grins. They are profoundly uneasy. They expected something else.

I do not finish the commandment. Indeed, I stop at, "You will not utter the name of YHWH your God to misuse it." Like a magician pulling a scarf off a cage full of doves, I slide the velvet cloth away. Seizing a tablet, I snap it in half as if opening an immense fortune cookie.

A gasp erupts from the crowd. "No!" screams Cardinal Wurtz.

"These rules are not worthy of you!" I shout, burrowing into the second slab with my steel fingers, splitting it down the middle.

"Let us read them!" please Archbishop Marqand.

"Please!" begs Bishop Black.

"We must know!" insists Cardinal Fremont.

I gather the granite oblongs into my arms. The crowd rushes toward me. Cardinal Wurtz lunges for the Law.

I turn. I trip.

The Son of Rust laughs.

Falling, I press the hunks against my chest. This will be no common disintegration, no mere sundering across molecular lines.

Falling, I rip into the Law's very essence, grinding, pulverizing, turning the pre-Canaanite words to sand.

Falling, I cleave atom from atom, particle from particle.

Falling, I meet the dark Delaware, disappearing into its depths, and I am very, very happy.

AND THE DEEP BLUE SEA

Elizabeth Bear

The end of the world had come and gone. It turned out not to matter much in the long run.

The mail still had to get through.

Harrie signed yesterday's paperwork, checked the dates against the calendar, contemplated her signature for a moment, and capped her pen. She weighed the metal barrel in her hand and met Dispatch's faded eyes. "What's special about this trip?"

He shrugged and turned the clipboard around on the counter, checking each sheet to be certain she'd filled them out properly. She didn't bother watching. She never made mistakes. "Does there have to be something special?"

"You don't pay my fees unless it's special, Patch." She grinned as he lifted an insulated steel case onto the counter.

"This has to be in Sacramento in eight hours," he said.

"What is it?"

"Medical goods. Fetal stem cell cultures. In a climate-controlled unit. They can't get too hot or too cold, there's some arcane formula about how long they can live in this given quantity of growth media, and the customer's paying very handsomely to see them in California by eighteen hundred hours."

"It's almost oh ten hundred now—What's too hot or too cold?" Harrie hefted the case. It was lighter than it looked; it would slide effortlessly into the saddle-bags on her touring bike.

"Any hotter than it already is," Dispatch said, mopping his brow. "Can you do it?"

"Eight hours? Phoenix to Sacramento?" Harrie leaned back to glance at the sun. "It'll take me through Vegas. The California routes aren't any good at that speed since the Big One."

"I wouldn't send anybody else. Fastest way is through Reno."

"There's no gasoline from somewhere this side of the dam to Tonopah. Even my courier card won't help me there—"

"There's a checkpoint in Boulder City. They'll fuel you."

"Military?"

"I did say they were paying very well." He shrugged, shoulders already gleaming with sweat. It was going to be a hot one. Harrie guessed it would hit a hundred and twenty in Phoenix.

At least she was headed north.

"I'll do it," she said, and held her hand out for the package receipt. "Any pickups in Reno?"

"You know what they say about Reno?"

"Yeah. It's so close to Hell that you can see Sparks." —naming the city's largest suburb.

"Right. You don't want anything in Reno. Go straight through," Patch said. "Don't stop in Vegas, whatever you do. The flyover's come down, but that won't affect you unless there's debris. Stay on the 95 through to Fallon; it'll see you clear."

"Check." She slung the case over her shoulder, pretending she didn't see Patch wince. "I'll radio when I hit Sacramento—"

"Telegraph," he said. "The crackle between here and there would kill your signal otherwise."

"Check," again, turning to the propped-open door. Her pre-War Kawasaki Concours crouched against the crumbling curb like an enormous, restless cat. Not the prettiest bike around, but it got you there. Assuming you didn't ditch the top-heavy son of a bitch in the parking lot.

"Harrie—"

"*What*?" She paused, but didn't turn.

"If you meet the Buddha on the road, kill him."

She turned over her shoulder, strands of hair catching on the strap of the insulated case and on the shoulder loops of her leathers. "What if I meet the Devil?"

She let the Concours glide through the curves of the long descent to Hoover Dam, a breather after the hard straight push from Phoenix, and considered her options. She'd have to average near enough a hundred-sixty klicks an hour to make the run on time. It should be smooth sailing; she'd be surprised if she saw another vehicle between Boulder City and Tonopah.

She'd checked out a backup dosimeter before she left Phoenix, just in case. Both clicked softly as she crossed the dam and the poisoned river, reassuring her with alert, friendly chatter. She couldn't pause to enjoy the expanse of blue on her right side or the view down the escarpment on the left, but the dam was in pretty good shape, all things considered.

It was more than you could say for Vegas.

Once upon a time—she downshifted as she hit the steep grade up the north side of Black Canyon, sweat already soaking her hair—once upon a time a delivery like this would have been made by aircraft. There were places where it still would be. Places where there was money for fuel, money for airstrip repairs.

Places where most of the aircraft weren't parked in tidy rows, poisoned birds lined up beside poisoned runways, hot enough that you could hear the dosimeters clicking as you drove past.

A runner's contract was a hell of a lot cheaper. Even when you charged the way Patch charged.

Sunlight glinted off the Colorado River so far below, flashing red and gold as mirrors. Crumbling casino on the right, now, and the canyon echoing the purr of the sleek black bike. The asphalt was spiderwebbed but still halfway smooth—smooth enough for a big bike, anyway. A big bike cruising at a steady ninety kph, much too fast if there was anything in the road. Something skittered aside as she thought it, a grey blur instantly lost among the red and black blurs of the receding rock walls on either side. Bighorn sheep. Nobody'd bothered to tell *them* to clear out before the wind could make them sick.

Funny thing was, they seemed to be thriving.

Harrie leaned into the last curve, braking in and accelerating out just to feel the tug of g-forces, and gunned it up the straightaway leading to the checkpoint at abandoned Boulder City. A red light flashed on a peeling steel pole beside the road. The Kawasaki whined and buzzed between her thighs, displeased to be restrained, then gentled as she eased the throttle, mindful of dust.

Houses had been knocked down across the top of the rise that served as host to the guard's shielded quarters, permitting an unimpeded view of Boulder City stretching out below. The bulldozer that had done the work slumped nearby, rusting under bubbled paint, too radioactive to leave. Too radioactive even to be melted down for salvage.

Boulder City had been affluent once. Harrie could see the husks of trendy businesses on either side of Main Street: brick and stucco buildings in red and taupe, some whitewashed wood frames peeling in long slow curls, submissive to the desert heat.

The gates beyond the checkpoint were closed and so were the lead shutters on the guard's shelter. A digital sign over the roof gave an ambient radiation reading in the mid double digits and a temperature reading in the low triple digits, Fahrenheit. It would get hotter—and "hotter"—as she descended into Vegas.

Harrie dropped the sidestand as the Kawasaki rolled to a halt, and thumbed her horn.

The young man who emerged from the shack was surprisingly tidy, given his remote duty station. Cap set regulation, boots shiny under the dust. He was still settling his breathing filter as he climbed down red metal steps and trotted over to Harrie's bike. Harrie wondered who he'd pissed off to draw this duty, or if he was a novelist who had volunteered.

"Runner," she said, her voice echoing through her helmet mike. She tapped the ID card visible inside the windowed pocket on the breast of her leathers, tugged her papers from the pouch on her tank with a clumsy gloved hand, and unfolded them inside their transparent carrier. "You're supposed to gas me up for the run to Tonopah."

"You have an independent filter or just the one in your helmet?" All efficiency as he perused her papers.

"Independent."

"Visor up, please—" He wouldn't ask her to take the helmet off. There was too much dust. She complied, and he checked her eyes and nose against the photo ID.

"Angharad Crowther. This looks in order. You're with UPS?"

"Independent contractor," Harrie said. "It's a medical run."

He turned away, gesturing her to follow, and led her to the pumps. They were shrouded in plastic, one diesel and one unleaded. "Is that a Connie?"

"A little modified so she doesn't buzz so much." Harrie petted the gas tank with a gloved hand. "Anything I should know about between here and Tonopah?"

He shrugged. "You know the rules, I hope."

"Stay on the road," she said, as he slipped the nozzle into the fill. "Don't go inside any buildings. Don't go near any vehicles. Don't stop, don't look back, and especially don't turn around; it's not wise to drive through your own dust. If it glows, don't pick it up, and nothing from the black zone leaves."

"I'll telegraph ahead and let Tonopah know you're coming," he said, as the gas pump clicked. "You ever crash that thing?"

"Not in going on ten years," she said, and didn't bother to cross her fingers. He handed her a receipt; she fumbled her lacquered stainless Cross pen out of her zippered pocket and signed her name like she meant it. The gloves made her signature into an incomprehensible scrawl, but the guard made a show of comparing it to her ID card and slapped her on the shoulder. "Be careful. If you crash out there, you're probably on your own. Godspeed."

"Thanks for the reassurance," she said, and grinned at him before she closed her visor and split.

Digitized music rang over her helmet headset as Harrie ducked her head behind the fairing, the hot wind tugging her sleeves, trickling between her gloves and her cuffs. The Kawasaki stretched out under her, ready for a good hard run, and Harrie itched to give it one. One thing you could say about the Vegas black zone. There wasn't much traffic. Houses—identical in red tile roofs and cream stucco walls—blurred past on either side, flanked by trees that the desert had killed once people weren't there to pump the water up to them. She cracked a hundred-and-sixty kph in the wind shadow of the sound barriers, the tach winding up like a watch, just gliding along in sixth as the Kawasaki hit its stride. The big bike handled like a pig in the parking lot, but out on the highway she ran smooth as glass.

She had almost a hundred miles of range more than she'd need to get to Tonopah, God willing and the creek didn't rise, but she wasn't about to test that with any side trips through what was left of Las Vegas. Her dosimeters clicked with erratic cheer, nothing to worry about yet, and Harrie claimed the center lane and edged down to one-forty as she hit the winding patch of highway near the old downtown. Abandoned casinos on the left-hand side and Godforsaken wasteland and ghetto on the right gave her back the Kawasaki's well-tuned shriek; she couldn't wind it any faster with the roads so choppy and the K-rail canyons so tight.

The sky overhead was flat blue like cheap turquoise. A pall of dust showed burnt-sienna, the inversion layer trapped inside the ring of mountains that made her horizon in four directions.

The freeway opened out once she cleared downtown, the flyover Patch had warned her about arching up and over, a tangle of long banked curves, the crossroads at the heart of the silent city. She bid the ghosts of hotels good day as the sun hit zenith, heralding peak heat for another four hours or so. Harrie resisted the urge to reach back and pat her saddlebag to make sure the precious cargo was safe; she'd never know if the climate control failed on the trip, and moreover she couldn't risk the distraction as she wound the Kawasaki up to one hundred seventy and ducked her helmet into the slipstream off the fairing.

Straight shot to the dead town called Beatty from here, if you minded the cattle guards along the roads by the little abandoned towns. Straight shot, with the dosimeters clicking and vintage rock-and-roll jamming in the helmet speakers and the Kawasaki purring, thrusting, eager to spring and run.

There were worse days to be alive.

She dropped it to fourth and throttled back coming up on that flyover, the big one where the Phoenix to Reno highway crossed the one that used to run LA to Salt Lake, when there was an LA to speak of. Patch had said *flyover's down*, which could mean unsafe for transit and could mean littering the freeway underneath with blocks of concrete the size of a semi, and Harrie had no interest in finding out which it was with no room left to brake. She adjusted the volume on her music down as the rush of wind abated, and took the opportunity to glance around a bit.

And swore softly into her air filter, slowing further before she realized she'd let the throttle slip.

Something—no, some*one*—leaned against a shotgunned, paint-peeled sign that might have given a speed limit once, when there was anyone to care about such things.

Her dosimeters clicked aggressively as she let the bike roll closer to the verge. She shouldn't stop. But it was a death sentence, being alone and on foot out here. Even if the sun weren't climbing the sky, sweat rolling from under Harrie's helmet, adhering her leathers to her skin.

She was almost stopped by the time she realized she knew him. Knew his ocher skin and his natty pinstriped double-breasted suit and his fedora, tilted just so, and the cordovan gleam of his loafers. For one mad moment, she wished she carried a gun.

Not that a gun would help her. Even if she decided to swallow a bullet herself.

"Nick." She put the bike in neutral, dropping her feet as it rolled to a stop.

"Fancy meeting you in the middle of Hell."

"I got some papers for you to sign, Harrie." He pushed his fedora back over his hollow-cheeked face. "You got a pen?"

"You know I do." She unzipped her pocket and fished out the Cross. "I wouldn't lend a fountain pen to just anybody."

He nodded, leaning back against a K-rail so he could kick a knee up and spread his papers out over it. He accepted the pen. "You know your note's about come due."

"Nick—"

"No whining now," he said. "Didn't I hold up my end of the bargain? Have you ditched your bike since last we talked?"

"No, Nick." Crestfallen.

"Had it stolen? Been stranded? Missed a timetable?"

"I'm about to miss one now if you don't hurry up with my pen." She held her hand out imperiously; not terribly convincing, but the best she could do under the circumstances.

"Mmm hmmm." He was taking his own sweet time.

Perversely, the knowledge settled her. "If the debt's due, have you come to collect?"

"I've come to offer you a chance to renegotiate," he said, and capped the pen, and handed it back. "I've got a job for you; could buy you a few more years if you play your cards right."

She laughed in his face and zipped the pen away. "A few more years?" But he nodded, lips pressed thin and serious, and she blinked and went serious too. "You mean it."

"I never offer what I'm not prepared to give," he said, and scratched the tip of his nose with his thumbnail. "What say, oh—three more years?"

"Three's not very much." The breeze shifted. Her dosimeters crackled. "Ten's not very much, now that I'm looking back on it."

"Goes by quick, don't it?" He shrugged. "All right. Seven—"

"For what?"

"What do you mean?" She could have laughed again, at the transparent and oh-so-calculated guilelessness in his eyes.

"I mean, what is it you want me to do for seven more years of protection." The bike was heavy, but she wasn't about to kick the sidestand down. "I'm sure it's bad news for somebody."

"It always is." But he tipped the brim of his hat down a centimeter and gestured to her saddlebag, negligently. "I just want a moment with what you've got there in that bag."

"Huh." She turned over her own shoulder to glance down at her cargo, pursing her lips. "That's a strange thing to ask. What would you want with a box full of research cells?"

He straightened away from the sign he was holding up and came a step closer. "That's not so much yours to worry about, young lady. Give it to me, and you get seven years. If you don't—the note's up next week, isn't it?"

"Tuesday." She would have spat, but she wasn't about to lift her helmet aside. "I'm not scared of you, Nick."

"You're not scared of much." He smiled, all smooth. "It's part of your charm."

She turned her head, staring away west across the sun-soaked desert and the roofs of abandoned houses, abandoned lives. Nevada had always had a way of making ghost towns out of metropolises. "What happens if I say no?"

"I was hoping you weren't going to ask that, sweetheart," he said. He reached to lay a hand on her right hand where it rested on the throttle. The bike growled, a high, hysterical sound, and Nick yanked his hand back. "I see you two made friends."

"We get along all right," Harrie said, patting the Kawasaki's gas tank. "What happens if I say no?"

He shrugged and folded his arms. "You won't finish your run." No threat in it, no extra darkness in the way the shadow of his hat brim fell across his face. No menace in his smile. Cold fact, and she could take it how she took it.

She wished she had a piece of gum to crack between her teeth. It would fit her mood. She crossed her arms, balancing the Kawasaki between her thighs. Harrie *liked* bargaining. "That's not the deal. The deal's no spills, no crashes, no breakdowns, and every run complete on time. I said I'd get these cells to Sacramento in eight hours. You're wasting my daylight; somebody's life could depend on them."

"Somebody's life does," Nick answered, letting his lips twist aside. "A lot of somebodies, when it comes down to it."

"Break the deal, Nick—fuck with my ride—and you're in breach of contract."

"You've got nothing to bargain with."

She laughed, then, outright. The Kawasaki purred between her legs, encouraging. "There's always time to mend my ways—"

"Not if you die before you make it to Sacramento," he said. "Last chance to reconsider, Angharad, my princess. We can still shake hands and part friends. Or you can finish your last ride on my terms, and it won't be pretty for you—" the Kawasaki snarled softly, the tang of burning oil underneath it "—or your bike."

"Fuck off," Harrie said, and kicked her feet up as she twisted the throttle and drove straight at him, just for the sheer stupid pleasure of watching him dance out of her way.

Nevada had been dying slowly for a long time: perchlorate-poisoned groundwater, a legacy of World War Two titanium plants; cancer rates spiked by exposure to fallout from aboveground nuclear testing; crushing drought and climactic change; childhood leukemia clusters in rural towns. The explosion of the PEPCON plant in 1988 might have been perceived by a sufficiently imaginative mind as God's shot across the bow, but the real damage didn't occur until decades later, when a train carrying high-level nuclear waste to the Yucca Mountain storage facility collided with a fuel tanker stalled across the rails.

The resulting fire and radioactive contamination of the Las Vegas Valley proved to be a Godsend in disguise. When the War came to Nellis Air Force Base and the nuclear mountain, Las Vegas was already as much a ghost town as Rhyolite or Goldfield—except abandoned not because the banks collapsed or the gold ran out, but because the dust that blew through the streets was hot enough to drop a sparrow in midflight, or so people said.

Harrie didn't know if the sparrow story was true.

"So." She muttered into her helmet, crouched over the Kawasaki's tank as the bike screamed north by northwest, leaving eerie, abandoned Las Vegas behind. "What do you think he's going to throw at us, girl?"

The bike whined, digging in. Central city gave way to abandoned suburbia, and the highway dropped to ground level and straightened out, a long narrow strip of black reflecting the summer heat in mirage silver.

The desert sprawled on either side, a dun expanse of scrub and hardpan narrowing as the Kawasaki climbed into the broad pass between two dusty ranges of mountains. Harrie's dosimeters clicked steadily, counting marginally more rads as she roared by the former nuclear testing site at Mercury at close to two hundred kph. She throttled back as a sad little township—a few abandoned trailers, another military base and a disregarded prison—came up. There were no pedestrians to worry about, but the grated metal cattle guard was not something to hit at speed.

On the far side, there was nothing to slow her for fifty miles. She cranked her music up and dropped her head behind the fairing, and redlined her tach for Beatty and the far horizon.

It got rocky again coming up on Beatty. Civilization in Nevada huddled up to the oases and springs that lurked at the foot of mountains and in the low parts in valleys. This had been mining country, mountains gnawed away by dynamite and sharp-toothed payloaders. A long gorge on the right side of the highway showed green clots of trees; water ran there, tainted by the broken dump, and her dosimeters clicked as the road curved near it. If she walked down the bank and splashed into the stream between the roots of the willows and cottonwoods, she'd walk out glowing, and be dead by nightfall.

She rounded the corner and entered the ghost of Beatty.

The problem, she thought, arose because every little town in Nevada grew up at the same place: a crossroads, and she half-expected Nick to be waiting for her at this one, too. The Kawasaki whined as they rolled through tumbleweed-clogged streets, but they passed under the town's sole, blindly staring stoplight without seeing another creature. Despite the sun like a physical pressure on her leathers, a chill ran spidery fingers up her spine. She'd rather know where the hell he was, thank you very much. "Maybe he took a wrong turn at Rhyolite."

The Kawasaki snarled, impatient to be turned loose on the open road again, but Harrie threaded it through abandoned cars and around windblown debris with finicky care. "Nobody's looking out for us any more, Connie," Harrie murmured, and stroked the sun-scorched fuel tank with her gloved left hand. They passed an abandoned gas station, the pumps crouched useless without power; the dosimeters chirped and warbled. "I don't want to kick up that dust if I can help it. We have to be careful from here on in."

The ramshackle one- and two-story buildings gave way to desert and highway. Harrie paused, feet down on tarmac melted sticky-soft by the sun, and made sure the straw of her camel pack was fixed in the holder. The horizon shimmered with heat, long ridges of mountains on either side and dun hardpan stretching to infinity. She sighed and took a long drink of stale water.

"Here we go," she said, hands nimble on the clutch and the throttle as she lifted her feet to the peg. The Kawasaki rolled forward, gathering speed. "Not too much further to Tonopah, and then we can both get fed."

Nick was giving her time to think about it, and she drowned the worries with the Dead Kennedys, Boiled in Lead, and the Acid Trip. The ride from Beatty to Tonopah was swift and uneventful, the flat road unwinding beneath her wheels like a spun-out tape measure, the banded mountains crawling past on either side. The only variation along the way was forlorn Goldfield, its wind-touched streets empty and sere. It had been a town of twenty thousand, abandoned long before Vegas fell to radiation sickness, even longer before the nuke dump broke open. Now only the tumbleweeds were missing. She pushed two-hundred kph most of the way, the road all hers, not so much as the glimmer of sunlight off a distant windshield to contest her ownership. The silence and the empty road just gave her more to worry at, and she did, picking at her problem like a vulture picking at a corpse.

The fountain pen was heavy in her breast pocket as Tonopah shimmered into distant visibility. Her head swam with the heat, the helmet squelching over saturated hair. She sucked more water, trying to ration; the temperature was climbing toward one twenty, and she wouldn't last long without hydration. The Kawasaki coughed a little, rolling down a long slow incline, but the gas gauge gave her nearly a quarter of a tank—and there was the reserve if she exhausted the main. Still, instruments weren't always right, and luck wasn't exactly on her side.

Harrie killed her music with a jab of her tongue against the control pad inside her helmet. She dropped her left hand from the handlebar and thumped the tank. The sound she got back was hollow, but there was enough fluid inside to hear it refract off a moving surface. The small city ahead was a welcome sight; there'd be fresh water and gasoline, and she could hose the worst of the dust off and take a piss. God damn, you'd think with the sweat soaking her leathers to her body, there'd be no need for that last, but the devil *was* in the details, it turned out.

Harrie'd never wanted to be a boy. But some days she really wished she had the knack of peeing standing up.

She was only about half a klick away when she realized that there was something wrong about Tonopah. Other than the usual; her dosimeters registered only background noise as she came up on it, but a harsh reek like burning coal rasped the back of her throat even through the dust filters, and the weird little town wasn't the weird little town she remembered. Rolling green hills rose around it on all sides, thick with shadowy, leafless trees, and it was smoke haze that drifted on the still air, not dust. A heat shimmer floated over the cracked road, and the buildings that crowded alongside it weren't Tonopah's desert-weathered construction but peeling white shingle-sided houses, a store-front post office, a white church with the steeple caved in and half the facade dropped into a smoking sinkhole in the ground.

The Kawasaki whined, shivering as Harrie throttled back. She sat upright in the saddle, letting the big bike roll. "Where the hell are we?" Her voice reverberated. She startled; she'd forgotten she'd left her microphone on.

"Exactly," a familiar voice said on her left hand. "Welcome to Centralia." Nick wore an open-faced helmet and straddled the back of a Honda Goldwing the color of dried blood, if blood had gold dust flecked through it. The Honda hissed at the Kawasaki, and the Connie growled back, wobbling in eager challenge. Harrie restrained her bike with gentling hands, giving it a little more gas to straighten it out.

"Centralia?" Harrie had never heard of it, and she flattered herself that she'd heard of most places.

"Pennsylvania." Nick lifted his black-gloved hand off the clutch and gestured vaguely around himself. "Or Jharia, in India. Or maybe the Chinese province of Xinjiang. Subterranean coal fires, you know, anthracite burning in abandoned mines. Whole towns abandoned, sulfur and brimstone seeping up through vents, the ground hot enough to flash rain to steam. Your tires will melt. You'll put that bike into a crevasse. Not to mention the greenhouse gases. Lovely things." He grinned, showing shark's teeth, four rows. "Second time asking, Angharad, my princess."

"Second time saying no." She fixed her eyes on the road. She could see the way the asphalt buckled, now, and the dim glow from the bottom of the sinkhole underneath the church. "You really are used to people doing your bidding, aren't you, Nick?"

"They don't usually put up much of a fight." He twisted the throttle while the clutch was engaged, coaxing a whining, competitive cough from his Honda.

Harrie caught his shrug sideways, but kept her gaze trained grimly forward. Was that the earth shivering, or was it just the shimmer of heat-haze over the road? The Kawasaki whined. She petted the clutch to reassure herself.

The groaning rumble that answered her wasn't the Kawasaki. She tightened her knees on the seat as the ground pitched and bucked under her tires, hand clutching the throttle to goose the Connie forward. Broken asphalt sprayed from her rear tire. The road split and shattered, vanishing behind her. She hauled the bike upright by raw strength and nerved herself for a glance in her mirrors; lazy steam rose from a gaping hole in the road.

Nick cruised along, unperturbed. "You sure, Princess?"

"What was that you said about Hell, Nick?" She hunkered down and grinned at him over her shoulder, knowing he couldn't see more than her eyes crinkle through the helmet. It was enough to draw an irritated glare.

He sat back on his haunches and tipped his toes up on the footpegs, throwing both hands up, releasing throttle and clutch, letting the Honda coast away behind her. "I said, welcome to it."

The Kawasaki snarled and whimpered by turns, heavy and agile between her legs as she gave it all the gas she dared. She'd been counting on the refuel stop here, but compact southwestern Tonopah had been replaced by a shattered sprawl of buildings, most of them obviously either bulldozed or vanished into pits that glared like a wolf's eye reflecting a flash, and a gas station wasn't one of the remaining options. The streets were broad, at least, and deserted, not so much winding as curving gently through shallow swales and over hillocks. Broad, but not intact; the asphalt rippled as if heaved by moles and some of the rises and dips hid fissures and sinkholes. Her tires scorched; she coughed into her filter, her mike amplifying it to a hyena's bark. The Cross pen in her pocket pressed her breast over her heart. She took comfort in it, ducking behind the fairing to dodge the stinking wind and the clawing skeletons of ungroomed trees. She'd signed on the line, after all. And either Nick had to see her and the Kawasaki safe or she got back what she'd paid.

As if Nick abided by contracts.

As if he couldn't just kill her, and get what he wanted that way. Except he couldn't keep her, if he did.

"Damn," she murmured, to hear the echoes, and hunched over the Kawasaki's tank. The wind tore at her leathers. The heavy bike caught air coming over the last rise. She had to pee like she couldn't believe and the vibration of the engine wasn't helping, but she laughed out loud to set the city behind.

She got out easier than she thought she would, although her gauge read empty at the bottom of the hill. She switched to reserve and swore. Dead trees and smoking stumps rippled into nonexistence around her, and the lone and level sands stretched to ragged mountains east and west. Back in Nevada, if she'd ever left it, hard westbound now, straight into the glare of the afternoon sun. Her polarized faceplate helped somewhat, maybe not enough, but the road was smooth again before and behind and she could see Tonopah sitting dusty and forsaken in her rear-view mirror, inaccessible as a mirage, a city at the bottom of a well.

Maybe Nick could only touch her in the towns. Maybe he needed a little of man's hand on the wilderness to twist to his own ends, or maybe it amused him. Maybe it was where the roads crossed, after all. She didn't think she could make it back to Tonopah if she tried, however, so she pretended she didn't see the city behind her and cruised west, toward Hawthorne, praying she had enough gas to make it but not expecting her prayers to be answered by anybody she particularly wanted to talk to.

The 95 turned northwest again at the deserted Coaldale junction; there hadn't been a town there since long before the War, or even the disaster at Vegas. Mina was gone too, its outskirts marked by a peeling sign advertising a long-abandoned crawfish farm, the "Desert Lobster Facility."

Harrie's camel bag went dry. She sucked at the straw forlornly one last time and spat it out, letting it sag against her jaw, damp and tacky. She hunkered down and laid a long line of smoking road behind, cornering gently when she had to corner, worried about her scorched and bruised tires. At least the day was cooling as evening encroached, as she progressed north and gained elevation. It might be down into the double digits, even, although it was hard to tell through the leather. On her left, the Sarcophagus Mountains rose between her and California.

The name didn't amuse her as much as it usually did.

And then they were climbing. She breathed a low sigh of relief and patted the hungry, grumbling Kawasaki on the fuel tank as the blistering blue of Walker Lake came into view, the dusty little town of Hawthorne huddled like a crab on the near shore. There was nothing moving there either, and Harrie chewed her lip behind the filter. Dust had gotten into her helmet somehow, gritting every time she blinked; long, weeping streaks marked her cheeks behind the visor. She hoped the dust wasn't the kind that was likely to make her glow, but her dosimeters had settled down to chicken-like clucking, so she might be okay.

The Kawasaki whimpered apologetically, and died as she coasted into town.

"Christ," she said, and flinched at the echo of her own amplified voice. She reached to thumb the mike off, and, on second thought, left it alone. It was too damned quiet out here without the Kawasaki's commentary. She tongued her music back on, flipping selections until she settled on a tune by Grey Line Out.

She dropped her right foot and kicked the stand down on the left, then stood on the peg and slung her leg over the saddle. She ached with vibration, her hands stiff claws from clutching the handlebars. The stretch of muscle across her ass and thighs was like the reminder of a two-day-old beating but she leaned into the bike, boot sole slipping on grit as she heaved it into motion. She hopped on one foot to kick the stand up, wincing.

It wasn't the riding. It was the standing up, afterwards.

She walked the Kawasaki up the deserted highway, between the deserted buildings, the pavement hot enough to sear her feet through the boot leather if she stood still for too long. "Good girl," she told the Kawasaki, stroking the forward brake handle. It leaned against her heavily, cumbersome at a walking pace, like walking a drunk friend home. "Gotta be a gas station somewhere."

Of course, there wouldn't be any power to run the pumps, and probably no safe water, but she'd figure that out when she got there. Sunlight glimmered off the lake; she was fine, she told herself, because she wasn't too dehydrated for her mouth to wet at the thought of all that cool, fresh water.

Except there was no telling what kind of poison was in that lake. There was an old naval base on its shore, and the lake itself had been used as a kind of kiddie pool for submarines. Anything at all could be floating around in its waters. Not, she admitted, that there wasn't a certain irony to taking the long view at a time like this.

She spotted a Texaco station, the red and white sign bleached pink and ivory, crazed by the relentless desert sun. Harrie couldn't remember if she was in the Mojave or the Black Rock desert now, or some other desert entirely. They all ran together. She jumped at her own slightly hysterical giggle. The pumps *were* off, as she'd anticipated, but she leaned the Kawasaki up on its kickstand anyway, grabbed the climate-controlled case out of her saddlebag, and went to find a place to take a leak.

The leather was hot on her fingers when she pulled her gloves off and dropped her pants. "Damned, stupid… First thing I do when I get back to civilization is buy a set of leathers and a helmet in white, dammit." She glanced at the Kawasaki as she fixed herself, expecting a hiss of agreement, but the long black bike was silent. She blinked stinging eyes and turned away.

There was a garden hose curled on its peg behind one of the tan-faced houses huddled by the Texaco station, the upper side bleached yellow on green like the belly of a dead snake. Harrie wrenched it off the peg one-handed. The rubber was brittle from dry rot; she broke it twice trying to uncoil a section, but managed to get about seven feet clean. She pried the fill cap off the underground tank with a tire iron and yanked off her helmet and air filter to sniff, checking both dosimeters first.

It had, after all, been one of those days.

The gas smelled more or less like gasoline, though, and it tasted like fucking gasoline too, when she got a good mouthful of it from sucking it up her impromptu siphon. Not very good gasoline, maybe, but beggars and choosers. The siphon wouldn't work as a siphon because she couldn't get the top end lower than the bottom end, but she could suck fuel up into it and transfer it, hoseful by hoseful, into the Kawasaki's empty tank, the precious case leaning against her boot while she did.

Finally, she saw the dark gleam of fluid shimmer through the fill hole when she peered inside and tapped the side of the tank.

She closed the tank and spat and spat, wishing she had water to wash the gasoline away. The lake glinted, mocking her, and she resolutely turned her back on it and picked up the case.

It was light in her hand. She paused with one hand on the flap of the saddlebag, weighing that gleaming silver object, staring past it at her boots. She sucked on her lower lip, tasted gas, and turned her head and spat again. "A few more years of freedom, Connie," she said, and stroked the metal with a black-gloved hand. "You and me. I could drink the water. It wouldn't matter if that was bad gas I fed you. Nothing could go wrong…."

The Kawasaki was silent. Its keys jangled in Harrie's hip pocket. She touched the throttle lightly, drew her hand back, laid the unopened case on the seat. "What do you say, girl?"

Nothing, of course. It was quiescent, slumbering, a dreaming demon. She hadn't turned it on.

With both thumbs at once, Harrie flicked up the latches and opened the case.

It was cool inside, cool enough that she could feel the difference on her face when she bent over it. She kept the lid at half-mast, trying to block that cool air with her body so it wouldn't drift away. She tipped her head to see inside: blue foam threaded through with cooling elements, shaped to hold the contents without rattling. Papers in a plastic folder, and something in sealed culture plates, clear jelly daubed with ragged polka dots.

There was a sticky note tacked on the plastic folder. She reached into the cool case and flicked the sticky note out, bringing it into the light. Patch's handwriting. She blinked.

"Sacramento next, if these don't get there," it said, in thick, black, definite lines. "Like Faustus, we all get one good chance to change our minds."

If you meet the Buddha on the road—

"I always thought there was more to that son of a bitch than met the eye," she said, and closed the case, and stuffed the note into her pocket beside the pen. She jammed her helmet back on, double-checking the filter that had maybe started leaking a little around the edges in Tonopah, slung her leg over the Kawasaki's saddle, and closed the choke.

It gasped dry when she clutched and thumbed the start button, shaking between her legs like an asthmatic pony. She gave it a little throttle, then eased up on it like easing up on a virgin lover. Coaxing, pleading under her breath. Gasoline fumes from her mouth made her eyes tear inside the helmet; the tears or something else washed the grit away. One cylinder hiccuped. A second one caught.

She eased the choke as the Kawasaki coughed and purred, shivering, ready to run.

Both dosimeters kicked hard as she rolled across the flat open plain toward Fallon, a deadly oasis in its own right. Apparently Nick hadn't been satisfied with a leukemia cluster and perchlorate and arsenic tainting the ground water; the trees Harrie saw as she rolled up on the startling green of the farming town weren't desert cottonwoods but towering giants of the European forest, and something grey and massive, shimmering with lovely crawling blue Cherenkov radiation, gleamed behind them. The signs she passed were in an alphabet she didn't understand, but she knew the name of this place.

A light rain was falling as she passed through Chernobyl.

It drove down harder as she turned west on the 50, toward Reno and Sparks and a crack under the edge of the clouds that glowed a toxic, sallow color with evening coming on. Her tires skittered on slick, greasy asphalt.

Where the cities should have been, stinking piles of garbage crouched against the yellowing evening sky, and nearly naked, starvation-slender people picked their way over slumped rubbish, calling the names of loved ones buried under the avalanche. Water sluiced down her helmet, soaked her saddle, plastered her leathers to her body. She wished she dared drink the rain. It didn't make her cool. It only made her wet.

She didn't turn her head to watch the wretched victims of the garbage slide. She was one hour out of Sacramento, and in Manila of fifty years ago.

Donner Pass was green and pleasant, sunset staining the sky ahead as red as meat. She was in plenty of time. It was all downhill from here.

Nick wasn't about to let her get away without a fight.

The big one had rerouted the Sacramento River, too, and Harrie turned back at the edge because the bridge was down and the water was on fire. She motored away, a hundred meters, two hundred, until the heat of the burning river faded against her back. "What's that?" she asked the slim man in the pinstriped suit who waited for her by the roadside.

"Cuyahoga river fire," he said. "1969. Count your blessings. It could have been Bhopal."

"Blessings?" She spared him a sardonic smile, invisible behind her helmet. He tilted the brim of his hat with a grey-gloved finger. "I suppose you could say that. What is it really?"

"Phlegethon."

She raised her visor and glanced over her shoulder, watching the river burn. Even here, it was hot enough that her sodden leathers steamed against her back. The back of her hand pressed her breast pocket. The paper from Patch's note crinkled; her Cross poked her in the tit.

She looked at Nick, and Nick looked at her. "So that's it."

"That's all she wrote. It's too far to jump."

"I can see that."

"Give me the case and I'll let you go home. I'll give you the Kawasaki and I'll give you your freedom. We'll call it even."

She eyed him, tension up her right leg, toe resting on the ground. The great purring bike shifted heavily between her legs, lithe as a cat, ready to turn and spit gravel from whirring tires. "Too far to jump."

"That's what I said."

Too far to jump. Maybe. And maybe if she gave him what was in the case, and doomed Sacramento like Bhopal, like Chernobyl, like Las Vegas... maybe she'd be damning herself even if he gave it back to her. And even if she wasn't, she wasn't sure she and the Kawasaki could live with that answer.

If he wanted to keep her, he had to let her make the jump, and she could save Sacramento. If he was willing to lose her, she might die on the way over, and Sacramento might die with her, but they would die free.

Either way, Nick lost. And that was good enough for her.

"Devil take the hindmost," she said under her breath, and touched the throttle one more time.

THE GOAT CUTTER

Jay Lake

The Devil lives in Houston by the ship channel in a high-rise apartment fifty-seven stories up. They say he's got cowhide sofas and a pinball machine and a telescope in there that can see past the oil refineries and across Pasadena all the way to the Pope in Rome and on to where them Arabs pray to that big black stone.

He can see anyone anywhere from his place in the Houston sky, and he can see inside their hearts.

But I know it's all a lie. Except about the hearts, of course. Cause I know the Devil lives in an old school bus in the woods outside of Dale, Texas. He don't need no telescope to see inside your heart, on account of he's already there.

This I know.

Central Texas gets mighty hot come summer. The air rolls in heavy off the Gulf, carries itself over two hundred miles of cow shit and sorghum fields and settles heavy on all our heads. The katydids buzz in the woods like electric fans with bad bearings, and even the skeeters get too tired to bite most days. You can smell the dry coming off the Johnson grass and out of the bar ditches.

Me and my best friend Pootie, we liked to run through the woods, climbing bob wire and following pipelines. Trees is smaller there, easier to slip between. You gotta watch out in deer season, though. Idiots come out from Austin or San Antone to their leases, get blind drunk and shoot every blessed thing that moves. Rest of the time, there's nothing but you and them turkey vultures. Course, you can't steal beer coolers from turkey vultures.

The Devil, he gets on pretty good with them turkey vultures.

So me and Pootie was running the woods one afternoon somewhere in the middle of summer. We was out of school, waiting to be sophomores in the fall, fixing to amount to something. Pootie was bigger than me, but I already got tongue off Martha Dempsey. Just a week or so ago back of the church hall, I even scored a little titty squeeze inside her shirt. It was over her bra, but that counts for something. I knew I was coming up good.

Pootie swears he saw Rachel MacIntire's nipples, but she's his cousin. I reckoned he just peeked through the bathroom window of his aunt's trailer house, which ain't no different from me watching Momma get out of the shower. It don't count. If there was anything to it, he'd a sucked on 'em, and I'd of never heard the end of *that*. Course I wouldn't say no to my cousin Linda if she offered to show me a little something in the shower.

Yeah, that year we was big boys, the summer was hot, and we was always hungry and horny.

Then we met the Devil.

Me and Pootie crossed the bob wire fence near the old bus wallow on county road 61, where they finally built that little bridge over the draw. Doug Bob Aaronson had that place along the south side of 61, spent his time roasting goats, drinking tequila and shooting people's dogs.

Doug Bob was okay, if you didn't bring a dog. Three years back, once we turned ten, he let me and Pootie drink his beer with him. He liked to liquor up, strip down to his underwear and get his ass real warm from the fire in his smoker. We was just a guy and two kids in their shorts drinking in the woods. I'm pretty sure Momma and Uncle Reuben would of had hard words, so I never told.

We kind of hoped now that we was going to be sophomores, he'd crack some of that *Sauza Conmemorativo Anejo* for us.

Doug Bob's place was all grown over, wild rose and stretch vine and beggar's lice everywhere, and every spring a huge-ass wisteria wrapped his old cedar house with lavender flowers and thin whips of wood. There was trees everywhere around in the brush, mesquite and hackberry and live-oak and juniper and a few twisty old pecans. Doug Bob knew all the plants and trees, and taught 'em to us sometimes when he was less than half drunk. He kept chickens around the place and a mangy duck that waddled away funny whenever he got to looking at it.

We come crashing through the woods one day that summer, hot, hungry, horny and full of fight. Pootie'd told me about Rachel's nipples, how they was set in big pink circles and stuck out like little red thumbs. I told him I'd seen that picture in *Hustler* same as him. If'n he was gonna lie, lie from a magazine I hadn't stole us from the Triple E Grocery.

Doug Bob's cedar house was bigger than three double wides. It set at the back of a little clearing by the creek that ran down from the bus wallow. He lived there, fifty feet from a rusted old school bus that he wouldn't never set foot inside. Only time I asked him about that bus, he cracked me upside the head so hard I saw double for days and had to tell Uncle Reuben I fell off my bike.

That would of been a better lie if I'd of recollected that my bike'd been stolen three weeks gone. Uncle Reuben didn't beat me much worse than normal, and we prayed extra long over the Bible that night for forgiveness.

Doug Bob was pretty nice. He about never hit me, and he kept his underpants on when I was around.

That old smoker was laid over sidewise on the ground, where it didn't belong. Generally, Doug Bob kept better care of it than anything except an open bottle of tequila. He had cut the smoker from a gigantic water heater, so big me and Pootie could of slept in it. Actually, we did a couple of times, but you can't never get ash out of your hair after.

And Pootie snored worse than Uncle Reuben.

Doug Bob roasted his goats in that smoker, and he was mighty particular about his goats. He always killed his goats hisself. They didn't usually belong to him, but he did his own killing. Said it made him a better man. I thought it mostly made him a better mess. The meat plant over in Lockhart could of done twice the job in half the time, with no bath in the creek afterward.

Course, when you're sweaty and hot and full of piss and vinegar, there's nothing like a splash around down in the creek with some beer and one of them big cakes of smelly purple horse soap me and Pootie stole out of barns for Doug Bob. Getting rubbed down with that stuff kind of stings, but it's a good sting.

Times like that, I knew Doug Bob liked me just for myself. We'd all smile and laugh and horse around and get drunk. Nobody got hit, nobody got hurt, everybody went home happy.

Doug Bob always had one of these goats, and it was always a buck. Sometimes a white Saanen, or maybe a creamy La Mancha or a brown Nubian looked like a chubby deer with them barred goat eyes staring straight into your heart. They was always clean, no socks nor blazes nor points, just one color all over. Doug Bob called them *unblemished*.

And Doug Bob always killed these goats on the north side of the smoker. He had laid some rocks down there, to make a clear spot for when it was muddy from winter rain or whatever. He'd cut their throats with his jagged knife that was older than sin, and sprinkle the blood all around the smoker.

He never let me touch that knife.

Doug Bob, he had this old gray knife without no handle, just rags wrapped up around the end. The blade had a funny shape like it got beat up inside a thresher or something, as happened to Momma's sister Cissy the year I was born. Her face had that funny shape until Uncle Reuben found her hanging in the pole barn one morning with her dress up over her head.

They puttied her up for the viewing at the funeral home, but I recall Aunt Cissy best with those big dents in her cheek and jaw and the one brown eye gone all white like milk in coffee.

Doug Bob's knife, that I always thought of as Cissy's knife, it was kind of wompered and shaped all wrong, like a corn leaf the bugs been at. He'd take that knife and saw the head right off his goat.

I never could figure how Doug Bob kept that edge on.

He'd flay that goat, and strip some fatback off the inside of the hide, and put the head and the fat right on the smoker where the fire was going, wet chips of mesquite over a good hot bed of coals.

Then he'd drag the carcass down to the creek, to our swimming hole, and sometimes me and Pootie could help with this part. We'd wash out the gut sack and clean off the heart and lungs and liver. Doug Bob always scrubbed the legs specially well with that purple horse soap. We'd generally get a good lot of blood in the water. If it hadn't rained in a while, like most summers, the water'd be sticky for hours afterward.

Doug Bob would take the carcass and the sweetbreads—that's what he called the guts, sweetbreads. I figured they looked more like spongy purple and red bruises than bread, kind of like dog food fresh outta the can. And there wasn't nothing sweet about them.

Sweetbreads taste better than dog food, though. We ate dog food in the winter sometimes, ate it cold if Uncle Reuben didn't have work and Momma'd been lazy. That was when I most missed my summers in the woods with Pootie, calling in on Doug Bob.

Doug Bob would drag these goat parts back up to the smoker, where he'd take the head and the fat off the fire. He'd always give me and Pootie some of that fat, to keep us away from the head meat, I guess. Doug Bob would put the carcass and the sweetbreads on the fire and spit his high-proof tequila all over them. If they didn't catch straight away from that, he'd light 'em with a bic.

We'd watch them burn, quiet and respectful like church on account of that's what Doug Bob believed. He always said God told him to keep things orderly, somewhere in the beginning of Leviticus.

Then he'd close the lid and let the meat cook. He didn't never clean up the blood around the smoker, although he would catch some to write Bible verses on the sides of that old school bus with.

The Devil lives in San Francisco in a big apartment on Telegraph Hill. Way up there with all that brass and them potted ferns and naked women with leashes on, he's got a telescope that can see across the bay, even in the fog. They say he can see all the way to China and Asia, with little brown people and big red demon gods, and stare inside their hearts

The Devil, he can see inside everybody's heart, just about.

It's a lie, except that part about the hearts. There's only one place in God's wide world where the Devil can't see.

Me and Pootie, we found that smoker laying over on its side, which we ain't never seen. There was a broken tequila bottle next to it, which ain't much like Doug Bob neither.

Well, we commenced to running back and forth, calling out "Doug Bob!" and "Mr. Aaronson!" and stuff. That was dumb cause if he was around and listening, he'd of heard us giggling and arguing by the time we'd crossed his fence line.

I guess we both knew that, cause pretty quick we fell quiet and starting looking around. I felt like I was on TV or something, and there was a bad thing fixing to happen next. Them saloon doors were flapping in my mind and I started wishing mightily for a commercial.

That old bus of Doug Bob's, it was a long bus, like them revival preachers use to bring their people into town. I always thought going to Glory when you died meant getting on one of them long buses painted white and gold, with Bible verses on the side and a choir clapping and singing in the back and some guy in a powder blue suit and hair like a raccoon pelt kissing you on the cheek and slapping you on the forehead.

Well, I been kissed more than I want to, and I don't know nobody with a suit, no matter the color, and there ain't no choir ever going to sing me to my rest now, except if maybe they're playing bob wire harps and beating time on burnt skulls. But Doug Bob's bus, it sat there flat on the dirt with the wiry bones of tires wrapped over dented black hubs grown with morning glory, all yellow with the rusted old metal showing through, with the windows painted black from the inside and crossed over with duct tape. It had a little vestibule Doug Bob'd built over the double doors out of wood from an old church in Rosanky. The entrance to that vestibule was crossed over with duct tape just like the windows. It was bus number seven, whatever place it had come from.

And bus number seven was covered with them Bible verses written in goat's blood, over and over each other to where there was just red-brown smears on the cracked windshield and across the hood and down the sides, scrambled scribbling that looked like Aunt Cissy's drool on the lunch table at Wal-Mart. And they made about as much sense.

I even seen Doug Bob on the roof of that bus a few times, smearing bloody words with his fingers like a message to the turkey vultures, or maybe all the way to God above looking down from His air-conditioned heaven.

So I figured, the smoker's tipped, the tequila's broke, and here's my long bus bound for glory with Bible verses on the side, and the only choir is the katydids buzzing in the trees and me and Pootie breathing hard. I saw the door of the wooden vestibule on the bus, that Doug Bob never would touch, was busted open, like it had been kicked out from the inside. The duct tape just flapped loose from the door frame.

I stared all around that bus, and there was a new verse on the side, right under the driver's window. It was painted fresh, still shiny and red. It said, "Of the tribe of Reuben were sealed twelve thousand."

"Pootie."

"Huh?" He was gasping pretty hard. I couldn't take my eyes off the bus, which looked as if it was gonna rise up from the dirt and rumble down the road to salvation any moment, but I knew Pootie had that wild look where his eyes get almost all white and his nose starts to bleed. I could tell from his breathing.

Smelled like he wet his pants, too.

"Pootie," I said again, "there ain't no fire, and there ain't no fresh goat been killed. Where'd the blood come from for that there Bible verse?"

"Reckon he talking 'bout your Uncle?" Pootie's voice was duller than Momma at Christmas.

Pootie was an idiot. Uncle Reuben never had no twelve thousand in his life. If he ever did, he'd of gone to Mexico and to hell with me and Momma. "Pootie," I tried again, "where'd the blood come from?"

I knew, but I didn't want to be the one to say it.

Pootie panted for a little while longer. I finally tore my eyes off that old bus, which was shimmering like summer heat, to see Pootie bent over with his hands on his knees and his head hanging down. "It ain't his handwritin' neither," Pootie sobbed.

We both knew Doug Bob was dead.

Something was splashing around down by the creek. "Aw, shit," I said. "Doug Bob was—is our friend. We gotta go look."

It ain't but a few steps to the bank. We could see a man down there, bending over with his bare ass toward us. He was washing something big and pale. It weren't no goat.

Me and Pootie, we stopped at the top of the bank, and the stranger stood up and turned around. I about shit my pants.

He had muscles like a movie star, and a gold tan all the way down, like he'd never wore clothes. The hair on his chest and his short-and-curlies was blonde, and he was hung good. What near to made me puke was that angel's body had a goat head. Only it weren't no goat head you ever saw in your life.

It was like a big heavy ram's head, except it had *antlers* coming up off the top, a twelve point spread off a prize buck, and baby's eyes—big, blue and round in the middle. Not goat's eyes at all. That fur kind of tapered off into golden skin at the neck.

And those blue eyes blazed at me like ice on fire.

The tall, golden thing pointed to a body in the creek. He'd been washing the legs with purple soap. "Help me with this. I think you know how it needs to be done." His voice was windy and creaky, like he hadn't talked to no one for a real long time.

The body was Doug Bob, with his big gut and saggy butt, and a bloody stump of a neck.

"You son of a bitch!" I ran down the bank, screaming and swinging my arms for the biggest punch I could throw. I don't know, maybe I tripped over a root or stumbled at the water's edge, but that golden thing moved like summer lightning just as I slipped off my balance.

Last thing I saw was the butt end of Doug Bob's ragged old knife coming at me in his fist. I heard Pootie crying my name when my head went all red and painful.

The Devil lives in your neighborhood, yours and mine. He lives in every house in every town, and he has a telescope that looks out the bathroom mirror and up from the drains in the kitchen and out of the still water at the bottom of the toilet bowl. He can see inside of everyone's heart through their eyes and down their mouth and up their asshole.

It's true, I know it is.

The hope I hold secret deep inside my heart is that there's one place on God's green earth the Devil can't see.

I was naked, my dick curled small and sticky to my thigh like it does after I've been looking through the bathroom window. A tight little trail of cum itched my skin. My ass was on dirt, and I could feel ants crawling up the crack. I opened my mouth to say, "Fine," and a fly buzzed out from the inside. There was another one in the left side of my nose that seemed ready to stay a spell.

I didn't really want to open my eyes. I knew where I was. My back was against hot metal. It felt sticky. I was leaning against Doug Bob's bus and part of that new Bible verse about Uncle Reuben under the driver's window had run and got Doug Bob's heart blood all down my back. I could smell mesquite smoke, cooked meat, shit, blood, and the old oily metal of the bus.

But in all my senses, in the feel of the rusted metal, in the warmth of the ground, in the stickiness of the blood, in the sting of the ant bites, in the touch of the fly crawling around inside my nose, in the stink of Doug Bob's rotten little yard, there was something missing. It was an absence, a space, like when you get a tooth busted out in a fight, and notice it for not being there.

I was surrounded by absence, cold in the summer heat. My heart felt real slow. I still didn't want to open my eyes.

"You know," said that windy, creaky voice, sounding even more hollow and thin than before, "if they would just repent of their murders, their sorceries, their fornication, and their thefts, this would be a lot harder."

The voice was sticky, like the blood on my back, and cold, coming from the middle of whatever was missing around me. I opened my eyes and squinted into the afternoon sun.

Doug Bob's face smiled at me. Leastwise it tried to. Up close I could tell a whole lot of it was burnt off, with griddle marks where his head had lain a while on the smoker. Blackened bone showed through across the cheeks. Doug Bob's head was duct-taped to the neck of that glorious, golden body, greasy black hair falling down those perfect shoulders. The head kept trying to lop over as he moved, like it was stuck on all wompered. His face was puffy and burnt-up, weirder than Doug Bob mostly ever looked.

The smoker must of been working again.

The golden thing with Doug Bob's head had Pootie spread out naked next to the smoker. I couldn't tell if he was dead, but sure he wasn't moving. Doug Bob's legs hung over the side of the smoker, right where he'd always put the goat legs. Cissy's crazy knife was in that golden right hand, hanging loose like Uncle Reuben holds his when he's fixing to fight someone.

"I don't understand…" I tried to talk, but burped up a little bit of vomit and another fly to finish my sentence. The inside of my nose stung with the smell, and the fly in there didn't seem to like it much neither. "You stole Doug Bob's head."

"You see, my son, I have been set free from my confinement. My time is at hand." Doug Bob's face wrinkled into a smile, as some of his burnt lip scaled away. I wondered how much of Doug Bob was still down in the creek. "But even I can not walk the streets with my proud horns."

His voice got sweeter, stronger, as he talked. I stared up at him, blinking in the sunlight.

"Rise up and join me. We have much work to do, preparations for my triumph. As the first to bow to my glory you shall rank high among my new disciples, and gain your innermost desire."

Uncle Reuben taught me long ago how this sweet bullshit always ends. The old Doug Bob liked me. Maybe even loved me a little. He was always kind to me, which this golden Doug Bob ain't never gonna be.

It must be nice to be loved a lot.

I staggered to my feet, farting ants, using the ridges in the sheet metal of the bus for support. It was hot as hell, and even the katydids had gone quiet. Except for the turkey vultures circling low over me, I felt like I was alone in a giant dirt coffin with a huge blue lid over my head. I felt expanded, swollen in the heat like a dead coyote by the side of the road.

The thing wearing Doug Bob's head narrowed his eyes at me. There was a faint crinkling sound as the lids creased and broke.

"Get over here, *now*." His voice had the menace of a Sunday morning twister headed for a church, the power of a wall of water in the arroyo where kids played.

I walked toward the Devil, feet stepping without my effort.

There's a place I can go, inside, when Uncle Reuben's pushing into me, or he's using the metal end of the belt, or Momma's screaming through the thin walls of our trailer the way he can make her do. It's like ice cream without the cone, like cotton candy without the stick. It's like how I imagine Rachel MacIntire's nipples, sweet and total, like my eyes and heart are in my lips and the world has gone dark around me.

It's the place where I love myself, deep inside my heart.

I went there and listened to the little shuffling of my pulse in my ears.

My feet walked on without me, but I couldn't tell.

Cissy's knife spoke to me. The Devil must of put it in my hand.

"We come again to Moriah," it whispered in my heart. It had a voice like its metal blade, cold from the ground and old as time.

"What do you want?" I asked. I must of spoke out loud, because Doug Bob's burned mouth was twisting in screaming rage as he stabbed his golden finger down toward Pootie, naked at my feet next to the smoker. All I could hear was my pulse, and the voice of the knife.

Deep inside my heart, the knife whispered again. "Do not lay a hand on the boy."

The golden voice from Doug Bob's face was distant thunder in my ears. I felt his irritation, rage, frustration building where I had felt that cold absence.

I tried again. "I don't understand."

Doug Bob's head bounced up and down, the duct tape coming loose. I saw pink ropy strings working to bind the burned head to his golden neck. He cocked back a fist, fixing to strike me a hard blow.

I felt the knife straining across the years toward me. "You have a choice. The Enemy promises anything and everything for your help. I can give you nothing but the hope of an orderly world. You choose what happens now, and after."

I reckoned the Devil would run the world about like Uncle Reuben might. Doug Bob was already dead, and Pootie was next, and there wasn't nobody else like them in my life, no matter what the Devil promised. I figured there was enough hurt to go around already and I knew how to take it into me.

Another one of Uncle Reuben's lessons.

"Where you want this killing done?" I asked.

The golden thunder in my ears paused for a moment, the tide of rage lapped back from the empty place where Doug Bob wasn't. The fist dropped down.

"Right here, right now," whispered the knife. "Or it will be too late. Seven is being opened."

I stepped out of my inside place to find my eyes still open and Doug Bob's blackened face inches from my nose. His teeth were burnt and cracked, and his breath reeked of flies and red meat. I smiled, opened my mouth to speak, but instead of words I swung Cissy's knife right through the duct tape at the throat of Doug Bob's head.

He looked surprised.

Doug Bob's head flew off, bounced into the bushes. The golden body swayed, still on its two feet. I looked down at Pootie, the old knife cold in my hands.

Then I heard buzzing, like thunder made of wires.

I don't know if you ever ate a fly, accidental or not. They go down fighting, kind of tickle the throat, you get a funny feeling for a second, and then it's all gone. Not very filling, neither.

These flies came pouring out of the ragged neck of that golden body. They were big, the size of horseflies. All at once they were everywhere, and they came right at me. They came pushing at my eyes and my nose and my ears and flying right into my mouth, crawling down my throat. It was like stuffing yourself with raisins till you choke, except these raisins crawled and buzzed and bit at me.

The worst was they got all over me, crowding into my butt crack and pushing on my asshole and wrapping around my balls like Uncle Reuben's fingers right before he squeezed tight. My skin rippled, as if them flies crawled through my flesh.

I jumped around, screaming and slapping at my skin. My gut heaved, but my throat was full of flies and it all met in a knot at the back of my mouth. I rolled to the ground, choking on the rippling mess I couldn't spit out nor swallow back down. Through the flies I saw Doug Bob's golden body falling in on itself, like a balloon that's been popped. Then the choking took me off.

I lied about the telescope. I don't need one.

Right after, while I was still mostly myself, I sent Pootie away with that old knife to find one of Doug Bob's kin. They needed that knife, to make their sacrifices that would keep me shut away. I made Pootie seal me inside the bus with Doug Bob's duct tape before he left.

The bus is hot and dark, but I don't really mind. There's just me and the flies and a hot metal floor with rubber mats and huge stacks of old Bibles and hymnals that make it hard for me to move around.

It's okay, though, because I can watch the whole world from in here.

I hate the flies, but they're the only company I can keep. The taste grows on me.

I know Pootie must of found someone to give that old knife to. I try the doors sometimes, but they hold firm. Somewhere one of Doug Bob's brothers or uncles or cousins cuts goats the old way. Someday I'll find him. I can see every heart except one, but there are too many to easily tell one from another.

There's only one place under God's golden sun the Devil can't see into, and that's his own heart.

I still have my quiet place. That's where I hold my hope, and that's where I go when I get too close to the goat cutter.

·ON THE ROAD TO
NEW EGYPT

Jeffrey Ford

One day when I was driving home from work, I saw him there on the side of the road. He startled me at first, but I managed to control myself and apply the brakes. His face was fixed with a look somewhere between agony and elation. That thumb he thrust out at an odd angle was gnarled and had a long nail. The sun was setting and red beams danced around him. I stopped and leaned over to open the door.

"You're Jesus, right?" I said.

"Yeah," he said and held up his palms to show the stigmata.

"Hop in," I told him.

"Thanks, man," he said as he gathered up his robe and slipped into the front seat.

As I pulled back onto the road, he took out a pack of Camel Wides and a dark blue Bic lighter. "You don't mind, do you?" he asked, but he already had a cigarette in his mouth and was bringing a flame to it.

"Go for it," I said.

"Where you headed?" he asked.

"Home, unless you're here to tell me different," I said, forcing a laugh.

"Easy, easy," he said.

After a short silence, Christ took a couple of deep drags and blew the smoke out the partially opened window.

"Where are *you* going?" I asked.

"You know, just up the road a piece."

We stopped at a red light and I looked over at him. That crown of thorns must have itched like hell. I shook my head and said, "Wait till I tell my wife about this."

"She religious?" he asked.

"Not particularly, but still, she'll get the impact."

He smiled and flicked some ashes into his palm.

We drove on for a while through the vanishing light, past fields of pumpkins and dried corn stalks. A few minutes later, night fell, and I turned on the headlights. I didn't see it at first, but a possum darted out into the road right in front of the car. *Bump, bump,* we were over it in a microsecond. I looked at Christ.

He shrugged as if to say, "What can you do?"

"… and Heaven?" I asked as the car traveled into a valley where the trees from either side of the road had, above, grown together into a canopy.

"Angels, blue skies, your relatives are all there. The greats are there. Basically everybody is there. It gets a little tense sometimes, a little close."

"You said that 'basically' everybody is in Heaven," I said. "Who isn't?"

"You know," he said, "those other people."

We kept going past the fences of the horse farms, the edges of barren fields, until Christ had me stop as McDonald's and order him a quarter pounder with cheese, and a chocolate shake. I paid for it with my last couple of dollars.

He said, "I'll pay you back in indulgences."

"Hey, it's on me," I said.

He wolfed down the burger like the Son of Man that he was.

"So what have you seen in your travels?" I asked.

"You name it," he said, sucking at his shake. "The human drama."

"Do you ever stop anywhere?"

"Sometimes. I'm always on the look-out for an old Howard Johnson." There was a short pause and then he said, "Could you step on it a little, have to be in New Egypt by eight."

"Sure thing," I said and put down the pedal. "You meeting someone?"

"I've been seeing this woman there on and off for the past couple of years. Every once in a while I'll appear, give her a little push and then split by sunup."

"She must be pretty special."

"Yeah," he said, and took out a flattened wallet. "Here she is."

He showed me an old photo of this forty-five-year-old ex-blonde-bombshell in a leopard bikini.

"Nice," I said.

"Nice isn't the word for it," he said, with a wink.

"What's she do?" I asked.

"A little of this, a little of that," he said.

"No, I mean, where does she work?"

"At the funeral parlor. She sews mouths and lids shut. She lives in a small house in the center of town. When I get there, she's usually in bed. I step out of the armoire, minus the robe, and slip between the sheets with her. We eat of the fruit of the knowledge of good and evil for a few hours and then lay back, have a smoke."

"Does she know who you are?"

"I hope by this time she's figured it out," he said.

"She'll end up going to the tabloids with the story," I warned.

"Screw it, she already has. We were in that one recently with Bigfoot on the cover and the story about the woman who turned to stone on page three."

"I missed that one, but I remember the cover."

All of a sudden Christ sat straight up and pointed out the windshield. "Whoa, whoa," he said, "pull over like you're going to pick this guy up."

Only when he spoke did I see the shadowy figure up ahead on the side of the road. I could see it was a guy and that he was hitchhiking. I passed by him a few feet and then pulled over to the shoulder. We could hear him running toward the car.

"Okay, peel out," Christ said.

I did and we left that stranger in the dust.

"I love that one," said the savior.

A few minutes passed and then I heard a hatchet of a voice from the back seat. "You fuckers," it said. I looked in the rearview mirror and there was the Devil—horns, red skin, cheesy whiskers in a goatee. As I looked at him his grin turned into a wide smile.

Jesus reached back and offered a hand.

"Who's the stiff at the wheel?" asked the Devil.

"You mean fat boy here?" Christ said and they both burst out laughing. "He's cool."

"Nice to meet you," said the Devil.

I reached back and shook a hand that was a tree branch with the power to grip. "Name's Jeff," I said.

"I am Legion," he hissed.

Then he stuck his head in the space between us and shot a little burp of flame into the air. Christ doubled over with silent laughter. "I got a bag of Carthage Red on me, you got any papers?" the Devil asked, putting his hand on Christ's shoulder.

"Does the Pope shit in the woods?" asked the Son of God.

The Devil got the papers and started rolling one in the back seat. "Jeff, you ever try this shit?"

"I never heard of it."

"It's old, man, it'll make you see God."

"By the way," Christ said, interrupting, "what ever happened with that guy in Detroit?"

"I took him," said the Devil. "Mass murderer, just reeking evil. He hung himself in the jail cell. They conveniently forgot to remove his belt."

"I thought I told you I wanted him," said Christ.

"I thought I cared," said the Devil. "Anyway, you get that old woman from Tampa. She's going to make canonization. I guarantee it."

"I guess that's cool," he said.

"Eat me if it isn't," said the Devil. They both started laughing and each patted me on the back. The Devil lit up the enormous joint he had created and the odd pink smoke began to permeate the car.

It tasted like cinnamon and fire and even with only the first toke, I was stunned. Paranoia set in instantly, and I slowed the car down to about thirty. I drove blindly while in my head I saw the autumn afternoon woods of my childhood, where it was so still and the leaves silently fell. I thought of home and it was far away.

When my mind returned to me at a red light, I realized that the radio was on. New Age music, a piano, some low moaning formed a backdrop to the conversation of my passengers.

"What do you think?" Christ had just asked.

"I think this music has to go," said the Devil. His fingers grew like snakes from the back seat, and he kept pressing the scan button on the radio until he came to the oldies station. "Back seat memories," he said.

Somehow it was decided that we would go to Florida and check out the lady who was going to become a saint. "Maybe she'll pop a miracle," said the Devil.

"No sweat," said Christ.

"My wife's expecting me home around nine," I said.

The Devil laughed really loud. "I'll tell you what I'll do," he said. "I'll split myself in two, and half of me will go to your house and boff your wife till we get back."

Christ leaned over and put his hand on my knee. "Don't be an idiot," he said to me with a smile. "I have to be in New Egypt by eight."

"You can do things?" I asked.

"Look," said Christ, nodding toward the windshield. "We're there. Just make a right at this corner. It's the third house on the left."

I looked up and saw that we were in a suburban neighborhood with palm trees lining the side of the road. The houses were all one-story ranch styles and painted in pastel colors. When I pulled the car over in front of the house, I could hear crickets singing quickly in the night heat.

Before we got out, the Devil leaned toward the front seat and said to Christ, "I'll make you a bet she doesn't do a miracle while we're here."

"Bullshit," said Christ.

"What do you want to bet?" asked the Devil.

"How about *him*," said the savior and pointed that weird thumb at me.

"Quite the high roller," said the Devil.

As we were walking up the driveway to the front door, the Devil lagged a little behind us. I leaned over and, in a whisper, asked Christ if he thought she would perform.

He shrugged and rolled his eyes. "Have faith, man," he said. "Sometimes you win, sometimes you lose."

"I heard that," said the Devil. "I don't like whispering."

We walked right through the front door and into the living room where a woman was sitting in front of the television. At first, I thought she was deaf, but it soon became clear that we were completely invisible to her.

The Devil walked up behind me and handed me a sixteen-ounce Rolling Rock. "There she is in all her splendor," he said, as he handed a beer to Christ. "Doesn't look like much of an opportunity here unless she's gonna get better looking."

We stood and stared at her. She was about sixty-five with short hair dyed brown and wearing a flowered bathrobe. On the coffee table in front of her sat an ashtray with a lit cigarette in one of the holders. In her left hand she held a glass of ark wine. As the daily reports of mayhem and greed came through the box, she shook her head from time to time and sipped her drink.

"What's she done?" I asked.

"She brought a kid back from the dead a few months ago," said the Devil. "A girl was hit by a car outside a local grocery store. Mrs. Lumley, here, was present and just touched the girl's hand. The kid got right up off the stretcher and walked away."

"Strange shit," said Christ. "We don't really know how it works."

"You mean," I said, "that you can't make her do a miracle?"

"Not exactly," said Christ.

"That's a bitch, isn't it?" said the Devil. "Now drink your beer and calm down."

The Devil walked around behind Mrs. Lumley's chair and used two fingers to make horns behind her head. Christ went to pieces over that one. I even had to laugh while we watched her pick her nose. She was at it for a good five minutes. Christ applauded her every strategy, and the Devil said, "The one that got away."

"We better sit down. This may take a few minutes," said Christ.

The Devil and I sat down on the couch and Christ took an old rocker across from us. The evil one rolled another huge joint and listened intently to the report on television of a murder/suicide in California. Mrs. Lumley began singing "The Whispering Wind" to herself in between sips of wine while Christ hummed in a duet with her.

"I've had more fun in church," said the Devil, as he passed me the joint. Again, I tasted the cinnamon and fire, and I took big gulps of beer to soothe my throat.

Christ begged off and just rocked contentedly in his chair.

The news eventually ended and *Jeopardy* came on the television. "Wait till I get my hooks into *this* asshole," the Devil said, nodding toward the host of the show.

"He's yours," said Christ. "It's on me." Then he pointed his finger at Mrs. Lumley and made her change the channel to a *Star Trek* rerun.

While we waited for something to happen, the Devil showed me a trick. He took a big draw of Carthage Red and then exhaled it in a perfect globe of smoke. The globe hovered in the air before my eyes and turned crystal clear. Then it was filled with an image of my wife and kids reading bedtime stories. When I reached for it, the globe popped like a soap bubble.

"Parlor tricks," said Christ.

Eventually, Mrs. Lumley got up, turned off the set, and went into her bedroom. We followed her as far as the door, where we looked in at her. She was kneeling next to the bed, saying her prayers.

"I hope you like the heat," the Devil said to me.

Then Christ said, "Look."

Mrs. Lumley lay on the floor, her body twitching. A steady groan escaped through her clenched teeth. In seconds, her skin had become a metallic blue and her head had doubled in size. Fangs, claws, gills, audibly popped from her features. She turned her head to face us, and I could feel she was actually seeing us with her expanding eyes.

"Shit," said the Devil, and turned and ran toward the door.

"Let's get out of here," said Christ, and he too turned and ran. I followed close behind.

By the time we got outside, the Devil was sticking his head out of the back-seat window of the car. "Move your asses," he yelled.

I ran around the front of the car and climbed in the driver's seat as fast as I could. Mrs. Lumley, now some kind of rapidly changing blue creature, growled from the front lawn. I turned on the ignition and hit the gas.

"What the fuck was that supposed to be?" said Christ, catching his breath as he passed us each a cigarette.

"Your old man is out of his mind," said the Devil. "It's all getting just a little too strange."

"Tell me about it," said Christ. "Remember, I warned you back when they first walked on the moon."

"This is some really evil shit, though," said the Devil.

"The whole ball of wax is falling apart," said Christ.

"I actually had a break-out in the ninth hole of Hell last week," said the Devil. "A big bastard—he smashed right through the ice. Killed one demon with his bare hands and broke another one's back."

"Did you get him?" I asked.

"One of my people said she saw him in Chicago."

"Purgatory is spreading like the plague," said Christ.

The Devil leaned up close behind me and put his claw hand on my shoulder. I could feel his hot breath on the back of my neck. "His old man is reading Nietzshe," he whispered, his tongue grazing my earlobe.

"What's he saying?" Christ asked me.

"Which way am I supposed to turn to get out of this development?" I asked.

Just then there was an abrupt bump on the top of the car. It startled me and I swerved, almost hitting a garbage can.

"You gotta check this out," said the Devil. "Saint Lumley of the Bad Trips is flying over us."

"Punch the gas," yelled Christ, and I floored it. I drove like a maniac, screeching around corners as the pastel ranches flew by.

"We're starting to lose her," the Devil called out.

"What are you carrying?" Christ asked.

"I've got a full minute of fire," said the Devil. "What have you got?"

"I've got the Machine of Eden," said Christ.

"Uhh, not *The* fucking Machine of Eden," said the Devil, and slammed the back of my seat.

"What do you mean?" said Christ.

"When was the last time that thing worked?"

"It works," said Christ.

"Pull off and go through the gate up on your right," said the Devil. "We've got to take her out or she'll dog us for eternity."

"I don't like this at all," said Christ.

After passing the gate, I drove on a winding gravel road that led to the local landfill. There were endless moonlit hills of junk and garbage. I parked the car and we got out.

"We've got to get to the top of that hill before she gets here," said Christ, pointing to a huge mound of garbage.

I scrabbled up the hill, clutching at old car seats and stepping on dead appliances. Startled rats scurried through the debris. When I reached the top I was sweating and panting. Christ beat me, but I had to reach down and help the Devil up the last few steps.

"It's the hooves," he said, "they're worse than high heels."

"There's some cool stuff here," said Christ.

"I saw a whole carton of *National Geographics* I want to snag on the way out," said the Devil.

Off in the distance, I saw the shadow of something passing in front of the stars. It was too big to be a bird. "Here she comes," I yelled and pointed. They both spun around to look. "What do I do?" I asked.

"Stay behind us," said Christ. "If she gets you, it's going to hurt."

The next thing I knew, Mrs. Lumley had landed and we three were backed against the edge of the hill with a steep drop behind us. Her blue skin shone in the moonlight like armor, but there were tufts of hair growing from it. She had this amazing aqua body and an eight-foot wingspan, but with the exception of the gills and fangs, she still had the face of a sixty-five-year-old woman. She moved slowly toward us, burping out words that made no sense.

When she came within a few feet of us, Christ said, "Smoke 'em if you got 'em," and the Devil stepped forward. Tentacles began to grow from her body toward him. One managed to wrap itself around his left horn when he opened his mouth to assault her with a minute of fire. The flame discharged like a blowtorch and stopped her cold. When she was completely engulfed in the blaze, the tentacles retracted, but she would not melt.

As soon as the evil one finished, coughing out great clouds of gray smoke, Mrs. Lumley opened her eyes and the tentacles began to grow again from her sides. I looked over and saw that Christ was holding something in his right hand. It appeared to be a remote control, and he was furiously pushing its buttons.

The Devil had jumped back beside me, his hand clutching my arm. He had real fear in his serpent eyes, yet he could not help but laugh at Christ messing around with the Machine of Eden.

"What's with the cosmic garage door opener," he shouted.

"It works," said Christ, as he continued to nervously press buttons. I felt one of the tentacles wrap itself around my ankle. Mrs. Lumley opened her mouth and crowed like a rooster. Another of the blue snake appendages entwined itself around the Devil's midsection. We both screamed as she pulled us toward her.

"Three," Christ yelled, and a beam of light shot out of the end of the Machine. I then heard the sound of celestial voices singing in unison. Mrs. Lumley took the blast full in the chest and began instantly to shrivel. Before my eyes, like the special effects in a crappy science fiction movie, she turned into a tree. Leaves sprouted, pink blossoms grew, and as the singing faded, pure white fruit appeared on the lower branches.

"Not fun," said the Devil.

"I thought she was going to suck your face off," said Christ.

"What exactly was she," I asked, "an alien?"

Christ shook his head. "Nah," he said, "just a fucked-up old woman."

"Is she still a saint?" I asked.

"No, she's a tree," he said.

"You and your saints," said the Devil and plucked a piece of fruit. "Take one of these," he said to me. "It's called the *Still Point of the Turning World*. Only eat it when you need it."

I picked one of the white pears off the tree and put it in my pocket before we started down the junk hill. The Devil found the box of magazines and Christ came up with a lamp made out of seashells. We piled into the car and I started it up.

I heard Christ say, "Holy shit, it's 8:00!"

The next thing I knew I was on my usual road back in Jersey. The car was empty but for me, and I was just leaving New Egypt.

THAT HELL-BOUND TRAIN

Robert Bloch

When Martin was a little boy, his daddy was a Railroad Man. Daddy never rode the high iron, but he walked the tracks for the CB&Q, and he was proud of his job. And every night when he got drunk, he sang this old song about That Hell-Bound Train.

Martin didn't quite remember any of the words, but he couldn't forget the way his Daddy sang them out. And when Daddy made the mistake of getting drunk in the afternoon and got squeezed between a Pennsy tank-car and an AT&SF gondola, Martin sort of wondered why the Brotherhood didn't sing the song at his funeral.

After that, things didn't go so good for Martin, but somehow he always recalled Daddy's song. When Mom up and ran off with a traveling salesman from Keokuk (Daddy must have turned over in his grave, knowing she'd done such a thing, and with a passenger, too!) Martin hummed the tune to himself every night in the Orphan Home. And after Martin himself ran away, he used to whistle the song softly at night in the jungles, after the other bindlestiffs were asleep.

Martin was on the road for four-five years before he realized he wasn't getting anyplace. Of course he'd tried his hand at a lot of things—picking fruit in Oregon, washing dishes in a Montana hash-house, stealing hubcaps in Denver and tires in Oklahoma City—but by the time he'd put in six months on the chain gang down in Alabama he knew he had no future drifting around this way on his own.

So he tried to get on the railroad like his daddy had and they told him that times were bad. But Martin couldn't keep away from the railroads. Wherever he traveled, he rode the rods; he'd rather hop a freight heading north in sub-zero weather than lift his thumb to hitch a ride with a Cadillac headed for Florida. Whenever he managed to get hold of a can of Sterno, he'd sit there under a nice warm culvert, think about the old days, and often as not he'd hum the song about That Hell-Bound Train. That was the train the drunks and the sinners rode—the gambling men and the grifters, the big-time spenders, the skirt-chasers, and all the jolly crew. It would be really fine to take a trip in such good company, but Martin didn't like to think of what happened when that train

196

finally pulled into the Depot Way Down Yonder. He didn't figure on spending eternity stoking boilers in Hell, without even a Company Union to protect him. Still, it would be a lovely ride. If there was such a thing as a Hell-Bound Train. Which, of course, there wasn't.

At least Martin didn't think there was, until that evening when he found himself walking the tracks heading south, just outside of Appleton Junction. The night was cold and dark, the way November nights are in the Fox River Valley, and he knew he'd have to work his way down to New Orleans for the winter, or maybe even Texas. Somehow he didn't much feel like going, even though he'd heard tell that a lot of those Texas automobiles had solid gold hubcaps.

No sir, he just wasn't cut out for petty larceny. It was worse than a sin—it was unprofitable, too. Bad enough to do the Devil's work, but then to get such miserable pay on top of it! Maybe he'd better let the Salvation Army convert him.

Martin trudged along humming Daddy's song, waiting for a rattler to pull out of the Junction behind him. He'd have to catch it—there was nothing else for him to do.

But the first train to come along came from the other direction, roaring toward him along the track from the south.

Martin peered ahead, but his eyes couldn't match his ears, and so far all he could recognize was the sound. It was a train, though; he felt the steel shudder and sing beneath his feet.

And yet, how could it be? The next station south was Neenah-Menasha, and there was nothing due out of there for hours.

The clouds were thick overhead, and the field mists rolled like a cold fog in a November midnight. Even so, Martin should have been able to see the headlight as the train rushed on. But there was only the whistle, screaming out of the black throat of the night. Martin could recognize the equipment of just about any locomotive ever built, but he'd never heard a whistle that sounded like this one. It wasn't signaling; it was screaming like a lost soul.

He stepped to one side, for the train was almost on top of him now. And suddenly there it was, looming along the tracks and grinding to a stop in less time than he'd believed possible. The wheels hadn't been oiled, because they screamed too, screamed like the damned. But the train slid to a halt and the screams died away into a series of low, groaning sounds, and Martin looked up and saw that this was a passenger train. It was big and black, without a single light shining in the engine cab or any of the long string of cars; Martin couldn't read any lettering on the sides, but he was pretty sure this train didn't belong on the Northwestern Road.

He was even more sure when he saw the man clamber down out of the forward car. There was something wrong about the way he walked, as though one of his feet dragged, and about the lantern he carried. The lantern was dark, and the man held it up to his mouth and blew, and instantly it glowed redly. You don't have to be a member of the Railway Brotherhood to know that this is a mighty

198 • ROBERT BLOCH

peculiar way of lighting a lantern.

As the figure approached, Martin recognized the conductor's cap perched on his head, and this made him feel a little better for a moment—until he noticed that it was worn a bit too high, as though there might be something sticking up on the forehead underneath it.

Still, Martin knew his manners, and when the man smiled at him, he said, "Good evening, Mr. Conductor."

"Good evening, Martin."

"How did you know my name?"

The man shrugged. "How did you know I was the Conductor?"

"You are, aren't you?"

"To you, yes. Although other people, in other walks of life, may recognize me in different roles. For instance, you ought to see what I look like to the folks out in Hollywood." The man grinned. "I travel a great deal," he explained.

"What brings you here?" Martin asked.

"Why, you ought to know the answer to that, Martin. I came because you needed me. Tonight, I suddenly realized you were backsliding. Thinking of joining the Salvation Army, weren't you?"

"Well—" Martin hesitated.

"Don't be ashamed. To err is human, as somebody-or-other-once said. Reader's Digest, wasn't it? Never mind. The point is, I felt you needed me. So I switched over and came your way."

"What for?"

"Why, to offer you a ride, of course. Isn't it better to travel comfortably by train than to march along the cold streets behind a Salvation Army band? Hard on the feet, they tell me, and even harder on the eardrums."

"I'm not sure I'd care to ride your train, sir," Martin said. "Considering where I'm likely to end up."

"Ah, yes. The old argument." The Conductor sighed. "I suppose you'd prefer some sort of bargain, is that it?"

"Exactly," Martin answered.

"Well, I'm afraid I'm all through with that sort of thing. There's no shortage of prospective passengers anymore. Why should I offer you any special inducements?"

"You must want me, or else you wouldn't have bothered to go out of your way to find me."

The Conductor sighed again. "There you have a point. Pride was always my besetting weakness, I admit. And somehow I'd hate to lose you to the competition, after thinking of you as my own all these years." He hesitated. "Yes, I'm prepared to deal with you on your own terms, if you insist."

"The terms?" Martin asked.

"Standard proposition. Anything you want."

"Ah," said Martin.

"But I warn you in advance, there'll be no tricks. I'll grant you any wish you can name—but in return, you must promise to ride the train when the time comes."

"Suppose it never comes?"

"It will."

"Suppose I've got the kind of a wish that will keep me off forever?"

"There is no such wish."

"Don't be too sure."

"Let me worry about that," the Conductor told him. "No matter what you have in mind, I warn you that I'll collect in the end. And there'll be none of this last-minute hocus-pocus, either. No last-hour repentances, no blonde frauleins or fancy lawyers showing up to get you off. I offer a clean deal. That is to say, you'll get what you want, and I'll get what I want."

"I've heard you trick people. They say you're worse than a used-car salesman."

"Now, wait a minute—"

"I apologize," Martin said, hastily. "But it is supposed to be a fact that you can't be trusted."

"I admit it. On the other hand, you seem to think you have found a way out."

"A sure-fire proposition."

"Sure-fire? Very funny!" The man began to chuckle, then halted. "But we waste valuable time, Martin. Let's get down to cases. What do you want from me?"

Martin took a deep breath. "I want to be able to stop Time."

"Right now?"

"No. Not yet. And not for everybody. I realize that would be impossible, of course. But I want to be able to stop Time for myself. Just once, in the future. Whenever I get to a point where I know I'm happy and contented, that's where I'd like to stop. So I can just keep on being happy forever."

"That's quite a proposition," the Conductor mused. "I've got to admit I've never heard anything just like it before—and believe me, I've listened to some lulus in my day." He grinned at Martin. "You've really been thinking about this, haven't you?"

"For years," Martin admitted. Then he coughed. "Well, what do you say?"

"It's not impossible, in terms of your own subjective time-sense," the Conductor murmured. "Yes, I think it could be arranged."

"But I mean really to stop. Not for me just to imagine it."

"I understand. And it can be done."

"Then you'll agree?"

"Why not? I promised you, didn't I? Give me your hand."

Martin hesitated. "Will it hurt very much? I mean, I don't like the sight of blood, and—"

"Nonsense! You've been listening to a lot of poppycock. We already have made our bargain, my boy. I merely intend to put something into your hand. The ways and means of fulfilling your wish. After all, there's no telling at just what moment you may decide to exercise the agreement, and I can't drop everything and come running. So it's better if you can regulate matters for yourself."

"You're going to give me a Time-stopper?"

"That's the general idea. As soon as I can decide what would be practical." The Conductor hesitated. "Ah, the very thing! Here, take my watch."

He pulled it out of his vest-pocket; a railroad watch in a silver case. He opened the back and made a delicate adjustment; Martin tried to see just exactly what he was doing, but the fingers moved in a blinding blur.

"There we are." The Conductor smiled. "It's all set, now. When you finally decide where you'd like to call a halt, merely turn the stem in reverse and unwind the watch until it stops. When it stops, Time stops, for you. Simple enough?" And the Conductor dropped the watch into Martin's hand.

The young man closed his fingers tightly around the case. "That's all there is to it, eh?"

"Absolutely. But remember—you can stop the watch only once. So you'd better make sure that you're satisfied with the moment you choose to prolong. I caution you in all fairness; make very certain of your choice."

"I will." Martin grinned. "And since you've been so fair about it, I'll be fair, too. There's one thing you seem to have forgotten. It doesn't really matter what moment I choose. Because once I stop Time for myself, that means I stay where I am forever. I'll never have to get any older. And if I don't get any older, I'll never die. And if I never die, then I'll never have to take a ride on your train."

The Conductor turned away. His shoulders shook convulsively, and he may have been crying. "And you said I was worse than a used-car salesman," he gasped, in a strangled voice.

Then he wandered off into the fog, and the train-whistle gave an impatient shriek, and all at once it was moving swiftly down the track, rumbling out of sight in the darkness.

Martin stood there, blinking down at the silver watch in his hand. If it wasn't that he could actually see it and feel it there, and if he couldn't smell that peculiar odor, he might have thought he'd imagined the whole thing from start to finish—train, Conductor, bargain, and all.

But he had the watch, and he could recognize the scent left by the train as it departed, even though there aren't many locomotives around that use sulphur and brimstone as fuel.

And he had no doubts about his bargain. That's what came of thinking things through to a logical conclusion. Some fools would have settled for wealth, or power, or Kim Novak. Daddy might have sold out for a fifth of whiskey.

Martin knew that he'd made a better deal. Better? It was foolproof. All he needed to do now was choose his moment.

He put the watch in his pocket and started back down the railroad track. He hadn't really had a destination in mind before, but he did now. He was going to find a moment of happiness...

Now young Martin wasn't altogether a ninny. He realized perfectly well that happiness is a relative thing; there are conditions and degrees of contentment, and they vary with one's lot in life. As a hobo, he was often satisfied with a warm handout, a double-length bench in the park, or a can of Sterno made in 1957 (a vintage year). Many a time he had reached a state of momentary bliss through such simple agencies, but he was aware that there were better things. Martin determined to seek them out.

Within two days he was in the great city of Chicago. Quite naturally, he drifted over to West Madison Street, and there he took steps to elevate his role in life. He became a city bum, a panhandler, a moocher. Within a week he had risen to the point where happiness was a meal in a regular one-arm luncheon joint, a two-bit flop on a real army cot in a real flophouse, and a full fifth of muscatel.

There was a night, after enjoying all three of these luxuries to the full, when Martin thought of unwinding his watch at the pinnacle of intoxication. But he also thought of the faces of the honest johns he'd braced for a handout today. Sure, they were squares, but they were prosperous. They wore good clothes, held good jobs, drove nice cars. And for them, happiness was even more ecstatic—they ate dinner in fine hotels, they slept on innerspring mattresses, they drank blended whiskey.

Squares or no, they had something there. Martin fingered his watch, put aside the temptation to hock it for another bottle of muscatel, and went to sleep determined to get himself a job and improve his happiness-quotient.

When he awoke he had a hangover, but the determination was still with him. Before the month was out Martin was working for a general contractor over on the South Side, at one of the big rehabilitation projects. He hated the grind, but the pay was good, and pretty soon he got himself a one-room apartment out on Blue Island Avenue. He was accustomed to eating in decent restaurants now, and he bought himself a comfortable bed, and every Saturday night he went down to the corner tavern. It was all very pleasant, but—

The foreman liked his work and promised him a raise in a month. If he waited around, the raise would mean that he could afford a second-hand car. With a car, he could even start picking up a girl for a date now and then. Other fellows on the job did, and they seemed pretty happy.

So Martin kept on working, and the raise came through and the car came through and pretty soon a couple of girls came through.

The first time it happened, he wanted to unwind his watch immediately. Until he got to thinking about what some of the older men always said. There was a guy named Charlie, for example, who worked alongside him on the hoist. "When you're young and don't know the score, maybe you get a kick out of running around with those pigs. But after a while, you want something better. A nice girl of your own. That's the ticket."

Martin felt he owed it to himself to find out. If he didn't like it better, he could always go back to what he had.

Almost six months went by before Martin met Lillian Gillis. By that time he'd had another promotion and was working inside, in the office. They made him go to night school to learn how to do simple bookkeeping, but it meant another fifteen bucks extra a week, and it was nicer working indoors.

And Lillian was a lot of fun. When she told him she'd marry him, Martin was almost sure that the time was now. Except that she was sort of—well, she was a nice girl, and she said they'd have to wait until they were married. Of course, Martin couldn't expect to marry her until he had a little more money saved up, and another raise would help, too.

That took a year. Martin was patient, because he knew it was going to be worth it. Every time he had any doubts, he took out his watch and looked at it. But he never showed it to Lillian, or anybody else. Most of the other men wore expensive wristwatches and the old silver railroad watch looked just a little cheap.

Martin smiled as he gazed at the stem. Just a few twists and he'd have something none of these other poor working slobs would ever have. Permanent satisfaction, with his blushing bride—Only getting married turned out to be just the beginning. Sure, it was wonderful, but Lillian told him how much better things would be if they could move into a new place and fix it up. Martin wanted decent furniture, a TV set, a nice car.

So he started taking night courses and got a promotion to the front office. With the baby coming, he wanted to stick around and see his son arrive. And when it came, he realized he'd have to wait until it got a little older, started to walk and talk and develop a personality of its own.

About this time the company sent him out on the road as a trouble-shooter on some of those other jobs, and now he was eating at those good hotels, living high on the hog and the expense-account. More than once he was tempted to unwind his watch. This was the good life… Of course, it would be even better if he just didn't have to work. Sooner or later, if he could cut in on one of the company deals, he could make a pile and retire. Then everything would be ideal. It happened, but it took time. Martin's son was going to high school before he really got up there into the chips. Martin got a strong hunch that it was now or never, because he wasn't exactly a kid anymore.

But right about then he met Sherry Westcott, and she didn't seem to think he was middle-aged at all, in spite of the way he was losing hair and adding stomach. She taught him that a toupee could cover the bald spot and a cummerbund could cover the pot-gut. In fact, she taught him quite a lot and he so enjoyed learning that he actually took out his watch and prepared to unwind it.

Unfortunately, he chose the very moment that the private detectives broke down the door of the hotel room, and then there was a long stretch of time when Martin was so busy fighting the divorce action that he couldn't honestly say he was enjoying any given moment.

When he made the final settlement with Lil he was broke again, and Sherry didn't seem to think he was so young, after all. So he squared his shoulders and went back to work.

He made his pile, eventually, but it took longer this time, and there wasn't much chance to have fun along the way. The fancy dames in the fancy cocktail lounges didn't seem to interest him anymore, and neither did the liquor. Besides, the Doc had warned him off that.

But there were other pleasures for a rich man to investigate. Travel, for instance—and not riding the rods from one hick burg to another, either. Martin went around the world by plane and luxury liner. For a while it seemed as though he would find his moment after all, visiting the Taj Mahal by moonlight. Martin pulled out the battered old watch-case, and got ready to unwind it. Nobody else was there to watch him—

And that's why he hesitated. Sure, this was an enjoyable moment, but he was alone. Lil and the kid were gone, Sherry was gone, and somehow he'd never had time to make any friends. Maybe if he found new congenial people, he'd have the ultimate happiness. That must be the answer—it wasn't just money or power or sex or seeing beautiful things. The real satisfaction lay in friendship.

So on the boat trip home, Martin tried to strike up a few acquaintances at the ship's bar. But all these people were much younger, and Martin had nothing in common with them. Also they wanted to dance and drink, and Martin wasn't in condition to appreciate such pastimes. Nevertheless, he tried.

Perhaps that's why he had the little accident the day before they docked in San Francisco. "Little accident" was the ship's doctor's way of describing it, but Martin noticed he looked very grave when he told him to stay in bed, and he'd called an ambulance to meet the liner at the dock and take the patient right to the hospital.

At the hospital, all the expensive treatment and the expensive smiles and the expensive words didn't fool Martin any. He was an old man with a bad heart, and they thought he was going to die.

But he could fool them. He still had the watch. He found it in his coat when he put on his clothes and sneaked out of the hospital.

He didn't have to die. He could cheat death with a single gesture—and he intended to do it as a free man, out there under a free sky.

That was the real secret of happiness. He understood it now. Not even friendship meant as much as freedom. This was the best thing of all—to be free of friends or family or the furies of the flesh.

Martin walked slowly beside the embankment under the night sky. Come to think of it, he was just about back where he'd started, so many years ago. But the moment was good, good enough to prolong forever. Once a bum, always a bum.

He smiled as he thought about it, and then the smile twisted sharply and suddenly, like the pain twisting sharply and suddenly in his chest. The world began to spin and he fell down on the side of the embankment.

He couldn't see very well, but he was still conscious, and he knew what had happened. Another stroke, and a bad one. Maybe this was it. Except that he wouldn't be a fool any longer. He wouldn't wait to see what was still around the corner.

Right now was his chance to use his power and save his life. And he was going to do it. He could still move, nothing could stop him. He groped in his pocket and pulled out the old silver watch, fumbling with the stem. A few twists and he'd cheat death, he'd never have to ride that Hell-Bound Train. He could go on forever. Forever.

Martin had never really considered the word before. To go on forever—but how? Did he want to go on forever, like this; a sick old man, lying helplessly here in the grass?

No. He couldn't do it. He wouldn't do it. And suddenly he wanted very much to cry, because he knew that somewhere along the line he'd outsmarted himself. And now it was too late. His eyes dimmed, there was a roaring in his ears...

He recognized the roaring, of course, and he wasn't at all surprised to see the train come rushing out of the fog up there on the embankment. He wasn't surprised when it stopped, either, or when the Conductor climbed off and walked slowly toward him.

The Conductor hadn't changed a bit. Even his grin was still the same.

"Hello, Martin," he said. "All aboard."

"I know," Martin whispered. "But you'll have to carry me. I can't walk. I'm not even really talking anymore, am I?"

"Yes you are," the Conductor said. "I can hear you fine. And you can walk, too." He leaned down and placed his hand on Martin's chest. There was a moment of icy numbness, and then, sure enough, Martin could walk after all.

He got up and followed the Conductor along the slope, moving to the side of the train.

"In here?" he asked.

"No, the next car," the Conductor murmured. "I guess you're entitled to ride Pullman. After all, you're quite a successful man. You've tasted the joys of wealth and position and prestige. You've known the pleasures of marriage and father-hood. You've sampled the delights of dining and drinking and debauchery, too, and you traveled high, wide, and handsome. So let's not have any last-minute recriminations."

"All right," Martin sighed. "I can't blame you for my mistakes. On the other hand, you can't take credit for what happened, either. I worked for everything I got. I did it all on my own. I didn't even need your watch."

"So you didn't," the Conductor said, smiling. "But would you mind giving it back to me now?"

"Need it for the next sucker, eh?" Martin muttered.

"Perhaps."

Something about the way he said it made Martin look up. He tried to see the Conductor's eyes, but the brim of his cap cast a shadow. So Martin looked down at the watch instead.

"Tell me something," he said, softly. "If I give you the watch, what will you do with it?"

"Why, throw it into the ditch," the Conductor told him. "That's all I'll do with it." And he held out his hand.

"What if somebody comes along and finds it? And twists the stem backward, and stops Time?"

"Nobody would do that," the Conductor murmured. "Even if they knew."

"You mean, it was all a trick? This is only an ordinary, cheap watch?"

"I didn't say that," whispered the Conductor. "I only said that no one has ever twisted the stem backward. They've all been like you, Martin—looking ahead to find that perfect happiness. Waiting for the moment that never comes."

The Conductor held out his hand again.

Martin sighed and shook his head. "You cheated me after all."

"You cheated yourself, Martin. And now you're going to ride that Hell-Bound Train."

He pushed Martin up the steps and into the car ahead. As he entered, the train began to move and the whistle screamed. And Martin stood there in the swaying Pullman, gazing down the aisle at the other passengers. He could see them sitting there, and somehow it didn't seem strange at all.

Here they were: the drunks and the sinners, the gambling men and the grifters, the big-time spenders, the skirt-chasers, and all the jolly crew. They knew where they were going, of course, but they didn't seem to give a damn. The blinds were drawn on the windows, yet it was light inside, and they were all living it up—singing and passing the bottle and roaring with laughter, throwing the dice and telling their jokes and bragging their big brags, just the way Daddy used to sing about them in the old song.

"Mighty nice traveling companions," Martin said. "Why, I've never seen such a pleasant bunch of people. I mean, they seem to be really enjoying themselves!"

The Conductor shrugged. "I'm afraid things won't be quite so jazzy when we pull into that Depot Way Down Yonder."

For the third time, he held out his hand. "Now, before you sit down, if you'll just give me that watch. A bargain's a bargain—"

Martin smiled. "A bargain's a bargain," he echoed. "I agreed to ride your train if I could stop Time when I found the right moment of happiness. And I think I'm about as happy right here as I've ever been."

Very slowly, Martin took hold of the silver watch-stem.

"No!" gasped the Conductor. "No!"

But the watch-stem turned.

"Do you realize what you've done?" the Conductor yelled. "Now we'll never reach the Depot! We'll just go on riding, all of us—forever!"

Martin grinned. "I know," he said. "But the fun is in the trip, not the destination. You taught me that. And I'm looking forward to a wonderful trip. Look, maybe I can even help. If you were to find me another one of those caps, now, and let me keep this watch—"

And that's the way it finally worked out. Wearing his cap and carrying his battered old silver watch, there's no happier person in or out of this world—now and forever—than Martin. Martin, the new Brakeman on That Hell-Bound Train.

THE GOD ⊙F
DARK LAUGHTER
Michael Chabon

Thirteen days after the Entwhistle-Ealing Bros. circus left Ashtown, beating a long retreat toward its winter headquarters in Peru, Indiana, two boys out hunting squirrels in the woods along Portwine Road stumbled on a body that was dressed in a mad suit of purple and orange velour. They found it at the end of a muddy strip of gravel that began, five miles to the west, as Yuggogheny County Road 22A. Another half mile farther to the east and it would have been left to my colleagues over in Fayette County to puzzle out the question of who had shot the man and skinned his head from chin to crown and clavicle to clavicle, taking ears, eyelids, lips, and scalp in a single grisly flap, like the cupped husk of a peeled orange. My name is Edward D. Satterlee, and for the last twelve years I have faithfully served Yuggogheny County as its district attorney, in cases that have all too often run to the outrageous and bizarre. I make the following report in no confidence that it, or I, will be believed, and beg the reader to consider this, at least in part, my letter of resignation.

The boys who found the body were themselves fresh from several hours' worth of bloody amusement with long knives and dead squirrels, and at first the investigating officers took them for the perpetrators of the crime. There was blood on the boys' cuffs, their shirttails, and the bills of their gray twill caps. But the country detectives and I quickly moved beyond Joey Matuszak and Frankie Corro. For all their familiarity with gristle and sinew and the bright-purple discovered interior of a body, the boys had come into the station looking pale and bewildered, and we found ample evidence at the crime scene of their having lost the contents of their stomachs when confronted with the corpse.

Now, I have every intention of setting down the facts of this case as I understand and experienced them, without fear of the reader's doubting them (or my own sanity), but I see no point in mentioning any further *anatomical* details of the crime, except to say that our coroner, Dr. Sauer, though he labored at the problem with a sad fervor was hard-put to establish conclusively that the victim had been dead before his killer went to work on him with a very long, very sharp knife.

207

The dead man, as I have already mentioned, was attired in a curious suit—the trousers and jacket of threadbare purple velour, the waistcoat bright orange, the whole thing patched with outsized squares of fabric cut from a variety of loudly clashing plaids. It was on account of the patches, along with the victim's cracked and split-soled shoes and a certain undeniable shabbiness in the stuff of the suit, that the primary detective—a man not apt to see deeper than the outermost wrapper of the world (we do not attract, I must confess, the finest police talent in this doleful little corner of western Pennsylvania)—had already figured the victim for a vagrant, albeit one with extraordinarily big feet.

"Those cannot possibly be his real shoes, Ganz, you idiot," I gently suggested. The call, patched through to my boarding house from that gruesome clearing in the woods, had interrupted my supper, which by a grim coincidence had been a Brunswick stew (the specialty of my Virginia-born landlady) or pork and *squirrel*. "They're supposed to make you laugh."

"They *are* pretty funny," said Ganz. "Come to think of it." Detective John Ganz was a large-boned fellow, upholstered in a layer of ruddy flesh. He breathed through his mouth, and walked with a tall man's defeated stoop, and five times a day he took out his comb and ritually plastered his thinning blond hair to the top of his head with a dime-size dab of Tres Flores.

When I arrived at the clearing, having abandoned my solitary dinner, I found the corpse lying just as the young hunters had come upon it, supine, arms thrown up and to either side of the flayed face in a startled attitude that fuelled the hopes of poor Dr. Sauer that the victim's death by gunshot had preceded his mutilation. Ganz or one of the other investigators had kindly thrown a chamois cloth over the vandalized head. I took enough of a peek beneath it to provide me with everything that I or the reader could possibly need to know about the condition of the head—I will never forget the sight of that monstrous, fleshless grin—and to remark the dead man's unusual choice of cravat. It was a giant, floppy bow tie, white with orange and purple polka dots.

"Damn you, Ganz," I said, though I was not in truth addressing the poor fellow, who, I knew, would not be able to answer my question anytime soon. "What's a dead clown doing in my woods?"

We found no wallet on the corpse, nor any kind of identifying objects. My men, along with the better part of the Ashtown Police Department, went over and over the woods east of town, hourly widening the radius of their search. That day, when not attending to my other duties (I was then in the process of breaking up the Dushnyk cigarette-smuggling ring), I managed to work my way back along a chain of inferences to the Entwhistle-Ealing Bros. Circus, which, as I eventually recalled, had recently stayed on the eastern outskirts of Ashtown, at the fringe of the woods where the body was found.

The following day, I succeeded in reaching the circus's general manager, a man named Onheuser, at their winter headquarters in Peru. He informed me over the phone that the company had left Pennsylvania and was now en route to Peru, and I asked him if he had received any reports from the road manager of a clown's having suddenly gone missing.

"Missing?" he said. I wished that I could see his face, for I thought I heard the flatted note of something false in his tone. Perhaps he was merely nervous about talking to a county district attorney. The Entwhistle-Ealing Bros. Circus was a mangy affair, by all accounts, and probably no stranger to pursuit by officers of the court. "Why, I don't believe so, no."

I explained to him that a man who gave every indication of having once been a circus clown had turned up dead in a pinewood outside Ashtown, Pennsylvania.

"Oh, no," Onheuser said. "I truly hope he wasn't one of mine, Mr. Satterlee."

"It is possible you might have left one of your clowns behind, Mr. Onheuser?"

"Clowns are special people," Onheuser replied, sounding a touch on the defensive. "They love their work, but sometimes it can get to be a little, well, too much for them." It developed that Mr. Onheuser had, in his younger days, performed as a clown, under the name of Mr. Wingo, in the circus of which he was now the general manager. "It's not unusual for a clown to drop out for a little while, cool his heels, you know, in some town where he can get a few months of well-earned rest. It isn't *common*, I wouldn't say, but it's not unusual. I will wire my road manager—they're in Canton, Ohio—and see what I can find out."

I gathered, reading between the lines, that clowns were high-strung types, and not above going on the occasional bender. This poor fellow had probably jumped ship here two weeks ago, holing up somewhere with a case of rye, only to run afoul of a very nasty person, possibly one who harbored no great love of clowns. In fact, I had an odd feeling, nothing more than a hunch, really, that the ordinary citizens of Ashtown and its environs were safe, even though the killer was still at large. Once more, I picked up a slip of paper that I had tucked into my desk blotter that morning. It was something that Dr. Sauer had clipped from his files and passed along to me. *Coulrophobia: morbid, irrational fear of or aversion to clowns.*

"Er, listen, Mr. Satterlee," Onheuser went on. "I hope you won't mind my asking. That is, I hope it's not a, well, a confidential police matter, or something of the sort. But I know that when I do get through to them, out in Canton, they're going to want to know.

I guessed, somehow, what he was about to ask me. I could hear the prickling fear behind his curiosity, the note of dread in his voice. I waited him out.

"Did they—was there any—how did he die?"

"He was shot," I said, for the moment supplying the least interesting part of the answer, tugging on that loose thread of fear. "In the head."

"And there was... forgive me. No... no harm done? To the body? Other than the gunshot wound, I mean to say."

"Well, yes, his head *was* rather savagely mutilated," I said brightly. "Is that what you mean to say?"

"Ah! No, no, I don't—"

"The killer or killers removed all the skin from the cranium. It was very skillfully done. Now, suppose you tell me what you know about it."

There was another pause, and a stream of agitated electrons burbled along between us.

"I don't know anything, Mr. District Attorney. I'm really sorry. I really must go now. I'll wire you when I have some—"

The line went dead. He was so keen to hang up on me that he could not even wait to finish his sentence. I got up and went to the shelf where, in recent months, I had taken to keeping a bottle of whiskey tucked behind my bust of Daniel Webster. Carrying the bottle and a dusty glass back to my desk, I sat down and tried to reconcile myself to the thought that I was confronted—not, alas, for the first time in my tenure as chief law-enforcement officer of Yuggogheny County—with a crime whose explanation was going to involve not the usual amalgam of stupidity, meanness, and singularly poor judgment but the incalculable intentions of a being who is genuinely evil. What disheartened me was not that I viewed a crime committed out of the promptings of an evil nature as inherently less liable to solution than the misdeeds of the foolish, the unlucky, or the habitually cruel. On the contrary, evil often expresses itself through refreshingly discernible patterns, through schedules and syllogisms. But the presence of evil, once scented, tends to bring out all that is most irrational and uncontrollable in the public imagination. It is a catalyst for pea-brained theories, gimcrack scholarship, and the credulous cosmologies of hysteria.

At that moment, there was a knock on the door to my office, and Detective Ganz came in. At one time I would have tried to hide the glass of whiskey, behind the typewriter or the photo of my wife and son, but now it did not seem to be worth the effort. I was not fooling anyone. Ganz took note of the glass in my hand with a raised eyebrow and a school-marmish pursing of his lips.

"Well?" I said. There had been a brief period, following my son's death and the subsequent suicide of my dear wife, Mary, when I had indulged the pitying regard of my staff. I now found that I regretted having shown such weakness. "What is it, then? Has something turned up?"

"A cave," Ganz said. "The poor bastard was living in a cave."

The range of low hills and hollows separating lower Yuggogheny from Fayette County is rotten with caves. For many years, when I was a boy, a man named Colonel Earnshawe operated penny tours of the iridescent organ pipes and jagged stone teeth of Neighborsburg Caverns, before they collapsed in the mysterious earthquake of 1919, killing the Colonel and his sister Irene, and putting to rest many strange rumors about that eccentric old pair. My childhood friends and I, ranging in the woods, would from time to time come upon the root-choked mouth of a cave exhaling its cool plutonic breath, and dare one another to leave the sunshine and enter that world of shadow—that entrance, as it always seemed to me, to the legendary past itself, where the bones of Indians and Frenchmen might lie moldering. It was in one of these anterooms of buried history that the beam of a flashlight, wielded by a deputy sheriff from Plunkettsburg, had struck the silvery lip of a can of pork and beans. Calling to his companions, the deputy plunged through a curtain of spiderweb and found himself in the parlor, bedroom, and kitchen of the dead man. There were some cans of chili and hash, a Primus stove, a lantern, a bedroll, a mess kit, and an old Colt revolver, Army issue, loaded and apparently not fired for some time. And there were also books—a Scout guide to roughing it, a collected Blake, and a couple of odd texts, elderly and tattered: one in German called "Über das Finstere Lachen," by a man named Friedrich von Junzt, which appeared to be religious or philosophical in nature, and one a small volume bound in black leather and printed in no alphabet known to me, the letters sinuous and furred with wild diacritical marks.

"Pretty heavy reading for a clown," Ganz said.

"It's not all rubber chickens and hosing each other down with seltzer bottles, Jack."

"Oh, no?"

"No, sir. Clowns have unsuspected depths."

"I'm starting to get that impression, sir."

Propped against the straightest wall of the cave, just beside the lantern, there was a large mirror, still bearing the bent clasps and sheared bolts that had once, I inferred, held it to the wall of a filling-station men's room. At its foot was the item that had earlier confirmed to Detective Ganz—and now confirmed to me as I went to inspect it—the recent habitation of the cave by a painted circus clown: a large, padlocked wooden makeup kit, of heavy and rather elaborate construction. I directed Ganz to send for a Pittsburgh criminalist who had served us with discretion in the horrific Primm case, reminding him that nothing must be touched until this Mr. Espy and his black bag of dusts and luminous powders arrived.

The air in the cave had a sharp, briny tinge; beneath it there was a stale animal musk that reminded me, absurdly, of the smell inside a circus tent.

"Why was he living in a cave?" I said to Ganz. "We have a perfectly nice hotel in town."

"Maybe he was broke."

"Or maybe he thought that a hotel was the first place they would look for him."

Ganz looked confused, and a little bit annoyed, as if he thought I were being deliberately mysterious.

"*Who* was looking for him?"

"I don't know, Detective. Maybe no one. I'm just thinking out loud."

Impatience marred Ganz's fair, bland features. He could tell that I was in the grip of a hunch, and hunches were always among the first considerations ruled out by the procedural practices of Detective John Ganz. My hunches had, admittedly, an uneven record. In the Primm business, one had very nearly got both Ganz and me killed. As for the wayward hunch about my mother's old crony Thaddeus Craven and the strength of his will to quit drinking—I suppose I shall regret indulging that one for the rest of my life.

"If you'll excuse me, Jack…" I said. "I'm having a bit of a hard time with the stench in here."

"I was thinking he might have been keeping a pig." Ganz inclined his head to one side and gave an empirical sniff. "It smells like pig to me."

I covered my mouth and hurried outside in the cool, dank pinewood. I gathered in great lungfuls of air. The nausea passed, and I filled my pipe, walking up and down outside the mouth of the cave and trying to connect this new discovery to my talk with the circus man, Onheuser. Clearly, he had suspected that this clown might have met with a grisly end. Not only that, he had known that his fellow circus people would fear the very same thing—as if there were some coulrophobic madman with a knife who was as much a part of circus lore as the prohibition on whistling in the dressing room or on looking over your shoulder when you marched in a circus parade.

I got my pipe lit, and wandered down into the woods, toward the clearing where the boys had stumbled over the dead man, following a rough trail that the police had found. Really, it was not a trail so much as an impromptu alley of broken saplings and trampled ground that wound a convoluted course down the hill from the cave to the clearing. It appeared to have been blazed a few days before by the victim and his pursuer; near the bottom, where the trees gave way to open sky, there were grooves of plowed earth that corresponded neatly with encrustations on the heels of the clown's giant brogues. The killer must have caught the clown at the edge of the clearing, and then dragged him along by the hair, or by the collar of his shirt, for the last twenty-five yards, leaving this furrowed record of the panicked, slipping flight of the clown. The presumed killer's footprints were everywhere in evidence, and appeared to have been made by a pair of long and pointed boots. But the really puzzling thing was a third set of prints, which Ganz had noticed and mentioned to me, scattered here and there along the cold black mud of the path. They seemed to have been made by a barefoot child of eight or nine years. And damned, as Ganz had concluded his report to me, if that barefoot child did not appear to have been dancing!

I came into the clearing, a little short of breath, and stood listening to the wind in the pines and the distant rumble of the state highway, until my pipe went out. It was a cool afternoon, but the sky had been blue all day and the woods were peaceful and fragrant. Nevertheless, I was conscious of a mounting sense of disquiet as I stood over the bed of sodden leaves where the body had been found. I did not then, nor do I now, believe in ghosts, but as the sun dipped down behind the tops of the trees, lengthening the long shadows encompassing me, I became aware of an irresistible feeling that somebody was watching me. After a moment, the feeling intensified, and localized, as it were, so I was certain that to see who it was I need only turn around. Bravely—meaning not that I am a brave man but that I behaved as if I were—I took my matches from my jacket pocket and relit my pipe. Then I turned. I knew that when I glanced behind me I would not see Jack Ganz or one of the other policemen standing there; any of them would have said something to me by now. No, it was either going to be nothing at all or something that I could not even allow myself to imagine.

It was, in fact, a baboon, crouching on its hind legs in the middle of the trail, regarding me with close-set orange eyes, one hand cupped at its side. It had great puffed whiskers and a long canine snout. There was something in the barrel chest and the muttonchop sideburns that led me to conclude, correctly, as it turned out, that the specimen was male. For all his majestic bulk, the old fellow presented a rather sad spectacle. His fur was matted and caked with mud, and a sticky coating of pine needles clung to his feet. The expression in his eyes was unsettlingly forlorn, almost pleading, I would have said, and in his mute gaze I imagined I detected a hint of outraged dignity. This might, of course, have been due to the hat he was wearing. It was conical, parti-colored with orange and purple lozenges, and ornamented at the tip with a bright-orange pompom. Tied under his chin with a length of black ribbon, it hung from the side of his head at a humorous angle. I myself might have been tempted to kill the man who had tied it to my head.

"Was it you?" I said, thinking of Poe's story of the rampaging orang swinging a razor in a Parisian apartment. Had that story had any basis in fact? Could the dead clown have been killed by the pet or sidekick with whom, as the mystery of the animal smell in the cave now resolved itself, he had shared his fugitive existence?

The baboon declined to answer my question. After a moment, though, he raised his long crooked left arm and gestured vaguely toward his belly. The import of this message was unmistakable, and thus I had the answer to my question—if he could not open a can of franks and beans, he would not have been able to perform that awful surgery on his owner or partner.

"All right, old boy," I said. "Let's get you something to eat." I took a step toward him, watching for signs that he might bolt or, worse, throw himself at me. But he sat, looking miserable, clenching something in his right paw. I crossed the distance between us. His rancid-hair smell was unbearable. "You need a bath, don't you?" I spoke, by reflex, as if I were talking to somebody's tired old dog. "Were you and your friend in the habit of bathing together? Were you there when it happened, old boy? Any idea who did it?"

The animal gazed up at me, its eyes kindled with that luminous and sagacious sorrow that lends to the faces of apes and mandrills an air of cousinly reproach, as if we humans have betrayed the principles of our kind. Tentatively, I reached out to him with one hand. He grasped my fingers in his dry leather paw, and then the next instant he had leapt bodily into my arms, like a child seeking solace. The garbage-and-skunk stench of him burned my nose. I gagged and stumbled backward as the baboon scrambled to wrap his arms and legs around me. I must have cried out; a moment later a pair of iron lids seemed to slam against my skull, and the animal went slack, sliding, with a horrible, human sigh of disappointment, to the ground at my feet.

Ganz and two Ashtown policemen came running over and dragged the dead baboon away from me.

"He wasn't—he was just—" I was too outraged to form a coherent expression of my anger. "You could have hit *me!*"

Ganz closed the animal's eyes, and laid its arms out at its sides. The right paw was still clenched in a shaggy fist. Ganz, not without some difficulty, managed to pry it open. He uttered an unprintable oath.

In the baboon's palm lay a human finger. Ganz and I looked at each other, wordlessly confirming that the dead clown had been in possession of a full complement of digits."

"See that Espy gets that finger," I said. "Maybe we can find out whose it was."

"It's a woman's," Ganz said. "Look at that nail."

I took it from him, holding it by the chewed and bloody end so as not to dislodge any evidence that might be trapped under the long nail. Though rigid, it was strangely warm, perhaps from having spent a few days in the vengeful grip of the animal who had claimed it from his master's murderer. It appeared to be an index finger, with a manicured, pointed nail nearly three-quarters of an inch long. I shook my head.

"It isn't painted," I said. "Not even varnished. How many women wear their nails like that?"

"Maybe the paint rubbed off," one of the policemen suggested.

"Maybe," I said. I knelt on the ground beside the body of the baboon. There was, I noted, a wound on the back of his neck, long and deep and crusted over with dirt and dried blood. I now saw him in my mind's eye, dancing like a barefoot child around the murderer and the victim as they struggled down the path to the clearing. It would take a powerful man to fight such an animal off. "I can't believe you killed our only witness, Detective Ganz. The poor bastard was just giving me a hug."

This information seemed to amuse Ganz nearly as much as it puzzled him.

"He was a monkey, sir," Ganz said. "I doubt he—"

"He could make signs, you fool! He told me he was *hungry.*"

Ganz blinked, trying, I supposed, to append to his personal operations manual this evidence of the potential usefulness of circus apes to police inquiries.

"If I had a dozen baboons like that one on my staff," I said, "I would never have to leave the office."

That evening, before going home, I stopped by the evidence room in the High Street annex and signed out the two books that had been found in the cave that morning. As I walked back into the corridor, I thought I detected an odd odor—odd, at any rate, for that dull expanse of linoleum and buzzing fluorescent tubes—of the sea: a sharp, salty, briny smell. I decided that it must be some new disinfectant being used by the custodian, but it reminded me of the smell of blood from the specimen bags and sealed containers in the evidence room. I turned the lock on the room's door and slipped the books, in their waxy protective envelope, into my briefcase, and walked down High Street to Dennistoun Road, where the public library was. It stayed open late on Wednesday nights, and I would need a German-English dictionary if my college German and I were going to get anywhere with Herr von Junzt.

The librarian, Lucy Brand, returned my greeting with the circumspect air of one who hopes to be rewarded for her forebearance with a wealth of juicy tidbits. Word of the murder, denuded of most of the relevant details, had made the Ashtown *Ambler* yesterday morning, and though I had cautioned the unlucky young squirrel hunters against talking about the case, already conjectures, misprisions, and outright lies had begun wildly to coalesce; I knew the temper of my home town well enough to realise that if I did not close this case soon things might get out of hand. Ashtown, as the events surrounded the appearance of the so-called Green Man, in 1932, amply demonstrated, has a lamentable tendency toward municipal panic.

Having secured a copy of Köhler's Dictionary of the English and German Languages, I went, on an impulse, to the card catalogue and looked up von Junzt, Friedrich. There was no card for any work by this author—hardly surprising, perhaps, in a small-town library like ours. I returned to the reference shelf, and consulted an encyclopedia of philosophical biography and comparable volumes of philologic reference, but found no entry for any von Junzt—a diplomate, by the testimony of his title page, of the University of Tübingen and of the Sorbonne. It seemed that von Junzt had been dismissed, or expunged, from the dusty memory of his discipline.

It was as I was closing the Encyclopedia of Archaeo-Anthropological Research that a name suddenly leapt out at me, catching my eye just before the pages slammed together. It was a word that I had noticed in von Junzt's book: "Urartu." I barely managed to slip the edge of my thumb into the encyclopedia to mark the place; half a second later and the reference might have been lost to me. As it turned out, the name of von Junzt was also contained—sealed up—in the sarcophagus of this entry, a long and tedious one devoted to the work of an Oxford man by the name of St. Dennis T.R. Gladfellow, "a noted scholar," as the entry had it, "in the field of inquiry into the beliefs of the ancient, largely unknown peoples referred to conjecturally today as proto-Urartians." The reference lay buried in a column dense with comparisons among various bits of obsidian and broken bronze:

G's analysis of the meaning of such ceremonial blades admittedly was aided by the earlier discovered of Friedrich von Junzt, at the site of the former Temple of Yrrh, in north central Armenia, among them certain sacrificial artifacts pertaining *to the worship of the proto-Urartian deity Yê-Heh, rather grandly (though regrettably without credible evidence) styled "the god of dark or mocking laughter" by the German, a notorious adventurer and fake whose work, nevertheless, in this instance, has managed to prove useful to science.*

The prospect of spending the evening in the company of Herr von Junzt began to seem even less appealing. One of the most tedious human beings I have ever known was my own mother, who, early in my childhood, fell under the spell of Madame Blavatsky and her followers and proceeded to weary my youth and deplete my patrimony with her devotion to that indigestible caseation of balderdash and lies. Mother drew a number of local simpletons into her orbit, among them poor old drunken Thaddeus Craven, and burnt them up as thoroughly as the earth's atmosphere consumes asteroids. The most satisfying episodes of my career have been those which afforded me the opportunity to prosecute charlatans and frauds and those who preyed on the credulous; I did not now relish the thought of sitting at home with such a man all evening, in particular one who spoke only German.

Nevertheless, I could not ignore the undeniable novelty of a murdered circus clown who was familiar with scholarship—however spurious or misguided—concerning the religious beliefs of proto-Urartians. I carried the Köhler's over to the counter, where Lucy Brand waited eagerly for me to spill some small ration of beans. When I offered nothing for her delectation, she finally spoke.

"Was he a German?" she said, showing unaccustomed boldness, it seemed to me.

"Was *who* a German, my dear Miss Brand?"

"The victim." She lowered her voice to a textbook librarian's whisper, though there was no one in the building but old Bob Spherakis, asleep and snoring in the periodicals room over a copy of *Grit*.

"I—I don't know," I said, taken aback by the simplicity of her inference, or rather by its having escaped me. "I suppose he may have been, yes."

She slid the book across the counter toward me.

"There was another one of them in here this afternoon," she said. "At least, I think he was a German. A Jew, come to think of it. Somehow he managed to find the only book in Hebrew we have in our collection. It's one of the books old Mr. Vorzeichen donated when he died. A prayer book, I think it is. Tiny little thing. Black leather."

This information ought to have struck a chord in my memory, of course, but it did not. I settled my hat on my head, bid Miss Brand good night, and walked slowly home, with the dictionary under my arm and, in my briefcase, von Junzt's stout tome and the little black-leather volume filled with sinuous mysterious script.

I will not tax the reader with an account of my struggles with Köhler's dictionary and the thorny bramble of von Junzt's overheated German prose. Suffice to say that it took me the better part of the evening to make my way through the introduction. It was well past midnight by the time I arrived at the first chapter, and nearing two o'clock before I had amassed the information that I will now pass along to the reader, with no endorsement beyond the testimony of those pages, nor any hope of its being believed.

It was a blustery night; I sat in the study on the top floor of my old house's round tower, listening to the windows rattle in their casements, as if a gang of intruders were seeking a way in. In this high room, in 1885, it was said, Howard Ash, the last living descendant of our town's founder, General Hannaniah Ash, had sealed the blank note of his life and dispatched himself, with postage due, to his Creator. A fugitive draft blew from time to time across my desk and stirred the pages of the dictionary by my left hand. I felt, as I read, as if the whole world were asleep—benighted, ignorant, and dreaming—while I had been left to man the crow's nest, standing lonely vigil in the teeth of a storm that was blowing in from a tropic of dread.

According to the scholar or charlatan Friedrich von Junzt, the regions around what is now northern Armenia had spawned, along with an entire cosmology, two competing cults of incalculable antiquity, which survived to the present day: that of Yê-Heh, the God of Dark Laughter, and that of Ai, the God of Unbearable and Ubiquitous Sorrow. The Yê-Hehists viewed the universe as a cosmic hoax, perpetrated by the father-god Yrrh for unknowable purposes: a place of calamity and cruel irony so overwhelming that the only possible response was a malevolent laughter like that, presumably, of Yrrh himself. The laughing followers of baboon-headed Yê-Heh created a sacred burlesque, mentioned by Pausanias and by one of the travellers in Plutarch's dialogue "On the Passing of the Oracles," to express their mockery of life, death, and all human aspirations. The rite involved the flaying of a human head, severed from the shoulders of one who had died in battle or in the course of some other supposedly exalted endeavor. The clown-priest would don the bloodless mask and then dance, making a public travesty of the noble dead. Through generations of inbreeding, the worshippers of Yê-Heh had evolved into a virtual subspecies of humanity, characterized by distended grins and skin as white as chalk. Von Junzt even claimed that the tradition of painted circus clowns derived from the clumsy imitation, by noninitiates, of these ancient kooks.

The "immemorial foes" of the baboon boys, as the reader may have surmised, were the followers of Ai, the God Who Mourns. These gloomy fanatics saw the world as no less horrifying and cruel than did their archenemies, but their response to the whole mess was a more or less permanent wailing. Over the long millennia since the heyday of ancient Urartu, the Aiites had developed a complicated physical discipline, a sort of jujitsu or calisthenics of murder, which they chiefly employed in a ruthless hunt of followers of Yê-Heh. For they believed that Yrrh, the Absent One, the Silent Devisor who, an eternity ago, tossed the cosmos over his shoulder like a sheet of fish wrap and wandered away leaving not a clue as to his intentions, would not return to explain the meaning of his inexplicable and tragic creation until the progeny of Yê-Heh, along with all copies of the Yê-Hehist sacred book, "Khndzut Dzul," or "The Unfathomable Ruse," had been expunged from the face of the earth. Only then would Yrrh return from his primeval hiatus—"bringing what new horror or redemption," as the German intoned, "none can say."

All this struck me as a gamier variety of the same loony, Zoroastrian plonk that my mother had spent her life decanting, and I might have been inclined to set the whole business aside and leave the case to be swept under the administrative rug by Jack Ganz had it not been for the words with which Herr von Junzt concluded the second chapter of his tedious work:

While the Yê-Hehis gospel of cynicism and ridicule has, quite obviously, spread around the world, the cult itself has largely died out, in part through the predation of foes and in part through chronic health problems brought about by inbreeding. Today [von Junzt's book carried a date of 1849] it is reported that there may be fewer than 150 of the Yê-Hehists left in the world. They have survived, for the most part, by taking on work in travelling circuses. While their existence is known to ordinary members of the circus world, their secret has, by and large, been kept. And in the sideshows they have gone to ground, awaiting the tread outside the wagon, the shadow on the tent-flap, the cruel knife that will, in a mockery of their own long-abandoned ritual of mockery, deprive them of the lily-white flesh of their skulls.

Here I put down the book, my hands trembling from fatigue, and took up the other one, printed in an unknown tongue. "The Unfathomable Ruse"? I hardly thought so; I was inclined to give as little credit as I reasonably could to Herr von Junzt's account. More than likely the small black volume was some inspirational text in the mother tongue of the dead man, a translation of the Gospels perhaps. And yet I must confess there were a few tangential points in von Junzt's account that caused me some misgiving.

There was a scrape then just outside my window, as if a finger with a very long nail were being drawn almost lovingly along the glass. But the finger turned out to be one of the branches of a fine old horse-chestnut tree that stood outside the tower, scratching at the window in the wind. I was relieved and humiliated. Time to go to bed, I said to myself. Before I turned in, I went to the shelf and moved to one side the bust of Galen that I had inherited from my father, a country doctor. I took a quick snort of good Tennessee whiskey, a taste for which I had also inherited from my old man. Thus emboldened, I went over to the desk and picked up the books. To be frank, I would have preferred to leave them there—I would have preferred to burn them, to be really frank—but I felt that it was my duty to keep them about me while they were under my watch. So I slept with the books beneath my pillow, in their wax envelopes, and I had the worst dream of my life.

It was one of those dreams where you are a fly on the wall, a phantom bystander, disembodied and unable to speak or intervene. In it, I was treated to the spectacle of a man whose young son was going to die. The man lived in a corner of the world where, from time to time, evil seemed to bubble up from the rusty red earth like a black combustible compound of ancient things long dead. And yet, year after year, this man met each new outburst of horror, true to his code, with nothing but law books, statutes, and county ordinances, as if sheltering with only a sheet of newspaper those he had sworn to protect, insisting that the steaming black geyser pouring down on them was nothing but a light spring rain. That vision started me laughing, but the cream of the jest came when, seized by a spasm of forgiveness toward his late, mad mother, the man decided not to prosecute one of her old paramours, a rummy by the name of Craven, for driving under the influence. Shortly thereafter, Craven steered his old Hudson Terraplane the wrong way down a one-way street, where it encountered, with appropriate cartoon sound effects, an oncoming bicycle ridden by the man's heedless, darling, wildly pedalling son. That was the funniest thing of all, funnier than the amusing ironies of the man's profession, than his furtive drinking and his wordless, solitary suppers, funnier even than his having been widowed by suicide: the joke of a father's outliving his boy. It was so funny that, watching this ridiculous man in my dream, I could not catch my breath for laughing. I laughed so hard that my eyes popped from their sockets, and my smile stretched until it broke my aching jaw. I laughed until the husk of my head burst like a pod and fell away, and my skull and brains went floating off into the sky, white dandelion fluff, a cloud of fairy parasols.

Around four o'clock in the morning, I woke and was conscious of someone in the room with me. There was an unmistakable tang of sea in the air. My eyesight is poor and it took me a while to make him out in the darkness, though he was standing just beside my bed, with his long thin arm snaked under my pillow, creeping around. I lay perfectly still, aware of the tips of this slender shadow's fingernails and the scrape of his scaly knuckles, as he riled the contents of my head and absconded with them through the bedroom window, which was somehow also the mouth of the Neighborsburg Caverns, with tiny of Colonel Earnshaw taking tickets in the booth.

I awakened now in truth, and reached immediately under the pillow. The books were still there. I returned them to the evidence room at eight o'clock this morning. At nine, there was a call from Dolores and Victor Abbott, at their motor lodge out on the Plunkettsburg Pike. A guest had made an abrupt departure, leaving a mess. I got into a car with Ganz and we drove out to get a look. The Ashtown police were already there, going over the buildings and grounds of the Vista Dolores Lodge. The wastebasket of Room 201 was overflowing with blood-soaked bandages. There was evidence that the guest had been keeping some kind of live bird in the room; one of the neighboring guests reported that it had sounded like a crow. And over the whole room there hung a salt smell that I recognized immediately, a smell that some compared to the smell of the ocean, and others to that of blood. When the pillow, wringing wet, was sent up to Pittsburgh for analysis by Mr. Espy, it was found to have been saturated with human tears.

When I returned from court, late this afternoon, there was a message from Dr. Sauer. He had completed his postmortem and wondered if I would drop by. I took the bottle from behind Daniel Webster and headed on down to the county morgue.

"He was already dead, the poor son of a biscuit eater," Dr. Sauer said, looking less morose than he had the last time we spoke. Sauer was a gaunt old Methodist who avoided strong language but never, so long as I had known him, strong drink. I poured us each a tumbler, and then a second. "It took me a while to establish it because there was something about the fellow that I was missing."

"What was that?"

"Well, I'm reasonably sure that he was a hemophiliac. So my reckoning time of death by coagulation of the blood was all thrown off."

"Hemophilia," I said.

"Yes," Dr. Sauer said. "It is associated with inbreeding, as in the case of royal families in Europe."

Inbreeding. We stood there for a while, looking at the sad bulk of the dead man under the sheet.

"I also found a tattoo," Dr. Sauer added. "The head of a grinning baboon. On his left forearm. Oh, and one other thing. He suffered from some kind of vitiligo. There are white patches on his nape and throat."

Let the record show that the contents of the victim's makeup kit, when it was inventoried, included cold cream, rouge, red greasepaint, a powder puff, some brushes, cotton swabs, and five cans of foundation in a tint the label described as "Olive Male." There was no trace, however, of the white greasepaint with which clowns daub their grinning faces.

Here I conclude my report, and with it my tenure as district attorney for this blighted and unfortunate county. I have staked my career—my life itself—on the things I could see, on the stories I could credit, and on the eventual vindication, when the book was closed, of the reasonable and skeptical approach. In the face of twenty-five years of bloodshed, mayhem, criminality, and the universal human pastime of ruination, I have clung fiercely to Occam's razor, seeking always to keep my solutions unadorned and free of conjecture, and never to resort to conspiracy or any kind of prosecutorial woolgathering. My mother, whenever she was confronted by calamity or personal sorrow, invoked cosmic emanations, invisible empires, ancient prophecies, and intrigues; it has been the business of my life to reject such folderol and seek the simpler explanation. But we were fools, she and I, arrant blockheads, each of us blind to or heedless of the readiest explanation: that the world is an ungettable joke, and our human need to explain its wonders and horrors, our appalling genius for devising such explanations, is nothing more than the rim shot that accompanies the punch line.

I do not know if that nameless clown was the last, but in any case, with such pursuers, there can be few of his kind left. And if there is any truth in the grim doctrine of those hunters, then the return of our father Yrrh, with his inscrutable intentions, cannot be far off. But I fear that, in spite of their efforts over the last ten thousand years, the followers of Ai are going to be gravely disappointed when, at the end of all we know and everything we have ever lost or imagined, the rafters of the world are shaken by a single, terrible guffaw.

THE KING OF THE DJINN

David Ackert

and Benjamin Rosenbaum

Grinding and roaring, the sixteen-wheeler crested a great dune, and Musa rejoiced: there on the horizon, the Mediterranean glittered, blue as Heaven. "God is great!" he shouted as he shifted into second for the downgrade.

Each week, Musa made this trip, carrying a ton of devilish black carbonated soda from the bottling plant of El-Nasr to the decadent tongues of Cairo. And each week, when he reached the open road, his heart threw off its burdens.

In the town, the nights were empty and cold. He'd awaken again and again to the sudden emptiness of his house—his wife Suha dead, his son Jamal away at university. The days were full of packing and loading and tinkering, activity and worry. The men of the bottling plant were always asking Musa for blessings, for amulets, for the resolution of disputes. They'd found out, somehow, that he'd once studied Qur'an and Hadith in the great merkab in Cairo. Sometimes he even had the odd sense that they knew about his meetings with the King of the Jinn. He never knew what to say to them.

On the road, Musa was with God alone. He prayed without words as he drove, using only his breath, opening himself to God as the great bounty of the world came into focus. Every blinding white grain of sand reflected God's glory at Musa; the blue vault of the heavens was filled with God's breath. The roaring engine of the semi and the black ribbon of the highway testified to the great genius God had entrusted in man. Whenever Musa saw a camel or a goat or a date tree in the sand beyond the highway, it was full of life, full to bursting, and the life in it reached out into Musa's heart and whispered to him: we are one.

The King of the Jinn had been right. It was he who had told Musa to abandon the academy, that his soul was starving. Musa had given his inheritance to charity, dropped out of the merkab, and found this simple work. For forty years, he had devoted himself to the secret path of the breath. He slowed down enough for God to find him, and God took Musa in the palm of His hand and held him there. Even at Suha's death, God's love of Musa never wavered; Musa cried like a woman at her graveside, and God held him with strong arms and kept him safe from despair.

Now Musa could see tiny white flecks against the sea's blue. Whitecaps dancing. The road turned parallel to the shore.

As for the King of the Jinn: Musa was not sure, of course, that he really was the King of the Jinn. That was just a guess. He called himself "Gil".

But since 1952, when they had met in a café in the student quarter, Musa had become an old man, and Gil had not aged a day. Gil looked like a Persian, but he spoke a fluent and elegantly complex classical Arabic, the way no one had spoken it since the time of the Prophet. And in Gil's eyes, Musa saw the kind of fearlessness men had only when they were young and arrogant, or old and dying. Yet Gil possessed it all the time.

Given his instrumental role in turning Musa to the true knowledge of God, it was possible that Gil was an angel. But Gil did not act like an intimate of God's. Whenever he showed up, every few years, Gil would ask for Musa to talk of his discoveries, hanging hungrily on every word. It was the hunger of an unmarried youth asking about sex, or a poor man asking about luxury. There was something that kept Gil from embracing God's presence, from accepting God's love as Musa did. For this, Musa pitied him. Even so, Gil also had a majesty about him, an admirable depth and power. To call him just a Jinn seemed meager. Surely he was the King of the Jinn.

When Musa's thoughts turned to Gil like this, it was often a sign that he would be visiting soon. Musa's heart beat happily at the thought. If he had a friend in this world, with Suha gone, it was Gil.

The motor coughed a particularly agonized cough, and Musa looked quickly at the temperature gauge. It was in the red. Musa had no clock; he used the motor's periodic overheating to time his daily prayers. He pulled the truck off the road into a patch of sand packed down by the tracks of many tires.

Musa sloshed the remaining water in his canteen skeptically. He had drunk too much that morning; there was not enough for drinking and purification both. He clambered out of the cab and, in the shadow of the truck, did the ablutions with sand. Then he performed the prayers. How it lifted his heart, to be one with the millions of the faithful, all yearning towards the city where God had spoken to his best and final prophet. Thus had God completed the work of filling the world with his bounty: air to breathe, water to drink, food to eat, people to love, and finally the gentle and firm rules and the great poetry and wisdom of the Word of God.

His prayers done, his motor still smoking, Musa sat cross-legged in the shadow of the truck, on the sand, and allowed his soul to rise.

His soul ascended and saw the sand and the date palms, the ribbon of highway and the truck, the sea and cliffs beyond. It swept higher and he saw the fertile valley of the Nile and the teeming cities and the ships and cars and airplanes.

His soul descended into Cairo and flew through the streets, yearning for his only son Jamal. It was a Tuesday, when his son had no classes at the University. He would probably be watching soccer and drinking coffee at his favorite café.

Musa's soul entered the café. But there was no laughter, no shouting and no urging on of players running after a ball. The men sat in silence. The room was choked in anger.

On the television, Zionists were committing their atrocities in the camps of Palestine. Tanks fired at young men. Bulldozers tore houses open. Old women, old men, and children ran bleeding through the devastated and smoking streets.

Musa's soul found Jamal sitting in the corner, his fist clenched around his coffee glass. Jamal was full of fury. Why?, Jamal's heart cried. How can we bear our weakness, how can we bear to see the innocents suffer!

My son, Musa's soul called to him, do not be taken by hopelessness. There are always evildoers in the world, as long as men are weak. Take heart, God is great—

But Jamal's heart did not listen. It went on suffering and raging in its own misery and shame. I sit here in Cairo, it said, studying engineering, while America buys bullets to kill the children of Palestine. While my father delivers America's soda pop! To earn the money with which I buy this coffee. We are all slaves!

Musa's soul was struck as if his son had kicked him. It flew out of the café and out of Cairo, and back into his body where it sat by the road.

Musa prayed that his son would not be swept away by hatred and bitterness. As he prayed, his heart galloped like a horse, and he was aware of the thousands of bottles of Pepsi sitting in their crates in his truck, and he prayed that his son would not despise him.

At the sound of a car stopping, Musa opened his eyes. There, in the glare of the desert sun beyond the shadow of the truck, was the King of the Jinn getting out of a Jeep.

Musa got quickly to his feet. He bowed deeply in greeting.

The King of the Jinn walked into the shadow of the truck and bowed back. He was wearing a European-style suit and carrying a briefcase. Beneath his calm smile Musa could feel a great, empty yearning.

"It is good to see you," Musa said as they shook hands. He resisted the urge to embrace the King of the Jinn.

"And you."

Musa's heart was still thundering from his encounter with his son, and he was dizzy and sweating from the heat. He looked at the smile of the creature in the suit, and all of a sudden he found himself asking the question that was always on his tongue, but which he had told himself he would never ask. And so stupidly—he had not inquired as to the health of the other, had not offered him water or coffee or apologized for his inability to provide proper hospitality, had not told or heard any stories, had exchanged neither compliments nor proverbs. His stupid tongue simply jumped up and asked rudely: "are you a Jinn?" Then he clapped his hands to his mouth in horror.

Gil grinned. As if he approved of the question, was proud of Musa for asking it. He squinted and pursed his lips as if deciding how to answer.

"I don't know what I am," he said finally. "But that is the best proposal I have heard so far."

Musa stood transfixed with embarrassment. He coughed and tried to think of what to say to return the conversation to its proper course.

"And since I am, for lack of a better word, a Jinn," said Gil, "I should offer you wishes."

"Oh no!" said Musa. "I could not accept!"

"Musa," said Gil, "our encounters have been valuable to me over the years. You deserve at least one wish. Would you like it for yourself, or for your son?"

"For my son!" gulped Musa. Old fool!, he shouted at himself silently. You did not even refuse three times! And yet he was so worried about Jamal.

"Very well," said Gil, smiling and handing Musa the briefcase. "Here is what your son wants most in the world."

A chill went through Musa's hands. He set the briefcase down in the sand and looked at the latches. They were shiny and brass.

"Well?" said Gil.

Musa reached out with shaking hands to open the latches.

Most of the contents of the briefcase were covered with a cloth of fine dark silk. But on top of the silk was a blue plastic booklet with a picture of an eagle, and western letters on it. An American passport. Musa opened it. There was his son's picture. He looked up at Gil, confused. Was this what Jamal wanted? To go to America? Musa did not know what to think. There would be dangers, temptations—but at the same time Jamal would learn much, and perhaps—

Gil's eyes were sad—though Musa thought, again, that the sadness was on the surface, like a mask; that beneath it was emptiness—and he gestured back to the briefcase.

Musa looked down again. He moved aside the black cloth.

The rest of the briefcase was filled with thick yellow cylinders of something that looked like clay, connected with electrical tape and wires.

"No!" shouted Musa. "No!"

With that passport, Jamal could go through the border at Taba, into Israel. He could go to the busiest cafe, the most crowded corner in Tel Aviv, and murder himself and a hundred Zionists—Zionists in baby carriages, Zionists in bridal gowns, Zionists with canes and false teeth—and join the Palestinian martyrs in their struggle.

But surely Jamal would never get through! He would be searched at the border. They would find the bomb, they would punish him! But the stillness in Gil's eyes told Musa that the King of the Jinn had granted far greater wishes, and that Jamal would not fail.

Musa prostrated himself at Gil's feet, burying his face in his hands. "No!" he cried. "Please! Please, sir—Gil—whatever you are—do not do this!"

"Musa, you have become complacent," Gil said. "You have a special gift, a special connection to God. But it is too easy for you. You drive your truck and have visions and take it for granted that it is enough. But God requires more. Sometimes God requires sacrifice."

Musa struggled to his feet, looked wildly around. "This isn't what God wants!

Don't tell me God wants my only child martyred! To murder innocents along with the guilty, as the oppressors themselves do! Is that how the Prophet fought?"

"Musa," said Gil, and in his voice was an ancient, ancient cold, with ten thousand years of emptiness behind it, "there is nothing you can do about that. Here is what you can do."

Musa waited, watching Gil's bottomless, glittering eyes.

"Write an amulet," Gil said. "For the protection and redemption of your son's soul. If you think he is going into sin—write an amulet to protect him."

Musa wanted to protest more, to plead. But he found himself going to the cab of his truck and getting in, and taking his parchment and pens and ink out of the dashboard compartment. His tears mixed with the ink as he wrote the declaration of faith and he prayed, fervently, fervently. He no longer felt God's grace in every grain of sand. He felt as though God's grace was hidden at the end of a very long tunnel.

Gil came and took the amulet from him. "Thank you, Musa," he said, and walked to his Jeep and got in.

Musa started his motor. He would rush to Cairo, too, and talk to Jamal. He would persuade him of the wrongness of his actions. He released the clutch and eased onto the road as the Jeep pulled out ahead of him.

But Jamal would not listen. Musa could hear his arguments now. How else to strike at the powerful oppressor, he would say, but the only way we can? Could Musa say for certain he was wrong? But not my son!, Musa's heart shouted. God, God, not my only son! Jamal would look at him with contempt. Driver of sodas.

The road began a long, steep downgrade. Musa took his foot off the gas, lightly tapped the brake as he followed. The Jeep sped on ahead.

Jamal would not listen. He would be gone, and Musa's life would be empty. If Jamal could only get through this period of youth and fiery blood, if he could only learn patience and humility, learn to trust God and endure injustice… but he would not have time. The briefcase in the Jeep ahead would see to that.

Help me, God, help me, Musa prayed, with all his heart.

Was it God? Or was it His Adversary? Or simply desperation? Something took Musa's foot off the brake and slammed it down onto the gas and held it there.

The truck groaned and shuddered as it surged down the downgrade. It gained on the Jeep.

The distance closed.

Gil looked back over his shoulder, and in that instant Musa realized he loved the King of the Jinn as a dog loves his master, and he slammed on the brake. But the inertia of a ton of Pepsi would not entertain such indecision. The wheels of the cab locked and skidded, the trailer behind slammed it forward, and the nose of the semi smashed into the Jeep, flipping it into the air. Musa was thrown into the wheel; his jaw snapped and blood fountained across the windshield. He felt the truck fishtail off the road, and then roll; he heard the sound of ten thousand shattering Pepsi bottles fill the desert.

Then it stopped.

Then came the sound of ten thousand bottles slowly reassembling themselves.

The droplets of blood swam slowly back through the air into Musa's veins.

The glass of the windshield reassembled, each piece flying silently, gracefully, back to meet its brothers, glinting in the sunlight. Behind them, the sky rolled back to its proper place above Musa.

The Jeep swung down out of the sky, kissed the cab of the truck, and moved forward onto the road. The trailer of the rig drew back and the cab settled down. Musa's foot left the brake and landed on the gas.

Musa had never known what a gift the gentle movement of time was, the succession of each moment in its turn, each moment a wide open field of freedom and of choice. He felt his heart beat backwards, his breath move backwards through his lungs. He wanted to shout, to cry, to escape the cab, but he could not: his limbs moved in their predetermined course as the Jeep and the truck crept backwards up the hill. Slowly, time dragged its Musa puppet back through the seconds, until he was in his cab parked at the side of the road handing the amulet to Gil. Then it released him.

Gil gasped and spat into the sand. He was shaking. So was Musa. The King of the Jinn looked up at him with a wild, feral grin.

Musa gripped the wheel, his heart exploding in terror.

"You surprised me, Musa," Gil said. "I'm amazed. It's been a very long time since any of my collection surprised me." He looked out over the desert horizon. "I think I've had you on too loose a leash. Your talents make you too hard to control."

Musa watched this King of the Djinn in silent terror. This creature who played with time as a child plays with dolls. Was this Satan himself?

Gil glanced back and saw Musa's face, and for a moment the chill, benign mask of the King of the Djinn slipped, and Musa saw what was under it: desperate rage. Then Gil smiled coolly again.

"You're a fool, Musa. I'm not Time's master. I'm its victim."

He looked down at the amulet and stroked it once, gently. Then he slipped it into his pocket.

He threw the briefcase into the Jeep but did not get in. He stood and watched Musa. "Well," he said finally, "There's nothing you can do to save Jamal. And you won't see me again. So all your earthly attachments are gone now, Musa. You're free to find God." Gil pointed out into the empty desert. "He's that way."

Musa looked in the direction the Djinn had pointed.

God's presence was everywhere, in every grain of sand. It was the same huge, infinite, bountiful light.

But how could he have misjudged it before, to think it gentle? It was alien, inhuman, immense beyond reason. If every human was burned alive, if every creature on earth was swallowed in the fire, the Divine Presence would not blink.

Musa began to walk.

He walked until his throat was dry and his breathing shallow. Then, after a while, he was crawling. It was only a spiritual exercise.

The sand was hot against his cheek.

The Sahara was a vast white page, and Musa's body one tiny, bent black letter written on it. Seen from above, seen from very far away.

SUMMON, BIND, BANISH

Nick Mamatas

Alick, in Egypt, with his wife, Rose. Nineteen aught-four. White-kneed tourists. Rose, several days into their trip, starts acting oddly, imperiously. She has always wanted to travel, but Alick's Egypt is not the one she cares for. She prefers the Sphinx from the outside, tea under tents, tourist guides who haggle on her behalf for dates and carpeting. She wanted to take a trip on a barge down the Nile, but there weren't any. At night, she spreads for Alick, or sometimes takes to her belly, and lets him slam and grind till dawn. Mother was wrong. There is no need to think of the Empire, or the men in novels. There's Alick's wheezing in her ear, the thick musk of an animal inside the man, and waves of pleasure that stretch a moment into an aeon. But she doesn't sleep well because the Egypt morning is too hot.

A ritual Alick performs fails. The ambience of Great Pyramid cannot help but inspire, but the shuffling travelers and their boorish gawking profanes the sacred. The sylphs he promised to show his wife—"This time, it will work, Rose. I can feel it," Alick had said, his voice gravel—do not appear. But Rose enters a trance and stays there, smiling slightly and not sweating even under the brassy noon sky for the rest of the trip.

"They're waiting for you!" she says. And under her direction Alick sits in the cramped room of his pension and experiences the presence of Aiwaz, the minister of Hoor-paar-kraat, Crowley's Holy Guardian Angel, and the transmitter of Liber AL vel Legis, sub figura CCXX, The Book of the Law, as delivered by XCIII=418 to DCLXVI.

Alick doesn't turn around. He never turns around over the course of those three days of hysterical dictation. But he feels Aiwaz, and has an idea of how the spirit manifests. A young man, slightly older than Alick, but dark, strong, and active. As ancient in aspect and confident in tone as Alick wishes he was. The voice, he's sure, is coming from the corner of the room, over his left shoulder. He writes for an hour a day, for three days.

See, people, here's the thing about Crowley. He was racist and sexist and sure hated the Jews. Real controversial stuff, sure, but you know what, he was

229

actually in the dead center of polite opinion when it came to the Negroes and the swarthies and money-grubbing kikes and all those other lovely stereotypes. Crowley and the Queen could have had tea and, with pinkies raised, tittered over some joke about big black Zulu penises. Except. Except Crowley loved the penis. His sphincter squeaked like an old shoe as he performed the most sacred of his magickal rituals. That's where it all comes from, really. The Book of the Law, Aiwaz, the whole deal with the HGA, it's buggery. That dark voice over the left shoulder is a spirit, all right, but it's the spirit of Herbert Charles Pollitt, who'd growl and bare his teeth and sink them into the back of Crowley's neck after bending the wizard over and penetrating him.

You ever get that feeling? The feeling of a presence, generally at night, alone, in a home that's quiet except for the lurch and hum of an old fridge, or the clock radio mistuned to be half on your favorite radio station and half in the null region of frizzy static. It's not all in your head, by definition, as you willed your anxieties and neuroses three feet back and to the left. And that's a good thing. Because the last thing you want is for it to be in your skull with you. The last thing you want is for me to be in your skull with you. Crowley pushed it out, out into the world.

Alick in Berlin, fuming at being passed over for a position in British Intelligence. He may be a beast, a fornicator, a bugger, and ol' 666 himself, but he had been a Cambridge man, bloody hell, and that used to mean something. He didn't betray Great Britain, it was Great Britain that betrayed him. Rose did as well, the fat old cow of a whore. So he works for the Hun, in Germany, writing anti-British propaganda: "For some reason or other the Germans have decided to make the damage as widespread as possible, instead of concentrating on one quarter. A great deal of damage was done in Croydon where my aunt lives. Unfortunately her house was not hit. Count Zeppelin is respectfully requested to try again. The exact address is Eton Lodge, Outram Road." But the old home still tugs at him, so he declares himself Supreme and Holy King of Ireland, Iona, and all other Britons within the sanctuary of the Gnosis.

The winter is damp and the water stays in his lungs. The doctor gives him heroin and Alick dreams in his small bed that his teeth are falling out. Awake again, he files a few into points, so dosed on his medication that he sees not himself in the mirror, but another man both in and before the mirror. The real Alick, the young boy whose mother called him the Beast for masturbating, stands in the well of the doorway, watching and feeling only the slightest cracking pain, in sympathy with the actions of the Alick he's watching. Those fangs will find a wrist one day.

I reached enlightenment in the way most people do these days; in my mother's basement, which I converted into a mockery of an apartment thanks to a dorm fridge, a hot plate I never used, and a half-bath my father put in for me after I promised to go back to school and at least get my Associates degree. The only good thing about community college is that it gave me access to the library at the state college, and like any library of size, it had a fairly decent collection of occult materials. I'm from a pretty conservative area too, so the books had been left on the shelf, unmolested in their crumbling hardcovers, for years. Old-looking occult books are the most frequently stolen from libraries, after classic art books that could pass for porn, but out here in Bucks County even the metalheads couldn't care less, so I was the one who got to swipe them.

Mostly they stayed under my futons, infusing the dust bunnies with dark wisdom. I really have to credit my metaphysical sensitivities to my old television. It's a black-and-white number with knobs and everything, one for VHF and one for UHF. Small, it had been on my grandmother's bureau for years, off entirely except on Sundays, when she'd tune in to Channel 67 and watch the Polish language programming. After she died my mother's brothers and sisters swarmed all over her tiny room, snagging gaudy jewelry—lots of silver and amethysts, and broaches the size of small turtles—the fancy sheets she hadn't used in the entire time I'd been alive, the passbooks and checkbooks, and then, finally, the dense Old World furniture she'd kept after selling her own place and moving in with us.

By 3 PM that afternoon, when I got home from class, the only things left in grandma's room were her TV (on the floor in a dusty rectangle where the dresser had been), a doily (still atop the TV) and the smell of her, half-perfume, half-sausage (everywhere). I stood around while my mother cried and father frowned, but I felt nothing except the presence. Grandma on the steps, walking down into the living room. Grandma on the big easy chair, tiny feet in beige stockings poking up on the ottoman, her lips smacking as she turned the page in a newspaper. The sharp wheeze before she spoke to ask for something, her voice a crackling song on a 78 RPM record, tinny and distant. I'd always cringe a bit when she walked into the room, and was cringing now that she was gone. Because she wasn't.

Alick in Italy, at the height of his powers. The Scarlet Woman, Leah Hirsig, is with him. Two points pierce her flesh just past her palms, like a tiny stigmata run dry. The UK is still out of the question, and Germany, an economic basketcase: Theodor Reuss and the other members of the Ordo Templi Orientis are pushing wheelbarrows full of scrip to the store to buy their daily bread. New York reeks of piss and Irishmen, and Leah's family up in the Bronx would not understand that she has become Alostrael, the womb of God. Paris has gaping cunts and asses aplenty, but the magus needs time and space enough to remove himself from the world. And Cefalu, in Palermo, Sicily, is cheap and far from the bald old bugger Mussolini. The weather does his lungs good, but the taste of opium, the sizzle of heroin boiling, never leaves his tongue or nostrils.

Sometimes Alick fancies himself the Lord of the Manor when a peasant knocks on the door and offers him a goat. "Milk good yes," the man says, likely the only English he knows. Twenty minutes later, staggering drunk around the courtyard, eyes crossed, goat following the rope lead in his hand like a reluctant dog, does Alick realize the goat is a male. No milk there. Leah declares, time and again, till she believes it: "I dedicate myself wholly to the great work. I will work for wickedness, I will kill my heart, I will be shameless before all men, I will freely prostitute my body to all creatures." Alick, for a moment, decides to test her on the peasant, but in the end takes the goat.

The ritual is cramped. Alick had gathered around home a mess of bohemians, whores, and thrillseekers, but there's real magic to be had, he's sure of it. Alostrael bends over the altar, and Alick nods for the goat to be brought in. Its phallus is huge and swings low, so Alick himself masturbates it, and then, with his other hand on one of the goat's horns, leads the animal to Leah. The penetration is clumsy, he misses twice and Leah squirms—Christ, Alick hates it when women squirm, and that's why he's always preferred men, and to be the one presenting his anus. He can do it right. Just lay there, bitch!—but finally it is achieved. Leah is a wild woman, all hips and twisted back, and Alick watches her closely. At the moment of orgasm, her orgasm, not the goat's, he'll slit the beast's throat. But the bucking bitch comes too quickly and Alick can't let go of the goat to reach the knife, so he wraps his thick hands around its neck, fingers searching under the coarse hair to find the vein and throat, and starts to squeeze and crush.

I didn't get very good reception in the basement, but I had nothing else to do but try, and leaf through some of the books: Liber Ala, 777, but I wasn't in the right state of mind for them. My reception was as poor of that of the television. I played with the UHF knob for a bit and found, I thought, the station that played the Polish-language programming grandma liked, but it didn't come through clearly. With a bit of pressure I managed to balance the knob between two stations and got two signals at once, both indistinct and distant under the wall of frizzling static. I sat on the floor, back to the edge of my futon and watched, and then it came to me.

There are two universes. The one we all live in, the one you're familiar with. Ever stub your toe or have an orgasm or eat a sandwich or have sand in the crack of your ass after a day at the beach or an afternoon in your garden? That's the universe of Choronzon, the dweller in the Abyss, the dark being who stands between us and our perfect, enlightened selves. Choronzon is not really a being, he is our being, all our flaws and hidden shames, the swirling chaos that we keep down deep in ourselves, and the moments of avoidance and denial we manage to come up with to keep it at bay.

The second universe, that's the good stuff.

Alick in London, on the wrong side of history. Mussolini had deported him as if the Sicilian countryside wasn't already full of goatfuckers. Leah's womb betrayed him, with a girl that died and a miscarriage. The womb of God, the holy grail, was filled with tainted blood. Alick's bankrupt too, having lost a libel case against bohemian writer Nina Hamnett, who dared call him a "black magician."

The Germans went crazy again, reveling in the secrets of the Black Lodge, in the evil reflection of Logos known as Da'ath to the Hebrews. The Hebrews being broiled and gassed by Hitler. Rudolph Hess lands in Scotland and a peasant with a pitchfork captures him with ease. Ian Fleming has an idea: send Alick to interview the superstitious Hess. The Nazis were steeped in the occult, and even based some of their troop movements on astrology. Fleming's superiors nix the plan, but Alick knows Hess. He can sense the German across the moors and miles, twitching and counting on his fingers, dictating plaintive letters to phantom secretaries in his cell, crying for his friend, Hitler.

Alick isn't the wickedest man in the world anymore; he doesn't even rank in the top twenty.

Okay, so now I am going to enlighten you all. Liber XV O.T.O. Ecclesiæ Gnosticæ Catholicæ Canon Missæ describes the Gnostic mass. Here's the big secret: in the same way a Catholic or Eastern Orthodox practitioner takes communion and thus eats the body of Christ, the Logos made flesh, the worshippers of the Gnostic mass eat Da'ath. By the way, just knowing this makes you an initiate of the Ninth Degree, so enjoy it and welcome to the club.

Alick in Hastings, nineteen forty-seven. It's cold. Alick is fat now, and needn't shave his head to keep up his mien of bald menace. Menace, like a bone-white old man who spends fifteen hours a day in bed is a menace. His Will is gone; he can't even rouse his own member anymore, much less the members of any of the innumerable little sects and cults that have kept up the chants and the publications of this or that inane ritual. Really, Alick was just pulling it all out of his bum half the time. The other half, well, most of that was just for the opium and the cock, and, rarely, a cunt. And the tiny fraction left over? Well, Alick decides, some of that was almost real.

There's a presence, closer now than it has ever been. No longer is it the Holy Guardian Angel, or a young boy heavy with promises weighing on Alick's back. It's in his chest. His lungs are drowning in mucus and scum. Alick wishes the loo would expire, so that a plumber would be called. Alick would summon him into the room like a minor goetic spirit, and demand that the worker take his snake and jam it down Alick's throat, and pull out the aeons of black muck he's sure are living in his chest. Regrets? Alick has a few.

"Sometimes, I hate myself," he says, then he dies, closed like a window.

My name is Ron Jankowaik, and I am thirty-two years old. I work as an underwriter for Jefferson Insurance Partners Ltd. in Danbury, Connecticut. In the last election, I voted for Joseph Lieberman even though he left the Democratic Party. I liked his guts for standing up for what he believes in, even if I don't necessarily agree with everything he says. I felt that the other guy was too much of a loose canon. I also believe that marriage is something between a man and a woman.

I'm married to Marie Jankowaik. She likes to joke that she knew it was love when she would no longer cringe at the idea of having the last name Jankowaik. We met when I was tending bar in New Haven. She went to U. Conn and I had drifted up there from Pennsylvania, poking around in cheap apartments and reading a lot, mostly, and we hooked up right away. Been seven years and still going strong. Once we qualify for a mortgage, and if we can find a place for less than a quarter mil around here, we're definitely going to start a family.

Marie likes it from behind, which is fine with me as she is a bit on the hippy side. She's quiet, grunts and whimpers, never screams or moans. When we're together like that I often find my mind wandering. Her wide back is like a blank canvas, or a movie screen the second before the lights go down. And just under the skin, Da'ath, the abyss. And beyond that seeming infinity The Tree of Life, the Sephirot, pulses. With every thrust, electricity shoots up the spine and across her nervous system.

Look, people, I know what you're thinking. You're expecting this story to end with some tedious murder. I slide my forearm down and around Marie's neck, and then at the moment of orgasm I jerk, and yank, separating her skull from her vertebrae like my grandmother used to do with goats when she was a kid. No. Here's how the story ends.

I feel a presence over my shoulder and to the left, when I bend over my desk at work in my little cube, or when I'm idling in my car at a red light that's taking its sweet time changing to green, or when I'm fucking my wife with nothing but the creak of bedsprings and the hum of our well-wired ranch house encaging us.

Sometimes I turn around and it's a co-worker. Marc, eager to buttonhole me in the break room and tell me about the college Spring Break when he went to Boystown and took in the donkey show. Two guys have to work together to tie the donkey's front legs, and lift him up so that one of the strippers can blow him, then she straddles and fucks. Crowley was deported and derided for years in the press, chased from his home and nearly burnt out of the boarding houses he was reduced to living in. Marc tells his story for laughs, and bonded well enough with the regional manager over it that now he's my supervisor.

Sometimes I turn around and it's a woman in the car behind me, hunched over the wheel, her face a twist of aggravation, one hand clenched like talons, the other reaching over and smacking the kid in the car seat next to her. A white woman, middle class, the nice part of Danbury. (Yes, you were wondering what color she was.) Crowley cried when his first baby girl died, and when the other was born dead. This woman just wants the shrieking to stop.

And at night, when I have Marie bent over the corner of the bed, and I let my mind wander, I feel that presence back and to the left, and I see myself. A better me, fucking a better Marie, atop a better bedspread in a better universe. Through the abyss I'll crawl one day and leave all the detritus of this world behind. I'll walk into and through the wall of white static and into that better reality. We have to live through this world of horrors, eat all it offers, and then we can transcend.

I squeeze her flesh, gasp, and come.

THE BOTTLE IMP
Robert Louis Stevenson

There was a man of the Island of Hawaii, whom I shall call Keawe; for the truth is, he still lives, and his name must be kept secret; but the place of his birth was not far from Honaunau, where the bones of Keawe the Great lie hidden in a cave. This man was poor, brave, and active; he could read and write like a schoolmaster; he was a first-rate mariner besides, sailed for some time in the island steamers, and steered a whaleboat on the Hamakua coast. At length it came in Keawe's mind to have a sight of the great world and foreign cities, and he shipped on a vessel bound to San Francisco.

This is a fine town, with a fine harbour, and rich people uncountable; and in particular, there is one hill which is covered with palaces. Upon this hill Keawe was one day taking a walk with his pocket full of money, viewing the great houses upon either hand with pleasure. "What fine houses these are!" he was thinking, "and how happy must those people be who dwell in them, and take no care for the morrow!" The thought was in his mind when he came abreast of a house that was smaller than some others, but all finished and beautified like a toy; the steps of that house shone like silver, and the borders of the garden bloomed like garlands, and the windows were bright like diamonds; and Keawe stopped and wondered at the excellence of all he saw. So stopping, he was aware of a man that looked forth upon him through a window so clear that Keawe could see him as you see a fish in a pool upon the reef. The man was elderly, with a bald head and a black beard; and his face was heavy with sorrow, and he bitterly sighed. And the truth of it is, that as Keawe looked in upon the man, and the man looked out upon Keawe, each envied the other.

All of a sudden, the man smiled and nodded, and beckoned Keawe to enter, and met him at the door of the house.

"This is a fine house of mine," said the man, and bitterly sighed. "Would you not care to view the chambers?"

So he led Keawe all over it, from the cellar to the roof, and there was nothing there that was not perfect of its kind, and Keawe was astonished.

"Truly," said Keawe, "this is a beautiful house; if I lived in the like of it I should be laughing all day long. How comes it, then, that you should be sighing?"

"There is no reason," said the man, "why you should not have a house in all points similar to this, and finer, if you wish. You have some money, I suppose?"

"I have fifty dollars," said Keawe; "but a house like this will cost more than fifty dollars."

The man made a computation. "I am sorry you have no more," said he, "for it may raise you trouble in the future; but it shall be yours at fifty dollars."

"The house?" asked Keawe.

"No, not the house," replied the man; "but the bottle. For, I must tell you, although I appear to you so rich and fortunate, all my fortune, and this house itself and its garden, came out of a bottle not much bigger than a pint. This is it."

And he opened a lockfast place, and took out a round-bellied bottle with a long neck; the glass of it was white like milk, with changing rainbow colours in the grain. Withinsides something obscurely moved, like a shadow and a fire.

"This is the bottle," said the man; and, when Keawe laughed, "You do not believe me? Try, then, for yourself. See if you can break it."

So Keawe took the bottle up and dashed it on the floor till he was weary; but it jumped on the floor like a child's ball, and was not injured.

"This is a strange thing," said Keawe. "For by the touch of it, as well as by the look, the bottle should be of glass."

"Of glass it is," replied the man, sighing more heavily than ever; "but the glass of it was tempered in the flames of hell. An imp lives in it, and that is the shadow we behold there moving; or so I suppose. If any man buy this bottle the imp is at his command; all that he desires—love, fame, money, houses like this house, ay, or a city like this city—all are his at the word uttered. Napoleon had this bottle, and by it he grew to be the king of the world; but he sold it at last, and fell. Captain Cook had this bottle, and by it he found his way to so many islands; but he too sold it, and was slain upon Hawaii. For, once it is sold, the power goes and the protection; and unless a man remain content with what he has, ill will befall him."

"And yet you talk of selling it yourself?" Keawe asked.

"I have all I wish, and I am growing elderly," replied the man. "There is one thing the imp cannot do—he cannot prolong life; and, it would not be fair to conceal from you, there is a drawback to the bottle; for if a man die before he sells it, he must burn in hell for ever."

"To be sure, that is a drawback and no mistake," cried Keawe. "I would not meddle with the thing. I can do without a house, thank God; but there is one thing I could not be doing with one particle, and that is to be damned."

"Dear me, you must not run away with things," returned the man. "All you have to do is to use the power of the imp in moderation, and then sell it to someone else, as I do to you, and finish your life in comfort."

"Well, I observe two things," said Keawe. "All the time you keep sighing like a maid in love, that is one; and, for the other, you sell this bottle very cheap."

"I have told you already why I sigh," said the man. "It is because I fear my health is breaking up; and, as you said yourself, to die and go to the devil is a pity for anyone. As for why I sell so cheap, I must explain to you there is a peculiarity about the bottle. Long ago, when the devil brought it first upon earth, it was extremely expensive, and was sold first of all to Prester John for many millions of dollars; but it cannot be sold at all, unless sold at a loss. If you sell it for as much as you paid for it, back it comes to you again like a homing pigeon. It follows that the price has kept falling in these centuries, and the bottle is now remarkably cheap. I bought it myself from one of my great neighbours on this hill, and the price I paid was only ninety dollars. I could sell it for as high as eighty-nine dollars and ninety-nine cents, but not a penny dearer, or back the thing must come to me. Now, about this there are two bothers. First, when you offer a bottle so singular for eighty-odd dollars, people suppose you to be jesting. And second—but there is no hurry about that—and I need not go into it. Only remember it must be coined money that you sell it for."

"How am I to know that this is all true?" asked Keawe.

"Some of it you can try at once," replied the man. "Give me your fifty dollars, take the bottle, and wish your fifty dollars back into your pocket. If that does not happen, I pledge you my honour I will cry off the bargain and restore your money."

"You are not deceiving me?" said Keawe.

The man bound himself with a great oath.

"Well, I will risk that much," said Keawe, "for that can do no harm." And he paid over his money to the man, and the man handed him the bottle.

"Imp of the bottle," said Keawe, "I want my fifty dollars back." And sure enough he had scarce said the word before his pocket was as heavy as ever.

"To be sure this is a wonderful bottle," said Keawe.

"And now, good morning to you, my fine fellow, and the devil go with you for me!" said the man.

"Hold on," said Keawe, "I don't want any more of this fun. Here, take your bottle back."

"You have bought it for less than I paid for it," replied the man, rubbing his hands. "It is yours now; and, for my part, I am only concerned to see the back of you." And with that he rang for his Chinese servant, and had Keawe shown out of the house.

Now, when Keawe was in the street, with the bottle under his arm, he began to think. "If all is true about this bottle, I may have made a losing bargain," thinks he. "But perhaps the man was only fooling me." The first thing he did was to count his money; the sum was exact—forty-nine dollars American money, and one Chili piece. "That looks like the truth," said Keawe. "Now I will try another part."

The streets in that part of the city were as clean as a ship's decks, and though it was noon, there were no passengers. Keawe set the bottle in the gutter and walked away. Twice he looked back, and there was the milky, round-bellied bottle where he left it. A third time he looked back, and turned a corner; but he had scarce done so, when something knocked upon his elbow, and behold! it was the long neck sticking up; and as for the round belly, it was jammed into the pocket of his pilot coat.

"And that looks like the truth," said Keawe.

The next thing he did was to buy a cork-screw in a shop, and go apart into a secret place in the fields. And there he tried to draw the cork, but as often as he put the screw in, out it came again, and the cork as whole as ever.

"This is some new sort of cork," said Keawe, and all at once he began to shake and sweat, for he was afraid of that bottle.

On his way back to the port-side, he saw a shop where a man sold shells and clubs from the wild islands, old heathen deities, old coined money, pictures from China and Japan, and all manner of things that sailors bring in their sea-chests. And here he had an idea. So he went in and offered the bottle for a hundred dollars. The man of the shop laughed at him at the first, and offered him five; but indeed, it was a curious bottle—such glass was never blown in any human glass-works, so prettily the colours shown under the milky white, and so strangely the shadow hovered in the midst; so, after he had disputed awhile after the manner of his kind, the shopman gave Keawe sixty silver dollars for the thing, and set it on a shelf in the midst of his window.

"Now," said Keawe, "I have sold that for sixty which I bought for fifty—so, to say truth, a little less, because one of my dollars was from Chili. Now I shall know the truth upon another point."

So he went back on board his ship, and, when he opened his chest, there was the bottle, and had come more quickly than himself. Now Keawe had a mate on board whose name was Lopaka.

"What ails you?" said Lopaka, "that you stare in your chest?"

They were alone in the ship's forecastle, and Keawe bound him to secrecy, and told all.

"This is a very strange affair," said Lopaka; "and I fear you will be in trouble about this bottle. But there is one point very clear—that you are sure of the trouble, and you had better have the profit in the bargain. Make up your mind what you want with it; give the order, and if it is done as you desire, I will buy the bottle myself; for I have an idea of my own to get a schooner, and go trading through the islands."

"That is not my idea," said Keawe; "but to have a beautiful house and garden on the Kona Coast, where I was born, the sun shining in at the door, flowers in the garden, glass in the windows, pictures on the walls, and toys and fine carpets on the tables, for all the world like the house I was in this day—only a storey higher, and with balconies all about like the king's palace; and to live there without care and make merry with my friends and relatives."

"Well," said Lopaka, "let us carry it back with us to Hawaii, and if all comes true, as you suppose, I will buy the bottle, as I said, and ask a schooner."

Upon that they were agreed, and it was not long before the ship returned to Honolulu, carrying Keawe and Lopaka, and the bottle. They were scarce come ashore when they met a friend upon the beach, who began at once to condole with Keawe.

"I do not know what I am to be condoled about," said Keawe.

"Is it possible you have not heard," said the friend, "your uncle—that good old man—is dead, and your cousin—that beautiful boy—was drowned at sea?"

Keawe was filled with sorrow, and, beginning to weep and to lament he forgot about the bottle. But Lopaka was thinking to himself, and presently, when Keawe's grief was a little abated, "I have been thinking," said Lopaka. "Had not your uncle lands in Hawaii, in the district of Kau?"

"No," said Keawe, "not in Kau; they are on the mountain-side—a little way south of Hookena."

"These lands will now be yours?" asked Lopaka.

"And so they will," said Keawe, and began again to lament for his relatives.

"No," said Lopaka, "do not lament at present. I have a thought in my mind. How if this should be the doing of the bottle? For here is the place ready for your house."

"If this be so," cried Keawe, "it is a very ill way to serve me by killing my relatives. But it may be, indeed; for it was in just such a station that I saw the house with my mind's eye."

"The house, however, is not yet built," said Lopaka.

"No, nor like to be!" said Keawe, "for though my uncle has some coffee and ava and bananas, it will not be more than will keep me in comfort; and the rest of that land is the black lava."

"Let us go to the lawyer," said Lopaka; "I have still this idea in my mind."

Now, when they came to the lawyer's, it appeared Keawe's uncle had grown monstrous rich in the last days, and there was a fund of money.

"And here is the money for the house!" cried Lopaka.

"If you are thinking of a new house," said the lawyer, "here is the card of a new architect, of whom they tell me great things."

"Better and better!" cried Lopaka. "Here is all made plain for us. Let us continue to obey orders."

So they went to the architect, and he had drawings of houses on his table.

"You want something out of the way," said the architect. "How do you like this?" and he handed a drawing to Keawe.

Now, when Keawe set eyes on the drawing, he cried out aloud, for it was the picture of his thought exactly drawn.

"I am for this house," thought he. "Little as I like the way it comes to me, I am in for it now, and I may as well take the good along with the evil."

So he told the architect all that he wished, and how he would have that house furnished, and about the pictures on the wall and the knick-knacks on the tables; and he asked the man plainly for how much he would undertake the whole affair.

The architect put many questions, and took his pen and made a computation; and when he had done he named the very sum that Keawe had inherited.

Lopaka and Keawe looked at one another and nodded.

"It is quite clear," thought Keawe, "that I am to have this house, whether or not it comes from the devil, and I fear I will get little good by that; and of one thing I am sure, I will make no more wishes as long as I have this bottle. But with the house I am saddled, and I may as well take the good along with the evil."

So he made his terms with the architect, and they signed a paper; and Keawe and Lopaka took ship again and sailed to Australia; for it was concluded between them they should not interfere at all, but leave the architect and the bottle imp to build and to adorn that house at their own pleasure.

The voyage was a good voyage, only all the time Keawe was holding in his breath, for he had sworn he would utter no more wishes, and take no more favours from the devil. The time was up when they got back. The architect told them that the house was ready, and Keawe and Lopaka took a passage in the Hall, and went down Kona way to view the house, and see if all had been done fitly according to the thought that was in Keawe's mind.

Now, the house stood on the mountain-side, visible to ships. Above, the forest ran up into the clouds of rain; below, the black lava fell in cliffs, where the kings of old lay buried. A garden bloomed about that house with every hue of flowers; and there was an orchard of papaia on the one hand and an orchard of breadfruit on the other, and right in front, toward the sea, a ship's mast had been rigged up and bore a flag. As for the house, it was three storeys high, with great chambers and broad balconies on each. The windows were of glass, so excellent that it was as clear as water and as bright as day. All manner of furniture adorned the chambers. Pictures hung upon the wall in golden frames: pictures of ships, and men fighting, and of the most beautiful women, and of singular places; nowhere in the world are there pictures of so bright a colour as those Keawe found hanging in his house. As for the knick-knacks, they were extraordinary fine: chiming clocks and musical boxes, little men with nodding heads, books filled with pictures, weapons of price from all quarters of the world, and the most elegant puzzles to entertain the leisure of a solitary man. And as no one would care to live in such chambers, only to walk through and view them, the balconies were made so broad that a whole town might have lived upon them in delight; and Keawe knew not which to prefer, whether the back porch, where you got the land breeze, and looked upon the orchards and the flowers, or the front balcony, where you could drink the wind of the sea, and look down the steep wall of the mountain and see the Hall going by once a week or so between Kookena and the hills of Pele, or the schooners plying up the coast for wood and ava and bananas.

When they had viewed all, Keawe and Lopaka sat on the porch.

"Well," asked Lopaka, "is it all as you designed?"

"Words cannot utter it," said Keawe. "It is better than I dreamed, and I am sick with satisfaction."

"There is but one thing to consider," said Lopaka; "all this may be quite natural, and the bottle imp have nothing whatever to say to it. If I were to buy the bottle, and got no schooner after all, I should have put my hand in the fire for nothing. I gave you my word, I know; but yet I think you would not grudge me one more proof."

"I have sworn I would take no more favours," said Keawe. "I have gone already deep enough."

"This is no favour I am thinking of," replied Lopaka. "It is only to see the imp himself. There is nothing to be gained by that, and so nothing to be ashamed of; and yet, if I once saw him, I should be sure of the whole matter. So indulge me so far, and let me see the imp; and, after that, here is the money in my hand, and I will buy it."

"There is only one thing I am afraid of," said Keawe. "The imp may be very ugly to view; and if you once set eyes upon him you might be very undesirous of the bottle."

"I am a man of my word," said Lopaka. "And here is the money betwixt us."

"Very well," replied Keawe. "I have a curiosity myself. So come, let us have one look at you, Mr. Imp."

Now as soon as that was said, the imp looked out of the bottle, and in again, swift as a lizard; and there sat Keawe and Lopaka turned to stone. The night had quite come, before either found a thought to say or voice to say it with; and then Lopaka pushed the money over and took the bottle.

"I am a man of my word," said he, "and had need to be so, or I would not touch this bottle with my foot. Well, I shall get my schooner and a dollar or two for my pocket; and then I will be rid of this devil as fast as I can. For to tell you the plain truth, the look of him has cast me down."

"Lopaka," said Keawe, "do not you think any worse of me than you can help; I know it is night, and the roads bad, and the pass by the tombs an ill place to go by so late, but I declare since I have seen that little face, I cannot eat or sleep or pray till it is gone from me. I will give you a lantern, and a basket to put the bottle in, and any picture or fine thing in all my house that takes your fancy—and be gone at once, and go sleep at Hookena with Nahinu."

"Keawe," said Lopaka, "many a man would take this ill; above all, when I am doing you a turn so friendly, as to keep my word and buy the bottle; and for that matter, the night and the dark, and the way by the tombs, must be all tenfold more dangerous to a man with such a sin upon his conscience, and such a bottle under his arm. But for my part, I am so extremely terrified myself, I have not the heart to blame you. Here I go then; and I pray God you may be happy in your house, and I fortunate with my schooner, and both get to heaven in the end in spite of the devil and his bottle."

So Lopaka went down the mountain; and Keawe stood in his front balcony, and listened to the clink of the horse's shoes, and watched the lantern go shining down the path, and along the cliff of caves where the old dead are buried; and all the time he trembled and clasped his hands, and prayed for his friend, and gave glory to God that he himself had escaped out of that trouble.

But the next day came very brightly, and that new house of his was so delightful to behold that he forgot his terrors. One day followed another, and Keawe dwelt there in perpetual joy. He had his place on the back porch; it was there he ate and lived, and read the stories in the Honolulu newspapers; but when anyone came by they would go in and view the chambers and the pictures. And the fame of the house went far and wide; it was called Ka-Hale Nui—the Great House—in all Kona; and sometimes the Bright House, for Keawe kept a Chinaman, who was all day dusting and furbishing; and the glass and the gilt, and the fine stuffs, and the pictures, shown as bright as the morning. As for Keawe himself, he could not walk in the chambers without singing, his heart was so enlarged; and when ships sailed by upon the sea, he would fly his colours on the mast.

So time went by, until one day Keawe went upon a visit as far as Kailua to certain of his friends. There he was well feasted; and left as soon as he could the next morning, and rode hard, for he was impatient to behold his beautiful house; and, besides, the night then coming on was the night in which the dead of old days go abroad in the sides of Kona; and having already meddled with the devil, he was the more chary of meeting with the dead. A little beyond Honaunau, looking far ahead, he was aware of a woman bathing in the edge of the sea; and she seemed a well -grown girl, but he thought no more of it. Then he saw her white shift flutter as she put it on, and then her red holoku; and by the time he came abreast of her she was done with her toilet, and had come up from the sea, and stood by the track-side in her red holoku, and she was all freshened with the bath, and her eyes shone and were kind. Now Keawe no sooner beheld her than he drew rein.

"I thought I knew everyone in this country," said he. "How comes it that I do not know you?"

"I am Kokua, daughter of Kiano," said the girl, "and I have just returned from Oahu. Who are you?"

"I will tell you who I am in a little," said Keawe, dismounting from his horse, "but not now. For I have a thought in my mind, and if you knew who I was, you might have heard of me, and would not give me a true answer. But tell me, first of all, one thing: Are you married?"

At this Kokua laughed aloud. "It is you who ask questions," said she. "Are you married yourself?"

"Indeed, Kokua, I am not," replied Keawe, "and never thought to be until this hour. But here is the plain truth. I have met you here at the roadside, and I saw your eyes, which are like the stars, and my heart went to you as swift as a bird. And so now, if you want none of me, say so, and I will go on to my own place; but if you think me no worse than any other young man, say so, too, and I will turn aside to your father's for the night, and tomorrow I will talk with the good man."

Kokua said never a word, but she looked at the sea and laughed.

"Kokua," said Keawe, "if you say nothing, I will take that for the good answer; so let us be stepping to your father's door."

She went on ahead of him, still without speech; only sometimes she glanced back and glanced away again, and she kept the string of her hat in her mouth.

Now, when they had come to the door, Kiano came out on his verandah, and cried out and welcomed Keawe by name. At that the girl looked over, for the fame of the great house had come to her ears; and, to be sure, it was a great temptation. All that evening they were very merry together; and the girl was as bold as brass under the eyes of her parents, and made a mock of Keawe, for she had a quick wit. The next day he had a word with Kiano, and found the girl alone.

"Kokua," said he, "you made a mock of me all the evening; and it is still time to bid me go. I would not tell you who I was, because I have so fine a house, and I feared you would think too much of that house and too little of the man that loves you. Now you know all, and if you wish to have seen the last of me, say so at once."

"No," said Kokua; but this time she did not laugh, nor did Keawe ask for more.

This was the wooing of Keawe; things had gone quickly; but so an arrow goes, and the ball of a rifle swifter still, and yet both may strike the target. Things had gone fast, but they had gone far also, and the thought of Keawe rang in the maiden's head; she heard his voice in the breach of the surf upon the lava, and for this young man that she had seen but twice she would have left father and mother and her native islands. As for Keawe himself, his horse flew up the path of the mountain under the cliff of tombs, and the sound of the hoofs, and the sound of Keawe singing to himself for pleasure echoed in the caverns of the dead. He came to the Bright House, and still he was singing. He sat and ate in the broad balcony, and the Chinaman wondered at his master, to hear how he sang between the mouthfuls. The sun went down into the sea, and the night came; and Keawe walked the balconies by lamplight, high on the mountains, and the voice of his singing startled men on ships.

"Here am I now upon my high place," he said to himself. "Life may be no better; this is the mountain top; and all shelves about me towards the worse. For the first time I will light up the chambers, and bathe in my fine bath with the hot water and the cold, and sleep alone in the bed of my bridal chamber."

So the Chinaman had word, and he must rise from sleep and light the furnaces; and as he wrought below, beside the boilers, he heard his master singing and rejoicing above him in the lighted chambers. When the water began to be hot the Chinaman cried to his master; and Keawe went into the bathroom; and the Chinaman heard him sing as he filled the marble basin; and heard him sing, and the singing broken, as he undressed; until of a sudden, the song ceased. The Chinaman listened, and listened; he called up the house to Keawe to ask if all were well, and Keawe answered him "Yes," and bade him go to bed; but there was no more singing in the Bright House; and all night long, the Chinaman heard his master's feet go round and round the balconies without repose.

Now the truth of it was this: as Keawe undressed for his bath, he spied upon his flesh a patch like a patch of lichen on a rock, and it was then that he stopped singing. For he knew the likeness of that patch, and knew that he was fallen in the

Chinese Evil. Now, it is a sad thing for any man to fall into this sickness. And it would be a sad thing for anyone to leave a house so beautiful and so commodious, and depart from all his friends to the north coast of Molokai between the mighty cliff and the sea-breakers. But what was that the case of the man Keawe, he who had met his love but yesterday, and won her but that morning, and now saw all his hopes break, in a moment, like a piece of glass?

Awhile he sat upon the edge of the bath; then sprang, with a cry and ran outside; and to and fro, to and fro, along the balcony, like one despairing.

"Very willingly could I leave Hawaii, the home of my fathers," Keawe was thinking. "Very lightly could I leave my house, the high-placed, the many-windowed, here upon the mountains. Very bravely could I go to Molokai, to Kalaupapa by the cliffs, to live with the smitten and to sleep there, far from my fathers. But what wrong have I done, what sin lies upon my soul, that I should have encountered Kokua coming cool from the sea water in the evening? Kokua, the soul ensnarer! Kokua, the light of my life! Her may I never wed, her may I look upon no longer, her may I no more handle with my living hand; and it is for this, it is for you, O Kokua! that I pour my lamentations!"

Now you are to observe what sort of a man Keawe was, for he might have dwelt there in the Bright House for years, and no one been the wiser of his sickness; but he reckoned nothing of that, if he must lose Kokua. And again, he might have wed Kokua even as he was; and so many would have done, because they have the souls of pigs; but Keawe loved the maid manfully, and he would do her no hurt and bring her in no danger.

A little beyond the midst of the night, there came in his mind the recollection of that bottle. He went round to the back porch, and called to memory the day when the devil had looked forth; and at the thought ice ran in his veins.

"A dreadful thing is the bottle," thought Keawe, "and dreadful is the imp, and it is a dreadful thing to risk the flames of hell. But what other hope have I to cure the sickness or to wed Kokua? What!" he thought, "would I beard the devil once, only to get me a house, and not face him again to win Kokua?"

Thereupon he called to mind it was the next day the Hall went by on her return to Honolulu. "There must I go first," he thought, "and see Lopaka. For the best hope that I have now is to find that same bottle I was so please to be rid of."

Never a wink could he sleep; the food stuck in his throat; but he sent a letter to Kiano, and about the time when the steamer would be coming, rode down beside the cliff of the tombs. It rained; his horse went heavily; he looked up at the black mouths of the caves, and he envied the dead that slept there and were done with trouble; and called to mind how he had galloped by the day before, and was astonished. So he came down to Hookena, and there was all the country gathered for the steamer as usual. In the shed before the store they sat and jested and passed the news; but there was no matter of speech in Keawe's bosom, and he sat in their midst and looked without on the rain falling on the houses, and the surf beating among the rocks, and the sighs arose in his throat.

"Keawe of the Bright House is out of spirits," said one to another. Indeed, and so he was, and little wonder.

Then the Hall came, and the whaleboat carried him on board. The after-part of the ship was full of Haoles who had been to visit the volcano, as their custom is; and the midst was crowded with Kanakas, and the forepart with wild bulls from Hilo and horses from Kau; but Keawe sat apart from all in his sorrow, and watched for the house of Kiano. There it sat, low upon the shore in the black rocks and shaded by the cocoa palms, and there by the door was a red holoku, no greater than a fly, and going to and fro with a fly's busyness.

"Ah, queen of my heart," he cried, "I'll venture my dear soul to win you!"

Soon after, darkness fell, and the cabins were lit up, and the Haoles sat and played at the cards and drank whisky as their custom is; but Keawe walked the deck all night; and all the next day, as they steamed under the lee of Maui or of Molokai, he was still pacing to and from like a wild animal in a menagerie.

Towards evening they passed Diamond Head, and came to the pier of Honolulu. Keawe stepped out among the crowd and began to ask for Lopaka. It seemed he had become the owner of a schooner—none better in the islands—and was gone upon an adventure as far as Pola Pola or Kahiki; so there was no help to be looked for from Lopaka. Keawe called to mind a friend of his, a lawyer in the town (I must not tell his name), and inquired of him. They said he was grown suddenly rich, and had a fine new house upon Waikiki shore; and this put a thought in Keawe's head, and he called a hack and drove to the lawyer's house.

The house was all brand-new, and the trees in the garden no greater than walking-sticks, and the lawyer, when he came, had the air of a man well pleased.

"What can I do to serve you?" said the lawyer.

"You are a friend of Lopaka's," replied Keawe, "and Lopaka purchased from me a certain piece of goods that I thought you might enable me to trace."

The lawyer's face became very dark. "I do not profess to misunderstand you, Mr. Keawe," said he, "though this is an ugly business to be stirring in. You may be sure I know nothing, but yet I have a guess, and if you would apply in a certain quarter I think you might have news."

And he named the name of a man, which, again, I had better not repeat. So it was for days, and Keawe went from one to another, finding everywhere new clothes and carriages, and fine new houses and men everywhere in great contentment, although, to be sure, when he hinted at his business their faces would cloud over.

"No doubt I am upon the track," thought Keawe. "These new clothes and carriages are all the gifts of the little imp, and these glad faces are the faces of men who have taken their profit and got rid of the accursed thing in safety. When I see pale cheeks and hear sighing, I shall know that I am near the bottle."

So it befell at last that he was recommended to a Haole in Beritania Street. When he came to the door, about the hour of the evening meal, there were the usual marks of the new house, and the young garden, and the electric light shining in the windows; but when the owner came, a shock of hope and fear ran through Keawe; for here was a young man, white as a corpse, and black about the eyes, the hair shedding from his head, and such a look in his countenance as a man may have when he is waiting for the gallows.

"Here it is, to be sure," thought Keawe, and so with this man he no ways veiled his errand. "I am come to buy the bottle," said he.

At the word, the young Haole of Beritania Street reeled against the wall.

"The bottle!" he gasped. "To buy the bottle!" Then he seemed to choke, and seizing Keawe by the arm carried him into a room and poured out wine in two glasses.

"Here is my respects," said Keawe, who had been much about with Haoles in his time. "Yes," he added, "I am come to buy the bottle. What is the price by now?"

At that word the young man let his glass slip through his fingers, and looked upon Keawe like a ghost.

"The price," said he; "the price! you do not know the price?"

"It is for that I am asking you," returned Keawe. "But why are you so much concerned? Is there anything wrong about the price?"

"It has dropped a great deal in value since your time, Mr. Keawe," said the young man, stammering.

"Well, well, I shall have the less to pay for it," said Keawe. "How much did it cost you?"

The young man was as white as a sheet. "Two cents," said he.

"What?" cried Keawe, "two cents? Why, then, you can only sell it for one. And he who buys it—" The words died upon Keawe's tongue; he who bought it could never sell it again, the bottle and the bottle imp must abide with him until he died, and when he died must carry him to the red end of hell.

The young man of Beritania Street fell upon his knees. "For God's sake buy it!" he cried. "You can have all my fortune in the bargain. I was mad when I bought it at that price. I had embezzled money at my store; I was lost else; I must have gone to jail."

"Poor creature," said Keawe, "you would risk your soul upon so desperate an adventure, and to avoid the proper punishment of your own disgrace; and you think I could hesitate with love in front of me. Give me the bottle, and the change which I make sure you have all ready. Here is a five-cent piece."

It was as Keawe supposed; the young man had the change ready in a drawer; the bottle changed hands, and Keawe's fingers were no sooner clasped upon the stalk than he had breathed his wish to be a clean man. And, sure enough, when he got home to his room and stripped himself before a glass, his flesh was whole like an infant's. And here was the strange thing: he had no sooner seen this miracle, than his mind was changed within him, and he cared naught for the Chinese Evil, and little enough for Kokua; and had but the one thought, that here he was bound to the bottle imp for time and for eternity, and had no better hope but to be a cinder for ever in the flames of hell. Away ahead of him he saw them blaze with his mind's eye, and his soul shrank, and darkness fell upon the light.

When Keawe came to himself a little, he was aware it was the night when the band played at the hotel. Thither he went, because he feared to be alone; and there, among happy faces, walked to and fro, and heard the tunes go up and down, and saw Berger beat the measure, and all the while he heard the flames crackle, and saw the red fire burning in the bottomless pit. Of a sudden the band played Kiki-au-ao; that was a song that he had sung with Kokua, and at the strain courage returned to him.

"It is done now," he thought, "and once more let me take the good along with the evil."

So it befell that he returned to Hawaii by the first steamer, and as soon as it could be managed he was wedded to Kokua, and carried her up the mountain side to the Bright House.

Now it was so with these two, that when they were together, Keawe's heart was stilled; but so soon as he was alone he fell into a brooding horror, and heard the flames crackle, and saw the red fire burn in the bottomless pit. The girl, indeed, had come to him wholly; her heart leapt in her side at sight of him, her hand clung to his; and she was so fashioned from the hair upon her head to the nails upon her toes that none could see her without joy. She was pleasant in her nature. She had the good word always. Full of song she was, and went to and fro in the Bright House, the brightest thing in its three storeys, carolling like the birds. And Keawe beheld and heard her with delight, and then must shrink upon one side, and weep and groan to think upon the price that he had paid for her; and then he must dry his eyes, and wash his face, and go and sit with her on the broad balconies joining in her songs, and, with a sick spirit, answering her smiles.

There came a day when her feet began to be heavy and her songs more rare; and now it was not Keawe only that would weep apart, but each would sunder from the other and sit in opposite balconies with the whole width of the Bright House betwixt. Keawe was so sunk in his despair, he scarce observed the change, and was only glad he had more hours to sit alone and brood upon his destiny and was not so frequently condemned to pull a smiling face on a sick heart. But one day, coming softly through the house, he heard the sound of a child sobbing, and there was Kokua rolling her face upon the balcony floor, and weeping like the lost.

"You do well to weep in this house, Kokua," he said. "And yet I would give the head off my body that you (at least) might have been happy."

"Happy!" she cried. "Keawe, when you lived alone in your Bright House, you were the word of the island for a happy man; laughter and song were in your mouth, and your face was as bright as the sunrise. Then you wedded pour Kokua; and the good God knows what is amiss in her—but from that day you have not smiled. Ah!" she cried, "what ails me? I thought I was pretty, and I knew I loved him. What ails me that I throw this cloud upon my husband?"

"Poor Kokua," said Keawe. He sat down by her side, and sought to take her hand; but that she plucked away. "Poor Kokua," he said, again. "My poor child—my pretty. And I thought all this while to spare you! Well, you shall know all. Then, at least, you will pity poor Keawe; then you will understand how much he loved you in the past—that he dared hell for your possession—and how much he loves you still (the poor condemned one), that he can yet call up a smile when he beholds you."

With that, he told her all, even from the beginning.

"You have done this for me?" she cried. "Ah, well then what do I care!"—and she clasped and wept upon him.

"Ah, child!" said Keawe, "and yet, when I consider the fire of hell, I care a good deal!"

"Never tell me," said she; "no man can be lost because he loved Kokua, and no other fault. I tell you, Keawe, I shall save you with these hands, or perish in your company. What! you loved me, and gave your soul, and you think I will not die to save you in return?"

"Ah, my dear! you might die a hundred times, and what difference would that make?" he cried, "except to leave me lonely till the time comes of my damnation?"

"You know nothing," said she. "I was educated in a school in Honolulu; I am no common girl. And I tell you, I shall save my lover. What is this you say about a cent? But all the world is not American. In England they have a piece they call a farthing, which is about half a cent. Ah! sorrow!" she cried, "that makes it scarcely better, for the buyer must be lost, and we shall find none so brave as my Keawe! But, then, there is France; they have a small coin there which they call a centime, and these go five to the cent or thereabout. We could not do better. Come, Keawe, let us go to the French islands; let us go to Tahiti, as fast as ships can bear us. There we have four centimes, three centimes, two centimes one centime; four possible sales to come and go on; and two of us to push the bargain. Come, my Keawe! kiss me, and banish care. Kokua will defend you."

"Gift of God!" he cried. "I cannot think that God will punish me for desiring aught so good! Be it as you will, then; take me where you please: I put my life and my salvation in your hands."

Early the next day Kokua was about her preparations. She took Keawe's chest that he went with sailoring; and first she put the bottle in a corner; and then packed it with the richest of the clothes and the bravest of the knick-knacks in the house. "For," said she, "we must seem to be rich folks, or who will believe in the bottle?" All the time of her preparation she was as gay as a bird; only when she looked upon Keawe, the tears would spring in her eye, and she must run and kiss him. As for Keawe, a weight was off his soul; now that he had his secret shared, and some hope in front of him, he seemed like a new man, his feet went lightly on the earth, and his breath was good to him again. Yet was terror still at his elbow; and ever and again, as the wind blows out a taper, hope died in him, and he saw the flames toss and the red fire burn in hell.

It was given out in the country they were gone pleasuring to the States, which was thought a strange thing, and yet not so strange as the truth, if any could have guessed it. So they went to Honolulu in the Hall, and thence in the Umatilla to

San Francisco with a crowd of Haoles, and at San Francisco took their passage by the mail brigantine, the Tropic Bird for Papeete, the chief place of the French in the south islands. Thither they came, after a pleasant voyage, on a fair day of the Trade Wind, and saw the reef with the surf breaking, and Motu Iti with its palms, and the schooner riding withinside, and the white houses of the town low down along the shore among green trees, and overhead the mountains and the clouds of Tahiti, the wise island.

It was judged the most wise to hire a house, which they did accordingly, opposite the British Consul's, to make a great parade of money, and themselves conspicuous with carriages and horses. This it was very easy to do, so long as they had the bottle in their possession; for Kokua was more bold than Keawe, and whenever she had a mind, called on the imp for twenty or a hundred dollars. At this rate they soon grew to be remarked in the town; and the strangers from Hawaii, their riding and their driving, the fine holokus and the rich lace of Kokua, became the matter of much talk.

They got on well after the first with the Tahitian language, which is indeed like to the Hawaiian, with a change of certain letters; and as soon as they had any freedom of speech, began to push the bottle. You are to consider it was not an easy subject to introduce; it was not easy to persuade people you were in earnest, when you offered to sell them for four centimes the spring of health and riches inexhaustible. It was necessary besides to explain the dangers of the bottle; and either people disbelieved the whole thing and laughed or they thought the more of the darker part, became overcast with gravity, and drew away from Keawe and Kokua, as from persons who had dealings with the devil. So far from gaining ground, these two began to find they were avoided in the town; the children ran away from them screaming, a thing intolerable to Kokua; Catholics crossed themselves as they went by; and all persons began with one accord to disengage themselves from their advances.

Depression fell upon their spirits. They would sit at night in their new house, after a day's weariness, and not exchange one word, or the silence would be broken by Kokua bursting suddenly into sobs. Sometimes they would pray together; sometimes they would have the bottle out upon the floor, and sit all evening watching how the shadow hovered in the midst. At such times they would be afraid to go to rest. It was long ere slumber came to them, and if either dozed off, it would be to wake and find the other silently weeping in the dark, or perhaps, to wake alone, the other having fled from the house and the neighbourhood of that bottle, to pace under the bananas in the little garden, or to wander on the beach by moonlight.

One night it was so when Kokua awoke. Keawe was gone. She felt in the bed and his place was cold. Then fear fell upon her, and she sat up in bed. A little moonshine filtered through the shutters. The room was bright, and she could spy the bottle on the floor. Outside it blew high, the great trees of the avenue cried aloud, and the fallen leaves rattled in the verandah. In the midst of this Kokua was aware of another sound; whether of a beast or of a man she could scarce tell, but it was as sad as death, and cut her to the soul. Softly she arose, set the door ajar, and looked forth in the moonlit yard. There, under the bananas, lay Keawe, his mouth in the dust, and as he lay he moaned.

It was Kokua's first thought to run forward and console him; her second potently withheld her. Keawe had borne himself before his wife like a brave man; it became her little in the hour of weakness to intrude upon his shame. With the thought she drew back into the house.

"Heavens!" she thought, "how careless have I been—how weak! It is he, not I that stands in this eternal peril; it was he, not I, that took the curse upon his soul. It is for my sake, and for the love of a creature of so little worth and such poor help, that he now beholds so close to him the flames of hell—ay, and smells the smoke of it, lying without there in the wind and moonlight. Am I so dull of spirit that never till now I have surmised my duty, or have I seen it before and turned aside? But now, at least, I take upon my soul in both the hands of my affection; now I say farewell to the white steps of heaven and the waiting faces of my friends. A love for a love, and let mine be equalled with Keawe's! A soul for a soul, and be it mine to perish!"

She was a deft woman with her hands, and was soon apparelled. She took in her hands the change—the precious centimes they kept ever at their side; for this coin is little used, and they had made provision at a Government office. When she was forth in the avenue clouds came on the wind, and the moon was blackened. The town slept, and she knew not whither to turn till she heard one coughing in the shadow of the trees.

"Old man," said Kokua, "what do you here abroad in the cold night?"

The old man could scarce express himself for coughing, but she made out that he was old and poor, and a stranger in the island.

"Will you do me a service?" said Kokua. "As one stranger to another, and as an old man to a young woman, will you help a daughter of Hawaii?"

"Ah," said the old man. "So you are the witch from the eight islands, and even my old soul you seek to entangle. But I have heard of you, and defy your wickedness."

"Sit down here," said Kokua, "and let me tell you a tale." And she told him the story of Keawe from the beginning to the end.

"And now," said she, "I am his wife, whom he bought with his soul's welfare. And what should I do? If I went to him myself and offered to buy it, he would refuse. But if you go, he will sell it eagerly; I will await you here; you will buy it for four centimes, and I will buy it again for three. And the Lord strengthen a poor girl!"

"If you meant falsely," said the old man, "I think God would strike you dead."

"He would!" cried Kokua. "Be sure he would. I could not be so treacherous—God would not suffer it."

"Give me the four centimes and await me here," said the old man.

Now, when Kokua stood alone in the street, her spirit died. The wind roared in the trees, and it seemed to her the rushing of the flames of hell; the shadows tossed in the light of the street lamp, and they seemed to her the snatching hands of evil ones. If she had had the strength, she must have run away, and if she had had the breath she must have screamed aloud; but, in truth, she could do neither, and stood trembling in the avenue, like an affrighted child.

Then she saw the old man returning, and he had the bottle in his hand.

"I have done your bidding," said he. "I left your husband weeping like a child; tonight he will sleep easy." And he held the bottle forth.

"Before you give it me," Kokua panted, "take the good with the evil—ask to be delivered from your cough."

"I am an old man," replied the other, "and too near the gate of the grave to take a favour from the devil. But what is this? Why do you not take the bottle? Do you hesitate?"

"Not hesitate!" cried Kokua. "I am only weak. Give me a moment. It is my hand resists, my flesh shrinks back from the accursed thing. One moment only!"

The old man looked upon Kokua kindly. "Poor child!" said he, "you fear; your soul misgives you. Well, let me keep it. I am old and can never more be happy in this world, and as for the next—"

"Give it me!" gasped Kokua. "There is your money. Do you think I am so base as that? Give me the bottle."

"God bless you, child," said the old man.

Kokua concealed the bottle under her holoku, said farewell to the old man, and walked off along the avenue, she cared not whither. For all roads were not the same to her, and led equally to hell. Sometimes she walked, and sometimes ran; sometimes she screamed out loud in the night, and sometimes lay by the wayside in the dust and wept. All that she had heard of hell came back to her; she saw the flames blaze, and she smelt the smoke, and her flesh withered on the coals.

Near the day she came to her mind again, and returned to the house. It was even as the old man said—Keawe slumbered like a child. Kokua stood and gazed upon his face.

"Now, my husband," said she, "it is your turn to sleep. When you wake it will be your turn to sing and laugh. But for poor Kokua, alas! that meant no evil—for poor Kokua no more sleep, no more singing, no more delight, whether in earth or heaven."

With that she lay down in the bed by his side, and her misery was so extreme that she fell in a deep slumber instantly.

Late in the morning her husband woke her and gave her the good news. It seemed he was silly with delight, for he paid no heed to her distress, ill though she dissembled it. The words stuck in her mouth, it mattered not; Keawe did the speaking. She ate not a bite, but who was to observe it? for Keawe cleared the dish. Kokua saw and heard him, like some strange thing in a dream; there were times when she forgot or doubted, and put her hands to her brow; to know herself doomed and hear her husband babble, seemed so monstrous.

All the while Keawe was eating and talking, and planning the time of their return, and thanking her for saving him, and fondling her, and calling her the true helper after all. He laughed at the old man that was fool enough to buy that bottle.

"A worthy old man he seemed," Keawe said. "But no one can judge by appearances. For why did the old reprobate require the bottle?"

"My husband," said Kokua, humbly, "his purpose may have been good."

Keawe laughed like an angry man.

"Fiddle-de-dee!" cried Keawe. "An old rogue, I tell you; and an old ass to boot. For the bottle was hard enough to sell at four centimes; and at three it will be quite impossible. The margin is not broad enough, the thing begins to smell of scorching—brrr!" said he, and shuddered. "It is true I bought it myself at a cent, when I knew not there were smaller coins. I was a fool for my pains; there will never be found another, and whoever has that bottle now will carry it to the pit."

"O my husband!" said Kokua. "It is not a terrible thing to save oneself by the eternal ruin of another? It seems to me I could not laugh. I would be humbled. I would be filled with melancholy. I would pray for the poor holder."

Then Keawe, because he felt the truth of what she said, grew the more angry. "Heighty-teighty!" cried he. "You may be filled with melancholy if you please. It is not the mind of a good wife. If you thought at all of me, you would sit shamed."

Thereupon he went out, and Kokua was alone.

What chance had she to sell that bottle at two centimes? None, she perceived. And if she had any, here was her husband hurrying her away to a country where there was nothing lower than a cent. And here—on the morrow of her sacrifice—was her husband leaving her and blaming her.

She would not even try to profit by what time she had, but sat in the house, and now had the bottle out and viewed it with unutterable fear, and now, with loathing, hid it out of sight.

By-and-by, Keawe came back, and would have her take a drive.

"My husband, I am ill," she said. "I am out of heart. Excuse me, I can take no pleasure."

Then was Keawe more wroth than ever. With her, because he thought she was brooding over the case of the old man; and with himself, because he thought she was right, and was ashamed to be so happy.

"This is your truth," cried he, "and this your affection! Your husband is just saved from eternal ruin, which he encountered for the love of you—and you take no pleasure! Kokua, you have a disloyal heart."

He went forth again furious, and wandered in the town all day. He met friends, and drank with them; they hired a carriage and drove into the country, and there drank again. All the time Keawe was ill at ease, because he was taking this pastime while his wife was sad, and because he knew in his heart that she was more right than he; and the knowledge made him drink the deeper.

Now there was an old brutal Haole drinking with him, one that had been a boatswain of a whaler, a runaway, a digger in gold mines, a convict in prisons. He had a low mind and a foul mouth; he loved to drink and to see others drunken; and he pressed the glass upon Keawe. Soon there was no more money in the company.

"Here, you!" said the boatswain, "you are rich, you have been always saying. You have a bottle or some foolishness."

"Yes," said Keawe, "I am rich; I will go back and get some money from my wife, who keeps it."

"That's a bad idea, mate," said the boatswain. "Never you trust a petticoat with dollars. They're all as false as water; you keep an eye on her."

Now, this word struck in Keawe's mind; for he was muddled with what he had been drinking.

"I should not wonder but she was false, indeed," thought he. "Why else should she be so cast down at my release? But I will show her I am not the man to be fooled, I will catch her in the act."

Accordingly, when they were back in town, Keawe bade the boatswain wait for him at the corner, by the old calaboose, and went forward up the avenue alone to the door of his house. The night had come again; there was a light within, but never a sound; and Keawe crept about the corner, opened the back door softly, and looked in.

There was Kokua on the floor, the lamp at her side, before her was a milk-white bottle, with a round belly and a long neck; and as she viewed it, Kokua wrung her hands.

A long time Keawe stood and looked in the doorway. At first he was struck stupid; and then fear fell upon him that the bargain had been made amiss, and the bottle had come back to him as it came at San Francisco; and at that his knees were loosened, and the fumes of the wine departed from his head like mists off a river in the morning. And then he had another thought; and it was a strange one, that made his cheeks burn.

"I must make sure of this," thought he.

So he closed the door, and went softly round the corner again, and then came noisily in, as though he were but now returned. And, lo! by the time he opened the front door no bottle was to be seen; and Kokua sat in a chair and started up like one awakened out of sleep.

"I have been drinking all day and making merry," said Keawe. "I have been with good companions, and now I only come back for money, and return to drink and carouse with them again."

Both his face and voice were as stern as judgement, but Kokua was too troubled to observe.

"You do well to use your own, my husband," said she, and her words trembled.

"O, I do well in all things," said Keawe, and he went straight to the chest and took out money. But he looked besides in the corner where they kept the bottle, and there was no bottle there.

At that the chest heaved upon the floor like a sea billow, and the house spun about him like a wreath of smoke, for he saw he was lost now, and there was no escape. "It is what I feared," he thought. "It is she who bought it."

And then he came to himself a little and rose up; but the sweat streamed on his face as thick as the rain and as cold as the well-water.

"Kokua," said he, "I said to you today what ill became me. Now I return to carouse with my jolly companions," and at that he laughed a little quietly. "I will take more pleasure in the cup if you forgive me."

She clasped his knees in a moment; she kissed his knees with flowing tears.

"O," she cried, "I asked but a kind word!"

"Let us never one think hardly of the other," said Keawe, and was gone out of the house.

Now, the money that Keawe had taken was only some of that store of centime piece they had laid in at their arrival. It was very sure he had no mind to be drinking. His wife had given her soul for him, now he must give his for hers; no other thought was in the world with him.

At the corner, by the old calaboose, there was the boatswain waiting.

"My wife has the bottle," said Keawe, "and, unless you help me to recover it, there can be no more money and no more liquor tonight."

"You do not mean to say you are serious about that bottle?" cried the boatswain.

"There is the lamp," said Keawe. "Do I look as if I was jesting?"

"That is so," said the boatswain. "You look as serious as a ghost."

"Well, then," said Keawe, "here are two centimes; you must go to my wife in the house, and offer her these for the bottle, which (if I am not much mistaken) she will give you instantly. Bring it to me here, and I will buy it back from you for one; for that is the law with this bottle, that it still must be sold for a less sum. But whatever you do, never breathe a word to her that you have come from me."

"Mate, I wonder are you making a fool of me?" asked the boatswain.

"It will do you no harm if I am," returned Keawe.

"That is so, mate," said the boatswain.

"And if you doubt me," added Keawe, "you can try. As soon as you are clear of the house, wish to have your pocket full of money, or a bottle of the best rum, or what you please, and you will see the virtue of the thing."

"Very well, Kanaka," said the boatswain. "I will try; but if you are having your fun out of me, I will take my fun out of you with a belaying pin."

So the whaler-man went off upon the avenue; and Keawe stood and waited. It was near the same spot where Kokua had waited the night before; but Keawe was more resolved, and never faltered in his purpose; only his soul was bitter with despair.

It seemed a long time he had to wait before he heard a voice singing in the darkness of the avenue. He knew the voice to be the boatswain's; but it was strange how drunken it appeared upon a sudden.

Next, the man himself came stumbling into the light of the lamp. He had the devil's bottle buttoned in his coat; another bottle was in his hand; and even as he came in view he raised it to his mouth and drank.

"You have it," said Keawe. "I see that."

"Hands off!" cried the boatswain, jumping back. "Take a step near me, and I'll smash your mouth. You thought you could make a cat's-paw of me, did you?"

"What do you mean?" cried Keawe.

"Mean?" cried the boatswain. "This is a pretty good bottle, this is; that's what I mean. How I got it for two centimes I can't make out; but I'm sure you shan't have it for one."

"You mean you won't sell?" gasped Keawe.

"No, sir!" cried the boatswain. "But I'll give you a drink of the rum, if you like."

"I tell you," said Keawe, "the man who has that bottle goes to hell."

"I reckon I'm going anyway," returned the sailor; "and this bottle's the best thing to go with I've struck yet. No, sir!" he cried again, "this is my bottle now, and you can go and fish for another."

"Can this be true?" Keawe cried. "For your own sake, I beseech you, sell it me!"

"I don't value any of your talk," replied the boatswain. "You thought I was a flat; now you see I'm not; and there's an end. If you won't have a swallow of the rum, I'll have one myself. Here's your health, and goodnight to you!"

So off he went down the avenue toward town, and there goes the bottle out of the story.

But Keawe ran to Kokua light as the wind; and great was their joy that night; and great, since then has been the peace of all their days in the Bright House.

TWO ⊙ OLD MEN

Kage Baker

It was Sunday, January 26, 1961, and Markie Souza was six years old. He sat patiently beside his mother in the long pew, listening to Father Gosse talk about how wonderful it was to have a Catholic in the White House at last. Markie knew this was a good thing, in a general kind of way, because he was a Catholic himself; but it was too big and too boring to think about, so he concentrated his attention on wishing his little sister would wake up.

She was limp on his mother's ample shoulder, flushed in the unseasonable heat, and the elastic band that held her straw hat on was edging forward under her chin. Any minute now it was going to ride up and snap her in the nose. Markie saw his opportunity and seized it: he reached up and tugged the band back into place, just incidentally jostling the baby into consciousness. Karen squirmed, turned her head and opened her eyes. She might have closed them again, but just then everybody had to stand up to sing *Tantum Ergo Sacramentum*. The little girl looked around in unbelieving outrage and began to protest. Markie put his arms up to her.

"I'll take her out, Mama," he stage-whispered. His mother gratefully dumped the baby into his arms without missing a note. He staggered out of the pew and up the strip of yellow carpet that led to the side door. There was a little garden out there, a couple of juniper bushes planted around a statue of a lady saint. She was leaning on a broken ship's wheel. It had been explained to Markie that she was the patron saint of sailors and fishermen. Markie's daddy was a fisherman, and when he'd lived with them his mother had used to burn candles to this saint. Karen's daddy wasn't a fisherman, though, he only cut up fish at the big market on the other side of the harbor, and Markie assumed this was why Mama had stopped buying the little yellow votive candles any more.

Karen tottered back and forth in front of the statue, and Markie stood with his hands in his pockets, edging between her and the juniper bushes when she seemed likely to fall into them, or between her and the parked cars when she'd make a dash for the asphalt. It was a dumb game, but it was better than sitting inside. Every so often he'd look away from the baby long enough to watch the progress of a big ship that was working its way across the horizon. He wondered

257

if his daddy was on the ship. The baby was quick to make use of an opportunity too, and the second she saw his attention had wandered would bolt down the narrow walkway between the church and the rectory. He would run after her, and the clatter of their hard Sunday shoes would echo between the buildings.

After a while there was singing again and people started filing out of the church, blinking in the light. Markie got a firm grip on Karen's fat wrist and held on until Mama emerged, smiling and chatting with a neighbor. Mama was a big lady in a flowered tent dress, blonde and blue-eyed like Karen, and she laughed a lot, jolly and very loud. She cried loud too. She was usually doing one or the other; Mama wasn't quiet much.

She swept up Karen and walked on, deep in her conversation with Mrs. Avila, and Markie followed them down the hill from the church. It was hot and very bright, but the wind was fresh and there were seagulls wheeling and crying above the town. Their shadows floated around Markie on the sidewalk, all the way down Hinds Street to the old highway where the sidewalk ended and the dirt path began. Here the ladies in their Sunday dresses shouted their goodbyes to each other and parted company, and Markie's Mama swung round and began a conversation with him, barely pausing to draw breath.

"Got a letter from Grandpa, honey, and he sent nice presents of money for you and the baby. Looks like you get your birthday after all! What do you want, you want some little cars? You want a holster and a six-shooter like Leon's got? Whatever his damn mother buys him, honey, you can have better."

"Can I have fishing stuff?" Markie didn't like talking about presents before he got them—it seemed like bad luck, and anyway he liked the idea of a surprise.

"Or I'll get you more of those green soldiers—what? No, honey, we talked about this, remember? You're too little and you'd just get the hooks in your fingers. Wait till you're older and Ronnie can show you." Ronnie was Karen's daddy. Markie didn't want to go fishing with Ronnie; Ronnie scared him. Markie just put his head down and walked along beside Mama as she talked on and on, making plans about all the wonderful things he and Ronnie would do together when he was older. She was loud enough to be heard above the cars that zoomed past them on the highway, and when they turned off the trail and crossed the bridge over the slough her voice echoed off the water. As they neared their house, she saw Mrs. O'Farrell hanging out a laundry load, and hurried ahead to tell her something important. Markie got to walk the rest of the way by himself.

Their house was the third one from the end in a half-square of little yellow cottages around a central courtyard. It had been a motor court, once; the rusted neon sign still said it was, but families like Markie's paid by the week to live here year in and year out. It was a nice place to live. Beside each identical clapboard house was a crushed-shell driveway with an old car or truck parked in it, and behind each house was a clothesline. In front was a spreading lawn of Bermuda grass, lush and nearly indestructible, and beyond that low dunes rose, and just beyond them was the sea.

Off to the south was a dark forest of eucalyptus trees, and when Markie had been younger he'd been afraid of the monster that howled there. Now he knew it was just the freight train, he'd seen where its tracks ran. To the north was the campground, where the people with big silver trailers pulled in; then the bridge that crossed the slough, and the little town with its pier and its general store and hotels.

It was a good world, and Markie was in a hurry to get back to it. He had to change his clothes first, though. He didn't like going into the house by himself, but Mama looked like she was going to be talking to Mrs. O'Farrell a while, so he was careful not to let the rusty screen bang behind him as he slipped inside.

Ronnie was awake, sitting up in bed and smoking. He watched Markie with dead eyes as Markie hurried past the bedroom door. He didn't say anything, for which Markie was grateful. Ronnie was mean when he had that look in his eyes.

Markie's room was a tiny alcove up two stairs, with his bed and a dresser. He shed the blue church suit and the hard shoes, and quickly pulled on a pair of shorts and a cotton shirt. Groping under the bed he found his knapsack. His father had bought it at an Army Surplus store and it had an austere moldy smell, like old wars. He loved it. He put it on, adjusting the straps carefully, and ran from the house.

"Bye, Ma," he shouted as he ran past, and she waved vaguely as she continued telling Mrs. O'Farrell about the fight the people in the next house had had. Markie made for the big state campground. It was the place he always started his search.

There were certain places you could always find pop bottles. Ditches by the side of highways, for example: people pitched them out of speeding cars, in fact a lot of interesting stuff winds up in ditches. Bottles got left in alleyways between houses, and in phone booths, and in flower planters where the flowers had died, and in bushes on the edges of parking lots. The very best place to look was at the campground, just after one of the big silver trailers had pulled away from a space, before the park attendant had emptied the trash can. Beer bottles were worthless, but an ordinary pop bottle was worth two cents on deposit, and the big Par-T-Pak bottles were worth a nickel. Five empty Coca-Cola bottles could be redeemed for ten cents, and ten cents bought a comic book or a soda, or two candy bars—three if you went to Hatta's News, Cigars and Sundries, which carried three-cent Polar Bars. Ten cents bought two rolls of Lifesavers or one box of Crackerjacks, or ten Red Vines, or five Tootsie Roll Pops. Markie knew to the penny what he could do with his money, all right.

The original point of getting the money, though, had been to hand it to Mama in triumph. For a moment he'd completely have her attention, even if she were talking with the other women in the court; she'd yell out that he was her little hero, and engulf him in a hug, and briefly things would be the way they'd been before Karen had been born. Lately this had begun to lose its appeal to him, but the hunt had become more interesting as he got older and better at it, and then one day an idea had hit him like a blow between the eyes—buried treasure! He could save all those dimes in a box and keep it buried somewhere. He was still incredulous at how long it had taken him to think of this, especially since he lived at the beach, which was where people buried treasure.

He thought seriously about this as he scuttled between the campsites, scoring a Bireley's bottle from one trash can and two Frostie Rootbeer bottles from another. The Playtime Arcade had little treasure chests you could buy with blue tickets, real plastic ones with tiny brass locks, but he was too little to play the games that gave out blue tickets and scared to go in the arcades by himself anyway. Still, there were cigar boxes and glass jars and tin cans. Any of those might do for a start.

He spotted a good-sized cache of Nehi bottles at one campsite, but the campers were still there: an elderly man and woman seated in folding chairs, talking sadly and interminably about something. He decided to go into the dunes a while, to give them time to leave. Sometimes people wandered into the dunes with pop bottles, too, though usually all there was to find were beer bottles or little whiskey bottles in screwed-up paper bags. Once in a while the sand would drift away from old, old bottles, purple from time and the sun, and those could be sold to the old lady who ran the junk shop on Cypress Street. She'd pay ten cents per bottle, very good money.

So he struggled through the willow thicket, which was swampy and buzzing with little flies, and emerged into the cooler air of the dunes. Trails wound here through the sand, between the lawns of dune grass and big, leaning, yellow flowers. He knew all the labyrinths between the rows of cypress or eucalyptus trees that had been planted there, a long time ago, when somebody had built a big hotel on the sands. There was a story that one night a storm had come up and blown away the big dune from under the hotel, and the hotel had tipped over like a wrecked ship in the sand. Sometimes the winter storms would blow away enough sand to uncover some of the lost stuff from long ago: old machinery, a grand piano, a box of letters, a Model T Ford.

All the last storm seemed to have uncovered was clamshells. Markie wandered out from the edge into the full sunlight and the sea wind blew his hair back from his forehead. He couldn't hear the waves at all, though they were crashing white with the spray thrown back from their tops. He couldn't hear any sound, though there were little kids playing at the edge of the water, and their mouths were opening as they yelled to one another. He looked around him in confusion.

He was in the place at the edge of the dunes where the trees had died, a long time ago, and they were leafless and silver from fifty years of salt spray, with their silver branches still swept backward from the winds when they were alive. There was a little line of bright water running in a low place beyond the edge, with some green reeds and a big white bird with a crest standing motionless, or moving its neck to strike at a silver fish or a frog. On the other side of the water the high dunes started, the big mountains of sand where there were no trees, only the sand changing color, white or pink or pale gold, and the sky and the pale floating clouds and their shadows on the sand. That was where the old man was sitting. He was looking at Markie.

"Come here, boy," he said, and his voice was so loud in the silence Markie jumped. But he came, at least as far as the edge of the water. The white bird ignored him. The old man was all in white, a long robe like saints wore, and his hair and beard were long and white too. His eyes were as scary as Ronnie's eyes.

"I want you to run an errand for me, boy," he said. His voice was scary, too.

"Okay," said Markie.

"Go into the town, to the arcade with the yellow sign. Ask for Smith."

"Okay," said Markie, though he was scared to go inside the arcades.

"Give him a message for me. Ask him how he likes this new servant of mine. Say to him: My servant has set himself to feed and clothe the poor, and to break the shackles of the oppressed, and to exalt the wise even to the stars. He has invoked the names of the old kings and the days of righteousness. Why should he not succeed? You go to Smith, boy, and you ask him just that. And go along the beach, it'll be faster. Do it, boy."

"Okay," said Markie, and he turned and fled. He made no sound floundering through the hot sand, but as he got to the hard wet sand there was noise again: the roar of the surf, the happy screaming of the little kids playing in the water. He ran up the beach toward the town and never looked back once.

By the time he reached the town and climbed up the ramp from the beach, he had decided to turn in his pop bottles at Hatta's and go home along the state highway. Just as he'd made up his mind on this, however, he passed the yard where the Anderson's big dog slept on its tether, in the shade under a boat up on sawhorses. The dog woke and leapt up barking, as it often did; but to Markie's horror the tether snapped, and the dog came flying over the fence and landed sprawling, right behind him. Markie ran so fast, jolting along the hot sidewalk, that a bottle flew out of his knapsack and broke. The dog stopped, booming out furious threats, but Markie kept going until he got around the corner onto Cypress Street and felt it was safe to slow down.

"Okay," he gasped, "Okay. I'm just going to turn in my bottles and *then* I'm going to the arcade, okay?"

There was a rumble like thunder, but it was only somebody starting up a motorcycle in front of Harry's Bar.

Markie limped into Hatta's News, Cigars and Sundries, grateful for the cool linoleum under his feet. Mr. Hatta wasn't there; only sulky Mary Beth Hatta, who had lately started wearing lipstick. She barely looked up from her copy of *Calling All Girls* as he made his way back to the counter. "Deposit on bottles," he mumbled, sliding his pack off and setting the bottles out one by one.

She gave a martyred sigh. "Eight cents," she told him, and opened the cash register and counted a nickel and three pennies into his sweaty palm. On his way out he slowed longingly by the comic book rack, but her voice came sharply after him:

"If you're not going to buy one of those, don't read them!"

Ordinarily he'd have turned and responded in kind, lifting the tip of his nose or maybe the corners of his eyes up with his fingers; but he remembered the old man in the dunes and it made him feel cold all over, so he hurried out without word or gesture.

At the corner of Pomeroy Avenue he turned and stared worriedly down the street. This was the Bad Part of town. There on the corner was the Peppermint Twist Lounge, and beyond it was the Red Rooster Pool Room, and beyond that the Roseland Ballroom, where fights broke out every Saturday night. Further down toward the pier were the penny arcades: Playland, with its red sign, and the other one with no name. Its yellow sign just said ARCADE.

Markie wasn't ever supposed to go over here, but he did. For a while after his daddy had moved out Markie had been able to see him by walking past the Red Rooster, looking quickly in through the door into the darkness. His daddy would be at the back, leaning listlessly against the wall with a beer bottle or a pool cue in his hand. If he saw Markie he'd look mad, and Markie would run. Then one day his daddy hadn't been there any more, nor had he been there since.

Markie looked in, all the same, as he trotted down the street. No daddy. Markie kept going, all the way down the street, to stand at last outside the doors of the arcade with the yellow sign. He drew a deep breath and went in.

The minute he crossed the threshold into darkness, he wanted to clap his hands over his ears. It was the loudest place he'd ever heard. In a corner there was a jukebox booming, telling him hoarsely that Frankie and Johnny were lovers. Next to that was a glass booth in which a marionette clown jiggled, and as its wooden jaw bobbed up and down a falsetto recording of *The Farmer in the Dell* played nearly as loud as the jukebox. From the back came the monotonous thunder of the skee-ball lanes, and the staccato popping of the shooting gallery: somebody had trapped the grizzly bear in his sights and it stood and turned, stood and turned, bellowing its pain as the ducks and rabbits kept racing by. There were pinball machines ringing and buzzing, with now and then a hollow double knock as a game ended, and a shout of disgust as a player punched a machine or rattled it on its legs. In a booth fixed up with a seat and steering wheel, somebody was flying as grey newsreel skies from the last World War flickered in front of them, and the drone of bomber engines played from a speaker. There were big boys standing around, with slicked-back hair and cigarettes, and some of them were shouting to each other; most of them were silent at their games, though, and dead-eyed as the waxen lady in the booth who swung one arm in a slow arc along her fan of playing cards.

Markie stood shivering. Big boys were scary. If you were lucky they ignored you or just flicked their cigarette butts at you, but sometimes they winked at their friends and grabbed you by the arm and said Hey, Shrimp, C'mere, and then they told you jokes you couldn't understand or asked you questions you couldn't answer, and then everybody would laugh at you. He turned to run outside again, but at that moment a car backfired right outside the door. With a little yelp he ran forward into the gloom.

Then he had to keep going, so he pretended he'd meant to come in there all along, and made for a small machine with a viewscope low enough for him to reach. Silver letters on a red background read IN THE DAYS OF THE INQUI-SITION. He didn't know what the last word was, but underneath it in smaller letters were the words *One Cent*, so he dug in his pocket for a penny and dropped it in the slot, and looked through the little window.

Clunk, a shutter dropped, and by yellow electric light he saw a tiny manne-quin with its head on a block. Whack, another mannequin all in black dropped a tiny axe on its neck, as a third mannequin robed in brown burlap bobbed back and forth in a parody of prayer. The head, no bigger than a pencil eraser, dropped into a tiny basket. Just before the light went out Markie could see the head coming back up again on a thread, to snap into place until the next penny was dropped into the slot.

Markie stepped back and looked around. There were other penny machines in this part of the arcade, with titles like SEE YOURSELF AS OTHERS SEE YOU and THE PRESIDENT'S WIFE. He felt in his pocket for more pennies, but a hand on his shoulder stopped him. He turned and stared up at someone very tall, whose face was hideous with lumps and pits and sores.

"Whatcha lookin' for, peanut?" the person shouted.

"Are you Smith?" Markie shouted back. "I got to say something to Smith."

The person jerked a thumb behind them. "Downstairs," he told Markie. Markie followed the direction of the thumb and found himself descending into dark-ness on a carpeted ramp, booming hollowly under his feet, that led to a long low room. It was a little quieter down here. There were dim islands of light over pool tables, and more dead-eyed boys leaned by them, motionless until an arm would suddenly flash with movement, shoving a cuestick forward. Markie was too short to see the colored balls rolling on the table, but he could hear the quiet clicking and the rumble as they dropped into darkness.

At the back of the room were more pinball machines, brightly lit up, and these did not feature little race horses or playing cards, like the ones upstairs. There were naked ladies and leering magicians on them, instead. There was an old man seated between two machines, resting his arms on the glass panels. Markie approached cautiously.

This was a wizened old man, heavily tattooed, in old jeans and a T-shirt color-less with dust. The dust seemed to be grained in his skin and thick in his hair and straggly beard. He wore pointed snakeskin boots and a change belt full of nickels, and he was smoking a cigarette. His eyes were heavy-lidded and bored.

"Are you Smith?" Markie asked him. The old man's eyes flickered over him.

"Sure," he replied. It was hard to hear him, so Markie edged closer.

"I talked to this other man, and he said I was supposed to tell you something," he said, loudly, as though the old man were deaf. Smith took a long drag on his cigarette and exhaled. It smelled really bad. Markie edged back a pace or two.

"Oh yeah?" Smith studied his cigarette thoughtfully. "What's he got to say to me, kid? He bitching about something again?"

"No, he says—" Markie scratched a mosquito bite, trying to remember. "He wants to know how you like his new servant, the one that breaks chains and stuff. He says he talks about old kings and rightness? You know? And he wants to know why he shouldn't, um, s—s-succeed."

"He does, huh?" Smith stuck his cigarette behind one ear and scratched his beard. "Huh. He's baiting me again, isn't he? Jeeze, whyn't he ever leave well enough alone? Okay. Why shouldn't this servant succeed?" He removed the cigarette and puffed again, then stabbed the air with it decisively. "*Here's* why. His father was unrighteous, and his sins are visited on his kids, right, unto the third and fourth generation? Aren't those the rules? So there, that's one reason. And this man is an adulterer and lusts after the flesh, right? Reason Number Two. Hmmm…" Smith pondered a moment; then his eyes lit up. "And when his son was born dead he despaired in his heart! Sin, Sin and Sin again. That's why his big-shot servant should fail, and you can tell him so from me. Okay, kid? Now beat it."

Markie turned and ran, up the ramp and out through shrieking darkness, and into the clean daylight at the foot of the pier. He pounded to a stop beside the snack stand and caught his breath, looking back fearfully at the arcade. After a moment he wandered out on the pier and looked south toward the dunes. They seemed far away, and full of strange shifting lights. He shrugged and ventured further along the pier, stopping to watch with interest as a fisherman reeled in a perch and gutted it there on the spot. There were four telescopes ranged along the pier at intervals, and he stopped and climbed the iron steps to look into the eyepiece of each one, and check the coin slot to see if anyone had jammed a dime in there. No such luck. Further on, he stopped at the bait stand and bought a bag of peanuts for five cents. Just beyond the bait stand was a bench with a clean spot, and he settled down and proceeded to eat the peanuts, dropping the shells through the gaps between the pier planks and watching the green water surge down below.

The last shell felt funny and light, and when he opened it he found inside a little slip of paper printed in red ink. GET GOING, it said.

He jumped up and ran, heart in mouth, and clattered down the stairway to the beach. Near the bottom of the Ocean View Avenue ramp he had to slow down, hobbling along clutching at his side, but he was too scared to stop.

All the way down the beach he watched the place with the silver trees, and he couldn't see the old man's white robes anywhere. The same little kids were still playing on the sand, though, and when he put down his head and plodded across the soft sand the same silence fell over everything; so he was not really much surprised, coming to the foot of the first dune, to lift his head and see the old man leaning against one of the dead trees.

"All right, boy, tell me what his answer was," said the old man without pre-amble.

Markie gulped for air and nodded. "He says—your servant should be failed because of his father, and the rule about the two and three generations. And he's committed adultery about the flesh, and his son died, and that's why." Markie sank down on the sand, stretching out his tired legs. The old man put his head on one side and stared fixedly into space for a moment.

"Hmm," he said. "Point taken. Very well. Go back and find Smith. Tell him he may therefore afflict my servant with wasting disease, and set scandal to defile his good name. Further, that he may confound his judgment among the nations. Go, boy, and tell him that."

Markie didn't want to go anywhere, and he was just tired enough to open his mouth in protest. Before he could make a sound he felt the soft sand begin to run and sink under him, and in terror he scrambled away on all fours. It didn't seem wise not to keep going once he'd started, so once he reached the hard sand he got to his feet and limped away down the beach, muttering to himself.

He left the beach and had started up the ramp at Ocean View before he remembered that the Andersons' dog was loose. Turning, he picked his way along the top of the seawall, balancing precariously and stepping around the loose bricks. Jumping from the end, he wandered through the courtyard of another small motel, pausing to duck into its row of phone booths and carefully checking to see if any change had been left in the Coin Return compartment. If none had, sometimes a punch at the Coin Return lever sent a couple of nickels cascading down; this was another good way to get money. The third booth rewarded his efforts mightily. Not only did he coax a nickel out of the phone, somebody had dropped a dime and it had fallen and stuck between the booth's ventilation slits near the floor. Markie's fingers were little enough to prize it out. He pocketed his small fortune and strolled on along the seafront, feeling pleased with himself.

At the snackbar at the foot of the pier he paused and bought a bottle of Seven-Up. The laconic counterman took off the bottlecap for him and thrust a straw down the neck. Markie carried the bottle carefully to the railings above the sand and sat with his legs dangling through the rails, sipping and not thinking. When the bottle was empty he held it up to his eye like a telescope and surveyed the world, emerald green, full of uncertain shapes. The view absorbed him for a while. He was pulled back to earth by the sound of shouting. One of the shouting voices belonged to Ronnie. Markie scrambled back from the railings and turned around quickly.

Ronnie and another man were over in the parking lot, standing one on either side of a big red and white convertible, yelling across it at one another.

"You were drunk!" the other man was telling Ronnie.

"*Fuck* you!" Ronnie told the man. "I haven't had a drink in two years. Fuck you!"

"Oh, that's some great way to talk when you want your job back," the man laughed harshly, pulling open the car door and getting inside. "It sure is. So you haven't had a drink in two years? So what exactly was that you puked up all over Unit Three, you goddam bum?" He slammed the door and started up his car.

"Come on, man!" Ronnie caught hold of the car door. "You can't do this. I've got an old lady and a kid, for Christ's sake!" But the man was backing up his car, shaking his head, and as he drove away uptown Ronnie ran after him, yelling pleas and threats.

Markie slunk into the arcade, and for a moment the din was almost welcome. At least nobody was fighting in there. He squared his shoulders and marched down the ramp, down into the room where there was no day or night.

Smith was waiting for him, leaning forward with his elbows on his knees. His cigarette was canted up under his nose at a jaunty angle.

"You deliver my answer?" he inquired. Markie nodded. Smith leaned back and exhaled slowly, two long jets of smoke issuing from his nose. He closed his eyes for a moment and when he opened them his attention was riveted on Markie, suddenly interested. "Hey. What's your name, kid?"

"Markie Souza."

"Souza, huh?" Smith narrowed his eyes and pulled at his beard. "So you're a Portugee, huh? Boy, your people have been cheated by some experts. You know it was the Portuguese who discovered the New World really? And a lot of other places, too. They never get credit for it, though. The Spanish and the Italians grabbed all the glory for themselves. Your people used to have a big empire, kid, did you know that? And it was all stolen from them. Mostly by the English, but the Spanish had a hand in that too. Next time you see some Mexican kid, you ought to bounce a rock off his head. You aren't all Portuguese, though, are you, with that skin?" Smith leaned forward again, studying Markie. "What are you? What's your mother, kid?"

"She's Irish," Markie told him.

"Well, Irish!" Smith grinned hugely. His teeth were yellow and long. "Talk about a people with good reasons to hate! Kid, I could sit here for three days and three nights telling you about the injustices done to the Irish. You got some scores to settle, kid, you can't grow up fast enough. Any time you want to know about Irish history, you just come down here and ask me."

"Okay," said Markie faintly. The smoke was making him sick. "But the man said to tell you some other stuff."

"What'd he say?"

"That you can do bad things to his servant. Waste and disease, and, uh, scandal. And something about confining his judgment of nations."

"All right," Smith nodded. "All right, that's fair. Will do." He made a circle out of his thumb and index finger and held it up in an affirmative gesture. "But... ask him if he doesn't think we ought to up the ante a little. So what if I punish one sinner with good intentions? He's the leader of a whole people, right? Aren't all his people jumping on his little bandwagon with their Camelot bullshit? How seriously do they believe in what they're saying? Shouldn't they be tested too?"

Markie didn't know what to say, so he nodded in agreement. Smith stuck his cigarette back between his teeth and laced his gnarled fingers together, popping the knuckles.

"O-kay! We got a whole nation suddenly figuring out that racial injustice is bad, and poverty is bad, and reaching for the stars is good, right? Except they damn well knew that already, they just didn't bother to do anything about it until a pretty boy in the White House announced that righting all wrongs is going to be the latest thing. *Fashion*, that's the only reason they care now. So what'll they do if this servant of his is taken out of the picture? My bet is, they won't have the guts to hang on to those high ideals without a figurehead. What's he want to bet? You go ask him, kid. Does he want to test these people?"

Markie nodded and ran. It was a lot to remember and the words kept turning in his head. He emerged into the brilliant sunlight and stood, dazzled, until he realized that he was still clutching the empty Seven-Up bottle. With a purposeful trot he started up Pomeroy Avenue. The phone booth behind the Peppermint Twist lounge yielded a Nesbitts bottle, and there were two Coca-Cola bottles in the high grass next to the Chinese restaurant, and three pennies lying on the sidewalk in plain view right in front of the Wigwam Motor Inn. He was panting with triumph as he marched into Hatta's, and the cool green linoleum felt good under his bare feet. He lined the bottles up on the counter. Mary Beth looked up from her magazine. She was reading *Hit Parade* now.

"Eight cents," she announced. "Are you ever going to buy anything in here, junior?"

"Okay," he said cheerfully, and moved down the counter to the candy display next to the big humidor case. The front of the display was tin rolls of Lifesavers, carefully enameled to look like the real thing. He pretended to grab up a roll of Butter Rum and tugged in feigned surprise when it remained riveted in place. The patience in Mary Beth's eyes was withering, so he stopped playing and picked out five wax tubes filled with colored juice. Mary Beth gave him his three cents in change and took up her magazine again. He stepped out on the hot pavement and hurried down to the beach.

There was supposed to be a way to bite holes in the wax tubes and play music, once you'd sucked out the sweet juice. All the way down the beach he experimented without success, and his teeth were full of wax by the time he looked up and noticed that he'd reached the silver trees again. He plodded across the sand. The old man was standing by the little stream, watching in silence as the big white bird speared a kicking frog.

"Tell me what he said this time," said the old man, without looking up.

"He said Okay," Markie replied, staring at the dying frog in fascination. "And he wants to bet with you about the people with Camelot and everything. And Fashion. He says, what if the man gets taken out of the picture. You want to test them? I think that was what he said."

"A test!" The old man looked up sharply. "Yes! Very well. Let it be done as he has said; let the people be tested. When he has done unto my servant as I have permitted, let him do more. Let him find a murderer. That man's heart shall I harden, that he may strike down my servant. Let the wife be a widow; let the children weep for their father, and his people mourn. Will they bury righteousness with my servant, and return to their old ways? Or will they be strong in the faith and make his works live after him? We'll see, won't we? Go back to Smith, boy. Tell him that."

"Okay," Markie turned and plodded away across the sand. His legs were getting tired. He needed more sugar.

He stopped in at Hatta's on his way back down Cypress Street. Mary Beth looked up at him in real annoyance, but he dug a nickel and five pennies out of his pocket and smacked them down on the counter.

"I'm *buying* something, ha ha ha," he announced, and after a great deal of forethought selected a Mars Bar. As he wandered back down Pomeroy he ate the bar in layers, scraping away the nougat with his teeth and crunching up the almonds in their pavement of hard chocolate. When the candy was gone you could always chew on the green waxed paper wrapper, which tasted nice and felt interesting between the teeth. He was still chewing on it when he passed the Red Rooster and spotted Ronnie inside, ghastly pale under a cone of artificial light, leaning over a green table and cursing as his shot went wrong. Markie gulped and ran.

Down in the underground room, Smith was watching a fly circle in the motionless air. As Markie approached him, he made a grab for it and missed.

"Shit," he said tonelessly. He noticed Markie and grinned again.

"Well? Did he take me up on it?"

Markie nodded and sat down, rubbing his legs. The red carpet felt sticky.

"He says—yes, test. He says he'll let you find a murderer and he'll make his heart hard. He says let his children cry. He says we'll see about the people and faith."

"So *I'm* supposed to get him a murderer?" Smith leaned back. "That figures. I don't have anything else to do, right? Okay, I'll get him his murderer. This will take some work to get it just right… but, Hell, I like a challenge. Okay." He unrolled his shirtsleeve and took out a pack of cigarettes, and lit one; Markie didn't see just how, because the cloud of smoke was so immediate and thick. Smith waved it away absently and stared into space a moment, thinking. Markie got up on all fours and staggered to his feet, drawing back Smith's attention.

"I bet he's not paying you anything to run all these messages, is he?" Smith inquired. "Hasn't even offered, huh?"

"Nope," Markie sighed.

"That's him all over. Well, here's something for you." Smith leaned down and fished out something from a brown paper bag under his stool. He held up a brown bottle. "Beer! Big kids like beer."

Markie backed away a pace, staring at it. Ronnie had made him taste some beer once; he had cried and spit it out. "No, thank you," he said.

"No? Nobody'll know. Come on, kid, you must be thirsty, the way he's made you run around." Smith held it out. Markie just shook his head. Smith's eyes got narrow and small, but he smiled his yellow smile again.

"You sure? It's yours anyhow, you've earned it. What do you want me to do with it?"

Markie shrugged.

"You want me to give it to somebody else?" Smith persisted. "What if I give it to the first guy I meet when I go home tonight, huh, kid? Can I do that?"

"Okay," Markie agreed.

"Well, okay then! Now go deliver my message. Tell him I'll get him his murderer. Go on, kid, make tracks!"

Markie turned and limped out. He went slowly down the stairs to the beach, holding on to the sticky metal handrail. It was late afternoon now and a chilly wind had come up. All along the beach, families were beginning to pack up to go home, closing their striped umbrellas and collecting buckets and sand spades. Mothers were forcing hooded sweatshirts on protesting toddlers and fathers were carrying towels and beach chairs back to station wagons. The tide was out; as Markie trudged along shivering he saw the keyholes in the sand that meant big clams were under there. Ordinarily he'd stop and dig up a few, groping in the sand with his toes. He was too tired this afternoon.

The sun was red and low over the water when he got to the dead trees, and the dunes were all pink. The old man was pacing beside the water, in slow strides like the white bird. He turned his bright glare on Markie.

"He says okay," Markie told him without prompting. "He'll get a murderer."

The old man just nodded. Markie thought about asking the old man for payment of some kind, but one look into the chilly eyes was enough to silence him.

"Now, boy," said the old man briskly, "Another task. Go home and open the topmost drawer of your mother's dresser. You'll find a gun in there. Take it into the bathroom and drop it into the water of the tank behind the toilet. Go now, and let no one see what you've done."

"But I'm not supposed to go in that drawer, ever," Markie protested.

"Do it, boy." The old man looked so scary Markie turned and ran, stumbling up the face of the dune and back into the thicket. He straggled home, weary and cold.

Mama was sitting on the front steps with two of the other mothers in the courtyard, and they were drinking beers and smoking. Mama was laughing uproariously at something as he approached.

"Hey! Here's my little explorer. Where you been, boyfriend?" she greeted him, carefully tipping her cigarette ash down the neck of an empty beer bottle.

"Hanging around," he replied, stopping and swatting at a mosquito.

"You seen Ronnie?" Mama inquired casually, and the other two mothers gave her a look, with little hard smiles.

"Uh-uh." He threaded his way through them up the steps.

"Well, that's funny, because he was going to give you a ride home if he saw you," Mama replied loudly, with an edge coming into her voice. Markie didn't know what he was supposed to say, so he just shrugged as he opened the screen door.

"He's probably out driving around looking for you," Mama stated. She raised her voice to follow him as he retreated into the dark house. "I don't want to start dinner until he gets back. Whyn't you start your bath? Don't forget you've got school tomorrow,"

"Okay," Markie went into the bathroom and switched on the light. When he saw the toilet, he remembered what he was supposed to do. He crept into Mama's bedroom.

Karen was asleep in the middle of the bed, sprawled with her thumb in her mouth. She did not wake up when he slid the dresser drawer open and stood on tiptoe to feel around for the gun. It was at the back, under a fistful of Ronnie's socks. He took it gingerly into the bathroom and lifted the lid of the toilet tank enough to slip it in. It fell with a splash and a clunk, but to his great relief did not shoot a hole in the tank. He turned on the water in the big old claw-footed tub and shook in some bubble flakes. As the tub was filling, he slipped out of his clothes and climbed into the water. All through his bath he half-expected a sudden explosion from the toilet, but none ever came.

When he got out and dressed himself again, the house was still dark. Mama was still outside on the steps, talking with the other ladies. He was hungry, so he padded into the kitchen and made himself a peanut butter and jelly sandwich and ate it, sitting alone at the kitchen table in the dark. Then he went into his little room and switched on the alcove light. He pulled out the box of comic books from under his bed and lay there a while, looking at the pictures and reading as much as he knew yet of the words.

Later he heard Mama sobbing loudly, begging the two other mothers to stay with her, and their gentle excuses about having to get home. Heart thudding, he got up and scrambled into his cowboy pajamas, and got under the covers and turned out the light. He lay in a tense knot, listening to her come weeping through the house, bumping into the walls. Was she going to come in and sit on his bed and cry again? No; the noise woke up Karen, who started to scream in the darkness. He heard Mama stumbling into the bedroom, hushing her, heard the creaking springs as she stretched out on the bed beside the baby. Markie relaxed. He was going to be left in peace. Just before he fell asleep, he wondered where Ronnie was.

Ronnie had played badly in the back room of the Red Rooster, all afternoon. He'd come out at last and lingered on the streetcorner, not wanting to have to go home and explain why he wasn't going in to work the next day. As he'd stood there, an old man had come up and pressed a bottle of beer into his hand and walked quickly on, chuckling. Ronnie was too surprised to thank him for the gift, but he was grateful. He went off and sat on the wall behind the C-Air Motel, sipping his beer and watching the sun go down. From there he went straight into Harry's Bar and had more, and life was good for a while.

But by the time he crawled into his truck and drove out to the old highway, he was in a bad mood again. He was in a worse mood when he climbed from his truck after it ran into the ditch. As he made his way unsteadily through the darkness, a brilliantly simple solution to his problems occurred to him. It would take care of the truck, the lost job, Peggy and the baby, everything. Even the boy. All their problems over forever, with no fights and no explanations. It seemed like the best idea he'd ever had.

He crept into the house, steadying himself by sliding along the wall. Once in the bedroom he groped around in the dresser drawer for a full two minutes before he realized his gun wasn't in there. Peggy was deep unconscious on the bed, and didn't hear him. He stood swaying in the darkness, uncertain what to do next. Then he got mad. All right; he'd show them, and they'd be sorry.

So he left the house, falling noisily down the front steps, but nobody heard him or came to ask if he was all right. Growling to himself he got up and staggered out to the woods, and lay down on the train tracks with a certain sense of ceremony. He passed out there, listening to the wind in the leaves and the distant roar of breakers.

The freight train came through about twenty minutes later.

...WITH BY GOOD INTENTIONS

Carrie Richerson

"So, Mr. Sandoval—your company has won the bid for my little project. I suppose I don't need to tell you that you had some... *fierce*... competition?"

The client smiles at Roy.

A smile from the Big Man is a fearsome sight. It makes Roy want to run far, far away, very fast. Fortunately for his status as low-bidder on this project, certain portions of his anatomy are not cooperating. Inside his steel-capped work boots, all ten toes have begun to gibber and moan among themselves, and to try to slither back up inside his feet. (He is aware that other parts are trying to slither up inside elsewhere.) The toes are blocked in their efforts because the feet have swiftly and silently turned to stone. Rooted to the spot, Roy decides there is nothing to do but act like the professional he is.

"*Sí*, and I guarantee we'll bring this project in on time and within budget."

"You are aware, I trust, of the... *penalties*... that accrue for nonperformance?"

Now the client is beaming. Fangs glint in the ruddy light.

Ice crawls up Roy's legs to his knees, which begin to quiver like an underdone flan. He tries to imagine a steel rebar shoring up his spine so he does not simply fall to the simmering ground and scream.

"*Sí*. We'll be getting started now," he forces himself to say. "There's just one thing, *Señor*," he adds, as the Big Man starts to turn away.

"And that is... ?" The client's tone is silky; the gaze he fixes on Roy could strip the flesh from his bones.

"You're required to supply me with a copy of the approved Environmental Impact Statement before we can start," Roy manages to choke out past a tongue that wants only to flap in abject terror.

"I'm *required*?" The Big Man is suddenly a lot bigger. A lot redder. A lot hotter. He looms over Roy like doom personified. He is almost as terrifying as Roy's *abuela*, Maria Luisa Carmina Portillo de Santiago, when she is voicing her *disappointment* in her grandson. Steam rises from Roy's sodden clothes, but he plunges ahead. "*Sí*. Section 47 of the contract, page 64: 'Contractee agrees to obtain and

272

provide contractor with certified approval of project from the Environmental Protection Agency, and any and all local approvals and licenses, before work can commence. Approved EIS must be available for public inspection at all times at the contractor's site headquarters. Failure of the contractee to obtain such approvals shall not be counted against contractor's performance. Failure to obtain such approvals within a timely fashion shall cause this contract to terminate without prejudice against contractor," Roy quotes from memory. He pulls his damp copy of the contract from his jacket pocket in case the client is not convinced. The moment stretches out. The Big Man contemplates Roy, and Roy stares back, bug- and cross-eyed, unable even to wipe away the sweat that pours down his forehead. Then the client shrugs.

"I can see that you are indeed the right man for the job, Mr. Sandoval. Here is your copy of the EIS." He snaps his fingers and a thick document materializes in his hand. He hands it to Roy; fingerprints smolder in the margins.

Roy checks the EIS carefully. It has all the correct stamps and approvals, and is signed by the commissioner of the EPA herself. Somehow Roy is not surprised to see the Big Man has that kind of pull. Appended to the document are all the necessary local approvals and waivers. He is acutely aware of the client hovering impatiently over him as he reads the papers, in part because of the overpowering reek of sulfur coming off the client's body. For a moment he considers mentioning to the client that there are deodorants to help such a manly Big Man with body odor, then he thinks better of the idea.

"Everything appears to be in order, *Señor*."

"Then you had better get started, hadn't you?" The client points a razored talon to the sun, already well above the eastern horizon. "Tick tock, Mr. Sandoval. Sundown on the seventh day comes apace." He vanishes in a cloud of fume and ash. Only a smoking hoofprint remains.

Roy gasps with relief and almost sags to the ground as his lower extremities unpetrify. He swings around and waves to his crew. "*¡Ándale, hombres!*" Dozens of diesel engines cough to life and begin to puff black exhaust into the clear morning air. The biggest 'dozer, under the command of Roy's gang boss Felipe, spins with almost dainty grace in a half circle and charges toward the survey flags marking the beginning of the route. The blade bangs down and bites into hardpan. Behind Felipe's 'dozer, a conga line of dump trucks, front-end loaders, spreaders, graders, and rollers forms up. Rock crushers, slurry mixers, water trucks, sprayers, asphalt cookers, and all the support vehicles—cooks' RV, first aid RV, Roy's office RV, and the bunk RVs needed for construction far from civilization—organize to the side. The project is underway. Roy whistles over a dump truck and swings into the cab beside the driver. He has a project, a budget, a deadline. A most inflexible deadline.

The first two days they bust rock, tons and tons of it. The demolition crews rove ahead of the 'dozers, blowing the largest boulders and rock ledges apart. The bulldozers blade the beginnings of a roadway through the rubble while front-end loaders shovel the debris into dump trucks, which take it to the crushers. More trucks bring the crushed product back to the route, where spreaders and graders form it into road base. The work proceeds with practiced smoothness.

Roy employs the best demo expert in the business. It is widely acknowledged that Kath can trim dynamite sticks to the millimeter by eye, and juggle a dozen blasting caps at once, stone sober (which everyone knows is much harder than juggling them drunk). She brings the mountains low and levels valleys, makes the rough places smooth and plain as they follow the ruler-straight line of survey flags westward.

On the morning of the third day, out past Kingdom Come, Kath brings Roy the bad news. "Survey flags disappeared last night, boss." Roy has been expecting trouble since the moment they started the project; he is almost relieved that something definite has finally happened so his stomach can stop winding itself in knots. This problem will be easy to solve; he expects more serious attempts at delay to follow.

"Get Jorge and his crew out there with the transit. And Kath—set guards tonight." She nods and goes off to rouse the surveyors and to unlock the armory.

The heat mounts by the hour, and by noon it is unbelievable. Roy makes sure his people have plenty to drink, but most shrug off the temperature. *No es nada,* they say, and work on stoically. Felipe pushes back his Stetson and spits into the dust. "This is nothin', *Jefe*. El Paso in July—now that's *muy caliente.*"

The afternoon brings a spot of good news. Roy's nephew, Ramón Benitez, brings him a sample of a new slurry. Ramón is Roy's sister's son, the first in the extended Sandoval *familia* to get a college degree. At Texas A&M University he studied chemical engineering and agronomy, and he is fond of saying "*El Dios* never made a better chemical engineering factory than the brown Jersey cow." His great ambition is to own a small dairy herd of his own; for now he makes Roy's job easier by constant tinkering with the many surfacing, binding, and weather-proofing chemicals used in paving operations.

He shows Roy a capped jar of thick, gray sludge, and a chunk of sulfurous, flaking rock. "It's this local brimstone, *Tío* Roy, from Hell's Half Acre. We can crush it and use it instead of fly ash. It saves us a lot of money, the slurry spreads easier, and sets up faster and harder." Roy examines the test plot. The reformulated slurry has set up into a smooth, hard surface full of tiny glittering flakes. "*¿Qué es?*" he asks.

"Iron pyrite, *Tío*. Fool's gold," Ramón answers. Roy okays the change. It will save them more than money; it will save time they would have had to spend trucking in the fly ash from power plants back in East Texas. They start spreading the new slurry that afternoon. The first section will be ready to tar by the next morning.

That night only a few survey flags disappear. Guards with rifles patrol the route, setting off road flares every few hundred feet. They report vague shapes skulking in the darkness just outside the circles of light, but only one sharpshooter connects with a target, and a skull-jangling howl greets his success. Morning reveals the corpse of a wolf-like creature four times the size of a Great Dane. "Hellhound," Kath says, pushing the animal's lip back with the barrel of her rifle to show a fang as long as her hand.

Kath brings the news to Roy, who is watching his tar boss roll on the first layer of asphalt sealer. Roy is an asphaltenophile, a connoisseur of heavy hydrocarbons. He knows his tars, from Athabascan bitumen to Trinidadian pitch. "I love the smell of asphalt in the morning," he tells Kath. "It smells like... progress." He is in too good a humor to be dismayed by Kath's report of the Hellhound. He agrees with her plan to handle the beasts if they return.

Roy has been running his crews in shifts from first light in the morning until full dark. He knows that toward the end, his people will have to work all night, under lights, but in these first days, he has let them get as much rest as possible for the sprint to come. It is during second shift lunch, right at noon on the fourth day, when the plague of snakes arrives.

They are rattlesnakes, sidewinders as long as gravel trucks and with hides armored like a Caterpillar. They bite two lunching workers and an assistant cook, while bullets from side arms and rifles bounce off harmlessly. The toll would be higher, but for their habit of coiling before a strike. As one huge head, jaws agape and fangs dripping corrosive venom, weaves back and forth above her, Kath pitches a lit stick of dynamite into the gullet. *BLAM!* When the smoke and the rain of snake parts clears away, so have the snakes. Deep scores in the rock show the fleeing trails. Roy sends scouts armed with RPGs after the surviving snakes. They destroy two more and report the rest have vanished.

Quick action in the emergency RV saves the workers' lives. Roy has had his medics stock up on Holy Water as well as antivenom for just such contingencies. He directs the cleanup of the site and the careful butchering of the remains of the snakes. That evening the workers feast on rattlesnake *fajitas*, with mounds of corn tortillas and roasted *chiles*. "¡Delicioso!" They salute the cooks. "¡Tastes like *pollo!*"

That night the Hellhounds return, but this time Kath has sent her teams out equipped with night-vision goggles, laser sights, and teflon-coated bullets. All night long Roy's dreams are punctuated with the crack of rifle fire, and in the morning he swings up the side of a dump truck to view a reeking pile of carcasses. "Treat them like *el coyote*," he tells Kath.

Ramón has come to report on the progress of his asphalt crews and overhears Roy's instruction. "What is she going to do with them, *Tío* Roy?"

"Wait and see, nephew."

A few hours later, Roy stops his pickup beside the canopy where Ramón has set up his headquarters for the day. As the radio dispatcher coordinates asphalt spreaders and rollers, Roy opens the truck door and motions Ramón inside. "Come, nephew. Let us ride the route and see how work is progressing."

Behind the asphalt team, at the beginning of the route, crews are already building forms for the concrete, while at the far end of the route, the slurry teams are finishing the road base. Every few miles, Kath's hunters have hung up a Hellhound carcass beside the roadway. "Is that what you meant, *Tío*?"

"*Sí.* With *el coyote*, you kill one and hang him up in the yard to warn the others. Figure it will work with Hellhounds, too. Remember this, nephew, for when you run the company—though let us hope you never have a project like *this*." Roy grins at his nephew, then turns serious.

"Ramón, even if we survive this, your mother my sister may never speak to me again for bringing you onto this project. If we fail, we lose everything—not just our lives, but our very hope of *Paraíso*."

Ramón squints into the sun dazzle out the windshield. "We won't fail, *Tío* Roy. This is the best road-building crew ever assembled, and they know what we stand to win. We won't fail you."

Roy drops Ramón back at his dispatch hut. "We work the night through, nephew. Tell your people."

"*Sí, Tío* Roy."

That night, as the asphalt crews hasten to seal the road base ahead of the form construction teams, swarms of vampire bats, so thick they blot out the stars, swoop down to feast. But the cooks have been adding bushels of garlic to the daily *menudo* and *posole*, and the bats flutter away in confusion. The ultrasonic cries of so many might have damaged the workers' hearing, but Roy has told his bosses to enforce the rule requiring earplugs on the job. At the height of the attack, Felipe turns on the ultrahigh-frequency broadcaster. Stunned bats rain from the sky; the crews kick them off the roadway and work on.

Ramón asks Roy, "Why didn't Felipe turn the power high enough to kill them, *Tío*?"

Roy sips his coffee and smiles. "Think, nephew. Where do we get most of our paving contracts? From the Legislature in Austin. We don't need to acquire a bad reputation with those bat-huggers."

Just before dawn, Roy sends everyone but the forms construction teams for a few hours' sleep. As the sun rises he sees maroon and purple clouds massing overhead. He tells the foremen to mount rain canopies over the RVs and heavy equipment and to move all other vehicles and tools under shelter. Then he turns in for a few hours of sleep himself.

The rain of blood begins midmorning and continues all day. Under the canopies they have fashioned from the Hellsnake skins, the concrete crews begin pouring. Roy and the sleeping workers are lulled by the patter and hiss of smoking drops on the impervious hides.

By early afternoon Roy wakes. He dons a chemical protection suit to go out into the bloody downpour to check the progress of the pour. They are using a quick-setting formulation of Portland cement and crushed brimstone that would harden even under water; the rain of blood has no effect on it except to tint the topmost layer a bright pink. Roy chats with the workers for a time as they swing the concrete chutes about and level and smooth the slabs. They swap stories of rains of blood past. "I was in a hurricane of blood once in Veracruz...."

"That's nothing! I was in a blood tornado!"

"My *abuelo* told me he was working cattle on a *rancho* near Harlingen once when there was a flash blood flood, and that's how come Santa Gertrudis cattle are red."

By nightfall the blood eases off to a drizzle and by midnight it is over. Felipe reports to Roy that the first aid unit has treated a few burns, and everyone has a headache from the noxious smell, but no equipment has been lost, and they are still on the timetable.

"Rain of blood—*no problemo, Jefe.* Now a rain of frogs—*that* would have been nasty!"

All night and all the next morning the concrete crews pour slabs, while the finishers follow behind smoothing, edging, cutting expansion joints and filling them with asphalt so the concrete can expand and contract through the blazing days and freezing nights without heaving.

The construction teams, having finished making concrete forms, start building the tollbooths and toll plaza.

By the time lunch is over, the concrete work is done, there have been no more problems, and Roy is getting more and more tense as he anticipates some further disaster. Only the finish work is left. The stripers load up with paint and start out at one o'clock. Behind them, crews set the adhesive reflectors to mark the roadway center lines and lane lines. The construction teams finish the tollbooths and the electronics crew installs and tests the automatic toll counters.

We are going to make it, Roy thinks, as he watches the sun slide down the sky. *We are going to win the biggest payoff of all.*

And then Felipe is at his side. "*Jefe,* we gotta problem."

No, thinks Roy. *Not now. Now when we were so close.*

"It's the striping paint, *Jefe,* the midline yellow. We were running low, so I sent some boys to the depot in Lubbock. The supplier was out, said somebody came in yesterday and bought up every barrel. And there's no time to order some delivered from Houston."

"How much do we need?"

"I figure we'll be short only about a hundred and fifty feet. About two quarts."

One hundred and fifty feet, Roy thinks. *It might as well be a mile. Or the distance between Paraíso and Infierno.*

Roy looks at the sun. The bottom edge of the disc is touching the horizon. A sulfurous wind is rising, and inside his head he hears a vast voice intone softly, *Tick, tock.*

He has never failed to bring a project in on time. He isn't going to start now. "Follow me!" he yells at Felipe as he swings into his pickup and floors it, racing for the striper as it approaches the end of the route. He slams to a stop behind the slow-moving machine and swings up onto the fender. At his gesture, Felipe jumps up beside him. Roy pries the lid off the paint reservoir; the last dregs of yellow paint are draining toward the outlet to the roller. "Steady me," Roy orders Felipe as he yanks his edging tool from his belt. He shoves his arm into the reservoir and slashes open his wrist.

"Keep going!" Felipe yells to the driver as yellow fluid pours out of Roy's arm into the reservoir. Roy wraps his free arm around a handhold and leans over the reservoir. "Whatever happens," he tells Felipe, "don't stop short."

Distant voices float through the blackness.

"*Tío* Roy, can you hear me? Is he going to be okay, Felipe?"

"Sure, *muchacho. A* few days of your *mamá's barbacoa* and some *cervezas*, he'll be *bien. El tigre*, that's your *tío*."

The blackness is starting to lighten to gray. Roy can feel he is lying down; something cold is being pressed to his forehead.

Then there is another voice, and Roy must, now *must*, open his eyes.

"Well, well, Mr. Sandoval. That was very clever of you. It was something I did not anticipate, and that is saying a lot."

There is a crowd around him, but Roy knows the owner of that voice. "All Sandovals bleed highway-marking yellow, *Señor*. Paving is in our blood. Help me up," he says to his crew. Ramón protests, but Felipe and Kath shush him and haul Roy to his feet.

Roy feels as empty as a broken *piñata*. Someone has bound his wrist tightly with a bandana. He leans on Felipe and raises his eyes anxiously to the horizon—the last sliver of a scarlet sun disappears as he looks.

"Yes, Mr. Sandoval. You have completed the project as per the specifications. Your payment is being credited to your account even as we speak."

Roy straightens and turns to look at the client. The Big Man does not look happy, but now Roy is not afraid.

"And our bonus?" he asks.

"Here." The client hands over a thick sheaf of documents. "'Get Out Of Hell Free' passes for everyone on your crew. And their families. Now I suggest you had all better be going, while I am still in the mood to honor our contract."

The heavy equipment and RVs are waiting for Roy's signal. The first souls are already lining up at the tollbooths. As each passes through, a sepulchral wail rings out.

Roy turns to leave, then turns back. "If I may ask one question, *Señor*."

The client glowers. "One."

"Why a divided six-lane superhighway? There's not going to be any return traffic, *no*?"

The Big Man regards Roy as dispassionately as though he is just another mote already broiling in Hell's infernos. "I appreciate the irony, Mr. Sandoval." He turns to watch the ever-lengthening lines at the tollbooths. "I expect my… guests… will appreciate it also, though not perhaps with the same pleasure. Now go." He stamps a hoof and disappears with a sulfurous blast.

"*Vaya con Dios, Señor*," Roy whispers, "though you would not thank me to hear me say it."

Roy turns to his crew crowded around, and his heart swells with pride in these men and women. "*¡Vamanos con Dios, amigos!*" he cries, lifting the sheaf of passes into the air. Cheering, whistling, and clapping greet his announcement before the crew scatters to their vehicles.

The conga line forms up again, heading back to civilization. Roy limps to Felipe's pickup and climbs wearily into the passenger seat. As the truck joins the end of the line of departing machinery, Roy turns to take what he trusts will be his last look at the entrance ramp to Hell. Someone on the crew has taken the time to erect the customary project notification:

THIS CAPITAL IMPROVEMENT PROJECT COMPLETED BY:

SANDOVAL PAVING CO.

ROY SANDOVAL, PROP.

YOUR TAX DOLLARS AT WORK

Someone has crossed out the "Sandoval" before "Paving" and carefully lettered "*Buenos Intenciones.*" Roy laughs, and Felipe raises an eyebrow at him. "Want me to fix it, *Jefe?*"

"Hell, no!" Roy says. "I think I'll change it permanently!"

Felipe grins. "*¡No problemo!*" he whoops and floors the accelerator.

NINE SUNDAYS IN A ROW

Kris Dikeman

If you wanta learn you somethin', go on down to a place where two roads cross. Get there Saturday 'round midnight, and wait there 'til Sunday morning—do that for nine Sundays, all in a row. The dark man, he'll send his dog to watch on you while you wait. And on the ninth morning, the dark man will meet you. And he will learn you—anything you wanta learn. But you remember this: that dark man, he don't work for free.

FIRST SUNDAY

I'm hunkered down in the tall grass, tail down, ears back. She leans back against the oak tree, wiggling her toes in the grass, big ugly boots beside her, moonlight throwing up shadows all around. Sat herself right in the center of the hard-packed and pebbly crossroads the better part of an hour before the soft weedy patch by the roadside and the oak's wide trunk wooed her over. That makes her luckier than that fool boy from Kansas, that one who nodded off three Sundays in. Never heard that turnip truck coming, stupid little bastard. Smashed flatter than flat, and all those turnips spread across the road to hell and breakfast and the driver dead with his back broke.

I hate turnips. Nasty mealy things.

She starts rummaging in that bag of hers, leather bag still reeking of dead cow's fright. Other bad smells too, stinky things, and plastic things. Mebbe a sandwich down close to the bottom, but not a meat sandwich. Good brown bread smell, but no meat. Not a bit.

She comes up with a conjure bag, and even hunkered way back here in the verbena my nose can twitch it out: store bought. The girl has brought a store bought conjure bag to the crossroads. I take a long whiff. No graveyard earth; no dead man's piss; no John the Conqueror root; no blood from a lady's monthly. Just some tired old oregano and a little mustard powder. Bag isn't even flannel.

Silly girl. Ugly thing, short hair like a boy, little scrawny body, looking like no girl I ever saw. Can't hardly tell she's female. I got better to do than sit here babysitting. Nine Sundays is a long time, and she don't have near the tenacity it's gonna take to see this through. Waste of my time.

280

The night is full of good smells; honeysuckle and butterfly lilies, lantana and night-blooming jasmine. There's a breeze from the river and the fireflies are all bunched up in the oak tree, moving through the leaves, little flicky-flick candle flames. Go home, girl. I've got my own business. There's a fox down by the river needs me to show him who's in charge.

She sets the conjure bag aside and pulls out the sandwich. Nope, no meat in there, not a speck. Tomatoes mostly, and green things. Waste of good brown bread. She settles back further against the tree, takes out a thumbed-up old book and starts reading by moonlight. I settle into the verbena. It's a long ways 'til sunrise.

SECOND SUNDAY

She's back under the oak tree, I'm back in the verbena. No breeze tonight, it's hot and close, and Mr. Moon is half the fella he used to be. She's got a lantern, makes a little circle of light, drawing every skeeter in ten counties, big cloud of buzz and bother. She's all over coated up with some unguent from a plastic bottle. Nasty smellin' stuff, and not hardly working by the way she's cussing and slapping.

She cusses like a man, and she's wearing those big old boots again. I expect she wishes she were beautiful. That's what I'd wish for, if I was an ugly woman.

A skeeter lights on my ear and I take a scratch. She stops reading and looks back at where I'm hiding.

"Is someone there?" she says. She holds up the lantern. The skeeter cloud rises up with it, like the mist around Mr. Moon.

"Hello?" she says. She sounds small.

I stay still as still, still as death. Nobody here but us bad things, sugar.

She listens to the night noise for a while, then settles back down, slaps at the skeeters, eats her sandwich. Brown bread again, and eggs this time. I like eggs. Raw is better, but cooked is fine too.

The dawn comes, finally. I'm achy all over from lying still so long. She packs up her stinky bag, looks back at where I'm hiding, walks down the road towards town, scratching at her arms.

I start for home. I'm almost to the shack when Red Rooster steps out of the grass in front of me.

Hear you got a task, he says, strutting up and down like he does. Since the Dark Man gave him those fighting spurs, Red Rooster thinks he's the prettiest trick around.

I'm keeping watch on a girl at the crossroads, I say, trying to slip past him. Keep her from harm, just in case she lasts all nine Sundays.

You think she'll make it? Red Rooster juts his head out and back, up and down, and shakes his big haughty tail. In the dawn, his feathers glow like foxfire. He swaggers a little ways past me and turns back, like he's giving me a show.

The skeeters like to eat her alive tonight, I tell him. I don't know if she'll be back.

And what is it to you, I want to say, but I've got to stay on his sweet side. The

Dark Man, he loves Red Rooster, and I'm not allowed to chase him, or bullyrag him, or nothing.

You better leave off that scratching, unless you want to frighten her away, he says.

You spying on me? I ask, and my hackles rise up. The Dark Man set me to watch over her. You mind your own business.

The Dark Man's business is my business, dog. Remember that. And he turns and struts back into the five-finger grass, impertinent as you please, and I go on home. I am not allowed to chase Red Rooster.

THIRD SUNDAY

Three Sundays in a row, that's more than some, less than many. I don't scratch the skeeters when they come, and she does not hear me.

She'll stop soon.

FOURTH SUNDAY

It's pissing down rain and the skeeters are all off somewhere. She's wearing some outlandish thing, great big piece of plastic with her head poking through the middle. No sandwich tonight, just an apple while she huddles under the oak, lamp in the grass at her feet. Down by the river, something big splashes into the water and she jumps.

Bet you have a nice warm home to go to, I think. The rain is soaking in my fur, and the verbena patch stinks, a skunk having expressed her vehement displeasure somewhere very near. Here we both sit, wet and miserable, because what you have is not enough, you want more and won't work to get it, you want the Dark Man to just hand it over to you. Greedy thing.

Sunrise comes, and she gathers up her things slowly and starts back to town. I go home.

The Dark Man is there, fussing around in the cupboard.

She's still waiting for me, he says.

Yes, boss, I say. This one's not giving up easy.

You're keeping her safe for me, he says, and takes down a mason jar, wipes off the dust with a grubby old rag.

Yes, boss. No harm comes to her.

You are a good dog, he says, and my tail thumps against the table leg.

He holds the jar in the candle flame, tipping it to and fro, watches what's inside beat against the glass.

Red Rooster struts on in.

You stink of skunk, he says to me, and the Dark Man laughs.

I know what that means. I go on out of the shack and crawl underneath the porch to a spot where it's mostly dry. Red Rooster comes out and sashays back and forth a while, those spurs clickety-click on the tired gray boards above my head. The Dark Man calls him inside and shuts the door.

FIFTH SUNDAY

She's sick.

Snuffling and hacking like an old hound, standing up a ways from the lantern. The skeeters have returned, and brought all their kin besides. The verbena still stinks, so I've changed my hiding spot, still downwind of the oak but across the road now in a clump of switchgrass, catty-corner like. She's racked with coughing now, bent over double with little ropy strings of bad-smelling nastiness jumping out of her. My vigil's over soon. She'll go back to her warm house, I'll go back to chasing rabbits and worrying that fox—

Something stealing through the grass. Something low and sly. Rattlesnake. Diamondback, by the smell. Ireful and ill-tempered, moving right to her with murder on its spiteful little mind.

I know where it comes from. I know who sends it. He's looking to reshuffle this deck, steal her away from my master.

You are keeping her safe for me, I hear the Dark Man say, and I tear on out of the high grass and across the road like perdition's flames. The girl sees me coming and lets out a scream, so high and sharp it pains my ears. The rattler sees me too, and lets fly as I come up, but he is just a sorry crawling vermin and I am the Dark Man's Good Dog, and I catch him behind his head and crush his bones in one bite. I whip him back and forth a bit, 'til I'm sure he knows he's dead, and drop him in the road. Then I look around.

She's crouched down behind the oak tree, staring at me, eyes all wide and frightened. She starts in coughing, holding on to the oak to stay upright. I sit down in the road. No point in going back to the high grass now.

"You're his dog," she whispers when her breath comes back. "The black dog. You're real. It's real."

Stupid woman. Why you been sitting out here five Sundays in a row, catching your death of the ague if you don't believe? People only believe the things they can see, and touch, and have. Like that man, that fool from Memphis, handed the Dark Man his guitar and then grabbed his arm, squeezed him like, just to see if he was solid.

The Dark Man don't like to be touched.

She coughs some more, then pulls out a bottle, honey and cold tea and cheap whiskey. She hunkers down beside the oak, swigging and coughing and staring at me, and we spend the rest of the night that way, she and I and the skeeters, and come the dawn I pick up the rattler and go home and her still sitting there, stunned-like.

SIXTH SUNDAY

The Dark Man pours the powder out of the packet. It sifts down into my fur, spilling all around me on the porch. I can smell all the things that went into it, and my nose wrinkles up. Sweet and kinda spoiled, like honey and curdled milk mixed up.

Remember, she can hear you in there, so no talking, he says.

Yes, boss.

He runs his finger across the diamond-patterned skin tacked out on the door, gives the rattle a flick with his finger, and smiles. It's just a little smile, but he knows I see it.

Go on now, he says.

I take off out the shack and down the road. It's close on to midnight. Mr. Moon is still fat and bright, and my shadow chases me all the way to the crossroads.

It's a hot night, muggy like, but she's all wrapped up in a raggedy shawl. She coughs, and it racks her. There's circles under her eyes, and she's all pale and peaked, a sight thinner than she was when all this started. That cold is a long time going. She leaves off coughing, catches her breath, looks up and sees me.

"Dog," she says. Then she stretches out her hand, waggling her fingers. "C'mere dog."

Usually they don't touch me right away. One time, this boy from Charleston wouldn't even let me near and I had to chase him through the grass, all the way to the riverbank. That was a treat.

I go on over and sit near her and I don't put my ears back or growl or show my teeth or nothing. She puts her hand right on my head. She's not a bit afraid.

"Good dog," she says, and my tail thumps in spite of me. "Good dog that saved my life." Her hand moves to the back of my ears. I turn my head a little, and she runs her hand down my spine. Then she finds a sweet spot on my shoulder and commences scratching, and my mutinous left hind foot starts to dance, tappity tap against the dirt.

She rummages around in her stinky bag, comes up with a sandwich.

"You want some of my chicken sandwich?"

Stupid woman. I grab the sandwich out of her hand, gulp it down so fast she don't see it go. Chicken is good. Best when you catch it yourself, but good any way you get it.

"Hey!" she says, and I duck my head away from her hand. She laughs, and scratches behind my ear again. "That was my supper, dog, but I guess you earned it, killing that bad old snake."

Supper? That little bit of chicken and brown bread?

She yawns, and leans back against the tree. "I'm so sleepy," she says. "But I guess I can rest a while, with you here to watch over me." And she with her hand on my back, she closes her eyes and drifts away, down into dreamland, and I go with.

We're standing outside a little tottery tarpaper house. Raggedy curtains drooping in the front window, front yard all mud and junk; an old water pump, a pile of car tires, door off a chicken coop. Clothes on the line, tired sheets and towels and a pair of man's coveralls, ripped and faded. Somewhere here, someplace not right now, I can hear a child crying.

She's beside me in the road, and she looks different. Stronger, more meat on her bones. Ugly boots gone, good walking shoes on her feet, big backpack, all shiny and new-smelling hooked on her shoulder. And something else, something I can't determinate.

"Here I go," she says, and turns her back on the house. She starts down the road, big long steps, and she doesn't look back, but I do. There's a face staring at us from that front window, looking angry and sad both at once, and then the tatty curtains twitch, and the face is gone.

"Dog! You coming?" she says, and I run to catch up.

We walk a long time. Mr. Moon lights the way. There's honeysuckle in the air, thick and sweet, and the further we get from that house the happier she is. Her step gets lighter, like she's shucking off some burden, and she starts in laughing from time to time.

We walk on and on. I flush a fat rabbit and chase it a while. She takes a big meat sandwich out of her bag and gives me half, and we drink our fill from a spring running by the road. She picks up an old stick and throws it as she walks along, and I bring it on back and she throws it again.

By and by the road under our feet changes, from hard-packed dirt to blacktop, smooth and oily and smelling from tar. The sky is changed now, the wind is dry and hot, the trees and brush all gone. And it's a puzzlement to me; I can smell the desert spread out all around us, sand and heat and open sky, but there's water up ahead too, a powerful lot of it.

"Look, dog. There it is." Off in the distance I can see a city, tall buildings and lights shining and blinking, and cars, and people—more than I've ever seen. And something else, a thick, rank smell the Dark Man taught me. Money. Bright lights and noise and money, that's the place her heart yearns for.

She pulls a pack of cards from her pocket, does a one-hand shuffle like she was born with the pasteboards in her hands. She spreads the cards out to make a fan and flutters them back and forth, and the ace of spades jumps out and dances along above us in that hot dry wind a second before she catches it neat as neat and slides it back in.

"They do what I tell them, now," she says. "I'm going to be the queen of the tables, dog, how's that sound to you?"

That's what's different about her, what I couldn't place. This dream is the future, after the Dark Man learns her what she wants to learn.

"Cards? You doing all of this to learn cards?" I ask.

"I'm going to be a queen," she says again, not paying me any mind. She's shuffling the cards again, makes the joker jump up this time. The breeze picks the card and pulls it up out of the deck, and it lands on the blacktop at my feet before she can catch it. The joker is the Dark Man, and he winks up at me. She makes a little *tch* sound and picks up the card, puts it back in the deck.

Her clothes are changed. She's wearing a dress, shiny spangles and beads, her hair is long and kind of curly, on her feet little bitty shoes with tall heels, and her fingers all covered in rings.

You're going to end up in the cupboard with all the rest, I think. But I won't speak. He'll beat me enough for what I've said already, I don't want more than that. No more. Nope.

Nope.

"Listen," I say. "Don't you understand? He don't work for free. You gonna lose your—"

Off in the desert comes a sound, raucous and ugly. It throws my mind into confusion and perplexes my tongue.

A rooster crowing.

Just like that we're back under the oak tree, air all moist and close, skeeters and no-see-ums digging at us. She's skinny again, and tired and sick, and I am just a dumb dog.

She jumps up and grabs her bag. "Three more Sundays, dog, and I'll leave this place forever." She runs on down the road, back to that tarpaper house.

Across the river, Red Rooster crows again. I head on home.

SEVENTH SUNDAY

My back hurts, and my head. The chain is too tight, and it's rubbing off all the fur about my neck.

Just after sunrise, Red Rooster comes strutting down the road like he owns it. He's been to the crossroads. I pick my head up slowly. My ear bleeds, little weepy drops.

"Was she there? She still sick?" I say.

He struts on past, like I'm not there.

I'm hungry.

EIGHTH SUNDAY

The Dark Man takes the chain off and gives me dinner.

Thank you, boss, I say.

Red Rooster has just come back from the crossroads again. He tosses his head, comb waggling. The Dark Man squints at him and Red Rooster finds elsewhere to be, quick as he can.

The Dark Man lays his hand on my head, and it hurts less.

Have you learned your lesson? He asks.

Yes boss, I'm sorry, I say.

He gives a little grunt and goes back into the shack. I wait until the door shuts. I go up onto the porch and sniff around 'til I find the spot where he poured the dream dust on me. There it is, sweet and spoiled-milky, settled into the cracks of the boards. Mebbe enough. Mebbe not.

The Dark Man will go to her at the ninth sunrise; she's got one Sunday still to wait. Next week Mr. Moon is ripe and full. Mebbe a big moon can help a little bit of powder do its work.

NINTH SUNDAY

The Dark Man is rearranging jars in the cupboard.

Boss? I ask.

Yes, he says, not turning around.

Boss, how come that cupboard never gets full? How many jars can that old cupboard hold?

He laughs, tosses the jar in his hand up in the air and catches it. Inside, something wretched flutters, then goes still.

It's a funny thing, he says. There's always room in this cupboard for one more.

He glances at me over his shoulder.

It's an hour 'til sunrise. You can go if you want, he says. Say goodbye to her.

Why I need to do that, Boss? I ask. She'll be back here soon enough.

He laughs at that, sets the jar down and touches my head.

You are my good dog, he says, my creature.

That I am and nothing else, I say.

Go on and catch a rabbit, he says, and takes up the jar again.

Yes boss. Thank you, boss.

I go out and pause on the porch to take a back scratch against the rough old boards. A good long scratch.

I run down the road, stop just before I reach the crossroad. I know he's here.

Come on out, Fussybritches, I say.

Red Rooster bustles out of the grass, all puffed up with vexation. He hates that name.

What do you want, dog? I'm busy on the Dark Man's task. I got this girl to watch for him, he says.

Do tell, I think. I expect a dumb dog like me wouldn't know much about it.

The Dark Man wants you to fetch him up some John the Conqueror root, I say.

I'm not the fetch-it boy round here, he says.

The Dark Man says you pick it nice and clean, like he needs it. But if you don't want to go—

He's off and down the road at a trot. When that big waving flag of a tail disappears over the hill, I run on to the crossroads.

So thin. Like she's the one been chained up all those days.

"Dog! You're back! Where'd you go? Bad dog, not coming to see me. I had to sit here all alone, with a nasty rooster staring at me all the time. He wouldn't move, not even when I threw rocks at him."

I wish you had better aim, I think.

She's petting me, but we don't have time. I shake myself hard, throwing up dream powder all around us. She sneezes, and I do too. We sneeze again and she commences laughing, then coughing, so hard she can't stop. I'm still sneezing—that bad milk smell is all up in my nose—and when I stop, she's breathing like she's just run a race, with a big smear of blood across her lip.

Oh, Mr. Moon. Help this dumb dog.

"What've you been rolling in?" she says, and coughs again. Then her eyes do a flutter. "I'm so tired, dog. I think now you're here, I'll close my eyes…."

And just like that we're out on the dream road, not near the house, but not near the city either. We're somewhere in between, where we took our walk and she threw that stick. She's strong again, and pretty, all done up in her sparkly dress.

"You listen to me, girl," I say. "You get on outta here, straight you wake up. The Dark Man wants your soul for his cupboard. You stay here, he'll get you for sure."

"He's going to help me." She smiles and takes the cards out again. She starts that fancy one-handed shuffle.

"How far you going to get sick as you are? What good playing cards do you in the graveyard? He means to have your soul, and he'll get it if you tarry here."

"He can't take my soul, dog."

"He's the Dark Man and it's Sunday number nine. He can take what he pleases now."

"No, dog." She bends down to me. "My soul was taken long ago," she says, and hikes up her long skirt for me to see a cicatrix of scars across her belly and thighs. She's been mistreated, this girl has.

"He can't hurt me any more than I been hurt," she says and I can see the beatings and the screams and bad times, swimming just below her skin.

You're a child and you're wrong, so wrong you can't imagine. You don't know about souls and what they worth. Don't know how much you can lose. You ain't seen the cupboard.

I say it, but no sound comes out.

No need for Red Rooster now; envious time has fled. The light is changing. It's dawn, and we're back at the crossroads.

The Dark Man steps from the high grass, takes off his best hat and gives her a bow. His coat is brushed, his boots polished to a killing shine.

Good morning, my dear, he says.

"Good morning sir. My name is Sally," she says.

Hello, Sally. How may I help you?

She hands over the cards, and he begins to shuffle. I know what comes next, and head to the oak tree to lie down.

The lesson takes about an hour. All that waiting, for an hour in his company. He hands the cards back to her one last time, and she shows him what she's learned. He applauds.

A pleasure to meet you, Sally, he says, I hope to see you again. He takes off his right glove and extends his hand to her.

I turn my head away as she reaches her hand over. They shake. Down by the river, Red Rooster screams in triumph.

"Thank you, but I'm heading west," Sally says, and picks up her bag. She slings it onto her shoulder, coughs with the effort. Then she looks the Dark Man right in the eye.

"Your dog is coming with me," she says.

He smiles. I don't believe that's so, Sally. He can be trouble, that dog, but he is mine.

"He's coming with me," she says. "We're going to take care of each other."

The Dark Man looks over at me, all quiet in the grass.

Is that so, dog? he asks. You leaving Red Rooster and me for greener pastures?

I look at her. Sally. She pats her thigh in a come-on gesture. I put my head down again.

No boss, I say to him. I am your good dog.

Sally calls me, pats her thigh again. I don't look up. The Dark Man laughs.

Good day, Miss, I think we will meet again soon, he says. Sooner than you might think.

She calls me one more time. I stand up and walk over to the Dark Man. He grabs me by the back of my neck, where my skin's rubbed all raw, but I don't wince. Not a bit. We watch Sally turn and walk down the road, stopping now and then to cough and shift that stinky bag from one shoulder to another. We walk home.

She's dying. She was a skinny thing at the start, and now that cold has turned on her, rotting out her lungs. I don't even think she knows it yet, but I can smell the death coming out of her when she breathes. She won't get even halfway to that bright city before she goes and then her soul's gonna come flying right on back here, and he'll put her in a jam jar and lock her away.

And me? Gonna be bad for me. He's gonna beat me and starve me and send that swaggering fowl to lord it over me. And I'll have to bear it. Because I know, someday, there'll be one second he won't be watching, one moment when I can get close. Mebbe some night when Mr. Moon is full so there's light for her to fly away by.

I'll tip that cupboard over, see if I don't.

LULL

by Kelly Link

There was a lull in the conversation. We were down in the basement, sitting around the green felt table. We were holding bottles of warm beer in one hand, and our cards in the other. Our cards weren't great. Looking at each others' faces, we could see that clearly.

We were tired. It made us more tired to look at each other when we saw we weren't getting away with anything at all. We didn't have any secrets.

We hadn't seen each other for a while and it was clear that we hadn't changed for the better. We were between jobs, or stuck in jobs that we hated. We were having affairs and our wives knew and didn't care. Some of us were sleeping with each others' wives. There were things that had gone wrong, and we weren't sure who to blame.

We had been talking about things that went backwards instead of forwards. Things that managed to do both at the same time. Time travelers. People who weren't stuck like us. There was that new movie that went backwards, and then Jeff put this music on the stereo where all the lyrics were palindromes. It was something his kid had picked up. His kid Stan was a lot cooler than we had ever been. He was always bringing things home, Jeff said, saying, You have got to listen to this. Here, try this. These guys are good.

Stan was the kid who got drugs for the other kids when there was going to be a party. We had tried not to be bothered by this. We trusted our kids and we hoped that they trusted us, that they weren't too embarrassed by us. We weren't cool. We were willing to be liked. That would have been enough.

Stan was so very cool that he hadn't even minded taking care of some of us, the parents of his friends (the friends of his parents), although sometimes we just went through our kids' drawers, looked under the mattresses. It wasn't that different from taking Halloween candy out of their Halloween bags, which was something we had also done, when they were younger and went to bed before we did.

Stan wasn't into that stuff now, though. None of the kids were. They were into music instead.

You couldn't get this music on CD. That was part of the conceit. It came only on cassette. You played one side, and then on the other side the songs all played backwards and the lyrics went forwards and backwards all over again in one long endless loop. La allah ha llal. Do, oh, oh, do you, oh do, oh, wanna?

Bones was really digging it. "Do you, do you wanna dance, you do, you do," he said, and laughed and tipped his chair back. "Snakey canes. Hula boolah."

Someone mentioned the restaurant downtown where you were supposed to order your dessert and then you got your dinner.

"I fold," Ed said. He threw his cards down on the table.

Ed liked to make up games. People paid him to make up games. Back when we had a regular poker night, he was always teaching us a new game and this game would be based on a TV show or some dream he'd had.

"Let's try something new. I'm going to deal out everything, the whole deck, and then we'll have to put it all back. We'll see each other's hands as we put them down. We're going for low. And we'll swap. Yeah, that might work. Something else, like a wild card, but we won't know what the wild card was, until the very end. We'll need to play fast—no stopping to think about it—just do what I tell you to do."

"What'll we call it?" he said, not a question, but as if we'd asked him, although we hadn't. He was shuffling the deck, holding the cards close like we might try to take them away. "DNA Hand. Got it?"

"That's a shitty idea," Jeff said. It was his basement, his poker table, his beer. So he got to say things like that. You could tell that he thought Ed looked happier than he ought to. He was thinking Ed ought to remember his place in the world, or maybe Ed needed to be reminded what his place was. His new place. Most of us were relieved to see that Ed looked okay. If he didn't look okay, that was okay too. We understood. Bad things had happened to all of us.

We were contemplating these things and then the tape flips over and starts again.

It's catchy stuff. We could listen to it all night.

"Now we chant along and summon the Devil," Bones says. "Always wanted to do that."

Bones has been drunk for a while now. His hair is standing up and his face is shiny and red. He has a fat stupid smile on his face. We ignore him, which is what he wants. Bones's wife is just the same, loud and useless. The thing that makes the rest of us sick is that their kids are the nicest, smartest, funniest, best kids. We can't figure it out. They don't deserve kids like that.

Brenner asks Ed if he's found a new place to live. He has.

"Off the highway, down by that Texaco, in the orchards. This guy built a road and built the house right on top of the road. Just, plop, right in the middle of the road. Kind of like he came walking up the road with the house on his back, got tired, and just dropped it."

"Not very good feng shui," Pete says.

Pete has read a book. He's got a theory about picking up women, which he's always sharing with us. He goes to Barnes & Noble on his lunch hour and hangs around in front of displays of books about houses and decorating, skimming through architecture books. He says it makes you look smart and just domesticated enough. A man looking at pictures of houses is sexy to women.

We've never asked if it works for him.

Meanwhile, we know, Pete's wife is always after him to go up on the roof and gut the drains, reshingle and patch, paint. Pete isn't really into this. Imaginary houses are sexy. Real ones are work.

He did go buy a mirror at Pottery Barn and hang it up, just inside the front door, because otherwise, he said, evil spirits go rushing up the staircase and into the bedrooms. Getting them out again is tricky.

The way the mirror works is that they start to come in, look in the mirror, and think a devil is already living in the house. So they take off. Devils can look like anyone—salespeople, Latter-day Saints, the people who mow your lawns—even members of your own family. So you have to have a mirror.

Ed says, "Where the house is, is the first weird thing. The second thing is the house. It's like this team of architects went crazy and sawed two different houses in half and then stitched them back together. Casa Del Guggenstein. The front half is really old—a hundred years old—the other half is aluminum siding."

"Must have brought down the asking price," Jeff says.

"Yeah," Ed says. "And the other thing is there are all these doors. One at the front and one at the back and two more on either side, right smack where the aluminum siding starts, these weird, tall, skinny doors, like they're built for basketball players. Or aliens."

"Or palm trees," Bones says.

"Yeah," Ed says. "Sure. Palm trees. And then one last door, this vestigial door, up in the master bedroom. Not like a door that you walk through, for a closet, or a bathroom. It opens and there's nothing there. No staircase, no balcony, no point to it. It's a Tarzan door. Up in the trees. You open it and an owl might fly in. Or a bat. The previous tenant left that door locked—apparently he was afraid of sleepwalking."

"Fantastic," Brenner says. "Wake up in the middle of the night and go to the bathroom, you could just pee out the side of your house."

He opens up the last beer and shakes some pepper in it. Brenner has a thing about pepper. He even puts it on ice cream. Pete swears that one time at a party he wandered into Brenner's bedroom and looked in a drawer in a table beside the bed. He says he found a box of condoms and a pepper mill. When we asked what he was doing in Brenner's bedroom, he winked and then put his finger to his mouth and zipped his lip.

Brenner has a little pointed goatee. It might look silly on some people, but not on Brenner. The pepper thing sounds silly, maybe, but not even Jeff teases Brenner about it.

"I remember that house," Alibi says.

We call him Alibi because his wife is always calling to check up on him. She'll say, So was Alec out shooting pool with you the other night, and we'll say, Sure he was, Gloria. The problem is that sometimes Alibi has told her some completely different story and she's just testing us. But that's not our problem and that's not our fault. She never holds it against us and neither does he.

"We used to go up in the orchards at night and have wars. Knock each other down with rotten apples. There were these peacocks. You bought the orchard house?"

"Yeah," Ed says. "I need to do something about the orchard. All the apples are falling off the trees and then they just rot on the ground. The peacocks eat them and get drunk. There are drunk wasps, too. If you go down there you can see the wasps hurtling around in these loopy lines and the peacocks grab them right out of the air. Little pickled wasp hors d'oeuvres. Everything smells like rotting apples. All night long, I'm dreaming about eating wormy apples."

For a second, we're afraid Ed might tell us his dreams. Nothing is worse than someone telling you their dreams.

"So what's the deal with the peacocks?" Bones says.

"Long story," Ed says.

So you know how the road to the house is a private road, you turn off the highway onto it, and it meanders up some until you run into the house. Some day I'll drive home and park the car in the living room.

There's a big sign that says private. But people still drive up the turnoff, lost, or maybe looking for a picnic spot, or a place to pull off the road and fuck. Before you hear the car coming, you hear the peacocks. Which was the plan because this guy who built it was a real hermit, a recluse.

People in town said all kinds of stuff about him. Nobody knew. He didn't want anybody to know.

The peacocks were so he would know when anyone was coming up to the house. They start screaming before you ever see a car. So remember, out the back door, the road goes on down through the orchards, there's a gate and then you're back on the main highway again. And this guy, the hermit, he kept two cars. Back then, nobody had two cars. But he kept one car parked in front of the house and one parked at the back so that whichever way someone was coming, he could go out the other way real fast and drive off before his visitor got up to the house.

He had an arrangement with a grocer. The grocer sent a boy up to the house once every two weeks, and the boy brought the mail too, but there wasn't ever any mail.

The hermit had painted in the windows of his cars, black, except for these little circles that he could see out of. You couldn't see in. But apparently he used to drive around at night. People said they saw him. Or they didn't see him. That was the point.

The real estate agent said she heard that once this guy had to go to the doctor. He had a growth or something. He showed up in the doctor's office wearing a woman's hat with a long black veil that hung down from the crown, so you couldn't see his face. He took off his clothes in the doctor's office and kept the hat on.

One night half of the house fell down. People all over the town saw lights, like fireworks or lightning, up over the orchard. Some people swore they saw something big, all lit up, go up into the sky, like an explosion, but quiet. Just lights. The next day, people went up to the orchard. The hermit was waiting for them—he had his veil on. From the front, the house looked fine. But you could tell something had caught fire. You could smell it, like ozone.

The hermit said it had been lightning. He rebuilt the house himself. Had lumber and everything delivered. Apparently kids used to go sneak up in the trees in the orchard and watch him while he was working, but he did all the work wearing the hat and the veil.

He died a long time ago. The grocer's boy figured out something was wrong because the peacocks were coming in and out of the windows of the house and screaming.

So now they're still down in the orchards and under the porch, and they still came in the windows and made a mess if Ed forgot and left the windows open too wide. Last week a fox came in after a peacock. You wouldn't think a fox would go after something so big and mean. Peacocks are mean.

Ed had been downstairs watching TV.

"I heard the bird come in," he says, "and then I heard a thump and a slap like a chair going over and when I went to look, there was a streak of blood going up the floor to the window. A fox was going out the window and the peacock was in its mouth, all the feathers dragging across the sill. Like one of Susan's paintings."

Ed's wife, Susan, took an art class for a while. Her teacher said she had a lot of talent. Brenner modeled for her, and so did some of our kids, but most of Susan's paintings were portraits of her brother, Andrew. He'd been living with Susan and Ed for about two years. This was hard on Ed, although he'd never complained about it. He knew Susan loved her brother. He knew her brother had problems.

Andrew couldn't hold down a job. He went in and out of rehab, and when he was out, he hung out with our kids. Our kids thought Andrew was cool. The less we liked him, the more time our kids spent with Andrew. Maybe we were just a little jealous of him.

Jeff's kid, Stan, he and Andrew were thick as thieves. Stan was the one who found Andrew and called the hospital. Susan never said anything, but maybe she blamed Stan. Everybody knew Stan had been getting stuff for Andrew.

Another thing that nobody said: what happened to Andrew, it was probably good for the kids in the long run.

Those paintings—Susan's paintings—were weird. None of the people in her paintings ever looked very comfortable, and she couldn't do hands. And there were always these animals in the paintings, looking as if they'd been shot, or gutted, or if they didn't look dead, they were definitely supposed to be rabid. You worried about the people.

She hung them up in their house for a while, but they weren't comfortable paintings. You couldn't watch TV in the same room with them. And Andrew had this habit, he'd sit on the sofa just under one portrait, and there was another one too, above the TV. Three Andrews was too many.

Once Ed brought Andrew to poker night. Andrew sat awhile and didn't say anything, and then he said he was going upstairs to get more beer and he never came back. Three days later, the highway patrol found Ed's car parked under a bridge. Stan and Andrew came home two days after that, and Andrew went back into rehab. Susan used to go visit him and take Stan with her—she'd take her sketchbook. Stan said Andrew would sit there and Susan would draw him and nobody ever said a word.

After the class was over, while Andrew was still in rehab, Susan invited all of us to go to this party at her teacher's studio. What we remember is that Pete got drunk and made a pass at the instructor, this sharp-looking woman with big dangly earrings. We were kind of surprised, not just because he did it in front of his wife, but because we'd all just been looking at her paintings. All these deer and birds and cows draped over dinner tables, and sofas, guts hanging out, eyeballs all shiny and fixed—so that explained Susan's portraits, at least.

We wonder what Susan did with the paintings of Andrew.

"I've been thinking about getting a dog," Ed says.

"Fuck," we say. "A dog's a big responsibility." Which is what we've spent years telling our kids.

The music on the tape loops and looped. It was going round for a second time. We sat and listened to it. We'll be sitting and listening to it for a while longer.

"This guy," Ed says, "the guy who was renting this place before me, he was into some crazy thing. There's all these mandalas and pentagrams painted on the floors and walls. Which is also why I got it so cheap. They didn't want to bother stripping the walls and repainting; this guy just took off one day, took a lot of the furniture too. Loaded up his truck with as much as he could take."

"So no furniture?" Pete says. "Susan get the dining room table and chairs? The bed? You sleeping in a sleeping bag? Eating beanie weenies out of a can?"

"I got a futon," Ed says. "And I've got my work table set up, the TV and stuff. I've been going down to the orchard, grilling on the hibachi. You guys should come over. I'm working on a new video game—it'll be a haunted house—those are really big right now. That's why this place is so great for me. I can use every-thing. Next weekend? I'll fix hamburgers and you guys can sit up in the house, keep cool, drink beer, test the game for me. Find the bugs."

"There are always bugs," Jeff says. He's smiling in a mean way. He isn't so nice when he's been drinking. "That's life. So should we bring the kids? The wives? Is this a family thing? Ellie's been asking about you. You know that retreat she's on, she called from the woods the other day. She went on and on about this past life. Apparently she was a used-car salesman. She says that this life is karmic payback, being married to me, right? She gets home day after tomorrow. We get together, maybe Ellie can set you up with someone. Now that you're a free man, you need to take some advantage."

"Sure," Ed says, and shrugs. We can see him wishing that Jeff would shut up, but Jeff doesn't shut up.

Jeff says, "I saw Susan in the grocery store the other day. She looked fantastic. It wasn't that she wasn't sad anymore, she wasn't just getting by, she was radiant, you know? That special glow. Like Joan of Arc. Like she knew something. Like she'd won the lottery."

"Well, yeah," Ed says. "That's Susan. She doesn't live in the past. She's got this new job, this research project. They're trying to contact aliens. They're using household appliances: satellite dishes, cell phones, car radios, even refrigerators. I'm not sure how. I'm not sure what they're planning to say. But they've got a lot of grant money. Even hired a speechwriter."

"Wonder what you say to aliens," Brenner says. "Hi, honey, I'm home. What's for dinner?"

"Your place or mine?" Pete says. "What's a nice alien like you doing in a galaxy like this?"

"Where you been? I've been worried sick," Alibi says.

Jeff picks up a card, props it sideways against the green felt. Picks up another one, leans it against the first. He says, "You and Susan always looked so good together. Perfect marriage, perfect life. Now look at you: she's talking to aliens, and you're living in a haunted house. You're an example to all of us, Ed. Nice guy like you, bad things happen to you, Susan leaves a swell guy like you, what's the lesson here? I've been thinking about this all year. You and Ellie must have worked at the same car dealership, in that past life."

Nobody says anything. Ed doesn't say anything, but the way we see him look at Jeff, we know that this haunted house game is going to have a character in it who walks and talks a lot like Jeff. This Jeff character is going to panic and run around on the screen of people's TVs and get lost.

It will stumble into booby traps and fall onto knives. Its innards will sloop out. Zombies are going to crack open the bones of its legs and suck on the marrow. Little devils with monkey faces are going to stitch its eyes open with tiny stitches and then they are going to piss ribbons of acid into its eyes.

Beautiful women are going to fuck this cartoon Jeff in the ass with garden shears. And when this character screams, it's going to sound a lot like Jeff screaming. Ed's good at the little details. The kids who buy Ed's games love the details. They buy his games for things like this.

Jeff will probably be flattered.

Jeff starts complaining about Stan's phone bill, this four-hundred-dollar cell phone charge that Stan ran up. When he asked about it, Stan handed him a stack of twenties just like that. That kid always has money to spare.

Stan also gave Jeff this phone number. He told Jeff that it's like this phone sex line, but with a twist. You call up and ask for this girl named Starlight, and she tells you sexy stories, only, if you want, they don't have to be sexy. They can be any kind of story you want. You tell her what kind of story you want, and she makes it up. Stan says it's Stephen King and sci-fi and the *Arabian Nights* and *Penthouse Letters* all at once.

Ed interrupts Jeff. "You got the number?"

"What?" Jeff says.

"I just got paid for the last game," Ed says. "The one with the baby heads and the octopus girlies, the Martian combat hockey. Let's call that number. I'll pay. You put her on speaker and we'll all listen, and it's my treat, okay, because I'm such a swell guy."

Bones says that it sounds like a shit idea to him, which is probably why Jeff went and got the phone bill and another six-pack of beer. We all take another beer.

Jeff turns the stereo down—

Madam I'm Adam
Oh Madam my Adam

—and puts the phone in the middle of the table. It sits there, in the middle of all that green, like an island or something. Marooned. Jeff switches it on speaker. "Four bucks a minute," he says, and shrugs, and dials the number.

"Here," Ed says. "Pass it over."

The phone rings and we listen to it ring and then a woman's voice, very pleasant, says hello and asks if Ed is over eighteen. He says he is. He gives her his credit card number. She asks if he was calling for anyone in particular.

"Starlight," Ed says.

"One moment," the woman says. We hear a click and then Starlight is on the line. We know this because she says so. She says, "Hi, my name is Starlight. I'm going to tell you a sexy story. Do you want to know what I'm wearing?"

Ed grunts. He shrugs. He grimaces at us. He needs a haircut. Susan used to cut his hair, which we used to think was cute. He and Andrew had these identical lopsided haircuts. It was pretty goofy.

"Can I call you Susan?" Ed says.

Which we think is strange.

Starlight says, "If you really want to, but my name's really Starlight. Don't you think that's sexy?"

She sounds like a kid. A little girl—not even like a girl. Like a kid. She doesn't sound like Susan at all. Since the divorce, we haven't seen much of Susan, although she calls our houses sometimes, to talk to our wives. We're a little worried about what she's been saying to them.

Ed says, "I guess so." We can tell he's only saying that to be polite, but Starlight laughs as if he's told her a joke. It's weird hearing that little-kid laugh down here.

Ed says, "So are you going to tell me a story?"

Starlight says, "That's what I'm here for. But usually the guy wants to know what I'm wearing."

Ed says, "I want to hear a story about a cheerleader and the Devil."

Bones says, "So what's she wearing?"

Pete says, "Make it a story that goes backwards."

Jeff says, "Put something scary in it."

Alibi says, "Sexy."

Brenner says, "I want it to be about good and evil and true love, and it should also be funny. No talking animals. Not too much fooling around with the narrative structure. The ending should be happy but still realistic, believable, you know, and there shouldn't be a moral although we should be able to think back later and have some sort of revelation. No *and suddenly they woke up and discovered that it was all a dream*. Got that?"

Starlight says, "Okay. The Devil and a cheerleader. Got it. Okay."

The Devil and the Cheerleader

So the Devil is at a party at the cheerleader's house. They've been playing spin the bottle. The cheerleader's boyfriend just came out of the closet with her best friend. Earlier the cheerleader felt like slapping him, and now she knows why. The bottle pointed at her best friend who had just shrugged and smiled at her. Then the bottle was spinning and when the bottle stopped spinning, it was in her boyfriend's hand.

Then all of a sudden an egg timer was going off. Everyone was giggling and they were all standing up to go over by the closet, like they were all going to try to squeeze inside. But the Devil stood up and took the cheerleader's hand and pulled her backwards-forwards.

So she knew what exactly had happened, and was going to happen, and some other things besides.

This is the thing she likes about backwards. You start out with all the answers, and after a while, someone comes along and gives you the questions, but you don't have to answer them. You're already past that part. That was what was so nice about being married. Things got better and better until you hardly even knew each other anymore. And then you said good night and went out on a date, and after that you were just friends. It was easier that way—that's the dear, sweet, backwards way of the world.

Just a second, let's go back for a second.

Something happened. Something has happened. But nobody ever talked about it, at least not at these parties. Not anymore.

Everyone's been drinking all night long, except the Devil, who's a teetotaler.

He's been pretending to drink vodka out of a hip flask. Everybody at the party is drunk right now and they think he's okay. Later they'll sober up. They'll think he's pretentious, an asshole, drinking air out of a flask like that.

There are a lot of empty bottles of beer, some empty bottles of whiskey. There's a lot of work still to be done, by the look of it. They're using one of the beer bottles, that's what they're spinning. Later on it will be full and they won't have to play this stupid game.

The cheerleader guesses that she didn't invite the Devil to the party. He isn't the kind of guy that you have to invite. He'll probably show up by himself. But now they're in the closet together for five minutes. The cheerleader's boyfriend isn't too happy about this, but what can he do? It's that kind of party. She's that kind of cheerleader.

They're a lot younger than they used to be. At parties like this, they used to be older, especially the Devil. He remembers all the way back to the end of the world. The cheerleader wasn't a cheerleader then. She was married and had kids and a husband.

Something's going to happen, or maybe it's already happened. Nobody ever talks about it. If they could, what would they say?

But those end-of-the-world parties were crazy. People would drink too much and they wouldn't have any clothes on. There'd be these sad little piles of clothes in the living room, as if something had happened, and the people had disappeared, disappeared right out of their clothes. Meanwhile, the people who belonged to the clothes would be out in the backyard, waiting until it was time to go home. They'd get up on the trampoline and bounce around and cry.

There would be a bottle of extra-virgin olive oil and sooner or later someone was going to have to refill it and go put it back on the pantry shelf. You'd have had these slippery naked middle-aged people sliding around on the trampoline and the oily grass, and then in the end all you'd have would be a bottle of olive oil, some olives on a tree, a tree, an orchard, an empty field.

The Devil would stand around feeling awkward, hoping that it would turn out he'd come late.

The kids would be up in their bedrooms, out of the beds, looking out the windows, remembering when they used to be older. Not that they ever got that much older.

But the world is younger now. Things are simpler. Now the cheerleader has parents of her own, and all she has to do is wait for them to get home, and then this party can be over.

Two days ago was the funeral. It was just how everyone said it would be.

Then there were errands, people to talk to. She was busy.

She hugged her aunt and uncle good-bye and moved into the house where she would live for the rest of her life. She unpacked all her boxes, and the Salvation Army brought her parents' clothes and furniture and pots and pans, and other people, her parents' friends, helped her hang her mother's clothes in her mother's closet. (Not this closet.) She bunched her mother's clothes up in her hand and sniffed, curious and hungry and afraid.

She suspects, remembering the smell of her mother's monogrammed sweaters, that they'll have fights about things. Boys, music, clothes. The cheerleader will learn to let all of these things go.

If her kids were still around, they would say I told you so. What they did say was, Just wait until you have parents of your own. You'll see.

The cheerleader rubs her stomach. Are you in there?

She moved the unfamiliar, worn-down furniture around so that it matched up old grooves in the floor. Here was the shape of someone's buttocks, printed onto a seat cushion. Maybe it would be her father's favorite chair.

She looked through her father's records. There was a record playing on the phonograph, it wasn't anything she had ever heard before, and she took it off, laid it back in its empty white sleeve. She studied the death certificates. She tried to think what to tell her parents about their grandchildren, what they'd want to know.

Her favorite song had just been on the radio for the very last time. Years and years ago, she'd danced to that song at her wedding. Now it was gone, except for the feeling she'd had when she listened to it. Sometimes she still felt that way, but there wasn't a word for it anymore.

Tonight, in a few hours, there will be a car wreck and then her parents will be coming home. By then, all her friends will have left, taking away six-packs and boyfriends and newly applied coats of hair spray and lipstick.

She thinks she looks a bit like her mother.

Before everyone showed up, while everything was still a wreck downstairs, before the police had arrived to say what they had to say, she was standing in her parents' bathroom. She was looking in the mirror.

She picked a lipstick out of the trash can, an orangey red that will be a favorite because there's just a little half-moon left. But when she looked at herself in the mirror, it didn't fit. It didn't belong to her. She put her hand on her breastbone, pressed hard, felt her heart beating faster and faster. She couldn't wear her mother's lipstick while her mother lay on a gurney somewhere in a morgue: waiting to be sewn up; to have her clothes sewn back on; to breathe; to wake up; to see the car on the other side of the median, sliding away; to see her husband, the man that she's going to marry someday; to come home to meet her daughter.

The recently dead are always exhausted. There's so much to absorb, so many things that need to be undone. They have their whole lives ahead of them.

The cheerleader's best friend winks at her. The Devil's got a flashlight with two dead batteries. Somebody closes the door after them.

Soon, very soon, already now, the batteries in the Devil's flashlight are old and tired and there's just a thin line of light under the closet door. It's cramped in the closet and it smells like shoes, paint, wool, cigarettes, tennis rackets, ghosts of perfume and sweat. Outside the closet, the world is getting younger, but in here is where they keep all the old things. The cheerleader put them all in here last week.

She's felt queasy for most of her life. She's a bad time traveler. She gets time-sick. It's as if she's always just a little bit pregnant, are you in there? and it's worse in here, with all these old things that don't belong to her, even worse because the Devil is always fooling around with time.

The Devil feels right at home. He and the cheerleader make a nest of coats and sit down on them, facing each other. The Devil turns the bright, constant beam of the flashlight on the cheerleader. She's wearing a little flippy skirt. Her knees are up, making a tent out of her skirt. The tent is full of shadows—so is the closet. The Devil conjures up another Devil, another cheerleader, mouse-sized, both of them, sitting under the cheerleader's skirt. The closet is full of Devils and cheerleaders.

"I just need to hold something," the cheerleader says. If she holds something, maybe she won't throw up.

"Please," the Devil says. "It tickles. I'm ticklish."

The cheerleader is leaning forward. She's got the Devil by the tail. Then she's touching the Devil's tail with her pompoms. He quivers.

"Please don't," he says. He giggles.

The Devil's tail is tucked up under his legs. It isn't hot, but the Devil is sweating. He feels sad. He's not good at being sad. He flicks the flashlight on and off. Here's a knee. Here's a mouth. Here's a sleeve hanging down, all empty. Someone knocks on the closet door.

"Go away," the cheerleader says. "It hasn't been five minutes yet. Not even."

The Devil can feel her smile at him, like they're old friends. "Your tail. Can I touch it?" the cheerleader says.

"Touch what?" the Devil says. He feels a little excited, a little nervous. Old enough to know better, brand-new enough, here in the closet, to be jumpy. He's taking a chance here. Girls—women—aren't really domestic animals at the moment, although they're getting tamer, more used to living in houses. Less likely to bite.

"Can I touch your tail now?" the cheerleader says.

"No!" the Devil says.

"I'm shy," he says. "Maybe you could stroke my tail with your pompom, in a little bit."

"We could make out," the cheerleader says. "That's what we're supposed to do, right? I need to be distracted because I think I'm about to have this thought. It's going to make me really sad. I'm getting younger, you know? I'm going to keep on getting younger. It isn't fair."

She puts her feet against the closet door. She kicks once, like a mule.

She says, "I mean, you're the Devil. You don't have to worry about this stuff.

In a few thousand years, you'll be back at the beginning again and you'll be in good with God again, right?"

The Devil shrugs. Everybody knows the end of that story.

The cheerleader says, "Everyone knows that old story. You're famous. You're like John Wilkes Booth. You're historical—you're going to be really important. You'll be Mr. Bringer-of-Light and you'll get good tables at all the trendy restaurants, choruses of angels and maître d's, et cetera, la, la, la, they'll all be singing hallelujahs forever, please pass the vichyssoise, and then God unmakes the world and he'll put all the bits away in a closet like this."

The Devil smirks. He shrugs. It isn't a bad life, hanging around in closets with cheerleaders. And it gets better.

The cheerleader says, "It isn't fair. I'd tell him so, if he were here. He'll unhang the stars and pull Leviathan right back out of the deep end of the vasty bathwater, and you'll be having Leviathan tartare for dinner. Where will I be, then? You'll be around. You're always around. But me, I'll get younger and younger and in a handful of years I won't be me at all, and my parents will get younger and so on and so on, whoosh! We'll be gone like a flash of light, and you won't even remember me. Nobody will remember me! Everything that I was, that I did, all the funny things that I said, and the things that my friends said back to me, that will all be gone. But you go all the way backwards. You go backwards and forwards. It isn't fair. You could always remember me. What could I do so that you would remember me?"

"As long as we're in this closet," the Devil says, he's magnanimous, "I'll remember you."

"But in a few minutes," the cheerleader says, "we'll go back out of the closet and the bottle will spin, and then the party will be over, and my parents will come home, and nobody will ever remember me."

"Then tell me a story," the Devil says. He puts his sharp, furry paw on her leg. "Tell me a story so that I'll remember you."

"What kind of story?" says the cheerleader.

"Tell me a scary story," the Devil says. "A funny, scary, sad, happy story. I want everything." He can feel his tail wagging as he says this.

"You can't have everything," the cheerleader says, and she picks up his paw and puts it back on the floor of the closet. "Not even in a story. You can't have all the stories you want."

"I know," the Devil says. He whines. "But I still want it. I want things. That's my job. I even want the things that I already have. I want everything you have. I want the things that don't exist. That's why I'm the Devil." He leers and it's a shame because she can't see him in the dark. He feels silly.

"Well, what's the scariest thing?" says the cheerleader. "You're the expert, right? Give me a little help here."

"The scariest thing," the Devil says. "Okay, I'll give you two things. Three things. No, just two. The third one is a secret."

The Devil's voice changes. Later on, one day the cheerleader will be listening to a preschool teacher say back the alphabet, with the sun moving across the window, nothing ever stays still, and she'll be reminded of the Devil and the closet and the line of light under the door, the peaceful little circle of light the flashlight makes against the closet door.

The Devil says, "I'm not complaining," (but he is) "but here's the way things used to work. They don't work this way anymore. I don't know if you remember. Your parents are dead and they're coming home in just a few hours. Used to be, that was scary. Not anymore. But try to imagine: finding something that shouldn't be there."

"Like what?" the cheerleader says.

The Devil shrugs. "A child's toy. A ball, or a night-light. Some cheap bit of trash, but it's heavier than it looks, or else light. It shines with a greasy sort of light or else it eats light. When you touch it, it yields unpleasantly. You feel as if you might fall into it. You feel light-headed. It might be inscribed in a language which no one can decipher."

"Okay," the cheerleader says. She seems somewhat cheered up. "So what's the next thing?"

The Devil shines the flashlight in her eyes, flicks it on and off. "Someone disappears. Gone, just like that. They're standing behind you in a line at an amusement park—or they wander away during the intermission of a play—perhaps they go downstairs to get the mail—or to make tea—"

"That's scary?" the cheerleader says.

"Used to be," the Devil says. "It used to be that the worst thing that could happen was, if you had kids, and one of them died or disappeared. Disappeared was the worst. Anything might have happened to them."

"Things are better now," the cheerleader says.

"Yes, well." The Devil says, "Things just get better and better nowadays. But— try to remember how it was. The person who disappeared, only they didn't. You'd see them from time to time, peeking in at you through windows, or down low through the mail slot in your front door. Keyholes. You might see them in the grocery store. Sitting in the backseat of your car, down low, slouching in your rearview mirror. They might pinch your leg or pull your hair when you're asleep. When you talk on the phone, they listen in, you hear them listening."

The cheerleader says, "Like, with my parents—"

"Exactly," says the Devil. "You've had nightmares about them, right?"

"Not really," the cheerleader says. "Everyone says they were probably nice people. I mean, look at this house! But, sometimes, I have this dream that I'm at the mall, and I see my husband. And he's just the same, he's a grown-up, and he doesn't recognize me. It turns out that I'm the only one who's going backwards. And then he does recognize me and he wants to know what I've done with the kids."

The last time she'd seen her husband, he was trying to grow a beard. He couldn't even do that right. He hadn't had much to say, but they'd looked at each other for a long time.

"What about your children?" the Devil says. "Do you wonder where they went when the doctor pushed them back up inside you? Do you have dreams about them?"

"Yes," the cheerleader says. "Everything gets smaller. I'm afraid of that."

"Think how men feel!" the Devil says. "It's no wonder men are afraid of women. No wonder sex is so hard on them."

The cheerleader misses sex, that feeling afterwards, that blissful, unsatisfied itch.

"The first time around, things were better," the Devil says. "I don't know if you remember. People died, and no one was sure what happened next. There were all sorts of possibilities. Now everyone knows everything. What's the fun in that?"

Someone is trying to push open the closet door, but the cheerleader puts her feet against it, leaning against the back of the closet. "Oh, I remember!" she says, "I remember when I was dead! There was so much I was looking forward to. I had no idea!"

The Devil shivers. He's never liked dead people much.

"So, okay, what about monsters?" the cheerleader says. "Vampires? Serial killers? People from outer space? Those old movies?"

The Devil shrugs. "Yeah, sure. Boogeymen. Formaldehyde babies in Mason jars. Someday someone is going to have to take them out of the jar, unpickle them. Women with teeth down there. Zombies. Killer robots, killer bees, serial killers, cold spots, werewolves. The dream where you know that you're asleep but you can't wake up. You can hear someone walking around the bedroom picking up your things and putting them down again and you still can't wake up. The end of the world. Spiders. *No one was with her when she died.* Carnivorous plants."

"Oh goody," the cheerleader says. Her eyes shine at him out of the dark. Her pompoms slide across the floor of the closet. He moves his flashlight so he can see her hands.

"So here's your story," the cheerleader says. She's a girl who can think on her feet. "It's not really a scary story. I don't really get scary."

"Weren't you listening?" the Devil says. He taps the flashlight against his big front teeth. "Never mind, it's okay, never mind. Go on."

"This probably isn't a true story," the cheerleader says, "and it doesn't go backwards like we do. I probably won't get all the way to the end, and I'm not going to start at the beginning, either. There isn't enough time."

"That's fine," the Devil says. "I'm all ears." (He is.)

The cheerleader says, "So who's going to tell this story, anyway? Be quiet and listen. We're running out of time."

She says, "A man comes home from a sales conference. He and his wife have been separated for a while, but they've decided to try living together again. They've sold the house that they used to live in. Now they live just outside of town, in an old house in an orchard.

The man comes home from this business conference, and his wife is sitting in the kitchen and she's talking to another woman, an older woman. They're sitting on the chairs that used to go around the kitchen table, but the table is gone. So is the microwave, and the rack where Susan's copper-bottomed pots hang. The pots are gone, too.

The husband doesn't notice any of this. He's busy looking at the other woman. Her skin has a greenish tinge. He has this feeling that he knows her. She and the wife both look at the husband, and he suddenly knows what it is. It's his wife. It's his wife, two of her, only one is maybe twenty years older. Otherwise, except that this one's green, they're identical: same eyes, same mouth, same little mole at the corner of her mouth.

"How am I doing so far?"

"So-so," the Devil says. The truth (the truth makes the Devil itchy) is, he only likes stories about himself. Like the story about the Devil's wedding cake. Now that's a story.

The cheerleader says, "It gets better."

It Gets Better

The man's name is Ed. It isn't his real name. I made it up. Ed and Susan have been married for ten years, separated for five months, back together again for three months. They've been sleeping in the same bed for three months, but they don't have sex. Susan cries whenever Ed kisses her. They don't have any kids. Susan used to have a younger brother. Ed is thinking about getting a dog.

While Ed's been at his conference, Susan has been doing some housework. She's done some work up in the attic which we won't talk about. Not yet. Down in the spare bathroom in the basement, she's set up this machine, which we get around to later, and this machine makes Susans. What Susan was hoping for was a machine that would bring back Andrew. (Her brother. But you knew that.) Only it turns out that getting Andrew back requires a different machine, a bigger machine. Susan needs help making that machine, and so the new Susans are going to come in handy after all. Over the course of the next few days, the Susans explain all this to Ed.

Susan doesn't expect Ed will be very helpful.

"Hi, Ed," the older, greenish Susan says. She gets up from her chair and gives him a big hug. Her skin is warm, tacky. She smells yeasty. The original Susan—the Susan Ed thinks is original, and I have no idea if he's right about this, and, later on, he isn't so sure, either—sits in her chair and watches them.

Big green Susan: am I making her sound like Godzilla? She doesn't look like Godzilla, and yet there's something about her that reminds Ed of Godzilla, the way she stomps across the kitchen floor—leads Ed over to a chair and makes him sit down. Now he realizes that the kitchen table is gone. He still hasn't managed to say a word. Susan, both of them, is used to this.

"First of all," Susan says, "the attic is off-limits. There are some people working up there. (I don't mean Susans. I'll explain Susans in a minute.) Some visitors. They're helping me with a project. About the other Susans, there are five of me at the moment—you'll meet the other three later. They're down in the basement. You're allowed in the basement. You can help down there, if you want."

Godzilla Susan says, "You don't have to worry about who is who, although none of us are exactly alike. You can call us all Susan. We're discovering that some of us may be more temporary than others, or fatter, or younger, or greener. It seems to depend on the batch."

"Are you Susan?" Ed says. He corrects himself. "I mean, are you my wife? The real Susan?"

"We're all your wife," the younger Susan says. She puts her hand on his leg and pats him like a dog.

"Where did the kitchen table go?" Ed says.

"I put it in the attic," Susan says. "You really don't have to worry about that now. How was your conference?"

Another Susan comes into the kitchen. She's young and the color of green apples or new grass. Even the whites of her eyes are grassy. She's maybe nineteen, and the color of her skin makes Ed think of a snake. "Ed!" she says, "How was the conference?"

"They're keen on the new game," Ed says. "It tests real well."

"Want a beer?" Susan says. (It doesn't matter which Susan says this.) She picks up a pitcher of green foamy stuff, and pours it into a glass.

"This is beer?" Ed says.

"It's Susan beer," Susan says, and all the Susans laugh.

The beautiful, snake-colored nineteen-year-old Susan takes Ed on a tour of the house. Mostly Ed just looks at Susan, but he sees that the television is gone, and so are all of his games. All his notebooks. The living room sofa is still there, but all the seat cushions are missing. Later on, Susan will disassemble the sofa with an ax.

Susan has covered up all the downstairs windows with what looks like sheets of aluminum foil. She shows him the bathtub downstairs where one of the Susans is brewing the Susan beer. Other Susans are hanging long, mossy clots of the Susan beer on laundry racks. Dry, these clots can be shaped into bedding, nests for the new Susans. They are also edible.

Ed is still holding the glass of Susan beer. "Go on," Susan says. "You like beer."

"I don't like green beer," Ed says.

"You like Susan, though," Susan says. She's wearing one of his T-shirts, and a pair of Susan's underwear. No bra. She puts Ed's hand on her breast.

Susan stops stirring the beer. She's taller than Ed, and only a little bit green. "You know Susan loves you," she says.

"Who's up in the attic?" Ed says. "Is it Andrew?"

His hand is still on Susan's breast. He can feel her heart beating. Susan says,

"You can't tell Susan I told you. She doesn't think you're ready. It's the aliens."

They both stare at him. "She finally got them on the phone. This is going to be huge, Ed. This is going to change the world."

Ed could leave the house. He could leave Susan. He could refuse to drink the beer.

The Susan beer doesn't make him drunk. It isn't really beer. You knew that, right?

There are Susans everywhere. Some of them want to talk to Ed about their marriage, or about the aliens, or sometimes they want to talk about Andrew. Some of them are busy working. The Susans are always dragging Ed off to empty rooms, to talk or kiss or make love or gossip about the other Susans. Or they're ignoring him. There's one very young Susan. She looks like she might be six or seven years old. She goes up and down the upstairs hallway, drawing on the walls with a marker. Ed isn't sure whether this is childish vandalism or important Susan work. He feels awkward asking.

Every once in a while, he thinks he sees the real Susan. He wishes he could sit down and talk with her, but she always looks so busy.

By the end of the week, there aren't any mirrors left in the house, and the windows are all covered up. The Susans have hung sheets of the Susan beer over all the light fixtures, so everything is green. Ed isn't sure, but he thinks he might be turning green.

Susan tastes green. She always does.

Once Ed hears someone knocking on the front door. "Ignore that," Susan says as she walks past him. She's carrying the stacked blades of an old ceiling fan, and a string of Christmas lights. "It isn't important."

Ed pulls the plug of aluminum foil out of the eyehole, and peeks out. Stan is standing there, looking patient. They stand there, Ed on one side of the door, and Stan on the other. Ed doesn't open the door, and eventually Stan goes away. All the peacocks are kicking up a fuss.

Ed tries teaching some of the Susans to play poker. It doesn't work so well, because it turns out that Susan always knows what cards the other Susans are holding. So Ed makes up a game where that doesn't matter so much, but in the end, it makes him feel too lonely. There aren't any other Eds.

They decide to play spin the bottle instead. Instead of a bottle, they use a hammer, and it never ends up pointing at Ed. After a while, it gets too strange watching Susan kiss Susans, and he wanders off to look for a Susan who will kiss him.

Up in the second-story bedroom, there are always lots of Susans. This is where they go to wait when they start to get ripe. The Susans loll, curled in their nests, getting riper, arguing about the end of some old story. None of them remember it the same way. Some of them don't seem to know anything about it, but they all have opinions.

Ed climbs into a nest and leans back. Susan swings her legs over to make room for him. This Susan is small and round. She tickles the soft part of his arm, and then tucks her face into his side.

Susan passes him a glass of Susan beer.

"That's not it," Susan says, "It turns out that he overdosed. Maybe even did it on purpose. We couldn't talk about it. There weren't enough of us. We were trying to carry all that sadness all by ourself. You can't do something like that! And then the wife tries to kill him. I tried to kill him. She kicks the fuck out of him. He can't leave the house for a week, won't even come to the door when his friends come over."

"If you can call them friends," Susan says.

"No, there was a gun," Susan says. "And she has an affair. Because she can't get over it. Neither of them can."

"She humiliates him at a dinner party," Susan says. "They both drink too much. Everybody goes home, and she breaks all the dishes instead of washing them. There are plate shards all over the kitchen floor. Someone's going to get hurt; they don't have a time machine. They can't go back and unbreak those plates. We know that they still loved each other, but that doesn't matter anymore. Then the police showed up."

"Well, that's not the way I remember it," Susan says. "But I guess it could have happened that way."

Ed and Susan used to buy books all the time. They had so many books they used to joke about wanting to be quarantined, or snowed in. Maybe then they'd manage to read all the books. But the books have all gone up to the attic, along with the lamps and the coffee tables, and their bicycles, and all Susan's paintings. Ed has watched the Susans carry up paperback books, silverware, old board games, and holey underwear. Even a kazoo. The Encyclopædia Britannica. The goldfish and the goldfish bowl and the little canister of goldfish food.

The Susans have gone through the house, taken everything they could. After all the books were gone, they dismantled the bookshelves. Now they're tearing off the wallpaper in long strips. The aliens seem to like books. They like everything, especially Susan. Eventually when the Susans are ripe, they go up in the attic too.

The aliens swap things, the books and the Susans and the coffee mugs for other things: machines that the Susans are assembling. Ed would like to get his hand on one of those devices, but Susan says no. He isn't even allowed to help, except with the Susan beer.

The thing the Susans are building takes up most of the living room, Ed's office, the kitchen, the laundry room—

The Susans don't bother with laundry. The washer and the dryer are both gone and the Susans have given up wearing clothes altogether. Ed has managed to keep a pair of shorts and a pair of jeans. He's wearing the shorts right now, and he folds the jeans up into a pillow, and rests his head on top of them so that Susan can't steal them. All his other clothes have been carried up to the attic

—and it's creeping up the stairs, spilling over into the second story. The house is shiny with alien machines.

Teams of naked Susans are hard at work, all day long, testing instruments, hammering and stitching their machine together, polishing and dusting and stacking alien things on top of each other. If you're wondering what the machine looks like, picture a science fair project involving a lot of aluminum foil, improvised, homely, makeshift, and just a little dangerous-looking. None of the Susans is quite sure what the machine will eventually do. Right now it grows Susan beer.

When the beer is stirred, left alone, stirred some more, it clots and makes more Susans. Ed likes watching this part. The house is more and more full of shy, loud, quiet, talkative, angry, happy, greenish Susans of all sizes, all ages, who work at disassembling the house, piece by piece, and, piece by piece, assembling the machine.

It might be a time machine, or a machine to raise the dead, or maybe the house is becoming a spaceship, slowly, one room at a time. Susan says the aliens don't make these kinds of distinctions. It may be an invasion factory, Ed says, or a doomsday machine. Susan says that they aren't that kind of aliens.

Ed's job: stirring the Susan beer with a long, flat plank—a floorboard Susan pried up—and skimming the foam, which has a stringy and unpleasantly cheese-like consistency, into buckets. He carries the buckets downstairs and makes Susan beer soufflé and Susan beer casserole. Susan beer surprise. Upside-down Susan cake. It all tastes the same, and he grows to like the taste.

The beer doesn't make him drunk. That isn't what it's for. I can't tell you what it's for. But when he's drinking it, he isn't sad. He has the beer, and the work in the kitchen, and the ripe, green fuckery. Everything tastes like Susan.

The only thing he misses is poker nights.

Up in the spare bedroom, Ed falls asleep listening to the Susans talk, and when he wakes up, his jeans are gone, and he's naked. The room is empty. All the ripe Susans have gone up to the attic.

When he steps out into the hall, the little Susan is out there, drawing on the walls. She puts her marker down and hands him a pitcher of Susan beer. She pinches his leg and says, "You're getting nice and ripe."

Then she winks at Ed and runs down the hall.

He looks at what she's been drawing: Andrew, scribbly crayon portraits of Andrew, all up and down the walls. He follows the pictures of Andrew down the hall, all the way to the master bedroom where he and the original Susan used to sleep. Now he sleeps anywhere, with any Susan. He hasn't been in their room in a while, although he's noticed the Susans going in and out with boxes full of things. The Susans are always shooing at him when he gets in their way.

The bedroom is full of Andrew. There are Susan's portraits of Andrew on the walls, the ones from her art class. Ed had forgotten how unpleasant and peculiar these paintings are. In one, the largest one, Andrew, life-sized, has his hands around a small animal, maybe a ferret. He seems to be strangling it. The ferret's mouth is cocked open, showing all its teeth. A picture like that, Ed thinks, you ought to turn it towards the wall at night.

Susan's put Andrew's bed in here, and Andrew's books, and Andrew's desk. Andrew's clothes have been hung up in the closet. There isn't an alien machine in the room, or for that matter, anything that ever belonged to Ed.

Ed puts a pair of Andrew's pants on, and lies down on Andrew's bed, just for a minute, and he closes his eyes.

When he wakes up, Susan is sitting on the bed. He can smell her, that ripe green scent. He can smell that smell on himself. Susan says, "If you're ready, I thought we could go up to the attic together."

"What's going on here?" Ed says. "I thought you needed everything. Shouldn't all this stuff go up to the attic?"

"This is Andrew's room, for when he comes back," Susan says. "We thought it would make him feel comfortable, having his own bed to sleep in. He might need his stuff."

"What if the aliens need his stuff?" Ed says. "What if they can't make you a new Andrew yet because they don't know enough about him?"

"That's not how it works," Susan says. "We're getting close now. Can't you feel it?"

"I feel weird," Ed says. "Something's happening to me."

"You're ripe, Ed," Susan says. "Isn't that fantastic? We weren't sure you'd ever get ripe enough."

She takes his hand and pulls him up. Sometimes he forgets how strong she is.

"So what happens now?" Ed says. "Am I going to die? I don't feel sick. I feel good. What happens when we get ripe?"

The afternoon light makes Susan look older, or maybe she just is older. He likes this part: seeing what Susan looked like as a kid, what she'll look like as an old lady. It's as if they got to spend their whole lives together. "I never know," she says. "Let's go find out. Take off Andrew's pants, and I'll hang them back up in the closet."

They leave the bedroom and walk down the hall. The Andrew drawings, the knobs and dials and stacked, shiny machinery watch them go. There aren't any other Susans around at the moment. They're all busy downstairs. He can hear them hammering away. For a minute, it's the way it used to be, only better. Just Ed and Susan in their own house.

Ed holds on tight to Susan's hand.

When Susan opens the attic door, the attic is full of stars. Stars and stars and stars. Ed has never seen so many stars. Susan has taken the roof off. Off in the distance, they can smell the apple trees, way down in the orchard.

Susan sits down cross-legged on the floor and Ed sits down beside her. She says, "I wish you'd tell me a story."

Ed says, "What kind of story?"

Susan says, "A bedtime story? When Andrew was a kid, we used to read this book. I remember this one story about people who go under a hill. They spend one night down there, eating and drinking and dancing, but when they come out, a hundred years have gone by. Do you know how long it's been since Andrew died? I've lost track."

"I don't know stories like that," Ed says. He picks at his flaky green skin and wonders what he tastes like. "What do you think the aliens look like? Do you think they look like giraffes? Like marbles? Like Andrew? Do you think they have mouths?"

"Don't be silly," Susan says. "They look like us."

"How do you know?" Ed says. "Have you been up here before?"

"No," Susan says. "But Susan has."

"We could play a card game," Ed says. "Or I Spy."

"You could tell me about the first time I met you," Susan says.

"I don't want to talk about that," Ed says. "That's all gone."

"Okay, fine." Susan sits up straight, arches her back, runs her green tongue across her green lips. She winks at Ed and says, "Tell me how beautiful I am."

"You're beautiful," Ed says. "I've always thought you were beautiful. All of you. How about me? Am I beautiful?"

"Don't be that way," Susan says. She slouches back against him. Her skin is warm and greasy. "The aliens are going to get here soon. I don't know what happens after that, but I hate this part. I always hate this part. I don't like waiting. Do you think this is what it was like for Andrew, when he was in rehab?"

"When you get him back, ask him. Why ask me?"

Susan doesn't say anything for a bit. Then she says, "We think we'll be able to make you, too. We're starting to figure out how it works. Eventually it will be you and me and him, just the way it was before. Only we'll fix him the way we've fixed me. He won't be so sad. Have you noticed how I'm not sad anymore? Don't you want that, not to be sad? And maybe after that we'll try making some more people. We'll start all over again. We'll do everything right this time."

Ed says, "So why are they helping you?"

"I don't know," Susan says. "Either they think we're funny, or else they think we're pathetic, the way we get stuck. We can ask them when they get here."

She stands up, stretches, yawns, sits back down on Ed's lap, reaches down, stuffs his penis, half-erect, inside of her. Just like that. Ed groans.

He says, "Susan."

Susan says, "Tell me a story." She squirms. "Any story. I don't care what."

"I can't tell you a story," Ed says. "I don't know any stories when you're doing this."

"I'll stop," Susan says. She stops.

Ed says, "Don't stop. Okay." He puts his hands around her waist and moves her, as if he's stirring the Susan beer.

He says, "Once upon a time." He's speaking very fast. They're running out of time.

Once, while they were making love, Andrew came into the bedroom. He didn't even knock. He didn't seem to be embarrassed at all. Ed doesn't want to be fucking Susan when the aliens show up. On the other hand, Ed wants to be fucking Susan forever. He doesn't want to stop, not for Andrew, or the aliens, or even for the end of the world.

Ed says, "There was a man and a woman and they fell in love. They were both nice people. They made a good couple. Everyone liked them. This story is about the woman."

This story is about a woman who is in love with somebody who invents a time machine. He's planning to go so far into the future that he'll end up right back at the very beginning. He asks her to come along, but she doesn't want to go. What's back at the beginning of the world? Little blobs of life swimming around in a big blob? Adam and Eve in the Garden of Eden? She doesn't want to play Adam and Eve; she has other things to do. She works for a research company. She calls people on the telephone and asks them all sorts of questions. Back at the beginning, there aren't going to be phones. She doesn't like the sound of it. So her husband says, Fine, then here's what we'll do. I'll build you another machine, and if you ever decide that you miss me, or you're tired and you can't go on, climb inside this machine—this box right here—and push this button and go to sleep. And you'll sleep all the way forwards and backwards to me, where I'm waiting for you. I'll keep on waiting for you. I love you. And so they make love and they make love a few more times and then he climbs into his time machine and whoosh, he's gone like that. So fast, it's hard to believe that he was ever there at all. Meanwhile she lives her life forward, slow, the way he didn't want to. She gets married again and makes love some more and has kids and they have kids and when she's an old woman, she's finally ready: she climbs into the dusty box down in the secret room under the orchard and she pushes the button and falls asleep. And she sleeps all the way back, just like Sleeping Beauty, down in the orchard for years and years, which fly by like seconds, she goes flying back, past the men sitting around the green felt table, now you can see them and now they're gone again, and all the peacocks are screaming, and the Satanist drives up to the house and unloads the truckload of furniture, he unpaints the pentagrams, soon the old shy man will unbuild his house, carry his secret away on his back, and the apples are back on the orchard trees again, and then the trees are all blooming, and now the woman is getting younger, just a little, the lines around her mouth are smoothing out. She dreams that someone has come down into that underground room and is looking down at her in her time machine. He stands there for a long time. She can't open her eyes, her eyelids are so heavy, she doesn't want to wake up just yet. She dreams she's on a train going down the tracks backwards and behind the train, someone is picking up the beams and the nails and the girders to put in a box and then they'll put the box away. The trees are whizzing past, getting smaller and smaller and then they're all gone too. Now she's a kid again, now she's a baby, now she's much smaller and then she's even smaller than that. She gets her gills back. She doesn't want to wake up just yet, she wants to get right back to the very beginning where it's all new and clean and everything is still and green and flat and sleepy and everybody has crawled back into the sea and they're waiting for her to get back there too and then the party can start. She goes backwards and backwards and backwards and backwards and backwards and backwards and backwards and backwards and backwards and backwards and backwards—

The cheerleader says to the Devil, "We're out of time. We're holding things up. Don't you hear them banging on the door?"

The Devil says, "You didn't finish the story."

The cheerleader says, "And you never let me touch your tail. Besides, there isn't any ending. I could make up something, but it wouldn't ever satisfy you. You said that yourself! You're never satisfied. And I have to get on with my life. My parents are going to be home soon."

She stands up and slips out of the closet and slams the door shut again, so fast the Devil can hardly believe it. A key turns in a lock.

The Devil tries the doorknob, and someone standing outside the closet giggles.

"Shush," says the cheerleader. "Be quiet."

"What's going on?" the Devil says. "Open the door and let me out—this isn't funny."

"Okay, I'll let you out," the cheerleader says. "Eventually. Not just yet. You have to give me something first."

"You want me to give you something?" the Devil says. "Okay, what?" He rattles the knob, testing.

"I want a happy beginning," the cheerleader says. "I want my friends to be happy too. I want to get along with my parents. I want a happy childhood. I want things to get better. I want them to keep getting better. I want you to be nice to me. I want to be famous, I don't know, maybe I could be a child actor, or win state-level spelling bees, or even just cheer for winning teams. I want world peace. Second chances. When I'm winning at poker, I don't want to have to put all that money back in the pot, I don't want to have to put my good cards back on top of the deck, one by one by—

Starlight says, "Sorry about that. My voice is getting scratchy. It's late. You should call back tomorrow night."

Ed says, "When can I call you?"

Stan and Andrew were friends. Good friends. It was like they were the same species. Ed hadn't seen Stan for a while, not for a long while, but Stan stopped him, on the way down to the basement. This was earlier. Stan grabbed his arm and said, "I miss him. I keep thinking, if I'd gotten there sooner. If I'd said something. He liked you a lot, you know, he was sorry about what happened to your car—"

Stan stops talking and just stands there looking at Ed. He looks like he's about to cry.

"It's not your fault," Ed said, but then he wondered why he'd said it. Whose fault was it?

Susan says, "You've got to stop calling me, Ed. Okay? It's three in the morning. I was asleep, Ed, I was having the best dream. You're always waking me up in the middle of things. Please just stop, okay?"

Ed doesn't say anything. He could stay there all night and just listen to Susan talk.

What she's saying now is, "But that's never going to happen, and you know it. Something bad happened, and it wasn't anyone's fault, but we're just never going to get past it. It killed us. We can't even talk about it."

Ed says, "I love you."

Susan says, "I love you, but it's not about love, Ed, it's about timing. It's too late, and it's always going to be too late. Maybe if we could go back and do everything differently—and I think about that all the time—but we can't. We don't know anybody with a time machine. How about this, Ed—maybe you and your poker buddies can build one down in Pete's basement. All those stupid games, Ed! Why can't you build a time machine instead? Call me back when you've figured out how we can work this out, because I'm really stuck. Or don't call me back. Good-bye, Ed. Go get some sleep. I'm hanging up the phone now."

Susan hangs up the phone.

Ed imagines her, going down to the kitchen to microwave a glass of milk. She'll sit in the kitchen and drink her milk and wait for him to call her back. He lies in bed, up in the orchard house. He's got both bedroom doors open, and a night breeze comes in through that door that doesn't go anywhere. He wishes he could get Susan to come see that door. The breeze smells like apples, which is what time must smell like, Ed thinks.

There's an alarm clock on the floor beside his bed. The hands and numbers glow green in the dark, and he'll wait five minutes and then he'll call Susan. Five minutes. Then he'll call her back. The hands aren't moving, but he can wait.

WE CAN GET THEM FOR YOU WHOLESALE

Neil Gaiman

Peter Pinter had never heard of Aristippus of the Cyrenaics, a lesser-known follower of Socrates who maintained that the avoidance of trouble was the highest attainable good; however, he had lived his uneventful life according to this precept. In all respects except one (an inability to pass up a bargain, and which of us is entirely free from that?), he was a very moderate man. He did not go to extremes. His speech was proper and reserved; he rarely overate; he drank enough to be sociable and no more; he was far from rich and in no wise poor. He liked people and people liked him. Bearing all that in mind, would you expect to find him in a lowlife pub on the seamier side of London's East End, taking out what is colloquially known as a "contract" on someone he hardly knew? You would not. You would not even expect to find him in the pub.

And until a certain Friday afternoon, you would have been right. But the love of a woman can do strange things to a man, even one so colourless as Peter Pinter, and the discovery that Miss Gwendolyn Thorpe, twenty-three years of age, of 9, Oaktree Terrace, Purley, was messing about (as the vulgar would put it) with a smooth young gentleman from the accounting department—*after*, mark you, she had consented to wear an engagement ring, composed of real ruby chips, nine-carat gold, and something that might well have been a diamond (£37.50) that it had taken Peter almost an entire lunch hour to choose—can do very strange things to a man indeed.

After he had made this shocking discovery, Peter spent a sleepless Friday night, tossing and turning with visions of Gwendolyn and Archie Gibbons (the Don Juan of the Clamages accounting department) dancing and swimming before his eyes—performing acts that even Peter, if he were pressed, would have to admit were most improbable. But the bile of jealousy had risen up within him, and by the morning Peter had resolved that his rival should be done away with.

Saturday morning was spent wondering how one contacted an assassin, for, to the best of Peter's knowledge, none were employed by Clamages (the department store that employed all three of the members of our eternal triangle, and, incidentally, furnished the ring), and he was wary of asking anyone outright for

315

fear of attracting attention to himself.

Thus it was that Saturday afternoon found him hunting through the Yellow Pages.

ASSASSINS, he found, was not between ASPHALT CONTRACTORS and ASSESSORS (QUANTITY); KILLERS was not between KENNELS and KINDERGARTENS; MURDERERS was not between MOWERS and MUSEUMS. PEST CONTROL looked promising; however closer investigation of the pest control advertisements showed them to be almost solely concerned with "rats, mice, fleas, cockroaches, rabbits, moles and rats" (to quote from one that Peter felt was rather hard on rats) and not really what he had in mind. Even so, being of a careful nature, he dutifully inspected the entries in that category, and at the bottom of the second page, in small print, he found a firm that looked promising.

"*Complete discreet disposal of irksome and unwanted mammals, etc.*" went the entry, "*Ketch, Hare, Burke and Ketch. The Old Firm.*" It went on to give no address, but only a telephone number.

Peter dialled the number, surprising himself by so doing. His heart pounded in his chest, and he tried to look nonchalant. The telephone rang once, twice, three times. Peter was just starting to hope that it would not be answered and he could forget the whole thing when there was a click and a brisk young female voice said, "Ketch Hare Burke and Ketch. Can I help you?"

Carefully not giving his name, Peter said, "Er, how big—I mean, what size mammals do you go up to? To, uh, dispose of?"

"Well, that would all depend on what size sir requires."

He plucked up all his courage. "A person?"

Her voice remained brisk and unruffled. "Of course, sir. Do you have a pen and paper handy? Good. Be at the Dirty Donkey pub, off Little Courtney Street, E3, tonight at eight o'clock. Carry a rolled-up copy of the *Financial Times*—that's the pink one, sir—and our operative will approach you there." Then she put down the phone.

Peter was elated. It had been far easier than he had imagined. He went down to the newsagent's and bought a copy of the *Financial Times*, found Little Courtney Street in his *A-Z* of London, and spent the rest of the afternoon watching football on the television and imagining the smooth young gentleman from accounting's funeral.

It took Peter a while to find the pub. Eventually he spotted the pub sign, which showed a donkey and was indeed remarkably dirty.

The Dirty Donkey was a small and more or less filthy pub, poorly lit, in which knots of unshaven people wearing dusty donkey jackets stood around eyeing each other suspiciously, eating crisps and drinking pints of Guinness, a drink that Peter had never cared for. Peter held his *Financial Times* under one arm as conspicuously as he could, but no one approached him, so he bought a half of shandy and retreated to a corner table. Unable to think of anything else to do while waiting, he tried to read the paper, but, lost and confused by a maze of grain futures and a rubber company that was selling something or other short (quite what the short somethings were he could not tell), he gave it up and stared at the door.

He had waited almost ten minutes when a small busy man hustled in, looked quickly around him, then came straight over to Peter's table and sat down.

He stuck out his hand. "Kemble. Burton Kemble of Ketch Hare Burke Ketch. I hear you have a job for us."

He didn't look like a killer. Peter said so.

"Oh, lor' bless us, no. I'm not actually a part of our workforce, sir. I'm in sales."

Peter nodded. That certainly made sense. "Can we—er—talk freely here?"

"Sure. Nobody's interested. Now then, how many people would you like disposed of?"

"Only one. His name's Archibald Gibbons and he works in Clamages account-ing department. His address is—"

Kemble interrupted. "We can go into all that later, sir, if you don't mind. Let's just quickly go over the financial side. First of all, the contract will cost you five hundred pounds—"

Peter nodded. He could afford that and in fact had expected to have to pay a little more.

"—although there's always the special offer," Kemble concluded smoothly.

Peter's eyes shone. As I mentioned earlier, he loved a bargain and often bought things he had no imaginable use for in sales or on special offers. Apart from this one failing (one that so many of us share), he was a most moderate young man. "Special offer?"

"Two for the price of one, sir."

Mmm. Peter thought about it. That worked out at only—250 each, which couldn't be bad no matter how you looked at it. There was only one snag. "I'm afraid I don't have anyone else I want killed."

Kemble looked disappointed. "That's a pity, sir. For two we could probably have even knocked the price down to, well, say four hundred and fifty pounds for the both of them."

"Really?"

"Well, it gives our operatives something to do, sir. If you must know"—and here he dropped his voice—"there really isn't enough work in this particular line to keep them occupied. Not like the old days. Isn't there just *one* other person you'd like to see dead?"

Peter pondered. He hated to pass up a bargain, but couldn't for the life of him think of anyone else. He liked people. Still, a bargain was a bargain—

"Look," said Peter. "Could I think about it and see you here tomorrow night?"

The salesman looked pleased. "Of course, sir," he said. "I'm sure you'll be able to think of someone."

The answer—the obvious answer—came to Peter as he was drifting off to sleep that night. He sat straight up in bed, fumbled the bedside light on, and wrote a name down on the back of an envelope, in case he forgot it. To tell the truth, he didn't think that he could forget it, for it was painfully obvious, but you can never tell with these late-night thoughts.

The name that he had written down on the back of the envelope was this: *Gwendolyn Thorpe.*

He turned the light off, rolled over, and was soon asleep, dreaming peaceful and remarkably unmurderous dreams.

Kemble was waiting for him when he arrived in the Dirty Donkey on Sunday night. Peter bought a drink and sat down beside him.

"I'm taking you up on the special offer," he said by way of greeting.

Kemble nodded vigorously. "A very wise decision, if you don't mind me saying so, sir."

Peter Pinter smiled modestly, in the manner of one who read the *Financial Times* and made wise business decisions. "That will be four hundred and fifty pounds, I believe?"

"Did I say four hundred and fifty pounds, sir? Good gracious me, I do apologize. I beg your pardon, I was thinking of our bulk rate. It would be four hundred and seventy-five for two people."

Disappointment mingled with cupidity on Peter's bland and youthful face. That was an extra—25. However, something that Kemble had said caught his attention.

"Bulk rate?"

"Of course, but I doubt that sir would be interested in that."

"No, no, I am. Tell me about it."

"Very well, sir. Bulk rate, four hundred and fifty pounds, would be for a large job. Ten people."

Peter wondered if he had heard correctly. "Ten people? But that's only forty-five pounds each."

"Yes, sir. It's the large order that makes it profitable."

"I see," said Peter, and "Hmm," said Peter, and "Could you be here at the same time tomorrow night?"

"Of course, sir."

Upon arriving home, Peter got out a scrap of paper and a pen. He wrote the numbers one to ten down one side and then filled it in as follows:

1).*Archie.*

2)..*Gwennie.*

3)..

and so forth.

Having filled in the first two, he sat sucking his pen, hunting for wrongs done to him and people the world would be better off without.

He smoked a cigarette. He strolled around the room.

Aha! There was a physics teacher at a school he had attended who had delighted in making his life a misery. What was the man's name again? And for that matter, was he still alive? Peter wasn't sure, but he wrote *The Physics Teacher, Abbot Street Secondary School* next to the number three. The next came more easily—his department head had refused to raise his salary a couple of months back; that the raise had eventually come was immaterial. *Mr. Hunterson* was number four.

When he was five, a boy named Simon Ellis had poured paint on his head while another boy name James somebody-or-other had held him down and a girl named Sharon Harsharpe had laughed. They were numbers five through seven, respectively.

Who else?

There was the man on television with the annoying snicker who read the news. He went on the list. And what about the woman in the flat next door with the little yappy dog that shat in the hall? He put her and the dog down on nine. Ten was the hardest. He scratched his head and went into the kitchen for a cup of coffee, then dashed back and wrote *My Great-Uncle Mervyn* down in the tenth place. The old man was rumoured to be quite affluent, and there was a possibility (albeit rather slim) that he could leave Peter some money.

With the satisfaction of an evening's work well done, he went off to bed.

Monday at Clamages was routine; Peter was a senior sales assistant in the books department, a job that actually entailed very little. He clutched his list tightly in his hand, deep in his pocket, rejoicing in the feeling of power that it gave him. He spent a most enjoyable lunch hour in the canteen with young Gwendolyn (who did not know that he had seen her and Archie enter the stockroom together) and even smiled at the smooth young man from the accounting department when he passed him in the corridor.

He proudly displayed his list to Kemble that evening.

The little salesman's face fell.

"I'm afraid this isn't ten people, Mr. Pinter," he explained. "You've counted the woman in the next-door flat *and* her dog as one person. That brings it to eleven, which would be an extra"—his pocket calculator was rapidly deployed—"an extra seventy pounds. How about if we forget the dog?"

Peter shook his head. "The dog's as bad as the woman. Or worse."

"Then I'm afraid we have a slight problem. Unless—"

"What?"

"Unless you'd like to take advantage of our wholesale rate. But of course sir wouldn't be—"

There are words that do things to people; words that make people's faces flush with joy, excitement, or passion. *Environmental* can be one; *occult* is another. *Wholesale* was Peter's. He leaned back in his chair. "Tell me about it," he said with the practised assurance of an experienced shopper.

"Well, sir," said Kemble, allowing himself a little chuckle, "we can, uh, *get* them for you wholesale, seventeen pounds fifty each, for every quarry after the first fifty, or a tenner each for every one over two hundred."

"I suppose you'd go down to a fiver if I wanted a thousand people knocked off?"

"Oh no, sir," Kemble looked shocked. "If you're talking those sorts of figures, we can do them for a quid each."

"One *pound?*"

"That's right, sir. There's not a big profit margin on it, but the high turnover and productivity more than justifies it."

Kemble got up. "Same time tomorrow, sir?"

Peter nodded.

One thousand pounds. One thousand people. Peter Pinter didn't even know a thousand people. Even so—there were the Houses of Parliament. He didn't like politicians; they squabbled and argued and carried on so.

And for that matter—

An idea, shocking in its audacity. Bold. Daring. Still, the idea was there and it wouldn't go away. A distant cousin of his had married the younger brother of an earl or a baron or something—

On the way home from work that afternoon, he stopped off at a little shop that he had passed a thousand times without entering. It had a large sign in the window—guaranteeing to trace your lineage for you and even draw up a coat of arms if you happened to have mislaid your own—and an impressive heraldic map.

They were very helpful and phoned him up just after seven to give him their news.

If approximately fourteen million, seventy-two thousand, eight hundred and eleven people died, he, Peter Pinter, would be *King of England.*

He didn't have fourteen million, seventy-two thousand, eight hundred and eleven pounds: but he suspected that when you were talking in those figures, Mr. Kemble would have one of his special discounts.

Mr. Kemble did.

He didn't even raise an eyebrow.

"Actually," he explained, "it works out quite cheaply; you see, we wouldn't have to do them all individually. Small-scale nuclear weapons, some judicious bombing, gassing, plague, dropping radios in swimming pools, and then mopping up the stragglers. Say four thousand pounds."

"Four thou—? That's in*cred*ible!"

The salesman looked pleased with himself. "Our operatives will be glad of the work, sir." He grinned. "We pride ourselves on servicing our wholesale customers."

The wind blew cold as Peter left the pub, setting the old sign swinging. It didn't look much like a dirty donkey, thought Peter. More like a pale horse.

Peter was drifting off to sleep that night, mentally rehearsing his coronation speech, when a thought drifted into his head and hung around. It would not go away. Could he—could he *possibly* be passing up an even larger saving than he already had? Could he be missing out on a bargain?

Peter climbed out of bed and walked over to the phone. It was almost 3 A.M., but even so—

His Yellow Pages lay open where he had left it the previous Saturday, and he dialled the number.

The phone seemed to ring forever. There was a click and a bored voice said, "Burke Hare Ketch. Can I help you?"

"I hope I'm not phoning too late—" he began.

"Of course not, sir."

"I was wondering if I could speak to Mr. Kemble."

"Can you hold? I'll see if he's available."

Peter waited for a couple of minutes, listening to the ghostly crackles and whispers that always echo down empty phone lines.

"Are you there, caller?"

"Yes, I'm here."

"Putting you through." There was a buzz, then "Kemble speaking."

"Ah, Mr. Kemble. Hello. Sorry if I got you out of bed or anything. This is, um, Peter Pinter."

"Yes, Mr. Pinter?"

"Well, I'm sorry it's so late, only I was wondering—How much would it cost to kill everybody? Everybody in the world?"

"Everybody? All the people?"

"Yes. How much? I mean, for an order like that, you'd have to have some kind of a big discount. How much would it be? For everyone?"

"Nothing at all, Mr. Pinter."

"You mean you wouldn't do it?"

"I mean we'd do it for nothing, Mr. Pinter. We only have to be asked, you see. We always have to be asked."

Peter was puzzled. "But—when would you start?"

"Start? Right away. Now. We've been ready for a long time. But we had to be asked, Mr. Pinter. Good night. It *has* been a *pleasure* doing business with you."

The line went dead.

Peter felt strange. Everything seemed very distant. He wanted to sit down. What on earth had the man meant? "We always have to be asked." It was definitely strange. Nobody does anything for nothing in this world; he had a good mind to phone Kemble back and call the whole thing off. Perhaps he had overreacted, perhaps there was a perfectly innocent reason why Archie and Gwendolyn had entered the stockroom together. He would talk to her, that's what he'd do. He'd talk to Gwennie first thing tomorrow morning—

That was when the noises started.

Odd cries from across the street. A catfight? Foxes probably. He hoped someone would throw a shoe at them. Then, from the corridor outside his flat, he heard a muffled clumping, as if someone were dragging something very heavy along the floor. It stopped. Someone knocked on his door, twice, very softly.

Outside his window the cries were getting louder. Peter sat in his chair, knowing that somehow, somewhere, he had missed something. Something important. The knocking redoubled. He was thankful that he always locked and chained his door at night.

They'd been ready for a long time, but they had to be asked—

DETAİLS

China Miéville

When the boy upstairs got hold of a pellet gun and fired snips of potato at passing cars, I took a turn. I was part of everything. I wasn't an outsider. But I wouldn't join in when my friends went to the yellow house to scribble on the bricks and listen at the windows. One girl teased me about it, but everyone else told her to shut up. They defended me, even though they didn't understand why I wouldn't come.

I don't remember a time before I visited the yellow house for my mother.

On Wednesday mornings at about nine o'clock I would open the front door of the decrepit building with a key from the bunch my mother had given me. Inside was a hall and two doors, one broken and leading to splintering stairs. I would unlock the other and enter the dark flat. The corridor was unlit and smelled of old, wet air. I never walked even two steps down that hallway. Rot and shadows merged, and it looked as if the passage disappeared a few yards from me. The door to Mrs. Miller's room was right in front of me. I would lean forward and knock.

Quite often there were signs that someone else had been there recently. Scuffed dust and bits of litter. Sometimes I was not alone. There were two other children I sometimes saw slipping in or out of the house. There were a handful of adults who visited Mrs. Miller.

I might find one or another of them in the hallway outside the door to her flat, or even in the flat itself, slouching in the crumbling dark hallway. They would be slumped over or reading some cheap-looking book or swearing loudly as they waited.

There was a young Asian woman who wore a lot of makeup and smoked obsessively. She ignored me totally. There were two drunks who came sometimes. One would greet me boisterously and incomprehensibly, raising his arms as if he wanted to hug me into his stinking, stinking jumper. I would grin and wave nervously, walk past him. The other seemed alternately melancholic and angry. Occasionally I'd meet him by the door to Mrs. Miller's room, swearing in a strong cockney accent. I remember the first time I saw him, he was standing there, his red face contorted, slurring and moaning loudly.

"Come on, you old slag," he wailed, "you sodding old *slag*. Come on, please, you cow."

His words scared me but his tone was wheedling, and I realized I could hear her voice, Mrs. Miller's voice, from inside the room, answering him back. She did not sound frightened or angry.

I hung back, not sure what to do, and she kept speaking, and eventually the drunken man shambled miserably away. And then I could continue as usual.

I asked my mother once if I could have any of Mrs. Miller's food. She laughed very hard and shook her head. In all the Wednesdays of bringing the food over, I never even dipped my finger in to suck it.

My mum spent an hour every Tuesday night making the stuff up. She dissolved a bit of gelatin or cornflour with some milk, threw in a load of sugar or flavorings, and crushed a clutch of vitamin pills into the mess. She stirred it until it thickened and let it set in a plain white plastic bowl. In the morning it would be a kind of strong-smelling custard that my mother put a dishcloth over and gave me, along with a list of any questions or requests for Mrs. Miller and sometimes a plastic bucket full of white paint.

So I would stand in front of Mrs. Miller's door, knocking, with a bowl at my feet. I'd hear a shifting and then her voice from close by the door.

"Hello," she would call, and then say my name a couple of times. "Have you my breakfast? Are you ready?"

I would creep up close to the door and hold the food ready. I would tell her I was.

Mrs. Miller would slowly count to three. On three, the door suddenly swung open a snatch, just a foot or two, and I thrust my bowl into the gap. She grabbed it and slammed the door quickly in my face.

I couldn't see very much inside the room. The door was open for less than a second. My strongest impression was of the whiteness of the walls. Mrs. Miller's sleeves were white, too, and made of plastic. I never got much of a glimpse at her face, but what I saw was unmemorable. A middle-aged woman's eager face.

If I had a bucket full of paint, we would run through the routine again. Then I would sit cross-legged in front of her door and listen to her eat.

"How's your mother" she would shout. At that I'd unfold my mother's careful queries. She's okay, I'd say, she's fine. She says she has some questions for you.

I'd read my mother's strange questions in my careful childish monotone, and Mrs. Miller would pause and make interested sounds, and clear her throat and think out loud. Sometimes she took ages to come to an answer, and sometimes it would be almost immediate.

"Tell your mother she can't tell if a man's good or bad from that," she'd say; "Tell her to remember the problems she had with your father." Or: "Yes, she can take the heart of it out. Only she has to paint it with the special oil I told her about." "Tell your mother seven. But only four of them concern her and three of them used to be dead."

"I can't help her with that," she told me once, quietly. "Tell her to go to a doctor, quickly." And my mother did, and she got well again.

"What do you not want to be when you grow up?" Mrs. Miller asked me one day.

That morning when I had come to the house the sad cockney vagrant had been banging on the door of her room again, the keys to the flat flailing in his hand.

"He's begging you, you old tart, please, you owe him, he's so bloody angry," he was shouting, "only it ain't you gets the sharp end, is it? *Please*, you cow, you sodding cow, I'm on me knees…"

"My door knows you, man," Mrs. Miller declared from within. "It knows you and so do I, you know it won't open to you. I didn't take out my eyes and I'm not giving in now. Go home."

I waited nervously as the man gathered himself and staggered away, and then, looking behind me, I knocked on the door and announced myself. It was after I'd given her the food that she asked her question.

"What do you not want to be when you grow up?"

If I had been a few years older her inversion of the cliché would have annoyed me. It would have seemed mannered and contrived. But I was only a young child, and I was quite delighted.

I don't want to be a lawyer, I told her carefully. I spoke out of loyalty to my mother, who periodically received crisp letters that made her cry or smoke fiercely, and swear at lawyers, bloody smartarse lawyers.

Mrs. Miller was delighted.

"Good boy!" she snorted. "We know all about lawyers. Bastards, right? With the small print. Never be tricked by the small print! It's right there in front of you, *right there in front of you*, and you can't even *see* it and then suddenly it *makes you notice it*! And I tell you, once you've seen it it's got you!" She laughed excitedly. "Don't let the small print get you. I'll tell you a secret." I waited quietly, and my head slipped nearer the door.

"The devil's in the details!" She laughed again. "You ask your mother if that's not true. The devil is in the details!"

I'd wait the twenty minutes or so until Mrs. Miller had finished eating, and then we'd reverse our previous procedure and she'd quickly hand me out an empty bowl. I would return home with the empty container and tell my mother the various answers to her various questions. Usually she would nod and make notes. Occasionally she would cry.

After I told Mrs. Miller that I did not want to be a lawyer she started asking me to read to her. She made me tell my mother, and told me to bring a newspaper or one of a number of books. My mother nodded at the message and packed me a sandwich the next Wednesday, along with the *Mirror*. She told me to be polite and do what Mrs. Miller asked, and that she'd see me in the afternoon.

I wasn't afraid. Mrs. Miller had never treated me badly from behind her door. I was resigned and only a little bit nervous.

Mrs. Miller made me read stories to her from specific pages that she shouted out. She made me recite them again and again, very carefully. Afterward she would talk to me. Usually she started with a joke about lawyers, and about small print.

"There's three ways not to see what you don't want to," she told me. "One is the coward's way and too damned painful. The other is to close your eyes forever which is the same as the first, when it comes to it. The third is the hardest and the best: You have to make sure *only the things you can afford to see* come before you."

One morning when I arrived the stylish Asian woman was whispering fiercely through the wood of the door, and I could hear Mrs. Miller responding with shouts of amused disapproval. Eventually the young woman swept past me, leaving me cowed by her perfume.

Mrs. Miller was laughing, and she was talkative when she had eaten.

"She's heading for trouble, messing with the wrong family! You have to be careful with all of them," she told me. "Every single *one* of them on that other side of things is a tricksy bastard who'll kill you as soon as *look* at you, given half a chance.

"There's the gnarly throat-tripped one... and there's old hasty, who I think had best remain nameless," she said wryly. "All old bastards, all of them. You *can't trust them* at all, that's what I say. I should know, eh? Shouldn't I?" She laughed. "Trust me, trust me on this: It's too easy to get on the wrong side of them.

"What's it like out today?" she asked me. I told her that it was cloudy.

"You want to be careful with that," she said. "All sorts of faces in the clouds, aren't there? Can't help noticing, can you?" She was whispering now. "Do me a favor when you go home to your mum: Don't look up, there's a boy. Don't look up at all."

When I left her, however, the day had changed. The sky was hot, and quite blue.

The two drunk men were squabbling in the front hall and I edged past them to her door. They continued bickering in a depressing, garbled murmur throughout my visit.

"D'you know, I can't even really remember what it was all *about*, now!" Mrs. Miller said when I had finished reading to her. "I can't remember! That's a terrible thing. But you don't forget the basics. The exact question escapes me, and to be honest I think maybe I was just being *nosy* or *showing off*... I can't say I'm proud of it but it could have been that. It could. But whatever the question, it was all about a way of seeing an answer.

"There's a way of looking that lets you read things. If you look at a pattern of tar on a wall, or a crumbling mound of brick or somesuch… there's a way of unpicking it. And if you know how, you can trace it and read it out and see the things hidden *right there in front of you*, the things you've been seeing but not noticing, all along. But you have to learn how." She laughed. It was a high-pitched, unpleasant sound. "Someone has to teach you. So you have to make certain friends. "But you can't make friends without making enemies.

"You have to open it all up for you to see inside. You have to make what you see into a window, and you see what you want through it. You make what you see a sort of *door*."

She was silent for a long time. Then: "Is it cloudy again?" she asked suddenly. She went on before I answered.

"If you look up, you look into the clouds for long enough and you'll see a face. Or in a tree. Look in a tree, look in the branches and soon you'll see them just so, and there's a face or a running man, or a bat or whatever. You'll see it all suddenly, a picture in the pattern of the branches, and you won't have *chosen* to see it. And you can't *unsee* it.

"That's what you have to learn to do, to read the details like that and see what's what and learn things. But you've to be damn careful. You've to be careful not to disturb anything." Her voice was absolutely cold, and I was suddenly very frightened.

"Open up that window, you'd better be damn careful that what's in the details doesn't look back and see you."

The next time I went, the maudlin drunk was there again wailing obscenities at her through the door. She shouted at me to come back later, that she didn't need her food right now. She sounded resigned and irritated, and she went back to scolding her visitor before I had backed out of earshot.

He was screaming at her that she'd gone too far, that she'd pissed about too long, that things were coming to a head, that there was going to be hell to pay, that she couldn't avoid it forever, that it was her own fault.

When I came back he was asleep, snoring loudly, curled up a few feet into the mildewing passage. Mrs. Miller took her food and ate it quickly, returned it without speaking.

When I returned the following week, she began to whisper to me as soon as I knocked on the door, hissing urgently as she opened it briefly and grabbed the bowl.

"It was an accident, you know," she said, as if responding to something I'd said. "I mean of *course* you know in *theory* that anything might happen, you get *warned*, don't you? But oh my… oh my *God* it took the breath out of me and made me cold to realize what had happened."

I waited. I could not leave, because she had not returned the bowl. She had not said I could go. She spoke again, very slowly.

"It was a new day." Her voice was distant and breathy. "Can you even imagine? Can you see what I was ready to do? I was poised... to change... to see everything that's hidden. The best place to hide a book is in a library. The best place to hide secret things is there, in the visible angles, in our view, in plain sight.

"I had studied and sought, and learnt, finally, to see. It was time to learn truths.

"I opened my eyes fully, for the first time.

"I had chosen an old wall. I was looking for the answer to some question that I told you I can't even *remember* now, but the question wasn't the main thing. That was the opening of my eyes.

"I stared at the whole mass of the bricks. I took another glance, relaxed my sight. At first I couldn't stop seeing the bricks as bricks, the divisions as layers of cement, but after a time they became pure vision. And as the whole broke down into lines and shapes and shades, I held my breath as I began to see.

"Alternatives appeared to me. Messages written in the pockmarks. Insinuations in the forms. Secrets unraveling. It was bliss.

"And then without warning my heart went tight, as I saw something. I made sense of the pattern.

"It was a mess of cracks and lines and crumbling cement, and as I looked at it, I saw a pattern in the wall.

"I saw a clutch of lines that looked just like something... terrible... something old and predatory and utterly terrible... staring right back at me.

"And then I saw it move."

"You have to understand me," she said. "*Nothing changed.* See? All the time I was looking I saw the wall. But that first moment, it was like when you see a face in the cloud. I just *noticed* in the pattern in the brick, I just *noticed* something, looking at me. Something angry.

"And then in the very next moment, I just... I just *noticed* another load of lines—cracks that had always been there, you understand? Patterns in broken brick that I'd seen only a second before—that looked exactly like that same thing, a little closer to me. And in the next moment a third picture in the brick, a picture of the thing closer still.

"Reaching for me."

"I broke free then," she whispered. "I ran away from there in terror, with my hands in front of my eyes and I was *screaming.* I ran and ran.

"And when I stopped and opened my eyes again, I had to run to the edges of a park, and I took my hands slowly down and dared to look behind me, and saw that there was nothing coming from the alley where I'd been. So I turned to the little snatch of scrub grass and trees.

"And I saw the thing again."

Mrs. Miller's voice was stretched out as if she was dreaming. My mouth was open and I huddled closer to the door.

"I saw it in the leaves," she said forlornly. "As I turned I saw the leaves in such a way... just a *chance conjuncture*, you understand? I noticed a pattern. I *couldn't not*. You don't choose whether to see faces in the clouds. I saw the monstrous thing again and it still reached for me, and I shrieked and all the mothers and children and fathers and children in the park turned and gazed at me, and I turned my eyes from that tree and whirled on my feet to face a little family in my way.

"And the thing was there in the same pose," she whispered in misery. "I saw it in the outlines of the father's coat and the spokes of the baby's pushchair, and the tangles of the mother's hair. It was just another mess of lines, you see? But you *don't choose what you notice*. And I couldn't help but notice *just the right lines* out of the whole, just the lines out of all the lines there, just the ones to see the thing again, a little closer, looking at me.

"And I turned and saw it closer still in the clouds, and I turned again and it was clutching for me in the rippling weeds in the pond, and as I closed my eyes I swear I felt something touch my dress.

"You understand me? You understand?"

I didn't know if I understood or not. Of course now I know that I did not.

"It lives in the details," she said bleakly. "It travels in that... in that perception. It moves through those chance meetings of lines. Maybe you glimpse it sometimes when you stare at clouds, and then maybe it might catch a glimpse of you, too.

"But it saw me *full* on. It's jealous of... of its place, and there I was peering through without permission, like a nosy neighbor through a hole in the fence. I know what it is. I know what happened.

"It lurks before us, in the everyday. It's the boss of *all the things* hidden in plain sight. Terrible things, they are. Appalling things. Just almost in reach. Brazen and invisible.

"It caught my glances. It can move through whatever I see.

"For most people it's just chance, isn't it? What shapes they see in a tangle of wire. There's a thousand pictures there, and when you look, some of them just appear. But now... the thing in the lines chooses the pictures for me. It can thrust itself forward. It makes me see it. It's found its way through. To me. Through what I see. *I opened a door into my perception.*"

She sounded frozen with terror. I was not equipped for that kind of adult fear, and my mouth worked silently for something to say.

"That was a long, long journey home. Every time I peeked through the cracks in my fingers, I saw that thing crawling for me.

"It waited ready to pounce, and when I opened my eyes even a crack I opened the door again. I saw the back of a woman's jumper and in the detail of the fabric the thing leapt for me. I glimpsed a yard of broken paving and I noticed just the lines that showed me the thing... *baying*.

"I had to shut my eyes quick.

"I *groped* my way home.

"And then I taped my eyes shut and I tried to think about things."

There was silence for a time.

"See, there was always the easy way, that scared me rotten, because I was never one for blood and pain," she said suddenly, and her voice was harder. "I held the scissors in front of my eyes a couple of times, but even bandaged blind as I was I couldn't bear it. I suppose I could've gone to a doctor. I can pull strings, I could pull in a few favors, have them do the job without pain.

"But you know I never… really… reckoned… that's what I'd do," she said thoughtfully. "What if you found a way to close the door? Eh? And you'd already put out your eyes? You'd feel such a *fool*, wouldn't you?

"And as you know it wouldn't be good enough to wear pads and eyepatches and all. I tried. You catch glimpses. You see the glimmers of light and maybe a few of your own hairs, and that's *the doorway right there*, when the hairs cross in the corner of your eye so that if you notice just a few of them in just the right way… they look like something coming for you. That's a doorway.

"It's… unbearable… having sight, but trapping it like that.

"I'm not giving up. See…" Her voice lowered, and she spoke conspiratorially. "*I still think I can close the door*. I learnt to see. I can unlearn. I'm looking for ways. I want to see a wall as… as bricks again. Nothing more. That's why you read for me," she said. "*Research*. Can't look at it myself of course, too many edges and lines and so on on a printed page, so you do it for me. And you're a good boy to do it."

I've thought about what she said many times, and still it makes no sense to me. The books I read to Mrs. Miller were school textbooks, old and dull village histories, the occasional romantic novel. I think that she must have been talking of some of her other visitors, who perhaps read her more esoteric stuff than I did. Either that, or the information she sought was buried very cleverly in the banal prose I faltered through.

"In the meantime, there's another way of surviving," she said slyly. "Leave the eyes where they are, but *don't give them any details*.

"That… thing can force me to notice its shape, but only in what's there. That's how it travels. You imagine if I saw a field of wheat. Doesn't even bear *thinking* about! A million million little bloody *edges*, a million lines. You could make pictures of damn *anything* out of them, couldn't you? It wouldn't take any effort at *all* for the thing to make me notice it. The damn *lurker*. Or in a gravel drive or, or a building site, or a lawn…

"But I can outsmart it." The note of cunning in her voice made her sound deranged. "Keep it away till I work out how to close it off.

"I had to prepare this blind, with the wrappings around my head. Took me a while, but here I am now. Safe. I'm safe in my little cold room. I keep the walls *flat white*. I covered the windows and painted them, too. I made my cloak out of plastic, so's I can't catch a glimpse of cotton weave or anything when I wake up.

"I keep my place nice and… simple. When it was all done, I unwrapped the bandages from my head, and I blinked slowly… and I was alright. Clean walls, no cracks, no features. I don't look at my hands often or for long. Too many creases. Your mother makes me a good healthy soup looks like cream, so if I accidentally look in the bowl, there's no broccoli or rice or tangled up spaghetti to make *lines and edges*.

"I open and shut the door so damned quick because I can only afford a moment. *That thing is ready to pounce.* It wouldn't take a second for it to leap up at me out of the sight of your hair or your books or whatever."

Her voice ebbed out. I waited a minute for her to resume, but she did not do so. Eventually I knocked nervously on the door and called her name. There was no answer. I put my ear to the door. I could hear her crying, quietly.

I went home without the bowl. My mother pursed her lips a little but said nothing. I didn't tell her any of what Mrs. Miller had said. I was troubled and totally confused.

The next time I delivered Mrs. Miller's food, in a new container, she whispered harshly to me: "It preys on my eyes, all the *white*. Nothing to see. Can't look out the window, can't read, can't gaze at my nails. Preys on my mind.

"Not even my memories are left," she said in misery. "It's colonizing them. I remember things… happy times… and the thing's waiting in the texture of my dress, or in the crumbs of my birthday cake. I didn't notice it then. But I can see it now. My memories aren't mine anymore. Not even my imaginings. Last night I thought about going to the seaside, and then the thing was there in the foam on the waves."

She spoke very little the next few times I visited her. I read the chapters she demanded and she grunted curtly in her response. She ate quickly.

Her other visitors were there more often now, as the spring came in. I saw them in new combinations and situations: the glamorous young woman arguing with the friendly drunk; the old man sobbing at the far end of the hall. The aggressive man was often there, cajoling and moaning, and occasionally talking conversationally through the door, being answered like an equal. Other times he screamed at her as usual.

I arrived on a chilly day to find the drunken cockney man sleeping a few feet from the door, snoring gutturally. I gave Mrs. Miller her food and then sat on my coat and read to her from a women's magazine as she ate.

When she had finished her food I waited with my arms outstretched, ready to snatch the bowl from her. I remember that I was very uneasy, that I sensed something wrong. I was looking around me anxiously, but everything seemed normal. I looked down at my coat and the crumpled magazine, at the man who still sprawled comatose in the hall.

As I heard Mrs. Miller's hands on the door, I realized what had changed. The drunken man was not snoring. He was holding his breath.

For a tiny moment I thought he had died, but I could see his body trembling, and my eyes began to open wide and I stretched my mouth to scream a warning, but the door had already begun to swing in its tight, quick arc, and before I could even exhale the stinking man pushed himself up faster than I would have thought him capable and bore down on me with bloodshot eyes.

I managed to keep as he reached me, and the door faltered for an instant, as Mrs. Miller heard my voice. But the man grabbed hold of me in a terrifying, heavy fug of alcohol. He reached down and snatched my coat from the floor, tugged at the jumper I had tied around my waist with his other hand, and hurled me hard at the door.

It flew open, smacking Mrs. Miller aside. I was screaming and crying. My eyes hurt at the sudden burst of cold white light from all the walls. I saw Mrs. Miller rubbing her head in the corner, struggling to her senses. The staggering, drunken man hurled my checked coat and my patterned jumper in front of her, reached down and snatched my feet, tugged me out of the room in an agony of splinters. I wailed snottily with fear.

Behind me, Mrs. Miller began to scream and curse, but I could not hear her well because the man had clutched me to him and pulled my head to his chest. I fought and cried and felt myself lurch as he leaned forward and slammed the door closed.

He held it shut.

When I fought myself free of him I heard him shouting.

"I told you, you slapper," he wailed unhappily. "I bloody told you, you silly old whore. I warned you it was time..." Behind his voice I could hear shrieks of misery and terror from the room. Both of them kept shouting and crying and screaming, and the floorboards pounded, and the door shook, and I heard something else as well.

As if the notes of all the different noises in the house fell into a chance meeting, and sounded like more than dissonance. The shouts and bangs and cries of fear combined in a sudden audible illusion like another presence.

Like a snarling voice. A lingering, hungry exhalation.

I ran then, screaming and terrified, my skin freezing in my T-shirt. I was sobbing and retching with fear, little bleats bursting from me. I stumbled home and was sick in my mother's room, and kept crying and crying as she grabbed hold of me and I tried to tell her what had happened, until I was drowsy and confused and I fell into silence.

My mother said nothing about Mrs. Miller. The next Wednesday we got up early and went to the zoo, the two of us, and at the time I would usually be knocking on Mrs. Miller's door I was laughing at camels. The Wednesday after that I was taken to see a film, and the one after that my mother stayed in bed and sent me to fetch cigarettes and bread from the local shop, and I made our breakfast and ate it in her room.

My friends could tell that something had changed in the yellow house, but they did not speak to me about it, and it quickly became uninteresting to them.

I saw the Asian woman once more, smoking with her friends in the park several weeks later, and to my amazement she nodded to me and came over, interrupted her companions' conversation.

"Are you alright?" she asked me peremptorily. "How are you doing?"

I nodded shyly back and told her that I was fine, thank you, and how was she?

She nodded and walked away.

I never saw the drunken, violent man again.

There were people I could probably have gone to to understand more about what had happened to Mrs. Miller. There was a story that I could chase, if I wanted to. People I had never seen before came to my house and spoke quietly to my mother, and looked at me with what I suppose was pity or concern. I could have asked them. But I was thinking more and more about my own life. I didn't want to know Mrs. Miller's details.

I went back to the yellow house once, nearly a year after that awful morning. It was winter. I remembered the last time I spoke to Mrs. Miller and I felt so much older it was almost giddying. It seemed such a vastly long time ago.

I crept up to the house one evening, trying the keys I still had, which to my surprise worked. The hallway was freezing, dark, and stinking more strongly than ever. I hesitated, then pushed open Mrs. Miller's door.

It opened easily, without a sound. The occasional muffled noise from the street seemed so distant it was like a memory. I entered.

She had covered the windows very carefully, and still no light made its way through from outside. It was extremely dark. I waited until I could see better in the ambient glow from the outside hallway.

I was alone.

My old coat and jumper lay spread-eagled in the corner of the room. I shivered to see them, went over, and fingered them softly. They were damp and mildewing, covered in wet dust.

The white paint was crumbling off the wall in scabs. It looked as if it had been left untended for several years. I could not believe the extent of the decay.

I turned slowly around and gazed at each wall in turn. I took in the chaotic, intricate patterns of crumbling paint and damp plaster. They looked like maps, like a rocky landscape.

I looked for a long time at the wall farthest from my jacket. I was very cold. After a long time I saw a shape in the ruined paint. I moved closer with a dumb curiosity far stronger than any fear.

In the crumbling texture of the wall was a spreading anatomy of cracks that—seen from a certain angle, caught just right in the scraps of light—looked in outline something like a woman. As I stared at it, it took shape, and I stopped noticing the extraneous lines, and focused without effort or decision on the relevant ones. I saw a woman looking out at me.

I could make out the suggestion of her face. The patch of rot that constituted it made it look as if she was screaming.

One of her arms was flung back away from her body, which seemed to strain against it, as if she was being pulled away by her hand, and was fighting to escape, and was failing. At the end of her crack-arm, in the space where her captor would be, the paint had fallen away in a great slab, uncovering a huge patch of wet, stained, textured cement.

And in that dark infinity of markings, I could make out any shape I wanted.

THE DEVIL DISINVESTS
By Scott Bradfield

"I don't think of it as laying off workers," the Devil told his Chief Executive Officer, Punky Wilkenfeld, a large round man with bloodshot eyes and wobbly knees. "I think of it as downsizing to a more user-friendly mode of production. I guess what I'm saying, Punky, is that we can't spend all eternity thinking about nothing more important than the bottom line. Maybe it's finally time to kick back, reflect on our achievements, and start enjoying some of that well-deserved R&R we've promised ourselves for so long."

As always, the Devil tried to be reasonable. But this didn't prevent his long-devoted subordinate from weeping copiously into his worsted vest.

"What will I *do*?" Punky asked himself over and over again. "Where will I *go*? All this time I thought you loved me because I was really, really evil. Now I realize you only kept me around because, oh God. For you it was just, just, it was just *business*."

The Devil folded his long forked tail into his belt and checked himself out in the wall-sized vanity mirror behind his desk. He was wearing a snappy handmade suit by Vuiton, gleaming Cordovan leather shoes, and prescription Ray-Bans. The Devil had long been aware that it wasn't enough to be good at what you did. In order for people to know it, you had to look good, as well.

Roger "Punky" Wilkenfeld lay drooped over the edge of the Devil's desk like a very old gardenia. The Devil couldn't help himself. He really loved this guy.

"What can I tell you, Roger?" the Devil said, as gently as he could. "Eventually it comes time for everybody to move on, and so in this particular instance, I'll blaze the trail, and leave you and the boys to pack things up in your own good time. Just be sure to lock up when you leave."

The Devil went to California. He rented a beachfront cottage on the Central Coast, sold off his various penthouses and Tuscan villas, and settled into the reflective life as easily as an anemone in a tide pool. Every day he walked to the local grocery for fresh fruits and vegetables, took long strolls into the dry amber hills, or rented one of the Nouvelle Vague classics he'd always meant to watch from Blockbuster. He disdained malls, televised sports, and corporate-owned franchise restaurants. He tore up his credit cards, stopped worrying about the bottom line, and never once opened his mail.

In his heyday, the Devil had enjoyed the most exotic pleasures that could be devised by an infinite array of saucy, fun-loving girls named Delilah. But until he met Melanie, he had never actually known true love.

"I guess it's because love takes time," the Devil reflected, on the night they first slept together on the beach. "And time has never been something I've had too much of. Bartering for souls, keeping the penitents in agony, stoking the infernos of unutterable suffering and so forth. And then, as if that's not enough, having to deal with all the endless constant whining. Oh *please,* Master, *please* take my soul, *please* grant me unlimited wealth and fame and eternal youth and sex with any gal in the office, I'll do *any*thing you ask, please *please.* When a guy's in the damnation game, he never gets a moment's rest. If I'd met you five years ago, Mel? I don't think I'd have stopped working long enough to realize what a wonderful, giving person you really are. But I've got the time now, baby. Come here a sec. I've definitely got lots of time for you now."

They moved in together. They had children—a girl and a boy. They shopped at the Health Food Co-Op, campaigned for animal rights, and installed an energy efficient Aga in the kitchen. They even canceled the lease on the Devil's Volvo, and transported themselves everywhere on matching ten-speed racing bikes. These turned out to be the most wonderful and relaxing days the Devil had ever known.

Then, one afternoon when the Devil was sorting recyclable materials into their appropriate plastic bins, he received a surprise visitor from his past. Melanie had just taken the kids to Montessori. The Devil had been looking forward all day to catching up with his chores.

"How they hanging, big boy? I guess I imagined all sorts of comeuppances for a useless old fart like yourself, but certainly never this. Wasting your once-awesome days digging through garbage. Cleaning the windows and mowing the lawn."

When the Devil looked up, he saw Punky Wilkenfeld climbing out of a two-door Corvette. Clad in one of the Devil's old suits, he looked slightly out of place amidst so much expensive retailoring. Some guys know how to hang clothes, the Devil thought. And some guys just don't.

"Why, Punky," the Devil said softly, not without affection. "It's you."

"It sure is, pal. But they don't call me Punky anymore."

"Oh no?" The Devil absently licked a bit of stale egg from his forepaw.

"Nope. These days, people call me *Mr.* Wilkenfeld. Or better yet, the Eternal Lord of Darkness and Pain."

"It's like this, Pop," Punky continued over Red Zinger tea in the breakfast room. "When you took off, you left a trillion hungry mouths to feed. Mouths with razor-sharp teeth. Mouths with multitudinously-forked tongues. Frankly,

I didn't know what to do, so I turned the whole kit-and-kaboodle over to the free-market-system and just let it ride. We went on the Dow in March, and by summer we'd bought out two of our closest rivals—Microsoft and ITT. I even hear Mr. Hot-Shot Heavenly Father's been doing a little diversifying. Doesn't matter to me, either. Whoever spends it, it's all money."

"It's always good to see a former employee make good, Punky," the Devil said graciously. "I mean, excuse me. *Mr.* Wilkenfeld."

Punky finished his tea with a long, parched swallow. "*Ahh,*" he said, and hammered the mug down with a short, rude bang. "I guess I just wanted you to know that I haven't forgotten you, Pops. In fact, I've even bought this little strip of beach you call home, and once we've finished erecting the new condos, we'll move on to offshore oil rigs, docking facilities, maybe even a yachting club or two. Basically, Pop, I'm turning your life into scrap metal. Nothing to do with business, either. I just personally hate your guts."

The Devil gradually grew aware of a dim beeping sound. With a sigh, Punky reached into his vest pocket and deactivated his digital phone with a brisk little flick.

"Probably my broker," Punky said. "He calls at least six times a day."

The Devil distantly regarded his former *chargé d'affaires,* whose soft pink lips were beaded with perspiration and bad faith. Poor Punky, the Devil thought. Some guys just never learn.

"And wanta know the best thing about this shoreline redevelopment project, Pop? There's absolutely nothing you can do about it. You take it to the courts—I own them. You take it to the Board of Supervisors—I own *them.* You organize eight million sit-down demonstrations and I pave the whole damn lot of you over with bulldozers. That's the real pleasure of dealing dirt to you born-again types, Pop. *You* gotta be *good.* But I don't."

The Devil watched Punky stand, brush himself off, and reach for his snakeskin briefcase. Then, as if seeking a balance to this hard, unaccommodating vision, he looked out his picture window at the hardware equipment littering his back yard. The Devil had been intending to install aluminum siding all week, and he hated to see unfulfilled projects rust away in the salty sea air.

"One second," the Devil said. "I'll be right back."

"Sorry, Pop, but this is one CEO who believes in full-steam-ahead, toot toot! Keep in touch, guy. Unless, that is, I keep touch with *you* first—"

But of course before Punky reached the front door the Devil had already returned from his back yard with the shearing scissors. And Punky, who had belonged to the managerial classes for more eons than he cared to remember, was slow to recognize any instrument used in the performance of manual labor.

"Hey, Pop, that's more like it," Punky said slowly, the wrong sun dawning from the wrong hills. "I could use a little grooming if only to remind us both who's boss. Here, see, at the edge of this cloven hoof? What does that look like to you? A hangnail?"

Punky had crouched down so low that it almost resembled submission.

At which point the Devil commenced to chop Punky Wilkenfeld into a million tiny bits.

"Seagulls don't mind what they eat," the Devil reflected later. He was standing at the end of a long wooden pier, watching white birds dive into the frothy red water. "Which is probably why they remind me so much of men."

The Devil wondered idly if his life had a moral. If it did, he decided, it was probably this:

Just because people change their lives for the better doesn't mean they're stupid.

Then, remembering it was his turn to do bouillabaisse, the Devil turned his back on the glorious sunset and went home.

FAUSTFEATHERS

A play by John Kessel

Cast of Characters:
Doctor John Faustus, professor of theology, University of Wittenberg
Wagner, his student and servant
Dicolini, a student at the university
Robin, another student
Frater Albergus, a spy for the Pope
Master Bateman, Albergus's henchman
Helen of Troy, a spirit
Mephistopheles, a demon from hell
Martin, a porter
The Clock
students, demons, a barmaid

The entire play takes place in Wittenberg, Germany in late December 1519.
Scene 1: Faustus's apartment, evening
Scene 2: Albergus's room at the Boar's Bollocks Inn, the next morning
Scene 3: Faustus's classroom, late morning
Scene 4: Faustus's apartment, afternoon
Scene 5: The tavern at the Boar's Bollocks Inn, late afternoon
Scene 6: Faustus's apartment, that evening
Scene 7: The tavern in the Boar's Bollocks Inn, after midnight

ACT ONE
Scene One
Spotlight downstage center. Enter Mephistopheles.
Mephistopheles: Know, ladies and gentlemen, that I am Mephistopheles, chief among lieutenants to our great Master Lucifer. For twenty-four years now I have been bound by magical contract as servant to the necromancer Doctor Faustus. But now the end draws nigh.

As all demons, in compensation for our damnation I am given the power to be in every place, and the power to render myself invisible (*renders himself invisible by draping his head and shoulders with tinsel).* I see you when you're sleeping, I see you when you wake, I know if you've been bad or good, so…

Excuse me. It is Christmas of 1519. All of Europe lies in turmoil over the heresies of Martin Luther. The Pope and the Roman Church attempt to keep repressed changes that cannot be repressed. To the West, a new world has been discovered. There is a rebirth of learning, a renewed quest for knowledge. It is an age of overreachers, where the certitudes of the Middle Ages have been challenged and in places, broken. New nations, new political movements, new commerce, new science, and old lusts. Vast opportunity for salesmen such as me.

Though you live some five centuries after the good doctor, you are bound as he by the self-same laws of the universe. There, but for the grace of God, go you.

Lights come up. We are in a medieval apartment, divided into three rooms. To stage right is a bedroom, center stage is a common room/dining room, and stage left is a library/laboratory/study. Of the furnishings of these rooms, the most bizarre is a human Clock *that stands in the corner of the commons room: a man in a modern business suit who calls out the hours aloud.*

The bedroom and laboratory are dark, but four men occupy the apartment. Wagner *is looking for something in the study. At the dining table, lingering over the remains of a dinner, are* Frater Albergus *,* Master Bateman *, and* Doctor Faustus. *Albergus is an imposing man of middle years, wearing somewhat elaborate medieval garb. Bateman is Albergus's henchman, a lascivious little man who has seen too much conniving and is cynically accustomed to it all. Wagner is Faustus's student at the university of Wittenberg, and his servant. He is waiting table at this dinner. Faustus looks exactly like Groucho Marx of the early Paramount Marx Brothers films. He wears gold wire-rimmed spectacles, a black academic gown over a loose white shirt, a sloppily tied black cravat, and tights.*

It is winter and a fire burns in the fireplace. At the rear of each room a latticed window looks out on the alley behind Faustus's apartment. At the beginning of the scene Wagner leaves the commons for his study and Albergus continues his conversation with Faustus.

Albergus: Of course the power that comes from the blood of unbaptized infants is only good during months without an "r" in them. My colleague Master Bateman, here, is an expert in such matters.

Bateman (smiling): I before e except after c.

Faustus: You know, to look at those teeth you'd swear they were real.

Wagner returns from the study.

Wagner: I cannot find them, Master.

Faustus: Of course you can't. Frater Albergus, meet my apprentice, Wagner. Don't let the feckless demeanor fool you. He really is a Renaissance dope.

Faustus exits.

Albergus: How long have you been Doctor Faustus's fag, my boy?

Wagner: Two years.

Albergus: Yet he treats you abominably. Why do you put up with it?

Wagner: I am a student of the magical arts. I seek knowledge.

Albergus: What sort of knowledge?

Wagner: The Meaning of Life.

Bateman: Big, beautiful, brown eyes are The Meaning of Life.

Albergus: He means magical knowledge. Am I right, son?

Wagner (*hesitates*): No. Learned sir, please keep my confidence. I have seen the most beautiful woman here, in Faustus's apartments. And yet she is *not* here, nor have I ever spied her entering or leaving. How I long to meet her! To get to converse with her.

Bateman: Have a friendly little chat. Discuss theology. Geometry. Anatomy.

Albergus: Was this woman Greek?

Wagner: How can one tell if a woman is Greek?

Bateman: There's a trick they do with…

Albergus: Enough, Bateman!

Faustus: Wagner! Get your sorry butt in here!

Exit Wagner

Albergus: We proceed apace, Bateman! See the way Faustus accepted our introduction from Doctor Phutatorious at face value. Now I must draw him out. The Pope will not tolerate these magical tricks any longer. We must expose this Faustus as a dealer with the devil, discover his contract, confiscate his magic book, and drag him before the Inquisition.

Clock: NINE O'CLOCK. THE TEMPERATURE IS TWELVE DEGREES. DO YOU KNOW WHERE YOUR CHILDREN ARE?

Bateman (*looking warily at Clock*): I don't know about you, but I'd rather not end up as a piece of furniture.

Albergus (*absorbed in his machinations*): And now hear what this slack fool says. This woman he speaks of must be Helen! But we need proof more positive than this. Now hurry and find us some students we can use as spies. Have them report to my rooms at the inn directly tomorrow morning.

Bateman leaves. Faustus and Wagner return from the study and Faustus sets down a box of cigars. Wagner sits on a stool in the corner. During the ensuing conversation he occasionally rises to refill their cups with wine.

Albergus: So tell me, learned Faustus, how you discovered the secret of this miraculous alembic.

Faustus: Never mind that, pick a card.

Faustus proffers a deck of tarot cards. When Albergus just stares he folds them away, leans forward over his glass of wine, places one end of a cigar into his mouth, lights the other from the candle flame. He puffs a few times, then exhales a plume of smoke across the table at Albergus. He pushes the wooden box forward.

Faustus: Sorry your friend had to leave so soon. Have a cigar.

As Albergus reaches out to take one…

Faustus: Just one.

Albergus: To be sure.

Albergus examines the cigar; he has never seen anything like this before and is not ready to take any chances with a magician like Faustus.

Albergus: Ah? What is the nature of this? This "see-gar" you burn here, Faustus? Albertus Magnus speaks of securing rooms against evil spirits by burning certain herbs, but he advocates the use of a brazier. Does not this smoke taste noxious to the palate?

Faustus: I've had better smokes, but you won't be able to get them for a couple of hundred years. I just burn these ropes to drive the bugs away.

Albergus (sniffs): There does not seem to be any hint of cinnabar. How did you come by these instruments?

Faustus: That's an interesting story. I was riding a double-decker down Broadway and when we took the corner to 42nd Street on two wheels (the driver was a dyspeptic Abyssinian) a young woman fell into my lap. Imagine my chagrin. Naturally I took her home with me and we became devoted friends. In the divorce settlement she got the Hemingway manuscripts, I got these stogies.

Albergus: In Nuremberg it is rumored you have had much success in conjuring the shades of historical figures.

Faustus: Hysterical figures. And I do mean figures. Remind me sometime to introduce you to Helen.

Wagner spills the wine.

Faustus: Try again, boy: cup *outside*, wine *inside*.

Albergus (pushing Wagner away as he tries to mop up the wine): Helen of Troy?

Faustus: Troy, Schenectady? One of those towns.

Albergus: So you have indeed raised the dead?

Faustus: She only acts that way in the mornings. Lithium deficiency.

Wagner finishes mopping the spilled wine.

Albergus: Have you heard the reports of the astounding incidents that took place recently in Rome? It is said that some sorceror, invisible, plucked food and drink right out of the Pope's mouth. Then, to humiliate the papists further, this same necromancer stole the heretic Bruno away from the Inquisition and whisked him off to Austria. A most clever trick. I only wish I'd been able to manage it myself. The person responsible for bearding the Antichrist's tool in his own den must be the most powerful mage in all of Europe. Who do you suppose that might be?

Faustus: Are you going to smoke that cigar or eat it? Go ahead! You can pay me later.

Albergus: Pay you? Alas, Faustus, I have but little coin in pocket.

Clock: NINE THIRTY. MAYBE YOU SHOULD CHECK YOUR WALLET.

Faustus: Money, money, money! I'm sick to death of this talk of money! It's destroying our marriage! These cigars would cost a couple of guilders on the open market. Of course it's closed now, so you're left to your own devices. You did bring your devices, didn't you?

Albergus: What sort of?

Faustus: If not, you'll have to get your brothers to help you.

Albergus: I have no brothers.

Faustus: Your father must have been relieved.

Albergus: My dear Faustus, do not insult me. I may only be an itinerant scholar, but I've come all the way from Nuremberg to sit at your feet and learn.

Faustus: As long as you're down there, how about shining those shoes.

Albergus: You do not mean what you say.

Faustus: Let me tell you a thing or two about what I mean.

FAUSTUS' SONG:

When I took this job
I told the dean
You play it nice
I'll play it mean
It don't pay to mess with the Wittenberg Man
The Greatest Scholar in all of Europe.
I'll clean your clock
I'll drink your hock
I'll be your friend
Until the end
Or something better comes along.
Wagner: It's true, it's true
He's beat me black and blue
Don't mess with the Wittenberg Man
The Wisest Guy in all of Europe.
Faustus: I've got my magical clock
And a book full of spells
I make deals with the spirits
I wear a cap with bells
I've got a dog with a bone
The philosopher's stone
So tell all your sages
All your magical mages
It don't pay to mess with the Wittenberg Man
The Faustest Doctor in all of Europe.
Albergus: Don't get me wrong, gentle colleague
I'm not here to try your patience
I've come to praise your great achievements
Learn to follow your investigations

Into the arcane hollows
Of these hallowed halls
The ivy covered walls
Of this great institution.
I won't dis the reputation of the Wittenberg Man
The most Powerful Professor in all of Europe.
Faustus: If you're looking, pal, for knowledge
Let me give you a clue
Don't go to college
It's the worst you could do
Take my word for it, buddy
I work here every day
Before your first semester
You'll begin to fester
In a most distressful way.
But if you must matriculate
Here's a tip I can relate:
Make a deal with the devil
Before you step through the door.
Don't worry about perdition
It's a faculty tradition
He'll get you grants galore
You'll publish oceans, magic potions
Win mysterious promotions
That a Chancellor can't ignore
Take a warlock's degree
Major in astrology
For a minor, sorcery
And a concentration in dissimulation.
For whatever the alumni say
About the university way
This fact is indisputable:
That it's a storehouse of knowledge
Because none of it ever leaks out.
Wagner: None of it ever leaks out
It's sealed in weighty books where
It's a heavy-duty obligation
To open even one
That old humanistic science
That new deconstructive fun
I've been searching for it full time
But a glimpse of a pretty ankle
Is all I've ever won.
Faustus: Take the kid's word, he should know

I'm the door that he can't peek through
Can't storm or even leak through
Can't speculate or guess, no
Students aren't here to be blessed, so
Forget the father confessor
I'm the universal professor.
Still I don't want to be inhospitable
'twould be pitiful, Bro' Albergus.
Leave ambition on the doorstep
And I'm the honcho, at your service.
But just don't mess with the Wittenberg Man
The Hottest Burgher in all of Germany.
He knows where your body's buried
Or meant to be.

Albergus: I take your point, noble Faustus. But my questions were entirely innocent.

Faustus: But late at night, lights turned low, when you're alone with your answers? That's a different story!

Albergus: My dear colleague! There's no need to treat me like a mountebank.

Faustus: Oh, so now it's high finance? Well, money means nothing here, friend.

Albergus: Why must you keep speaking of money?

Faustus: This is a public university. What else are we going to talk about? You'll learn soon enough that a little Latin goes a long way in this institution. There used to be a little Latin around here, but he went away. That's how I got this job. You look a little Latin yourself, and I wish you'd gone with him. You foreign scholars want to dance to the music without paying the piper. And what does it get you? Asparagus, or contract bridge. But a card like you could care less who maintains the bridge contract, as long as you can pass water under it. Speaking of contracts, what makes you think you're going to get your hands on mine?

Albergus: I'm sure I don't know what you're talking about.

Faustus: If you're so sure, why aren't you rich? You brute! No, don't try to apologize!

Albergus: I didn't come here to be insulted.

Faustus: This is a good place for it. Where do you usually go?

Albergus stands, throwing down his napkin.

Albergus: I *beg* your pardon?

Faustus: Don't grovel, I can't pardon you. You'll have to talk to the Pope. Too bad, I hear he's not much of an audience. Well, it's certainly been a pleasure talking to myself this evening. I must visit myself more often. As for you, sir, I want you to remember that scholarship is as scholarship does, and neither does my wife, if I had one, which I don't. Nor do my children, if I had any, who would be proud of me for saying so. Now get out!

Albergus leaves in a huff. Faustus goes to his side of the table, sits in his chair, takes a bite out of a chicken leg from Albergus's plate and sips his wine.

Clock: TEN O'CLOCK. ALL IS WELL.

Faustus holds out his cup to Wagner.

Faustus: More wine, boy.

Scene Two

Scene opens in Albergus's room at The Boar's Bollocks inn. Albergus is at his table composing a report for the Pope.

Albergus: When will those students arrive?

Bateman: They should be here soon.

Albergus: They're completely reliable men?

Bateman: As a logician, you realize as well as I that such judgments are necessarily subjective.

Albergus: Never mind logic. Stick to the facts.

Bateman: They're men. I would say that's a completely reliable statement.

Albergus seals the letter, hands it to Bateman.

Albergus: Fair enough. Send this off to the Pope.

Bateman leaves. A knock comes at the door.

Albergus: Enter.

The door opens and two sloppy men come in. The darker of the two, Dicolini, wears a black hat that comes to a point that hints at the pointed skull beneath it. His coat is shabby and two sizes too small. He wears an expression of small-minded guile. His companion Robin's face is round and empty as the full moon. His ragged clothes are even shabbier than Dicolini's if that is possible. He smells like a fishmonger and a mass of curly red hair explodes from beneath his floppy hat. They come forward in unison, hands extended.

Albergus: Noble Robin and gentle Dicolini, welcome!

Robin shakes his hand. Albergus recoils, draws back his hand and finds he is holding a dead fish. Robin contorts in silent laughter, slaps his knee. Albergus throws down the fish. Robin looks offended.

Dicolini: Atsa some joke, eh boss?

Albergus: Gentlemen, gentlemen. Let us speak of our business. I have called you here because you are brother scholars, acquainted with the university, and students of the renowned Doctor Faustus. I have also heard that you are available for delicate work and for a reasonable fee can keep your mouths shut. I trust I have not been mislead?

Dicolini: I keepa my mouth shut for nothing. Robin, his mouth cost extra.

Robin opens his mouth and sticks out his tongue, from which a price tag dangles.

Albergus: What I want you to do is keep an eye on Doctor Faustus for me.

Dicolini: Atsa different story. Eyes cost more.

Albergus: No, no. "Keep an eye on him"—that's just an expression.

Dicolini: You want the whole expression, it cost you a pretty penny. We give you a pretty expression, though.

Robin puffs out his cheeks, purses his lips and crosses his eyes. Albergus controls himself, ignores him.

Albergus: I want you to find out how Faustus spends his evenings. Does he practice black magic? Is he in league with infernal forces? And I need proof, the sooner the better. Should you do this for me, your investigation shall receive such thanks as fits aking's remembrance.

Dicolini: How much you gonna pay?

Albergus: I'll pay you ten silver pieces.

Dicolini: We a-no want no pieces. We want the whole thing.

Robin honks a horn and nods, surly.

Albergus: Another ten pieces then, if you provide me the information I need. That's all.

Dicolini: How do we know thatsa all?

Albergus: What?

Dicolini: Look, we shadow Faustus for you, how we gonna know when you give us ten pieces thatsa the whole thing?

Albergus: But I'm offering you twenty pieces for shadowing Faustus.

Dicolini: See what I mean? First you gotta ten pieces, now you gotta twenty pieces, but we no gotta the whole thing.

Albergus: You shadow Faustus for me, and then we'll talk about the whole thing.

Dicolini: You no understand. Suppose I drop a vase, itsa break. How many pieces I got? I don't know; I gotta count them. Now you give me ten pieces, you give me twenty pieces, I still don't have them all, maybe. I shatter vase, we shadow Faustus, itsa same thing: we no gonna do the job until we know we getta the whole thing.

As Albergus and Dicolini haggle, Robin creeps behind them. He draws another fish from the folds of his ragged cloak and slips it onto Albergus's chair. Albergus, arguing with Dicolini, draws a kerchief from his sleeve, mops his brow, and sits down. A moment later he lets out a strangled cry and leaps from the chair, cracking his knee on the table. He picks up the fish and holds it out at arm's length.

Albergus: What's this?

Robin whips a sword out and lunges, impaling the fish and the sleeve of Albergus's doublet. Albergus steps back and slips on the first fish. His arms fly up, jerking Robin toward him. Dicolini catches Albergus under the armpits, and Robin sprawls on top of him.

Dicolini: You no fool me, boss. Atsafish.

Albergus and Robin struggle to get up, but Robin's hand is caught in the guard. When they make it to their feet the pommel is wedged under the clasp that holds Albergus's cloak closed around his neck. The sword guard presses against his throat, and his arm stretches the length of the blade as if tied to a splint. Chin forced high into the air, Albergus whirls around like a manic signpost.

Dicolini: Don't worry, boss. We get you out.

Robin jumps on Albergus's back and shoves a hand down his collar. Dicolini pulls him over onto the table. He lies spread-eagled while Robin pulls the sword up through the collar, across his neck. Afraid they will cut his throat, he struggles, but Dicolini is sitting on his left arm.

Dicolini: Relax. We take care of everything.

Robin draws the sword completely out and the fish catches against Albergus's throat. Robin shakes hands with Dicolini. Albergus sits up, stands, tugs his clothes into order, trying to compose himself.

Albergus: Gentlemen. I trust we are in agreement now—you'll do this piece of work for me?

Dicolini: We do the whole thing.

Robin honks. Albergus steers them toward the door, his arms across their shoulders.

Albergus: Splendid. Remember now, should you meet me in public, I'm a stranger.

Dicolini: Stranger than who?

Albergus: Us. You and I—and your friend, of course. *Strangers.*

Dicolini: Hesa stranger than both of us put together.

Albergus: So I'm beginning to understand.

Dicolini: We gotta go now. We're gonna be late for the classes we wanna miss.

Albergus: My apologies for detaining you. Just make sure you get me something I can use against Faustus.

Robin pulls a red-hot poker out of the robe. He grips the iron in both hands, waving it under Albergus's nose. Albergus falls back; Robin offers him the poker. Dicolini shoves Robin.

Dicolini: Whatsa matter for you? You crazy? The boss no play poker!

Robin, hurt, puts the poker back in his robe.

Scene Three
Lights come up on a classroom. At the front is a raised platform with a table, a lectern and behind it a blackboard. A window to the streets of Wittenberg at the left, a doorway at right. Students gathering before class, Among them are Albergus, sitting in the front row, and Wagner, Faustus's fag, likewise in front.

Albergus: You seem melancholy today, young student. Did your master take last night's misunderstanding amiss?

Wagner: I don't think he misunderstood anything. He did make me pick a card. Something he calls three card monte.

Albergus: He predicted your future?

Wagner: Not exactly. But he won back my salary for the next six months. As long as it keeps me close to her, it doesn't matter.

Albergus: I see you are reading divine Homer. Practicing your Greek?

Wagner: Only dreaming of Helen, fairer than the evening air, clad in beauty of a thousand stars. Her lips suck forth my soul; see where it flies! Here will I dwell, for heaven be in these hips.

WAGNER'S SONG:

I came to work for Faustus seeking scientific sport
Over universal secrets to emote
But then one early evening as I was cleaning out his rooms
I caught a glimpse of Helen
And that was all she wrote
Yes it's true, I can't deny it
I'm in love with Helen's ghost
A spirit maiden, made of mist
My equanimity is toast
Her ectoplasmic thighs
Call from me so many sighs
That it isn't even funny
(Please don't laugh.)
Her hair it glows like golden wheat
Let's not talk about her feet
Skin of alabaster pure
A fleshy spirit, that's for sure
They say her face launched many ships
How I'd love to kiss those lips
Find a way to mingle fluids
(In a chaste way, sir, of course)
To assay those frosty tetons
That a climber never clumb.
Though I cannot speak a sound sir
Please don't tell me that I'm dumb
When I think of her posterior
Fully round and fully packed
I can't imagine one superior
My imagination's racked.
Though it's true she's Greek to me
Nonetheless I seek to be
Round her temple holy shrine
Long to comprehend she's mine.
It's not a problem that's she's dead, sir.
Though my love's an ancient queen
She's as fresh as any daisy
On at Spring morn, that you've seen.
But she comes, and then she goes

She's at Faustus's beck and call
And I've not said any word to her
Just espied her from the hall
At a distance, faintly glowing
Mist of moisture on her skin
Dewy smile, one earlobe showing
But he never lets me in
How I'd love to try her virtue
And to have her try my own
But I guess that it's not destined
And I'm stuck here all alone
Facing humiliation daily
Who'm I kidding, I'm a mess
As I try to do his bidding
A mass of horny male distress
And my grades are really suffering
And my shoes are getting old
And my soul has lost its stuffing
And my bed is still and cold
Do you think I like this pining
I'm a handsome, vital man!
But the barmaids and the co-eds
Cannot lend me any hand.
So my eyes are growing shaky
My complexion is at risk
If I brush my hair much longer
I'll be bald before I'm kissed.
Sex I've found's the greatest mystery;
In that ocean, down we sink
It's the cosmic bang that made us
It's the power that I seek.
I'm in love with Homer's Helen
Homer's Helen makes me mush
Blushing like the greenest sucker
Mooning for a succubus.

Faustus enters, wearing long black academic robes, puffing a cigar, in Groucho lope. Strides back and forth in front of the class, takes up a pointer, raps the lectern, turns and pulls down a chart of a human head with areas mapped out on it like a steer apportioned for slaughter. Except these parts are labelled "Imagination," "Love" "Sex" "Politics" "Sports" "Clothes" "Gambling" "Religion".

Faustus: Here we have a diagram of the astral mind in the fourth quarter of the phrenological year. You'll note the eruptions at the zenith. These eruptions can be cleared up with fulminate of mercury, but the woman only comes on

Tuesday afternoons. The rest of the week you have to take care of yourself, if you know what's good for you. Wagner, tell us what's good for you.

Wagner, startled, stumbles to his feet.

Wagner: Chastity, Doctor Faustus.

Faustus: Chastity, is it? What about obedience?

Wagner: Obedience. Of course.

Faustus: Poverty?

Wagner: That, too.

Faustus: Quit monking around, boy! Who do you think you're kidding? You'd better sit down and hibernate until that bonus in your codpiece goes away. Or is that a cod in your bonus piece?

With a crash, the door of the room slams open and in dash Robin and Dicolini. They trip over each other, get up, scramble into two seats in the front row. Dicolini sees Albergus, gives a doubletake.

Dicolini: Who's this guy? I never saw him before in my life.

He winks theatrically at Albergus. Faustus turns his ire on Dicolini.

Faustus: Late for class again, eh?

Dicolini: We a-no late.

Faustus: Why, the town clock struck not five minutes ago. It's half past ten!

Dicolini: No it's not.

Robin pulls an hourglass from out of his bottomless cloak. All the sand is in the bottom. He waves it at Faustus.

Dicolini: See, we're right on time.

Faustus: Not according to that.

Dicolini: Atsa run a little fast. Shesa use quicksand.

Faustus: Oh no. You can't fool me that easily. By that hourglass, it must be eleven o'clock.

Dicolini: Then class is over. Let's go, Robbie.

Faustus: Hold on, Macduff. I'm not done lecturing.

Dicolini: Too bad. We're done listening.

Faustus: Well, you can forget about leaving until *my* clock strikes eleven. Time is money, and my time is worth at least a couple of marks. You boys look like a couple of marks. Are you brothers?

Robin is insulted. He comes out of his seat, huffing and puffing as if he is about to go berserk.

Dicolini: My friend, hesa get pretty mad. You watch out or he give you a piece of his mind.

Faustus: No thanks. I wouldn't want to take the last piece.

Dicolini: Atsa okay. He won't notice.

Faustus: Well, if you say so. Come here, young man.

Faustus reaches for Robin's arm but somehow finds himself holding his thigh. He pushes it away in disgust.

Faustus: Let's take a look at your skull.

Robin pulls a glowing skull from his cloak and presents it to Faustus. The class recoils. Faustus pops open its mouth and relights his cigar from the candle burning inside. He tosses the skull out the window, stands Robin in front of the chart, and backs off a step to appraise him. Moon-faced Robin looks about as intelligent as a hardboiled egg. Faustus taps his pointer against Robin's skull.

Faustus: The astral mind is responsible for contact with the spiritual world without the intervention of either seraphim or cherubim. You all know what a seraph is, don't you?

Dicolini (standing): Sure. On my pancakes, I like a maple seraph.

Faustus: No, no. Cherubs, seraphs.

Dicolini: I no like a cherub. I like amaple.

Faustus: These aren't food—they're angels.

Dicolini: I no like angel food, either.

Faustus: Well, that takes the cake. Where was I?

Robin is rubbing against the chart like a cat.

Faustus: Let's forget about the astral mind. That's obviously not relevant with this subject. Don't let me wake you, now. I'm not offending you by talking, am I?

Robin honks.

Faustus: Gesundheit. Moving south from the astral mind, we come to the inferior regions of the intellect. And when I say inferior, I mean inferior. The inferior mind, as you'll remember from our last lecture, is responsible for worldly thought, for instance, how did your nose get that way, and wasn't that a great plague we had last month. Worldly thought, of course, must be processed by one of the other organs before it becomes definable in emotional terms. The heart, for instance, controls affection, the liver, love, and the spleen, anger. Who can tell us what the kidneys control?

Dicolini (rising again): The kid knees keep their legs from bending backwards.

Faustus leans toward Albergus.

Faustus: Do you hear voices?

Dicolini turns around, raises his fists to accept the accolades of his fellow students. Faustus turns on him.

Faustus: A kid's knees already bend backwards. Do you have any other bright ideas?

Dicolini: Not right now. I let you know.

Faustus: Do that. Drop me a postcard to warn me when you'll arrive. If I had a couple more students like you boys I could change gold into lead.

Wagner sighs. He's thinking of fair Helen. Meanwhile, Robin has moved to Faustus's lectern and opens Faustus's magic book. A small cloud of dust billows out. Robin pulls a kerchief out of his sleeve with a flourish, sneezes, then blows his nose with a loud honk. There is a flash of light and a smell of sulfur. When the smoke clears there is an imp standing on the edge of the podium. The class is astounded. Albergus stands up. Faustus stubs his cigar out on Dicolini's hat.

Robin, delighted, holds his hand out to the imp, which crawls up his arm onto his shoulder.

Faustus: Oh, no you don't!

Dicolini: Come on, Robbie!

Faustus and Robbie dance back and forth on opposite sides of the lectern. Robin dashes for the door with Dicolini, who slams it in Faustus's face. Faustus whips it open, looks out, comes back to the lectern and whirls on Wagner.

Faustus: As your punishment, you will retrieve that imp for me by midnight.

Wagner: But Magister, I didn't do anything!

Faustus: Since when has that made any difference around here?

Scene Four

We are back in Faustus's apartment, in the study. Faustus is there, idly leafing through a copy of Esquire. *With him is monstrous Mephistopheles, a demon from Hell and Faustus's servant.*

Mephistopheles moves to stage front at points during this scene, addressing the audience directly in asides. Whenever he does, Faustus freezes in place in the background until Mephisto returns and takes up his place in the conversation.

Mephisto (aside): Better to rule in Hell than serve in Heaven, Lucifer told us. Little did I know that I would end up spending twenty-four years playing mindless practical jokes for a man purported to be the wisest scholar in Europe. When I fell from heaven, I knew I was in for a poorer class of associate, but I never thought it could get this bad. Why *this* is hell, nor am I out of it.

Clock: FOUR O'CLOCK. HOW MUCH LONGER DO I HAVE TO KEEP DOING THIS?

Mephisto: Midnight tonight, noble Faustus. Then do the jaws of hell open to receive thee.

Faustus: How late do they stay open?

Mephisto: Long enough to swallow thee up, soul and socks.

Faustus (holding up cigar): Light it.

The cigar magically flares up, and Faustus takes a few speculative puffs.

Faustus: And what happens after that?

Mephistopeles points to the wall, and a Gustave Doré engraving of Hell and demons is projected onto it.

Mephisto: Here is Dis, the city of Hell. You will be thrown into this perpetual torture-house. These are the furies, tossing damned souls on burning forks; their bodies boil in lead. Over here are humans broiling on coals that can never die. These souls that are fed with sops of burning fire were gluttons in their lives who laughed to see the poor starve at their gates. You shall see ten thousand tortures more horrid.

Faustus: You're not much of a travel agent. "See Dis and die."

Mephisto: Usually it's the other way around.

Faustus: You're right. Dis ain't no joke.

Mephisto: Fools that will laugh on earth must weep in hell.

Faustus: You won't settle for a moan in Cologne?

Mephisto (*aside*): Grubs on the eyeballs. Perhaps I'll start him with that. But no sense doing the other side's work for it. He might still repent.

Mephistopheles dissolves the vision of hell.

Faustus: By the way, have you seen Helen lately?

Mephisto: In your closet.

Faustus: In my closet! What's she doing in there?

Mephisto: You told her to stay in it.

Faustus: I did? Oh, yes. Literal girl. Thank heaven for literal girls.

Mephisto: Heaven had nothing to do with it.

Faustus: Well, what am I supposed to do, swing both ways?

Mephisto: Shall I have her dress?

Faustus: It wouldn't fit you. Work on your thighs.

Mephisto (*aside*): When he tires, I'll strap him to a bed of razors.

Faustus (*pacing*): So she's in the closet, eh? And here I stand bantering with the help. Get her out here pronto. If she won't come, call for me, and I'll go in after her. If I don't come back, you can have my alembic.

Mephisto: This is no game, Faustus.

Faustus: It isn't? I thought it was the alembic games.

Mephisto: Worry not about Helen, magister. If she disobeys you, I'll cull thee out the wildest Frauleins in the north of Europe.

Faustus: The cull of the wild, eh? Sounds like a bunch of dogs to me. And who's going to clean up after them, tell me that. If I gave you half a chance you'd wreck this happy home.

Faustus whips out a book of raffle tickets and proffers them.

Faustus: How about half a chance? Cost you ten marks.

Mephsito (*aside*): An eon up to his chin in boiling manure. (*to Faustus*) Just now I don't feel lucky.

Faustus: So? Never mind that, pick a card.

Mephistopheles begins to beat his head against the table.

Faustus: Hey, watch that finish! Okay, look, just keep an eye on Wagner for me, then. He wants to examine Helen's thesis. Can you imagine the consequences if she managed to seduce that boy? Why, she's been dead for two thousand years! What would his mother say? What would I say?

Mephisto: What *would* you say?

Faustus: Is it true that you wash your hair in clam broth?

Mephisto (*aside*): A codpiece of burning iron.

MEPHISTO'S SONG:

I was once an angel bright, lived by heaven's wall
Never had no problems, never took on city hall

Then Lucifer sought out my help in his election bid
To revolutionize God's government; don't ask me how we did.
Then I was proud to be a demon, didn't care if I was damned
Frolicked in the brimstone pools, surfed the Styx's strand
A sophisticated soul from Dante's seventh circle down
Until the day I found myself working for this clown.
Now I'm Faustus's fool
There's not a thing I can do
My fate's intolerably cruel
Each day it hits me anew
(If I were alive I would kill myself.)
Smuggled off to Rome to swipe the Papal second course
Riding on a bale of hay changed into a horse
Lighting his cigars, cleaning up his mess
Playing tricks on ostlers, IQs forty-three or less
Scaring up a bowl of grapes on January first
Mixing up a stupid drink to quench a stupid thirst
Chasing down new girls for him to catechise unsightly
Doing stupid card tricks watching stupid card tricks nightly.
I'm only Faustus's tool
There's no one that I can sue
Stuck in this backwater school
Feeling so battered and blue.
(Please sir, may I have another Tylenol?)
There's no kind of man I haven't tempted in my days
I've hung with every ex-seraphim this side of Hades
Sent Alexander a mosquito, taught Cleopatra how to kiss
Told Lao Tzu to quit his job, and now I'm down to this.
They say the Lord of Heaven's ways work quite mysteriously
Pal, I'm here to tell you what they say they say it justly.
Just one thought has kept me sane for twenty-seven years
That's at the stroke midnight I'll be drying all my tears
For now I'm Faustus's fool
Trapped within his arena
Doing hops through his hoops
I ain't seen nothing obscener.
(Bet your dog can't dance like this.)
Clock: You think you've got it bad, let's switch jobs awhile, Sam
At least you get to walk around, I'm frozen on this stand
What's more I can't remember why he strapped me to this block
I must have pissed him off some way. Bong! It's five o'clock.
Mephisto: Five o'clock! That means he's only seven hours away
From a certain course of exercise I'm planning from this day
I'll whip him into shape, I'll take a pound of flesh or more

He'll be twice the man he is today and I'll be half as sore.
No longer Faustus's fool
There'll be some things I can do
I'll be intolerably cruel
He'll end up scholarly stew.
(Wizard guts—they're not just for breakfast anymore!)

While Faustus and Mephisto banter in the study, the door to Faustus's apartments opens silently and Wagner sneaks in. He goes to the study door, listens, hears their voices, music. Sniffs the air. As Faustus comes to open the door he rushes across the common room into the bedroom, looks around frantically, then hides in the closet, where he trips over some shoes and bumps into Helen. The closet is cut away, so we can view the inside. Dim light. Hanging robes. Heaps of shoes, boots. Helen, bored.

Wagner: Mmmph! Who is it?

Helen (helping him up): It is I, Helen.

Wagner: Helen! Just who I've been looking for. I must see you.

Helen: And here I am without a candle.

Wagner: No one can hold a candle to you! I need you, Helen. You cannot know the torture I've been through imagining what Faustus has been doing with you.

Helen: Is that why you came into the closet?

Wagner: Faustus sent me on a fool's errand, but now that I'm with you I'll never play the fool again. He expects me to find an imp he lost. I snuck in to search his books for a spell to help me. I don't know why he can't do it himself.

Helen: He knows how to do it himself. But sometimes he'd rather not. Look at me.

Faustus and Mephistopheles enter the bedroom. Fausts makes Mephistopheles go down on all fours and begins to use him as a card table, laying out a solitaire hand with his tarot deck. Steam begins to rise from Mephisto's collar.

Wagner: I wish I could. Say, do you smell burning sulfur?

Helen: You should never eat radishes.

Wagner: Who can he have out there with him?

Helen: Some visiting scholar, surely. I'm so glad you found me. I didn't even suspect you knew of my existence. I've been so bored, cooped up in here. It's worse than life with Menelaus ever was. And Sparta was heaven compared to this! I'm still a young woman. I want to sing, I want to dance, I want to enjoy every particle of life! Can you help me, dear student?

She kisses him passionately. Steam begins to rise from Wagner's collar, too. Outside in the bedroom, Faustus is coughing from the gathering smoke in the room; he gathers up his cards, waves the billowing clouds of smoke away and retreats to the common room. Mephisto rises and follows.

Wagner: I'll do my best. You have to realize I'm not very experienced at…

Helen: Don't worry. Troy wasn't ruined in a day. But now you must go.

Wagner: Go? But I just got here.

Helen: Nevertheless. If Faustus found you here his jealously would know no bounds. Come back later, fair student. Tonight! Faustus will be gone until midnight. Return at eleven, and I will show you arts of which I alone am mistress. Until then you must do his bidding.

Wagner: Eleven? How can I wait that long, thinking of you?

Helen: Troilus recommended strenuous exercise and cold baths. Until eleven, my love!

She propels him out the door.

Scene Five
In the Boar's Bollocks Inn. Albergus sits at a table with Bateman plotting Faustus's destruction. A buxom barmaid serves their beers. Albergus is indifferent, but Bateman inspects her avidly.

Albergus: A half-witted student merely looks into that book and is able to conjure up an imp! Can you imagine the power that volume must contain?

Bateman: A guy could have a hot time with that book.

Albergus: It is all a matter of knowing the right words. Faustus's book must contain the language of UrCreation.

Bateman (watching waitress): Or even the language of procreation?

Albergus: You see, Bateman, most language is just empty words. You've sat outside on a splendid fall afternoon, and the sun warmed your limbs, the sweet breeze caressed your cheek, you lay back and watched the skies, the bullocks, the squirrels?

Bateman:—the thighs, the buttocks, the girls—

Albergus:—it's a total sensory experience—

Bateman: I'll say.

Albergus:—and there is no way that ordinary language can capture even one thousandth of it.

Bateman: Preach it, brother!

Albergus:—But that's ordinary language. What about extraordinary language? What about the language of God, Bateman? In what language did God originally say, "Let There Be Light!"

Bateman: French?

Albergus: He said it, Bateman, in that mystic, UrCreative language, the language of ultimate truth. The language that came *before* reality. If a man could grasp that grammar of creation, he could control all that exists! And that language, Bateman, I am convinced, is written in Faustus's book. Can you imagine it? Faustus has his hand upon the axis of the universe! Yet to what use does he put this power?

Bateman: Well he turned that guy into a clock. And there's those cigar things?

Albergus: Precisely. A total waste. The man has no more business owning that book than a rabbit.

Bateman: I don't think he owns a rabbit.

Albergus: That book belongs to he who can make use of it.

Bateman: Uh, speaking of grammar, I think that's supposed to be "to him," boss?

Albergus: To *me*, Bateman. And I aim to get it. Think of the things I might accomplish—strictly for the good of mankind, Bateman, the good of mankind!

ALBERGUS'S SONG:

Power!
I want power!
Enough power to allow
My unique know how to flower.
The world around is aching
For a wise hand to administer a braking
To this runaway cart
The ungovernable heart.
And I can do it.
Why cast my pearls before swine
Why waste my life drinking cheap wine
When I might have champagne
Which, given my intellect,
I deserve
Most royally.
Truth!
Is all I pursue, forsooth!
Not like Faustus, that uncouth pretender.
I must water the tender
Bud of my curiosity
So that my incipient virtuosity
Might grow into a prowess so vital
That it will delight all
And a vision acute
To boot.
Knowledge!
I need knowledge
Not for my own aggrandizement,
But for the advisement, see,
Of those rulers who so ignorantly
Mistake the proper course
Of action. I'll be the source
Of expedient counsel
A man like me, responsible,

Will make them realize
That to do otherwise than I suggest
Would not be best
For the health of the common folk
Or their own.
Bateman: Love!
Liebschaft!
Amour!
Is what I suggest you initially explore.
I'll help you out, select moral subjects
For your experiments
In passion philters
Affection smelters
And aphrodisiac science.
Don't risk your priceless mind:
I'll selflessly bind myself through rigorous paces
Endure numerous embraces
Test my tender body against feminine wiles
Quaff wild potions out of wilder vials
In Aphrodite's clinical trials.
This barmaid, here, for instance
Could no doubt benefit
From our ministrations
Don't you think?
Boss?
Albergus: No greed
Or seed
Of self-concern will tarnish my discerning need
To do what must be done
I'll take no bad advice
Or advice at all, indeed.
For it would not be nice
To be swayed
By the paltry parade
Of unenlightended folk who'll seek for my largess
My relief from their distress
The gratitude's store
Which I shall dispense
Selflessly, more
Or less.

You see, Bateman? That man is an imposter; I shall be the true Faustus! But now, how to break in to his study? Who knows what risks that would entail?

Wagner enters, looks around, goes to him.

Wagner: Pardon me, sir. I am looking for my fellow students, Robin and Dicolini. Have you seen them?

Albergus: Not since they fled your master's lecture.

Wagner: I've exhausted myself searching. I thought they were my friends, but it seems they are more interested in other matters now.

Albergus: A sad breach of faith. Is there anything a fellow scholar can do?

Wagner: Nothing. Unless you can retrieve the imp that Robin called up.

Albergus: I am not without some magical prowess. Perhaps I can locate it. Not only that, but if you'll tell me when Faustus is away, I can deposit the creature—caged—in his rooms. It would make a good joke, don't you think? Especially after the shameful way he treated you today.

Wagner: If you could do that, my gratitude would surpass Goneril's to her father!

Albergus: You have only to ask.

Wagner: Yes, good Frater, please. Faustus told me he would not be home until midnight tonight. If you can arrive before then—

Albergus: I shall be there at ten.

Wagner: Uh—better make it eleven. Eleven-thirty—I have affairs—uh—business. I will let you in.

Albergus: Leave it to me. I will be discreet.

Wagner: Thank you, thank you.

Wagner pumps Albergus's hand vigorously and leaves, as excited as a groom on his wedding day.

Albergus: So, we have our entry into Faustus's rooms! Once there, I will discover the satanist's iniquities. Bateman, you must go to the Bishop of Wittenberg and tell him at once to assemble an ecclesiastical tribunal. We will arrest Faustus by the dawn, have him convicted by noon and roasting at the stake by vespers. And for good measure, we'll roast this slack fool Wagner along with him.

But wait! I must not be compromised by being associated with the disappearance of Faustus's magic book. (*snaps fingers*) Aha! A disguise! (*writes a hurried note*) Bateman, after you speak to the bishop I want you to fetch me the following items.

Albergus hands Bateman the note and the latter exits. Albergus sips his tankard of ale, throws a couple of coins onto the table, then departs himself. As soon as he does Robin and Dicolini crawl out from beneath the table. Dicolini drains the remainder of Albergus's ale in a gulp. Robin picks up one of the coins and bites through it. He chews thoughtfully, pulls a salt shaker from his robe, sprinkles the remainder on the coin and pops it into his mouth.

Dicolini: You hear that, Robbie? That Icebergus, hesa cross-double us. Hesa break the case himself and keep alla pieces. We gonna have to get tough.

Robin thrusts a fist under Dicolini's nose, grimacing and breathing heavily; his other arm goes into a windmill windup. Dicolini kicks him in the butt.

Dicolini: Whatsa matter for you! Getta tough with him, not me. Now listen, we gotta move fast and get to Faustus's place before the boss, before Wagner, before anybody. We get there so early we be there before we arrive!

Robin honks. They exit. Wagner returns carrying a bundle of clothes. He addresses the barmaid.

Wagner: Have you a bath here

Barmaid: No, sir. In the summer, some guests use the rain barrel in the lower court. But of course it is frozen…

Wagner: Perfect. I want you to chop a hole in the ice for me. I need to keep cool.

Barmaid: You must be very hot.

Wagner (beginning to unlace his boots): You cannot imagine.

Barmaid: What clothing is that?

Wagner: You know Doctor Faustus? Well, a certain young woman I know is expecting to see him tonight. Imagine her surprise when she finds me in his place!

Scene Six

Upstage left, lights come up on alley behind Faustus's study. Dicolini and Robin wheel a wooden cart or barrow full of paraphernalia up below Faustus's second-floor bedroom window. Dicolini throws a rope over a rafter protruding out below the eaves, then ties one end around his chest.

Clock (from above): ELEVEN O'CLOCK. IT'S COLDER THAN A WITCH'S BICYCLE SEAT OUT THERE.

Dicolini: Okay, Robbie. You tug onna rope, and I'll get in through Faustus's window. Keep a look out. If anybody comes, whistle.

Robin nods, spits into his palms, leaps high into the air and grabs the rope. The rope hauls Dicolini two feet above the ground, and Robin hands two feet above the ground on the opposite end; they struggle and flop together like hooked fish. Lights go down halfway, leaving them in stage left, and come up upstage right on the entrance to Faustus's apartments, where the porter, Martin, sits on a stool against the wall snoring, drunk as usual. Wagner comes up, sees Martin, then puts on a Faustus costume: black academic gown, mortarboard hat, greasepaint mustache, wire rimmed spectacles. He then strides up to Martin, who wakes woozily as Wagner salutes him and goes inside.

Lights go down upstage, come up downstage to reveal the inside of Fausuts's apartment. Wagner enters through common room door, then hurries to the bedroom and the wardrobe. He opens the door and stands on the threshhold.

Wagner: Helen!

Helen: Darling!

Wagner is overwhelmed by her ardor, even perhaps a little scared.

Wagner: Don't worry—it's me, Wagner! You can come out of the closet, now.

Helen: Oh!

Wagner: What's wrong?

Helen: I thought you were Faustus. I forgot to tell you that I can't come out until he says I can. After all, I am his to command. Won't you come in?

Wagner: But—

Clock: ELEVEN FIFTEEN. I WONDER HOW THE METS ARE DOING?

A sound from the commons room. It's Faustus, who has come from his study toward the bedroom, followed by Mephistopheles. Wagner climbs into the closet just as Faustus and the demon enter.

Faustus: I wish you'd stop following me around. I want to get ready for bed.

Mephisto: You shall not sleep this night, Faustus.

Faustus: I certainly won't if you keep pestering me. Go away.

Mephistopheles disappears in a cloud of sulfurous smoke and flame. Faustus goes to the closet.

Faustus: Now where's my nightshirt? I thought I left it lying around here. (*To Helen*) Are you still in there?

Helen: Who?

Faustus: Unless you're keeping an owl, Helen of Troy.

Wagner nudges Helen frantically. She gets flustered.

Helen: What owl? There's no owl in here.

Faustus: Owl take your word for it. Does one of you birds want to hand me my nightshirt?

Wagner fumbles among the clothes, gives Helena nightshirt. She opens the door a crack and hands it out. Faustus peeks in.

Faustus: Hope it's not too boring in there.

Helen: Not yet. I wouldn't mind some fresh air once in a while.

Faustus (sniffs): The air in there smells pretty fresh already. Or maybe it's my undershirt. (*Hauls out tarot deck*) Would you like to take a card?

Helen: No, thank you.

Faustus closes the door, takes the nightshirt and leaves. The rathaus clock strikes and Wagner jumps.

Wagner: You said Faustus would be out tonight!

Helen: Did I?

Helen embraces Wagner. He forgets his annoyance and begins to nuzzle her. They fumble around in the cramped closet, and Helen finally pushes him away.

Wagner: Noble queen?

Helen: I'm sorry, but I can't get into the mood lying on old shoes. Can't you find some way to let me out?

Wagner: Wait here. Faustus's magic book must be around somewhere. I'll find a spell of unbinding.

Wagner leaves the closet and sneaks out of the bedroom toward Faustus's study. The lights fade downstage and come up upstage right on the entrance to the building, where Martin still sits. Albergus enters in a blizzard of impatience. He dons a Faustus disguise of robe, greasepaint mustache, spectacles and mortarboard and approaches Martin. Martin gives a woozy double take as Albergus enters.

Lights go down upstage right, come up downstage on Faustus's apartment. Wagner has gone into Faustus's study. Albergus enters the common room, considers the study but goes into the bedroom. He rifles through the bedside table, the trunk at the end of the bed. It's full of clothes, including a nightshirt or two that he throws onto the bed. He tries the closet door. As soon as he opens it Helen throws her arms around him.

Helen: Darling! Let me out of the closet! Then will I fulfill your every desire.

Albergus (stumbling back, hauling out across): Back, hell-fiend!

He slams the closet door on Helen. He wipes his brow, shaken. Just then there is a rattling from the window. Albergus hurries from the room. The window opens, and Dicolini climbs in, unties the rope. He peeks out the bedroom door, then hesitates. He ponders, sees the nightshirt on the bed, snaps his fingers. He takes off his boots, rolls up his pants, dons the nightshirt and a stocking cap. From the bedside table he takes some makeup and smears a greasepaint mustache over his lip, puts on some spare spectacles. Just as he's about to leave the room he hears a voice.

Helen: Is that you?

Dicolini: Maybe.

Helen: Please let me out of here.

Dicolini: Who are you?

Helen: Don't be silly. You know who I am.

Dicolini: Itsa slip my mind.

Helen (sarcastically): Well, I'm the most beautiful woman in history.

Dicolini: Never mind coming out. I come in.

Dicolini opens the closet door. Helen throws her arms around his neck.

Helen: Darling!

Lights fade on the bedroom, come up on the study. Wagner is frantically searching through the papers on Faustus's desk. He finds an impressive contract, Faustus's deal with the devil. He tries to puzzle it out, reading aloud.

Wagner: ... party of the first part shall be called the party of the first part... contractee reserves the right to a speedy conviction, the right to a free lunch, the right to sing the blues, the right... in the event of a change of political party, the once in a blue moon, when hell freezes over, if the pope is Catholic, and bears sit in the woods... rights to knowledge including but not confined to THE MEANING OF LIFE and any related subsidiary meanings, notions, ideas, quips, lemmas and passing fancies...

Clock: ELEVEN THIRTY. IT'S LATER THAN YOU THINK.

Albergus, in common room, and Wagner in the study both jump. The door to the hall opens and Faustus re-enters; Albergus immediately enters the study. When the study door opens Wagner stuffs the contract into his shirt and dashes under the desk. Albergus comes to the desk, rifles through the papers, finds nothing and goes to the ranks of bookshelves toward the back of the study.

In the bedroom, Dicolini and Helen are doing a combination wrestling match and waltz as he tries to maneuver her toward the bed. She begins to realize that this is not Faustus, and resists.

In the common room, Faustus is searching through shelves and cabinets looking for something. Finally he gives up.

Faustus (to clock): Have you seen my cigars anywhere?

Clock: What, am I the maid, too?

In the study Wagner is about to sneak out from beneath the desk when Faustus gives up on the commons and enters the study. Wagner dashes back under the desk. Albergus watches warily from behind a bookshelf. In the bedroom Dicolini is pressing Helen toward the bed.

Dicolini: Bella felissima ronzoni, allapacino.

Helen: My lord, you know I don't understand Latin.

Dicolini: Atsa not Latin, atsa Italian.

Helen: I don't understand Italian, either.

Dicolini: Atsa okay. Neither do I.

Lights down in bedroom, up on alley upstage left. Robin is freezing. He tears a picture of a fire from a book and pins it to the cart, trying to warm his hands before it. He stomps around, flapping his arms. The imp, in his cloak, awakes, pops out, leaps onto the rope and scrambles up through the window. Robin runs around frantically. He stops, snaps his fingers. He rummages through the cart, gets out a nightshirt, glasses, nightcap. He smears black grease from the cart axle under his nose as a mustache. Thus dressed he goes upstage right to where Martin keeps the entrance. Martin gives a double-take, Robin enters.

Lights go down on exterior and up on interior. Robin rushes in through the common room door and races to the bedroom. Inside he skids to a stop when he sees Dicolini and Helen on the bed. Helen has the upper hand. She's got her foot on his neck and is about to bash him with the chamber pot. Dicolini sees Robin.

Dicolini: Faustus!

Robin looks over his shoulder. Helen releases Dicolini, who runs from the room. She smiles tentatively at Robin. Robin smiles back. She throws her arms around his neck.

Helen: Darling!

Robin leaps atop her, horn honking.

In the commons, Dicolini is heading toward the door when Mephistopheles materializes in light and smoke directly in front of him. They collide and sprawl across the dining table, scattering crockery and candlesticks.

Mephisto: You time is nigh, mortal. You will pay dearly for your sins.

Dicolini: I never touched her, boss. Shesa better man than I am.

Mephisto: You insist on playing the fool, even now?

Dicolini: No. Hesa still down inna alley.

Mephistopheles, furious, stomps into the bedroom to talk to Helen. He finds her with Robin on the bed. Once again she has the upper hand, stomping on his horn, which honks. Robin looks up to see Mephisto's glowing eyes. He leaps from the bed and hides in the closet.

Mephisto: It will avail Faustus nothing to hide.

Helen: I don't think that's Faustus.

Mephisto: Who is it, then?

Helen: I don't know, but I've seen a lot of him lately.

Mephisto: Don't tell me you've succumbed to Faustus. Are you doing his bidding?

Helen: You find him and I'll try.

Mephisto: Where is he?

Helen: Hang around a while. He'll turn up. Or else somebody just as good.

Mephisto: This Faustus is devilishly clever and these dopplegangers make my job harder. I don't want to get the wrong man.

Helen: In my experience, not many men aren't the wrong one.

Mephisto: "Better to rule in Hell than serve in Heaven." Ha!

Mephistopheles renders himself invisible, then goes into the commons, deep in thought. Meanwhile, Dicolini has fled from the commons to the study. Faustus, seeing his double enter, gets up from behind the table.

Faustus: So it's you, is it?

Dicolini: Atsa crazy. Itsa no me. Itsa you.

Faustus: How do I know it's me?

Dicolini: I just told you. I'm not here.

Faustus: If you're me, how come you're not smoking a cigar?

Dicolini: You no give me one.

Faustus whips out a cigar and gives it to him.

Faustus: There you go. Let's see you get out of that one.

Dicolini: You got a match?

Faustus: Never mind.

Faustus takes back the cigar. Wagner, meanwhile, is trying to crawl out while they bicker. Faustus spots him.

Faustus: Hold on there! I can't get away from me that easily!

Wagner gets up and runs out of the room. Faustus tries to chase him, but gets tangled up with Dicolini. Meanwhile, Albergus sneaks out of the common room in the confusion. In the course of the next action he is searching through the room for Faustus's magic book, which he finally finds, just before the climax, with the assistance of Robin's imp. Mephistopheles, invisible, observes him doing this.

Wagner rushes through the commons directly into the bedroom, He shoves the door open and, not seeing Helen, jumps into the closet, tearing off his clothes. He embraces Robin.

Wagner: Dearest, I couldn't find the book, but—

Robin's horn honks. Wagner is nonplussed.

Helen: What are you doing in there?

Wagner opens the door and pulls Robin out by his collar. Robin's face splits in a shy smile of love. Wagner pushes him out the bedroom door and turns to Helen.

Wagner: Helen?

Helen: Darling!

She throws her arms around his neck and draws him toward the bed.

Clock: ELEVEN FORTY-FIVE. LATE LATE LATE.

Mephistopheles, roused by the clock, makes a decision. He goes from the commons into the study. The instant he enters, Faustus and Dicolini speak as one.

Faustus & Dicolini: Oh, so you're back, eh?

Mephisto: Your doom is at hand.

Faustus fans out his deck of tarot cards.

Faustus: Never mind that. Pick a card.

Dicolini (*taking one*): So, what am I got?

Faustus: You've got one, I've still got seventy-seven.

Dicolini: You wrong. Itsa ace of wands.

Faustus: Wandaful. (*gesturing to Mephistopheles*) Does your wormy friend want to try his luck?

Dicolini: Hesa outside in the alley.

At this, Robin enters munching a slice of bread. He goes to the alchemical table and smears the bread with some noxious chemicals, takes a bite. He offers the bread to Faustus.

Faustus: No, thanks. It's bad enough being damned. Indigestion I don't need.

Clock: IT'S MIDNIGHT. BONG. BONG. BONG… (*continues throughout following action.*)

Mephisto: Enough! Which one of you is the real Faustus?

At that moment, Albergus, who has found the magic book, strides into the room.

Albergus: Ha ha! Fools! Now at last ultimate knowledge is mine! My time has come, and I am become the true Faustus!

Mephisto: Good enough for me.

With that he snaps his fingers and a horde of misshapen demons erupt from the corners of the room. They seize Albergus, and in an explosion of light and smoke, drag him off to Hell. As the air clears the last stroke of midnight dies away. In the next room, the clock moves for the first time in the play. It stretches, shakes its aching legs and arms, gives a little hop of exhilaration.

Clock exits. In the bedroom, Wagner finds he is embracing empty air. He stumbles to the closet, but it is empty.

Wagner: Helen?

Following the smell of smoke, he enters the study. Faustus and Dicolini are seated around a bonfire smoking cigars. Robin, using Mephistopheles's pitchfork, is shoveling books into the fire.

Dicolini: Atsa good smoke.

Wagner: Where is she?

Faustus gestures at Wagner's drooping trousers.

Faustus: Cut is the branch that might have grown full straight.

He pulls the sweaty contract off Wagner's chest and adds it to the fire.

Wagner: What have you done with her?

Dicolini: She was one helluva wrestler, eh, partner?

Robin leans on his pitchfork and gives a long, low whistle.

Wagner: But it's not fair! We were only getting to know each other!

Faustus: My boy, she was a scarlet woman and you're nothing but a green student. She would have made you blue someday.

Dicolini: If you didn't turn yellow first.

Faustus (offering a hot dog): Meanwhile, how about a little roast scholar?

Dicolini: Atsa no roast, atsa friar.

Wagner stumbles from the room. Lights go down.

Scene Seven

Lights come up on the Boar's Bollocks, where Wagner, moping, is seated at a table telling his story to the barmaid. At the next table a man sits with his back to the audience.

Wagner: ... and when I came to, she was gone! Did my master Faustus care? Did Dicolini and Robin, my closest friends, care?

Barmaid: I care.

Wagner: The story of mankind is a sad story. The saddest story I know.

Barmaid: Poor Wagner! Were you hurt?

Wagner: Emotional loss means nothing to the true intellectual.

Barmaid (touching his chest): Let me help you.

Wagner: The world is a cold place.

Barmaid: But you told me you were hot.

Wagner (standing, beginning to orate): And I've learned much from all this. The beginning of wisdom is mine. I've learned that despite the centuries that have passed since the beginning of time, despite the wars, heresies and degradations, the corruptions of institutions and loss of faith, the ages of bad behavior, one thing remains. People are, for better or worse, still human. That has not changed. Good and evil co-exist. Some souls are saved, others are lost. The appetites of the body and the mind conflict. Men aspire to the stars, women abandon them, scholars seek knowledge, students...

The barmaid seizes him by the shoulder, bends him over and gives him a furious kiss. They fall off the bench, under the table. Bateman enters.

Bateman: Has anyone seen my master Albergus?

The man at the next table turns and hails him. It is the Clock.

Clock: He's busy. Will be for a while. Meanwhile, could you tell me what time it is?

Lights down in tavern. Mephistopheles comes out to address the audience.

Mephisto: These our revels now are done.
All my power's overthrown.
Wagner's found a girl at last
History has swallowed past.
For me, I'm off to warmer climes
And giving up these wretched ryhmes.
Plagiarize I can no more
From better writers' magic store
Of characters, ideas, words,
Comic mishaps *très absurd*..
With brothers Marx's sweet inventions
To tell of Faustus was our intention.
Now you must tell us if our play
Justified such rude display
A laugh's the end we're hoping for
Please don't send us back for more.
But if our humor's fit your plans
You may release us with your hands.

Curtain

THE PROFESSOR'S TEDDY BEAR

Theodore Sturgeon

"Sleep," said the monster. It spoke with its ear, with little lips writhing deep within the folds of flesh, because its mouth was full of blood.

"I don't want to sleep now. I'm having a dream," said Jeremy. "When I sleep, all my dreams go away. Or they're just pretend dreams. I'm having a real dream now."

"What are you dreaming now?" asked the monster.

"I am dreaming that I'm grown up—"

"Seven feet tall and very fat," said the monster.

"You're silly," said Jeremy. "I will be five feet, six and three eighth inches tall. I will be bald on top and will wear eyeglasses like little thick ashtrays. I will give lectures to young things about human destiny and the metempsychosis of Plato."

"What's a metempsychosis?" asked the monster hungrily.

Jeremy was four and could afford to be patient. "A metempsychosis is a thing that happens when a person moves from one house to another."

"Like when your daddy moved here from Monroe Street?"

"Sort of. But not that kind of a house, with shingles and sewers and things. *This* kind of a house," he said, and smote his little chest.

"Oh," said the monster. It moved up and crouched on Jeremy's throat, looking more like a teddy bear than ever. "Now?" it begged. It was not very heavy.

"Not now," said Jeremy petulantly. "It'll make me sleep. I want to watch my dreams some more. There's a girl who's not listening to my lecture. She's thinking about her hair."

"What about her hair?" asked the monster.

"It's brown," said Jeremy. "It's shiny, too. She wishes it were golden."

"Why?"

"Somebody named Bert likes golden hair."

"Go ahead and make it golden then."

"I can't! What would the other young ones say?"

"Does that matter?"

369

"Maybe not. Could I make her hair golden?"

"Who is she?" countered the monster.

"She is a girl who will be born here in about twenty years," said Jeremy. The monster snuggled closer to his neck.

"If she is to be born here, then of course you can change her hair. Hurry and do it and go to sleep."

Jeremy laughed delightedly.

"I changed it," said Jeremy. "The girl behind her squeaked like the mouse with its leg caught. Then she jumped up. It's a big lecture-room, you know, built up and away from the speaker-place. It has steep aisles. Her foot slipped on the hard step."

He burst into joyous laughter.

"Now what?"

"She broke her neck. She's dead."

The monster sniggered. "That's a very funny dream. Now change the other girl's hair back again. Nobody else saw it, except you?"

"Nobody else saw," said Jeremy. "There! It's changed back again. They never even knew she had golden hair for a little while."

"That's fine. Does that end the dream?"

"I s'pose it does," said Jeremy regretfully. "It ends the lecture, anyhow. The young people are all crowding around the girl with the broken neck. The young men all have sweat under their noses. The girls are all trying to put their fists into their mouths. You can go ahead."

The monster made a happy sound and pressed its mouth hard against Jeremy's neck. Jeremy closed his eyes.

The door opened. "Jeremy, darling," said Mummy. She had a tired, soft face and smiling eyes. "I heard you laugh."

Jeremy opened his eyes slowly. His lashes were so long that when they swung up, there seemed to be a tiny wind, as if they were dark weather fans. He smiled, and three of his teeth peeped out and smiled too. "I told Fuzzy a story, Mummy," he said sleepily, "and he liked it."

"You darling," she murmured. She came to him and tucked the covers around his chin. He put up his hand and kept the monster tight against his neck.

"Is Fuzzy sleeping?" asked Mummy, her voice crooning with whimsy.

"No," said Jeremy. "He's hungering himself."

"How does he do that?"

"When I eat, the—the hungry goes away. Fuzzy's different."

She looked at him, loving him so much that she did not—could not think. "You're a strange child," she whispered, "and you have the pinkest cheeks in the whole wide world."

"Sure I have," he said.

"What a funny little laugh!" she said, paling.

"That wasn't me. That was Fuzzy. He thinks you're funny."

Mummy stood over the crib, looking down at him. It seemed be the frown that looked at him, while the eyes looked past. Finally she wet her lips and patted his head. "Good night, baby."

"Good night, Mummy." He closed his eyes. Mummy tiptoed out. The monster kept right on doing it.

It was naptime the next day, and for the hundredth time Mummy had kissed him and said, "You're so *good* about your nap, Jeremy!" Well, he was. He always went straight to bed at nap-time, as he did at bedtime. Mummy didn't know why, of course. Perhaps Jeremy did not know. Fuzzy knew.

Jeremy opened the toy-chest and took Fuzzy out. "You're hungry, I bet," he said.

"Yes. Let's hurry."

Jeremy climbed into the crib and hugged the teddy bear close. "I kept thinking about that girl," he said.

"What girl?"

"The one whose hair I changed."

"Maybe because it's the first time you've changed a person."

"It is not! What about the man who fell into the subway hold?"

"You moved the hat. The one that blew off. You moved it under his feet so that he stepped on the brim with one foot and caught his toe in the crown, and tumbled in."

"Well, what about the little girl I threw in front of the truck?"

"You didn't touch her," said the monster equably. "She was on roller skates. You broke something in one wheel so it couldn't turn. So she fell right in front of the truck."

Jeremy thought carefully. "Why didn't I ever touch a person before?"

"I don't know," said Fuzzy. "It has something to do with being born in this house, I think."

"I guess maybe," said Jeremy doubtfully.

"I'm hungry," said the monster, settling itself on Jeremy's stomach as he turned on his back.

"Oh, all right," Jeremy said. "The next lecture."

"Yes," said Fuzzy eagerly. "Dream bright, now. The big things that you say, lecturing. Those are what I want. Never mind the people there. Never mind you, lecturing. The things you say."

The strange blood flowed as Jeremy relaxed. He looked up to the ceiling, found the hairline crack that he always stared at while he dreamed real, and began to talk.

"There I am. There's the—the room, yes, and the—yes, it's all there, again. There's the girl. The one who has the brown, shiny hair. The seat behind her is empty. This must be after that other girl broke her neck."

"Never mind that," said the monster impatiently. "What do you say?"

"I—" Jeremy was quiet. Finally Fuzzy nudged him. "Oh. It's all about yesterday's unfortunate occurrence, but, like the show of legend, our studies must go on."

"Go on with it then," panted the monster.

"All right, all right," said Jeremy impatiently. "Here it is. We come now to the Gymnosophists, whose ascetic school has had no recorded equal in its extremism. Those strange gentry regarded clothing and even food as detrimental to purity of thought. The Greeks also called them Hylobioi, a term our more erudite students will notice as analogous to the Sanskrit *Vana-Prasthas*. It is evident that they were a profound influence on Diogenes Laërtius, the Elysian founder of pure skepticism…"

And so he droned on and on. Fuzzy crouched on his body, its soft ears making small masticating motions; and sometimes when stimulated by some particularly choice nugget of esoterica, the ears drooled.

At the end of nearly an hour, Jeremy's soft voice trailed off, and he was quiet. Fuzzy shifted in irritation. "What is it?"

"That girl," said Jeremy. "I keep looking back to that girl while I'm talking."

"Well, stop doing it. I'm not finished."

"There isn't any more, Fuzzy. I keep looking and looking back to that girl until I can't lecture any more. Now I'm saying all that about the pages in the book and the assignment. The lecture is over."

Fuzzy's mouth was almost full of blood. From its ears, it sighed. "That wasn't any too much. But if that's all, then it's all. You can sleep now if you want to."

"I want to watch for a while."

The monster puffed out its cheeks. The pressure inside was not great. "Go on, then." It scrabbled Jeremy's body and curled up in a sulky huddle.

The strange blood moved steadily through Jeremy's brain. With his eyes wide and fixed, he watched himself as he would be, a slight, balding professor of philosophy.

He sat in the hall, watching the students tumbling up the steep aisles, wondering at the strange compulsion he had to look at that girl, Miss—Miss—what was it?

Oh. "Miss Patchell!"

He stared, astonished at himself. He had certainly not meant to call out her name. He clasped his hands tightly, regaining the dry stiffness which was his closest approach to dignity.

The girl came slowly down the aisle steps, her widest eyes wondering. There were books tucked under her arm, and her hair shone. "Yes, Professor?"

"I—" He stopped and cleared his throat. "I know it's the last class today, and you are no doubt meeting someone. I shan't keep you very long… and if I do," he added, and was again astonished at himself, "you can see Bert tomorrow."

"Bert? Oh!" She colored prettily. "I didn't know you knew about—how *could* you know?"

He shrugged. "Miss Patchell," he said. "You'll forgive an old—ah—middle-aged man's rambling, I hope. There is something about you that—that—"

"Yes?" Caution, and an iota of fright in her eyes. She glanced up and back at the now empty hall.

Abruptly he pounded the table. "I will *not* let this go on for another instant without finding out about it. Miss Patchell, you are becoming afraid of me, and you are wrong."

"I th-think I'd better…" she said timidly, and began backing off.

"*Sit down!*" he thundered. It was the first time in his entire life that he had thundered at anyone, and her shock was not one whit greater than his. She shrank back and into a front-row seat, looking a good deal smaller than she actually was, except about the eyes, which were much larger.

The professor shook his head in vexation. He rose, stepped down off the dais, and crossed to her, sitting in the next seat.

"Now be quiet and listen to me." The shadow of a smile twitched his lips and he said, "I really don't know what I am going to say. Listen, and be patient. It couldn't be more important."

He sat a while, thinking, chasing vague pictures around in his mind. He heard, or was conscious of, the rapid but slowing beat of her frightened heart.

"Miss Patchell," he said, turning to her, his voice gentle. "I have not at any time looked into your records. Until—ah—yesterday, you were simply an-other face in the class, another source of quiz papers to be graded. I have not consulted the registrar's files for information about you. And, to my almost certain knowledge, this is the first time I have spoken with you."

"That's right, sir," she said quietly.

"Very good, then." He wet his lips. "You are twenty-three years old. The house in which you were born was a two-story affair, quiet old, with a leaded bay window at the turn of the stairs. The small bedroom, or nursery, was directly over the kitchen. You could hear the clatter of dishes below you when the house was quiet. The address was 191 Bucyrus Road."

"How—oh yes! How did you know?"

He shook his head, and then put it between his hands. "I don't know. I don't know. I lived in that house, too, as a child. I don't know how I knew that you did. There are things in here—" He rapped his head, shook it again. "I thought perhaps you could help."

She looked at him. He was a small man, brilliant, tired, getting old swiftly. She put a hand on his arm. "I wish I could," she said warmly. "I do wish I could."

"Thank you, child."

"Maybe if you told me more—"

"Perhaps. Some of it is—ugly. All of it is cloudy, long ago, barely remembered.

And yet—"

"Please go on."

"I remember," he half-whispered, "things that happened long ago that way, and recent things I remember—twice. One memory is sharp and clear, and one is old and misty. And I remember, in the same misty way, what is happening now—and what will happen!"

"I don't understand."

"That girl. That Miss Symes. She—died here yesterday."

"She was sitting right behind me," said Miss Patchell.

"I know it! I knew what was going to happen to her. I knew it mistily, like an old memory. That's what I mean. I don't know what I could have done to stop it. I don't think I could have done anything. And yet, down deep I have the feeling that it's my fault—that she slipped and fell because of something I did."

"Oh, no!"

He touched her arm in mute gratitude for the sympathy in her tone, and grimaced miserably. "It's happened before," he said. "Time and time and time again. As a boy, as a youth, I was plagued with accidents. I led a quiet life. I was not very strong and books were always more my line than baseball. And yet I witnessed a dozen or more violent, useless deaths—automobile accidents, drownings, falls, and one or two—" his voice shook—"which I won't mention. And there were countless minor ones—broken bones, maimings, stabbings… and every time, in some way, it was my fault, like the one yesterday… and I—I—"

"Don't," she whispered. "Please don't. You were nowhere near Elaine Symes when she fell."

"I was nowhere near any of them! That never mattered. It never took away the burden of guilt. Miss Patchell—"

"Catherine."

"Catherine. Thank you so much! There are people called by insurance actuaries, 'accident prone.' Most of these are involved in accidents through their own negligence, or through some psychological quirk which causes them to defy the world, or to demand attention, by getting hurt. But some are simply present at accidents, without being involved at all—catalysts of death, if you'll pardon a flamboyant phrase. I am, apparently, one of these."

"Then—how could you feel guilty?"

"It was—" He broke off suddenly, and looked at her. She had a gentle face, and her eyes were filled with compassion. He shrugged. "I've said so much," he said. "More would sound no more fantastic and do me no more damage."

"There'll be no damage from anything you tell me," she said, with a sparkle of decisiveness.

He smiled his thanks this time, sobered, and said, "These horrors—the maimings, the deaths—they were *funny*, once, long ago. I must have been a child, a baby. Something taught me, then, that the agony and death of others was to be promoted and enjoyed. I remember, I—almost remember when that stopped. There was a—a toy, a—a—"

Jeremy blinked. He had been staring at the fine crack in the ceiling for so long that his eyes hurt.

"What are you doing?" asked the monster.

"Dreaming real," said Jeremy. "I am grown up and sitting in the big empty lecture place, talking to the girl with the brown hair that shines. Her name's Catherine."

"What are you talking about?"

"Oh, all the funny dreams. Only—"

"Well?"

"They're not so funny."

The monster scurried over to him and pounced on his chest. "Time to sleep now. And I want to—"

"No," said Jeremy. He put his hands over his throat. "I have enough now. Wait until I see some more of this real-dream."

"What do you want to see?"

"Oh, I don't know. There's something…"

"Let's have some fun," said the monster. "This is the girl you can change, isn't it?"

"Yes."

"Go ahead. Give her an elephant's trunk. Make her grow a beard. Stop her nostrils up. Go on. You can do anything." Jeremy grinned briefly, then said, "I don't want to."

"Oh, go on. Just see how funny…"

"A toy," said the professor. "But more than a toy. It could talk, I think. If I could only remember more clearly!"

"Don't try so hard. Maybe it will come," she said. She took his hand impulsively. "Go ahead."

"It was—something—" the professor said haltingly, "—something soft and not too large, I don't recall…"

"Was it smooth?"

"No. Hairy—fuzzy. *Fuzzy!* I'm beginning to get it. Wait, now… A thing like a teddy bear. It talked. It—why, of course! It was alive!"

"A pet, then. Not a toy."

"Oh, no," said the professor, and shuddered. "It was a toy, all right. My mother thought it was, anyway. It made me dream real."

"You mean, like Peter Ibbetson?"

"No, no. Not like that." He leaned back, rolled his eyes up. "I used to see myself as I would be later, when I was grown. And before. Oh. Oh—I think it was then—Yes! It must have been then that I began to see all those terrible accidents. It was! It was!"

"Steady," said Catherine. "Tell me quietly."

He relaxed. "Fuzzy. The demon—the monster. I know what it did, the devil. Somehow it made me see myself as I grew. It made me repeat what I had learned. It—it ate knowledge! It did; it ate knowledge. It had some strange affinity for me, for something about me. It could absorb knowledge that I gave out. And it—it changed the knowledge into blood, the way a plant changes sunlight and water into cellulose!"

"I don't understand," she said again.

"You don't? How could you? How can I? I know that that's what it did, though. It made me—why, I was spouting my lectures here to the beast when I was four years old! The words of them, the sense of them, came from *now* to me *then*. And I gave it to the monster, and it ate the knowledge and spiced it with the things it made me do in my real dreams. It made me trip a man up on a hat, of all absurd things, and fall into a subway excavation. And when I was in my teens, I was right by the excavation to see it happen. And that's the way with all of them! All the horrible accidents I have witnessed, I have half-remembered before they happened. There's no stopping, any of them. What am I going to do?"

There were tears in her eyes. "What about me?" she whispered—more, probably, to get his mind away from his despair than for any other reason.

"You. There's something about you, if only I could remember. Something about what happened to that—that toy, that beast. You were in the same environment as I, as that devil. Somehow, you are vulnerable to it and—Catherine, Catherine, I think that something was done to you that—"

He broke off. His eyes widened in horror. The girl sat beside him, helping him, pitying him, and her expression did not change. But—everything else about her did.

Her face shrank, shrivelled. Her eyes lengthened. Her ears grew long, grew until they were like donkey's ears, like rabbit's ears, like horrible, long hairy spider's legs. Her teeth lengthened into tusks. Her arms shrivelled into jointed straws, and her body thickened.

It smelled like rotten meat.

There were filthy claws scattering out of her polished open-toed shoes. There were bright sores. There were—other things. And all the while she—it—held his hand and looked at him with pity and friendliness.

The professor—

Jeremy sat up and flung the monster away. "It isn't funny!" he screamed. "It isn't funny, it isn't, it isn't, it *isn't!*"

The monster sat up and looked at him with its soft, bland, teddy-bear expression. "Be quiet," it said. "Let's make her all squashy now, like soft-soap. And hornets in her stomach. And we can put her—"

Jeremy clapped his hands over his ears and screwed his eyes shut. The monster talked on. Jeremy burst into tears, leapt from the crib and, hurling the monster to the floor, kicked it. It grunted. "That's funny!" screamed the child. "Ha, ha!" he cried, as he planted both feet in its yielding stomach. He picked up the twitching mass and hurled it across the room. It struck the nursery clock. Clock and monster struck the floor together in a flurry of glass, metal, and blood. Jeremy stamped it all into a jagged, pulpy mass, blood from his feet mixing with blood from the monster, the same strange blood which the monster had pumped into his neck...

Mummy all but fainted when she ran in and saw him. She screamed, but he laughed, screaming. The doctor gave him sedatives until he slept, and cured his feet. He was never very strong after that. They saved him, to live his life and to see his real-dreams; funny dreams, and to die finally in a lecture room, with his eyes distended in horror while horror froze his heart, and a terrified young woman ran crying, crying for help.

THE HEIDELBERG CYLINDER

by Jonathan Carroll

It began the day our new refrigerator was delivered. A big silver thing that looked like a miniature Airstream trailer turned on its side. But Rae loved it. We had bought it a few days before. In January I told her as soon as my raise comes in, you get your fridge. And I kept my promise, all six hundred and thirty-nine dollars of it.

Two puffing deliverymen came in the pouring rain to curse and shove it into place in our kitchen. Both guys were in big bad moods, that was plain. But no wonder—who wants to deliver appliances in a ripping thunderstorm? When they were finished and I'd signed the delivery papers, Rae offered coffee. That perked them up. After they'd done stirring and sipping and settling into the chairs one guy, "Dennis" it said on his shirt, told a strange story that got us thinking.

For the past few days while driving around making deliveries, they'd seen piles of furniture all over town stacked in the middle of sidewalks. That didn't seem so strange to me. But Dennis said they saw it at least ten times overall: big piles of furniture heaped up, just sitting there unguarded usually.

"No that's not true," his partner Vito piped in. "Remember when we saw the man and woman standing next to a pile up on Lail Avenue, arguing? They were really fighting! Arms flying, pointing fingers at each other. It was like one had thrown the other outta the house with all their stuff, but you couldn't tell who'd thrown who."

"Just furniture? Nothing else? No moving vans there or anything? No people guarding the stuff?"

"Nope, that's the weird part. These piles of furniture and boxes, like whole households, stacked up and no one around. Go figure."

The four of us sat there drinking coffee, thinking it over. Then Dennis said, "We saw another pile coming over here today. Remember that nice blue leather couch and TV I pointed to? Jeez, stuff looked brand-new. Big screen TV... Just sitting out in the rain getting drenched.

"Times are tough. Maybe it's coincidence, but I hear a lotta people are being

378

thrown out of their houses by the banks."

"All at the same time? I don't think so, partner," Vito said sarcastically to him and winked at me.

Dennis straightened up and threw him a black look. "You got a better explanation, genius?"

"Nope. Just that it's weird. Never in my life have I seen stuff that nice left out alone on the street unguarded. And so many times. In the rain? Makes the whole town look like a big yard sale."

Right then Chapter Two began but none of us knew it yet. Before anyone had a chance to say more, the doorbell rang. I looked at Rae to see if she was expecting someone. She shook her head. Who now?

I got up to answer it. A second after opening that door I wished I hadn't. Standing on my porch were two guys looking like wet seals. One glimpse and you wanted to say, "No thanks to whatever you've got," slam the door in their faces and run for cover.

Naturally they were smiling. But you know the kind—totally fake. No one smiles like that without putting too much face into it. Or they got a gun stuck in their back. These guys were wearing identical brown suits freckled dark all over with rain. Bright yellow plastic nametags were pinned on their breast pockets. White shirts with the top button buttoned but no ties. Both had bowl haircuts that made them look like monks or The Beatles gone bad. And they smelled. I'm sorry to have to say that, but they did. They smelled like they'd lived in their buttoned-up rayon shirts way too long.

"Good morning, sir! I'm Brother Brooks and this is Brother Zin Zan."

"Brother who? You want to say all that again?" I stood back and gave them a lot of room, just in case they exploded and their crazy went all over my porch.

"Brooks and Zin Zan. Would you have a few moments to spare? It may just change your life!"

I knew where this was leading and was just about to adios them, but a thunderclap shook the house and rain came down like a tidal wave. What could I do, shove them back out in that flood? Really unhappily I asked, "You want to come in a minute?

Their faces lit up like Yankee Stadium for a night game. "We certainly would. Thank you very much."

In for a penny, in for a pound. "Want some coffee? Looks like you could use it."

"No thank you, sir. But it's certainly kind of you to offer."

"Well, come on in." They stepped into the hall and I closed the door. They both wore black basketball sneakers with a brand name written in white on the side that I couldn't make out. I thought it was kind of strange that Bible guys would be wearing sneakers. Much less underneath a suit.

"Bill, who was it?" Rae called out.

"Brooks Brothers and Sen Sen." I couldn't resist saying. And you know what?

Brooks started laughing.

"That's very funny, sir. People always make that mistake. But actually, it's Brother Brooks. And Brother Zin Zan. He's from New Zealand."

"New Zealand. Is that right? You're pretty far from home. Sorry for the mistake. Come on in."

I went first to see what would happen. When Rae and the delivery guys caught a view of who was following me, they got exactly the same look on their faces—Whaaat?

"Everybody, this is Brother Brooks and Brother Zin Zan. They say they can change our lives." I said it like I was introducing an act in Las Vegas.

Picking right up on it Dennis said, "Sounds good to me. Anything to stop delivering refrigerators!"

Rae stared at me like I'd gone nuts. Both of us hate door-to-door preachers with their ridiculous speeches and too many teeth. Her face asked, why had I let these guys in? Suddenly our house was like the dog pound—every stray in town under one roof, dripping on her carpets. I sat down but the Brothers kept standing. To my surprise, Zin Zan started talking. He had a strong accent. Then I remembered he was from New Zealand. The whole time he spoke, Brooks gave him an all-attention smile that looked as phony as a tinfoil Christmas tree.

"We represent a brotherhood called The Heidelberg Cylinder. Our avatar is a man named Beeflow."

"Beef-low?" Dennis looked at his partner and me, then wiggled his eyebrows and O'd his mouth.

"No, sir, Bee-flow. We believe we are entering the Second Diaspora. It will formally begin with the Millennium and continue for another 16,312 years."

"Sixteen thousand, you say? With or without intermission?"

My sweet wife tried to smooth that one over. "Would you two like some juice?"

"Thank you, Ma'am, but we don't drink anything but water. Beeflow says—"

"Who's this Beeflow?"

"Our spiritual master. Chosen avatar by—"

"What's an avatar? Sounds like that new model Honda."

Brother Brooks liked that one too. He smiled and for the first time it looked real. "No sir, an avatar is an incarnation of a deity. A kind of God in human form, you could say."

"What did your Mr. Beeflow do before he became God?"

Maybe it was the way Rae said it, so respectful and serious. Or maybe because Dennis and I were watching each other when she spoke. Whatever, as soon as my wife asked her question so gently, the three of us guys cracked up. I mean big time. We laughed so hard we choked.

"He was a travel agent."

"Good career move!" I said, which brought down the house again. Except for Rae. She FedExed me her stone face and I knew what that meant. I shut up fast.

"So what do you guys believe in? I mean, like a quick wrap-up of your religion?"

"We believe in rent control, a river view when possible, and forced air heating."

The living room got silent fast. Real silent.

"Say that again?"

"Room, sir. We believe in the just and proper distribution of room. Human space. Apartments, houses, it makes no difference. A civilized place to live."

"Geodesic domes," Zin Zan added, nodding.

"What the Hell are you talking about? I'm not following you here, Brother Brooks."

"Well sir, have you noticed all the furniture out on the streets of the city recently? Piles of it, looking like it's waiting to be picked up?"

"We were just talking about that!"

"It's the first sign of the beginning of the Diaspora."

"What's that?"

"A Diaspora is the breaking up and scattering of a people. The forced settling of people far from their ancestral homelands."

"You mean they're being moved out?"

"Yes, exactly."

"By who? Who's moving them?"

"Satan."

I cleared my throat and snatched a quick glimpse of Rae. She gave me a look that said, "Don't make trouble with these guys." So instead of cracking wise about the Satanic Moving Company, I looked at the others to see if they were going to snap at the bait.

"All those piles of stuff out on the streets are there because the Devil's throwing people out of their houses? Why's he doin' that?"

Zin Zan picked it up. "Because Hell is filled to overflowing, sir, and Satan needs the room. He plans to re-populate the Earth with the fallen."

I didn't know about the others but I was so embarrassed by the direction this conversation was taking that I could only stare at the floor and hope those Brothers would evaporate by the time I looked up again.

"So you're saying that if I was bad and die now, there's no room for me in Hell and I may end up back here living next door?" Vito said in a voice full of "you gotta be shittin' me."

My eyes still down, I heard Zin Zan's thick accent field the question. "Why do you think the world's in such bad straits, sir? New fatal diseases being discovered every day, crime the likes of which defy human imagination. How do you explain people's vast and unfailing indifference to one another?

"Because so many of them are dead. They have no souls. This has been going on for some time. The dead bring death back with them when they return to Earth."

What can you say to something looney-tuney like that? I felt like taking a nap. I felt like getting up from where I was sitting, maybe or maybe not giving a wave to everyone in the room, and walking right out of there into the bedroom and my pillow and about an hour nighty-night. My brain felt tired and like it had had something lousy and too heavy for lunch.

"Yeah? Well prove it, Brothers." Dennis spoke like he was spitting and said that last word like a Black soul brother. You know, he said it "bruddas" and there wasn't any respect in the word.

Not that it touched the Heidelberg Cylinder boys. They smiled on like two Ken dolls on a date with Barbie. Brooks politely asked, "What do you mean, sir?"

Dennis pointed an "it's your fault" finger at him and shook it. "You know exactly what I mean. Guys like you have been coming to my door for years, talking about how the world's gonna end tomorrow. God's gonna kick my butt for sinning unless I repent. Armageddon's coming so watch out! Well you know what? Arma-geddon pretty damned sick of hearing that stuff from your like. If you think you're so right about what you're saying, prove it. That's all—show us it's true. You say the Devil's on Earth moving dead people out of their houses? Show me!"

Vito put a thumbs up. "I agree! Show me too!"

I kind of felt like doing it too. I myself was sick of gleamy-eyed wackos coming to my house with their cheap pamphlets and "God's-gonna-get-you" threats. Having the big fat nerve to tell me I'd done everything wrong with my life. And I'd better start dancing to their tune or else. Oh yeah? How do you know; you been watching my every move?

What I resented most was how damned sure people like this were that they were right. Hey, maybe they were, but how could they be so convinced? I admit I wasn't sure of anything in life, much less how His Majesty upstairs in heaven makes things work. But at least I admit it. Listening to these dudes talk, or others like them who'd appeared over the years with their own smudged magazines and weird smiles, God was as easy to understand as the baseball scores.

"Well?"

The not-so Righteous Brothers blinked at the same time and smiled again. But kept their traps shut.

"Huh? Can you prove you're right? Or are you going to tell me to wait till Judgment Day rolls around to find out?"

"Oh no sir, we can show you right now. That's not a problem." Brooks spoke and his voice was nice as rice. I mean he spoke like what Dennis had just asked was the easiest favor in the world to grant. You want me to show you Satan? You want me to open up the back of the big clock and show you how it ticks? Follow me, sir—this way to Satan. Just like that. Simple.

"What the fuck are you guys talking about?"

Rae caught her breath hearing my words, but I couldn't help myself. I was suddenly as hot and sizzling as a frying chicken. I didn't like where this conversation was going. And I sure didn't believe what was just said. All eyes were on me like the kid who just farted in class. Dennis and Vito's faces said ha-ha, but Rae's was uh-oh because she knows my temper. The Brothers were calm as usual.

"You can sit there with a straight face and say you'll show me Satan this minute?"

"We can show you proof, sir. All the proof you'll need. We just have to go up to Pilot Hill."

"What's on Pilot Hill?"

"The proof you want."

"What proof?"

The brothers stood up. "We can go right now. We'll give you a thousand dollars each if you're not happy with our proof."

The room went stone quiet for the second time in ten minutes.

Rae said in a wiggly voice, "A thousand dollars?"

"Oh yes, ma'am. We have no desire to waste your valuable time." Brooks reached into his pocket and pulled out a roll of bills as thick as a Big Mac. So help me God, that man's hands contained more cash than I'd ever seen one person hold, outside of a bank teller.

Vito whistled one note low and asked what I'm sure we were all wondering: "How much you got there?"

Brooks looked at his hand. "I think ten thousand dollars. How much do you have, Brother Zin Zan?"

Zin stuck out his lower lip and nodded. "Ten thousand." He patted his pocket.

"Each of you guys is carrying ten grand?" Dennis's amazed voice cracked halfway through the sentence.

"That's the way we do things in our organization, sir. We want you to be happy with your decision, one way or the other."

Vito stood right up. "Well, I just made my decision—let's go!"

Dennis too. "I'm with you. Pilot Hill, here we come."

Rae looked at me and then stood up slowly. The Brothers did too. Only I stayed where I was sitting. To emphasize that fact even more I crossed my arms and went humph.

"What's the matter, Bill?"

"You know damn well what the matter is, Rae! This whole thing is nuts. The three of you are going out the door with these screwballs because they dangled some free money in front of you. Dangled but didn't give. Well how about this: I'll come too if you give me my thousand dollars right now, Brothers. Not later—this second. I'll give it back to you when we get there if I'm so convinced you're right."

"I'm fine with that, sir. It's no problem," Brooks said and without one second's hesitation peeled ten crisp new hundred-dollar bills off his Big Mac. "Here you go." He crossed the room and handed them to me.

"Hey, I want mine too if he's getting his now!"

"Me too."

"Yes, me too please." Rae said that. She is a shy, kind woman who doesn't even complain when someone big steps on her toe at the market. But now here she was wanting her thousand dollars up front just like everyone else. I was setting a bad example, but at least we were all a thousand dollars richer for it.

Then an evil thought came riding in. I looked suspiciously at the money in my hand. Maybe it was too fresh, too new? Was real money really that green? "How do we know this isn't fake? That it's not counterfeit or something?"

Brother Zin Zan was counting off hundreds while Brooks was handing Vito his share. "Oh we can stop at a bank on the way and have it checked if you like. But I guarantee you it's real."

I looked at my money like it might have something to say. This whole thing was so crazy, why shouldn't we just accept it at face value? Four thousand dollars was being handed out in that room and everyone was as cool as cucumbers about it. Like it happened to us every day and now was just the payoff hour. Rae wore a smile that was somewhere between happiness and crime.

"How do you want to go over there?"

"What do you mean?"

Dennis waved his hand around the room. "Well there's six of us. You want us all to go in your car?"

Zin Zan shook his head. "We don't have a car."

I shook mine. "We got a little Hyundai. We can barely get the two of us into it. It wouldn't know what to do with six people."

"It'd have a heart attack," Rae said, and it was like the first joke she'd made in five years.

All the guys smiled at her and I felt pretty proud to have a wisecracking wife. First she's putting out a greedy hand just like the others for a thousand dollars and now she was cracking jokes. She was suddenly a completely different woman from the one I knew, but I kind of liked it.

"Then I say we all go in the truck."

"What truck, yours? And ride in the back with the rest of the appliances?"

"Naah—you and your wife can sit up front with Dennis. Me and the Brothers will get in back."

Brooks and Zin Zan nodded to that and so did Rae. Who was I to argue? We put on our raincoats and waded out into the storm. Where I looked left and right but didn't see any furniture truck. "So where is it?"

"Right there. Right in front of you."

Right in front of me was a red truck. But on the side of it was a picture of a smiling white pig wearing a black baseball cap. The poor little guy was being roasted on a spit. Now I ask you, why would you put a baseball cap on a pig you were cooking? Even more, why would the pig be smiling while it died?

Above that dumbass picture was written "Lester's Meat." Which, when you thought about it, didn't sound very appetizing either. I made myself a mental note never to buy Lester's Meat.

"That's a meat truck."

"It's my uncle's. He lets me use it to make deliveries sometimes."

"You deliver appliances in a meat truck?"

"It's been known to happen." Vito and Dennis grinned at each other like they knew something we didn't.

"This is too weird. My new refrigerator was in there up alongside a side of beef?"

"No, the truck's empty now. He only lets me use it when it's empty."

"Yeah, but is my fridge going to smell of raw meat now?"

"I'm afraid we're going to have to walk," Brook said.

"Walk? Why?"

"Because members of the Heidelberg Cylinder are strict vegetarians. Not vegan but strict vegetarian. We don't eat anything with a face. We avoid contact with any form of meat."

"What the Hell are you talking about? You're not having contact with meat. We're going to Pilot Hill, like you wanted."

"I'm sorry, but we're not allowed contact with anything to do with meat. If there's a remnant in that truck it could contaminate us. No, it's out of the question. Brother Zin Zan and I will walk up to Pilot Hill and meet you there."

"It's three miles away. It'll take you an hour to get there! Look, I got a better idea. You guys get in the front and we'll all get in the back. I don't mind being contaminated by meat. Rae?"

She nodded. The Brothers looked at each other and shrugged that the idea was okay with them. Which is how we ended up standing inside a cold empty truck holding on for dear life while getting real intimate with the smell of fresh beef and etcetera. Then about three minutes after the ride began, the only little light bulb back there that lit anything flickered-flickered-flickered and went out. Poof—total blackness.

"Real cozy back here, huh?" Vito said from somewhere nearby in the blackness.

"I can't see a damned thing."

"Not much to see. Just a bunch of empty space."

"Bill?" Rae's voice was small, like she was far away.

"Yeah?"

"I'm scared now. I don't think I want to go."

"Why's that? You were fast enough taking their money," I threw in with a little twist-of-the-knife in my voice.

"I know, but I gotta bad feeling now."

"Why?"

"Because those men are so sure of themselves. They've got pockets full of money and can give away a thousand dollars just to prove they're right."

"Four thousand dollars."

Vito made his whistle again. "Four thousand smackers. Did you ever carry four thousand dollars in your pocket? From the way they talked, it sounds like these guys do it every day. Kind of tempting when you think about it, you know?"

The darkness felt like it was suddenly heavier. So did the silence that followed what he'd said.

"What's your point?"

Vito tried to sound light but I heard the rats gathering on the other side of his voice. "Well, there's twenty thousand dollars sitting up there next to the driver. That's a lot of money."

"Bill—"

A hand touched me on the elbow and I assumed it was Rae's. I patted it until I realized it was too damned big for her hand and that it was Vito's instead.

I gave him a fast hard poke that couldn't have felt good. "Just what the Hell are you doing?"

"Nothing, man. Take it easy. It's dark in here, in case you didn't notice. I'm just trying to get my bearings.

"Well, get them away from me."

Why was he touching my elbow in the dark like that? And why was he making suggestions like maybe we should do something criminal about the twenty thousand dollars sitting in the Brothers' pockets at that very minute?

"Bill?"

"What Rae?" I said it pretty harshly, and angry voices are not that woman's favorite music. Sure enough, her answer came back at me like a flame-thrower.

"Don't you talk to me like that, Bill Gallatin! I don't like any of this. I want to go home. They can have their money back. I don't care. I just want to go back home now."

"Well honey, wait till we stop and they let us out. There's not much we can do till then."

"But we should be there by now. It's not that far. How come we haven't gotten there yet?"

I took a deep breath and licked my tongue back and forth across my lips, which is usually my procedure when I'm trying hard to stay calm. When I was sure I had my temper back on its leash I spoke. "I don't know why we aren't there yet, sweetheart. Pilot Hill's on the other side of town, remember. It takes a little while to get there."

"I want to get out of this truck right now; it's creepy and weird."

"Well sure it is. It's pitch black and we're standing in the back of a meat truck!"

"I don't mean that."

"Well what do you mean, Rae?" I lost my composure and my voice came out sounding damned irritated.

The next thing I know, my good wife's crying because she's scared, while at the same time I'm realizing this is all my fault, basically. I was the one who invited Brother Brooks and Zin Zan into our house not one hour ago. Before them everything was fine—we had a new refrigerator, we were shooting the breeze with the movers, and finishing our coffee.

Before I had a chance to say anything more, the truck began slowing. Then it stopped with a jerk that sent us all flying, judging by the sound of things around me. Vito yelled "Hey!" and Rae squealed, but I was quiet because it was all I could do to stop from falling on my face. My mother used to say never try standing up when the bus is going around a corner. Now I had one to add to that—never try keeping your balance in the dark. You need to see stuff so you can judge angles and tilts. At that moment I couldn't see anything so I was groping out with my hands, basically reaching for whatever would have me.

Unfortunately I found something.

What's warm and furry and licks your hand in the dark? A dark that had gotten ten times darker because all of a sudden it was totally silent in there except for the sound of me being slurpy-licked by an eager tongue.

"Shit!" I yanked my hand and body back like they'd been in fire and doing so, lost my balance after touching something warm and furry. I didn't know where I was falling because it was whoa-whoa-whoa backward. But still it was away from the tongue and that was all that mattered.

I fell on my ass. One of those breath-death drops where you land bullseye on the tenderest part of your spine. It sent an atomic jolt of pain up to the tips of my ears and then shivered back down my body, gradually looking for a place to stop.

When I could breathe again around the pain, I said "Rae?" Nothing. Then I said "Vito?" Silence. Nothing but me, the dark and whatever thing had licked me.

"Mr. Gallatin? My name is Beeflow. I'll be your guide now."

The voice was right next to my ear. Right next to it. I was on my ass, remember. It was a nice voice—smooth and low—but without warning hearing it so close to me in that all-out darkness, know what my first thought was? The very first one?

Is it little?

Is this thing standing up, or bending down to talk into my ear? How big is it? Not what is it, or how did it suddenly get two inches from my ear. How big is it?

Then I tried sliding away from whatever it was.

"Don't be afraid."

"Get away from me! Where are the others? Rae?"

"You needn't worry; they're fine."

"Prove they're fine."

"Bill, we're fine."

"Rae?"

"Yes, sweetie, don't worry. I'm in Los Angeles."

"What? Where? What?"

"Yes! I'm at the Universal Studios tour with Vito. We're about to go into the *Back to the Future* ride. I'm so excited!"

Her voice sounded like she was talking on a telephone. In her background was a lot of noise—kids shouting and laughter, some sounds I didn't recognize. Then to my amazement, I heard the bold theme song to *Back to the Future*. I recognized it right away. We owned the video and would pop it in the machine pretty often because it was one of our favorites.

"Bill? We're going in now. I'll talk to you later, honey, and give you a full report. Do you have the tickets, Vito?"

"Got 'em right here."

The son of a bitch! Ever since we got married six years ago Rae and I have talked about going to L.A. and especially to the Universal Studios Tour to take that ride because we like the movie so much. Now here was some moving man I didn't even know accompanying my wife instead of me.

I was so angry at the thought that for a few seconds I forgot where I was and what had been going on.

"You see Mr. Gallatin, everything is all right. By the time your wife's ride is over, you'll know everything and the two of you will be back home again. But in the meantime she can be having the time of her life. Do something she's always wanted to do. Isn't that super? We try to make everybody happy."

"No it's not super! I was supposed to be there with her! How come Vito gets to go while I'm here with a sore ass talking to you in the dark? Who are you anyway? Can't you turn on some lights?"

"You wouldn't want that. You don't want to see me." He said it quietly and kind of to-himself sad.

"Why's that?"

It was quiet a minute. Then he said something that slammed shut every door in my head. "Do you ever look in the toilet after you go?"

"What?"

"Sneak a peek at what your body didn't want. Check to see what your stomach set free?"

"For God's sake! That's disgusting!"

"Tell the truth now, son."

"You're not my doctor! Why should I tell you that? I've had enough. I want out. How do I open this door?"

"If you open it you'll see me and that will be the end for you." The tone of his voice said this is the truth—don't doubt it. "I asked about looking in the toilet because in a way that's what I am. I'm everything about yourself you don't like, Mr. Gallatin. I am the shit you look at in the toilet. Once a delicious meal, now just brown stink."

I would have laughed in his face if I could have seen it. But since it was so dark, I barked out a loud phony one to give him the same effect. "You're nuts. And why did you lick me? What was that all about?"

Now he laughed. "That wasn't me—it was your old friend Cyrus. Who's right next to me. Remember him?"

"No. Who's Cyrus?"

"Why he's your soul, Mr. Gallatin. Don't you recognize it when you are touched by your own soul?"

"My soul's warm and furry and has a tongue like a dog? I don't think so, Mr. Beef-low."

"Beeflow. You disappoint me, sir. Shall I give you a demonstration?"

"You can give me the key out of here."

"All right."

Suddenly the truck door opened—bam—and I didn't think twice. I ran for the daylight and jumped off the lip of the back of the truck. Something smart told me don't look back. Was there really a Beeflow or a Cyrus or anything else to further cook my already-barbecued brain? I didn't want to find out. The only thing on my mind at the moment was to get the fuck out of there.

When my feet touched pavement I started running. I was so bent on getting someplace, anyplace away from there that I didn't really look around. Why should I? This was my town. I'd lived here all my life. All I had to do was grab a quick glimpse of what was around me and I'd know exactly where I was. And just when the thought of taking that quick glimpse came to me, I heard something coming up very fast behind me. The sound it made scared me right down to the basement of my blood cells.

And whatever it was got closer while I ran faster, as fast as I could. Just as I cried out because I knew I was caught, doomed, the thing jumped on my back and knocked me flat on my face.

It was heavy. Huge. Whatever hit me had a lot of weight and that fact made it a ton more scary.

So I stayed down, a mouse with a cat on its back, my cheek flat against the hot street asphalt. I could smell it, along with other things. Something in my mouth was bleeding, my nose honked hurt. I tasted blood; pain flew around my face. I smelled the hot street.

"Pose, get down boy. Come back here." The man's voice wasn't familiar but just hearing the thing on my back had a name, a name I understood, made me feel sort of better. But "Pose" stayed standing on me and did not move an inch of its heavy self.

"Damn it, dog, what'd I just say to you? Get over here!"

The weight left and I was free again. Looking up a little, I saw four large hairy paws moving away. Slowly I put my palms flat on the ground and pushed myself to my knees. My arms were shaking because I guess I wasn't finished being scared.

"Jeez buddy, I'm terribly sorry about that. Pose gets carried away sometimes when he sees someone running like you were. He wants to get in on the fun. Still pretty much a puppy." The voice tried to be friendly and apologizing at the same time. I was finally going to kick someone's ass: Pose's Daddy's.

Standing again, I brushed off my hands and looked up real slow, Clint Eastwood-style.

Five feet away a giant Irish wolfhound stood next to a nothing-looking man. Both of them were on fire. I mean, both man and dog were in big bright flames. The guy was smiling and came toward me. Before I could do anything he stuck out a burning hand to shake and said, "I'm Mel Shaveetz. Nice to meet you. We just moved in here a couple of days ago. Haven't met many people yet."

Taking one giant step back, I jammed both hands as deep into my pockets as they'd go. Through his flames Mel frowned until it dawned on him. "Oh for God's sake, I'm sorry!" He blew on his index finger. All the flames on him went out like he'd blown out a birthday candle. Like he was blowing himself out.

"I keep forgetting. Sorry about that."

"Who are you?"

Instead of answering, he reached down and squeezed the dog's nose. Its flames went out too. "Mel Shaveetz. And this is Posafega."

"You were on fire!"

"Yeah well, that happens where we come from."

"And where's that?"

"Hell."

"You mean you're dead?"

"Couldn't put on this kind of light show if I were alive. Did you think I was one of those monks who burn themselves alive?"

"You and the dog are dead?"

"No, I am. Pose is just a hound from Hell. He's my roommate."

"A Hellhound!"

"That's right."

"How come I didn't get burned when he was standing on my back?"

"Because you're not dead."

"It just looks like a big wolfhound to me."

Mel shrugged. "Nobody ever said what breed Hellhounds had to be. You want to come in the house and have a beer?"

"Which house do you mean? I know everyone who lives around here."

He pointed to a brown and white saltbox across the street. "You're looking at it—number eighty-eight."

"Eighty-eight? I know who lives in eighty-eight and it isn't you. Chris and Terry Rolfe live there."

He looked away and tried to make his eyes busy. "Yeah well, not anymore. They moved."

I remembered what our refrigerator movers had said about seeing piles of people's belongings left out on the street. And I remembered the Brothers saying that was because the dead were being moved back to earth from Hell.

"I went to school with Chris Rolfe. He's lived in this town as long as I have. I'd know if he was planning to leave."

"Look, you want that beer or not?"

I wanted to check out the inside of that house. I didn't believe for a minute what he was saying about Rolfe. As far as I knew, that house still belonged to a living guy I saw at least once a week for the past twenty years.

We walked slowly up to the front door, Posafega keeping us company all the way. Not only was that dog big, it was also seriously ugly. Its hair looked like stuffing out of an eighty-year-old mattress. Its face was thin enough to open a letter. The animal was so big that if it stood on its hind legs and had a good hook shot, it could have played pro basketball. So that was a Hellhound. I said the word inside my mouth to myself—Hellhound.

Just as we were walking in the door, I smelled smoke. Sure enough, Mel was beginning to go up in flames again. "Hey man, you're on fire."

"Yeah well, I'll fix it when we get inside." He kept moving while his flames kept rising. The big dog's, too.

Remember I said we loved the movie *Back to the Future*? Well my wife and I are just overall big movie fans so it isn't the only video we own. And that's where my next problem arrived. I wasn't about to pass up the chance to see the inside of a dead man's house and look around for Chris Rolfe. Plus the invitation was offered on a silver platter. But when I think about it now, maybe going in there wasn't the best idea I ever had. Because here's what happened next: opening the front door, Mel and flame-dog marched in, no big deal. A lot more carefully I followed but only got a few feet into the place before I froze and my jaw dropped below sea level.

I recognized what I saw immediately because I'd seen it so often before and had always wished I could go there. Now I was. The inside of Mel's house, the house that used to belong to Chris Rolfe, was now Rick's American Bar from the movie *Casablanca*.

While my brain tried to swallow that fact, Mel sat down at the white piano and began playing the movie's theme son, "As Time Goes By." He wasn't bad either. Then he began to sing it but I was walking around the room so I didn't pay much attention. The dog plumped down on the floor and went to sleep. I was in such shock that I didn't realize until later that both of them lost their flames as soon as we got into the house. Like once they were home they were normal again. Although my idea of normal that day had taken a vacation to another planet.

As far as I could see every detail in the room was perfect, right down to the ashtrays on the table and full bottles behind the bar. The room was empty except for us, which gave it a whole different feeling from what it was like in the movie. Other than that though, this definitely was Rick's place. If Humphrey Bogart had walked in at that minute I would not have been one bit surprised.

Mel finished playing with a big right-hand display—DONG!—and afterwards

392 • JONATHAN CARROLL

everything was very quiet in there. Naturally I was tempted to say real coolly, "Play it again, Sam," but I didn't.

Instead I asked, "What is all this?"

"It's Rick's. Don't you know *Casablanca*? The movie?

"Yes I know *Casablanca*! That wasn't my question. How come you live in this house now and it looks like a movie set instead of someone's living room?"

"Before we come back, they ask us what kind of décor we would like where we live. We get to choose."

"Choose what?"

"The décor! What'd I just tell you?"

"I'm very confused, Mel."

He took a deep breath like I was the stupidest being he'd ever met and my dumbness was using up his air supply. "Before we come back here, to Earth, they ask what kind of décor we'd like in the house they assign us. We get to choose. I said Rick's American Bar from the movie because that was the coolest place on Earth."

"How long ago did you die?"

"Last Friday."

"How?"

"I drowned in Aqaba, scuba diving. I stepped on a poisonous sea urchin and had an allergic reaction. Pretty pathetic way to go."

"And you went to Hell?"

"Straight to. Do not pass go, do not collect two hundred dollars."

"But you're back here a week later?"

"Not by choice, pal. Not by choice." The doorbell rang. Mel held up one finger for quiet. "Let me just get that. What kind of beer do you want? I've got everything here. There's even a good Polish one. Zee-veetch or some name like that."

He left the room and the animal followed. I wondered if it was some kind of satanic chaperone. What kind of visitors did the dead have? That thought grew so fast and so horror-movie-ugly in my head that in the minute or so it took Mel to return, I was almost hyperventilating. What kind of visitors DID the dead have? Good God, what if they were—

"It's for you."

I opened my mouth, closed it, opened again. "Me? No one knows I'm here."

"Yeah, well, obviously they do. They say they want to talk to you. Two goofy-looking guys with shaggy haircuts."

"Brooks and Zin Zan!"

"Whatever." Mel shrugged.

I started out but stopped short when I thought of something. "Were—were you on fire when they saw you?"

"Sure. Anytime I step out of this house I start to burn. One of the many drawbacks of being back on Earth again." He sounded angry about it, put out.

"Did you like it in Hell?"

"I can't say much about it because that's against the rules, you being alive and all." He looked left and right, as if some enemy might be listening. "But I will tell you this—ever think maybe that Hell stuff you've always heard is a bunch of crap? Maybe it's given all that bad press because they want to keep people OUT of there? That if people really knew what it was like, an awful lot of them might kill themselves to get there sooner?"

The dog started growling. It was not a sound you ever want to hear. Worse, it was staring at Mel while it snarled. That monster's lip was curled up and twitching like it was going to attack any second.

"Shut up, Pose. How about that cat you told the other day? Don't you think I was listening?"

"Whoa! You and the dog understand each other?"

"Different rules apply when you're dead. Yes we understand each other. He's pissed off at me for telling you about Hell. It doesn't matter. You'd better go see your friends. I'll get the beers." He went to the bar and I left the room.

Sure enough, Brooks and Zin Zan were standing just on the other side of the open doorway. They lit up when they saw me. I gotta admit I was happy to see them too, considering everything that had been happening.

"Hi guys, what are you doing here?"

Both opened their mouths and started talking but I didn't hear a thing. Their faces and hand movements were busy, too, but came with no soundtrack. After a while I pointed to my ears and made a face that said nothing's coming though. They seemed to understand and gestured for me to step outside.

Just as I was about to do exactly that, Mel Shaveetz's voice said from about five inches behind my ear, "I wouldn't go out there if I were you."

Still looking at the Brothers, I asked why not? I don't like being told what to do; especially not by dead people who live on movie sets with burning dogs.

"Because once you do, you can't come back in here again."

"Why would I want to?"

"Because the answers you need are in here, not out there with them." Mel's voice was snotty and know-it-all, all "You dumbbell—I'm smarter than you are" tone. Which I hate. Without even bothering to look back at the asshole, I stepped toward the Brothers. I heard a terrible savage growl from back in the house. The hairy Devil dog was coming for me again.

Adding to that, the Brothers' eyeballs widened till they almost popped out of their heads at whatever it was they saw coming up behind me. Then those holy cowards turned on their four heels and ran. Me too. Not that I expected to get very far. I knew how that giant could run. I'd felt its weight pressing down on my back. Now I knew any second it'd be on me again doing a lot worse than before.

I'm running and know I'll be caught but I'll fight back. What else could I do? For the first sprint I ran looking at the ground. That's how I always ran fastest as a kid. No distractions, just watch the ground straight in front of you and move like lightning in front of thunder.

But eventually I realized even through all the fear that nothing had caught or eaten me yet. So I looked up, wondering why not? The Brothers were a hundred feet ahead, standing still now and facing me. Why had they stopped when a moment ago they were so scared? And where was that Posafega?

I looked over my shoulder cringing because it might just be waiting to give me a nasty shock. But the only surprise was that that dog wasn't there. "What is going on?"

"We were afraid we wouldn't be able to get you out of there, sir. That would have been big trouble for all concerned. But here you are—you made it!"

Zin Zan looked like he was about to kiss me, he was so happy.

Instead of answering, I looked at Rolfe's house again to make sure we were talking about the same thing. Only when I was bringing my eyes back around to the Brothers did I see a street sign: Pilot Hill. That's where we'd been planning to go in the first place before all this other shit started happening.

"Is this what you wanted to show me? Rolfe's house? Is that what this is all about?"

"No sir, actually it was someone else's house we wanted to show you up here. But I don't think you need to see it now to believe what we were saying before."

"True. So who else lost their house on this street?"

They looked at each other to see which of them was going to drop the bad news bomb. Zin Zan said, "Everyone."

"What?"

"That's right." Brooks moved his arm in a way that took in the whole area. "Every house on Pilot Hill has been taken over."

"I don't believe it." I looked around again to make sure that dog wasn't sneaking up on me from some secret angle.

"It's true, Mr. Gallatin. If you'd like, go look in anyone's window here and you'll see."

"I will do exactly that." I crossed the street to my friend Carl Hull's house and looked in his window because I knew exactly what it looked like inside. What I noticed first was everything was black and white in there. Or I should say in black and white. I knew Carl's house and this wasn't it. I stepped back and looked at the façade. This was Hull's house, all right. So I looked in the window again. Carl's wife Naomi loves yellow things—furniture, pillows, rugs. But there wasn't an inch of yellow anything in there. No couch, curtains, nothing—only black and white.

The living room was full of old fat furniture; most of it covered in some thick material like velvet. Like your Grandma's house. Pure old people's furniture. The Hull house I knew had a few pieces of cheap yellow furniture, a round "Garfield" rug in front of a TV set as big as you could get. That machine was Carl's pride and you had to give the man credit—he didn't scrimp when it came to home entertainment. But where was that big Sony screen today?

"Sherlock Holmes."

I jumped. "Don't do that, Brooks! Don't sneak up on me. My eggs have been scrambled enough for one day. Besides, what are you talking about?"

"This house—the woman who moved in here chose the décor of the first Sherlock Holmes film. Starring Clive Brook, Ernest Torrence—"

"Where's Carl and Naomi?"

"At Lake of the Ozarks on vacation. They'll be coming back soon to this ugly surprise."

"Where's their stuff? Their belongings?"

"The new tenant had it hauled away this morning."

"Why is everything black and white in there?"

Brooks seemed surprised at my question. "Because that film was in black and white. The new occupant wanted things to look exactly like the film."

"Well, *Casablanca* was black and white too. But Mel's house was in color. You saw it."

Brooks nodded. "He chose the colorized version. He's not a purist. I hope you don't mind me saying this, Mr. Gallatin, but it would be very good if we got a move on."

"Where to now?"

"Back to your house."

"What's at my house that wasn't there an hour ago?"

"A moving van."

Three sets of eyes bounced back and forth, back and forth like Flubber for a while before any of the mouths connected to them had more to say.

"They're taking over my house now?"

"Yes sir. That's why we came to warn you this morning."

"You knew about this? You knew it would happen?" We started walking—fast.

"We always know it'll happen—just not when. We didn't think it would be so soon and in such large numbers. That's why we go door to door. The problem is no one ever believes what we say until it's too late. So Beeflow decided to change the way we do things because the situation is now getting critical."

"Was that really Beeflow who talked to me back in the truck?"

"Yes sir. Was Cyrus there too?"

"How do you know about that? I thought was my soul!"

"It is. Did it lick your hand in the dark?" He smiled and shook his head like he'd just found a fond memory in his pocket. "That's its way of greeting you, telling you it's there. It happens that way to us all. But 'Cyrus' is only Beeflow's nickname for it. The real name of the human soul is Kopum, pronounced Coe-poon. You'll learn all about that later."

"Then why does he call it Cyrus?"

"It's easier to accept in the beginning. The name sounds a lot less strange than Kopum. People like feeling safe, especially when it comes to their souls."

We hurried back and only when we were halfway home did I think about what I was doing or the fact I had accepted everything they'd told me as cold hard fact. The name of my soul was Cyrus, but not really because it's actually Kopum. Okay. Dead people were moving into my house? If you say so. The craziness of it all made me slow some but not stop. I'd seen and heard enough in the last hour to know parts of my world had suddenly gone seriously damned wobbly, but this? Could it really be true?

"Look at that."

I was so deep into thinking about all of this that my brain didn't click until my eyes saw the scene in front of us. And then the first thing I did was burst out laughing. There's this guy I know and work with named Eric Dickey. Just saying that name makes my lips squinch up like I ate something bad. I hate that son of a bitch. You don't want to get me started on him because I've got a whole alphabet of reasons why I do not wish him well—in this life or any other. It's enough to say that we started disliking each other in ninth grade and only got better at it as the years passed.

Anyway, Eric Dickey and his stumpy wife Sue live in a nice house a few blocks from ours. And I've got to admit it is a handsome place. Eric is a foreman at my company who knows how to kiss ass well enough to get promotions while the rest of us are worrying half the time about what will happen if there are layoffs. But the fact of the matter is the Dickeys to have a really nice house and at work Eric is always bragging about the new this or new that they bought for their place. They don't have any kids so they go all-out buying top of the line air conditioners, lawnmowers, gas grills—the kind of expensive things that can be seen from the street and coveted by the rest of us slobs. A real asshole.

So anyway, I'm laughing now because what do you know—old Dickey's stuff is piled on the street in front of his beautiful house. This time seeing a pile like that doesn't surprise me so much as make my heart throw a fist in the air and yell ALL RIGHT! Maybe this Hell business isn't so bad after all. But that feeling was short lived because just as I was relishing seeing kiss-ass Dickey's stuff dumped out on the street, who should walk around from the back of his house but a caveman!

So help me God. Tat sounds totally nuts but it is the truth. And you've seen him before in every caveman movie you ever watched. The fucker is hunched over in a sort of monkey scrunch and has got so much hair growing on his body you can't really make out where the head ends and the rest begins. I mean this fellow is ALL Hair and even when he looks at you, his face is hard to make out because everything is so completely covered in fur.

Now if that wasn't enough, this whatever it is, this creature looks at us and growls like a monster. No, he more like roars like a lion and it's one loud ugly sound. Then he threw up two furry arms that looked like a couple of tree trunks with brown moss growing on them. I was sure he was going to come charging at us because he thought we were going to steal his place from him. But as far as I was concerned, he was the best neighbor in town if he had evicted

Eric Dickey on his bragging ass. When I thought for sure Mr. Caveman was coming for us, I put up my hand—palm out. I was even about to say "How!" like cowboys do to Indians when they meet up on the prairie. Where that idea came from in my brain I do not know, except maybe I thought you greeted dinosaur eaters the same way you did Commanches. Even though the two groups were only about a few million years apart on the time line. When he roared again I thought it was time to get out of there so I started off.

"Wait, don't run. He can't bother you." Zin Zan called out. I stopped but my feet weren't convinced. They kept going up and down, sort of running in place just in case he was wrong. "How do you know that?"

"Because we're with you. We know how to keep him away. You're protected so long as you don't go into his house. That's why it was so dangerous when you went into that other man's place."

"But where's Dickey and his wife?"

"Hiding in their basement."

"No shit?" Ear to ear I was grinning. Ear to ear.

"You're going to have to stop using that kind of language, Mr. Gallatin. It just won't do."

I wanted to say "fuck you," but the picture of Eric hiding in his basement from a furry caveman, while all his high-priced possessions sat in a heap on the curb—that was happiness enough for the moment to keep my dirty words in my mouth. "So dead people from all the different ages are being sent back here? Not just recent ones like Mel?"

Brook shook his head and frowned. "That is correct. It's totally chaotic but only part of the problem we face. Look! That is exactly what I'm talking about!" From behind the house smoke and flame started coming around the corner. And not just "too many burgers on the barbecue" stuff—these were big impressive clouds of brown smoke and some yellow flame coming fast and scary toward us.

"What's happening?"

Zin Zan pointed at the caveman. "He probably started a fire back there. He can't help it—guys like him don't know any better."

"Should we do something about it?"

From the distance came faint siren sounds.

"No, someone's obviously called it in already. We've got to get to your house now."

"Yeah, but what's going to happen when the firetrucks get here and have to deal with Mr. One Million B.C.?" I pointed at you-know-who.

"That's their problem, not ours. Right now we've got to get you back home."

We started walking again but I kept turning around to look at that hairy guy standing in front of Eric's house. He didn't move. The sirens got louder, nearer. Were those voices coming from inside the house? Was someone shouting in there?

"Come on, Mr. Gallatin. There's no time."

I looked at the Brothers. I looked at the caveman. I looked at the house, the smoke behind him. I knew I was about to do something really stupid and probably unnecessary.

"We can't just go."

Both Brothers turned toward the siren sounds and gestured toward them. "They're coming now. They'll be here any minute."

"But what happens in the meantime? Maybe they'll die down there of smoke inhalation or whatever. Don't you watch those emergency rescue shows on TV? Every minute counts."

"Every minute counts for you too. You have to save your home! Do you understand that? They are taking your house!"

I lowered my head and started walking in the wrong direction. One of them touched my arm. I shook him off. Eric Dickey was a turd but I wasn't going to let him die. Maybe I was being stupid because he probably would have been saved just fine without my help. But I didn't want ugly things on my conscience. I didn't want to live the rest of my life with a picture pinned to the inside of my brain of a man and his weasel-eyed wife lying facedown forever in a smoky basement because I needed to get home.

"We won't be able to help if you go in there. We can't go with you!"

"Then just wait out here. I'll be right back." I kept walking. The caveman saw me but seemed to have his mind on other things. He lifted his head and sniffed the air like an animal—nose up high, making these little up and down jerks every now and again. Sniff-jerk-sniff-jerk. Then he turned and ran around the house to the back.

Which was just fine with me because it gave me free access to the front door. The moment B.C. disappeared from sight, I ran for it. Behind me the Brothers were hollering now, "Don't!" and, "Please come back!" But I was already there. The bad news was that the door was locked. The good news? An aluminum baseball bat was leaning against the house. Without a second's hesitation I picked it up. Not a second too soon because I heard a rough animal grunt behind me. Not too close but close enough to have me bringing that bat up to "play ball!" height by the time I'd swiveled around to face that grunt. In shock I almost dropped the damn thing seeing what I did.

The caveman was about ten feet away. In his hands was the charred body of what could only have been a dog. In fact it was definitely a dog because the head wasn't as grilled as the rest of the black, still-smoking body. I could make out that it was once upon a time a beagle or some such. That's what the fire behind the house probably started off being—he was cooking some poor sucker's Lassie or Snoopy. Rest in Peace, Snoopy. Bet you never thought you'd end up lunch.

I didn't have any time to think about it because B.C. dropped his Happy Meal and came at me. I swung the bat at his head. Lucky for him, he was able to turn a bit at the last second so instead of hitting a home run I only knocked him flat.

The clang of metal-on-head sounded like a cooking pot dropped on concrete. I knew I hadn't killed him because he was already dead, but also because he was twitching and frothing up ugly stuff out at the mouth. I stood over him a few seconds to see if he'd get up again. But most of him was on vacation and what wasn't, was busy jerking around.

So I swung that fine silver bat again, this time through one of the large windows into what I assumed was the Dickey living room. After the first crash of glass, I knocked out some slivers still stuck in the window frame and after a last glance at him just to be sure, I climbed in.

I've never been to a jungle. I've never been most places but that's okay because I don't speak other languages and the idea of a passport makes me nervous. But as soon as I put both feet down inside the Dickey's house I was hit by a wet tropical heat the likes of which I'd never experienced. Everything around me was like this 3-D green. A green so strong it almost hurt my eyes. When I took a step forward, I was hit in the face by some kind of nasty thick vine that was a whole new scare in itself. When I managed to push that out of the way I tried to get my bearings looking left and right but all I saw was green everything and sounds that screamed and screeched and cawed and pretty much made me deaf. I was in a jungle somehow and as that sunk into my brain I somehow remembered a line from school that just popped up out of nowhere but said it all—the forest primeval.

Mel Shaveetz had said they got to choose a décor when they came back to Earth. So of course a caveman would want one exactly like where he had been living. In the forest primeval. The Earth a million years ago or fifty thousand or whatever.

Instead of Eric Dickey's living room, I was back on Earth a zillion years ago, standing like a rabbit frozen in the headlights. And there were no walls in this "décor," it wasn't limited to a few closed-in rooms like Rick's Bar. Everywhere I looked was jungle that went out in every direction with no end in sight. This wasn't a room—this was forever. Right about then the next words came to my mind.

"Jurassic Park," I said out loud but couldn't hear very well for all the screeching going on around me.

"Dinosaurs!" Monsters with teeth as big as the baseball bat I still held. Walking houses with serious appetites for anything fleshy. I had to get out of here. In a panic I turned around, planning to go right back through the window into my world. But there was no window. Only trees and vines and green and noise.

Eventually my brain stopped its own screeching in fear. And although I was scared shitless of what might come stomping out of the trees at any minute, I was losing control so fast that there was only one thing left to do—close my eyes. A trick that almost always worked for me when things got so bad I could feel life unraveling. Close my eyes and say, "I am driving my life. I am steering this car. I CONTROL THINGS."

I started the "I am—" but it was drowned out by the terrible new sound of something very big—and near—coming my way through the jungle. THUMP THUMP THUMP. It was running! As huge as it sounded in the not-so-far distance, the speed of its footsteps said it was running at me. It was my turn to be lunch.

"What are the six questions?"

How did I hear that? The voice had spoken calmly and in no hurry. But I heard it clearly above everything else. What six questions? Who is this? Were they the last words I'd ever hear? WAS IT GOD?

"No, Mr. Gallatin, it's Beeflow. What are the six questions?"

Thump Thump Thump. I heard bushes crashing, birds crying out like they do when they're disturbed or attacked. This monster was closer, it was almost here.

"WHAT ARE THE SIX QUESTIONS?"

"I don't know what the fuck you're talking about! Get me out of here!"

And then the biggest shock of all—I heard him sigh! A disappointed sigh. The sigh of a teacher when you've answered a question wrong in class.

"All right, I'll help you this one time but not again. Name one experience from your past you wish you could repeat. That is the third question."

"Are you nuts? Now? The thing's coming! Get me out of here!"

"Then answer the question, and quickly."

"An experience I want to repeat? I don't know. Jeez, I don't know. Help me, willya?" My voice sounded like one of the scared birds up in the trees.

"No, help yourself—answer that question."

And when he said that, an answer came so clear and calm to my mind that I was surprised I hadn't known it immediately. "I wish I could have sex again for the first time with Rae. That was the best night of my life."

"Very very good. Now look in your hand."

I looked, even though the bushes nearby rustled hard which meant whatever monster was coming had arrived. Instead of the silver baseball bat, I held a black metal cylinder about two feet long. The dinosaur burst out at me like a rocket with legs. Its teeth were even bigger than I had thought they'd be. Its open mouth looked ten feet wide. I didn't even have a chance to raise the cylinder up to do whatever it might do to fight off the thing. Because it was there.

And then gone.

That's right—it whizzed right by me. Whatever kind of prehistoric piece of shit it was, the creature ran by and went crashing on into the jungle behind me. It didn't even stop to have a look or say hello. Not that I was disappointed. I stood there looking after it and then I looked at the black cylinder in my hand, trying to figure out how it played into all this. No answer came. It was just this metal thing that a while before had been a baseball bat.

I stood there listening while Tyrannosaurus-whatever galloped farther away into the jungle. And then it became quiet around me, or as quiet as a place like that is ever going to be. It took me some more time to detox from the scare that was still sending fireballs of adrenaline to all corners of my body. I stood a while longer and then sort of collapsed on the ground in a heap, dropping the cylinder as I did.

I looked at it and wondered what kind of magic had changed it from a baseball bat into this without my ever having felt it. I wondered if it had somehow saved me from being eaten. Or had answering Beeflow's question been the reason? What were the six questions he was talking about? What was this cylinder lying on the ground a foot away? How was I going to get out of the forest primeval and back to my world?

"Don't turn around,"

I didn't but sure was tempted. It was Beeflow again. "Why can't I look at you?"

"Because I told you before, Mr. Gallatin, I am everything ugly about you. I'm your shit in the toilet, the dark side of your moon, the worst lies you've told, the hurt you dropped on others. I am everything bad about you and if you want to look that square in the face then go ahead. But I warn you, looking your own evil in the eye is as bad as looking at Medusa. It will wreck you, turn part of you into stone."

"And you say you're me?"

"Only in part. I've chosen to take all that's bad in you for the time being so you can face challenges other than your own."

"Are you, uh, human?"

"I was once, but am no longer. Years ago I had a vision and it changed me forever."

"What kind of vision?"

"You're looking at it now."

I happened to be looking at the cylinder next to me. "That thing? The baseball bat?"

"Yes. I was in a flea market in London and on a table amongst other junk was a brass object. I worked as a travel agent but my great hobbies were inventing and the history of tools. So I was well versed in the function of all sorts of machinery, archaic tools, and the like. I was no newcomer to obscure gadgets. But for the life of me I could not understand what purpose this gizmo served. Written on the side of it in thick letters were the words 'Heidelberg Cylinder.' I picked it up and turned it over and over in my hands but its purpose still baffled me. I was perplexed and fascinated, so I paid three pounds and put it in my pocket.

"When I returned home to America and was able to look through the reference books in my library, I discovered something staggering: The Heidelberg Cylinder had been used in every great modern invention. The cotton gin, the first steam engine, the telephone, internal combustion engine. You name it and a version of the cylinder was one of the components. It was the essential piece in every one of those innovations. It was the things that made them all work. I was astonished and then utterly skeptical so I researched further. Different versions of the cylinder were used in the first telegraph, the television, computers. Sometimes it was made of a different metal, or Bakelite, then plastic, carbon—you get the point. It was the part that made these earth-shaking inventions work, Mr. Gallatin, but no one had ever noted the connection. One man-made object made all these things possible.

"I couldn't believe that no one had ever made the discovery. And then it hit me—no one was supposed to make the discovery! The Heidelberg Cylinder is meant to be invented again and again in its different guises and then put into the workings of whatever new different machines we dream up in the future.

"Because do you know what the Cylinder really is? The concrete proof of our immortality. The result of the human mind and spirit working as one to solve problems and overcome them. Any problems. Physical proof of the fact we can do anything we want, even live forever if we choose, if we set our minds to it."

I looked at it and rubbed my mouth. "That thing?"

"Yes, that thing."

I picked it up, turned it over. It was black and there was nothing written on it. Definitely not any "Heidelberg Cylinder."

"How come it's black and there's no writing on it?"

"Because once you realize what it is, it changes into something else. Something someone else will need to discover its importance. For me it was the brass object I described. For the person who had it before you it turned into a sixteenth-century Persian lock. For you it became a baseball bat."

"Then what is it now?"

"I don't know. Probably something from the future."

Reaching out to pick it up, I stopped when he said that. "But I didn't discover anything with the baseball bat. Definitely not any of that stuff you were saying about man's immortality: I just brained the caveman with it."

"Yes, but that's because I've chosen to intervene. There simply isn't enough time for it to happen in the slow and proper way it should. Mankind is in jeopardy and we must work quickly to avoid a catastrophe. I'll tell you the end of my story briefly and you will understand.

"When I grasped the extraordinary importance of the Heidelberg Cylinder, I became obsessed with my search and found it again and again the further I looked. But what was I to do with my discovery? Who should I tell and in what context?"

I had to interrupt. "When did you turn into, uh, what you are?"

"Once we've learned about the Cylinder, all of us change eventually."

That made me stand up. "What do you mean? Change how?"

"It varies from person to person. I can't say how it will affect you."

I was getting nervous again. "But what about Brooks and Zin Zan? They're both normal. They're weird but they're normal."

"For now, because both of them are new to the group. But sooner or later they will change and take on new forms. We call it 'hatching.' As I said, I can't tell you what forms either of them will take, but they will definitely metamorphose into something entirely different."

"Do they know that? Do they know they're going to change?"

"Of course Mr. Gallatin, and they welcome it."

"So does that mean now that I know, I'm going to change too?"

"Yes."

"But I don't want to change! I like my life."

"I'm afraid we need you more than you need your life. I want to show you something."

Before I had a chance to protest, everything changed. In an instant, a blink, half a breath, we went from jungle to paradise.

I'd heard it before but now I know it's true: paradise is what you want it to be. If you imagine angels with wings and harps sitting on gold clouds, that's what you'll see. Perfect gardens where lions dance the cha-cha while beautiful women serve you ice-cold rum? Then that's what it will be. I didn't know my paradise until I saw it. The moment I did, I knew this was it—nothing could be better.

An outdoor restaurant in the middle of the countryside somewhere. A few metal tables were set up under four big chestnut trees. The wind was blowing, tossing up the corners of the white tablecloths. The sun shone down through the leaves, flickering beautiful yellow, green and white light across everything.

A bunch of people were sitting at one of the tables having the best time laughing, eating and talking. A black guy was sitting at one end of the table playing a Gibson Hummingbird guitar softly but really well. A woman nearby kept jumping up from her place, hugging him and then sitting back down again.

The different colors and variety of food spread out for them across the table was amazing. All kinds of meats and salads, vegetables piled high, soups, cakes and pies. The breads alone would have kept you busy for days making sandwiches. Once you saw it you couldn't take your eyes off this—plenty. My mouth started watering. I knew it had to be the greatest food that ever was and to taste any bit of it would bring you to tears.

"Hey Bill, why're you standing over there like you're hypnotized? Get your ass over here and say hello." The man who spoke didn't just look like my father, it was him. He'd been dead eleven years.

I didn't move but just assumed Beeflow was nearby so I asked out loud, "Is it real? Is that really my Dad?"

"Yes. Look around the table. You know everyone there."

It was true. A girl I'd known and liked who'd died in a water skiing accident, my uncle Birmy next to my father, others. I did know everyone at that table.

Some better than others but I had known them all—when they were alive. When my father called out my name they looked over and smiled like seeing me was the best thing that had happened to them all day. It made me feel good and gave me the damned creeps at the same time.

"Welcome to Hell, Mr. Gallatin," Beeflow said.

Why did I already know that? How did I know that's what he was going to say and it wouldn't surprise me?

"It's the most wonderful place in the world because it's your most wonderful place. Everything is familiar here, you know everyone, the food is gorgeous—"

He was interrupted by the sound of the drowned girl laughing. It was the most beautiful, innocent, sexy laugh I'd ever heard. Her head was thrown back and she was laughing and all I could focus on was her long slim neck. Like everything else there, it was almost too much to take. Since when could the sight of a woman's bare neck send me over the moon?

"You see, it's already beginning to affect you. That's what is so splendid about it. Because everything here is yours, it would be so easy to slide right into this world and never want to go home."

"It really is Hell? This is where you go when you've been bad?"

"Yes. That's what Mel Shaveetz was saying to you and why the dog started growling at him. If people knew how marvelous this is, do you think they'd work hard at living? Or at being good, achieving something, working for one another? Too many of them would throw up their hands and just wait to die. Or they would kill themselves for the stupidest reasons just so they could come here earlier than planned."

"Everyone's Hell is this good?"

"Yes it is."

"Then what's Heaven like?"

"Infinitely better. But it is extremely hard to get into Heaven, Mr. Gallatin. It is almost impossible."

"But a person wins either way: Hell is great and Heaven is better."

"That should make no difference to you when you're alive. There is a purpose to living that is far more important than ending up comfortably dead."

"So what is the purpose of living?"

The people at the table seemed to have forgotten I was standing there and had gone back to enjoying their party. Some of them were singing now. The black guy was playing the Lovin' Spoonful song "Coconut Grove." Others were eating big fat chicken legs or steaks, slices of pie a la mode. More than anything I wanted to go over and join them. Like a hungry kid, I was itching to be at the table.

"Pay attention, Gallatin! Stop drooling over hamburgers. What I'm telling you is vitally important. People are alive because they have jobs to do. They are meant to improve and broaden the human experience as best they can. The Cylinder is concrete proof of that. After death, mankind comes here if they failed, or to Heaven if they succeeded. But if they knew about this, it would change everything.

"Dangerously few people would work hard, or dream, or love well and with all their hearts. Because no matter how they lived, they get this in the end.

"Mankind's progress has been slow but steady. But now Satan is attempting to change that. He says there is no more room in Hell and has begun moving the dead back to Earth in greater and greater numbers. Those who have already been sent were told the move wouldn't be permanent. Life on Earth is made as pleasant as possible for them by allowing them to create their environment.

"God cannot reason with Satan about this, but we know that is nothing new. This forced relocation has been going on for centuries, but until now God overlooked it because the few that were sent back to Earth were regarded by the living as lunatics and ignored. Not anymore."

"Why? Why is it happening?"

"Because Mankind no longer accepts the idea of Damnation. He no longer feels he deserves eternal suffering for what he did or did not do on Earth. Guilt has grown obsolete. In the past, people were so afraid of what would happen to them in the afterlife that they created the most frightening scenarios possible. So when they did die, naturally those things happened to them. They brought their worse nightmares along and they came true.

"No longer. For the common man today, a fire-and-brimstone Hell has become an old-fashioned idea, and Heaven is a child's dream."

"Because we live happier lives, we get to be happier dead?"

"Exactly, and Satan absolutely hates that. When suffering prevailed in Hell, he was satisfied. But since people create their own Hell from what they knew in life, in recent decades it has generally become a rather nice place. He cannot abide that. So he has changed the rules. He is sending the dead back to Earth en masse. And it is clear what effect that will have on things there."

"Why doesn't God stop him?"

"Because God wants us to stop him. It is part of our ongoing task."

"How? How are we supposed to stop the Devil?"

"We must come up with a plan. Perhaps many plans before one works effectively. Obviously some will work, others won't."

"Jeez, Bill, are we going to have to drag you over to the table with a rope? We even got your favorite over there—potato salad with extra horseradish in the sauce." My father was suddenly in front of me smiling that great old smile that had always made me want to climb in his lap and stay there forever.

"Dad, where's mom? Is she here?"

He smiled and threw a thumb over his shoulder for me to look there. Coming out of the restaurant was my mother. A cry rose up in my throat that I was just barely able to hold onto before it spilled out. There she was, looking like she did before the cancer ate her body. There she was in that red-and-white striped dress, all her black hair long and curly again. Best of all she was chubby like before—"pleasantly plump" as she called herself. Not the hairless stick-thin woman who turned to the wall one day while lying in her bed and never really turned back, choosing instead to disappear into her sickness and never come out again.

In her hands she held a whipped cream cake. Sort of pale pink on the sides, black bittersweet chocolate on the top. It was my favorite. She had always made it on special occasions. The last time I ever had it was on our wedding day. Rae got the recipe from her but was never able to make it right. All Moms have one secret recipe that can't be copied and this was hers. A whipped cream cake.

She went to the table and put it down in front of an empty seat. Reaching over, she arranged the silverware there. I knew she was setting it up for me. Come over and cut your cake, she was saying. Sit with your father and me and tell us what your life has been since we left. Tell us about Rae who we always liked and your job and how you've filled your days. Because we love you and want to hear everything. How many people on this Earth want to hear everything about you? How many people—

"They're dead, Mr. Gallatin."

I blinked, looking from my mother to my father. I was in a trance. My mother, my father, her cake, this place—

"They're dead, and you have things to do."

Beeflow's words struck my head like a hammer. They hurt that much. I didn't want to hear them. I didn't want this picture of my good parents to go away just because they were dead.

"What do you want from me? It's my parents! I haven't seen them—Can't I have five minutes together with my parents?"

"You're finding reasons to stay here. And the longer you stay, the more reasons you'll fine. It's very tricky that way. Very seductive. But everything here is from your life, Gallatin, it is from life, do you understand? How lucky you've been to amass all these fine memories? How good life has been to you? It's been a good friend. Don't you owe it something?"

Furious, I turned toward his voice without thinking. And when I saw him, when I saw what he was I began to cry. Because he'd told the truth—he was everything I didn't want to know about myself. He had no special shape or size. You couldn't say it's a man or a monster or a Devil or whatever. He was just it, them, all those things you try to ignore or cover up or argue against or justify or put up a million defenses against just to keep from saying there I am, that is part of me.

But then something amazing happened and I don't even know if I can take credit for it. I turned away. I turned away from Mr. Beeflow and looked back at that table, my parents, and the things that made my life big rather than small and shitty. I saw the good people, the good stuff on the table, the trees blowing in the wind and the smell of spring and food and life. Despite having "seen" Beeflow, I still had managed to survive and bring all of these beautiful things along to the death that would someday be mine. I was grateful. And I knew he was right—painful as it was, I had to give all this up for now and go back to do what I could to try and keep life as it had always been for everybody.

"Son?" Dad's voice.

I closed my eyes. "All right, Mr. Beeflow, I understand. Take me back."

Immediately something warm and familiar licked my hand. This time I didn't open my eyes. Whatever it was took the hand and pulled it gently to the left. Blind, I walked a few steps, trusting it, knowing that it was Cyrus. It made so much sense—once you made your mind up to go, only your own soul could lead you back to where you began.

"Not so fast, Monsieur. Who's going to pay for this meal, Bill? The bill, Bill. When you eat at my table, you pay for my cooking."

The Devil wore a chef's cap. One of those stupid high white ones that look like something put on the end of a lamb chop at a ritzy restaurant. He wore that white hat and all the rest of his clothes were white too. His face was nothing special—just a face surrounded by lots of white. No, that's not true—there was one strange-looking thing about him—he had two moustaches. Slim little things, they sat one right under the other like lines on paper.

"I see by your admiring eye that you're looking at my moustaches. Is this going to be the new trend or what?"

"It looks stupid if you ask me. Plus people can't grow two moustaches."

He shrugged and played with both of them. Top one, then the bottom. "But they can grow one really thick one and cut a space in the middle, making levels."

"It's still stupid."

"Every fool's entitled to his opinion. But let's get back to the facts—how do you plan on paying for this meal? P.S. I don't take Visa or Mastercard." He laughed and it sounded like someone unscrewing a tight plastic-on-plastic cap. I squinted at the sound but didn't look away. I guess my face said I was confused, so he took my arm. I tried to pull away but he wouldn't let me.

"You chose to come here, Bill boy, and now you want to leave, which, however, is a human no-no. Any person who sees this and wants to go back has to pay."

"Pay with what?"

"Something you love. I'll let you go back but the price for this meal, this little view you just had, is something you love in life. If you stay here you get to keep all this. But if you go back you've got to give me something from your life you never thought you could live without."

"Mr. Beeflow, are you there? Is this true?"

"Forget it, he can't help you. Anyway you saw what he looked like."

"You made Beeflow do this too?"

"Yup. He gave up his body. He was a handsome man. A very vain one too. Nothing he liked more than looking at himself in a mirror and admiring the view. I never thought he would do it but sometimes people surprise me."

Suddenly I remembered Cyrus and looked down at the hand he had been holding. No Cyrus—nothing was there. Only the ground. The ground in that beautiful Hell. Gathering myself together, gathering words in my mouth to make a sentence I never thought I would say in a million years, I took a deep breath and said, "Rae, take my love for Rae."

He didn't react immediately. He looked at me hard, like I was trying to trick him. But we both knew there was no way I could trick him.

"I thought you'd say something like that but it's not enough, Bill. Try again."

"I don't know anything else. That's about as bad as I can imagine. Not loving my wife anymore? What could be worse than not loving Rae?"

I climbed through the window of Eric Dickey's house back out into my world and my life. The first thing I smelled there was big thick smoke. It took only a second to remember I'd gone in there in the first place to save Eric and his wife from burning up in the caveman's fire. Jumping off the porch, I ran around to the back of the house. There was a high pile of wood and other things burning in the middle of their yard. Firemen had a hose turned on it, trying to get it under control. Both of the Dickeys were off to one side on their knees, taking oxygen. There was so much tussle and turmoil out there—people running around, fire being fought, police, firemen and the like. No one noticed me standing there. I couldn't help thinking that there had been absolutely no reason for me to go into that house because the fire had all been out here. But then if I hadn't gone in—

"Brother Bill?"

Brooks came up on one side of me, Zin Zan on the other. Neither of them was smiling and neither was I.

"Are you all right?"

A fireman rushed by us and knocked into me hard as he passed but I didn't react.

"Now I'm your Brother? Is that what you call me from now on? Brother Bill?"

"We don't have to call you anything if that's what you'd prefer. Are you all right?"

"You know where I just was, don't you?"

They both nodded.

"And you both went there once and saw the Devil?"

Again, slow nods.

In the smoke and the fire and the confusion and the running around and the noise that was a hundred kinds of noise, I saw something I hadn't seen all afternoon although it had been right in front of me the whole time.

"My God, you're Brooks Collins!"

Half a smile crossed Brother Brooks's face and then died. He nodded again.

"I have all your albums."

"Better take care of them—there won't be any more."

"You gave that up?" A few beats passed until I understood. "That's what you gave the Devil? Your talent?

"And the fame. He wasn't going to let me go just giving up the one. The world today is full of people who have no talent but are famous. No one recognizes me anymore. Only you, but that's because you've been to Hell. You perceive things other people don't."

"I guess we'd better get going."

It was not a far walk to my place but long enough to look around and appreciate things like I never had before. Now and then we'd pass a house and from just a glimpse, we knew if it had been taken over or not. But once I wasn't sure and crept to a window to look. I can't tell you how happy I was to see a normal family inside watching TV and eating popcorn.

"How come Mel Shaveetz and his dog were on fire when they left their house, but the caveman wasn't? All of them were dead."

"Because the Devil keeps changing the rules all the time. That's the reason why so many people are unhappy in life—the rules keep changing. There's really no way of knowing what will happen from one day to the next with this. That's why it's so hard for us to convince people of what's going on. And because it's happening so much faster now, that's why Beeflow has become more directly involved."

"Why doesn't the Devil stop him?"

"Arrogance. He doesn't see Beeflow or us as a threat. There's your house. Do you know what you're gonna do?"

"Stay here. I've got to see something."

They stood by a light pole while I went and opened the front door. Closing it quietly behind me as if someone nearby was sleeping and I didn't want to wake them, I just stood in the hallway a minute, being home, breathing home. My mother used to say after we'd come back from a trip, "At home, even the walls heal you." And that's just how I felt standing there, smelling my life in those near rooms, my eyes running over our possessions and photos on the walls that I knew the whole history of. Lucky me—all of them showed in different ways what a very good time I'd had right up until that day. Lucky me. But the Brothers had earlier said a moving van had been in front of my house. That's why I'd come back in here—to see who had taken over our house and how they had changed things. I needed to see what was different so I could prepare my wife and somehow protect her from what was happening. But why then was nothing different in here?

Then I heard it—the zhunk of furniture being shoved hard across a floor. Someone else was in my house. Someone upstairs from the sound of it. The back of my neck prickled and my eyes opened wide of their own doing. I wore sneakers so I was able to cross the floor and climb the stairs with very little sound. While climbing I heard that same sound a few more times, sometimes louder and longer, sometimes short and sharp. Zhunk-silence-zhuuunk. Like that. I couldn't figure out what it was but it was definitely real and I needed to find out about it.

At the top of the stairs I stood still and waited till the next time it came.

It was down the hall in our bedroom. Zhunk. From where I stood I could see that door was open about a third and something white was on the floor just inside the bedroom. I couldn't make out what it was. Tiptoeing down the hall, I kept trying to focus in on what that white thing was. It came to me in stages. A piece of clothing—a shirt—a white T-shirt. And just when I realized that's what it was, I heard the other sounds. Sex. A woman having sex and liking it a lot.

Rae doesn't like sex. That's been the major problem in our marriage. Once in a while she's sort of in the mood, but it's like when you're sort of in the mood for pizza but can easily do without it if there's none around. I always got the feeling she's doing me a favor when she said yes and I can't tell you how dry and lonely that made me feel. She's a woman I have always wanted to touch but is more than clear she doesn't want that.

A T-shirt was on the floor and when I looked I saw writing on it and knew it said "Hard Rock Café." It was my shirt but it was very big and Rae liked that so she often slept in it. Her sounds kept up and they would have made any man hot. I'd known them once but not for a long time. Still, I recognized them instantly. I walked as close to the door as I could and looked in.

My wife was on our bed naked, straddling a guy whose face I couldn't see. She was working him so hard that their banging bodies made the bed slide on the floor. Zhunk.

Even when we did have sex, she'd never do it like that with me because she didn't like me seeing her entirely naked. It was always in the dark and she'd wear some kind of clothes—a shirt or sweatshirt so she'd never be completely stripped. As if wearing something meant she was still distant from me and this act even when it was going on.

Did I watch? Yes. Did it make me hot? It sure did. I stood off to the side and watched her do whoever it was beneath her all the things I'd dreamt of her doing with me for as long as I could remember.

What had I given the Devil to come back here? Rae's love for me. My love for her wasn't enough, or so he'd said. So I said take hers then.

Our relationship wasn't the best. We never had sex anymore, and we seemed to fight more than we should have. Still, I knew she loved me in her scared, mysterious way. I could see it in her eyes when she looked at me.

Sometimes. Plus there were other things she did that overall made up for what was missing. You get along and sometimes you get along so well that you don't think about what you're missing because you just love them there in your life, whatever way they've chosen to be.

As I stood there watching my wife fuck another man, I knew the Devil had changed the rules again: no dead people had moved into my house. No *Casablanca* backgrounds or jungles were needed here. Everything was the same except for the fact that my wife's love for me was dead. What more proof did

I need than what was right in front of me?

There was nothing to take. I turned and went back down the hall, down the stairs. I was planning to go right back out of the house but when I touched the front doorknob I stopped. I walked back to the kitchen without thinking, kissed that new refrigerator. The thing that had started all this in the first place. That was all I wanted to do before leaving but don't ask me why. It just meant something to me and that was reason enough. I kissed our silver refrigerator and it was cool metal on my lips and then it was really time to go.

"Mr. Gallatin?" Beeflow's voice.

I stood and stared at the refrigerator. "What?"

"If it's of any comfort, he didn't make this happen. It's been going on for some time. Upstairs?"

"I know what you mean."

"You were never supposed to know about it. She was always very careful and discreet. But when you offered it to him, when you gave up her love for you—"

"I know what you're saying, Beeflow. I'm not that stupid. He shows me the truth, you show me the truth—both of you killing me with all this truth about my life. Was that the plan? Because what good does it do? Seeing the truth just shows you how wrong you were about things and how ugly they really are."

"Sometimes. And sometimes it brings the genuinely good things into better focus."

I threw up my hands in disgust. "I don't want to hear any more. Okay? Don't say another word." I left my house for the last time and started walking over to the Brothers, not really knowing if what Beeflow had said made things better or worse.

But I didn't have any time to think about it. Suddenly from down the street came all these screams and sounds of people running. *Lots* of people running. I'd just gotten to Brooks and Zin Zan when this crowd arrived. First came a bunch of men in Roman gladiator uniforms—swords, shields, sandals up to their knees, the whole bit. They came stampeding down the street slap-slap-slapping on their sandals. Every last one of them looked scared shitless. They all kept looking over their shoulders at what was after them.

When they were gone, a few moments passed and then came the second wave. Maybe a hundred wild-looking, screaming women in leather and animal skins, wearing headdresses made out of crazy-colored bird feathers, carrying spears and swords and all kinds of other ugly weapons, some of their faces covered in war paint, went barreling after those scared gladiators. It was clear they were going to catch up any minute.

After the last ones passed I said, "What the fuck was that?"

Brooks and Zin Zan started running after them. Brooks said, "Some dead fool chose the movie *Hercules and the Captive Women* to fill his house. But guess what—they escaped."

"And we're supposed to do something about it? Us? Just the three of us?"

We were already running after them when Zin Zan said, "Now it gets interesting."

MIKE'S PLACE
David J. Schwartz

The Devil got a job tending bar at Mike's Place. You'd think he'd be bitter about his change of fortune, but he just shrugs it off. He says a lot of big corporations have failed, and Hell, Inc. was no different, when you get down to it. As for exchanging seven figures annually for five an hour plus tips, he just laughs and says there aren't a lot of places that will hire a guy with horns.

For his part, the Devil doesn't discriminate. Used to be you just had to be sinful; now you just have to be thirsty. He says the only difference is that now the really bad ones get tossed out instead of in.

Not that a lot of people are eighty-sixed from Mike's. It happens, of course— Mike doesn't put up with fighting, for example. But he puts up with a lot. Too much, some of the waitresses might say. Like Ashes, who never lets a woman enter or leave the bar without putting his hands on her in some way. Or Little Tony, who sits in the corner talking to himself and never tips for his Diet Cokes. Or Beezle.

Beezle used to work with the Devil. I think we've all figured out his real name by now, but nobody cares to say it out loud. The Devil insists they aren't friends, and talks to him as little as possible. Nobody talks to Beezle if they can avoid it. You see, Beezle takes the form of a giant fly, four feet high not counting the legs. On his barstool he looks like sort of a big hairy throw pillow with wings. He only drinks those blended frou-frou drinks, which the Devil hates making. Strawberry daiquiris, mostly. Beezle doesn't have any fingers, so he picks up the glass with both of his front legs, takes a long sip from the straw, and sets the glass back down again. Twenty minutes later he's ready for another.

On the surface, though, the waitresses have no reason to get so upset about Beezle hanging around. He always sits at the bar (at the same stool, in fact, and no one else ever sits there), and he never talks to anyone but the Devil—he doesn't even come in on Mondays, when the Devil takes off and Mike's pal Gabe fills in. He doesn't smell any worse than anyone else in the place, and better than some. He doesn't grab the girls and he doesn't try to brush up against them when the place is crowded. He also doesn't attract a lot of smaller flies, surprisingly.

But Beezle makes everyone nervous. For one thing, he sees everything with those multi-faceted eyes, and for all we know he hears everything too, so you either have to learn to ignore him or resign yourself to quietly getting drunk. Which, to be fair, plenty of the regulars are happy to do. Most of them don't have anywhere else to be, since the Crisis.

Things were bad even before Heaven went out of business. Most people still refer to it as Heaven, or Heavenly Ventures, even though they changed the name to Heaventure when they spun the angels off into their own corporation. It's hard to say which was a worse mistake.

Heaventure. What kind of a word is that? The Devil says it sounds like Paradise with a sneeze attached. Heaventure. They claimed to have vetted it up and down, fed it to focus groups all across the mortal realm, but you know how that is. You give people fifty bucks, they tend to tell you what they think you want to hear. And the angels—I'm still waiting for someone to explain to me how getting rid of your most visible, most profitable product line is a good idea. The whole time Heaventure was "focusing on the aftercare of exceptional mortal souls," as they put it, the Seraphim Company was making money hand over wingtip. Angels were big business: porcelain figurines, inspirational posters, bumper stickers, plush toys, recordings of the heavenly chorus, branded school supplies, protection services... that last was a bit controversial. Apparently there was a big shakeup in the boardroom before that went into effect, but that was just a picketer in the path of a juggernaut, if you get my meaning.

Meanwhile by this time the guys upstairs were about to lose their halos. They managed to keep it quiet until Friday came around, but when there were no paychecks every cubicle-dweller in the Eternal City emailed everyone they knew. The Big Guy called a company-wide meeting to ask people to remain calm and not to release confidential company information, but that was like throwing a deck chair off the Titanic. The ship was already sinking.

The twenty-four hour cable channels were on the story all weekend, but most people stayed pretty calm, because no one really understood the implications. Religious services were pretty well attended, but the clergy didn't have much in the way of answers.

Monday morning three things happened. The first thing most people noticed was that the streets, the cafés and the unemployment offices were clogged with all the blessed who had thought their needs would be taken care of for all eternity. They'd been kicked out of Paradise because of the second thing, which was that Heaventure filed for bankruptcy and announced that it was liquidating assets, beginning with real estate. The third thing was that *The Wall Street Journal* broke the story that Hell, Inc. was heavily invested in Heaventure, and stood to lose half a billion dollars.

Long story short, things went from bad to worse to the nether regions in a matter of days. Hell, Inc. followed Heaventure into insolvency, and the damned joined the blessed in the bread lines and the shelters. Congress made a lot of speeches about corporate accountability but stopped short of scheduling hearings; I guess none of them wanted to cross the Big Guy. The Dow took daily plunges, often only open for thirty minutes or less before the circuit-breaker safeguards shut it down. Massive layoffs were announced in every sector of the economy. Some wag at NBC, asked if this was a second Great Depression, said it was more like an Existential Crisis, and the name stuck.

After a week in hiding, the Big Guy turned up on—of course—Larry King. He said that Heaventure was conducting an internal investigation into what appeared to be some misreportage of funds. He said he deeply regretted that Heaventure was no longer able to provide services for the blessed, but financial realities necessitated a shutdown of operations. He had no comment on most of the softball questions Larry lobbed at him, and he cut the interview short when he was pressed on the question of the Covenant.

That was the Devil's first night at Mike's, and he shook his head at his ex-boss's performance. "He's really not good at doing his own talking," he said, and twisted open another bottle of Bud.

Everybody likes the Devil. He's unpretentious, he's funny, and he tells it like it is. It's a funny thing about life after the Crisis. The damned, in general, are a lot easier to get along with than the blessed. Even the ones who were only suffering eternal torment for a few days are pretty well-behaved, when all is said and done, and they don't act like they're entitled to everything. I can't tell you how many times in the first few days a blessed walked up to me on the street and said "I'm hungry." As if not only was this the most unbelievable thing in the world, but they expected that once having realized it I would immediately fetch them a glass of sweet nectar or something. Nowadays they don't so much tell people their problems. Mostly they stand around in their beautiful white clothes, staring at their smooth, lazy hands and sulking.

The damned, on the other hand, are grateful for what they've got. There was no beer in hell, the Devil says, unless you were an alcoholic. He says the rule was nobody got anything unless they got too much of it. You'd think the damned who walked into Mike's would leave as soon as they saw the Devil, but most of them talk to him like an old friend. They steer clear of Beezle, though.

People—living, damned or blessed—come to Mike's because he lets them run a tab for weeks, sometimes months. The rumor is that Mike got a big severance package from some big company, so he can afford to extend credit to people who might not be able to pay for a while, or at all. Thing is, people do pay when they can. I don't know that the bar is making any money, but it's still open, which is more than you can say for a lot of places nowadays.

There's this couple that comes in to Mike's all the time—regulars. He's a Jack Coke and she's a naked dirty Absolut martini, but that's not the only difference between them. He was blessed, see, and she was damned. Before that, who knows? Maybe they didn't meet until the Crisis. It doesn't seem polite to ask about it.

They were there the night that Christ showed up. It was a Tuesday, and there weren't a lot of people in the place—the Seraphim Company was having a job fair the next morning. Anyway, Christ came in, announced he was back, and right away everybody had questions.

"Is everyone going to be saved?" asked the blessed man, holding hands with the damned woman.

"It's in negotiations," said Christ.

"Is it the Rapture?" asked Ashes, who is a Born Again Christian.

"We're workshopping the campaign," Christ said. "We'll have the nomenclature in a month or two."

"What about ze Zcripturez?" This from Beezle, who had left his Brandy Alexander at the bar and was flying drunkenly towards Christ. "What about ze way zings were zuppozed to happen?"

"Those were just projections," said Christ. "Admittedly we've fallen a bit short, but we really feel that things are going to keep getting better. We've made a lot of positive changes at Heaventure. It's not just business as usual."

He kept talking, but by that time we had figured out that it was just a PR stunt. Everyone turned back to their drinks, except for Beezle, who passed out in the hall next to the men's room. After a while the Devil asked Christ what he was drinking. They chatted until he finished his Cutty and Water, and then Christ left, saying he had a lot of stops to make.

"Asshole," Little Tony shouted from his corner.

"Hey, none of that," said the Devil. "We all got to make a living." He cleared Christ's glass, set it in the washer, and wiped the counter down with a towel.

THUS I REFUTE BEELZY

John Collier

"There goes the tea bell," said Mrs. Carter. "I hope Simon hears it." They looked out from the window of the drawing room. The long garden, agreeably neglected, ended in a waste plot.

Here a little summerhouse was passing close by beauty on its way to complete decay. This was Simon's retreat. It was almost completely screened by the tangled branches of the apple tree and the pear tree, planted too close together, as they always are in the suburbs. They caught a glimpse of him now and then, as he strutted up and down, mouthing and gesticulating, performing all the solemn mumbo jumbo of small boys who spend long afternoons at the forgotten ends of long gardens.

"There he is, bless him!" said Betty.

"Playing his game," said Mrs. Carter. "He won't play with the other children anymore. And if I go down there the temper! And comes in tired out!"

"He doesn't have his sleep in the afternoons?" asked Betty.

"You know what Big Simon's ideas are," said Mrs. Carter. "'Let him choose for himself,' he says. That's what he chooses, and he comes in as white as a sheet."

"Look! He's heard the bell," said Betty. The expression was justified, though the bell had ceased ringing a full minute ago. Small Simon stopped in his parade exactly as if its tinny dingle had at that moment reached his ear. They watched him perform certain ritual sweeps and scratchings with his little stick, and come lagging over the hot and flaggy grass toward the house.

Mrs. Carter led the way down to the playroom, or garden-room, which was also the tearoom for hot days. It had been the huge scullery of this tall Georgian house. Now the walls were cream-washed, there was coarse blue net in the windows, canvas-covered armchairs on the stone floor, and a reproduction of Van Gogh's Sunflowers over the mantelpiece.

Small Simon came drifting in, and accorded Betty a perfunctory greeting. His face was an almost perfect triangle, pointed at the chin, and he was paler than he should have been. "The little elf-child!" cried Betty.

Simon looked at her. "No," said he.

417

At that moment the door opened, and Mr. Carter came in, rubbing his hands. He was a dentist, and washed them before and after everything he did. "You!" said his wife. "Home already!"

"Not unwelcome, I hope," said Mr. Carter, nodding to Betty. "Two people canceled their appointments; I decided to come home. I said, I hope I am not unwelcome."

"Silly!" said his wife. "Of course not."

"Small Simon seems doubtful," continued Mr. Carter. "Small Simon, are you sorry to see me at tea with you?"

"No, Daddy."

"No, what?"

"No, Big Simon."

"That's right. Big Simon and Small Simon. That sounds more like friends, doesn't it? At one time, little boys had to call their father 'sir.' If they forgot a good spanking. On the bottom, Small Simon! On the bottom!" said Mr. Carter, washing his hands once more with his invisible soap and water.

The little boy turned crimson with shame or rage.

"But now, you see," said Betty, to help, "you can call your father whatever you like."

"And what," asked Mr. Carter, "has Small Simon been doing this afternoon? While Big Simon has been at work."

"Nothing," muttered his son.

"Then you have been bored," said Mr. Carter. "Learn from experience, Small Simon. Tomorrow, do something amusing, and you will not be bored. I want him to learn from experience, Betty. That is my way, the new way."

"I have learned," said the boy, speaking like an old, tired man, as little boys so often do.

"It would hardly seem so," said Mr. Carter, "if you sit on your behind all the afternoon, doing nothing. Had my father caught me doing nothing, I should not have sat very comfortably."

"He played," said Mrs. Carter.

"A bit," said the boy, shifting on his chair.

"Too much," said Mrs. Carter. "He comes in all nervy and dazed. He ought to have his rest."

"He is six," said her husband. "He is a reasonable being. He must choose for himself. But what game is this, Small Simon, that is worth getting nervy and dazed over? There are very few games as good as all that."

"It's nothing," said the boy.

"Oh, come," said his father. "We are friends, are we not? You can tell me. I was a Small Simon once, just like you, and played the same games you play. Of course, there were no airplanes in those days. With whom do you play this fine game? Come on, we must all answer civil questions, or the world would never go round. With whom do you play?"

"Mr. Beelzy," said the boy, unable to resist.

"Mr. Beelzy?" said his father, raising his eyebrows inquiringly at his wife.

"It's a game he makes up," said she.

"Not makes up!" cried the boy. "Fool!"

"That is telling stories," said his mother. "And rude as well. We had better talk of something different."

"No wonder he is rude," said Mr. Carter, "if you say he tells lies, and then insist on changing the subject. He tells you his fantasy; you implant a guilt feeling. What can you expect? A defense mechanism. Then you get a real lie."

"Like in These Three," said Betty. "Only different, of course. She was an unblushing little liar."

"I would have made her blush," said Mr. Carter, "in the proper part of her anatomy. But Small Simon is in the fantasy stage. Are you not, Small Simon? You just make things up."

"No, I don't," said the boy.

"You do," said his father. "And because you do, it is not too late to reason with you. There is no harm in a fantasy, old chap. There is nothing wrong with a bit of make-believe. Only you must learn the difference between daydreams and real things, or your brain will never grow. It will never be the brain of a Big Simon. So, come on. Let us hear about this Mr. Beelzy of yours. Come on. What is he like?"

"He isn't like anything," said the boy.

"Like nothing on earth?" said his father. "That's a terrible fellow."

"I'm not frightened of him," said the child, smiling. "Not a bit."

"I should hope not," said his father. "If you were, you would be frightening yourself. I am always telling people, older people than you are, that they are just frightening themselves. Is he a funny man? Is he a giant?"

"Sometimes he is," said the little boy.

"Sometimes one thing, sometimes another," said his father. "Sounds pretty vague. Why can't you tell us just what he's like?"

"I love him," said the small boy. "He loves me.

"That's a big word," said Mr. Carter. "That might be better kept for real things, like Big Simon and Small Simon."

"He is real," said the boy, passionately. "He's not a fool. He's real."

"Listen," said his father. "When you go down to the garden there's nobody there. Is there?"

"No," said the boy.

"Then you think of him, inside your head, and he comes."

"No," said Small Simon. "I have to make marks. On the ground. With my stick."

"That doesn't matter."

"Yes, it does."

"Small Simon, you are being obstinate," said Mr. Carter. "I am trying to explain something to you. I have been longer in the world than you have, so naturally I am older and wiser. I am explaining that Mr. Beelzy is a fantasy of yours. Do you hear? Do you understand?"

"Yes, Daddy."

"He is a game. He is a let's-pretend."

The little boy looked down at his plate, smiling resignedly.

"I hope you are listening to me," said his father. "All you have to do is to say, 'I have been playing a game of let's-pretend. With someone I make up, called Mr. Beelzy.' Then no one will say you tell lies, and you will know the difference between dreams and reality. Mr. Beelzy is a daydream."

The little boy still stared at his plate.

"He is sometimes there and sometimes not there," pursued Mr. Carter. "Sometimes he's like one thing, sometimes another. You can't really see him. Not as you see me. I am real. You can't touch him. You can touch me. I can touch you." Mr. Carter stretched out his big, white dentist's hand, and took his little son by the nape of the neck. He stopped speaking for a moment and tightened his hand. The little boy sank his head still lower.

"Now you know the difference," said Mr. Carter, "between a pretend and a real thing. You and I are one thing; he is another. Which is the pretend? Come on. Answer me. Which is the pretend?"

"Big Simon and Small Simon," said the little boy.

"Don't!" cried Betty, and at once put her hand over her mouth, for why should a visitor cry, "Don't!" when a father is explaining things in a scientific and modern way? Besides, it annoys the father.

"Well, my boy," said Mr. Carter, "I have said you must be allowed to learn from experience. Go upstairs. Right up to your room. You shall learn whether it is better to reason, or to be perverse and obstinate. Go up. I shall follow you."

"You are not going to beat the child?" cried Mrs. Carter.

"No," said the little boy. "Mr. Beelzy won't let him."

"Go on up with you!" shouted his father.

Small Simon stopped at the door. "He said he wouldn't let anyone hurt me," he whimpered. "He said he'd come like a lion, with wings on, and eat them up."

"You'll learn how real he is!" shouted his father after him. "If you can't learn it at one end, you shall learn it at the other. I'll have your breeches down. I shall finish my cup of tea first, however," said he to the two women.

Neither of them spoke. Mr. Carter finished his tea, and unhurriedly left the room, washing his hands with his invisible soap and water.

Mrs. Carter said nothing. Betty could think of nothing to say. She wanted to be talking for she was afraid of what they might hear.

Suddenly it came. It seemed to tear the air apart. "Good god!" she cried. "What was that? He's hurt him." She sprang out of her chair, her silly eyes flashing behind her glasses. "I'm going up there!" she cried, trembling.

"Yes, let us go up," said Mrs. Carter. "Let us go up. That was not Small Simon."

It was on the second-floor landing that they found the shoe, with the man's foot still in it, much like that last morsel of a mouse which sometimes falls unnoticed from the side of the jaws of the cat.

İNFERNO·: CANTO· XXXİV

by Dante Alighieri

TRANSLATED FROM THE ORIGINAL ITALIAN BY HENRY WADSWORTH LONGFELLOW

"'Vexilla Regis prodeunt Inferni'
  Towards us; therefore look in front of thee,"
  My Master said, "if thou discernest him."

As, when there breathes a heavy fog, or when
  Our hemisphere is darkening into night,
  Appears far off a mill the wind is turning,

Methought that such a building then I saw;
  And, for the wind, I drew myself behind
  My Guide, because there was no other shelter.

Now was I, and with fear in verse I put it,
  There where the shades were wholly covered up,
  And glimmered through like unto straws in glass.

Some prone are lying, others stand erect,
  This with the head, and that one with the soles;
  Another, bow-like, face to feet inverts.

When in advance so far we had proceeded,
  That it my Master pleased to show to me
  The creature who once had the beauteous semblance,

He from before me moved and made me stop,
  Saying: "Behold Dis, and behold the place
  Where thou with fortitude must arm thyself."

How frozen I became and powerless then,
  Ask it not, Reader, for I write it not,
  Because all language would be insufficient.

I did not die, and I alive remained not;
 Think for thyself now, hast thou aught of wit,
 What I became, being of both deprived.

The Emperor of the kingdom dolorous
 From his mid-breast forth issued from the ice;
 And better with a giant I compare

Than do the giants with those arms of his;
 Consider now how great must be that whole,
 Which unto such a part conforms itself.

Were he as fair once, as he now is foul,
 And lifted up his brow against his Maker,
 Well may proceed from him all tribulation.

O, what a marvel it appeared to me,
 When I beheld three faces on his head!
 The one in front, and that vermilion was;

Two were the others, that were joined with this
 Above the middle part of either shoulder,
 And they were joined together at the crest;

And the right-hand one seemed 'twixt white and yellow;
 The left was such to look upon as those
 Who come from where the Nile falls valley-ward.

Underneath each came forth two mighty wings,
 Such as befitting were so great a bird;
 Sails of the sea I never saw so large.

No feathers had they, but as of a bat
 Their fashion was; and he was waving them,
 So that three winds proceeded forth therefrom.

Thereby Cocytus wholly was congealed.
 With six eyes did he weep, and down three chins
 Trickled the tear-drops and the bloody drivel.

At every mouth he with his teeth was crunching
 A sinner, in the manner of a brake,
 So that he three of them tormented thus.

To him in front the biting was as naught
 Unto the clawing, for sometimes the spine
 Utterly stripped of all the skin remained.

"That soul up there which has the greatest pain,"
 The Master said, "is Judas Iscariot;
 With head inside, he plies his legs without.

Of the two others, who head downward are,
 The one who hangs from the black jowl is Brutus;
 See how he writhes himself, and speaks no word.

And the other, who so stalwart seems, is Cassius.
 But night is reascending, and 'tis time
 That we depart, for we have seen the whole."

As seemed him good, I clasped him round the neck,
 And he the vantage seized of time and place,
 And when the wings were opened wide apart,

He laid fast hold upon the shaggy sides;
 From fell to fell descended downward then
 Between the thick hair and the frozen crust.

When we were come to where the thigh revolves
 Exactly on the thickness of the haunch,
 The Guide, with labour and with hard-drawn breath,

Turned round his head where he had had his legs,
 And grappled to the hair, as one who mounts,
 So that to Hell I thought we were returning.

"Keep fast thy hold, for by such stairs as these,"
 The Master said, panting as one fatigued,
 "Must we perforce depart from so much evil."

Then through the opening of a rock he issued,
 And down upon the margin seated me;
 Then tow'rds me he outstretched his wary step.

I lifted up mine eyes and thought to see
 Lucifer in the same way I had left him;
 And I beheld him upward hold his legs.

And if I then became disquieted,
 Let stolid people think who do not see
 What the point is beyond which I had passed.

"Rise up," the Master said, "upon thy feet;
 The way is long, and difficult the road,
 And now the sun to middle-tierce returns."

It was not any palace corridor
 There where we were, but dungeon natural,
 With floor uneven and unease of light.

"Ere from the abyss I tear myself away,
 My Master," said I when I had arisen,
 "To draw me from an error speak a little;

Where is the ice? and how is this one fixed
 Thus upside down? and how in such short time
 From eve to morn has the sun made his transit?"

And he to me: "Thou still imaginest
 Thou art beyond the centre, where I grasped
 The hair of the fell worm, who mines the world.

That side thou wast, so long as I descended;
 When round I turned me, thou didst pass the point
 To which things heavy draw from every side,

And now beneath the hemisphere art come
 Opposite that which overhangs the vast
 Dry-land, and 'neath whose cope was put to death

The Man who without sin was born and lived.
 Thou hast thy feet upon the little sphere
 Which makes the other face of the Judecca.

Here it is morn when it is evening there;
 And he who with his hair a stairway made us
 Still fixed remaineth as he was before.

Upon this side he fell down out of heaven;
 And all the land, that whilom here emerged,
 For fear of him made of the sea a veil,

And came to our hemisphere; and peradventure
To flee from him, what on this side appears
Left the place vacant here, and back recoiled."

A place there is below, from Beelzebub
As far receding as the tomb extends,
Which not by sight is known, but by the sound

Of a small rivulet, that there descendeth
Through chasm within the stone, which it has gnawed
With course that winds about and slightly falls.

The Guide and I into that hidden road
Now entered, to return to the bright world;
And without care of having any rest

We mounted up, he first and I the second,
Till I beheld through a round aperture
Some of the beauteous things that Heaven doth bear;

Thence we came forth to rebehold the stars.

COPYRIGHT ACKNOWLEDGMENTS

"The King of the Djinn" by David Ackert and Benjamin Rosenbaum © 2008. Originally published in *Realms of Fantasy*, 2008. Reprinted by permission of the authors.

"The Power of Speech" by Natalie Babbitt © 1974. Originally published in *Cricket*, 1974. Reprinted by permission of the author.

"Two Old Men" by Kage Baker © 2000. Originally published in *Asimov's*, 2000. Reprinted by permission of the author and the author's agent Linn Prentis

"And the Deep Blue Sea" by Elizabeth Bear © 2005. Originally published in *Sci Fiction*, 2005. Reprinted by permission of the author.

"A Reversal of Fortune" by Holly Black © 2007. Originally published in *The Coyote Road: Trickster Tales* (2007). Reprinted by permission of the author.

"That Hell-Bound Train" © 1958 by Mercury Press, Inc., for *The Magazine of Fantasy and Science Fiction*, September 1958. Copyright © 1986 by Robert Bloch. Reprinted by permission of Sally Francy c/o Ralph M. Vicinanza, Ltd.

"The Devil Disinvests" by Scott Bradfield © 2000. Originally published in *The Magazine of Fantasy and Science Fiction*, 2000. Reprinted by permission of the author.

"Ash City Stomp" by Richard Butner © 2003. Originally published in *Trampoline* from Small Beer Press, 2003. Reprinted by permission of the author.

"The Heidelberg Cylinder" by Jonathan Carroll © 2000. Originally published by Mobius Interactive, 2000. Reprinted by permission of the author and The Richard Parks Agency.

Night Shade Books Is an Independent Publisher of Quality SF, Fantasy and Horror

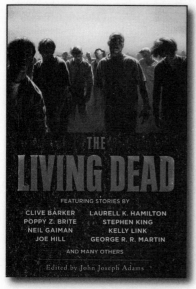

ISBN: 978-1-59780-143-0
Trade Paperback $15.95

Zombies have invaded popular culture, becoming the monsters that best express the fears and anxieties of the modern West. Zombies have been depicted as mind-controlled minions, the disintegrating dead, the ultimate lumpenproletariat, but in all cases, they reflect us, mere mortals afraid of death in a society on the verge of collapse.

Gathering together the best zombie literature of the last three decades from many of today's most renowned authors of fantasy, speculative fiction, and horror, including Stephen King, Harlan Ellison, George R. R. Martin, Clive Barker, Neil Gaiman, and Poppy Z. Brite, *The Living Dead* covers the broad spectrum of zombie fiction.

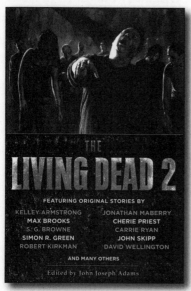

ISBN: 978-1-59780-190-4
Trade Paperback $15.99

Two years ago, readers eagerly devoured *The Living Dead*. *Publishers Weekly* named it one of the Best Books of the Year, and BarnesAndNoble.com called it "The best zombie fiction collection ever." Now acclaimed editor John Joseph Adams is back with 43 more of the best, most chilling, most thrilling zombie stories anywhere, including virtuoso performances by zombie fiction legends Max Brooks (*World War Z, The Zombie Survival Guide*), Robert Kirkman (*The Walking Dead*), and David Wellington (*Monster Island*).

The Living Dead 2 has more of what zombie fans hunger for — more scares, more action, more... brains.

Find these Night Shade titles and many others online at http://www.nightshadebooks.com or wherever books are sold.

Night Shade Books Is an Independent Publisher of Quality SF, Fantasy and Horror

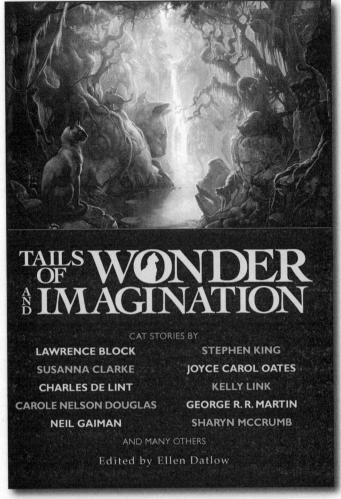

TAILS OF WONDER AND IMAGINATION

CAT STORIES BY

LAWRENCE BLOCK   STEPHEN KING

SUSANNA CLARKE   JOYCE CAROL OATES

CHARLES DE LINT   KELLY LINK

CAROLE NELSON DOUGLAS   GEORGE R. R. MARTIN

NEIL GAIMAN   SHARYN MCCRUMB

AND MANY OTHERS

Edited by Ellen Datlow

ISBN: 978-1-59780-170-6, Trade Paperback; $15.95

What is it about the cat that captivates the creative imagination? No other creature has inspired so many authors to take pen to page. Mystery, horror, science fiction, and fantasy stories have all been written about cats.

From legendary editor Ellen Datlow comes *Tails of Wonder and Imagination*, showcasing forty cat tales by some of today's most popular authors. With uncollected stories by Stephen King, Tanith Lee, Peter S. Beagle, and Theodora Goss, and a previously unpublished story by Susanna Clarke, plus feline-centric fiction by Neil Gaiman, Kelly Link, George R. R. Martin, Lucius Shepard, Joyce Carol Oates, Graham Joyce, and many others.

Tails of Wonder and Imagination features more than 200,000 words of stories in which cats are heroes and stories in which they're villains; people transformed into cats, cats transformed into people. And yes, even a few cute cats.

Night Shade Books Is an Independent Publisher of Quality SF, Fantasy and Horror

ISBN 978-1-59780-187-4, Trade Paperback; $15.95

Dragons: fearsome fire-breathing foes, scaled adversaries, legendary lizards, ancient hoarders of priceless treasures, serpentine sages with the ages' wisdom, and winged weapons of war.

Wings of Fire brings you all these dragons, and more, seen clearly through the eyes of many of today's most popular authors, including Peter S. Beagle, Holly Black, Orson Scott Card, Mercedes Lackey, Charles De Lint, Diana Wynne Jones, Ursula K Le Guin, George R. R. Martin, Anne McCaffrey, Garth Nix, and many others.

Edited by Jonathan Strahan (*The Best Science Fiction and Fantasy of the Year, Eclipse*), *Wings of Fire* collects the best short stories about dragons. From writhing wyrms to snakelike devourers of heroes; from East to West and everywhere in between, *Wings of Fire* is sure to please dragon lovers everywhere.